Trisha Telep is the editor of the bestselling Mammoth romance titles, including *The Mammoth Book of Vampire Romance, Love Bites, The Mammoth Book of Paranormal Romance* and *The Mammoth Book of Time Travel Romance*.

The Mammoth Book of Futuristic Romance

Edited by

TRISHA TELEP

RUNNING PRESS
PHILADELPHIA · LONDON

Constable & Robinson Ltd
55–56 Russell Square
London WC1B 4HP
www.constablerobinson.com

First published in the UK by Robinson,
an imprint of Constable & Robinson Ltd, 2013

A copy of the British Library Cataloging in Publication
Data is available from the British Library

UK ISBN: 978-1-78033-038-9 (paperback)
UK ISBN: 978-1-78033-043-3 (ebook)

1 3 5 7 9 10 8 6 4 2

First published in the United States in 2013 by Running Press Book Publishers,
A Member of the Perseus Books Group

Books published by Running Press are available at special discounts for bulk purchases
in the United States by corporations, institutions, and other organizations. For more
information, please contact the Special Markets Department at the Perseus Books Group,
2300 Chestnut Street, Suite 200, Philadelphia, PA 19103, or call (800) 810-4145,
ext. 5000, or e-mail special.markets@perseusbooks.com.

US ISBN: 978-0-7624-4601-8
US Library of Congress Control Number: 2011939128

9 8 7 6 5 4 3 2 1
Digit on the right indicates the number of this printing

Running Press Book Publishers
2300 Chestnut Street
Philadelphia, PA 19103-4371

Visit us on the web!
www.runningpress.com

Printed and bound in the UK

Contents

Copyright

Introduction

The future is friendly. Well, actually, the future is *more* than friendly. It's a bit *over*-friendly, if anything. Clumsy spacesuits and clunky helmets have done nothing to dampen our ardor, and even in those bleak dystopian visions where we keep up our wanton environmental destruction of the planet we call home, it's love that manages to provide some light at the end of the tunnel.

On space ships, on newly colonized planets, on versions of Earth that we may recognize, or not, and amidst our own and alien species, there is no shortage of love in the future. And that is a cause for celebration. Whatever lies ahead may be all-encompassing and vast, but we can be comforted by the knowledge that we'll always be falling in and out of love, being swept off our feet by meetings with handsome strangers, and longing, lusting and loving, far into an uncertain future. Whether we travel to new worlds or struggle to adapt to radical new changes on Earth, we can always expect to experience the warm, familiar feelings that make us human.

Although the setting might throw you, you'll feel right at home in the future. Meet hardy pioneers settling new planetary colonies, hoping for a fresh start on a new planet, complete with a government grant and a brand-new mate. Clashes with local, indigenous populations can lead to danger, adventure and inter-species love. Space is the newest new frontier, and the race to secure new territory brings all the old familiar faces out of the woodwork from Earth's dubious colonial past.

It's no surprise that big business plays a prominent role in the future, as does the military. Far-reaching corporations of limit-less wealth finance the exploration of new worlds, seeking the profit that new, untapped resources can supply. The military provides the muscle to fight the wars in space or dirtside, complete with genetic modifications and space-age nutritional supplements. In the future, peace seems even more elusive than it does today. The post-colonial world is over, and the race for new colonies has begun, bringing with it the same age-old aggression and ruthlessness.

But romance always saves the day, and there is a light-heart-edness to these future-set stories, with great lashings of humor and warmth. You'll meet former romantic partners trying to put the past behind them – and not succeeding – as they prepare to enter an intergalactic space race; time-traveling rebels out to romance the past; and great characters like Linnea Sinclair's recently deflowered bio-'cybe Kel-Paten, who makes living in space seem like a really good idea. Perhaps it's true that in space no one can hear you scream, but after sampling the stories here, you'll be sure that they must at least be able to hear you laugh.

Trisha Telep

Flying is Faster

Jeannie Holmes

For the human settlers of Maji – planet MAJ07, as it was officially designated in colony reports – Earth was a legend spoken of in the same reverent tones as Avalon, Nirvana, or Heaven. Wars, climate changes, and the decadent life of the ancient homeworlders had left only a blasted wasteland. Humans had had no choice but to take to the stars in search of new worlds.

The journey from Earth to Maji had taken hundreds of years. All settlers had been placed in cryogenic sleep, but small groups had been awakened along the way to run the ships, monitor the status of their fellow travelers, and procreate to ensure genetic diversity.

Ronan Frayne, like all inhabitants of New Denver settlement, had been born and educated on the colony transport. Upon reaching Maji, the towering mountains surrounding the settlement had both comforted and terrified him. Staring too long at their snowcapped peaks made his head swim and his stomach churn, but he loved the solidity they represented.

And solid ground was where Ronan desperately wanted to be. He clung to the ladder propped alongside the medical shelter's newest extension. One of the workers had been injured, and as the colony's doctor, it was Ronan's job to assess the damage.

"Don't look down," he told himself through clenched teeth. Concentrating on the roofline above him, he clasped the next rung and pushed with his shaky legs. "Four more and you're safe."

An eternity seemed to pass, but Ronan finally hoisted himself onto the roof and his stomach dropped. Large holes gaped across the incomplete structure, offering unfettered views of the debris scattered across the floor below. Groaning, he hooked his safety line to the cable skirting the construction zone and rose unsteadily to his feet.

"Over here," one of the workers called, waving his hand from the other side of a chasm.

Ronan nodded and shuffled his way through the discarded tools and building materials. All work had stopped and wouldn't resume until the injured worker was on the ground. He reached the two remaining workers and squatted. "What happened?"

"Laser welder malfunctioned," the injured worker said. He held a bloodied hand to the right side of his face. "Focusing crystal shattered."

Ronan set down his medikit and flipped it open. He grabbed the compact scanner and gently encouraged the man to lower his hand to reveal a deep cut over his brow. He swiped the scanner over the injury. "Was anyone else hit by the shrapnel?"

The other worker shook his head. "No one else was in the area."

Finishing his exam, Ronan reached for a dermal regenerator. "This may sting a bit," he murmured.

Blue light bathed the cut and the worker flinched.

"Hold still."

Several minutes passed before Ronan disengaged the regenerator. The worker's cut had mended, the flesh sealing itself and leaving only a thin pink line. He scanned the site once more. "That should take care of it, but you need to rest for the remainder of the day," he said, stowing his equipment. "If you feel any pain or dizziness, let me know immediately."

The worker grimaced but nodded. "Thanks, Doc."

A shadow passed over the men as the second worker helped the other to his feet. Ronan glanced skyward.

A winged creature flew overhead, silhouetted against the afternoon sun. It swooped and twirled along the thermal drafts rising from the valley.

"Budgie," one of the workers muttered.

Ronan frowned at the use of the slur. When human settlers had arrived on Maji, they'd been surprised to find it inhabited by a race of winged humanoids. The Auilans, as they were properly named, lived high in the surrounding mountains. Early contact with the tribal race had met with mixed results.

Most wanted little or no contact with the newcomers. However, one clan, the Azein, welcomed the humans and frequently visited the settlement.

Sunlight flashed off white-and-brown feathers as the Auilan soared overhead.

Ronan's frown turned to a smile. He knew that pattern well.

"It's Data." One of the workers groaned.

"Dotty," Ronan corrected his mispronunciation.

"Whatever."

One of the few female Azeins to venture into New Denver, Dah'Te was intelligent and curious about humans. Ronan looked forward to her visits and eagerly answered her questions in exchange for information on Auilan culture. He continued to watch as she circled.

Suddenly Dah'Te tucked her wings and plummeted toward the medical center.

He and the workers ducked as she unfurled her wings at the last possible moment and veered away, landing lightly on a nearby stack of steel girders.

A pair of great brown-and-white wings trailed down her back. His gaze drifted over her body, noting the elongated bird-like feet and four-fingered human-like hands ending in short talons. Dark hair framed her round face. Sunlight cast her skin in warm gold. Tribal tattoos traced up her arms and legs, and adorned her chest beneath a short toga-like covering.

"Ronan." She gasped his name. Larger-than-human amber eyes focused on him. Small abrasions marred her limbs and face. A cut along her shoulder wept blood and clear fluids. "Need help."

"What's wrong?"

"Linse and I hunt." Her breathing was erratic, her movements jerky, her hands never straying far from the short broad-blade sword at her side. "Linse hurt."

For the normally articulate Auilan to speak in clipped sentences, he knew her younger brother had to be in trouble. He gathered his equipment and stowed it in the medikit. "Where is Linse now?"

She pointed to the forest along the eastern mountains.

"What happened?"

"Talehons attack."

The Azein and Talehon clans had been warring over territory for almost a year. Linse was young, only in his early teens, and for Dah'Te to risk leaving him to seek Ronan's aid, the kid had to be in really bad shape.

Ronan grabbed his medikit and hurried for the ladder. Concern for the downed Auilan temporarily overcame his anxiety as he maneuvered around the roof's yawning pits. He ignored the calls of the workers, shouldered his kit, uncoupled his safety line, and swung onto the ladder, foregoing the rungs and sliding down the rails.

As soon as his booted feet hit the dry ground, he sprinted for one of the nearby solar-rovers. Dah'Te landed a few yards away, stirring a dust cloud with her wings as he climbed into the vehicle's open cab.

"Flying faster," she said.

Visions of free-falling to his death through a cloudless blue sky invaded his mind. His stomach clenched and he shook his head. "We'll need the rover to bring Linse back here."

She hesitated for a moment and then clambered onto the flatbed cargo area. Holding the roll bar, she pointed to a trail that sloped steadily upward into the mountains. "That way."

The rover lurched forward and bounced over the construction site's uneven turf.

It was foolish to head into the forest with dusk approaching, and even more so to go in search of an injured alien. But if the Talehons found Linse, they would surely kill him.

Ronan and Dah'Te sped through the forest trails, passing through swathes of deep shadow where the canopy thickened. More light filtered through the thinning trees the further they drove from New Denver. After what seemed like hours, Dah'Te tapped his shoulder and pointed to a small clearing. Ronan slowed the rover.

Broken branches littered the ground and the clean scent of fresh sap filled the air. Downy white-and-brown feathers drifted on the breeze to settle in clumps among the bright orange and blue wildflowers.

He stopped the rover, powered down the motor, and picked up his medikit. As he stepped from the vehicle, he hesitated, unsure about bringing the small plasma gun hidden beneath the dash. His oath as a doctor to cause no harm warred with his desire to help Dah'Te's brother. Sighing, he released the locks, pulled the gun free, and strapped it to his thigh.

Dah'Te crouched by a tree's base and he joined her. "I left Linse here," she said, her speech improving now that she'd had time to calm down a bit. She gestured to a dark patch of bark. "He was bleeding and his wing was broken."

Ronan studied their surroundings. "He can't have gone far."

"Unless the Talehons took him," she muttered, and stood.

"Don't think like that."

She shrugged and moved away. Her wing brushed his arm and he shivered as a small jolt shocked his spine. "I'm being realistic, Ronan." She glanced skyward from the clumps of feathers on the ground, and back to the feather trail. "Talehon clan won't hesitate to kill a youngling like Linse."

He heard the hitch in her voice as she spoke. "Dah'Te," he said softly and grabbed her arm to stop her. Like all Auilans, she was petite, the top of her head barely reaching Ronan's shoulder. He stooped to face her squarely.

Tears glimmered in the corners of her wide eyes.

"We'll find him." He cupped her cheek. "I promise."

She stepped close and slipped her arms around his waist, resting her cheek against his chest. Her wings folded to encircle him in a double embrace. "You shouldn't make an oath you may not honor."

The thrumming beat of wings drew Ronan's attention to the treetops in time to see three male Auilans plunging toward them.

"Down!" He pitched himself to the ground, pulling Dah'Te along with him as the men soared overhead in a flurry of black-and-red wings.

Dah'Te sprang to her feet, drawing her sword, and launched into the air in pursuit of the Talehon clan attackers.

He scrambled to his feet, calling and running after her. He hurdled fallen trees and sidestepped debris piles where vipers often hid. Brambles tugged at his pants. Branches slapped his arms and chest and left stinging welts. Ground-covering roots snagged his feet and slowed his chase.

Sharp bird-like cries and the metallic ring of clashing swords ricocheted through the forest. Shifting shadows underneath the sprawling canopy cloaked the Auilans' dark wings, making it difficult to pinpoint their locations. The sound of rushing water soon reached Ronan as he followed the trail of broken branches and drifting feathers.

A thrashing ball of wings and limbs crashed into Ronan, knocking him off balance. He tumbled into a bramble patch, thorns raking and slicing his skin, as he slid down a steep incline. His shoulder clipped a boulder, spinning him into the base of a large tree, which prevented him from falling into the swift current of the river below.

Groaning, he sat, braced his back against the tree, and pulled free the plasma gun. He searched for signs of his assailants or Dah'Te.

A flash of red to his right. A call from the left.

His instincts screamed for him to run. He forced himself to remain still.

Silver glinted as a black-and-red-winged Talehon dropped to the ground in front of him, swinging a short sword at his head.

He ducked, twisting to land on his back as he raised the gun, and fired. A bolt of superheated plasma lit the forest and skimmed the Auilan's side before tearing through an outstretched wing. Feathers blazed. The Talehon shrieked and retreated in a trail of charred feathers and smoke.

Ronan needed to find Dah'Te. He pushed to his feet.

Another Talehon swooped into view.

Ronan fired and missed.

The Auilan barreled into him. Taloned hands ripped into his shirt to grip flesh. With a few powerful wingstrokes, they were airborne and gliding over the river.

Ronan's stomach dipped and his head spun as the Auilan rose steadily higher. He briefly registered that he still had the pulse gun. He didn't dare use it, however, as an image of his own broken and twisted body floating away on the river's current danced before him.

A quickly moving shadow darted over them. The Talehon grunted and dropped several feet as something slammed into his back.

Ronan cried out in pain as one of the Auilan's hands tore free. He caught a brief glimpse of Dah'Te on the Talehon's back, ripping at his wings, before the Auilan released his grip, and Ronan was free-falling.

The icy river water shocked his breath. The rapid current tore the plasma gun from his hand. He kicked for the surface and gasped a fresh air supply before the flow pulled him under. His body slammed painfully into submerged boulders. The heavy medikit on his back weighed him down. He shrugged out of it only to have it also ripped from his hands as the current tossed him into another boulder.

He struggled through the water, broke free, and managed to grab a low hanging branch. Holding onto it, he kicked against the powerful flow and inched toward the safety of the bank. He pulled himself on shore, gasping and coughing to clear his lungs of water. His entire body ached. His chest and shoulders were on fire where the Auilan's talons had slashed him open. Darkness clouded his sight.

"Dah'Te . . ."

Shivering from the cold, he collapsed and allowed the shadows to consume him.

Night nibbled at daylight as Dah'Te followed the river, searching from aloft for evidence of Ronan. She'd seen him fall into the swiftly moving water as she grappled with the Talehon clansman.

When the first attack came, she'd pursued the Talehons. They had soon separated, the largest one turning on her. The battle had been brief. He'd outmatched her in strength, but her smaller size allowed for quicker strikes. She'd left him sprawled and lifeless on the forest floor.

She'd seen a second Talehon carrying away Ronan and attacked from above. Seeking to damage his wings and force him to land, she'd accomplished her goal, but Ronan had been lost to the river. The third attacker had vanished.

Guilt stabbed at her. It had been her suggestion to take her younger brother Linse hunting. When he'd challenged her to an aerial race, she'd joyfully accepted. But she'd been careless and hadn't noticed that they'd strayed into the territory at the heart of the dispute between Azein and Talehon clans.

The Talehons had attacked without warning. She and Linse had fought them off, but not before Linse had taken a strong hit in his left wing. He'd been grounded, injured, and she had been forced to leave him to seek help.

That she had thought to go to the humans – to Ronan – instead of her own clan surprised her. She liked the human healer. He freely answered her questions and asked only for his own to be answered in return. But, again, her carelessness had demanded a price, and now Ronan was lost.

She banked and dropped lower to the water. Her eyesight adjusted quickly to the gloaming, but it would still be easy to miss Ronan as darkness obscured the landscape.

Movement in the water pulled her into a dive. An object bobbed along the surface, caught in an eddy between two boulders. She swooped low, snatched her target from the current, and glided to shore. The red-and-white markings blazed in the dying sunlight.

It was Ronan's pack.

She spread her wings and ran for a large boulder near the shore. Using it as a springboard, she launched into the air. Ronan's pack weighed her down, forcing her to stay low to the river. Wing tips skimmed the water's surface as they bent and flexed to keep her aloft.

Her eyes scanned the shoreline. Twice she thought she saw a human form only to find it was a downed tree or rock outcrop. A third such shadowy form appeared to her left. She veered toward it and hope blossomed as light from the newly risen twin moons highlighted a shock of blond hair.

She landed in a run. "Ronan!"

He groaned as she slid to a stop beside him.

Carefully she rolled him onto his back. Deep wounds marred his chest and shoulders from the Talehon's claws.

"Ronan." She cradled his face. "Wake up."

He moaned but didn't open his eyes.

Dah'Te ripped away the remains of his shirt to expose the wounds. She grabbed his pack and dumped its waterlogged contents on the ground. Searching through the devices and supplies, despair crept into her heart. She wasn't a skilled healer. The contents spread before her meant nothing to her untrained eyes.

But she had to try.

She forced herself to be calm. She'd seen Ronan use his healer's tools. She only needed to remember.

Picking up a cylindrical device, she examined it. She tapped its ends with a talon. It remained silent. Laying it aside, she picked up a strange wand-like instrument. She pressed a small button on its side. Blue light filled the wand.

Recognition slammed into her.

She held the wand over a small cut on her arm. The skin beneath warmed, tingled, and then stitched itself together. She smiled and moved the wand to the worst of Ronan's wounds on his chest.

Long minutes passed before the first signs of healing showed, and the blue light was dimming. The wound closed slowly. The light flickered once. Twice. Vanished.

Dah'Te grunted in frustration. She shook the wand and pressed the button. No light showed. She smacked it against her palm. The light didn't return.

Ronan's chest wound was mostly healed. It still had a jagged and raw look but it no longer bled. The gashes along his shoulder weren't as severe, but required cleaning if they were to heal on their own.

She tore the rest of his shirt into strips and washed them in the river. Using the damp cloth, she cleansed the shoulder wound as best she could and rummaged through the remaining supplies. She found a packet of ointment that stung her nose when she smelled it. She smeared a fingertip's amount onto one of her own cuts.

It burned and stung and made her gasp, but after a moment the pain dulled.

She applied the remainder to Ronan's shoulder and a little to his chest. Using white cloth squares and strips of his shirt, she covered and bound his wounds.

Dah'Te gathered the pack's contents and returned them to their home. She drew her knees to her chest and wrapped her wings around herself like a cloak, watching the steady rise and fall of Ronan's chest as he slept beside her.

Ronan was unlike any Auilan man she'd known. Tall and lean, with a muscular frame. Golden hair cut close to his skull. No tribal markings. No wings. Small dark eyes that couldn't see the same distance as hers could. Physical appearances aside, his easy smile and laughter lightened her.

Something stirred within her as the twin moons moved overhead in their immortal dance with the stars. She longed for that familiar lightness to find her, to comfort her. She traced the shape of his mouth with her finger. On impulse she leaned forward and briefly pressed her lips to his.

He sighed. "Dah'Te . . ."

She stretched out on the ground next to him. The exertions of the day had weakened her, and fear for her brother chilled her. She laid her head on Ronan's chest, mindful to stay clear of his wounds.

He stirred, wrapping his arms around her.

Stretching her wings over them both for warmth, Dah'Te lay in the darkness and listened to the sound of Ronan's breath for a long time before sleep finally pulled her into its embrace.

Ronan awoke to sunshine and splashing water. He lifted his upper body, resting on his elbows, and grimaced as his muscles protested at the movement. Pain spread from his right shoulder, across his chest to the left, and choked his breath. He forced himself to sit and was surprised to find his chest, shoulder, and ribs wrapped in what could only be the remnants of his shirt.

Confusion fogged his mind but soon cleared as the memory of being carried away by an Auilan surfaced. Blinking against the bright dawn light, he studied his surroundings.

He sat on the riverbank, sunlight glistening off the water as it tumbled over rocks in a miniature waterfall. His medikit lay next to him. He frowned. Hadn't he lost it in the river?

Searching the pack, he found one of the seals had been damaged and water had seeped inside. Most of the sterile first-aid supplies were still intact. The bio-scanner wasn't so fortunate. Water had corroded the circuits, making it a useless paperweight. The dermal regenerator seemed to work, but the charge was expended so it was nonfunctional as well. He sighed and closed the kit.

Once more the sound of splashing water called to him.

He stood and waited for the world to stop its insane spin. A breeze swayed the trees, and a flutter of white drew him toward the river. Reaching the shore, he picked up the flimsy white material the wind had knocked loose from a branch. The splashing water sounds ceased and he glanced to his right.

Dah'Te stood in the river's shallows, the supple curve of her buttocks visible beneath the water. His eyes tracked the gentle curve of her spine upward to where her wings melded with flesh, and across her shoulders to the profiled swell of her bare breasts hidden by her arms. Her spiraling tattoos flowed with the contours of her muscles.

His gaze locked with hers. Heat rushed his face.

"You're staring," she said.

He dropped his gaze, trying to ignore the growing physical response of his body. "Sorry," he murmured, balling the thin fabric of her toga in his hands. "I didn't know you were, uh – didn't know you were bathing – were *here*."

Water sloshed.

He glanced at her in time to see her uncovered breasts as her wings folded around her like a cloak. "I should go," he said in a rush, and spun away.

"Ronan?"

He paused, back stiff, and body on fire with the urge to join her in the shallows.

"You have my clothes." Amusement made her musical voice sound all the more lyrical.

He whispered a curse and tightened his grip on the fabric. His head and body warred. He was a doctor. He'd seen naked people. Seeing Dah'Te shouldn't be any different from viewing a patient.

And yet he froze when he tried to face her.

A gentle touch on his back prickled his flesh and stuttered his breath.

Dah'Te traced the edge of his shoulder bandage as she moved to stand before him. "Your arm?"

He kept his eyes averted. "No pain."

Her other hand slipped up his opposite arm to rest on the second bandage. "Your chest?"

An ache pulsed under her touch. He met her gaze. "Hurts."

Worry knitted her brow. "The wound?"

He dropped the wad of fabric he held to cup her chin. "My heart," he whispered, and captured her lips with his own.

She opened to him. He reveled in her softness. Feathers trailed over his bare back as her wings caught him in an Auilan embrace. His arms snaked around her waist and drew her to him.

But it wasn't close enough.

Soon Ronan lay on his back with Dah'Te astride his hips as he moved inside her. Her soft moans spurred his rhythm. Sunlight silhouetted her wide-spread wings and lit her upturned face as her back bowed in ecstasy. Her climax shattered him and left him spent and trembling in her arms.

It took the better part of the morning for them to make their way back to the solar-rover. Dah'Te had argued that flying would be faster, but Ronan was adamant that his feet would remain on the ground. She didn't understand his fear of high places, but she accepted it. Staying grounded for too long made her anxious as well.

She glanced at Ronan's bare back as he bent over to check the rover's instruments. He muttered and fiddled with controls. Her gaze shifted downward to his buttocks and legs. Her mind drifted to their lovemaking and the excitement she'd felt when she'd discovered the strength hidden beneath his tender mannerisms. He hadn't left her wanting.

And yet, once they left the seclusion of their riverside camp, guilt had taken root in her mind. The closer she and Ronan had drawn to the place where she'd left her brother, the more that guilt had weighed on her, until she'd felt it would break her.

She forced herself to turn away and scan the skies for Talehon scouts. Two of the three who attacked them yesterday could've returned to their clan for reinforcements. She and Ronan would be outnumbered. Ronan and Linse, if he were found, would be killed. A kindness compared to her fate. If captured, her wings would be clipped and she would be made an amusement for Talehon warriors.

Dah'Te shuddered, her wings bristling. She wanted to find Linse and return to Azein clan territory. She rested an uneasy hand on the hilt of her sword. It was their only defense. Ronan had lost his weapon to the river.

Again her mind wandered and she silently chastised herself. She shouldn't have paired with Ronan. Not while Linse was still missing. What if the Talehons discovered her brother? He was a youngling, only ten and four winters, and no match for a Talehon warrior. Linse was her responsibility, and she'd forsaken him.

The solar-rover whirred to life behind her. Their plan was for Dah'Te to search for Linse from above while Ronan followed with the rover. They would need it to transport Linse back to New Denver colony for proper treatment.

Ronan's hand brushed her shoulder. "Are you ready?"

She met his gaze and nodded, unsure of her voice.

"The canopy here is too thick, so the rover doesn't have a full charge. Fly low and slow and I'll do my best to keep up."

She nodded again.

He gently kissed her lips.

She backed away.

He let her go.

Dah'Te spread her wings and jumped into the air. Her wings beat against the breeze, lifting her higher until she broke through the treetops. A quick survey of the landscape showed no signs of Talehon scouts. She dropped below the canopy and circled the area where she'd left Linse.

From above she could see the subtle signs of his passing. Disturbed brush. Dropped feathers. She followed the trail as it led away from the river and further up the mountainside. Occasionally she spiraled above the trees, checking for Talehons, but saw none.

Their absence should have allowed her to focus on the task of finding her brother. Instead, dread knotted her stomach. Urgency pushed her to fly faster, distancing herself from Ronan and the solar-rover.

She circled a dense thicket and her heart leapt as she spotted a flash of white near its border. Swooping low, she skimmed its edge and landed, sword at the ready. Peering into the shadows, she crept closer. "Linse?"

The drone of the rover's distant approach answered.

Dah'Te moved into the densely packed copse. Branches and vines tugged at her wings, making her wince and start. "Linse," she called again.

Shadows flashed white to her left.

She spun, bringing her sword to bear.

"Dah'Te!"

She halted her strike and stared into a grime-streaked and frightened face. "Linse," she breathed her brother's name.

He lay on the ground half-concealed by fallen leaves, in an obvious attempt to camouflage his presence. He shifted and grimaced as one wing shuddered, trailing useless at his side.

She dropped the sword as tears fell unbidden from her eyes. Kneeling, she pulled him into a tight embrace.

He buried his face in the hollow space between her neck and shoulder and sobbed. "I thought you'd forgotten about me."

"Never," she whispered. Her wings folded protectively around his trembling body.

"Talehons." He hiccupped. "Tracked me." He drew back. "Thought they would kill me." New tears spilled from his large yellow eyes.

She cradled his young face. "I'm so very sorry, Linse."

Beyond the thicket, the sound of the solar-rover intensified, slowed, and stopped. "Dah'Te!" Ronan called.

Linse jerked and his face paled. "Who is that?"

"Ronan," she answered, and stooped to gather her sword.

"The human healer?"

"Yes." She slipped her arm around his waist and slung his arm over her shoulder. Bearing most of his weight, she lifted and guided him through the thicket.

"Why did you go to the humans?"

She glanced at her brother. "Their colony is closer."

"No, it isn't."

Heat blossomed in her cheeks.

They broke from the thicket, and Ronan rushed to meet them. Moving carefully, the trio navigated the uneven terrain and settled Linse into the rover's cargo area. Dah'Te stayed close as Ronan examined the young Auilan. He was gentle in his handling of Linse. He asked brief questions and apologized if the young Auilan showed signs of pain or discomfort.

"The wing is definitely broken," Ronan announced. "Here." He indicated the long bone between the first joint and where the wing melded with Linse's back.

"How badly?" Dah'Te asked.

"Hard to say without a scanner, but there aren't any protruding bones. That's good. But I can feel it shifting, so it's more than a fracture."

Sweat slicked Linse's face and dampened his hair. His face was paler now than when Dah'Te had found him. His eyes were slits and his breathing ragged.

"I admit wings aren't my specialty," Ronan said, leveling his dark gaze on her. "But I know it needs to be stabilized."

Dah'Te knew what he meant and nodded. "Set the bone. Bind the wing. I'll keep him quiet."

While Ronan rummaged through his pack for suitable bindings, Dah'Te crouched beside Linse, gently stroking his cheek.

His eyelids fluttered, opened, but he seemed to have trouble focusing on her.

"Ronan is going to bind your wing," she explained. "Once we reach the human settlement, he can repair it."

Linse grunted and reached out his hand. She clasped it in both of hers.

He flinched as Ronan again touched his damaged wing.

She looked to Ronan.

He nodded, and twisted and pulled the wing.

Linse shrieked.

She did her best to keep Linse still as Ronan worked to align the fragile, hollow bones. She cooed, stroked her brother's cheek and hair, and wept. His cries lessened and were finally silenced when he slipped into unconsciousness. She continued to speak to him softly, apologizing, promising to take away his pain – saying anything to alleviate her own sense of guilt.

Ronan worked quickly to set the bone and immobilize the wing in a makeshift sling. He didn't believe the break was as damaging as it could've been, but infection was a concern. He was also worried that Linse was showing the first stages of shock. If they didn't reach New Denver soon, the injuries could prove deadly.

He tied the final support for the sling and knelt beside Dah'Te. His voice was soft as he spoke her name, his hands gentle as he covered hers.

She looked at him, tears tracking over her reddened cheeks as soon as they welled.

"I've done everything I can for Linse. We need to get him to New Denver."

She sniffled.

"I'll drive the rover and go slow so as not to jar him too much. I need you to fly ahead of us, direct me to the shortest but smoothest path. Do you understand?"

She nodded and moved into his arms.

He held her tightly, letting her melt into his embrace and absorb the warmth and comfort she needed. He wished he could reverse the sun and recapture their time beside the river. But that moment was gone, and they needed to focus on Linse.

Dah'Te seemed to sense his thoughts and pulled back, wiping her face and eyes to clear them.

He hopped down from the cargo bed and waited as she quickly kissed her brother's cheek and whispered in his ear.

"Remember, shortest and smoothest route," Ronan said when she rejoined him.

"I remember." As she prepared to take flight, a call sounded to their left. Another call from the right answered the first, followed by another. And another. And another.

"Talehons," Dah'Te whispered, her eyes widening.

"And we're surrounded."

She drew her sword and her wings bristled. Facing the forest, she dropped into a crouch.

Fear gripped Ronan and he grabbed her sword arm. "What are you doing?"

"Get Linse to your colony. Keep him safe."

"What? No! This is suicide."

"We don't have an option," she said, glaring at him.

"We could try reasoning with them."

She scoffed. "Talehons are brutes. They won't hesitate to kill you or Linse. Males have no value as prisoners or slaves."

"And females do?"

Her gaze shifted to the trees. She didn't answer, but he felt the tremor that shook her petite frame.

Anger flashed through Ronan. "You can't fight them all."

"Do you have a weapon? No, you don't."

"I will *not* let you sacrifice yourself."

She rounded on him. "*You* are the healer, Ronan. Linse needs *you*, not me."

"*I* need you, Dah'Te."

She stared at him in stunned silence.

"I can't lose you," he whispered. "There has to be another way."

Another series of calls rose from the forest. The Talehons were closing.

"The rover," Ronan said. "We can use it."

"It's too slow. It'll never outrun the Talehons."

"It doesn't have to outrun them. They'll be expecting us to use it for Linse. If I drive it toward the river, maybe they'll follow."

"What about Linse?"

A rueful smile tugged at his lips. "You're always saying flying is faster. You can take him to New Denver."

"So you'll sacrifice yourself instead?" She shook her head. "No."

"Dah'Te, we don't have time to argue."

"You're right. We don't." She lunged forward, wrapped him in a tight Auilan embrace, and kissed him.

Startled, his brain was still processing her kiss when she broke away.

"I'll find you. I promise," she whispered and launched into the air.

He reached for her but her wings had already carried her into the canopy. "Dah'Te!"

His shout was lost as she issued a long piercing shriek and zipped among the trees. He saw flashes of silver, cries rose in response, and black-winged shadows chased after retreating white-and-brown wings.

"You'd better," he whispered.

Dah'Te darted through the trees, using her smaller size to her advantage. She banked, turned, swooped, and pushed through tight gaps her pursuers were forced to circle. It pained her to leave Ronan and Linse, but drawing away the Talehons was truly the only way to save them.

A large Auilan dropped into view. His sword caught the light as he hurtled for her.

She met his charge. Their blades clashed, jarring her arms. He grabbed for her throat. She kicked away and pumped her wings, heading higher into the canopy.

Another Talehon glided toward her from above.

She folded her wings and dove for the ground.

The two clansmen weren't as nimble as she and collided, twisting and tumbling in a jumble of wings.

Dah'Te unfurled her wings, pulled out of the dive, and kicked off a large tree to change her direction and again propel herself into the canopy. Her back and shoulders were on fire from the exertion of flying, but she had to keep going.

A body slammed into her and spun her into a tree. The Talehon pinned her shoulder to the trunk with a taloned hand.

She cried out as the blow numbed the whole of her right arm. Her sword fell from her loosened grip.

The edge of the Talehon's blade pressed to her neck. He leered at her. "I'm going to enjoy plucking your wings, little one."

"Pluck this," she growled, and slashed her talons across his stomach. She felt the blade bite into her skin as he screeched. Pushing with all her strength, she shoved him back and pulled her wings in tight to her body. He recovered and swung the sword, but she'd already dropped like dead weight.

Dah'Te opened her wings and twisted, digging her talons into the trunk to slow her descent. She kicked away from the tree, bounced off another, glided to a third, and continued to bounce and glide until she'd regained enough altitude.

Her pursuer remained at her heels, and three more joined the chase.

While the confines of the forest gave her smaller size an advantage, it also required more physical strength. She'd lost her weapon, and she was tiring. She only had one option.

Sunlight momentarily blinded her as she broke through the trees. With the river glistening below her, Dah'Te led the Talehons in an open-air sprint for the mountains.

The solar-rover rattled over the uneven terrain, dipped into a hollow space, and threatened to overturn. Ronan risked a quick glance to the cargo bed.

Linse groaned but otherwise remained motionless.

Ronan had taken the precaution of using the rover's cargo straps to help secure the injured Auilan for the harrowing ride down the mountainside. The rover had been so slow on the incline that he hadn't fully considered the effects of a downward slope and momentum. The result was a significant increase in speed that would see them arriving in New Denver well ahead of the time he'd anticipated.

The rover bounced over a small rocky patch and skidded sideways into a log. He steered it through the skid and plowed forward.

They'd arrive all right, if his driving didn't kill them first, he thought.

A couple near-collisions with trees, several hard bounces, and a miniature rockslide later, the ground leveled out, and Ronan began to see familiar signs. He found the trail over which he and Dah'Te had traveled the day before, and as the trees thinned the rover gained speed.

He burst from the treeline, frightening several colonists working a garden plot. He wove through the settlement, gradually reducing speed, until he reached the medical center. The rover stopped in a billowing cloud of dust.

Several men who were working on the construction of the center's expansion called to him as he jumped from the rover.

"I've got an injured Auilan here," he said, ignoring their questions about where he'd been. He unbuckled the cargo straps securing Linse. "Help me get him inside."

No one moved, uncertainty evident on their faces.

"Now!"

Two men hurried forward, and under Ronan's direction they carried Linse into the medical center. Once they'd placed the youth in an exam room, Ronan started pulling supplies from cabinets and prepped a medical scanner.

"Hey, Doc," one of the men said.

Annoyed, Ronan looked up from his scanner.

"Yesterday, didn't you leave with that budgie girl? Ditty?"

He recognized the thin pink scar over the man's brow. Through clenched teeth, he said, "Her name is Dah'Te."

"Is she coming back?"

Hollowness threatened to steal his breath and cripple his mind. Glancing out the exam room's window toward the mountains, he whispered, "I wish I knew."

Dusk elongated and twisted the shadows outside the medical center into macabre caricatures of their original shapes. But Ronan only had eyes for the mountains as he sat on the center's roof, feet dangling over the edge. The usual dread he felt of heights had been replaced by a new terror: the fear of an empty sky.

Dah'Te hadn't returned. Worry screamed for him to search for her. Indecision froze him. He wanted to go back to the river, but he couldn't leave Linse yet. Infection had already begun to set into the damaged wing. While Ronan had repaired the break and started an antibiotic regime, the treatment required supervision for the first twenty-four hours to avoid reinjuring the wing.

He sighed and closed his eyes.

Dah'Te waited for him in the darkness. The memory of seeing her in the river's shallows haunted him. Every breeze was like the ghost of her touch.

He opened his eyes, focusing once more on the mountains.

The dying sun's light washed the snowcaps in pink, the treetops in gold, and illuminated a single darkly winged figure as it glided toward New Denver.

He stood, squinting to see the wing patterns. He tensed as it drew closer and banked to the right, heading straight for the medical center.

White-and-brown wings caught the final rays of the sun.

Ronan's heart soared as Dah'Te landed on the roof in a sprint. She leapt into his arms, wrapping him in an Auilan double embrace, and kissing him as though they'd been parted for years instead of hours.

When he finally pulled back, breathless, his elation was tarnished by the obvious bruising on her neck and the shallow cut and bandages. He gently probed the cut on her neck. Anger choked his voice. "The Talehons?"

"I told you they were brutes." She offered a wan smile. "But four brutes are no match for the entire Azein clan."

He grinned. "You led them to your clan?"

She nodded.

His mirth was shortlived, as thoughts of how they had parted clouded his mind. "Dah'Te, I—"

She pressed a fingertip to his lips. "It doesn't matter, Ronan. I'm here, just as I promised."

He crushed her against him and kissed her. When they broke, he cupped her cheek and she leaned into it, closing her eyes.

Suddenly she gasped and tensed. "Linse! Is he—"

"He's fine. Resting. I fixed the break. He had a minor infection that should clear up in a few days, but he'll need to stay in New Denver until he's well enough."

Her wings stroked his back. "What will we do until then?"

Ronan tightened his hold on her waist. "I know a great little campsite by the river . . ."

Star Crossed

Cathy Clamp

One

"There's a good chance you won't survive this mission." Navigator Rand Miflin heard the words and struggled not to roll his eyes or snort at Commander Berell.

He leaned back in a chair not meant for comfort. "When have I *ever* been expected to survive? The Stovians are out for blood."

Berell gave a little shrug and stood up against the backdrop of curtains carefully drawn to conceal a ravaged landscape. There was no denying the truth, but it was still hard to look at. Rand continued. "Earth is the first 'backward' planet that ever returned fire against them. We pissed them off."

And the emperor of the planet Stovia had responded with overwhelming force – wave after wave of troops and weapons that had turned every other conquered planet into a quivering mass of easily sold slaves. But Earthlings had learned far too quickly for the Great Leader's taste, thanks to captured technology.

Earth was on the verge of winning. It had been nearly a full month since humans had seen diron blasts redden the atmosphere.

"True, but this is different," Berell said. "The starfighter team taking on this job is going straight into the maw of the monster."

Rand felt his heart speed up a little, and he leaned forward. He wasn't sure if it was excitement or fear, but he'd lost the ability to separate the two reactions long ago. "You have my attention."

Berell paced the length of his office, hands clasped behind his back. "We need a navigator who can . . . think on his feet, Miflin. Steer the ship through unknown obstacles in a foreign, hostile environment." He paused for effect. "The ship will be striking a target in the center of Asort, the capital city of Stovia."

"That . . . wow." Rand tried to come up with a response that would let his dropped jaw do something useful. "That's going to take one hell of a pilot." Could he navigate it? Yeah, probably. But no pilot he'd ever met would be able to follow his instructions quick enough to keep them both from getting very dead, very fast.

Berell smiled. "I don't think that will be a problem. If you accept the assignment, your pilot will be E. L. Tyler."

As if on cue, the door opened. The short, broad man who entered wore a full zero-g suit, including a laser and a bullet-scarred face shield that hid his features. The helmet alone spoke of firefights most pilots could only imagine. Rand felt a rush of fear flow through him. Captain El Tyler was a legend. And not just a run-of-the-mill hometown legend, but a freaking *galactic* legend. Everyone from schoolkids to five-star generals spoke of him in hushed, reverent tones, like those reserved for dead presidents on old paper money, hall-of-fame rock stars and five-time winners of the Super Bowl. He'd been the primary sty in the emperor's eye for twenty-plus years. One-on-one starship dogfights, five to one, ten to one. He'd taken every job and had come back. Not always with a ship, and not always untouched, but never on his shield. Not only had Rand never met El Tyler, he'd never actually met anyone who *had* met him. Wow.

Rand stood in a rush, nearly knocking over the small table next to his chair. He held out his hand and stammered a greeting. "Captain Tyler. Wow. What an honor, sir." Then, to his great embarrassment, words just started coming out in a rush and he couldn't seem to stop. "I am such a huge fan! I've read stories of nearly every battle you've fought. The Venusian ring conflict, the Pluto stronghold attacks, and even that chase through the Sirian asteroid belt last month. That was *amazing*! I even dug up why everyone calls you 'El' instead of E. L. It's just such an *honor*."

And through it all, while he gushed his praise and held out his offering hand, Tyler just stood there, palms on hips, not even acknowledging his existence. Finally, after a long moment, Rand dropped his hand, feeling both like a fool and a chastised child.

The gravelly, metallic voice from behind the blast-shield cut Rand to the bone. "I don't know what you were thinking, Commander. I can't possibly fly with Miflin."

As Rand was about to open his mouth to protest the slur to his skills, Commander Berell growled what sounded suspiciously like an order. "You can and *will*, El. Miflin's the best, and you damned well know it. Don't make me pull rank."

"He was a smuggler, Walter – for sale to the highest bidder. He can't be trusted."

Rand felt his cheeks grow hot. But he couldn't deny his past. It had certainly been thrown in his face enough times. "That's behind me now. I'm in this for the long haul. I'm loyal to the Terran rebellion."

Now Tyler turned that shield to stare blankly at him. Rand could see his own head reflected in the mirrored surface. His face was a mix of emotions: angry, embarrassed, betrayed by a childhood hero; a thousand things. He adjusted his muscles until the expression that stared back in the reflection was calm and cold. But the words from behind the helmet quickly twisted them again. "For how long, Miflin? You've been *loyal* for what – six months now? I have stains in my coffee mug older than that."

"People change, El." Berell's voice was soft but matter-of-fact. "You did. I think it's time to show him how much. I'll vouch for him."

That made Rand's brows rise. *How had El "changed"?* He thought he knew everything about El Tyler's past. Perfect student, jet-fighter pilot in the last war between two minor Middle Eastern countries – back when there were only Americans, French, Greek, Iranians and other nationalities. Before the Stovians. Before the *real* world war began. But he'd never heard even a hint about any sort of shady past. There was nothing to change there, that he'd heard of.

"If one single word of this gets out, Miflin—" Tyler reached up and touched a spot on his helmet Rand hadn't noticed before. The voice behind the shield suddenly altered. It became higher-pitched, lighter. "Well, let's say nobody who matters will ever fly with you again . . ."

As Rand watched in amazement, the hands reached up and pulled off the helmet. Then Rand's mouth gaped so wide he could feel air on the back of his tongue. Blonde hair, the color of a sunflower, flowed down and down, past a heart-shaped jaw and a slender neck, to the heavy armor of a suit that he now realized obviously didn't fit a woman's slender frame. Worse, it wasn't just any woman. Officer Ellen Grayson was the cop who'd finally caught him and put him in jail. A cop, by the way, who had worked *for* the Stovians, after they'd taken over, before the rebellion started.

It couldn't be. The great Captain Tyler . . . a *woman*? No. There was no way El Tyler could be the same person as this cop. "You're *not* El Tyler." And he could prove it. Before he realized it, he was five steps forward, sticking a finger in her face. To her credit, she didn't flinch. "You were a beat cop, flying patrols, when the *real* Captain Tyler was running raids on the Stovians' moon base. You're the same age as me – too young to have been the pilot at the Pluto armory attack." Also too gorgeous. Damn, she had looked good in her tight black planetary police uniform. The shapeless mess she had on now wasn't worthy of that figure.

Her voice was calm when she responded. "Like the commander said . . . people change. Sometimes legends have to change, too." He wasn't sure how to take that comment, and neither she nor Berell elaborated. She paused and then accepted a glass of water the commander was holding out. "But you can be sure that I *am* El Tyler. I did fly in the Sirian asteroid battle and I kicked butt. And I am the best damned pilot you're ever likely to meet." She drank the water slowly, giving him time to think.

Did he trust her? No. But Berell did. And as much as he hated to admit it, she *was* the only one who had ever managed to catch him. If he had anyone to thank for being in the resistance, it was her.

Damn it.

"Fine. I'll do it. Just tell me where and when to be."

Commander Berell gave him a short nod and held out his hand to shake Rand's. Grayson, aka Tyler, didn't say a word. But he could swear he saw her smile before she put the helmet back over her face.

Two

Why had she agreed to this? Every warning signal in her head, plus several more scattered through her body, told her it was a bad idea. Yet here she was, squished less than a foot away from the most danger- ous man she'd ever met.

"Cozy, huh?" Rand Miflin whispered inches from her ear. The rush of warm air against her skin made her shiver. "Been waiting to get this close to you for a long time."

She didn't respond. Couldn't. After a long pause, he changed tack to try humor. "Should we have mentioned to the supply sergeant we're more than four feet tall?"

A safe topic. Good. El likewise kept her voice low enough not to be heard by any passing sound-detectors. The words came out in a gravelly baritone. "I know it's uncomfortable. But making the run in a Jupiter Javelin is the only chance we have to get close enough to Stovia for this to work."

Miflin grunted and struggled to extend his leg into a space not meant for a six-foot male. "Yeah, yeah. I read the briefing too. It's the only ship small enough to fit into the hold of the grain transport that makes regular runs to the planet. It's dense enough from the heavy metals that it'll look like an asteroid on scanners. But I *do* actually need to have feeling in my feet and hands in order to operate the equipment." He unlatched his restraints and crawled clumsily out of his seat. "I'm going to wiggle back to what's considered the lavatory on this heap. Don't . . . *wander off* while I'm gone." He chuckled at his own joke while El rolled her eyes.

As soon as he disappeared through the tiny doorway, she was able to take her first deep breath in the last hour. She hadn't dared to breathe normally while Rand was in the cockpit. That cologne he wore affected her just as badly as it had when she'd first met him. The vital-sign monitors would pick up her racing heart if she wasn't careful. She wished she could have lied and told him the Stovians had "human sniffers", so he couldn't wear the subtle, musky fragrance.

How in the hell was she going to concentrate on this mission if she couldn't think when he was close to her?

She raised her arms slightly, bumping the propulsion-indicator readout. A sigh escaped her. It wasn't just Rand's presence that was bothering her. The whole mission was risky, and probably suicide. It was better if she didn't dwell on it. She had to think positive. *I can do this. It's only two days. I just need to concentrate on the details. It's a critical job.* And it really was. The fate of Earth and every colony in the solar system hung in the balance.

She looked up automatically when a tone sounded above her. Miflin crawled through the doorway just as the transport's captain came over the com. "Captain Tyler? We just entered the wormhole. You'll have about five hours to stretch, talk and get something to eat before we enter the Polaris system. You're free to turn on the signal jammer. I'd rather not hear the details about why you're here. Bridge out."

"Well, at least he's honest." Rand shrugged one shoulder as best he could, and started to crawl backwards. "Let's get out of here into the main hold."

El pressed a button on the console before taking off her helmet and crawling out of her seat. One foot was completely numb. Even the pressure suits weren't enough to keep the blood flowing to all her limbs. At least Javelins had the advantage of mostly using hand controls. The only problem would be if they crashed. After a dozen more hours in the cockpit she didn't know if she'd be able to walk away. A beep sounded, indicating the signal jammer had finished its search of all available wavelengths, and had implemented a countersignal. They could now talk without being overheard.

She stepped down the gangplank to the overwhelming smell of wheat. When they'd arrived on the transport she'd closed her eyes and imagined she was back in Kansas, standing in her father's wheat field right at harvest. There was nothing quite like the scent of fresh-cut wheat. Her father had told her stories about wheat grown under blue skies and sunshine, instead of underground in hermetically controlled hydroponic farms housed in towering salt caverns. Maybe one day she'd have her own farm. Once the planet belonged to the humans again.

"You've got your eyes closed again. Thinking about a better place to be?" She opened them. Rand was sprawled on a beach lounger, eating a steaming ration of what smelled like beef stew.

"This bubble makes me nervous. There's more than a hundred tons of wheat surrounding us, held back by nothing but a thin sheet of plastic. One nick and we could be crushed." El shivered.

He looked up and around and then shrugged. "Then I wouldn't run with scissors." She felt her frown deepen when he smiled broadly; that damned infectious smile. He motioned to another antique metal-and-fabric lounger, folded up and leaning against the Javelin. "Pull up a chair and have some dinner. You got the Chicken à la King, and you'll be happy to know that no chickens were harmed in the making of the dish. Yum."

He really had pulled out a ration and started the heater inside. But as hungry as she was, she couldn't help but distrust him.

He noticed her staring with suspicion at the innocuous brown bag, and let out a small noise. "No, I didn't poison it. I'll trade if it'll make you happier."

She stared him down for a long moment. "Yeah, actually, it would." She held out her hand for the beef stew. "I'll take yours."

It took him aback. His sapphire-blue eyes showed honest shock. "Wow. You really *don't* trust me. I thought you were just objecting to the commander because you were afraid of being alone with me. You know, the whole sexual thing we've got going on."

She felt her face settle into a sneer and couldn't seem to stop it. "What *thing*? Why in the world would I be afraid of you? Besides your obvious odors, that is. I really don't trust you." It was such a reflex to deny it. She'd done it the last time they'd met, too.

What was wrong with admitting she was attracted? But no. There were too many good reasons not to get involved with someone like Rand Miflin. He was a criminal. There was no getting around that he didn't think the rules applied to him. People like him didn't change their basic nature. Sure, he was charismatic, and he even might believe he was being loyal, but there had to be something in this for him, and that made him dangerous. "Now, are you going to give me the stew, or do you want to admit you're trying to sabotage this mission?"

He shook his head and straddled the lounger. "From making you dinner to a Stovian saboteur in less than a minute. Screw this." Dumping the plastimetal fork into the bag, he tossed the meal at her hard. She barely managed to avoid wearing the stew, but tried to school her features so that she didn't look as embarrassed as she felt. He stood up and stalked to the top of the gangplank.

"Don't you want the chicken?" She didn't move from where she stood. She wasn't positive he was above punching her.

"Why would I? It's poisoned, right? I'm going to go inside and try to get some sleep. Shame there's only room for one to do that without using a zero-g bag. You can stay out here with the wheat." Before she could react, he pushed the code in the wall and the door slammed shut.

Terrific. Just her, a half-container of stew and a hundred tons of wheat. The moment she thought it, the transport made a course correction. The bubble bulged on one side and the top pressed inward until it was nearly touching the ship. *Oh, not good.*

But there was no way she was going to give in to her fear. The ship would actually withstand the weight of the wheat. It was the lack of air that would kill them if the bubble broke. She opened the one-way vents on her suit that sucked in oxygen to special bladder compartments. If the bubble failed, she'd at least have a day's worth of air to give the crew time to dig her out.

El moved the lounger until it was underneath the turanium gangplank, and pulled from a leg pocket the ancient device with the mission details. It would take forever to load. She took a bite of beef stew and grimaced. Probably no cows were harmed either.

A flash of credits appeared on the screen, a melding of a hundred long-defunct company logos in miniature, merged into one larger logo. *Who would have thought old analog technology would completely befuddle the best encryption breakers of the Stovian high command?* Bits and bytes, competing proprietary codes – hiding things in plain sight. It had been brilliant of the resistance to teach pilots a slew of early proprietary computer language. Xerox, Savin, Altos, Silex and a dozen others. Sort of like twentieth-century pilots learning Morse code.

She was going over the known maps of Stovia for the tenth time when she heard the door above her whoosh open and heavy boots take a few steps. "You really going to stay out here the whole time? I figured you'd be banging on the door to come in long before now."

El turned off the viewing pad and crawled out from under the gangplank to stretch. "You figured wrong. I need to learn these maps backward and forward in the time we've got. It doesn't matter whether that happens inside or outside the ship."

That seemed to interest him. "So you weren't scared? Not worried you'd be suffocated by the wheat?"

She couldn't help but shrug as she dragged the lounger out from underneath the plank and folded it. "Every second of every day I might die. Why be more scared of one thing over another? I took the precautions I could." When Rand raised his brows, seeming to question her, she elaborated. "Being under the gang-plank would give me a few seconds of shelter to put in my breathing tube and turn on my distress beacon. I've already stored up about a day's worth of air in the suit, which also gives me some crush protection. That's as good a chance as I'd have in the ship."

He was leaning against the doorway, just watching. She could feel his eyes on her, looking her up and down. It was as though his gaze was hands, flowing over her skin, making her shiver. Finally she couldn't stand it anymore and glanced at him. He pursed his lips and nodded. "Clever. I wondered what the suit was about – other than to hide your figure. Pity. It's a hell of a figure."

Had he ever noticed her figure? She honestly couldn't remember him ever commenting on it. She'd sure noticed his. Broad shoulders, narrow waist and oh, those sultry blue eyes and those dimples. Mmm-mmm. "I could say the same."

He froze and so did she. *Crap! Had she really said that out loud? Eek!* There was a long pause where neither said anything. Finally, she needed to break the silence . . . with something safe. "Part of the suit's bulk is the KevSix breastplate. Disrupts nearly every ranged weapon on the market – including the Stovian pulse rifles."

His voice was flat when he responded. "KevSix has only been on the market for about a year."

She sighed. Even though he'd dropped the subject in Berell's office, that discussion wasn't over. "Two for me. I've been the guinea pig. After all, whose rifle sight am I *not* in?"

There wasn't any way for him not to acknowledge that point, so he did with a slightly reluctant tip of his head. But then he dropped the bomb. "Rifle sights for a few years, sure. But *twenty*?"

She opened her mouth but was saved from responding when the captain of the transport announced, "We're about to come out of the hole. Two minutes to all quiet. Five minutes to launch."

It didn't give them much time. At least it was obvious Rand had done his homework too. He grabbed the loungers that El passed him and stowed them quickly and efficiently. There was economy of motion as he waved her inside the ship – not out of courtesy but because she had to be seated in order for him to get into his part of the cockpit.

She turned on the air scrubber first. If there were any error signals, the whole trip was off. There was no way they'd have enough air to make it to the return ship without the recirc filters working. After a long moment where both of them held their breaths, green light filled the tiny space. Her butterflies settled just a bit.

Now it was time to figure out whether they could save the human race.

Three

Did she have the right stuff to pull off this mission? Rand didn't know. Admittedly, Grayson had surprised him by staying cool under fire when he'd locked her out of the ship. But she shouldn't have admitted a weakness. It had almost been as though she was *asking* him to test her. Or had she expected it? Had she lied about her fear of being crushed? She didn't seem particularly upset. Was she playing him?

I just can't tell. And that bugged the crap out of him. It also bothered him that he couldn't find any evidence that she *wasn't* El Tyler. He had checked every record the night before they left, asked everyone he knew without actually mentioning Grayson's name. But while everybody *presumed* Tyler was male, nobody had ever officially seen the pilot without a helmet. "Like it's glued on," said his best source when he'd asked if Tyler's face had ever been seen. "Never outside the Joint Chiefs chamber, and maybe not in there either," the head of the Captain Tyler fan club claimed. *Asking her would do no good. He'd already made the accusation and she'd insisted she was the man himself. Worse, Berell had insisted it too, and he respected the hell out of Berell.*

So, fine. There were ways to learn the identity of a pilot. There were certain flying techniques that nobody had ever mastered as well as Tyler. He just had to figure out a way to force her into the maneuvers.

The add-on timer glued to the panel a scant meter from his nose flickered on and started the silent countdown from a hundred seconds as they plugged their grav suits into the vital sign monitors and adjusted the visual feeds into their helmets. When it reached zero, the lower hold doors opened and they fell into black, unforgiving space, where no human fighter ship had ever been. As they floated in the wake of the gravity fields of four planets, he watched as the grain ship's bay doors closed. The moment they latched, he knew the captain had pulled a level to release the air from the bubble. The wheat had probably already collapsed into the space where they'd been, leaving no evidence of their presence in the hold but a plastic floor liner that wouldn't be looked at twice when they offloaded.

There was no going back.

Well, at least not until they met up with the ship again on the return trip . . . if they lived that long.

He held his breath as the passive scanners pulled in signals from ships of all sizes as they brought supplies to the starving Stovian people. The war with Earth had taxed resources probably more than the emperor would like. Rumors had begun that food was being rationed on Stovia for the first time in the home planet's history.

A green light signaled the all-clear and they could speak again. He raised the face shield and his eyes adjusted to the darker space of the cabin. "Okay, so what's the plan?" He turned his head and still whispered just because it was habit. "We've got enough fuel for about fifteen hours." When he breathed in again, he caught a whiff of shampoo and sweat from the heavy helmet.

Grayson likewise raised her face shield, so her voice was back to a pleasant alto. "From the maps I've reviewed, take a course of 190.818 at sixteen degrees for about three hours. I'll be using the grav fields to steer as much as I can. That way we can save fuel and also not have the thrusters appear on scanners. Your job will be to keep us on course, so stay sharp."

He barely managed not to choke. *She was insane. Absolutely crazy.* "We'll use the thrusters *more* by trying to navigate only on gravity fields. Every time you move the stick, you'll go a thousand feet farther than you planned and have to hit the engines. We'll run out of fuel before we even get there. You planning on committing suicide?"

She reached backward awkwardly and pushed down his face shield. "Look in the lower left corner of the display."

He did. There was an object there, about ten times the size of their ship. "So? What am I looking at?"

"Asteroid. When I first met with the transport captain, he said there was a small asteroid field that circled Stovia, similar to Saturn but not as wide. He suggested that if we stayed in the wake of the biggest one, we could get within a few thousand kilometers of the planet and we'd look like just another dead rock in the sky."

So . . . crazy like a fox. "That's going to be a tricky bit of flying. You'll have to be within a few football fields of the surface of the asteroid to pull it off."

She turned her head and smiled. The white of her teeth turned green under the lights from the dash. "I can fly it if you can nav it. Easier than the Sirian belt firefight in April."

But the closer they got to the asteroid, the harder this whole mission looked. The asteroid appeared smooth and quiet from a distance, but close up was a tumbling, shifting mass of spiked ice and rock. Pieces the size of an aircraft carrier would occasionally break off and collide with a dozen other bits of rock before settling into an uneasy orbit around the planet. Yet the closer they got, the more stable Grayson's vital signs were. Her heart rate was slow and steady, her blood pressure what he would expect from a person sitting in a rocker with a cat in their lap.

She abruptly cranked the stick up and to the left and simultaneously hit the left thruster. Left on left caused the ship to spiral, and then another deft movement of her wrist caused them to do a neat flip around a frozen rock the size of a house. They landed back at nearly the exact spot they had started. The "Tyler Tip" – the one move that couldn't be faked. He wouldn't have believed it if he hadn't just experienced it. "You really are El Tyler." There was awe in his voice, and damned if he couldn't figure out how to keep it out.

"Yep." It was all the gravelly voice uttered before she went back to twitching the stick in ways that looked effortless, but Rand knew better. He was the one navigating, fingers moving on the antiquated keyboard to enter directions on the fly. Nothing about the Javelin was effortless. It was a heavy, cludgy ship that few pilots would even take on. The gravitational fields were affecting it in weird ways.

He started swearing quietly under his breath as another small stone hit the ship's hull. "There are just too many of them, El. All I can do is get out of the way of the biggest ones."

The next words out of her mouth stunned him. "I think we're going to have to land this beast."

"Land? Land *where*?" They were in an asteroid field. There weren't a lot of stable spots to navigate to. He turned his head as much as he could and stared at the side of her head.

She raised her hand enough to point out the front port. "Right there. It's not the biggest one, but it'll have to do."

He laughed. He couldn't help it. "Good one. Of course, *landing* sort of requires that you'll remain in one place with the power off."

"Oh, we will. Just steer me to the flat surface on this rock when it comes around again and I'll do the rest." She dropped her face shield. *Her vital signs might be stable, but he wasn't so sure about her brain.*

Still . . . the one thing that made Tyler a legend was thinking outside the box. He (or she) managed things that normal people wouldn't even contemplate. And hey, if he had to go out of this life, it might as well be doing something very cool. And riding an asteroid was something nobody had ever done.

He watched the screen in front of him while tapping on the keyboard to line up the ship with the correct pitch of the rock.

Tyler's gravel bass came over the mic in his helmet. "You don't make notes, do you? Most navigators I've met scribble with one hand and enter the numbers with the other."

He responded without looking up. "It's all eyes and fingers for me. I don't know that it actually goes through my brain. I see and my fingers just start moving. Always been that way, even when I was a kid."

"Yeah, I get that," she said. "For me, my eyes sort of convert images into numbers. I was a master at paint-by-numbers. I even used to make them for my friends. I knew a guy in grade school who could sketch outdoor scenes, and I'd add numbers based on what I saw. Got in trouble for it when a girl who couldn't paint won the talent show with one of our paint-by-numbers. The principal considered it cheating."

"Why didn't you become a navigator, then? Or why don't you do your own navigation?"

She gave a little laugh. "Because I can't both navigate and fly at the same time. I can do one or the other. Just not both . . . at least not fast enough to handle all the vectors. What about you? Why don't you fly?"

A snort erupted from him, sounding like a sneeze in his ears. "No dexterity, I'm afraid. I crashed the simulator so often that the techs banned me from the unit. I was actually messing up the software. I don't have a light enough touch. I go through keyboards pretty fast too. I even—"

"Hold that thought. We're coming up on our point. Bring me in flat so my nose is pointed toward the sun."

"You sure the nose is the best thing? Shouldn't we have the port wing toward the sun?"

Her voice snarled back. "Don't distract me! Just give me the figures."

He could see this ending badly, but his fingers flew over the keyboard to create the directions to land the ship. "Okay, start the touchdown in fifteen seconds, and . . . *mark*."

Rand's world narrowed to the sensation of movement from delicate blasts of the thrusters and the image of the rapidly approaching asteroid, lit only by the reflection from the nearest planet. They were about to touch down when something caught his attention from the corner of his eye. A large rock was break-ing off from the asteroid. It wasn't big enough to hurt them by itself, but it could definitely throw their trajectory off enough to crash. "Wait! Veer off. We've got a bogie to the left."

"No. We're too close. There's nowhere to go where we won't hit something. I can do this."

Crap. She was right. The closer they got, the more small objects were traveling in the wake of the asteroid that they hadn't noticed further back. His fingers hit the keys so hard as he typed that he could feel the vibration of the panel on his legs. Left, then right, up, over, twist. El moved the ship in ways he didn't know it would travel – totally dispelling the 'cludgy' rap the Javelin had from other pilots.

They hit the flat surface with a bounce and scrape and El scrambled to stop their forward movement before they shot right into an outcropping the size of an apartment block. "This isn't the way I wanted to do this!" Her voice was about an octave higher than normal. She reached forward in a rush and opened a panel he hadn't noticed. She slammed her fist down on the blue button underneath and he heard a muffled explosion underfoot. "Hang on!"

He was so tightly packed into the navpit, he couldn't imagine he could move. And yet he did. The ship made such a sudden stop that his head whiplashed against the inside of his helmet when it hit the neck support, making his teeth slam down on his tongue. "Ow!"

They had stopped, and he wasn't quite sure how. He watched the view port as their aspect shifted, turning the ship upside down. But they didn't drift. Then it occurred to him. "Harpoon anchor?"

She nodded. "Modified. It's an unstable platform, so we had to make it a tripod with quick-release breakaway."

Rand grabbed at his keyboard as it started to drop to the ceiling. He was starting to notice his head trying to keep up with the movements of the ship. "Upside down is going to be a problem. Another ten or so rotations and we're both going to be too dizzy to fly out of here if we need to."

"Agreed. We need to shut down and turn off the gravity. Then we'll be in the middle, and the ship can turn around us. It'll save on fuel – maybe enough to be able to take a second run at the weapon if we miss the first time."

He nodded, anxious to get out of the cramped navpit and move his legs. "We should try to get some sleep in the zero-g bags. It'll probably be four hours before we're close enough to the planet to risk charging the weapons." *And five hours until what would be the most challenging nav job of his life.*

Damn, what a rush . . .

Four

"It must be here somewhere!" She reached up and clenched a flashlight in her teeth while she dug through the tiny cabinet, turning over every box, and every container with one hand, keeping her balance with the other. Nothing.

She moved to the next one, tossing things behind her to float in mid-air.

Miflin's voice held both amusement and resignation, in nearly equal parts. "Give it up, Grayson. They only packed one zero-g sleep sack. They're bulky. We would have found the other by now."

She grabbed the flashlight to shine it into the very back corner of the space. "Don't be ridiculous. This is a two-person ship. They wouldn't pack only one sack." Nothing in cabinet number two. She pulled her way to the third.

He continued to connect the hooks to the wall latches, with near indifference to her growing panic. "Hey, here's a clue. Did you notice there's only one set of wall latches?"

She stopped and turned her head, her arm still deep in the bulkhead. "What?"

He pointed to the wall, and then patted above and below the single sack before batting away a rolled-up length of rope that floated near his head. "Only one set. Just one plug for a heater, too. I guess we're supposed to sleep together." He grinned. "Unless that would bother you, of course."

It was hard to deny her discomfort with a dozen containers of food and medicine, along with fluid packs, floating around the room. "Hardly. They probably expected the pilot and navigator to sleep in shifts. Someone is *normally* supposed to watch the position of the ship, after all."

"But *normally* the ship isn't attached to a hunk of ice in space with the power off. If we sleep in shifts, one of us won't survive the trip. Want to flip coins to see which of us freezes to death?"

It was sad that freezing to death was a viable option to crawling into a heated sleep sack with Rand Miflin. "You sleep first. I'll get the rest of these supplies stowed and go over the maps again."

He waggled a finger and kicked off from the wall, keeping a free hand up to protect his head. He wound up inches from her, close enough that her heart started to pound. "Oh, no. You forget – I'm not a pilot. I'm not going to get stuck out here after you freeze, not even knowing how to release the anchor from this rock. I swear I'll keep my hands to myself. We can even bundle up back to back. But we *are* both going to get in that bag. Even if I have to tie you up to do it."

The amusement had left his eyes. *He was dead serious. She'd never met a navigator who truly couldn't fly. She'd presumed he was just downplaying his skills, but maybe he wasn't kidding. And, admittedly, she didn't want to freeze. A quiet, anonymous death wasn't something she'd ever envisioned.* "Fine. But I'll hold you to your promise."

Stupidest thing he'd ever agreed to. The sensation of her legs twined around his as she snored softly made him crazy. Yeah, they'd started with their backs touching. But he hadn't been asleep for twenty minutes before he'd felt her hands all over him. He'd been both aroused and delighted – until he'd discovered she was sound asleep.

Damn it.

Apparently her subconscious mind was the only one willing to act on what she felt. Even helping her into the bag had made her crazy. She would make a low noise at the lightest touch but then deny she had. He'd presumed she'd give up on the charade once they were zipped in, but all she did was turn her back and not respond to a single thing he said.

If only she could keep her hands to herself. He'd been accused more than once by dates of being all hands. But he had nothing on El. Her hand slipped out of his again to travel toward his belt. He gasped at the sensation. *Crap.* He grabbed her hand again, and held it tight in sheer self-defense.

Stupid agreement.

Oh, the hell with it. That was it. He let go of her hands, raising his arms until his palms were under his head. One of her hands slipped under his shirt, started lightly scratching nails down his skin. He had to steady his breathing and interlock his fingers to keep from pulling her against him. When her other hand reached around his neck to tickle his ear, he let out a small moan.

He waited, enduring the torture until her hand left his chest, moving down until it was snugly locked over his raging erection.

Now.

"Grayson," he whispered. When she didn't respond, he said it louder. "*Grayson!*"

She woke with a start but the sack was tight enough against them that her hands didn't immediately move. "Huh? What?! What's wrong?"

He moved his head down until he was whispering in her ear. She shivered visibly. "Unless you plan to ravish me, move your hands."

She froze, consciousness finally arriving as she realized her position. One leg was wrapped around his, her arm around him, finger skimming his ear, other hand fondling him. And he was absolutely innocent of wrongdoing. "This isn't how it looks."

He chuckled and she winced. "Oh, don't worry. I can't see a thing. But the things I can *feel* are amazing."

She struggled to move to a safe position, but there was nowhere to go. He finally turned in the bag until he was facing her, nose to nose. He wormed his hand until he could push the hair away from her panicked eyes. He whispered softly. "Give it up, Grayson. Just let it happen." He leaned forward, pressed his lips against hers and she let out a little squeak. But she didn't stop him and he pushed forward, opening her mouth with his, letting their tongues tangle. *God, she tasted amazing.*

He ate at her mouth, let his hands roam to touch her silky skin. Arm, stomach, soft breast. There was no hope of sex, of course. There simply wasn't enough room to move. All he wanted to do was break down her barriers. Just a little.

They both came up gasping for air. The chill in the main bay actually felt good against his superheated skin. He grinned at her. "Now maybe we can *both* get some sleep."

He closed his eyes, but before they were fully shut he saw the surprise on her face.

Five

How was she supposed to sleep? Her entire body was aching, wanting more than her mind was willing to do. And Miflin was just snoring away.

Why had he kissed her? Worse, why had she let him?

Because you wanted him to, stupid. Since the first day you met him. There had been something about him, even then. A ne'er-do-well rake; that's what he would have been called in an earlier age. He smiled and women melted. Except her. She was the tough one. The perfect cop who had no emotions. More like the perfect patsy for a brutal overlord.

Miflin had managed to charm her, despite her carefully constructed walls – his black sense of humor, the fire in his eyes when he talked about getting the "product" to its destination.

And then she'd found out he was smuggling *kids*, getting them out of town before the Stovians arrived. She'd been shocked by the stories she'd heard, watched the terrified looks on the kids' faces when she'd sworn she'd get them back to their families. But they hadn't *wanted* to go home. Everybody there was already dead.

That was when she'd made her decision. The world didn't need more orphans. Order at the cost of lives wasn't what she wanted for her career.

So, really, it was Miflin who had caused her to defect, to change sides and join the resistance. But he hadn't followed. He'd stayed a freelance smuggler. And that had annoyed the hell out of her.

It wasn't easy to get out of the sleep sack without waking him. But the timer in the cockpit had gone off. It was time to start getting the ship ready to launch. She was sleepy when she slipped into what passed for a bathroom. There was no standing up straight and barely enough room to extend one arm. But at least she could clean off, brush her teeth and relieve herself.

Then it was to the cockpit to start the engines. The planet was massive in the view port. It looked similar to Earth but with rings of thick, dark clouds and far more land mass. It was surrounded by satellites bearing weaponry she didn't recognize. *Damn. How are we going to pull this off?*

It was when she was powering up the port thruster that the alarm sounded on the overhead panel. The passive sensor had come in contact with an active scanner.

Damn it. She couldn't decide whether to fire everything up and risk them showing up on scanners but in position to slip away, or shut everything down and try to pass by unnoticed. The problem was if they went much farther with the asteroid, they'd be right back at square one – waiting until the rock passed by the planet again on the next orbit. Except they didn't have that much food or water. It had to be now.

"Miflin!" She shouted the words and pressed a button that sounded an alarm in the back. She heard a thumping and then a body fall out onto the floor of the bay.

"What the hell! What's going on?" His voice was thick with sleep.

She already had her helmet on, so her voice came out deep. "Get suited up. We've been noticed."

She heard him utter several swear words, in interesting combinations, but at least he began to scramble around the bay, swearing more as he cracked his head on the ceiling while getting to the clothing storage. She turned to see him hopping to get into his suit. He called through the doorway. "How long?"

"The first scan was random. It'll take a little bit for them to hone in on us. I want to be gone by the time they do. I'm firing everything up, but it'll take a second to get to full charge. Five minutes to anchor release."

"Great. I have time to pee."

She rolled her eyes. Just like a man. She busied herself flicking on switches and pushing buttons, getting green lights all the way. At least the time in cold storage on the asteroid hadn't hurt any of their instruments. She was just about to release the anchor when a red light outside the view port caught her eye.

It was the last thing she remembered . . . other than the pain.

Red light filled the front cabin, spilling under the door to the bathroom. He was just zipping up when he noticed it, and then the scream came. Even with the voice modulator in the helmet, it was high and tortured. He bolted into the cockpit.

El's helmet was off and her face was . . . *smoking* under her hands. "Oh, God! It hurts. Oh my God!"

"What happened? Did something explode up here?"

"It's the weapon. It came from the surface, a red beam. Not diron or laser. Something else. It blinded me." She turned and grabbed at his flight suit. He finally saw her face. Her eyes were milky white, the lashes and eyebrows charred and falling in ashes onto her seat. "I'm *blind*, Rand!"

He pulled her out of her seat, supported her as he got her back into the sleep sack to examine her. His hands shook as he got out the med kit and used his teeth to open the package for a shot of morphine that included a high-strength antibiotic. He pressed the pressure needle against El's suit and heard her gasp as it injected into her arm. "Okay, just stay there for a second. I'm going to go shut down the ship except for the heat back here. The asteroid should mask the signature of this small ship."

She was crying when he got back. *He hated it when women cried, because it made him want to as well. The rough part was . . .*

she had reason. A pilot without eyes? What the hell were they going to do? His stomach threatened to expel what little he'd had to eat. "Hey," he said softly, as he approached, touching her hair lightly. "How you doing?"

"We can't go back, we can't go forward. How do you think I am? We're going to die out here."

He pulled a chair over from the wall. The sound made her jump and look around uselessly. He touched her again as he sat down. "We'll figure this out, El. We've passed the planet now. No ships have launched and no chatter has been picked up by the scanners. We have some time to think before the asteroid comes around again. Tell me what happened."

She did. There wasn't much to tell. He ran fingers through his hair. How could this happen? "So you think it was random? Just a test fire or something?"

She shook her head, her senses seeming to come back to her as the painkiller kicked in. "No, I think they know we're coming. It was targeted across the asteroid ring. They wouldn't risk blinding their own pilots or the transport ships—" She muttered a string of curse words. "The transport driver. He was a counteragent. But they don't know which rock we're on. They're probably just waiting until we're out of shipping lanes before they come and destroy the ship."

"Son of a bitch." She was right. That was the only way. "So what do you think this weapon is meant to do?"

"Exactly what it did. It blinds people. Even through blast shields. Think about it, Rand. How would we fight back if everyone . . . everyone on the whole *planet*, was blind?"

Shit. Earthlings would be easy pickings, easily sold as slaves for sex or hard labor where sight wasn't really required. Maybe the coal mines of Rigel or the diron mines on Pluto. "Why bother with underground lighting if everyone's blind? Damn."

"We have to take it out. I don't know how, but they can't be allowed to get this weapon onto an interstellar ship. You'll need to be the pilot. We don't have a choice."

He started shaking his head even though she couldn't see it. He stood up and walked to the bathroom and wet a strip of cloth to put on her forehead. *Better not to let her get too overheated in the sleep sack.* "You don't understand. I can't fly. It's not a question of confidence, or knowledge. My brain doesn't work that way.

Not everybody has the skill to fly a ship like El Tyler. It's rare, like it's part of your genes or something."

She laughed, a little high. But not hysterical. More drugged. "Genes. I guess you might say that. Granddad, Mom and me. The famous Tyler genes."

"Come again?" He put the cool cloth on her forehead and she calmed down.

"Granddad was E.L. Tyler. He was a pilot. Could fly anything . . . prop planes, jets, helicopters, even gliders. He spent his life in the sky. Until the Parkinson's set in. The stick started shaking, jerking. When he was called up for duty when the Stovians attacked, he couldn't do it."

It all finally made sense. "So you took his place?"

She waved a hand in the air wildly. Definitely feeling no pain now. "Pfft! I was *ten* when that happened. No, Mom was the next Tyler to pick up the stick. She insisted on going in his place. He said no. But she was stubborn. She challenged him to a race. Whoever won would go. She picked the planes, he set up the course." She paused, smiled, remembering. "She won. I was so *proud* of her. Granddad wasn't upset. She'd proved herself, and she was good. Damned good. He raised me while she flew. She was Lauren Tyler – still an 'L'. Only a very few in the upper hierarchy knew. She flew for the next decade. It broke her heart when I became a cop for the Stovians. She tried to convince me to resist, but I couldn't. It was all about *order*, y'know?" Now her voice was starting to slur. "All order, until I met *you*."

Wait. Huh?

"Remember those kids when we caught you? I broke them out of quarantine, flew them to safety, to the mountain base in Colorado. Then I went home and burned my black uniform. I asked my Mom where to sign up to fly. She was tired. Venus had taken a lot out of her. She couldn't use one foot anymore. But she challenged me to the course – a rite of passage."

He felt a smile come on, just a little one. "You beat her."

She nodded. "I was born Elle, E-L-L-E, not Ellen, and Mom gave me Tyler as a middle name. So still not a lie. El Tyler is a . . . a legend . . . you know." Her lids drifted closed over the ruined eyeballs. The muscles under the burned skin relaxed as she slept.

He reached down and pressed a gentle kiss against her temple, near the red, blistered skin of her forehead.

He moved the chair to a spot where he couldn't be seen from the front. More important, where he couldn't see out, in case they had a mobile version of the weapon. He started to go over the maps on Elle's reader. He hadn't really bothered much before, since it was pretty obvious they were going to have to wing it. *But she was right. They had to take out the weapon.*

When she woke up, four hours later, ready for another morphine shot, he had a plan. *It was reckless, insane – complete suicide.*

In other words, the perfect fit for a legendary smuggler and a legendary hero.

Six

"Okay, explain that to me again?" *She thought she must have heard wrong, because the idea was insanity.*

"We're going forward with the mission. You'll fly and I'll navigate. Then we'll land, hijack a ship capable of handling the wormhole, and go home. Easy-peasy."

She took the cloth off her forehead and flicked her eyelids over the milky orbs. It made her wince. "Somehow in that plan did you think how to get around the fact that I'm *blind*?! Are you insane, Miflin?"

"Not insane at all. In fact, it's the perfect defense." He pushed back the chair, scraping it across the patterned metal. "They've thrown all their eggs into one basket. They're planning that this weapon is the be-all and end-all. Don't you see, Elle? They're presuming that the beam was all they needed. They didn't send any follow-up ships because they didn't think they *had* to." He wished she could see his excitement. "That's our *in*. They presume a blind pilot can't fly."

"And they'd be right, Rand. I *can't* fly."

He nodded his head and took her hand in a tight grip. "No, but see – *you* can. Maybe *only* you. It's paint-by-numbers, all over again. I'll give you the numbers, you paint the picture. Like an instrument landing."

She held up a hand, trying to raise her body to a sitting position. Confusion was mixed with alarm on her face. "Wait. You want me to pilot the ship by *listening* to your navigation commands?"

"Why not? You said yourself . . . you think in numbers. The commands go from your eyes to your hands. Why not from your *ears* to your hands? But you'll have to trust me. Have to trust that I'll give you good data. I will. I swear I will, on the blood of everyone on Earth who's fought and died."

She mulled it over for long minutes and then finally responded. "Blind precision flying through surface defenses, and in dogfights? You're crazy."

"Yeah. I am. So are you. Smuggling kids through a blockade, fire fights in an asteroid field. We're both certifiable." She tipped her head, acknowledging the truth, so he pressed on. "Face facts, Tyler. We're dead anyway. The oxygen scrubbers will only last a week without servicing. We have food and water for two days, three with recycling. There's no way back if the transport captain is one of the bad guys. But if we pull it off – wow. We save the planet. We buy time for the resistence to prepare."

"And we send a message," she said after a pause, her neck muscles tightening, her face focused as though she could see him through the fog. "We can bring the war to *you*. We can find you, attack you. Maybe they even think we have a countermeasure to their superweapon. They probably don't have enough data on Earthlings anyway."

Rand found himself smiling when she smiled. *Reckless, talented, gorgeous – with or without blue eyes.* "I could fall in love with you, you know."

She reached out a hand. He took it. "If we survive this, I just may let you."

Elle sat in the cockpit, face shield down, meaningless. It hurt like fire, but she'd felt worse. She closed her eyes, which was redundant, but it helped her focus. She imagined the panel in front of her. She reached out and toggled a switch. The left thruster fired up on low. *Damn*. It should have been the right one, on high. She concentrated, tried to dredge up the flight here, through the asteroids – concentrating on the numbers on the display while her hands went to practiced spots.

"Give me coordinates, Rand. Any coordinates."

"It might help if we weren't still attached to the asteroid."

She let out a harsh breath, tried not to swear like her

grandfather. "Just do it, please. I need to see if we can do this before I discover I can't get back here."

"Okay, then. Good point. Let's go with . . ." He started typing hard. "197.824, left pitch 8.7, arc length 14.3."

"Skip the pitch and arc. The order of the numbers will tell me what they are. Just stick with initials for direction: 197.824, L 8.7, A 14.3. So . . . let's try this." She let the numbers fill her mind, let them flow through her to, as Miflin said, "paint the picture". The stick moved without her meaning to. The ship lurched, strained against the anchor. "Was that a real coordinate?"

"Yep, our first one," he said with far too much satisfaction in his voice. "Give 'er hell, Captain Tyler. Sir."

She smiled and pulled the anchor release. It didn't retract the anchor. It severed the connection at the ship. She felt the shudder as the ship eased away from the asteroid. She answered Rand's question before he asked it. "Less weight. We'll be able to maneuver quicker without it."

He tapped her shoulder lightly and she turned her head. "The rock's spinning again. We should probably get out of here."

One nod and she felt her hands dance over the controls. The thrusters reversed and she pulled up on the stick sharply. They tumbled and she felt the ship respond to the outcropping passing by the hull. "Tell me where to go next."

He did. Coordinate after coordinate, she stared where the screen would be and the numbers appeared in her mind as though her eyes were seeing them. He abbreviated easily after a few minutes. "184.2, L 87, A 14.2; 184, L 6, A. 9; 1922, L 13.3, A 12." She let her hands move, and soon it was as though she could see – at least as well as she normally could through the blast shield.

"Entering the planet's atmosphere. Remain on this course. Keep the nose steady. I'll let you know when you can let go."

She hated atmospheres. The stick vibrated wildly. Heat began to radiate through the cockpit. It would pass, but it made the blisters on her face sting, burn, made her skin melt and crackle even through the shields. "Damn it, Miflin. It hurts. I can't concentrate."

Rand reached back and put a hand on her shoulder. "Keep it steady, Elle. Just a few more minutes. We're nearly through. Don't let go. I can't do this for you. This is yours."

She wanted to let go. To put her hand to her face to shield her wounds from the heat. "I can't keep this up."

"You can. Trust me. Just another minute."

Did she trust him? Could she? "What's in this for you?" The drugs were wearing off and her eyeballs were swelling again. Her lids wouldn't close over them. She feared if she forced them, they wouldn't go up again. She needed distraction. "Tell me."

There was a long pause. It felt like forever as her face and hands crackled and crisped. "At first, it was the rush. I've always been an adrenaline junkie. Then it was the money. People who want to move things without suspicion will pay nearly anything. I tried the 'straight and narrow' route. Had a steady job with low pay and no future. Drove me nuts. So, you're right. I *was* for sale to the highest bidder."

Close now. She could feel the shaking lessen, but now was the most dangerous part. If they hit the stratosphere wrong, or the concentration of gases was too different from Earth, she could ricochet off, and they'd tumble and break up. Rand tightened his hand on her shoulder. His wrist was probably cramping from the angle. She asked him. "What changed?"

"There's always a line. A line you can't cross. To me, the line was kids. Who knew? Someone paid me to drive a freighter. I was told to ignore noises in the back. But I couldn't. They'd sealed them in without enough air holes. I broke it open. Not a one was more than ten. I didn't know where they were supposed to end up, and I didn't care. I dropped off the grid with them. Took them to the Mars colony's orphanage. I knew a group of nuns there who would care for them. A day later I joined the resistance."

Her muscles were getting so tired. "We must be going in wrong. It shouldn't take this long."

"It's a thick atmosphere. Hang in there. Nearly done. The clouds are getting lighter."

"So you joined the resistance to escape the wrath of your former clients?"

His voice turned hard as diamonds. "My *clients* were part of the Stovian high command. I discovered they preferred . . . *veal* for banquets."

Elle couldn't help but shudder. *Children as food.* "So that should make me trust you?"

"To stop Stovia from turning our whole planet into a slaughterhouse? Oh yeah. You can trust me." He took a deep breath and let it out slow.

Her voice took a teasing edge. "Not doing it for me?" *Why the hell did she ask that?* But it was spoken. She couldn't figure out how to take it back.

He tried to keep his voice light, but failed. "That, too. How would you get out of here if not for me? Breaking through the clouds now. Vector to 249.868, 14.87, 6.0, and stay straight as an arrow. Asort dead ahead, if the maps we have are accurate."

Dead ahead. Hopefully that wasn't prophetic.

The shaking of the stick stopped abruptly and the air began to cool. She let out a harsh breath she didn't know she was holding, and ripped off her gloves. She'd need finer control of the stick in the air. Rand patted her head and then let go to put his hands back on his keyboard. "Tell me where to go."

He did, and even described the scenery as they flew – so far with nobody noticing. "Weird trees here. They look like giant ferns. No, more like big stalks of celery. They're mostly brown and withering. Atmosphere sucks. Sort of like what they used to talk about in history books about the industrial age. Smog. Thick. Don't know if it's breathable to humans. At least, it can't be healthy." After a few minutes of silence, he started up again. "I think I see the place, up ahead. The complex is huge. How many bombs do we have, again?"

"Ten. Five bunker-busters and five diron fault-expanders." She reached forward to where the bay door-releases were located. Good. She recognized them by feel.

"Ten? On this tiny thing? Where?"

"It's why we don't have a galley or cargo bay. They were converted to munitions storage." One pull per release. If the complex was big, they might want to make two runs. Diron to shake things up, and then the bunker-busters to destroy anything underground.

The warning alarm sounded. "Uh-oh. We have company," she said. They were being targeted. "Move to atmosphere flight. Altimeter reading? Speed?"

"Thirty-five thousand feet, seven hundred knots. Shit! Incoming missile! Hard left roll. Now!"

She cranked the stick over and felt the ship slip into a barrel roll. The sizzling sound of a light missile went past her left ear. "Whew. That was close."

"Not as close as this one! Tyler Tip to right on two, one, *mark*!"

Her grandfather had taught her an old propeller-plane trick called an "Immelman". It was very close to a Tyler Tip, done in the atmosphere. The ship performed, just barely. She hadn't had the chance to test the Javelin in heavy air. It was sluggish, not nearly as light as in space. "That was too close. Let's get this done."

He gave the bearings and she dipped and wove around the towering trees, using Rand's rapid-fire coordinates. Her world narrowed to following the commands while trying to listen for the sound of the other planes outside the ship.

More enemy ships were launched as they got closer. "Get ready. Don't think about anything but releasing those bombs."

Now, why did he say that? His voice sounded strained. "Rand? What's wrong?"

"Nothing." His voice cracked. He was lying. She moved one hand back and touched his face. It was wet . . . and slippery. "You're bleeding. What happened?"

"Shrapnel came through the panel. All the instruments are working. I'll be fine. Just do your job. Don't worry about me."

Of course, the moment he said that, she started to. "What's your condition? If it's serious, we're breaking off until we can get you stabilized."

"I'm . . . okay. Just . . . a . . . little hard to—" He gasped. "Breathe."

The compartments had separate forced-air systems. So long as hers kept forcing air toward her helmet, she'd be fine. She reached up and yanked the cord on her suit, then handed the tube backwards. "Here. Don't argue. There's almost a day's worth of air here if you don't go crazy."

He pushed it away. "Can't. Need . . . to . . . talk, to direct . . . you."

Damn it. He was right. "But I can't afford for you to pass out, either." She pulled off her helmet and immediately her chest seized up from the horrible air quality. "Trade . . . me . . . helmets." Her head started to pound from the lack of oxygen.

Again Rand tried to wave it away but she insisted, pushing her helmet with the good line backwards. "I don't have to . . .

talk. I . . . can use . . . my suit." With that, she plugged the mouthpiece behind her lips and tossed the helmet entirely over her head.

After a long moment, she heard his voice again. "Damn you, Tyler. You can't afford to be low on air."

She just shrugged, not that he could see her. There wouldn't be any more talking until they were back in space. Then they could make repairs – provided they made it past the Stovian armada. The one nice thing was that the Javelin had speed. Once they dropped the weight, it would outrun anything the Stovians had.

She struggled not to pull air from the tube. It wasn't a forced-air system. But the toxic atmosphere had nearly overwhelmed her lungs. It was hard not to start coughing, and that could ruin her suit. She put her arm out of the cockpit and waved her hand in circles, telling Rand to *speed it up*.

It wasn't just the fuel, but her eyes were starting to swell again. This time, they were swelling inward. Probably the low oxygen wasn't helping. Her head was pounding. She tried not to be scared. *What would happen to them . . . to Rand, if she passed out?* She had to keep it together. She could collapse when they got away. *They had to get away.*

"Prepare to release." Rand's voice was hollow, sounded strange to her ears. Was it just the helmet's modulator, or something else? Worse, she couldn't ask. She fingered the control for the five-hundred-pounders and stretched her hand so her pinkie could flip the diron bomb controls. "On my mark, Elle. Five – four – three . . ." The pounding in her head was getting worse, all the way down one side to her neck now. But just a second longer. She could do this. "Two – one – MARK!"

She flipped both triggers and felt the Javelin soar upward like a deployed parachute when the weight dropped. The roar of turbine jets deafened her right ear as they shot upwards past the pursuers. She paused for a second to pull the air tube from her mouth. "Was it a hit?"

"Hit," came the weak reply. "Good . . . job, E—" Rand's voice stopped. She reached back and shook his shoulder.

"Rand?" No response. "Rand!" She had to put her air tube back in. But how was she going to be able to navigate back into space? Especially with followers? She thought back to the directions he'd given before they started darting through the trees. All she could do was pray and hope that the ship was already high enough in the atmosphere that there were no structures to hit. She pointed the nose up, put the thrusters on full, and threw off her restraints. They'd make it out or they wouldn't. But she had to find out how bad Rand's injuries were.

It was hard work to get him out of his seat. Dead weight was no picnic to move. Once he was in the rear cabin with the helmet off, she gingerly felt his face. He had a nasty cut over one temple that still had a piece of metal embedded. That was probably what had knocked him out. But could she remove it without damaging him further?

The ship shifted then, and something bounced heavily off their shield. Probably a smaller satellite. *Hopefully nothing bigger was in the way. But if there was* . . . No. she'd stay with Rand. Keep him safe until . . . She grabbed the piece of metal and pulled, praying it wasn't in too deep. It was stuck, but not in the bone, and came out easily, followed by a rush of blood.

Elle felt around in the med kit, hoping something would feel familiar. She couldn't think of anything in there that would *hurt* him, so she just grabbed what she hoped was an antibiotic and painkiller. Same as he'd given her. Or maybe a blood coagulant. She ripped open a package and fingered the trigger as she put it against his arm. She wouldn't think about what would happen if she failed. Mostly, she shouldn't care about anything other than the mission. Again her breathing tube was yanked out. "Damn you, Rand. Why in the hell did you make me care about you?"

A strong hand reached up and grabbed hers before she could push the plunger. "I could ask the same about you." His voice was weak but steady. "How about you don't give me a shot of estrogen, though. Okay?"

Crap! Was that what she'd grabbed? She let him take away the plunger and heard him rip open another package. The soft whoosh of the shot came to her ears and then another package was ripped open. She felt pressure against her arm. "Two for you. Anti-inflammatory and another painkiller. Then put your oxygen back in."

A voice came from the cockpit, causing both of them to turn their heads. "*Javelin One*, do you copy? Captain Tyler? This is the ESS *Discovery*. We've been instructed to grab the ship and get you home. We're being pursued, though, so we only have a minute if you want to hitch a ride."

Elle's heart started to pump wildly. *Home?* She pulled the helmet off Rand's head and moved forward to the cockpit, toggling the radio. "*Javelin One, Discovery.* You're welcome to grab us. Our controls are damaged, though. Can you collect us as we go by?"

After a pause, her heart soared. "Ten-Four, *Javelin One.* Prepare for forced capture. Strap yourself in tight."

Rand was right behind her, pushed her forward into her seat. He managed to climb back into the navpit. She gave him back the helmet. "But people will see your face," he said.

"You can give it back once we're on board. Or maybe Captain Tyler died. I don't know that there's any way I'll ever fly again." She tried to make it matter-of-fact, tried not to think of the implications. He covered her hand with his.

"You'll fly again. They're doing amazing things with implants. Until then, I'll be there, making sure you get whatever you need."

"What about the rebellion?" she asked softly. "The rush and the money?"

She could hear the smile in his voice as she put the oxygen tube back in. "Oh, I'll be supporting the rebellion. With your permission, I'll be ensuring the next incarnation of the Legend of El Tyler."

She reached back and clasped his hand. They felt the pull of the ESS *Discovery* and strapped themselves in for the long ride home.

Naturally Beautiful

Jamie Leigh Hansen

One

AD 2084, Shailene Mountains

"Remind me why we're doing this again?" Mike's irritable voice growled in his earpiece.

Lieutenant Reid Kincaid's lips twitched as he edged himself farther over the edge of the precipice at the top of the mountain. It was a very long fall to the dark depths of the valley below. It would be gorgeous when the sun rose, but for now there was just freezing air and the futile search for a heat signature. "Will you keep whining in my ear if I don't remind you?"

Mike huffed, the sound carrying easily through the earpiece, though he was a good distance away. "The guy's an ass who doesn't deserve our efforts to save him."

"I wonder if that's what you would have said last year when his miracle cure saved *you*." Reid gripped the rocks with his Caldy gloves, thankful for them and the matching sky suit. He could hold on to the edge of this rock all day if he had to, immune to the cold and the rocks trying to dig into his suit. Not that he wanted to, though. *Where was that damn helijet?*

"Last year, hell, that's basically what he said in the debate last night. What kind of spit-whack regrets curing all disease?"

"I don't know, but letting him die like a martyr for his cause will send this country up in flames." Not to mention leave one incredibly sexy daughter to grieve alone. Seeing her green eyes sparkle with sincerity from every screen was addictive. To see them teary and blurred with grief would suck beyond all telling.

There were no signs of humans below, but the ones responsible for the upcoming explosion were professionals. They would blow up the helijet and search for evidence to take back to their bosses that Dr Josiah Cross was dead at last. Until then, they were entrenched, and Reid would see no sign of their presence. Not that he could quit looking for them, anyway.

The helijet would enter from his left, winding through the valley in a laughable attempt to conceal its presence. But information was rarely secure anymore. Soon after a lock was built, there was a pick to open it. It was the way of the world.

"I hear sound." Reid edged away from the precipice, as the sky lightened from black to gray. When he rose, he'd be targeted. Only the sky suit could protect him, then. Lightweight, durable, temperature-controlled and, best of all, bulletproof. As long as they didn't throw a mag bomb his way, he'd be fine.

"Got your back, LT."

"Yep." They'd worked together too long for Reid to doubt it. The helijet hit his sight just as the sky lightened to a dark purple. Here at the top of the mountains, dawn was arriving quick.

"Just think, all those questions you have, you can ask in person in five . . ."

Reid rose, glancing at his watch and calculating as the jet flew closer, the bottom propellers not quite silent in the still morning air. "Four . . ."

Slightly faster than the jet, the sun peeked over the mountains, sending sparks of color to bloom across the landscape. "Three . . ."

The helijet hit the chosen point of reference, and Reid ran for the edge of the precipice. "Two . . ."

With each approaching step, he saw farther down the opposite mountain, the dark trees turning emerald, the wildflowers making an appearance as light splashed across them. His foot hit the last step. "One."

Reid launched into the air, his hands out, his feet together, his long body arching with the pressure of the wind. Straight down, the winding river gleamed a polished silver before his vision went black. Reid reached forward and made contact with the black jet. His gloves latched onto the smooth surface and he used his arms to guide himself over the side. Once he set his feet and had one hand wrapped around the outside handle, he pulled a retractable tool from his belt, zapped the door-lock, and released the tool to wind itself back to his belt. Moments later, he slid through the open door and faced the occupants. The pilot was safe, his emergency eject options in place. Dr Josiah Cross, his target. But when Reid's gaze clashed with wide, shocked, green eyes, the mission went to hell.

"Airborne 81, Dr Cross. This jet will explode in forty-five seconds."

Without hesitation, Dr Cross pushed his daughter into Reid's arms. "Take her."

"Father, no—"

Reid held her struggling form just so she wouldn't push him out of the jet. "Sir, my orders—"

"Don't matter," Cross snapped. The old man bent forward and grabbed a small case, unlocked his door and glanced at his daughter. "Nothing matters if I lose you, too, Jessica."

Jessica hesitated, meeting her father's gaze, and Reid was finally able to loosen his hold.

"Take this." Reid handed him a foam pellet, pressing it into the old man's hands. "Don't let go. You will be guided down. Mike, status 'Go'."

Cross nodded and Reid strapped Jessica's back to his front. She grabbed a large purse from the seat and he tried not to roll his eyes at the feminine habit. "Just make sure they're zipped and tucked very close to your body."

"Of course."

They assumed position at the doors. "Nice meeting you, Dr Cross. See you at the bottom."

"I love you, Daddy."

The old man nodded at them both, a strange glint in his eye, and then they jumped. Reid held Jessica's ankles together with his, falling with his back toward the ground. Above them, the jet disappeared in just seconds. The pilot wouldn't have long to eject, but he needed to get the jet away from them before he did. Reid curved his body around Jessica and guided them into position, their gazes now pointed at the swiftly approaching ground. She gripped his forearms against her chest, her fingernails hitting right at the split between his suit and his gloves. At least she wasn't screaming.

Reid released his wings: long, thin blades sewn into the back of his suit and magnetically controlled by his gloves. "Mike?"

"Got him in two . . ."

Slowed now, with his wings deployed, Reid looked to his right and slightly down to see Dr Cross become enveloped in a sphere of foam. Those tiny pellets had saved his own life more than once, though the foam they produced disintegrated quickly when deployed in the air. The doc would have only a few minutes before he had to land.

"One." Mike latched onto the top of the sphere, deploying his own wings almost immediately.

Reid's arms moved with the inhale of air his passenger finally took. The good doc wasn't completely safe yet, though. "Got him?"

"All good," Mike replied.

"Split in three."

"Two," Mike's voice came back.

"One," they said together, arching to opposite sides of the river. If the attackers needed proof of Dr Cross's death, they would have to split their own forces to figure out which of them had the old man. Hopefully. Every mission was planned with contingencies for anything that might go wrong, but no one could plan for absolutely everything.

Like the forceful wave of heat that washed over them as the helijet exploded.

Two

The ground rushed toward Jessica's face, stinging her eyes and playing havoc with her intestinal fortitude. Any second, they would land, and the only semblance of safety was the strength in the arms of the stranger holding her. The calm assurance in his voice as he spoke to his partner. The unflinching determination she'd glimpsed in his eyes just before her father had thrown her toward him. It wasn't enough.

She'd never done anything like this before. She didn't even go on the kiddie jumps at amusement parks. She worked in a high-rise building, looking down from the balcony outside her office calmly and comfortably, knowing all the safety features that went into it.

But there was no safety here. Screams built in her head, in her throat, and the only thing that kept them from coming out was the force of the air choking her whenever she opened her mouth.

Jessica gripped the stranger's wrist tighter and tighter the closer the ground came. Then it was there, and his longer legs were hopping along to slow them down while she raised her knees as far as she could to her chest. *If anything was going to break, let it be him first, please, God.* She squeezed her eyes shut, still screaming inside her head with each jarring bounce.

"Mike?" His voice sounded in her ear, irritatingly calm.

Barely loud enough for her to catch came the response, "We're good, LT."

"Good. Silence until rendezvous."

"Yes, sir."

Silence and dizziness overwhelmed her.

Jessica blinked her eyes open. *When had they sat on the ground? Was her father okay? When would the earth quit moving? Oh, God, she wanted to vomit. His calm voice as he spoke to whoever didn't help in the least. The fact that he held her upright, her back still to his chest, his legs bracing either side of hers and his arms locked tight around her – that* did *help. Kind of. At least something was still.*

She swallowed a few times before she could let any sound out. "Dad?"

"He's fine, sweetheart. They've landed safely and shall be heading north to our rendezvous point. You can see him for yourself once we get there."

"Doctor." She wasn't a "sweetheart", no matter how gently it was said. She was a fully accredited doctor, with a PhD and everything, damn it. She wasn't some adrenaline junkie who needed to defy death just to feel alive. And she would damn well set him straight on that as soon as she quit quaking from head to toe and wanting to vomit with every breath.

"Okay, Dr Sweetheart." Amusement colored his voice this time. "Try this."

Before she could ask what "this" was, it was at her lips and sliding in. Then she moaned. Chocolate melted over her tongue, instantly settling her stomach and going to work on her shakes. She could chastise him for what he called her *after* she could speak.

"Just take a deep breath and let the chocolate work its magic."

It took time, but the ground quit teetering and tottering.

The acidic nausea soothed beneath the effects of the chocolate. The slightly calmer adrenaline flowing through her cleared the fog of terror from her brain. And the warmth and strength holding her securely almost made her feel safe. But he was a stranger, and she needed to move. To stand on her own. *In just another minute. Or ten.*

Facing him would bring them too close, so she remained as she was, only lightening her death-clamp on his forearm. "How far is the rendezvous from here?"

"Six and a half clicks. Or about four miles."

"I see." *Well, barely.* She could see as far as the ground, maybe. "Who blew up our jet? Why do they want to kill my father? How did the military find out? What is at the rendezvous point, another jet or a building? Where are we supposed to go after we reach there? For how long?"

"Hey, Doc. Deep breaths."

Jessica took a deep breath. Her adrenaline had spiked with each question, and even more as each question led her deeper into problems that would need solutions.

"We don't have time to hash out everything. We don't know exactly who they are, but they will be coming for us."

And she was supposed to relax? Jessica sat straighter, looking around. Somehow, he'd carried her to a small area surrounded by trees and shrubs. Behind them was a hill of rock, and to the sides, impenetrable logs and green growth. There was a small clearing in front of them, easily surveyed from their position.

"So, we need to get up and run four miles?"

"Yes, Dr Sweetheart. The sooner the better."

Jessica rolled her eyes at his continued endearment/nickname and released his arm completely, then glanced around. "My briefcase?"

"Right here." He gave it to her.

Jessica leaned forward as he rose to his feet behind her. The waterproof leather briefcase was still locked closed and appeared none the worse for falling through the air with them. It had wide leather straps and a soft leather casing that zipped and locked closed. It resembled a large purse, but kept her work organized and protected. She pulled the strap over her shoulder and jumped to her feet.

Then rapidly buckled and fell, only stopping as the soldier's hard arm surrounded her. Jessica braced her hands against his chest and looked up into his midnight-blue eyes. "I apologize. I can do this. I promise."

"Of course you can. You just have to get used to standing again. Don't worry."

But even as he spoke to her in his low, calm voice and as he told her not to worry, he was scanning the area with a steady, hard gaze. That's right. *They*, whoever "they" were, would be looking for them. Jessica took another deep breath and willed strength to her legs. She pushed away from him, his chest barely moving.

"Okay. So, Airborne 81, what do I call you?"

"Lieutenant Reid Kincaid, Dr Sweetheart."

Then he smiled, and she could have sworn she was falling again.

Three

The ground tilted and vibrated beneath her feet, and the low hum of a helijet engine hit her from overhead like a forceful weight pressing her down. Then she was actually going down to squat with the lieutenant's arm guiding her from view. Between the muted dark camo of his uniform and the fronds of trees and bushes taller than them, they shouldn't be seen.

He eyed the sky, watching for the enemy's helijet. Before it reached them, it veered away, the force of the wind it stirred causing the leaves around them to flatten and spread so they could watch a clear path form as it left their area. A few seconds after it was gone, the lieutenant looked at her. "We need to get moving."

Jessica nodded, and he rose, tugging on her hand to help her up. Instead, she pulled him back down. "I can't go, yet."

Looking harassed and struggling with patience, he asked, "Why?"

Jessica slipped spiked heels off her feet and opened her briefcase. "I wear these for public appearances, but the shoes I prefer to wear are better for tramping quickly through a forest."

She felt his gaze lingering along the length of her legs, his features giving a silent thumbs-up to the heels. But when she held up her comfortable, lace-up shoes, his eyes brightened and he actually winked in approval. "Smart thinking, sweetheart."

She smirked as she slid them on her feet and tied them tight. "Geniuses tend to do that, Lieutenant."

He chuckled, visibly shrugging off her subtle reminder to

address her more respectfully. "Call me Reid," he said. And then added, "Ready?"

Grabbing one more item before she closed the case, Jessica stood, and slid the long strap of her bag diagonally across her body so it left her arms free. Arms she quickly raised to pull her long auburn hair back into a high, tight ponytail. "Now, I'm ready."

He nodded, scanning the area around them before leading her away.

She kept her voice low, but faced his back and spoke clearly. "What kind of traps are we looking for, Lieutenant?"

"Reid," he reminded, adding, "It's unknown where the men or women first touched ground, or how far ahead they've spread out, or how many of them we should look for."

Well, that made their job easy. "Then what *do* we look for?"

"We scan the trees for dark spots, pausing to make sure it's just thick leaves and branches. We scan the bushes lower to the ground for the same. Any lines, between our toes and the sky, that seem too straight to be natural, let me know. Otherwise, we just keep moving, listening for the sound of them, and stay clear of a straight view from the sky."

"Got it."

For the next hour, that's just what they did, communicating in simple, silent hand signals. Four miles could be run in an hour, easily, if she was on a straight track with relatively even ground. But between searching each dense tree or bush, and moving in a slow zigzag pattern to avoid anyone, one hour had only moved them a little over half a mile.

Pausing behind a tree, Jessica faced him. "Exactly how long do we have to reach the rendezvous?"

"Three hours from the jet exploding. It should have been plenty of time for two soldiers to get one old man in place."

"Am I holding you back?"

Reid looked at her, his eyebrows raised. "Actually, no. You seem to be keeping up quite easily. Why is that?"

She looked away. "I'm fit?"

"You *are* in optimal health."

Her mouth tightened, betraying her. Reid tugged her arm, returning her gaze to his face so he could search it. "You've taken TERA, haven't you?"

She pursed her lips. "No."

He scoffed. "Listen, sweetheart. Lies won't help us get out of here alive, placate your enemies, or help your father uninvent his miracle drug – for whatever insane reason he *wants* to do that. The force after him is a lot more determined than even we anticipated, and it's difficult to get past them."

Her eyes had narrowed at the word "insane" and irritation colored her voice now. "My father isn't insane. And I haven't 'taken' TERA. My mother had difficulty conceiving, and TERA fixed her fertility issues."

His eyes widened. "So you're the first generation born with it inside you."

It wasn't a question, but she confirmed anyway. "Yes. And for the record, there may be reasons he's regretted his invention, but he's never wanted to uninvent TERA. It has helped far too many people to live better lives."

"Exactly." Technologically Enhanced Rehabilitation Alleles were nanotechnology at a microscopic level: they traveled through the blood and repaired bodily damage at a cellular level. Congenital defects, genetic diseases and cancers were cured by delivering the proper rehabilitative information to cells. "Why regret that?"

She rolled her eyes. "He doesn't. But as with most inventions, there is the positive intention behind creating it, then the negative end of the spectrum. After diseases and many different health issues were cured, there were those who wanted to take it further. Ego, vanity and greed took control, and that wasn't what he wanted for his miracle cure."

"Okay, most everything gets misused—"

"Misused? That's like playing the wedding march at a funeral. Young girls are using TERA to change their hair and eye color – genetically. Being dissatisfied with their bodies and using anything available to reach an ideal appearance has all but eliminated ethnic differences and severely damaged the concept of health and beauty."

"True, the superficiality of some of its uses sucks, but the effects of aging, environmental influences and accidental traumas are practically reversible. It's a trade-off."

"And physical abilities have been optimized. Athletics associations want to treat it like steroid use, but the effects are everlasting and never leave your system, so any athlete who had a childhood illness, or a parent with fertility issues, wouldn't be able to play."

"Since that's practically all of them, there is no unfairness."

"Except to healthy people who've never had to take TERA, and now they are told that healthy isn't good enough. You must have this drug that optimizes every part of you, if not changes you completely."

"What's wrong with that?"

"There is a whole universe of psychological and philosophical issues. Super-soldiers, ethnic cleansing, conformist ideologies. Those are the biggest factors. Once laughed at and now all too real. And all that even before we learned of TERA's changes over time."

He couldn't argue with that. There were perfectionistic murmurings everywhere. Not just athletes and entertainment stars. Not just the military. It infiltrated society even at the grade-school level. That there might be unexpected changes was terrifying to contemplate. "What changes?"

"As you said, I am in the first generation born with TERA. I'm not even thirty years old. All of the effects aren't clear, yet, but how can we be expected to handle them when we don't even have the mental strength to embrace a world where people have different skin colors?"

Before he could say anything further, she darted away. Reid eyed their surroundings to see if she drew attention, found nothing, and dashed after her.

Four

Reid crouched directly behind her. "What kind of changes?"

She looked around them, her face strangely tight. "Well . . .You haven't noticed any strange appendages, have you?"

"What?" He paused, then he took in her dancing green eyes. She was probably getting him back for calling her "sweetheart". Oh, well. He'd have to do it even *more* now. "That's not funny, sweetheart. What changes?"

She exhaled an impatient sigh. "Nothing that will affect the next two hours, Lieutenant."

For what felt like the thousandth time, he snapped, "Reid."

"Fine, *Reid*, but we have to make up time. TERA is a very long, difficult debate, and we won't solve the concerns anytime soon. As for the changes, who knows? Are we headed toward the future from the *Terminator* movies, or the world of *X-Men*? All I do know is that the criminals searching for us right now have the same enhancements we do, so it's not like we have an advantage."

"Maybe not in that way, but I do have years of training and experience. So here's what we need to do." She was right. They needed to make up time, and stopping to debate the merits of a miracle cure was not a beneficial use of their resources.

Knowing she was born with TERA a part of her DNA, he was able to trust her civilian instincts a bit more, triple-check her less. At first, TERA had been created to focus on one illness at a time. Degenerative eye or nerve diseases, but not both. Being born with it in her system meant she had, naturally, a more general formula affecting the make-up of her entire body. Optimizing each organ and muscle and nerve. She truly could hear and see as well as he did, if not better. As long as she stayed in shape, which, eyeing her body, he had no doubt she did, she would be strong and fast. It was time to test his theory.

For the next hour, he pushed her, testing the limits of her speed and sight, no longer worrying about finding places to rest. Judging from the expression on her face, she loved it. How often did she get to push herself like this anywhere outside a gym? The fresh air and exertion had his heart pumping and racing as they climbed and dropped, ran across clearings, and hid from sight at a split-second's notice.

Their enemies were everywhere, it seemed. There shouldn't have been so many. His commanding officer said there had been a tip-off that the doctor would be attacked, but this seemed more than that. Was there a reverse tip that had betrayed military involvement in a rescue mission? That would explain the enemies' numbers, but not why they hadn't simply blown the jet apart sooner.

"Reid?" Jessica's voice was barely a breath of sound.

They'd climbed a tree, hoping to get more of an aerial view, only to find they were seconds from an ambush. Reid leaned against her back, pressing her closer to the trunk and hoping his camouflaged sky suit would block her clothes. Navy blue wasn't too bad, but it was still a clash with the environment and easier to spot. Angling his chin alongside her face, her melon-scented hair caught, tangling with his whiskers. He wanted to wrap his fingers around her ponytail and slide them down until he was free of the silky web, but he couldn't move. His hands were holding a branch above them and any movement to free himself could get him killed. So, instead, he inhaled and enjoyed the sweet scent.

Keeping his own whisper nearly silent, he replied, "Yes?"

"Why send so many if the explosion was meant to kill him?"

Good question. These men were sent to search. Was it really just to find a body and take a few pictures for proof? They wouldn't have needed so many for that. But if the military intel had been flawed, then that meant the doctor had been meant to survive to be captured. "Who knew you were flying with him?"

"It was a last-minute decision."

"Influenced by whom?" She held silent, so it had to be a good question. Letting her consider it, Reid returned his attention to the ground below him. One man was settled against a tree very close and slightly ahead of theirs. Reid could see his head, back and arms clearly. Nothing in his face or on his clothes pointed to an alliance, an ethnicity, or an identity of any kind. Only the taser in his hands hinted about his purpose.

Time crawled by, seconds becoming minutes until the scant amount of time they'd made up dwindled and they were just as far behind as they'd been. At this rate, there would be no rendezvous for them. What about Mike and the doc? Would they make it, at least? Mike had said they'd landed safely. A good pair of zoom lenses would have shown which doc had landed on which side of the river. Were there twice as many over there? Or could it be that Jessica was their true target?

Another man joined the one on the ground, sliding up beside him in well-practiced silence. The first man turned his head and the second man's hands began to move in a coded form of sign language. Reid's eyes widened. *Army, either current or past.*

The old doc has been captured, the new man signed.

The young doc is still evading us, the first man responded.

Are you sure we need them both?

Our orders were clear.

Have they passed this point already?

Maybe. No one ahead or behind has seen them either.

Ghosts.

Yes. That's the point.

We know the rendezvous. We should tighten formation and wait for them there.

The first man gazed around the clearing, looking at every tree but not behind him where Reid and Jessica were. With a sigh, he nodded. Both men gathered themselves and crept away. Reid watched them as far as he could, until they reached the darker depths and disappeared completely.

Reid rested his head on Jessica's shoulder, taking his first deep breath. His arms were beginning to shake from the effort of holding himself completely still. Jessica's had begun trembling against him awhile before. Standing motionless on a tree branch was not easy.

"What just happened?"

"Have you ever heard the term 'FUBAR'?"

"No."

"Soldiers created it over a hundred years ago to describe moments like this." *Fucked Up Beyond All Recognition. Yep, that was their situation now.*

"What does it mean?"

"It means they have the rendezvous, they have your dad and they have Mike. They just need us for a complete set."

Five

"What are you doing?" Jessica paused at the edge of the stream, her hands dripping cool water over her neck, as she tried not to flip out at the thought of her father being captured. The transition from dawn to early morning was unexpectedly hot, and her skirt and suit jacket felt heavy and smothering.

Reid poked around the saplings and bushes lining the stream and the base of the mountain. "According to my research, this mountain is riddled with caves."

She scowled, disbelief twisting her eyebrows. "You think hiding in a cave is the best move right now?"

"Not exactly. But sitting exposed while we hash out what to do next doesn't seem too genius."

Her skin suddenly chilled. "What's to hash? We rescue my father."

Reid continued his search, moving aside bushes and trees and even a few rocks. "By just walking in, getting him and leaving?"

If that's what it took, yes. Not *rescuing him was not an option.* "Why not? We've been walking right past these guys all morning."

"Okay, fine. Then what? Where do we hide him?"

"We're two miles away from the rendezvous point. How does hiding him this far back help?" Not having him face her was really annoying.

"The rendezvous is compromised. We need a new one. I'll call and set it up."

That silenced her for a moment. He turned back to searching and didn't see as she stalked right up behind him. At the last minute, he turned and she pushed him up against the boulders. In a low, deadly voice, she asked, "You'll *call?*"

He gave her a charming grin. "Yes. And no, I couldn't have done it sooner. Considering the mountains, the best reception is with the satellite in place and the sun up, so solar power can boost the signal."

"So we're going into a cave?" *In what world did that make sense?*

He tugged on her ponytail. "Good Lord, sweetheart. Trust me a little, will you?"

Jessica stared up at the man whose strength and determination had protected her all morning. He had rescued her from an exploding plane, even if it was by scaring her to death. It was his eyes and smile that calmed her when the enemy came too close. "Of course I trust you."

Just as his smile widened, she couldn't help but add, "A little."

He tweaked her nose and rolled his eyes. "Good. Now, behave yourself and crawl into the cave."

She glanced down where he pointed. The opening was tiny and shared with the stream. Raising her brows, she gave him a doubtful look. "You want me to do what?"

"I'll be right behind you." Before she could comment, he explained. "I need to cover the entrance."

Jessica sighed, but when he looked behind her and stiffened, she started moving, even before he gave her the order. "Now."

Thankfully, her skirt was long enough to cushion her knees as she crawled over rocks, through the water. She could hear Reid behind her, barely, but it was enough to comfort her as the darkness became complete. Her bag was on her back, safe from the water. She reached into it and felt for her safety ring. Feeling for the dangling unicorn pendant on her mother's old keyring, she identified her small pen light and switched it on.

The small tunnel lit up ahead of her, and she could see where the water seemed to stop. Jessica headed for that point. It seemed a little wider and they could at least sit on the side of the stream instead of in it. But once she reached it, she saw the water went down into a wider area, likely carved when the stream had been more than the trickle it was now. Carefully climbing down the few feet to the bottom, she chose a small dry area to the right. The water formed a pool in the center of a cavern barely tall enough for her to stand upright.

Reid joined her, stooping. "This looks like a good spot to stop."

Jessica nodded in agreement. Squatting beside the pool, she set the light on a rock and pulled off her wet jacket, using it to wipe dirt and debris from her arms and face. The surface of her skin felt nearly chilled now, but it was a welcome chill. She was able to quickly brush her hair into a neater ponytail and rinse her mouth out with water.

"Does that bag hold *everything*?" He sounded impressed.

Jessica glanced over her shoulder at him. He leaned against a boulder, fiddling with a small communications unit. "I can live out of it for two days, at least. Would you like a protein bar? They aren't as tasty as your chocolate, but they're filling."

"Sure."

She chose two from her bag and settled closer to him. The space was much wider than the tunnel, but that wasn't saying much. They couldn't sit side by side. Reid pulled her back to his front, between his legs, so she could lie back comfortably. "Rest a bit while we make contact."

She hated to appear weak, even for a second, but what the hell. He'd already seen her at her panicky worst that morning. And honestly, two hours of sneaking through a forest in the heat, tense with worry, made relaxing in a cool, dark cavern an irresistible temptation. And since they were waiting to talk to someone, she could do without guilt. Jessica adjusted her seat and fell back, letting his chest and arms cradle her.

Six

"Is the unit working?"

"It's all set up. I set a wireless signal outside the cave, it will amplify this unit. The call has gone out. As soon as the satellite catches the signal, they'll get it. Right now, we just have to wait for them to respond." He took a bite of his protein bar.

Jessica's fears showed in her voice. She swallowed a bite of her own bar before asking. "Do you think they're hurting my dad?"

"No."

Jessica angled her head up to face him. The flashlight cast enough of a glow that she could see his firm jaw already shading with the hint of whiskers. "Don't tell me the nice version. Be honest. I can handle it."

"Honestly," he angled down to meet her gaze. "He's seventy-nine years old, and whatever they need from him cannot and will not be gotten through force. He's a stubborn man and the kind of torture it would require would kill him. It would be a total failure when there are simpler ways."

Jessica narrowed her eyes. "Like threatening his only child, conceived late in life through a miracle intervention?"

His expression turned even grimmer. "If what they want is even his to give."

"What else could it be?"

He looked at her, his gaze prodding her to understand. "What if it's you they want? First generation born with TERA, genius ability and the experience of working with your father and the miracle drug?"

Her brows twisted in her confusion. "I thought this attack was politically motivated?"

Reid shrugged. "His allies want him on the speaking circuit. His detractors don't want a martyr catching the sympathy vote with his last wish. You weren't supposed to be on the jet. They already have your father, but are still searching for you. In force."

She nodded, resting the side of her face on his chest as she stared into blackness. "You're right. It doesn't add up."

"Do you have any idea why they would want you?"

"TERA is already widely available to anyone who wants it. I might be first generation, but I am far from the only one born with it inside me."

"What are you working on now?"

She shook her head. "That's clearance-only. Top level."

"Which means you and your father know, and who else?"

Jessica bit her lip, considering. "Our assistant, Sally. She is the one who encouraged me to go with Dad on this trip. I was worried about the stressful pace of the speaking engagements. Dad's very healthy. TERA helped him through heart malfunctions when I was in college, but he's been working hard and burning both ends for most of his life. It takes a toll."

Reid squeezed her close for a moment. "It's completely understandable that you would worry about him."

"Falcon, this is the Aerie. Over."

The sudden blast of speech made them both jump. The signal was clear, hardly any static.

"Hello, Aerie. This is Falcon. The fledgling and the eyas bated safely, but the flight was more turbulent than planned. Over."

Jessica frowned. If her father was the "fledgling", then she was the "eyas". She was *not* a downy baby chick, even if it made sense in falconry terms.

Reid grinned at her, running her ponytail through his fist as he listened.

"State your status, Falcon. Over."

"The fledgling and his dirt hawker are caught in a bow net."

A trap. Jessica nodded.

"Status. Over."

"The falcon and eyas are safe and laying down. Over."

"Wait on. Over."

"What does that mean?" Jessica frowned at him. "They want us to just sit here?"

Reid nodded. "For the moment, while they consider our situation."

"Why do they have to consider anything? You and I can just—"

He laughed. "Dr Sweetheart, if we want everyone to make it out alive, then we'll need reinforcements. Or, at the very least, a ride home. We just need to wait a minute."

Jessica huffed, glancing around their dimly lit cavern. The little flashlight was already fading and she dreaded attempting to crawl out of the cavern in complete darkness. Besides, the cooler air was no longer a pleasant break from a steamy morning, and with her wet jacket off and her skirt still drenched, it was getting downright cold. She shivered.

Reid reached between them and unzipped the front of his already dry suit, and then pulled her close, sharing his heat with her. "It won't be long."

Jessica huddled back against him, his undershirt soft against her cheek. She hadn't been this close to a man in a long while. Most of her relationships happened after a scientific breakthrough, when her work didn't consume her every conscious and unconscious thought and there were celebrations and fun to be had. Which meant her relationships were very few and far between.

Out of those few, not one had smelled quite like Reid. With him, there wasn't the overwhelming, cloying musk of cologne, or the too-sweet smell of scented laundry soap, or the grisly scent of sweat. He just smelled comfortable, safe, and she could almost imagine his arms belonged around her.

The voice from Aerie spoke, and she jumped. Reid responded with a complicated mix of military shorthand and falconry that barely made sense. All she caught was "*wing over*", "*dho-gazza*", and "*slip*". Jessica blinked in the dimness; the flashlight had faded even more. She looked up at Reid's face, waiting until he signed off. "I didn't follow all of that."

"They want us to change direction. Instead of racing for the rendezvous, they want us to set a trap that positions all of us to get rescued." He sounded too grim for her peace.

"What kind of trap?"

"The kind where I let you get caught."

Seven

The kind where I let you get caught.

Really? Jessica shoved the tail end of her hair out of her face and stormed back down the small tunnel to the outside – "stormed" as in carefully placed her knees on the rocks as she crawled as rapidly as possible, holding the nearly dead flashlight with her teeth. Reid was behind her because she'd refused to be left in that tomb-like cavern alone for even a nanosecond. Besides, if anyone was waiting for her once she emerged from the cave, it would all work out perfectly. She was *supposed* to be caught.

She didn't disagree with the plan, exactly, but something about it felt wrong. That ephemeral sliver of feeling left her irritable. Reaching the opening to the tunnels, Jessica slowed down, sliding through the water so she wouldn't make a loud splash.

When she emerged, she quickly pulled a pair of pajamas from her bag and slid them on, removing her wet skirt and shirt. She couldn't stand her soggy clothes another minute.

Reid finally crawled out of the cavern and retrieved his signal booster. "I still don't understand why this plan bothers you. It's a much more efficient way to find out where they are holding him."

"Yes, much more efficient. Are you ready?" She met his scrutiny with a detached impatience she'd had a long time to practice.

His square jaw firmed so hard he had to be grinding his teeth. "In three minutes, I will be. Be careful. I will be watching over you, but be careful anyway."

He started to walk away when she grabbed his arm and raised her gaze to his. "I know you will, but watch your back, too. They want something from us, so my father and I are relatively safe."

"If any of our assumptions about what they want are wrong, then we should assume they blew up the helijet with the intent to kill you." His grim expression underscored his words.

She nodded and looked down.

Which is why he caught her by surprise with a quick, hard kiss. She knew heat, firm lips, a slight scratch of whiskers, and then nothing, as he turned and walked away.

Jessica huffed and shook her head. "How like a man to be so dramatic."

Three minutes later, Lieutenant Reid Kincaid had claimed a high vantage point and watched as Jessica began to slip through the foliage. Her pale-blue pajamas stood out, much more than her suit had, from the darker greens and browns around her. It shouldn't take long for her to be picked up. He aimed his sights around him, focusing grimly.

To his surprise and shock, he'd apparently taught her *too* well. She slipped through two clearings and around numerous trees with no one the wiser. He grinned. She probably considered it a point of pride to not make it too easy for their enemies to capture her. Thankfully, she made an error before too much time passed.

One man held her wrist behind her back as another searched her purse.

The leader spoke clearly into his communications unit. "Command, I have the doc."

"And her guardian angel?"

"There appears to be no sign of him." The man gave Jessica a suspicious look.

Amazing woman that she was, she didn't hesitate to smear his name. "You mean the groping bastard that pulled me out of a helijet into the most terrifying minutes of my life? He's probably still on the ground, holding himself, praying for mercy. I do *not* like to be touched. You should remember that."

The soldier took in her proud stance, the arrogant tilt of her head, and the determination in the set of her shoulders. The commander spoke into his unit again. "She claims to have incapacitated him, sir."

Soon after, Reid watched them leave. Several others joined them, guarding their retreat. When they were out of sight, Reid descended the tree and watched the screen on his forearm bracers for the digital tracking arrow to match the one she'd placed inside her bra.

Aerie would've seen the signal as soon as she started to move. Now Reid just had to follow it, and map the details of the area for his reinforcements.

Jessica's heart hammered as she was led to the small clearing with a large cavern entrance at the back. Her father was visible, sitting on the floor in the cavern with his hands behind his back and a bandage wrapped around one ankle. He was pale and seemed to be in pain. She rushed forward, only to be jerked back by men who clearly did not understand *not* to touch her. At least they'd been mostly respectful up until now.

"Not so fast, doc. There's someone who would like to speak with you." The soldier tilted her to her left.

A familiar man approached her, though his clothing was far from the formal apparel she normally associated him with. His wavy blond hair was the same. His sparkling green eyes and charming grin. Stephen Carson had cornered both her and her assistant, Sally, at more than one public event. Only now did she see the seriousness behind his everyday good looks, and the sinister intent he'd hidden behind all those questions about TERA. She'd assumed he was faking an interest in her work in order to get closer to her. It had been vice versa and, though she'd resisted his advances, she now felt like a complete fool.

"Dr Cross." His gaze raked her thin nightwear, making her wish she wore heavier materials to bed.

"Mr Carson. Fancy meeting you here." Jessica trotted out their typical greeting, infusing it with bitter sarcasm.

"Don't be angry, Jessica. It had to happen this way."

"I truly doubt that, Stephen." Jessica crossed her arms. She'd purposefully tripped over branches and dragged her feet on her way to the clearing, giving Aerie time to arrive and position for their rescue. If she could delay even further by fighting with Stephen Carson, all the better. "If you have done anything to hurt my father, I *will* kill you."

The bastard laughed. Jessica glared at him until he stopped and cleared his throat. "He received some nicks and scrapes when he fell. I would never hurt him."

She snorted.

He gave her his most sincerely charming expression, spreading his hands palms up. "You don't understand. Neither of you were ever truly in danger. It just had to look as if you'd died. Your work must carry on. They were trying to stop it."

Jessica narrowed her eyes. "'They'?"

"The Naturalists, of course. TERA is too important, too life-changing. Your research must continue. We knew the army would catch wind of the assassination attempt and save you in time."

"If the government shuts us down, faking our deaths and kidnapping us won't help our research continue, Stephen." Jessica used her most biting tone, realising for certain what he wanted – a behind-the-scenes scientist who could continue research into unnatural ways to enhance a human body. To change people at a genetic level by playing God. That kind of research violated every medical ethic. But if she and her father were believed dead, they could continue that research and experimentation in secret, with no checks and balances to stop them. That was Stephen's intention and he actually thought she would be tempted by the offer.

Stephen gave her a look as if he'd just offered her an ice-cream sundae and a large spoon. "You know what I'm suggesting, Jessica. You could make this drug everything that it's truly meant to be."

In her peripheral vision came a movement she'd been expecting. Their time had run out. Before all hell descended into the clearing, she looked Stephen straight in the eye. "TERA is already what it was meant to be. A drug that cures disease and fixes physical impairments. Why is that never enough for people like you?"

Eight

Men began yelling and firing tasers. Stephen spun toward the commotion. Jessica ran to her father's side. Tears filled her eyes at his pain-filled face. There were scratches all over him and a bandage tight around his ankle. She began untying him. "Is this really from the fall?"

"Yes." He smiled at her, the love only shown for his work and for her shining in his eyes. "The blast made the foam disintegrate faster. Mike grabbed me before I could fall, but our position made landing awkward."

He nodded behind her and she turned to see an injured man lying on the ground. Her father continued, his voice suddenly grim. "Mike, on the other hand, was not hurt in the fall. All his traumas came after, when he wouldn't give up intel on your possible hiding spots."

Jessica pressed her lips together, glancing at the chaos outside the cave as she worked on the knots binding her father. Both sides of the conflict stayed well away from the cave. The scientists would be no good to any of them if they were injured.

Jessica freed her father and pulled him into her arms. She could have lost him today. It was a fear every day, of course, since he'd been forty-nine when she'd been born. After decades dedicated to medicine, one glimpse of her mother had shifted his focus. He'd been a loving husband and father until her mother had died. Afterwards, it had become the two of them, fighting the ills of the world together. But no matter how many medical advancements they made, the human body would only go so far before it quit.

The fighting was over and men were shouting and organizing.

Her father pulled away, taking in the anxiety on her face. "Airborne 81 out there?"

Warmth spread over her face. "Yes."

She caught the eye of the injured soldier on the ground. "Mike?"

Beautiful brown eyes peeked up at her. He grinned. "That's me."

"Are you bleeding?"

"No, ma'am. Sore ribs, broken leg, otherwise I'm fine." He winked.

Judging by the way the light hit his eyes and splashed across his face, a concussion and multiple cuts and contusions could be added to that list, but she nodded. "I'd better go check the others, then."

Mike frowned. "Be careful."

With a nod, Jessica headed to the entrance, trying not to be seen while she took in the status of their rescue. Before she made it inside, though, she ran headlong into a man who towered over her, his face shadowed by the setting sun behind him. She didn't need a clear sight of his face to recognize the man she'd been following all morning. Without warning, a rush of elation had her jumping up to her toes and hugging him close.

But Reid stood stiff, even as one of his hands patted her waist. Jessica pulled back. "Sorry. I was just so happy to see that you won."

Reid smiled at her, but it was a voice behind him that explained his reticence.

"Understandable, Dr Cross." Another soldier emerged from the shadows behind Reid. Reid's superior officer circled around Jessica to go straight to her father. "Good to see you doing so well, Dr Cross. You gave us all quite a scare."

"Nathan, it's good to see you. Is everything taken care of, now?"

Within minutes, the injured Mike, her father and Jessica were loaded onto another helijet. Seeing Reid appear in the doorway was almost déjà vu. This time, he spread a warm blanket over her and another over her father. Her pajamas weren't a complete lost cause yet, but they were thin, and cold air had covered the valley as soon as the sun had retreated. Reid sat across from them, his posture military perfect and his attitude properly withdrawn.

Jessica looked at her hands, twisting the blanket's ends in her fists. This had been the most eventful, dangerous day of her life and now she felt a connection to Reid. But did he feel the same for her? Or was that connection just the residual effect of an adrenalin rush they hadn't crashed down from yet? Did it really mean anything?

Jessica dreaded the answer.

Nine

Jessica hurried to set her flute of champagne on the waiter's tray as he passed by during the Eutopia fundraiser. *Eutopia.* She snorted. *Just another way of saying there were still issues that must be dealt with. Nothing was ever good enough. Cure illness, fine. Now there's poverty. Or political strife. Or too many hangnails.*

Considering the dark mood she'd had the last few months, alcohol was not a great idea. She and her father had testified against Stephen Carson and the men who'd blown up their helijet and attempted to kidnap them. She'd seen Reid once at the courthouse, from a distance. He hadn't spoken to her that day or any day since the helijet explosion. Normally, having someone pass in and out of her life didn't bother her. Other scientists, receptionists, medical interns – they usually had no effect.

A soldier who saved her life, then shared chocolate with her, should probably be the same. And maybe if Mike had been the one to rescue her, he would have been. But Reid's eyes haunted her. She'd stared into those expressive blue eyes so much that day, reading his directions as easily as reading a book. Not seeing him, except in her dreams, had become a painful, nagging weight she'd never experienced before.

Her mood was ruining everything right now. Jessica straightened, ready to avoid anyone asking her to dance. She just wanted to grab her purse and leave.

"What's wrong, Dr Sweetheart? Your experiments not turning out?"

Jessica's eyes widened and she spun to the voice at her back. The full skirt of her peach gown brushed against black-clad legs. Her gaze traveled up his formal long-tail tux to the three gold strips at his cuffs, and farther, to his broad shoulders decorated with stripes and stars and gold braid, and more ribbons than even she'd won for her doctorate research. Shock made her voice flatter than she intended. "Lieutenant."

Reid's face went from a charming half-smile to smooth and expressionless. "I didn't mean to bother you, Doctor. Just thought I'd be friendly."

He started to turn away and she panicked. *That was not what she wanted. Not at all.* Snagging his fingers, the tension in his hand and arm warned her not to attempt pulling on him. Jessica rushed in front of him and stared up into his face. "Friendly is an offer to dance."

He raised a brow. "I think not."

She tilted her chin up and raised a challenging brow. "Haven't you learned by now? Thinking should be left to the geniuses."

His lips twitched. Not quite a smile, but it would do. She tugged him onto the dance floor. It wasn't easy to talk, but it was not impossible, until his arms surrounded her again. He held her waist and hand at a discreet distance. She cast around for something more to say, but nothing seemed quite right. Too personal, to distant, too accusatory. As he stared over her shoulder, not seeming to be part of the dance at all, she went for the only tactic that seemed like it might work.

"Gee, save a girl's life, then don't talk to her again for three months. Is that the way with soldiers, Airborne 81?"

That brought his gaze back to her. "It *is* if the soldier in question is trying not to take advantage of a momentary attack of hero-worship."

Her eyes widened, then fell to the bow tie at his throat. "Oh."

As an incredibly good-looking man, he probably got that all the time. Desperate, needy, lonely women who had a day of excitement in their otherwise staid lives and refused to let it go. *Is that what she'd become?* Jessica tried to release her hand and step away but he wouldn't let her. She looked up, reading his eyes again.

The scary, expressionless look had gone, and he now seemed gentle, teasing. "Are you trying to abandon me? On a dance floor in front of hundreds of strangers? Now that is just cruel."

"No, of course I won't do that." Confused, she settled back into his grip. "Have you been well?"

Do you think of me? Dream of me? Remember holding me and maybe miss it? Desperate, foolish, whiny woman.

"My health is good. The weather is good. This event is good." His eyes mocked her attempt at innocuous conversation. "The case is closed."

She blinked. "The case?"

He raised a brow. "The one where I had to be debriefed, write reports, and speak to a jury in a completely unbiased manner."

"Oh." She nodded. "*That* case. It's closed for me, as well. Last week I finished signing the final paperwork."

"I know," he said meaningfully.

Jessica met his gaze again, but couldn't quite read him this time. "You know?"

"Now I can dance with you without any accusations of tampering with an investigation."

Jessica scowled. "Who would accuse you of that?"

"At this point, no one who matters. So, sweetheart, can I have your number?"

"Oh." Yes, that was genius thinking at work. She finally understood why he'd stayed away. And he wanted her number. Jessica's eyes darted to her purse, left at the table beside her father. Her father, whose twinkly eyes were focused on the two of them on the dance floor. Jessica looked back at Reid. "I don't have a pen, or my phone, or my business card with me."

He smiled. "I can get it from you before we say goodnight."

A glow she could actually feel spread across her face. "Yes, you can. But if you kiss me again, you'll have to promise to take your time."

He chuckled. "That's a promise."

A promise he fulfilled three hours later when he escorted her to her car. In the slowest of increments possible, he cupped the side of her face in one hand, slid the other arm around her waist, and did nothing short of caress her lips with his. Jessica closed her eyes and sank into him, one hand at the nape of his neck, playing with the smooth skin there. Her other hand reached around his back, pressing him even closer. This was exactly what she'd wanted, needed, dreamed about since his first abrupt kiss on the run.

Reid sucked her bottom lip between his and stroked his tongue lightly across it. Jessica shivered. This was absolutely worth jumping out of a jet for.

Seven Months of Forever

"Games of Command" Adventure

Linnea Sinclair

CAPTAIN'S OFFICE: UNITED COALITION
HUNTERSHIP REGALIA

Chatter strongly indicates the Triad Faction plans a significant move against the U-Cees. Attached is all I know right now. Target or targets have not been conclusively identified—

"One minute!" Captain Tasha Sebastian grumbled at the flashing green icon on her desk screen even though the icon couldn't hear her. But it made her feel that at least she wasn't ignoring the damned thing as she studied the information on enemy activity in the Far Reaches.

However, you shouldn't discount, Sass, that your name is high on the list. After all, you robbed the Faction of an expensive and irreplaceable asset.

It was that expensive and irreplaceable asset that now, via flashing green icon, wanted her attention. He would have to wait. The heavily encrypted packet from the Rebashee Underground took priority – and concentration. She was able to decrypt the data only because she had, after all, spent a good part of her early years as a raft-rat named Sass, and had been trained in the fine art of code-breaking – and ship hijacking – by a Rebashee mercenary.

The same mercenary who'd sent her this information in spite of the fact that the raft-rat was now a United Coalition huntership captain. The Rebashee had no love for either the U-Cees or the Triad Faction. But they hated the Faction more, especially with the recent assimilation of the Triad by the parasitic Ved'eskhar. "The new and *mullytrocking*-improved Triad, thanks to the Ved," Gund'jalar, her mercenary mentor had noted in a previous missive. If ruthless and morally bankrupt could be seen as an improvement. Sass doubted the thousands of Triad citizens psychically tortured saw it as such.

It took her ten more minutes to decrypt and process Gund'jalar's latest intel. The information *was* vague and felt as if the Ved-controlled Triad hadn't yet committed to a definitive course of action.

Or it's possible, she argued with herself, *that our friends in the resistance are finally causing trouble, forcing the Faction to scatter resources.* The U-Cees had hoped for that ever since the incursion of the Ved caused the collapse of the original U-Cee-Triad alliance over six months ago. Though she recognized she could be being overly optimistic.

But Gund'jalar wasn't an alarmist. This was something he wanted her to know now. She noted it.

My sources expect a more detailed update within a few shipdays if not hours. As soon as I know, so will you. Until then, my friend and best student, watch your back.

She closed the packet and filed it under three levels of encryption that, thanks to new security protocols Kel-Paten devised, could only be accessed by herself or Kel-Paten. There was still work to do with their personal protocols, but running a five-ship patrol group in the Far Reaches – right on the edge of the Triad border – had, understandably, taken precedence.

"Okay. Next?"

The flashing green icon was still there. She tapped it.

My office. Five minutes. Coffee awaits. BKP

A second box pulsed behind the first. *Impatience thy name is Branden Kel-Paten.* She opened that too with a swipe of her finger.

Your coffee's getting cold. We may have to explore other forms of heat . . .BKP

That made her grin in spite of the dire tone in the intel from Gund'jalar. For a man – she rarely thought of Branden as a bio-'cybe anymore – who was a virgin a mere seven months ago, he was a quick learner of these "other" forms of heat.

"The admiral beckons," she told the plump and purring black-and-white furzel sprawled across the corner of her desk. She hadn't intended to update Kel-Paten on Gund'jalar's information until she received the specifics promised in the second report. But Branden, a former Triad admiral, had been working with his own sources – Triad expats, for one – and a comparison of intel at this point might be advisable considering they *were* in the Far Reaches.

Looove Brandenfriend, was the telepathic furzel's answer. That and a furry bared belly. She gave Tank's belly a quick rub then headed for her office door. "Tell Branden I'm on my—"

The general quarters alarm whooped through the *Regalia's* corridors. Sass spun back toward her desk. "Tank, go blink! Blink to your kennel *now*." The furzel, well used to emergencies after their recent Faction-sponsored insanity in McClellan's Void, teleported – *blinked* – out of Sass's office and, according to the icon on her comp screen, into the safety of his personal lifepod in her quarters.

She slapped her shoulder comm link, connecting to the officer of the watch on the bridge. "Captain here. Status."

The information the OOW gave her as she jogged toward the lift made her gut clench: an interstellar thermal wave a few light-minutes out. It had sufficient power to turn a huntership like the *Regalia* – not to mention the two cruisers and two frigates traveling with her – into a ragged line of deep-space debris. The fact that she'd faced such a wave twice before only made her throat tighten.

Three times is never the charm it's purported to be.

She lunged out of the lift, colliding with a tall dark-haired man in freighter grays, his hands encased in black gloves. Admiral Branden Kel-Paten was a commanding presence even though he no longer wore an intimidating, black, enemy Triad uniform. He'd lost more than his virginity seven months earlier: with his defection from the Triad, Branden had lost his history, his home, his fleet, his commission. That the U-Cees' very formidable former enemy was still referred to as admiral was only because the half-human, half-cybernetic officer continued to earn it.

"We must be some kind of damned vortex magnet," Sass said tersely as Kel-Paten propelled her toward the bridge, one hand firmly grasping her forearm.

"Statistically improbable, Sass, but I won't disagree with you." The flat tone of his deep voice told her he was fully in his 'cybe function. That and the luminous glow of his eyes.

"Captain on deck," the officer of the watch sang out.

Sass waved the bridge crew back to their seats with a perfunctory, "As you were."

Kel-Paten slid into the chair next to hers in the center of the U-shaped bridge and, with a quick motion of his wrist, spiked into the ship's systems through the cybernetic interfaces that augmented his body. Collision alarms fell silent. Sass gleaned her data the old-fashioned way, studying what the screens and holographic master plot board before her told her. Yes, it was a thermal wave, but this time . . .

"McAbian residue readings are inconsistent with vortex formation," Kel-Paten announced over the low, tense rumble of voices around them. "No known binary-collision region in this sector. Energy signature is not indicative of an interstellar gas cavity."

"So it's not a star fart. Then what—?"

An object flashed onto the *Regalia's* short-range screens. A ship – less than three lightminutes out – impossibly, improbably hurtling through the blackness of deep space on a direct course for *Regalia's* patrol group.

"Deploy Starseekers. Forward shields full!" There was no jump gate here – no known and charted jump gate – but even if there was, no ship in her patrol group had logged a corresponding energy surge that preceded a gate transit. The unknown bogie had, to all intents and purposes, appeared out of nowhere.

And that was not good news.

Kel-Paten's frown told her he'd surmised that ugly fact, and likely more.

"We have ident on the bogie," her tactical officer called out without turning from her sensor station. "Fighter craft. Triad TZ-Four. Starseeker leader confirms configuration."

"A Teaser? We're being challenged by a godsdamned *Teaser*?" Teasers, like U-Cee Starseekers, were fast and efficient, yes. But a real threat only in fifteen-man squadrons that used the craft's speed and agility to attack and withdraw in repetitive waves, wearing down a ship's defensive shielding so the larger capital ships behind them could move in for the kill. A sole Teaser was little more than target practice for a ship like the *Regalia*. This meager effort couldn't possibly be what Gund'jalar's information alluded to, could it?

"TZ-Four, subclass Ada," Kel-Paten said as the *Regalia* adjusted course. "No accompanying battle group detected."

Yet.

"Where's the rest of the squadron?"

"Sensors aren't picking up anything right now, Captain," Tactical told her.

"Kel-Paten?"

His frown deepened. "Negative."

No battle group. No squadron. Just a lone Teaser on the edge of the Far Reaches . . .

"Scan for debris." The small fighter had to have been part of an attack group launched by the Triad Faction against Rebashee patrols. But why was it heading insystem, not for the Triad border? Unless the yet-to-be-located attack group was aimed at the patrol ships currently under her command? Gund'jalar's warning replayed in her mind. "Check all comm channels for distress signals, any kind of traffic. Scan the Teaser for life signs."

The pilot could be unconscious, the ship following a now-useless course. The ship's location could be a freak accident. Happenstance.

Except this freak accident was dumping a Teaser on her doorstep. And she was a firm disbeliever in happenstance.

However, espionage was something she was very familiar with.

"Your theories on using a vortex as a jumpgate," she said quietly, because even though this was *her* ship, Kel-Paten's work in that area was rightly deemed top secret. Especially as Kel-Paten had preliminary data that indicated a vortex's energies might also hold the key to the destruction of the Ved.

"Already scanned for telltales. Negative," he told her, equally as quietly.

That was good news and bad news. Good that the Faction hadn't beaten them to the punch in harnessing a vortex's power. Bad in that she still had no idea where the ship came from.

"No debris, no distress signals," Rembert, her first officer, reported.

Also not good.

"The *Hallmark* and the *Noble* report negative on debris and signals," Lieutenant Lucari at communications confirmed.

More not good. Sass was never happy when the not-goods ran in the plus column. "I don't like—"

"Distress signal active on Triad comm NB757." Kel-Paten's announcement interrupted her complaint. "Sending data to you now, Mr Rembert."

Triad comm NB757?

Her first officer swiveled back to his station to start his data analysis. "Got it, Admiral. Thanks."

"It's a coded squadron channel," Kel-Paten said before she could ask. "Short range. If the U-Cees even had it in their databases, it's likely been deleted as old intel. I haven't used it since I was a cadet."

Try as she might, Sass couldn't envision the dark-haired muscular man as a gangly twenty-year-old cadet.

"No life signs, Captain," Rembert called out. "No ship response to our hails, not even on that channel."

Something felt wrong, very wrong. Sass couldn't pin it down, other than a gut feeling. There were too many unexplained variables: a ship out of nowhere broadcasting on an old frequency in very short range . . .

"Tractor her in, Mr Rembert," Kel-Paten called out.

Sass's right hand shot up. "Belay that." She turned. "I don't like this. It's not a rescue. No one's alive aboard. Lock it in a tow if you want, but I don't want to risk—"

"Ship's breaking apart, Captain, Admiral!"

"Reel her in, Mr Rembert." Kel-Paten looked down at her. "We've suspected for months now that the Faction is moving assets across the border into this sector. If this is an error on their part, then this could get us information we need. Now."

"And if she's rigged with a bomb?"

"Shuttle Bay Eleven," Kel-Paten told Rembert. Then to Sass: "That will—"

"Okay. I don't like it, but . . ." She tightened her lips. Bay Eleven was triple-plated for just such situations. Somehow that didn't make her feel better.

"Got her! Eleven it is," Rembert replied.

Sass nodded her confirmation. "Call back our Seekers, Mr Rembert." She glanced over at Kel-Paten. "You'd better be right about this ship's threat potential."

A small smile quirked Kel-Paten's mouth as he spiked out, and his eyes shifted back to their normal pale-blue hue. "I always am." He rose. "Let's go see what our lucky find will reveal."

CORRIDOR UPPER BRIDGE DECK

It took Branden Kel-Paten's cybernetically enhanced mind all of three-point-six seconds to calculate the exact time it would take for the lift to travel from the upper level of the bridge to the lower shuttle docks on the *Regalia* and he knew – from that and from, well, experience – that that was exactly enough time to grab two decent kisses or one very excellent deep kiss from Captain Tasha Sebastian.

Never one to settle for anything less than perfection, he opted for the latter.

"Branden," Sass began as the lift doors *whooshed* closed, "I think—"

"Thinking not required," he rasped as he pulled her roughly against him and covered her already opening mouth – convenient, that – with his own. He took in her small *oomph* of breath and used that to let his tongue find hers. Then her hands splayed against his chest slid upward, curling around his neck, and Sass – *his* Sass, the woman he'd loved in secret for so very long – did her best to redefine his definition of an excellent kiss.

It had been seven months since his decades-old fantasies had become reality, but she still made his heart pound, made his hands tremble, made his body go electric in ways the cyber-surgeons who created him never imagined. They couldn't have. They'd created him for war, for death, for ugliness. What he had with Sass surpassed all descriptions of beauty.

He still woke by her side every ship morning fearing her presence was all a dream – or another Ved-induced hallucination like the one that had tortured them with bizarre alternate realities seven months before in McClellan's Void.

"My, oh my," she said, her voice breathy, when he broke their kiss one level before the shuttle decks.

"I haven't seen you since breakfast." That wasn't totally true. He could "see" her anytime he wanted simply by spiking into the ship's vid cams. But seeing her wasn't the same as feeling the heat of her skin on his. He needed that. Desperately. "It's almost dinner."

"And if someone else boarded the lift?"

"Not possible." Well, except for Tank, who could blink himself anywhere on the ship within seconds, and who had more than once shown up at some rather inopportune times. "I reprogrammed it before we left the bridge."

"Smart ass," she quipped as the lift doors opened. Three crewmembers waiting for the lift saluted and stepped aside.

"Thank you, Captain," he told her, motioning for her to exit first.

"My pleasure, Admiral."

"No, mine. Really."

The sound of the lift doors closing behind them was immediately followed by the sensation of a small hand smacking him on the rump. He grinned.

"Be careful with this so-called lucky find of yours, Branden. I don't like it. And my Rebashee contacts are getting chatter that something's in the works."

He sighed. "You and Gund'jalar grant the Faction capabilities I don't think they have. By the time I escaped, the Triad had lost most of the key officers, top personnel." Some escaped with him but far more were murdered. That was one of the many losses he felt keenly.

"And you don't feel the Ved'eskhar give them a definite advantage?"

"Granted, the Ved control those who remain. But that's exactly my point: they're alien creatures. Parasites. Their goal is to feed on humans' emotional reactions. The success of the Faction as a military and political entity is not their concern. I've believed all along they would get sloppy militarily. This could well be the first of many errors we'll find."

"Show me the rest of the squadron, or its debris, and I'll feel better. That kind of error I understand. But a ship just showing up with no logical explanation—"

"We don't know how long it's been traveling. The explanation could be just out of sensor range for us. I can access the Teaser's systems – I *know* a Teaser's systems – and find all that out and more."

Sass slowed as they approached Shuttle Bay Eleven. "I want one of our furzels to scan the ship for Ved resonances first."

"Agreed." Kel-Paten knew he could handle anything mechanical or cybernetic. He'd integrate his personal firewalls with the security blocks already resident in the U-Cee probes. But telepathic parasitic aliens were something he'd never been programmed for. Furzels, however, hunted them with great success. That was why there were virtually none of the small furry creatures in the Triad, and why every U-Cee ship and station housed them.

He followed Sass into the shuttle bay control room, and listened without comment while she requested a scanning furzel from the division chief on duty. The slender lines of the captured Triad ship – the Ada-class TZ-Four – drew him to the large viewport. Sleek, powerful, agile, adaptive, it was everything the Triad had been before the Faction. Yes, this one was battered, her hull caved in badly on her port side. But those flaws couldn't detract from her beauty, not even with the *Regalia*'s spiky security probes circling her, scanning for explosives and detonation devices.

He'd flown TZ-Twos in training and Threes in actual combat. "The Ada-class TZ-Four was released fifteen months ago," he told Sass and the chief as they watched the brown-striped furzel sniff the viewport, its fur-tufted ears cocked forward, long whiskers quivering. He couldn't hear its thoughts. He wasn't linked to it as he and Sass were to Tank. But he recognized the scanning posture.

"If the ship is a newer model then why was it broadcasting on an old comm channel?" Sass asked as the furzel disappeared from its perch in a blink, and then reappeared moments later.

He'd considered that question. "The NB757 comm was needed to integrate with older ships."

A plumy tail twitched. The furzel shook itself and stared with golden eyes up at the red-haired female ensign who was its teammate and handler. "Negative on Ved resonances, Captain," the woman said.

"Probes show negative on explosives," the chief added, pointing to the hovering holo screen with its rotating schematics of the craft.

Kel-Paten held back his "told you so" until the chief followed the ensign and the furzel out of the control room.

Sass snorted softly. "Just how long has it been since Teaser squadrons used NB757?"

Kel-Paten accessed his memory banks. "Twenty-one years, three months. TZ-Twos were the last official usage, though it existed on some early Threes because—"

"They had to talk to the older fighters. I know. But this is a TZ-Four."

"Exactly my point. I know her specs, defenses, and data structures because they're based on systems I'd developed for the *Vax*." That was another loss he felt keenly: The *Vaxxar*, his former Triad flagship, now little more than scrap, thanks to the Ved. He shook off the memory and tossed one of her trademark phrases at her: "Piece o' cake."

She responded with her green eyes narrowing in a clear warning. "Piece o' cake, my ass. Be careful. That's an order."

Kel-Paten dropped into the seat the chief had vacated and inserted one end of a makeshift data-spike into the access port. The *Regalia* was a U-Cee ship, not Triad. It might now be his home, but it was still foreign territory. Linking the other end to the ports in his wrist would grant him control of and access to the probes and through them the TZ-Four. A bit of home, a bit of familiarity. He hadn't realized how much he missed Triad tech until he'd seen the fighter.

"You hear me, flyboy?" She cuffed him lightly on the shoulder.

He held one end of the data-spike between gloved fingers and slanted a glance up at her, the woman he'd dubbed his "green-eyed vixen" more than a dozen years ago. "Sebastian." He paused deliberately. The name-and-pause was a ritual, also established long ago as a challenge to his patience. Now it held a distinctly sentimental and affectionate tone.

"Kel-Paten." She paused as well. Her mouth twitched.

He fought the urge to kiss those twitches; the world of hidden and forbidden Triad data beckoned him. For the past four shipweeks – ever since the *Regalia* had pulled him and what was left of his officers and crew off the dying hulk of his

flagship, the *Vaxxar* – he'd been living in an environment where
he really didn't belong. An environment where – in spite of
Sass – he was an outsider. His rank was a courtesy. His contri-
butions were appreciated, but as an adviser, not as part of the
team. Now, with this, a Triad ship, he knew he could make a
significant difference. Intel reports hinted that the Triad
Faction was amassing a secret battle group in the Far Reaches.
This TZ-Four had to have come from that – probably a
remnant of war games gone wrong. *He was going to use their
mistake to undermine them. Destroy them. Just as they'd destroyed
everything he'd once held sacred: his commission, his fleet, his flagship, his home.*

He activated his full 'cybe functions with a thought, and
clicked the end of the data-spike into his wrist. It took him
seven-point-three seconds to guide the probe to the access port
on the Teaser's hull, and another three-point-five seconds to
initiate a secure connection. Firewalls – his and the probes' –
shielded his entry. His mind slid down the datastream pathways
as if he were just another bit of code, which he was. Six seconds
more and he was at the main databanks.

If not for the years of training he'd been through, he would
have gasped aloud. *Luck? This was beyond luck. This was a verita-
ble mythical heaven of information on the Faction's fleet and its
movements. Its battle plans. Its . . . there. It had to be. More than just
battle plans. The Faction's security access codes. The U-Cees, the
Rebashee, hell, as far as he knew even the Illithians hadn't been able
to obtain these, though many had died trying.*

"This is incredible," he told Sass as he mentally surged toward
the databases, grabbing for . . .
Pain.
Blackness.
Nothing.

SICK BAY

Sass perched stiffly on the edge of a chair in Dr Caleb Monterro's
office, and turned her cold cup of coffee around in equally-as-
cold hands. Her throat was still tight from the screams she'd
held back when Branden had collapsed to the control-room

decking. Her chest ached from the shards of her breaking heart raking her insides raw.

But he was alive. The med-techs confirmed that when they arrived. Cal Monterro confirmed that when he hooked Kel-Paten up to the recently upgraded cyber-human diagnostics panel in sick bay's Room Six. But no one could say more than that, not even Lieutenant Jameson, the ship's leading cyber-tech, who was admittedly more used to dealing with military-issue computers than with a half-human Triadian bio-'cybe.

But Jameson, the cyber-tech, was all they had. The U-Cees had never been able to get full specs on Branden Kel-Paten. The few medical files they'd been able to retrieve a month ago from the *Vaxxar* were corrupted by the power spikes surging through the dying ship's failing systems. Though what they did know formed the basis for the instrumentation in Sick Bay Six.

Even with all that, they knew so little. And the only person who unequivocally had all the answers was unconscious in Cal's sick bay.

The one hope she had left was Captain Ralland Kel-Tyra, Branden's brother – well, they shared the same "paternal genetic donor", as Branden often put it. Though that fact was kept secret by the Triad for years. Like Branden, however, Kel-Tyra was a former high-ranking Triad officer who'd defected to the U-Cees when the Ved took control of the Triad. She knew Branden was integrating their personal security protocols with Kel-Tyra as a fail-safe – just as Kel-Tyra's were in a secure file on the *Regalia*. Sass kept staring at Cal's desk screen as if by thought alone she could will Kel-Tyra to answer. The officer of the watch – hell, the whole ship knew where she was. The minute Kel-Tyra responded to the *Regalia's* message, she would be alerted.

It had been more than three hours since that message had gone out. U-Cee controlled space was large, but military communications had been designed to account for that. An hour, two at most. She should have heard something – even if only a receipt confirmation. She hadn't.

A sickening thought made her hands go even colder. *Had the Faction's attack on Kel-Paten – and she and Jameson had no doubt the Teaser was a trap aimed specifically for him – been only a part of a larger plan to wipe out all "traitorous" former Triad officers and crew?*

The sound of footsteps made her jerk upright.

"No change," Cal told her as he angled around his desk, and then dropped tiredly into his chair. He tapped a screen icon. Data flashed against a white background. "The best Jameson can come up with is that we work from a worst-case scenario. When the admiral regains consciousness, we must assume he's been reprogrammed to harm this ship, you, the furzels, or all of the above."

"You're sure he will? Wake up, that is?"

"Jameson's very sure that if the Faction wanted him dead, he'd be dead."

Which meant they didn't want his death. They wanted a weapon. And there was no weapon quite as insidiously lethal as Branden Kel-Paten with his beyond-human strength, reflexes, and intellect. And his ability to kill with a touch.

"That's why I've posted security here in sick bay, and why I'm banning you from Room Six," Cal continued. "And don't try using your furzel to teleport you in there."

"Damn it, Cal, Branden wouldn't—"

"He can. He would."

"Jameson can't reprogram his reprogramming?"

"He's trying to."

"I gave you our list of code words." Kel-Paten would not be happy about that breach of personal security protocol. But he couldn't reprimand her until he woke up. And right now Sass would gladly face the stoniest of his reprimands, just to have him back. "His med files—?"

"Are more incomplete than we realized." Cal tapped his screen. "We not only ran through the key word list you gave Jameson. We mixed them up and threw in every other possible code we could think of to try and get him to respond. Ship names. Your name. Tank's. Captain Kel-Tyra's. Hell, we even uploaded images of winning hands in Starfield Doubles. His systems block everything."

She almost suggested they try a losing hand but, no. Branden Kel-Paten never lost.

Damn it! If only Kel-Tyra would answer.

"I'm not saying we're giving up. We will, right up to the last moment, try everything we can to restore him. But we're at a crossroads here, Captain. That's why I've come back – I'm sorry. You're not going to like what I must ask you now."

What could be worse than not permitting her to touch Branden? *Gods. No.*

Cal was tapping Branden's med-file data again. "Something that highly classified isn't in here. The Triad could never risk our finding out. But I suspect he's told you. We need that information or this entire ship is at risk."

Sass shut her eyes and forced the tremor threatening to surge through her body to stop. She knew what Cal wanted, what Security needed.

They needed to know the one vulnerability in Kel-Paten's synthderm mesh body.

They needed to know how to kill Branden.

SICK BAY ROOM 6

Nothing.
  Blackness.
  Pain.
  Cessation of pain.
  Power.

He came fully awake in a stark gray and white room and immediately cataloged his surroundings and their relative threat index. He ripped the data-feed cables from his wrist port. *Someone – the* enemy *– had tried to gain access to his systems.*

  Fools.

  But fools who had enough wisdom not to leave a human security guard in the room with him. That person would be dead before he could even raise his weapon.

He sat up, ran a second systems diagnostic and oriented himself. Med panels were all labeled in Standard, not Triadian. Definitely the enemy. But U-Cees, not the Rebashee or the Illithians. Not that that mattered much. His mission – it flooded him as soon as he came to consciousness – was to neutralize all enemy personnel, take control of the ship, and deliver it to the Triad.

  Piece o' cake.

  Piece o' cake? He shoved the uncharacteristic phrase away. *Residual data, likely something he'd overheard while unconscious. It sounded like the usual ridiculous U-Cee slang.*

Eight minutes and seventeen-point-two seconds later – according to the readout in the corner of his vision – the wall screen on his left flickered. Two humans in U-Cee tan uniforms stared at him. One – the male – wore the blue lab coat of a med-tech. The shorter female balanced an overweight black-and-white furzel in her arms.

His databanks brought up the humans' corresponding files: Dr Caleb Monterro, CMO. Captain Tasha Sebastian. Both assigned to the *Regalia*. The furzel was of no importance and, if necessary, easily terminated.

Excellent. He was exactly where he needed to be.

"How are you feeling, Admiral?" Sebastian asked. The furzel wiggled in her arms then slid down, out of view.

"Optimal." He plucked the useless data feed from the diagnostic bed and dropped it. "A waste of time. But you already know that, Sebastian."

Something flickered across Sebastian's face. He was programmed to unerringly interpret over one hundred and forty human facial expressions, and another sixty-seven nonhuman ones. He labeled what he saw in her face as "disappointment" and "grief".

Disappointed he was alive? Too bad.

Grief because perhaps before they trapped him in this sick-bay room, he'd killed someone she cared about? Good.

"Kel-Paten." She paused.

He stared at her. Waited. When she said nothing more, he continued to wait. *U-Cees and their infantile games.*

"Do you really need me to state name, rank, and serial number?" he asked curtly.

"We're not the enemy. I know you don't believe that right now, Branden. But we're not."

The use of his first name by this U-Cee trash annoyed him. He stated name, rank, and serial number.

The wall screen blanked.

Time to get to work. He had a mission to complete. And Bio-'cybernetic Kinetic Programmable Apparatus-Ten never failed.

DR CALEB MONTERRO'S OFFICE, SICK BAY

"Captain . . ."

The gentle tone in Cal's voice was exactly what Sass didn't need. *Damn it! She missed, really missed Doc Eden Fynn-Serafino, her former CMO, right now.* "Don't coddle me, Doctor. I can handle this." She stopped at his office door.

Tank leaned against her ankle. *Brandenfriend gone. Gone. Mommy sad.*

"Evacuate sick bay. Disable all equipment, especially data and comm feeds. Put a double containment field around the admiral's room. Then another pair around the sick bay itself. Yes." Her raised hand stilled Cal Monterro's comment. "He will get through those. Eventually. But it will slow him down. We need time, Cal. Time. We have to reach Captain Kel-Tyra. Since Tank couldn't make telepathic contact with Branden, Kel-Tyra's now our only chance of finding those key code words." She refused to voice her fear that Rall Kel-Tyra might already be dead.

"A security team—"

"In the corridor. Only. I'm not—" And she clenched her eyes shut for a moment. "I'm not ordering his . . . assassination. Not yet."

Cal's mouth tightened.

"Alert me when he breaches the first set of fields," Sass told him. Then she headed doggedly out into the *Regalia's* gray utilitarian corridor, Tank padding softly – and sadly – at her heels.

CAPTAIN TASHA SEBASTIAN'S OFFICE

Admiral Cayla "Ace" Edmonds's communication came in an hour and a half later. Right after the security update that Kel-Paten had already neutralized the first of Room Six's containment fields and was working steadily on the second.

"The shuttle Captain Kel-Tyra was traveling in came under attack by unknown bogies five hours ago, standard shiptime. We believe he made it to Lightridge Station, but Lightridge's commsat's ceased responding. I've got a battle group three lighthours out from station. It's a godsdamned *mullytrock*,

Sass. I'm sorry. As soon as I have something, you'll know. Edmonds out."

Sass gripped the edges of her office chair and shoved herself to her feet. *She had to try to save him. Brandon had more than once been willing to sacrifice his life for hers. He'd loved her in spite of what he was and who she was. She loved him because of what they were together.*

She knew better than to ask for sick bay's containment fields to be dropped. She settled for using the comm screen in CIC that – as it was her ship's Combat Information Center – had triple-secure emergency links to all key stations on the *Regalia*. It took a few minutes to re-establish sick bay's severed audio and video links. And that was a risk. Kel-Paten could spike in. But at least if he did, CIC's firewalls had the best chance of stopping him.

She didn't know how he knew that the screen in his room had come on quietly, only that he turned casually – if anything Kel-Paten did under full 'cybe power could be said to be casual – and raked her with a luminous icy-blue gaze, his expression unchanging and unreadable.

She didn't waste his time or hers. Her CIC commander was cutting the link at the five-minute mark.

"Branden, I know you're in there, inside whatever they've programmed into you. I need you to listen, to really listen to me. Ralland Kel-Tyra came under attack by the Triad Faction out by Lightridge. We have every reason to believe he made it to station. Your people are trying to kill him. They've already reprogrammed you. I am not your enemy. The U-Cees are not your enemy. Kel-Tyra is working with us, with the U-Cees, just as you have been for the past seven months. And now his life is threatened. We need your help, your knowledge."

His gaze didn't waver.

"Damn it all, flyboy, you have to remember!" Her voice rasped. The pain and fear she'd kept tamped down suddenly surfaced.

Something shifted in his hard expression. Sass didn't know what it was, only that there was a minuscule change, a slight tightening around his eyes. Then it was gone.

"If Kel-Tyra has turned traitor, I will deal with him after I take control of your ship."

The utter coldness in his tone made her gut clench. This would be her last chance to convince him. She could understand his not remembering her, but Branden and Ralland had spent almost their entire lives together. If anything could shatter Branden's reprogramming, it had to be Ralland. But there was no way she could now get Ralland here in person. This was her only other option.

She tapped the left side of her screen. A red icon expanded to a secondary screen showing the green-tinged bridge of the former Triad huntership, the *Vaxxar*, in total disarray. There was the U-shaped command center, the double-command sling and, in front of that, the curve of the railing. And a familiar tall dark-haired man, gloved hands braced against it.

The time stamp scrolling in the lower right showed a date four shipweeks past. *"United Coalition huntership* Regalia, *this is Branden Kel-Paten. I don't know if you can hear me. Our comm array is down. Life support is failing. We can't control the shields, though we're trying"* The image of Kel-Paten glanced over his left shoulder at a man sitting at a nearby station. Ralland Kel-Tyra, nodding.

"I repeat. Our comm array is down. Weapons banks, life support depleted. We're not a threat. We are . . . we are all that's left. The Triad is no more."

*"*Regalia, *if Tash – if Captain Sebastian is on board or anywhere in your Fleet, reach her. Please. Tell her I . . . tell her Branden Kel-Paten hopes – prays – her offer still stands. If you can hear me,* Regalia, *send us a signal. We have only two hours of air left—"*

A fat black-and-white furzel appeared suddenly on the wide railing in the green-tinged darkness, plumy tail flicking back and forth. Kel-Paten flinched, Ralland Kel-Tyra behind him rising swiftly from his seat. Then, in a blur of movement, Kel-Paten grabbed the furzel, clasping him tightly against his chest, relief and joy written starkly on his gaunt features . . .

Sass tapped the screen again and the playback stopped.

"A decent fabrication if a tad overly theatrical," Kel-Paten said. "But Captain Kel-Tyra doesn't sit nav on my ship. I suggest you reassign whatever intel officer gave you that erroneous data to the sanitation division. If you'll excuse me, I have work to do."

An alarm trilled shrilly behind her in CIC. "He's broken

through Room Six's second containment field, Captain," the CIC officer told her. "Kel-Paten now has complete access to sick bay."

CAPTAIN'S QUARTERS

Sass was tired, so godsdamned tired. The *Regalia* was well into third-shift, long past Sass's bedtime. She couldn't sleep. She paced the confines of the captain's quarters, alternately hugging her arms around her waist and thrusting her hands through her short-cropped hair, as she tried not to look at Branden's soft sweater thrown over the back of their couch. Or his new hiking boots tucked under their bedroom chair. She could bring him here, show him his own things mixed in with hers, but she knew he wouldn't believe her. If she even lived long enough to offer him the tour.

She really thought seeing the vid of himself and Ralland Kel-Tyra on the *Vax's* bridge would bring him back out of whatever cybernetic hell the Faction had shoved him into. All that effort had got her, though, was a derisive scoffing remark from him.

And an icy-blue stare she remembered far far too well, ever since they first met on the derelict freighter, the *Sarna Bogue*.

The captain had to make a decision soon. She knew that. The lives of her officers and crew hinged on it. Possibly the very fate of the United Coalition, if Kel-Paten commandeered her ship and handed over to the Faction all the intel the *Regalia* now held. She could not let the fact that she loved that man more than life itself stand in the way of what she knew had to be done.

Starting with the hard cold realization that the man she loved was no longer even there. *Someone, something else, inhabited Branden's body and cybernetically enhanced mind.*

When he breached the first of the two larger containment fields around the sick bay, she would have no choice but to give the order to kill him. She'd already provided the security team with the highly classified data on how to do that.

She hoped Ralland Kel-Tyra would forgive her. She knew she would never forgive herself.

I should have let you kidnap me. She'd told him that in McClellan's Void, when they had been trapped in another hell of the Faction's making – in a fabricated universe where all her sins as the infamous mercenary, Lady Sass, were paraded before Kel-Paten. She'd truly believed then that she'd lost him, that he was going to kill her.

But instead, he had admitted that at their first meeting on the decrepit *Sarna Bogue* twelve years ago he'd fallen in love with her. She'd been shocked. He'd said he'd known from that moment that, no matter who she was now or who she'd been, he wanted her in his life forever.

It was just a godsdamned *mullytrocking* shame that "forever" turned out to last only seven months.

She stared with all her might at her quarter's outer bulkhead, as if she could pierce her ship's hull with just her emotions, and send a message to the godsdamned *mullytrocking* Triad Faction – the same message she'd leveled at then-Captain Kel-Paten's *Vaxxar* a dozen years earlier:

Fuck you and the equinnard you rode in on.

It had certainly worked back then, changing her life and his. He'd told her more than once that it was a phrase he'd always associate with his "green-eyed vixen" . . .

She spun and bolted for her closet. "Tank, come! I need you now."

SICK BAY

Kel-Paten almost enjoyed dismantling the *Regalia*'s containment fields. They were a bit better than he'd anticipated, with a few unexpected twists and turns in the coding. It was a skillful pattern he'd come across only once before, a long time ago. That, too, was a pleasurable memory – as far as any 'cybe with emo-inhibitors could experience pleasure, that is. He tried recalling the details but they remained, oddly, elusive.

Unimportant, then. His programming automatically worked to a structured hierarchy. If and when that memory was needed to provide something of value, it would be there.

Until then . . .

There was a subtle change in the air currents. He spun to his right with unerring precision. Not toward the doors to the corridor. They were sealed. Not to any air duct or inner office door. Those posed no threat. But to . . .

"Captain Sebastian." He powered up fully. Even through his gloves, one touch would kill her. A brush of his fingers would render her unconscious. He could hold her hostage until he took control of her ship.

But how had she . . . ?

His brain searched, gathered, analyzed, redacted, gathered, analyzed, and redacted again. Two-point-seven seconds passed. She was unarmed. She had that fat furzel at her feet. She . . .

She was out of uniform, in patched and faded freighter grays, a ratty-looking red cap bearing the logo of a Kesh Valirr nighthouse perched askew on her short-cropped pale hair.

"*Vaxxar*, this is the *Sarna Bogue*," she said crisply. "Fuck you and the cquinnard you rode in on."

His body went rigid. His mind whirled, latching onto a coded sequence string of instructions that unpacked so quickly he was momentarily blinded in a blizzard of images and sounds and data.

Override. Execute. Override. Execute. Override. Execute.

His breath was sucked harshly out of his lungs. He bent over at the waist, gloved hands on his knees, and gasped for air, which suddenly tasted sweet and fresh – not stale and bitter as it had moments before.

He stared up at his green-eyed vixen. The galaxy slowly and elegantly righted itself.

Still hunched over, he focused his gaze on the name-patch above the single bar on her threadbare shirt. That insignia was the only part of her attire that was remotely regulation. He read her name and her rank aloud. "Lieutenant Sebastian."

She nodded, her mouth quivering slightly. "Captain Kel-Paten." Her voice, he noted, wavered. *Was she frightened of him? She needn't be. He could never, would never hurt her.*

He straightened, clearing his throat. "Where in hell am I?" This was not the bridge of the *Sarna Bogue*, though he could have sworn, moments ago, that that was where he was.

The furzel scampered across the decking and plopped down at his boots, then flipped onto its back, baring its very plump belly. A small high-pitched childlike voice exploded in Kel-Paten's head: *Brandenfriend! Tank loooves you. MommySass loooves you. Rub belly, please?*

He glanced down at the furry creature then back up at Lieutenant Sebastian. Tears trailed down her face – yet, illogically, she was grinning. He fought the urge to wipe those tears away. *He shouldn't touch her. He was Kel-Paten. She'd be afraid. Yet . . .*

She stepped toward him and he didn't try to stop her when she took his lethal gloved hand in her own, her fingers curling through his, flooding him with a surprising warmth.

"Sebastian?" He paused, embarrassed by the roughness of his voice.

"Kel-Paten." She paused too, and smiled up at him through her tears. "Welcome back, flyboy."

CAPTAIN'S QUARTERS

Branden Kel-Paten picked up the sweater he had no memory of wearing, then inspected the hiking boots he had no memory of acquiring, then cataloged the forty-six other items that were his in a closet he shared with . . .

A small hand rested lightly on his arm. "It's just a closet, Branden."

"Yes. Yes." A closet – a *cabin* he shared with Tasha Sebastian. "It's just that I don't fully remember much of this." Things were coming to him in snatches, like the twinkle of stars viewed dirtside – unlike stars in space, which didn't twinkle but were unchanging points of light.

His life right now felt like those dirtside twinkling stars working in triple overtime.

The best and the worst of it was Tasha. He remembered fully now their first meeting twelve years before on the *Bogue*, and in detail from there how he surreptitiously followed her career from lieutenant to commander on the *Asterion's Star*. He risked his own career paying agents exorbitant sums to keep track of her and obtain images of her. He even wrote her love letters that he never sent but kept securely buried in his very secure files, of course.

Though not all that secure. A few months ago, she had admitted finding them, when she was assigned to his flagship as part of the now-defunct U-Cee-Triad Alliance. He didn't remember any peace accord between the Triad and the U-Cees, short-lived though it was. Nor did he remember Tasha's attaining the rank of U-Cee captain. But he would remember, a Lieutenant Jameson assured him. Those rapidly twinkling stars of data would soon solidify into real chronological events. For now, his memory banks were in overload; his restore firmware still hunting and deleting the last vestiges of the coded worm the Faction had inserted into his mind through a devious trap within a rigged Trojan in the TZ-Four fighter's AI systems.

"At least you remembered the most important thing," she said with a wry smile, referring to the trigger phrase that had restored him to her. "It would have been nice, though, if you'd clued me in that you'd made that your override phrase."

He cleared his throat because the words he wanted to say – *I hate reminding you that I'm not fully human* – seemed to be stuck there, as they always were. He settled for: "It's not often I underestimate the enemy." And that enemy included himself – something he had admitted to an angry Ralland at Lightridge Station, in a brief conversation they had had an hour before.

"What worries me, Sass," Branden continued, his voice still rough, "is that right now the enemy knows me better than I know myself."

The hand on his arm moved to his waist. With a sigh, Tasha drew herself against him, head on his chest. "It'll all come back to you eventually, flyboy. Don't stress yourself out over it."

But while he waited for "eventually" to happen, he felt clumsy and stupid. He loved her so much. And she knew exactly how to move against him, how to touch him. Everything was so effortless when she did so.

He kept waiting for her to bolt away like the prosti on Mining Raft 309 when he'd been much younger, and drunk and shamed. The woman, seeing the scars on his chest and the synth-derm mesh on his hands, had recoiled, horrified.

Gingerly, he rested those same synth-derm mesh hands on Sass's shoulders.

Another sigh from her. "It's late." Her soft voice vibrated against his chest. "Actually, it's really early. We've missed a whole shipnight of sleep." She lifted her face. "Let's—"

"I don't need much sleep. But I've kept you awake too long. I can," and he motioned aimlessly toward the main room of their quarters, "spend time with my databases catching up on my, um, life."

Her hands slid down to grab the waistband of his pants. "Bed, Branden. Now."

Oh sweet gods. He had a very clear feeling that "bed" and "now" did not involve sleeping. And just because his body knew what she meant – and was announcing its intended cooperation with embarrassing enthusiasm – did not mean he had any skills, any methods, any godsdamned techniques in his databanks to honor her, to please her, to *love* her as he so very desperately wanted to do.

It would be – *he* would be an abysmal failure.

He cleared his throat. "Tasha." He paused.

"Branden." She paused.

"You need to understand that I've never been with . . . well, I've never wanted to. Not with anyone else. Just you. And you weren't . . . on my ship. We aren't – weren't on the same side. So I've never—"

"You have." She pinned him with a hard stare, but her mouth was twitching.

"I have?"

"*We* have. Lots of times in the past seven months." She stood on tiptoe, her breasts brushing his chest as she touched her lips to his. "*Lots.*"

His blood heated. His breath stuttered. His emo-inhibitors went fully offline. "What if I don't remember . . . how?"

She yanked on his waistband again and guided him down to the bed. "Then you'll be the only man in the history of the galaxy to lose his virginity twice," she said, straddling him as she worked on the seal-seam of his uniform shirt. "And I'll be the luckiest woman in the galaxy who gets to claim that honor. Twice."

"Sass?"

"Flyboy?"

"Make love to me."

"Is that an order, Admiral?"

"It is." He swallowed hard. *Oh, those clever, clever fingers of hers!*

"My pleasure."

"No, really." He gasped. "The pleasure is all mine."

Oooh. MommySass loooves Brandenfriend!

What? Telepathic furzels still startled him.

Tank! Sass telegraphed through that same link in his mind. *Privacy, please!*

Oops! O-kay. Tank go blink!

He reached for her face and brought it close to his. "Tasha," he murmured. "Come kiss."

Memories of Gravity

Patrice Sarath

The news of my grandfather's death reached me three months after the event, the transmission hindered by distance and garbled by the solar flares that mangled radio signals from Earth to the middle planets. Those of us on Bifrost Station in orbit around Jupiter were resigned to outdated mail and stale news; I preferred it that way. Piloting a shuttle between Bifrost and the research center on Ganymede required all my concentration, or so I told myself.

Still, the automated pinging of the transmitter with my code piqued my curiosity even as it triggered a strange reluctance. Who would be contacting me? I didn't have anyone on Earth I cared to correspond with, not since I'd been emancipated as a teen and made my own way in the solar system. I had left everything behind, and the only people who would care for me were dead. But I lived my life according to one principle: face the unpleasant head-on. That way you always see it coming.

After docking my shuttle and shedding my suit, I pushed toward my quarters to pick up the transmission. Still stinking of eight hours in a pressure suit, I sat down at my spartan desk in my spare quarters and called up my mail.

Transmission to: Captain Beatriz Sabatini, Bifrost Station
Date: 26 May 2237
From: Maher, Craven, Edelweiss, and Stroheim, Attorneys at Law
Dear Captain Sabatini,

We regret to inform you of the death of your grandfather, Richard Aldo Sabatini, on 10 May 2237.

Almost at once I was thrown back into my childhood, reliving memories I had tried so hard to bury – so hard that I had fled off-world from them, and halfway across the solar system. The adults at the funeral home had whispered over my head as I had sat kicking my chair, sad and frightened, not even the pretty dress and the shiny shoes making up for what I knew.

What will become of her, poor thing?

I heard the grandfather is taking her in.

Has anyone contacted her father?

Delicate laughter had followed, and I'd strained to make out the words: *Does anyone know which one he was?*

I forced myself to concentrate on the present and read the rest of the message. It was simple, text only. My grandfather had left me everything, but owing to ancient Earth laws, I had to return home to deal with my inheritance in person. I could not assign a proxy, nor could I engage a lawyer off-world to represent me in these matters.

I sat back, staring at the frozen text hanging in the air in front of me. Out of habit I lifted my hand to the scar that ran from my temple to my jawline, the last gift from my grandfather before I fled his presence.

"How far do I have to go to get away from you people?"

The bitter words hung in my small quarters much as the text did, unanswerable. In death my grandfather had as strong a hold on me as he had had in life. I imagined him glowering at me the way he had whenever I'd disappointed him, which was often.

"You are a Sabatini, Beatriz, and with that privilege comes great responsibility. We are not like other people. Let them misbehave, hmmm, child? Let them shirk their duties. Genes will tell, Beatriz. Genes will tell."

By other people, I knew he meant his daughter-in-law, my mother, and her dissolute lifestyle.

A small green light blinked patiently in the air at the end of the message, waiting to catch my attention. I touched the air where it blinked, and another message unfolded, this one an image transmission. I was surprised; that was expensive, even as tightly compressed as the message was.

The pixelated image resolved in front of me into a small bright scene: the family cemetery on Tern Island where I grew up. Generations of Sabatinis were laid to rest in the little overgrown grassy field, ancient gravestones weathering in the cold, wet island climate. My grandfather's grave was an upthrust obelisk in the center of the cemetery, shining and polished, surrounded by fresh dirt. I shook my head. *Typical.*

The image included a sensory file. The lawyers had really spared no expense. Pine trees soughed overhead, and I could feel the bright warmth of Sol on my shoulders. The waves broke on the shore and the whitecaps dazzled in the sunlight. I could smell the salt air and feel the breeze against my cheek. I shivered in the cold air.

The sensory file paused for a split second and then began again, and I shook my head in dismay. *As if I would be won over by warm sunlight on my shoulders.* I *liked* the sun where it was, I told myself, so far distant it was hardly bigger than a star.

I reached forward to close the image when something caught my eye and I paused. In the shadows on the farthest edge of the cemetery stood a figure. I couldn't make it out clearly but I could tell it was a child. Without thinking I leaned forward and my forehead brushed the image, sending it into a pixelated frenzy. Disgusted, I sat back and waited for it to resolve again. It was no use. The harder I looked, the blurrier the figure got, until finally it blended into the shadows and I couldn't see it any longer. No matter. I knew who it was, and who it was impossible that it could be. My grandfather was not the only ghost who haunted my nightmares.

Wet spray hit me in the face with salty seawater and I sputtered and gagged, my eyes stinging from the faceful of ocean. The wave had almost knocked me flat. I still had jelly legs even after exercising to rebuild muscles gone slack from zero-g. I wind-milled my arms and caught myself on the old fat posts lining the edge of the slippery wharf, waiting for the ferry to take me to Tern Island.

The sun was low in the sky on this wintry afternoon and I shivered in my coat and scarf.

I could see the ghostly lines of the massive near-Earth space station that was our closest satellite slowly rotating overhead, and I felt comforted. Space was not so far away after all, despite the weight of gravity that held me down.

"Well look who's here. Beatriz Sabatini, return of the prodigal daughter," someone called, laughter in his voice.

I turned cautiously, clutching my duffle bag and holding my hood down over my cap, recognition making my heart speed up with an unaccustomed happiness.

"Ethan Cardenas," I called back. "What are you doing here?"

"I'm your ride, darling," he said, and despite my misgivings I had to laugh at the double meaning. Ethan Cardenas, a ferry boat captain. I really was back on Earth.

Ethan waited for me in front of the rickety old office that perched on the rocks at the very edge of the wharf. He carried a thermos and was bundled in a yellow slicker, big black boots, and a wool watch cap. He was bulky, broad-shouldered, with creases around his eyes as if he spent his time peering into far distances. What I could see of his face was dark-skinned and clean-shaven.

I minced over to him cautiously. The soles of my boots clicked uselessly on the stone. They could be magnetized at need, but little good that did me here. He was laughing at me.

"Still got space legs," he said. He looked like he was enjoying my awkwardness, and I seethed. He was always teasing me when we were kids. He was handsome now and looked like he knew it, but he was just as infuriating. "When did you make landfall?"

"Three months ago," I said. Quarantine and mandatory re-immersion had taken that long. Once Earthside, I had to meet with my grandfather's attorneys and go over the will.

He snorted. "Took you long enough."

I didn't bother to reply. He had clearly never been off-world and didn't understand about launch windows and transfer points. He turned to give me an assessing look. I flushed and straightened under his gaze.

"My, you've grown, *Skinny*," he said, using his old nickname for me. I had been a gangly child, all arms and legs. Space and zero-g had only accentuated that. I managed to raise an eyebrow and give it back to him.

"Same with you, *Pudge*. Still the same jerkface kid you always were."

He just laughed, as if he knew his needling got to me. "Come on into the office. My mom wants to say hi."

He took the duffle bag from me and hefted it easily with a look of surprise. "This is all you've got?"

It was half my height and stuffed solid with my worldly possessions. I had taken little with me when I left Earth, and had accrued not much more. When every kilo is an extravagance, spacers learn to live lean.

"Yes," I said stiffly. "I travel light."

To my surprise, he said, "I hear that." There was a weighted undertone to his voice that made me wonder, but he didn't say anything more. I followed him into the office, and breathed a sigh when he closed the door on the winter day. The office was warm and well lit. Old charts were hung haphazardly on the wall in between sophisticated and modern transmitting and depth-sounding equipment. My eyes were drawn to the ancient twentieth-century phone that hung on the wall. Its twin was in the kitchen of the house on Tern Island. Mrs Dawes, the house-keeper, used to use the phone to call the office to put in the weekly grocery order.

Mrs Cardenas bustled out of the back room, a smile of pure delight gracing her broad face. She was a short, wide black woman, her hair only lightly frosted with gray.

"Little Beatriz, how you've grown. Come here, girl, let me give you a hug."

"Mrs Cardenas, it's wonderful to see you again." I hugged her back with delight. She had been so kind to a small, frightened child and a surly teenager – I felt a pang at the way I had thrust her out of my memory along with the rest of my childhood. She hadn't deserved that.

"Jupiter," she murmured, rubbing my back once more and then letting me go. "So far, Beatriz. It's good you've come home. Take off those wet things and sit awhile. I've got some soup and the rosemary biscuits you always loved so much. Goodness, child, you've gotten so skinny. They must not be feeding you well in space."

Ethan must have noticed that I moved slowly with fumbling hands to take off my coat and remove the scarf from my face. I unwound it and placed it on the hook, and put my coat and hat on top of it, gathering courage before turning around.

I could see their expressions as they took in the scar, a reminder of my life on Tern Island. Mrs Cardenas's lips parted; Ethan's face was unreadable. I tried to tell myself I didn't care. A little flirtation between old friends; that's all I wanted anyway.

"Oh, Beatriz," Mrs Cardenas said softly. "We should never have left you there."

"It's all right," I said. I managed a smile and touched my scar. "I survived. Every day it reminds me that life is good."

"Well," Mrs Cardenas said. "Let me get you some food."

While his mother went to bring back dinner, Ethan took off his coat and watch cap and hung them next to mine. He wore a knitted sweater and kept the scarf around his neck. All that clothing made me wonder what he looked like without it. Heat crawled up my cheeks and I looked away.

"Here you go," Mrs Cardenas said, bustling back in with bowls of soup, and balancing a basket of biscuits. Ethan grabbed the biscuits, and I cleared a spot on the long table that doubled as workspace. It was just like I remembered when we were kids, and I breathed deep, taking in the aroma of minestrone and rosemary biscuits. The first spoonful was heaven.

"You're right, Mrs Cardenas, there's nothing like this in space," I said, and she beamed.

"How long will you be staying?" Ethan asked, his voice neutral.

"Not very long," I said, feeling awful at the look on his mother's face. "I do plan to sell and return to Bifrost Station. I just needed to check on the place – I mean, I don't have to, but—" I quit my excuses. After all, I could hardly tell them I had seen a ghost.

"I see," Mrs Cardenas said. She glanced at her son. "Well, if you hurry, Ethan can get you there and back before dark."

"Oh no, I intend to stay the night," I blurted in a rush, just as Ethan said, "We can't do it in one afternoon, Ma."

We looked at each other.

"Not if you really want to see the place," he amended.

"Yes," I said firmly. "I do. Mrs Cardenas, the lawyers told me they prepared the house for my arrival and it's perfectly habitable. Surely Ethan ferried over the supplies and workers?" I looked over at him for support.

He nodded, but reluctantly. "It's all ready. They upgraded the

Stirling heat exchanger and fixed the roof and some other stuff."

I remembered the cranky old Stirling that used to creak and groan and keep me awake at night.

"So you see? Everything is set. In fact, the wind is kicking up. We should probably go before it gets worse," I said, then winced inwardly. I sounded as if I was eager to be rid of Mrs Cardenas, but I really just wanted to reassure her.

Mrs Cardenas didn't seem offended. She patted my hand. "I know you're anxious to be on your way, Bea, but I just think—" she didn't finish. "Ethan, perhaps you should stay, too."

"What?!" We both exclaimed. Ethan looked as shocked as I did. And perversely, that irritated me.

Despite her worry, Mrs Cardenas tried to keep from smiling. "I just think that Bea shouldn't be alone on Tern Island, especially so soon after returning from space."

"I'll be fine," I said. "Really. I appreciate your concern, but Ethan doesn't need to babysit me."

"Tell you what, Ma," Ethan said. He cast an anxious eye at the weather. "We'll see how it goes. If the weather is too bad, or if Bea doesn't feel comfortable about being by herself, we'll update accordingly."

Mrs Cardenas smiled up at her son and he kissed her on the cheek, and then picked up my duffle bag with an ease that I envied. She watched us from the window of the office while I trailed after him to his boat.

"What's the big deal about me staying alone on Tern Island?" I asked him. He looked at me and sighed.

"My mom, she thinks there's something not right about that house. And I don't know, Bea – you grew up there. You tell me."

I opened my mouth to say something and found I couldn't lie. Back then Ethan came and played with me whenever his father ferried over supplies, but he wasn't there every day, and his parents never let him stay overnight. Some of that was due to my grandfather, of course. At my expression, Ethan cocked an eyebrow as if to say, "See?"

"I don't believe in ghosts," I said finally. *And maybe it's about damn time that someone told the ghosts of Tern Island that.* As if he could hear that last unspoken bit, he snorted and shook his head.

We reached the ship, and my heart sank further. It wasn't a

ship but a mere boat, rusted and peeling, with a spray-soaked deck and a small pilothouse aft.

"Now, don't judge," he said, taking in my appraisal. "She's a good little ship, especially in weather like this."

"Not judging," I promised, and made a cross-my-heart gesture. He laughed and took my hand, helping me jump onto the swaying deck. He threw my duffle bag to me and hopped on board. He untied the lines and coiled them efficiently and once again beckoned me.

"Come into the wheelhouse with me – there's no heat, but it'll be warmer than on the deck." We all squeezed into the wheelhouse – him, the duffle bag, and me – and with the door closed it was warmer, though still dank. He started the engine, and I could smell the acrid chemical note of biodiesel.

The boat dipped and swayed as it pulled away from the wharf. He piloted with concentration, standing easily as we bounced along through the waves. I swallowed nausea. The odors from the engine and the sea were strong, and overwhelming me with scent memories.

"You can open the door if you need fresh air," he shouted over his shoulder. I shifted the duffle bag and opened the door a crack, and the fresh sea air rushed in, making my eyes water but relieving my stomach. I kept my gaze fixed firmly on the bow as it plowed through the waves, the ocean frothing over it like a scene out of *The Odyssey*. I, too, was going home to my island, but in my case there would be no welcoming dog, no waiting wife to recognize me. Unlike Ulysses, I intended to leave as soon as I had settled my affairs.

The island was just a dot at first, and then it steadily grew until the engine slowed and sputtered, and we puttered gently alongside the long jetty until Ethan cut the engine and we drifted.

"Give me a hand," he said, and I followed him out on deck. He jumped the distance between the deck and the jetty. I threw out the ropes, and he made his little boat fast with quick knots. I grabbed my duffle, threw it onto the jetty and followed more awkwardly, unaccustomed gravity complicating my movement. I slipped and he caught me, holding me close. His eyes had green flecks, and he had dimples around his mouth. I was staring and reddened. He steadied me and set me back a step, but he didn't let me go.

"Don't fall, Captain," he said softly, and the way he said it made it sound like a caress. "Water's cold."

"I remember," I said. You could only swim in August, and even then it was brutally cold. Ethan and I used to swim until our lips were blue and then run shivering into the house, where Mrs Dawes gave us hot chocolate and wrapped us in enormous towels.

At the same moment, we both realized he was still holding onto me. Ethan coughed and set me aside, and I turned to look at the house looming on a rise near the shore. I remembered its gables and roofs silhouetted against the wintry sky, a dark presence of stone and slate. The lighthouse thrust at the sky, white stone against a dark cloud. For a second it looked as if there were a light in the window, but I shut my eyes and looked again, and it was gone.

In a few minutes I would be alone in the house of my childhood. I could sense my own reluctance, and it irritated me. I steeled myself, picked up my duffle bag, and turned to Ethan.

"Well," I said. "Thank you."

"Look," he said. "I can come up with you, if you like." I could tell he didn't mean it, the way he cast an anxious look at his boat. The wind had picked up, and the waves crashing over the end of the jetty were increasing. The boat bobbed and bounced. I shook my head.

"I'll be okay." I attempted a smile. "They're not really ghosts, just memories, and they can't hurt me anymore." It was the first time I'd ever admitted it, I thought ruefully.

"If I were you, I'd burn the place down," he blurted. He caught himself. "Bea, if you need anything, just call, okay?"

"I will. You better be going. Weather's kicking up."

As if to emphasize my words, a wave crashed over the end of the jetty, spattering us with a curtain of spray and foam.

He surprised me with a comforting hug, and a kiss on my scarred cheek, kind and all the sweeter for it. Then he let me go and I hefted the duffle bag and headed up toward the house. Behind me the boat chugged into life and pulled away from the jetty.

I felt for the key in my coat pocket. The lawyers had sent it, along with a new set of keys, but this was the one that I remembered. It was ornate, tarnished brass. I had been fascinated with it as a child. At the door, I set down my duffle bag and pulled it out.

Something caught my attention and I turned sharply. The lighthouse was a dark shape in the gloom now, no longer white under the cloud. That's why the tiny flash of light was able to get my attention as much as it did. But when I looked straight at it, the tower stayed dark.

Some stars can only be seen out of the corner of the eye. But that's on a planet such as Earth, with an atmosphere. Out in space stars are defiantly bright. Still, I knew the trick of looking sidelong, and I knew that I would have to practice it, but later. I wanted – needed – to get inside. Deliberately, I turned my back on the lighthouse, put the key in the lock, and with some effort turned it. It scraped but the tumblers fell into place.

I took a deep breath and opened the door.

The house was warm, blessedly so, but gloomy, with very little light coming in through the high windows. I set my bag down, closed the door behind me, and touched the light plate where I remembered it. The warm glow that came up chased away the gloom, and I let out my breath.

The rich red carpet under the antique electric chandelier looked as warm as it had when I'd been a child, sitting in the ornate central medallion, playing with my toys. I remembered my grandfather thundering at me for leaving behind a sharp block that he had stepped on in the middle of the night in his wanderings.

His wanderings . . . I remembered those, too – the heavy-footed walkabouts in the night, creaking along the hallway, muttering to himself. I had asked the housekeeper Mrs Dawes about it once. She only told me to *hush*, that old men had to get up and about in the middle of the night, and there was nothing to be afraid of. And I knew that to be true, but then, why was my door always locked from the outside during the wanderings?

And one time it had stayed locked even past daylight, and I had shouted until I was hoarse and screamed and cried and wet myself, until at around mid-morning Mrs Dawes had come hurrying up the stairs, breathing hard, and scolded me for locking myself in, her eyes darting about the way people do when they lie.

I wandered around the house now, turning up the lights as I went. There was the parlor with the furniture covered with sheets. The dining room was shrouded as well. The kitchen was cheerful, though. The fridge hummed, and I peeked in. As the lawyers had promised and Ethan had confirmed, it was well stocked. The pantry was filled with dry goods, and someone had set out clean dishes for me. The kitchen smelled of freshness. I turned on the water and grabbed a glass, drinking the icy coldness of sweet water straight from the sky. I had forgotten how water tasted. In cities it was as filtered as it was on Bifrost Station.

I set the glass down on the farmhouse kitchen table and poked around a bit more. There was the ancient house phone that connected to the office on shore. There was the door to the root cellar, but it was locked. My grandfather used to store his wine and Scotch down there. I wondered if there was a stray bottle or two – a drink would be nice. I had left the other set of keys in my duffle bag, and I decided that despite my inclination for facing things head on, investigating the cellar could wait for morning.

I left the lights on and went up the stairs, turning on lights as I came across them. I looked into all the bedrooms except mine. There was grandfather's, with its lovely fireplace and mantel. Incongruously, there was a hospital bed in place of the massive four-poster that used to be there. I wondered why no one had come to remove it. It was sleek and white and shiny, still new with the latest med-tech.

The next bedroom was empty. Then there was a bathroom, with its tub big enough to swim in, and the tiles still bright blue and white, with dolphins cavorting in green waves. I suddenly wanted a bath. I had not had one since I left Earth. Here I could be as frivolous with water as I wished.

I saved my bedroom for last. I paused in front of the door, took a deep breath, and pushed it open. I fumbled for the light switch, and slowly the darkness gave way.

My grandfather had not changed a thing. There was the child's bed, too small for me when I left as a gawky teenager. There were my books and vids. The books were old relics of a previous age. I had a bright new reader but I preferred the books, even the musty-smelling ones. The vids had long gone dark, the gel memory having faded, but I picked one up and shook it, and for a moment a bright image of a horse galloping over a beach appeared in the air in front of me, and then ghosted away apologetically. I set it down on my bed and wandered around the room. The pictures on the walls stared down at me. Some were of animals – I remembered my owl phase – and there were the rock stars and the cute movie-star boys, young and non-threatening. I was far past that stage, and I thought of Ethan's green-flecked eyes and the dimples around his mouth, the strength in his arms as he had caught me. Gravity had its good points, I thought.

There was a dresser, my desk, and a clothes closet. I hesitated. The closet door was barely ajar. I remembered that it didn't like to stay closed. I hated it. I felt as if sometimes it moved from within, as if something watched me. One of my bedtime rituals had been to jam my desk chair under the doorknob to keep the door firmly closed. And once, when I thought I had closed it, I had woken in the middle of the night with the chair by the desk, and the closet door opening, ever so slightly, a tiny bit more as I stared at it. And my grandfather, wandering the halls, muttering and dragging his feet . . .

This was ridiculous. I reached out to yank open the closet door when I heard a loud *bang* from downstairs.

I jumped and gave a little shriek. My heart hammering so hard I was almost fainting, I backed out of the room and went to the top of the stairs.

"Who's there?" I shouted. It was an island for goodness' sakes. I was the only one home. I hadn't closed the front door completely, that's all.

Sure enough, I went downstairs and saw the front door wide open, banging against the wall with every gust of wind. Another gust drove rain onto the floor, wetting the flagstones and the rug, and cold air blasted the house. I cursed myself and went to push the door closed when another blink in the darkness caught my eye. I stood there, framed in the doorway, the house lights all blazing behind me, and stared at the dark lighthouse at the tip of the island. I could hear the crash of the waves and I was getting soaked with rain, and finally I saw it again. A light – a faded, barely visible light, fluttered weakly in the tower. I frowned. I couldn't understand what kind of light it was. It flickered and was barely bright and seemed to flutter . . .

Wait. Could it be candlelight?

The wind shrieked up around me and almost tore the door from my grasp. I came to my senses and pushed it closed and locked it for good measure, and the cold and the noise abated. I found myself hoping that Ethan had made it back to shore okay.

The steady thrumming from the Stirling heat exchanger in the basement eased my nerves. It sounded comforting and familiar, reminiscent of Bifrost Station, whose mechanical heartbeat was a sign that all was safe and sound.

I shivered in my wet clothes. It was time to change and settle in for the night.

The bathroom steamed up luxuriously, and I stripped out of my wet clothes and stepped into the full tub. I sank back and let my eyes close, enjoying the near sensation of weightlessness that the water gave me. The bath soothed my aching muscles and bones, so unaccustomed to one-g. Gravity was a burden, something we spacers have to relearn. There had been stories of people just returned who set a cup aside in mid-air and were surprised to see it drop. Worse were the spacers who pushed off of balconies or second stories without a single thought. Some of us have been exiled permanently, unable ever to return to Earth because of bones that have become so fragile that the forces of re-entry would turn them into dust.

I dozed, half-asleep, and ended up in the middle of a dream in which Ethan's ferry boat was crashing into the station and I was unable to stop it. The impact shuddered me, and the ferry broke apart in a bloom of fire, fed by the explosive decompression of station air.

I woke with a jerk and a splash, gasping as I sent cooled water up my nose. Disoriented, I wondered what had woken me, when I heard it again – a *bang*, much like the first time. The front door slamming open, and the rising sound of the storm as it wailed around and inside the house.

But I had locked the door.

I got up, heavy and clumsy as a mermaid on land, and fumbled for the big soft towel. I dried off hastily and then, cursing because I had forgotten to get dry clothes from my duffle bag, I struggled back into wet clothing and pulled on my boots once more. All the good the bath had done me vanished in a clammy moment.

At the top of the stairs, I could see the front door banging back and forth again, the storm flinging rain inside onto the red carpet of the hall.

I hurried down and closed it again, locked it again, and let my heartbeat subside as the warmth returned to the house.

"Beatriz Sabatini," I scolded myself out loud. "Get a hold of yourself. You are an experienced pilot and spacer with millions of miles of vacuum under your belt. Stop acting like a child."

I needed to change into dry clothes. With deliberation I went to pick up my duffle bag. It wasn't there. Confused, I turned all the way around. Nowhere. I certainly hadn't lugged it around with me when I'd first got in. I had dropped it just inside the entrance.

There was a large wet spot by the front door. A faint trail of wet gleamed across the wood floor where something large had been dragged.

Something steeled inside me. I grew calm, making my heartbeat slow and my breath even. I picked up a fire iron from the hearth, hefted it and followed the wet trail. I held my breath and listened for other breathing sounds, but the only background noise was the rhythmic movement of the Stirling.

The wet trail led to the kitchen, and now I could see small bare footprints. A child? The bag was heavy even if you didn't have zero-g muscles. How could a child drag it?

You know which child, I told myself. But I still didn't want to believe it.

The cellar door was open, cold musty wet air flowing up from it like air from an opened grave. Child or no child, I lifted the poker and called out.

"Come on out of there."

Nothing.

"Listen. You get your ass up those stairs right this instant, or I will call your mother."

There was a pause and then I heard a small giggle. I swallowed and swore all kinds of curses in my head. My mobile was in my duffle bag, and my duffle bag had been stolen. I eyed the antique phone. If ever there was an emergency, this was it. I didn't care if Ethan thought I was nuts. Maybe I *was* nuts. But I wasn't alone on Tern Island and someone was playing tricks. I picked up the house phone. There was static interference on the line, and then I heard a child sing slyly, "Beaaaa-uh."

"Who is this? Hello?"

The static increased and I had to move the phone away from my ear. The cellar door swung wildly and then slammed shut, making me jump. The latch fell into place.

Ethan, get me off this island now.

I brought the receiver back to my ear. The static was fainter now, and I could hear the ghost of other transmissions. I was straining to make sense of the words when I heard as clear as anything, "Bea, the lighthouse has the answers."

Static shrieked in my ear and I jumped back, dropping the phone to dangle by its twisted cord.

This was absurd. Someone was playing a sick joke and I had fallen for it. I looked at the closed cellar door. If there was a child down there – a preternaturally strong and clever child – I should still go down to find him or her. A child should be protected, after all. An uncomfortable memory came to me, of being locked in a dark, cramped place, and I shied away from it. Was it a memory or a nightmare?

I jiggled the latch of the cellar door and it creaked open. I felt for the string of the old-fashioned light unit, but when I tugged on it, nothing happened. The kitchen light barely illuminated the wooden stairs that disappeared into the gloom. The shelves that held my grandfather's wine and spirits were tucked beneath the stairs. There wasn't much space for anything else; just a small landing and some room to duck under the staircase and pull out a bottle of some fine '07 vintage. I couldn't see my duffle bag at all, so that's where my unseen adversary had probably hidden it.

Mrs Dawes had kept a flashlight and basic tools in the cupboard next to the sink. I checked it and sure enough there was a handheld torch of the simple wind-up kind that had amused me so much as a child. I wound it and a bluish light gleamed from the torch. I glanced back at the cellar door, uncomfortable at the thought of it slamming closed with me downstairs. Rummaging through the cupboard, I found the power screwdriver I was looking for. It didn't take long to take the cellar door off of its hinges and set it down on the floor of the kitchen.

"Little children who slam doors don't deserve to have them," I announced to the house. The only response was the wind.

The doorway yawned in front of me, and I shone the flashlight at it. The light had grown weaker and I quickly wound it up again.

Six steps into the ground. I walked down quickly, the air growing colder as soon as I left the kitchen. The thrumming of the Stirling was muffled; the heat exchanger lived on the other side of the house.

My duffle bag was not at the bottom of the stairs. Winding the light, I looked around and under the stairs. No duffle bag. No bottles either. Whoever had taken the duffle hadn't gone down the stairs. I went to go back up when something hit the back of my head and I pitched forward in a blinding flash of pain. The last thing I remembered was the flashlight rolling crazily, the smell of the ocean, and the fierce pain in the back of my head.

I woke up cold and stiff, with a pounding headache, thinking I was still on the Bifrost. But the rough wooden floor and the bitterly cold wind helped me remember that I had left Jupiter eighteen months ago. I was on Tern Island. I tried to get up but my legs didn't work. It was like when I first made planetfall. I gave up the attempt and lay there, trying to make sense of what was happening.

I blinked and opened my eyes hazily, seeing double. I was looking up at the night sky. The rain had stopped and the clouds had cleared. The stars flickered through the atmosphere, the spiral arm of the Milky Way a faint smudge against the void. I could see the massive armature of the station that orbited the Earth, its lights flashing rhythmically. I looked for Jupiter and saw her, a steady, reassuring point of light.

I turned my head, oh so carefully, almost overwhelmed by the pounding headache and the nausea. There was enough starlight for me to see the broken stone walls of the tower. Someone – no child, of course – had carried me to the top of the lighthouse. An enemy, I imagined. I struggled to come to terms with that. I had no enemies. Things like this simply didn't happen in space. People were – people were *chosen* for space, carefully vetted and analyzed and tested. They didn't hit pilots over the head with heavy objects and carry them to the top of dangerous towers. I would have felt more outrage if I hadn't been so sick and feeble.

I managed to push into a sitting position.

"Where are you?" I tried to shout, but my voice came out as a whisper. I was shivering from the cold and shock. I needed to get back to the house, despite the presence of my enemy. I wouldn't last the night up here.

A light caught my eye, the flickering of candlelight, a tiny reminder of danger. A candle doesn't light itself. I got to my hands and knees and then to my feet, swaying dangerously. The light waited, the little flame blowing sideways. I was drawn to it – I imagined I could even feel the tiny bit of heat it emitted. I tottered toward it, one step, then two.

A mighty gust of wind roared up out of the sky and battered me backwards. I couldn't even hear my own scream in the whirlwind that sent me to my rear on the wet, rough floor. My head pounded as if it were about to explode.

The wind abated as quickly as it had come up, taking the candlelight with it. I got my breath back and decided staying off my feet was best. I scooted over to the center of the tower, thinking I could find the stairs and the ladder down. The stars gave me enough light that my plan was rewarded. My boots found the trapdoor, and slow step by slow step I made it down the ladder.

This part of the tower was familiar to me. My grandfather had used it for storage of all kinds of junk. I didn't know who was playing with fire, but I knew where they had gotten the candles. I made my way to the cabinet with the emergency supplies and fumbled for a stub of my own. There were matches too, and after a few hasty tries I managed to light my candle. It flared and sputtered and the heat was uncomfortable, but it gave me light. I found a small lantern and fixed the candle inside it, holding it by the handle high above my head.

As I expected, no one was in sight. My headache had faded somewhat. I grabbed a wool blanket from the stack and wrapped it around myself. It smelled of urine and rat droppings but at least I stopped shivering. I could even, if I wanted, stay here for the night.

The lighthouse has the answers? I wasn't sure I wanted answers anymore. Someone had tried – was trying – to kill me. I wanted *off* Tern Island as much now as I had when I had been a teenager, when my grandfather had succumbed to his madness, calling me "Angelique", my mother's name, and cursing me for my bad blood, my defective genes, and for killing his son, my father. He had beaten me so badly that I still bore the scars on one side of my face. I had fled in the night, piloting a small fishing boat across the sound, setting a rough course by keeping the flickering light from the lighthouse at my back. I imagined I could still hear my grandfather screaming my name across the water. The Cardenas had sheltered me from his retribution, and then I had fled as far as I could.

I had gone all the way to the moons of Jupiter to escape his insanity, and here I was, back again, with no way to escape this time. Moving stiffly, I barricaded the door to the tower, constructing a deadfall of junk to warn me if anyone tried to get in. I cleared a lumpy old sofa and laid my aching body down, wrapped in the stinky blanket, and blew out the candle.

From where I lay, I could see a patch of starlight through the trapdoor in the ceiling. Jupiter burned bright, and I was comforted by her presence. I closed my eyes and slept.

I woke, plagued with a cold and stuffy nose, to birdsong and the wind in the pine trees. I sat up stiffly, waited for my headache to subside, and began the process of clearing out the deadfall at the door.

The sun was up but emitted no warmth. My breath misted as I made my way across the overgrown frost-rimed lawn to the house. I would call Mrs Cardenas and she would send Ethan, and once away from this place I would instruct my lawyers to sell the house and the island. I would begin the process of getting back into space. I never should have come.

The ocean was gray with whitecaps, the long stone jetty submerged by the tide. Despite my determination to leave and never come back, I paused to take in the island's harsh beauty. It was a stark place, unhealthy for a child to grow up in, but it was the only home I knew. And there was the cemetery, with its impossible image of a child who never existed. I knew I should walk away, and I knew I couldn't. It was an essential part of me, as much my DNA as the bad blood my grandfather had accused me of.

The rusty gate squealed as I pushed it open and entered the little graveyard. I looked around at the graves of my ancestors. There was my grandfather's – the massive, polished oblong thrusting into the sky. But it was not his grave I meant to see. Nestled in between the roots of the largest pine tree was a small, unassuming gravestone, its engraved name barely readable after eighty years of weather and time.

Bianca Fermes
29 April 2150 – 8 September 2161

I didn't believe in bad blood or bad genes, but I was beginning to believe in ghosts. Before me, at Tern Island, there had been another child, one whose grave was tucked furthermost under the pine trees in the cemetery. I was a lonely child, and before Ethan had come along, I had pretended she could play with me. I had only stopped when things became too real and the stories I made up about her became frightening, as if I hadn't been playing make-believe so much as narrating history.

"What happened to the little girl in the cemetery, the one who fell from the tower?" I remembered asking Mrs Dawes. And her only response had been to stutter and scold, telling me I was a bad girl for making up stories.

I stopped playing with Bianca and I never went back to the cemetery, but she was never far from my mind, especially at night when my grandfather hammered on my locked bedroom door and screamed at me.

I knelt awkwardly at the grave and put my hand on the rough stone. "I'm sorry I abandoned you," I said. "You must have been very lonely."

The pine trees stilled, and the cemetery grew silent.

"I went away to Jupiter," I went on, past the lump in my throat. "I tried to forget you and everything else that happened. But that wasn't fair, was it? It wasn't your fault."

When we go off-world, we leave our ghosts behind. They are too weighty to carry, these memories made of gravity. They won't fit in our small duffle bags and lean lives. But the ghosts remember us, and somehow that's worse.

"Dammit," a voice came from behind me. "You are hard to kill, Beatriz Sabatini."

I stood unsteadily. The man behind me had long brown hair and an untidy beard. His eyes were pale blue and red-rimmed. He wore an old worn coat and dirty jeans and pointed a gun at me. He did not look healthy, but he was stronger than I was. I had to remember that. I tried to will away my concussion. My life depended upon quick thought and action.

"You were supposed to fall off the tower," he went on. He gestured with the gun. "Practice until you get it right, I suppose. Move it."

I didn't move it. "And you are?" I inquired politely, retreating into icy, spacer calm. He sputtered.

"The rightful owner of this island," he said, advancing a step and waving the gun at me. I tried not to flinch. "And don't you forget it. You spacers with your attitude and your technology and your money and your fancy lives, you think you can just come back to Earth and take what belongs to others. I took care of this place when you took off. I took care of the old man all the time he was crazy, raving about you and some other whore and God knows what. Tern Island is mine, Spacer. You should have stayed in space where you belong."

Tell me about it, I thought.

"Where's my duffle bag?" I said.

"I don't know what you're talking about," he said. He gestured again with the gun. "Let's go."

I couldn't stall any longer. He fell in behind me and we made our way back to the tower. The sun was up and the ocean was blue and green, dazzling bright. Overhead the ghost armature of the space station was painted on the sky. The lighthouse with its broken stonework loomed above us.

The danger had cleared some of the fuzz from my mind. He couldn't just shoot me. He had to know that someone would come back to look for me. If it seemed like an accident, then no one would look for my killer. I wondered how he had managed to hide on the island in the eighteen months since my grandfather's death.

The lighthouse storage room gave me my answer. What I had not noticed last night in my concussed state was that the junk had been organized. There was a camp stove and pallets of canned foods. I felt sickened by the fact that I had spent the night in his lair.

"Where did you sleep last night?" I asked.

"The old man's room," he said smugly, and then caught himself. He jabbed me with the gun. "Shut up and climb."

Had he been in the house when I had bathed? I was repulsed by the thought. I climbed carefully, only partly taking my time to slow down the inevitable. I fumbled my way up the ladder, my boots slipping on the rungs. He was pressed up behind me, and I knew it was awkward for him too. I had to time my next move carefully. As my head cleared the trapdoor, I grabbed hold of the top of the ladder, engaged the magnets in my boots and kicked out. He grunted and his grip loosened. I felt the *clunk* as the magnets pulled the gun from his hand.

I flung myself up and out of the trapdoor, disengaged the magnetic soles and grabbed the gun as it dropped to the stone, aiming it at the attacker as he came barreling out of the trapdoor after me. He went stock still as he took in our reversal of fortune. My hand was shaking but I made myself calm.

"Back off," I ordered.

He swayed slightly, his head moving from side to side, his eyes darting in confusion. My sense of danger heightened.

He mumbled something and began to cry. "You can't do this to me!" he screamed. He stumbled forward and I backed up, turning along the curve of the broken tower wall. "I took care of that old bastard for three years while he went insane. He owes me!"

I didn't want to have to shoot him. "Stay where you are!" I said, my voice rising in panic. He took in my fear and in an instant he became sly.

"Oh, you don't want me to do this?" He took a step forward. I backed up instinctively, and he grinned, cruel. He did it again, and I backed up again, stumbling against the wall.

"Listen," I said. "I don't want to shoot. I will if I have to, though. So just stay where you are."

The gun was old and stiff, an antique. I wondered if he had found it in the storage room. I wondered if it even worked. I squeezed the trigger ever so slightly, and he saw the movement and stopped. I wondered how long I could hold it like that before I would shoot him. He began screaming and cursing at me, and despite myself I flinched. Perhaps it was because of my childhood, but I never could stand uncontrolled anger and rage. I licked my lips and held my ground, wishing for the peace and calm of space.

There was no warning when he charged me. I squeezed the

trigger reflexively and the report of the gun was loud and shocking. My outcry and his howl intermingled. I missed of course; the bullet ricocheted and sent a puff of concrete dust and stone into the air. He bowled into me, knocking me off my feet, and the gun flew from my hand to land a few feet away on the floor.

He grinned, his teeth dirty and unkempt. I started to speak but my eyes widened as I looked past him and made a sound. He snorted with disdain. "Really? That old tri—"

Ethan Cardenas bolted up through the trapdoor with one quick movement and brought a sizable chunk of old stonework down on my tormentor's head.

We sat in the sunlight and the cold air, enjoying the bright breeze, the dazzle on the sea, and the blue sky and scudding clouds. The space station wheeled silently overhead, creating spoke-wheeled shadows on the ocean. Ethan wrapped me in his warm wool pea coat and I leaned against him. My attacker groaned every now and then. From our vantage point we could see the three speed-boats with police flags coming our way, sending up a *vee* of white water from their bows.

"Why did you come back?" I asked. I felt warm and tired and safe.

His arm tightened around me. "You called. Or – someone did. The phone in the office rang. And when I answered it I couldn't hear anything except static and voices. The storm had come up pretty bad by then, so I couldn't get back before now. Sorry."

"Not your fault," I said, and leaned in closer. Ethan didn't seem to mind. He kissed the top of my head. It was like the kiss he had given me the day before, but somehow it held more promise.

"Maybe," he said, and there was guilt in his voice. I shifted to look up at him. "I never thought he'd still be on the island. After your grandfather died, it never occurred to me that Mike Dawes would have stayed."

"Mike Dawes," I repeated. "You mean—"

"The Dawes's grandson. After you left he came out to the island to help them take care of the place. They retired, and he stayed to look after your grandfather. As far as I knew he was a nice guy, but after a few years – well. He got more and more squirrelly. But I never thought he'd gone feral."

I didn't say that my grandfather had that effect on people. My gaze wandered over to the small candle that was still wedged firmly in the ruined tower wall. There was a sizable gap leading out into the air beside it. If I had continued walking toward the candle last night I would have gone right over the edge, just another spacer fallen victim to gravity. With me in my concussed state, had it not been for that wild gust of wind that had knocked me flat, it would have worked.

I knew better, though. That gust of wind was no coincidence. The last night I had spent on Tern Island, my grandfather had hammered on the locked door of my bedroom, screaming at me, calling me Bianca, Beatriz, even my mother's name, Angelique. I had curled up in my bed, terrified, until I had felt a small presence beside me. She had lain next to me, holding my hand as tight as possible, her small body pressed against mine, and we had hugged one another as the storm in my grandfather's head had raged just outside the door. It had lasted all night long, and when I had woken in the morning, drained and exhausted, there had been an impression on the bed next to me, but I had been alone.

"So what now?" Ethan said. "Are you going back to space?" His voice sounded cautiously neutral.

I would have thought I'd had enough of Earth. Ghosts, people trying to kill me, unpleasant memories. On the other hand, I lifted my face to the sun, its warmth giving me strength and energy. Maybe it was time to stop running from memories and face them head on, the way I had always prided myself that I did. I had ghosts to lay to rest after all, or at least one small ghost. It was the least I could do for Bianca Fermes, who had been one of my grandfather's victims long before I was born.

Space had been a respite, but it wasn't home. Even gravity no longer felt burdensome, as if my muscles were eager to regain strength. It helped that Ethan's arms around me felt good and strong, a reminder that gravity didn't just hold us down, it held us together, too.

"I don't know," I said honestly. "But I think I'll stay awhile and see if I can get used to one-g again."

His response was to give me a kiss, one that was neither kind nor comforting, but hungry and passionate. He broke off to whisper in my ear.

"Welcome home, Captain Sabatini. It's about time you came back down to Earth."

Fade Away and Radiate

Michele Lang

The only woman on an uninhabitable planet listened to the wail of the nightwind, alone in a research hut in the dead of the night. She studied her data outputs, and tried like hell not to think of Roberto. Because thinking of Roberto got her thinking about why she'd come to this desolate place. And thinking of her self-exile made her think of the man she was running away from . . .

There was a knock on the door.

It was the moment she had imagined a million times with dread, and yet now that it had come, she wasn't ready. With a gasp, Anika Bowman jumped from her chair, but before she could make any further moves, the door to her field lab swung open.

She glanced across the hut, to where her blaster lay hidden under her flat foam pillow. Her fingers itched to grab it, but it was too late now. Anika had bet her life on the simple fact that she was too far away from the rest of humanity to be murdered. If she survived the next few minutes, she would never make such a stupid mistake again.

Anika forced herself to look at the hulking figure filling up her doorway. Far away, outside the geodome in which she'd built the hut, the nightwind howled, hungry, unrequited. The haunting sound still pierced her heart.

"It's me," a muffled voice said, crackling over the spacesuit's interface.

For a single, agonizing moment, she imagined it was Roberto, come back to her across infinity. That behind that mirrored

helmet, Roberto was speaking to her now, that somehow he'd
returned, as he'd once promised.

A miracle. But, no.

Roberto was dead, just another casualty of the Glass Desert
war. Roberto hadn't come back to her in a box, or an urn, or
even on a memory stick or a download with a farewell
message. He'd just gotten vaporized, as if he'd never existed
in the first place.

Whoever this warrior was, hidden in his spacesuit, it wasn't
her husband. Roberto was never coming back. She was sure
of it.

Big square hands encased in spacegloves reached up to remove
the domed, mirrored helmet. She took a half-step back, her
heart pounding so hard in her chest it shook her with every beat.

Anika saw the man's face. She staggered backwards in her
shock. Roberto would have blown her away less.

"Billy Murphy, it's you," she managed to gasp. "Never
thought I'd see your face again."

Captain Billy Murphy grinned and looked her up and down in
a single glance. It was him: that thick, uncontrollable black hair.
(Much longer now since the last time she'd seen him.) The
deep-blue eyes, the spare, effective body. That face, even more
appealing for the marks inflicted by all the trouble he'd survived.

"Yep, me," Billy replied, and he laughed. "Took long enough for
me to find you, am I right? Like you didn't *want* me to find you."

She stared at him in wonder as he shut the door behind him,
clomped into the research hut, took a look around. Didn't take
more than a quick scan for Billy to see all there was to see.

The truth be told, she was relieved. Her life in the hut was
over, no matter what happened now between her and this man,
the last one to see her husband alive. And no matter how much
she'd once craved the solitude and the silence of this stony, dead
planet, Anika knew she couldn't live in this frozen hell forever.

"How did you find me?" Anika forced the words past the
lump in her throat. She would rather die than cry in front of
Billy Murphy. She'd already done too much crying in this man's
presence. She didn't dare do it again.

Billy laughed louder, and pulled the fingers of his gloves one
by one with his straight, white teeth to get them off. "Bet you
wanna know how I cracked your code."

He was like a tiger transformed into a man, pacing the little room in his armor, sizing up her potential as a meal. Both of them knew she was no warrior.

The floor shook under his boots as he walked, cracked his knuckles, and wiggled his fingers to get the circulation into them again. "Glad to see you're still in one piece."

For now, Anika couldn't help playing out what was going to happen next, going at a hundred times normal speed in her mind, like an end-of-life experience. The return to Earth. Her attempted, reattempted, and then final resignation from FortuneCorp – that place that had made her career, the place that wanted her soul along with her employment. A world corporation that intended to own this galaxy, that didn't let the little cogs in its mighty machine just break away.

So she would spurn the company, walk unaffiliated, unprotected, in New York. And one fine afternoon, walking along Broadway or riding the helobus, or reading newsfeeds in Petraeus Park, the end would come for her at last. A murderer would poison her, or kidnap her, or just wipe her out. It happened to genetic and nuclear scientists all the time. It had happened to Roberto. And if Billy was anywhere around, it would happen to him, too.

His expression softened when he saw her stricken face. "Listen, I made you a promise," he explained. "At Roberto's memorial. I swore, and I swore it to Robbo first. If anything happened to him in country, I was coming back after to watch out for you. You and I ain't got nobody else."

"I don't need watching." Anika cringed inside at the huskiness in her voice. She cleared her throat and stood straighter, not willing to yield to his charms. It was the same way she stood up to the fears that still stalked her every night. "I'm a big girl, and I've managed to survive just fine on my own all this time. I don't need your help."

Billy crossed his arms over his big, armored chest, and he shifted uneasily on his feet. It was as close as she'd ever come to seeing him losing his cool. "You're a good girl, and I know why Roberto loved you so hard. But you're lying to me. You're not surviving out here. You're lingering. Okay?"

The silence rose up like a ghost, and they stared at each other through the suddenly too-little space closing in between them.

Anika felt the damn tears coming, but she refused to shed them. Instead, she walked across the little room in three steps to her cot, and the blaster hidden there.

"I know you've traveled pretty far just to get here," she began.

"That would be an understatement."

She couldn't help smiling at that, at the way Billy tugged at her heart. "Yeah well, I think the best thing for you to do, Mr Spaceman, is stay the night, have some grub, and stock up on provisions. And head right back out in the morning. I'm assuming there's a craft in orbit waiting for you. No way you could head out to this quadrant all alone."

Billy laughed again, more gently this time. His thick, black hair stood on end, all messed up from his helmet. He pushed the buttons at his wrist points, and the exoskeleton of his suit softened. He pulled the suit down and stepped out of it, looking like a man now and not a robotic killer.

He looked vulnerable.

But Anika wasn't fooled. She knew what Billy really was, what Roberto had been before he'd gotten snuffed.

K-Ops. Genetically modified soldiers in the United States Army, technology owned by FortuneCorp, the soldiers serving their country. Sent by the US military to do what regular soldiers didn't have the physical or mental stamina to do.

Roberto never spoke of what he'd done as a soldier out in the Glass Desert. He had wanted to leave the war behind when he had come home to her, and she hadn't needed to know the details of his job. She'd wanted to love those memories away until he had to go back and make more of them.

But the last time he'd come home, Anika could tell something had changed. Roberto had changed. As if he knew the next time he went back to the Glass Desert, he wouldn't be coming back.

"I didn't come all this way just to say hello." Billy broke into her thoughts, his voice a little too calm.

A jolt of fear shot down the length of Anika's back. She didn't want to hear any more, but she owed it to Billy to hear him out. He had come to the edge of the known world to find her.

"Do you know how Roberto died?" Billy asked.

Anika's mouth was dry as sand. She licked her lips and shrugged her shoulders. "It's war," she managed to say. "Soldiers die in war. You don't need to tell me more than that."

He squinted at her, as if he were trying to figure out how much she already knew. "But you need to know. If you don't already."

Anika tried to relax but couldn't. Billy took a seat on Anika's desk chair, set in front of an ancient roll-top desk that looked ridiculously out of place on an uninhabitable planet at the back end of nowhere.

Billy's hands rested on the arms of her chair. She watched his strong fingers caressing the old-fashioned realwood, and wondered where he hid his own weapons.

She knew he was armed. She scanned his spare, hard body for the weapons – traveling from those strong, knowing hands up to his muscular arms encased in dark-blue flight silk, across the defined shoulders, the curve of his neck . . .

She realized, belatedly, that Billy had stopped talking. Anike tore her gaze from Billy's insanely beautiful body and forced herself to stare right into his eyes.

Eyes the color of midnight, of desolation. He seemed to pin her to the cot like a butterfly. Those eyes spoke of suffering she would understand, like Roberto's. And yet his voice, vibrating inside her chest, remained gentle, kind.

"Roberto didn't die in the field, you know."

"I know," Anika whispered. Miserable now, remembering. Billy was the one who had told her, after the memorial, in a low, quick undertone, far away from everybody else. The details were dangerous, she knew.

"Somebody got inside the barracks, somebody who knew they wanted Roberto specifically. They got past all of us – genmod soldiers – and killed him and escaped before we could do anything. And, Annie. I didn't tell you this. There was no investigation. Nothing. We were told to act like it had never happened."

Annie swallowed hard. "I figured he didn't die the official way, the way the government told me."

"What did you think?"

She shook her head as if she could negate the truth away. "Both of us worked for FortuneCorp, not like you soldiers. He never told you, did he?"

"Nope. As far as anybody on the team knew, he was just another soldier."

"Well, he wasn't. We worked together on genetic research,

human and ecological modifications. He was a geneticist, I'm a biologist. Together we worked on eco-transformative research. How to mutate human beings, and climates."

Billy nodded, not looking too surprised. "Roberto was way smarter than me," he said. "A million times smarter. But didn't have as much horse-sense. And you don't just need a killer instinct to survive the Glass Desert, Annie girl. You need prey instinct, too. Roberto just wore his smarts out in the open, and it cost him."

The lump in Anika's throat all but choked her. She shrugged and tried to laugh. "I always warned him to watch his back. Doing our kind of research is so dangerous. Rival corporations will kill scientists, kidnap them and extract their knowledge. And Roberto put himself outside of FortuneCorp's protection, going to war. But he wanted to understand what it was like to undergo genetic modification himself, and the only way to find out was to become a soldier. Like you."

"Roberto didn't fool nobody. I figured out after a while that he was a scientist, not a grunt."

"Ah, yes. He told you his motto? 'Geneticist, modify yourself.'"

Billy grinned sadly at the memory, and at Anika's imitation of Roberto's Spanish-inflected voice. For a moment, it was like Roberto was there with them, sharing the joke.

Anika smiled, and Billy looked into her soul again. But this time, his gaze felt more like a caress.

"I suppose a rival corporation got Roberto. Espionage. That's what I figured when I heard he was gone."

Billy stared at her for a long moment, and then he withdrew his gaze, looked into the middle distance, his open face suddenly unreadable. "After the memorial, I went back for six more months.

"Hard months, Annie. Hard, hard months. The whole team died out there, one by one. The genmod can help – infrared vision, limb regeneration – and it will keep you alive in the field, but the morale went bad."

Billy shifted in his chair, and looked into the distance, like he saw the pictures drawn by his words. She willed herself into complete silence. And Billy kept telling her the secrets of his war.

"Soldiers are superstitious, modified or not. And after Roberto was murdered on the base, our luck seemed to go with him. We knew some kind of bullshit was going on, okay? But we had no way to prove it. I figured with his scientist background, he made some bad enemies. Maybe he was even a spy, yeah? We didn't know for sure.

"I got the Murphy luck, ya know. Bad luck that gets you to the other side every time. But the other guys – their luck was just bad."

He leaned back in the chair and sighed. And Anika trembled, only then realizing that she had been holding her breath as he spoke.

"I'm so sorry," she whispered, watching the pain play over Billy's face like a shadow. "It must have been awful."

"Worse for you," he replied, his eyes still closed. "I'm the luckiest man alive, to get out of the desert. But you think he died because of you."

Anika took a huge gulp of air then, the guilt twisting like a knife in her chest. It was true. Roberto died because of the work they had done together.

Before she could say anything, Billy opened his eyes and looked at her. "Everybody in a war feels guilty for surviving, Annie. That's just part of the gig."

He looked ordinary again, the smart-ass kid from Southie that he'd once been, before he joined the Army to get the genmod. But that street kid was gone forever too, and both of them knew it.

"It's funny," he said. "You run with a pack in the war, and once those guys are gone, it's like you're missing a limb."

She nodded. That pain she knew all about. Still felt it, every day.

"I'll tell you how I tracked you down," he said. His voice was soft now, his Boston accent faded. "My tour ended and I was a lone wolf. So I come back to the Rotten Apple, and the first thing I do in New York is look you up, like I promised you. And him."

They exchanged a long, low glance, and Anika knew he was thinking of the memorial, too. The things he'd said to her. The way he'd sworn to protect her, the way he'd held her in his arms as she'd cried. That was a long, long time ago now.

"But you were gone," he continued. "Six months after the memorial, and your house was all locked up, I couldn't find you online. At first, I figured you was dead too, and why not? So was everybody else. But you took care of everything too neat. You disappeared too perfect."

She'd tried like hell to stay away from Billy. Because if a rival corporation had killed Roberto like she suspected, then a rival corporation would likely want to kill her too. After all, she and Roberto had worked as a scientific team. She had told her FortuneCorp regional supervisor about her fears, and they had told her the matter was under investigation. But, like Billy, she'd heard nothing more.

And that silence had terrified her. Both she and Roberto had done research on classified techniques for human genetic modification and ecological re-engineering. Those techniques were worth billions. Now that Roberto was dead, Anika had been the only one who could complete the research track they had started together.

Anika had run off-world, all the way to AlphaZed3, to escape the reach of any other corporation. Her new technology, the Bowman eco-drive, would serve as a living legacy of her husband's vision. And Anika had believed the remoteness of this posting would protect her from deadly visitors.

Billy's appearance put the lie to that notion. She knew to her core that Billy would never hurt her, that he had sworn to Roberto that he would protect her. But if Billy could make it way out here, anybody could. And the blaster under her pillow wouldn't save her.

The tears spilled over Anika's cheeks, onto her lips, tasting of regret and loss and fear. And loneliness, such terrible aching loneliness, so deep that she didn't dare surrender to it.

Billy got out of his chair and covered the space between them in a couple of bounding steps. He kneeled next to her low cot, and he was so tall that, even kneeling, his eyes were level with hers.

They were only centimeters apart now. Her breath caught in her throat.

Anika couldn't care less about her legacy now. All she could see in her mind was the wisteria, the morning glories, and the snapdragons climbing the glass windows of her bedroom in

Forest Hills, where she had once said goodbye to Roberto before he left for war for the last time.

"You aren't safe out here," Billy said gently. His eyes flashed with the tears he never shed, never. As he'd told her at the memorial, Billy Murphy didn't do tears.

The unshed tears in Billy's eyes flashed silver into midnight, lightning over a summer sea.

A rush of panic spread through Anika's body. "I have to hide. You understand why."

"I know you believe it was a rival corporation that murdered Roberto, to shut him up. To shut down your research. But think about it, Annie. Why didn't they murder you in New York?"

The question hovered in the air between them. Billy's hands reached for her and caressed her shoulders. And the shock of that touch roared through her like an ion storm. "I told you, Annie, that I love you. The night of the memorial I knew. And I told you. I knew it was too soon. You had to let him go, and I told you I'd wait, as long as it took. I fell for you the second I saw you. Roberto told me that I would."

Anika tried to speak, but she couldn't manage a word.

"Wait up, hear me out. The genmod does funny stuff, you know that. It gave Roberto some precog, he knew when stuff was going to happen."

Anika swiped the tears off her face, as if she could wipe Billy's words away. His fingers tightened over her shoulders, and she took a big, shuddering breath, fighting not to let go, not to release her true feelings.

"He had changed, by the end," she finally said. "Maybe it was the genmod. Or maybe it was just the war."

"Roberto told me he was going to die, the night before he was murdered. He told me he was planning to speak out about the stuff he'd seen in the war. But it was too late. And he told me I was going to save your life, just in time. And here I am, before it's too late, just like he said."

His arms slipped around her, protecting her, and Anika melted into him. After two years of running away from Roberto's killers, she'd finally turned around and faced the past, the grief of not just losing Roberto, but Billy too.

"I'm safe out here, I think," she said, her voice muffled from inside Billy's arms. "As long as I just do my work and don't cause any trouble, I don't think any other corporation can get through FortuneCorp's sectors. FortuneCorp runs the whole show out here."

"It's not safe. It wasn't safe for Roberto, surrounded by his brothers. It's not safe for you, out here all alone. I came to get you out of here."

Anika cried then, remembering. Billy just held her, his silence saying so much more than words ever could. The tears slipped away after a while, though she knew, like the tides, they'd return. They rolled in every night, as she stretched out on her cot, her fingers touching the blaster for courage.

But that time was done, now that Billy was here. He could still leave in the morning. If she had her way, he'd go when daylight came, free and alive. Free of his obligation to her. But everything had changed because he had found her. Even after he went back to his life, Anika would remember that he had come.

"One night," Anika insisted. "Stay the night and you'll go in the morning. Just like I first said. And as long as I stay here working, and as long as you don't poke the powers that be and just go your way, we should both be okay."

Billy's smile flashed across his face, banishing the shadows. "I got the Murphy luck, Annie. Too late to stay out of trouble, too late the day I was born. But I'm here."

He knew as well as she did that a night could last forever, that anything could happen between this moment they shared, and daybreak.

Reunions are funny, time-bending things. After only a few minutes more, Billy and Anika had recovered from their emotion. Anika took Billy into the jungle to show him her artistry.

She beamed her arc-light torch skyward and dappled shadows filtered through the broad leaves stretching over their heads. "Those are tiny weeds back at home," she whispered. "My technology grows crabgrass into trees, clovers into climbing vines. I grew this jungle in a single growing season. It would take fifty years, a hundred, for any other terraformer."

Anika crouched down and dug around in the sandy dirt until she found what she was looking for. She pulled the black tube out of the ground to show Billy. "This is what the trouble is all about," she said. "The Bowman eco-drive."

"Could anybody just take it and grow stuff?"

"You need the expertise, of course. But if you had the secret of it . . ."

She left the rest unspoken. Such a technological revolution was worth espionage, murder. To steal it, to control it, or at least to stop it.

They shared their dinner, eating picnic-style on the floor by the side of her bed, leaning against it.

Anika took a sip of protein gel. It didn't taste like much, but it did the job of nourishing her. And all she cared about was Billy, anyway. Getting as much of him as she could before he had to go away again.

She was hungry for the human contact, for the simple pleasure of talking to somebody. But it was more than that. This was Billy, the man who populated her secret dreams and kept her company in her memories. As Roberto faded away, Billy became more vivid, and she held on to him like a talisman, like a soldier's good-luck charm.

Never mind that he had the Murphy backwards luck he mentioned. She wanted all of him: that lopsided smile, that incandescent stare that made the rest of the universe disappear. It sounded idiotic, but she wanted to protect him. And if she couldn't protect him by staying away from him, she wanted to give him a place of sanctuary, where he could let go of the banter, let go of the war, and find a peaceful garden to lay his head.

But it wasn't that simple.

Anika put these thoughts away. Here with Billy, she was Annie, not Anika, and for the moment she could leave the beleaguered scientist behind, and be Annie, Billy's girl, at least for a single night.

"So how did you get from the Jobs Prize to planet AlphaZed3?"

She sighed and leaned back against the cot, feeling the heat of his arm all along her side, even though they didn't touch. "I don't know how I ended up here, really," she said, wrenching herself away from the tangled mess of her thoughts to look at him, in the flesh, next to her. "But making this planet habitable means big money for FortuneCorp," she said.

"You wanna know how I found you out here? I knew you and Roberto worked for FortuneCorp, first off. And that aside from all your science, you love growing things. So I thought to myself – 'Self, what would a scientist who loves growing things do for FortuneCorp?' Grow new worlds, of course. After that, I hacked into the employee database of off-world employees, tapped into a few contacts, and I was hot on your trail."

Annie's dinner congealed into a hard, cold pit in her stomach. "Nice little felony you committed there, Murph. And don't you realize they have a whole sheriff's division at FortuneCorp that'll trace your virtual tracks and hunt you down in the meatworld?"

Billy's smile got small and quiet and dangerous. "It was worth it, Annie. I found out who killed Roberto in the database, too – the information was right in his dossier. In yours."

The silence thundered between them.

"Don't worry about me. I have my ways of getting in and out of virtual space alive. My contacts. My brothers."

Annie nodded at him, numb to her bones. "So you know who killed him."

"You want to know."

"I'm not so sure. What can I do about it, even if I do know?"

Billy didn't answer her. Instead, he guzzled the rest of his own protein gel and crushed the titanium can between his fingers. He kept crushing it into a tiny cube, as Annie watched.

"Once I found out where you were and who killed Roberto, I had to find you," he said.

"So here I am, you found me," she said, a little waver in her voice. "Growing this ball of ice into something habitable."

Billy turned his head to look at the flimsy synthwood door to the hut, and Annie knew he could look right through it with his modified eyes. "That Bowman eco-drive is incredible. No other worldcorp has technology anything like it, not yet anyway. You grew a whole world."

"Well, a few hundred square meters worth. But we have to make it more than a few kliks wide for a colony to settle here and get to work. The precious metals frozen inside the ice are worth trillions. Once it's habitable, we can extract that ore and conquer the whole quadrant. We can use this as a regional base."

She still spoke of "we": what she and FortuneCorp could do together. It was a habit she had, maybe a bad one, but she wanted to belong to something – anything that was bigger than her and her fears.

Billy kept staring at the door, and didn't look away even when Annie dared to touch his shoulder. When he didn't respond to her, she squinted at the door as if she could see through it too, through sheer orneriness.

Nope.

Before she could say anything, Billy whispered directly into her mind: *What's that?*

Those two little words sparked the shakes in her, from deep inside, working out to the tips of her fingers, to the ends of her hair. For two reasons.

One, Billy spoke directly into her mind. How did he do that? She wasn't genmod in any way. Not even Roberto could do it, whisper into her soul. And he had tried.

So, what just happened?

The other reason was that Billy seemed to have seen something lurking in the jungle she'd grown, outside the perimeter of her research hut. But she hadn't introduced any fauna to her flora, not yet.

So, what the bloody hell was out there?

Billy must have picked up on her fear, for he rose silently to his feet, and put her behind him. He took a blaster out of his boot (so *that* was where it was) and walked to the door, step by soundless step.

Once he reached the frame, he motioned Annie back, and she decided not to argue. Before she could take cover behind her desk, Billy reached forward lightning fast, and swung the door open.

In a flash, Annie saw the hummingbird-fast metal wings and screamed, "Don't shoot!"

Billy reached forward and pinched Violet out of the air and into one of his big, square palms. Violet squeaked, and the gears ground audibly in the joints of her translucent wings.

"That's my lab assistant," Annie said, shaking so hard she reached for the top of her desk to keep from toppling over. "Violet. That's what I call her."

Billy brought the wriggling AI to her desk, opened the roll-top with an elbow, and pinned its metallic little body against the realwood surface.

"Looks like a killer drone to me," Billy growled.

"Violet's FortuneCorp-issued. And yes, they make the drones. But her directive is to assist me. She does growth measurements around the dome's perimeter, to see how permeable the dome membrane is at the edges. To see if we can extend the geodome biosphere. I should've warned you about her. Sorry, I'm such a ninny."

Billy snorted at that, sighed, and let Violet go. She buzzed on her back for a minute, like a metallic dragonfly, and then she found her footing and swung onto her furry-looking titanium feet.

"What's that?" Violet asked in her high-pitched, buzzing voice.

Annie restrained a sigh. "This is my old friend, Billy Murphy. He was, erm, in the neighborhood, and decided to stop by and say hello."

Violet's compound eyes took in Billy and Annie in a single glance. And for the first time, those jeweled, all-seeing eyes unnerved her.

They seemed to see right through her. Seemed to know who killed Roberto. And why.

But Annie's dangerous days were done. She was a frontier gardener now, she wanted to tell Violet. And that's all she wanted to be.

Violet joined them for the rest of their little picnic. Billy no longer looked at Annie or said much of anything. He just watched Violet. And Violet watched Annie.

"I need to return to my monitoring duties," Violet finally announced. "Are you sure you are okay here, boss?"

Annie smiled at her. Oh, she knew Violet was programmed, and didn't grow spontaneously out of carbon-based life, but she'd never cared. Violet knew an endless supply of silly jokes, entertained her and diverted her through long days of data analysis, eco-development, and heat generation under the geodome. Violet distracted her, on long, lonely, dark nights balanced on the edge of forever.

Her smile faded, though, as Violet's wings buzzed into life. For the first time, Annie saw a creature created by FortuneCorp, one whose loyalty extended through her to her mother – the corporation. But Annie only said, "Goodnight, Violet. All's well. As usual, mark me as off duty until sunrise."

"Will do, boss."

And with a buzz and blur of wings, Violet was gone into the night.

"You are in terrible danger," Billy whispered, after Violet was well and truly gone.

"I know," Annie whispered back.

"No. You don't know who killed Roberto. Who is likely to kill you, too."

Annie was afraid to know the truth. The truth was too horrible to hear.

Billy slid closer, put an arm around her, and leaned his head against hers.

Warmth flooded through her, and after a moment of basking in the pure human contact, Annie realized with a jolt that it wasn't just emotional warmth she felt. Her body seemed to have connected with Billy's. Their consciousness seemed to have merged.

Roberto had once described the mental union he'd felt with his team, the way the genmod made it possible for them to fight as one. And now she felt that merging for herself. Billy spoke into her now, the way he'd once spoken into his team.

FortuneCorp.

Was all that Billy said. He said it into her mind.

That was all it took, to strip the willful blindness from her eyes.

FortuneCorp.

It was FortuneCorp that had known about her background and profited from it. FortuneCorp that knew she'd refused to go off-world while Roberto still served in the Glass Desert. He was their employee, but he was also a US citizen. He had undergone the genmod without their express permission, and FortuneCorp knew that not even the corporation could recall Roberto from the field of war.

So FortuneCorp had killed Roberto.

Not a dying radiation-poisoned terrorist, as the government had told her. She hadn't believed that for a minute, but she'd assumed it was some corporate rival, some other worldcorp, killing Roberto to kill his value to his own company.

But FortuneCorp, her employer and Roberto's, had murdered him. So that it could post her off-world like it wanted. To test the Bowman eco-drive, gain that competitive edge.

Now she understood. As long as she worked on the Bowman eco-drive and asked no questions, FortuneCorp got what it wanted out of her. But if she quit, if she betrayed the company's loyalty, her value to FortuneCorp was gone. And if FortuneCorp couldn't have her talents, nobody could.

Her life was balanced on a razor's edge. She opened her mouth to speak, but Billy stopped her with a kiss. A kiss so mind-blowing in its intensity that all the devastating truth melted in its wake.

She surrendered to the fire of it, and it burned away the fear, the grief, the pain. The "we" was gone, was never more than a lie. Only an incandescent rage remained. And for the first time, an acceptance of the fact that Roberto was truly, forever, gone.

Billy whispered from inside that fire, into her mind. *I am getting you out of here. Alive. I swear.*

Annie made a little sound, and didn't bother trying to get her brain cells to respond in words. Instead, she wrapped her arms around him, and just kissed Captain Billy Murphy back.

He caressed her gently with his fingers, their tips feathering down the back of her neck and against the length of her arms. With a sigh, she surrendered to him, let the molten flood of feeling crest over all of her defenses.

His kiss became more insistent, and she opened her mouth to his, curling into his arms as they twined together on the floor. She ran her fingers through that thick hair, felt the stubble along the edge of his jaw, and that inner sensation of openness and vulnerability was almost more than she could bear.

She almost pulled away then, begged off, asked for more time, made some excuse and slipped out of his fingers. But Billy sighed too, and to her shock her heart surged inside of her. Began beating in tandem with Billy's heart, throbbing together in a single rhythm.

I will never leave you, he whispered into her, and all she could do was make a little sigh of gratitude in response. He kept kissing her even as he set her full length along the ground, and pressed his body against hers.

The warmth of him spread, and their shared fire rose up in

her. His hands found her bare skin, under her tunic, and she trembled under his gentle but insatiable touch.

Their hearts beat together, faster and faster. And then, at the same moment, their eyes opened. And it was like she was inside of Billy's body, staring back at herself. She simultaneously looked into him, and he looked into her. This communion was more intimate than even the act of sex; they mingled souls as well as their bodies.

From that double vantage, she could see what he saw when he looked at her. Feel what he felt. And the tears sprung up in her eyes. She was beautiful!

Billy kissed Annie again, as if he could kiss his life force right into her. She was the only woman who could slip through his fingers and right into his heart. He'd felt closer to her just hunting her in the cyberworld, and then the farthest quadrants of space, than to any other woman he'd ever known.

This little freckled blonde woman, who had run away from him to save him, had stolen his heart forever.

Annie couldn't get enough of his lips, the velvet skin at the nape of his neck. She kissed down the side of his face, and she whispered, "Just this night. And then you go. Please."

I will never leave you.

And she gave up trying to convince this man, who had the force of a hurricane, to do anything he didn't want to do. She knew he wanted to kiss her, and for one night she'd gladly take every last kiss that Billy Murphy had to give.

I'm going to take your kisses in return, Annie. Make you mine, forever. But first I want to make sure you are safe.

With a sigh, Annie did the thing she never did, and accepted things for what they were. Bit by bit, her consciousness receded from his, then with a sudden *snap* she was back in her body, and Billy Murphy was back in his.

They lay together in a sweaty, intertwined heap of longing. "I want you, so bad," Annie said.

"No kidding, right?" Billy said out loud, and laughed. "But I'm not getting naked with you, no way tonight. By this time tomorrow, though . . ."

By this time tomorrow, if Annie had her way, Billy would be safely gone. Her desire pulled hard, deep in the base of her belly. Annie licked her lips, and tasted the sweat and tears mixed together. And she was surprised to find the taste sweet.

They turned off the lights. Instead of lying in the cot, Billy insisted they sleep behind the bed, pressed up together on the floor against the flimsy back wall of the hut.

"Trust me," he said. "Sweet dreams."

His voice, so everyday and cordial, such a contrast to the raw passion they had just shared.

"But what about Violet?" she asked.

"I'll take care of that little bitch."

She got that he didn't trust Violet. But how could a little, unarmed lab AI do her any harm?

Annie soon found out.

Somehow Annie fell into sleep, tucked inside Billy's sheltering arms. He smelled like cinnamon and musk. She dreamed of far-off gardens filled with spices and wild creatures, fierce and beautiful.

Billy's face hovered over hers in her dream, open, finally at peace. The war was over . . .

Annie awoke to furious buzzing and violent curses, flailing arms, and the hoarse cries of a man fighting for his life.

She rolled under the cot to get out of the way, and the battle royal raged above. She heard the crash of furniture, the desk smashing to the ground, Billy's angry roar, the whine of Violet's wings.

She reached up and felt for the blaster still hidden under her pillow.

No! Annie!

And she drew her hand back just as fast. As if Billy had smacked her.

A second later silence thundered down over them, as if the battle had never happened.

"Billy?" she whispered, suddenly full of a terrible foreboding. "Billy!"

No answer, and after another minute Annie decided she was done with hiding.

She hesitated, waiting for Billy to yell into her mind again.
Nothing.

She crawled out from under the cot and flicked on the bare bulb that hung over the smashed remains of her desk.

Billy lay sprawled across the floor, utterly still. With a cry, she rushed forward and rolled him over with an adrenaline-fueled strength, searching his body for wounds. Violet buzzed up into her face, like a fat, lost cicada in Forest Hills in August.

She slapped the insectoid AI away from her. "Stand down!" she ordered. But instead of responding, Violet buzzed away from her, drunkenly banging into the flimsy synthwood door over and over again.

As Annie watched in horrified fascination, Violet fell to the ground and crawled away through the crack between the door and the threshold.

"Billy." She turned back to him, racking her brain, trying to figure out how a tiny AI could fell a big lug like Murphy. How could Violet have killed him without any firepower at all?

She checked for a heartbeat and found it, faint but steady. She let her hand rest against his chest. She listened to his breathing, so tentative that it seemed it might stop again at any moment.

Come back to me, she whispered inside his mind, not realizing she'd done it until he stirred under her, responding to her words with movement.

She stretched out next to him, warmed his cold body with her own, restraining her panic like a ravening dog on a leash.

"Back," Billy said aloud a minute later, words slurring. "It was poison. Little viper."

He opened his eyes, and Annie looked into him, disappeared into him. If he lived, she had to get him out of here.

She blinked hard to break their connection, and looked around the ruined hut. She could see beyond the circle of light shed by the bare bulb overhead.

Daylight. They'd survived the night.

"Do you . . . do you need an antidote?" Annie stuttered, though she didn't have one, nor any knowledge of how to concoct one.

"Nah. The genmod. Comes in . . . handy." With a groan, Billy sat up, his sides heaving. "That poison, though . . . it woulda worked on you. Easy."

Poison. Annie shuddered. "Violet."

"*Hells* yeah, Violet. She didn't have bullets or lasers inside her. I knew to check for that, before. But they stored poison in her. I'm not a drone specialist or I woulda known."

With growing amazement, Annie realized he was *apologizing* to her. "You saved my life. You realize that, I hope."

He shrugged. "She never woulda come after you if I hadn't showed up. Violet's here to make sure you stay here, working. But now she realizes I'm taking you away from here, away from FortuneCorp. And her real job is to kill you rather than allow you to get off-world with that Bowman drive. If they can't have your genius, nobody can."

Annie's stomach did a slow flip. *She'd always thought Violet worked for her. She was wrong. Annie worked for Violet, and if she messed up, she'd be terminated. For good.*

"She used up her first strike on your pillow because your face wasn't there," Billy said. "She had to move fast to get past me, she knew that. Didn't have the time to register you weren't sleeping in your usual place. But man, her reserve dose was enough to do the job, too. Ow."

Annie stared and stared at her pillow. The cover was shredded apart, and a thick, brown liquid puddled on the synthfoam padding.

She tore her gaze away and turned her attention to Billy's wounds. Annie could see the vicious punctures slashed into his palm.

"She got away," Annie said, and pointed to the door.

"She's probably got an emergency beacon signal programmed in 'er," Billy said, getting to his feet. "Time for us to get out of here, wicked fast. I hear FortuneCorp is working on a wormhole drive. If they've perfected it, then they can get here in two hours, not two days. Gotta go."

A sick dismay settled over Annie like a thundercloud, a terrible certainty of doom. The room did a slow spin, and she felt like she was going to puke. "But go where? FortuneCorp owns this whole sector. I can't hide from them, Billy. You came all the way out here to find me, but it's too late, no matter what Roberto told you. I think you can save yourself if you get out of here fast enough."

Billy's laugh shattered her. He drew to his full height, magnificent, alive, and unbroken, and she looked up from the floor at him in wonder.

"I don't work for FortuneCorp. I don't belong to them. Never did. The US Army broke me down and built me over as a genmod freakazoid. But FortuneCorp can go suck it."

He reached down for her with his bitten, bloody hand. Annie held on and pulled herself to her feet.

"Remember those brothers I told you about? The ones that helped me find you? They got free of FortuneCorp, just like you're gonna. They set up their own planet, with their own ways and their own freedom. And I'm taking you there."

"But . . ." Annie's resolve to sacrifice herself faded in the blaze of Billy's furious stare.

"No buts. I know, I know, you want me to go and save myself. I ain't built that way, and you know it. You wanna save me? Then come with me. Because if you're not leaving, then I'm staying, and we'll deal with FortuneCorp here, together."

He pulled her to the door, and this time Annie didn't hesitate. She left her past, her fear and her determination to hide, lying on the floor behind them.

"Sully's on the way to pick us up," Billy said. "We could use a gardener out there where we're going, on that new planet. You're just the woman we need."

They walked away from the trashed hut and into the jungle that had grown out of Annie's vision, through her patient fingers and over time, with careful tending.

After a moment's hesitation, Annie decided to speak her last misgiving. "How is it you can talk inside my soul?" she asked. "Roberto never could do it. He tried. It seems like, I don't know, cheating somehow. Like it wasn't right I couldn't commune with him like that. And here we are, you and me . . ."

Billy stopped walking and turned to face her. "Yeah, my bro Roberto was possessed of many gifts," he said with a sigh. "You guys were good together. But, Annie girl, Roberto's gone. And he left your protection to me."

They stood in a clearing surrounded by gently drooping vines, along a pathway of soft moss. The sun filtered weakly through the dome, arching high above both their heads.

"I was the team leader you know, and Roberto worked under me," Billy continued. "I called my brothers into union. That was my strength. Roberto could see ahead. But I could speak into his heart. And you can speak into mine, Annie. You know what that means."

She did know. It meant that despite Billy's physical strength, his horse-sense – as he called it – and his ability to survive anything, his love for Annie ruled him.

The jungle grew up around them, rich and green and fragrant.

When Annie looked around, she saw only the two of them walking alone in the garden. But she knew, despite all appearances to the contrary, they didn't walk alone. For one thing, Violet, the killer, still hunted them out there.

But Annie reached for Billy's hand and squeezed, and despite the terrible urgency that they get off AlphaZed3 now, he waited for her, the way he always had.

Annie closed her eyes, took a deep breath, and saw with her inner sight the place where Billy spoke to her. And she saw that in truth three of them walked in the jungle at dawn.

Goodbye, Roberto, she said inside of her, knowing that Billy could hear her too. *I will love you forever.*

Adios, mi corazon, Roberto replied. *Anika will stay with me, Annie goes with Billy. You go on, and I will too. We will meet again, in that place beyond the edge of forever.*

Annie kissed Roberto in her mind, and finally let him go. The whisper of his goodbye echoed over her as he faded away, speaking into her for the first time, and the last.

She watched him go, blinked the vision away, and took a look around. Only a moment had passed, but all had changed.

She was still in the clearing. Billy still waited for her. For the first time, Annie believed she could be free. *Free of FortuneCorp, free of the past, free of herself and her fears.*

"I never spoke with Roberto like that, you know, in the soul," she whispered. "I don't know if I really want to say goodbye to him."

She waited for the faithful tears to appear, but for the first time, they didn't come.

Billy spoke out loud, gently, with a sort of reverence. "Aw, you spoke to him without words, always, Annie. You have the soul of a healer. A grower of seeds, right? Anybody who could grow a world like this has the power to whisper into a heart. And what I heard was Roberto saying goodbye to you. He let you go, he wants you to go, you're free. He still loves you."

He took her hand and quietly pulled her forward through the little Eden she had cultivated. And she only paused to pull the Bowman eco-drive out of the ground. To take it with them, to grow a new world.

And they came to the perimeter, behind the research hut,

where Billy had moved through the barrier between her fledgling paradise and the ice.

"I don't have a cold-weather suit for you," Billy said. "You can't go out there yet."

They stared beyond the clear barrier between Annie's warm, unfurling garden and the frozen hell howling outside. Dimly, she could see the landing pod Billy had used to come down to her. It was already half-buried in the swirling snow and clouded ice of the native world.

And then she saw it. The rebel ship breaking through the ice planet's orbit, hovering over the frozen surface. She read the words painted crudely on the battered hull: *The Sullivan*.

A warm cascade of light shot from the belly of the ship to Billy's landing pod, then traveled along the ice to the permeable plexisurface of the geodome, seeking Billy. His soul.

The light poured through the clear membrane, warming her like the sun of her childhood. Annie put her hands up against the plexi, feeling the cool membrane yielding to the pressure of her fingertips.

And then right before Annie walked through into the protective light of *The Sullivan*'s waybeam, Violet rose up from underfoot. Beating her wings into the ground, like a homicidal mechanical hummingbird with a hypodermic needle for a beak, stabbing Annie's shoe again and again and again.

Her poison vial, now empty.

Billy looked down, then scraped Violet off her foot with his boot, and stomped until the AI was no more than a cluster of crushed gears.

"I bet the beacon inside the AI still works," Billy said. "We're getting out of here, just in time."

With that, they pressed through the membrane and walked up the pathway of light and into the belly of the ship that waited for them.

And Annie looked back one last time, to the garden she had grown, to the illusion of safety she was leaving behind. The dome glowed in the morning sunlight, iridescent as a soap bubble, the blasted frozen whiteness surrounding it.

Roberto wasn't there.

A huge weight suddenly rolled off her shoulders, a burden she'd never realized she carried, until it was released. After a

long, barren season, she was ready. It was time for Annie to let
the grief move through her, radiate and fade away, though not
the love, never the love. *She'd never forget him, would love him
always, but now she knew she was strong enough to carry the loss
forward into the future.*

Annie turned, kept walking into the light. And Billy Murphy
walked beside her. She'd never run away again.

New Earth Twelve

Mandy M. Roth

One

Delta Quadrant 2948, on board Expedition Vessel Rhea

Olivia Blu punched the last sequence of coordinates into the ship's control panel. She double-checked her course, waiting for the display screen to give her a visual of the destination of her choosing. As her destination appeared, a level of enthusiasm that couldn't be tempered rushed through her. Olivia's gaze went to one of the many cameras mounted throughout the huge transport vessel. The camera made a tiny noise and zoomed in on her. She smiled, obviously pleased. "That's it. Twelve is less than a week away. We did it."

"No," a deep, totally masculine voice said from the communication unit in the bridge. "You did it, Livia."

She snorted, pushing her long dark hair back from her face. She tied it in a loose bun and ran her fingers over the display screen showing the planet they were approaching. As a Goldilocks planet, it was situated among the stars in such a way that it could possibly support human life. Its atmospheric pressure was within the necessary range to be able to hold water, and by all accounts and probe readings, it had breathable air and everything needed for survival. The only thing they didn't have were clear images of the entire surface. The series of probes they'd launched over the course of the journey had malfunctioned mysteriously, giving only half the data required. Like the recon team sent over thirty years ago, the probes had vanished.

It wasn't the first planet humans had tried to colonize. She doubted it would be the last. The first eleven tries had been met with one failure or another. Sickness. War. Alien races that were unwelcoming. The list went on and on. The twelfth try would be different. She was sure of it. It had felt like this day might never come. But there it was on her screen – planet Twelve.

"I was thirteen when I woke up. I think we both know that without your guidance and help I'd have been put out an airlock long ago," she said casually.

The man controlling the cameras was quiet for a moment. "I wouldn't have allowed that to happen."

"Cam," she said respectfully, her attention still pulled to the sight of Twelve. "Let's be honest here. Quincy would have found a way to override your control of the vessel, and he'd have ejected me out an airlock had you not been there to walk me through what to do, and had you not activated all the androids on board to assist."

"I wasn't there, Livia," he said, sounding overwrought. She wondered if he had as much remorse as it sounded like he did. "I've never been able to actually be there."

"In physical form, no," she agreed. It was true. He'd been a voice for the past ten years of her journey – a guiding voice, but a voice all the same. "Cameron, you've been there in all the other ways that matter."

She touched the image of Twelve on the screen. She didn't want to dwell on the negative, on all that couldn't be altered. She wanted to try her best to focus on their future, even though it meant changes on the horizon. "We did it. In less than a week we'll be in Twelve's orbit. A lot of things will be different, won't they?"

He fell silent for a moment. "You know, my pre-set orders for pod release have started. I'll be able to be there physically very soon, Livia."

Olivia bent her head. Emotions welled in her. She should be elated by the news he'd be up and about soon. She wasn't. She liked having his undivided attention, and that would end the minute he woke from stasis. She knew it was selfish, but she couldn't stop the way she felt.

"I take it you're not happy about having me there physically," he said, a certain sadness to his voice.

She lifted her head and wiped her cheeks quickly, coming away with tears. She hated how easily she broke down over seemingly nothing. "No. I'm happy. I am. It's just, well, everyone else is going to wake up, too, and Oli is going to be so upset. So many people will be."

"Your brother will adjust fine."

She wasn't so sure. Oliver was stubborn and fiercely protective of her. Eleven years ago he'd tucked her safely into the pod next to his, kissed her forehead and told her it would feel like a dream and before she knew it – they'd be awake and on Twelve. That hadn't been the case. One year into the journey, all hell had broken loose and everything for her had changed. It hadn't been a quick dream. It had been ten long years. She'd aged. Her brother hadn't. "He went into suspended animation next to me when I was thirteen and he was twenty-six. He's going to wake up still twenty-six only to find I'm no longer thirteen. Ten years have passed for me."

"He'll come to terms with that," Cameron soothed. "The alternative isn't something he'd have wanted."

"You mean the lot of us 'pod-rejects' dead?"

"Pod-rejects?" Cameron questioned, laughing slightly. He'd never been fond of what the children of the ordeal had taken to calling themselves years ago. It had sort of stuck.

"Beats 'pod-kids'. You vetoed that one long ago."

"You're not kids anymore, Livia," he reminded. "You haven't been for a long time."

"I know, but the name fits," she returned. She sniffled again, her cheeks flushing quickly, flooded with shame. She shouldn't want him all to herself. She should be happy he could wake and, in turn, wake the rest of the passengers on board *Rhea*. "And everyone is going to get up, and they're going to demand your attention and your time. I think we've all got used to getting your undivided attention all these years."

"We?" a perky, short blonde asked from the doorway to the bridge. She wore tan fatigue pants and a light-pink tank top, showing off her curves. "Try *you*."

"Cara," Olivia said, wiping her face again to remove the signs she'd let her emotions get the better of her once more. "Stop.

Cameron has been there as a guiding voice and interface with the ship's computer for years."

"I know," Cara supplied, still grinning. "But have you ever noticed he goes by 'Doctor Cameron' to the rest of us, but to you he answers to 'Cam'?"

Olivia hadn't really ever thought about it. She and Cameron had grown close over the years. Even though he wasn't physically there, she considered him her closest friend.

She shrugged. "I'm not sure I'm following you."

"Livia, I've sat with you next to his stasis pod before. I'm very aware he's a good-looking guy." Cara entered the bridge. She had a mischievous grin on her face. "Tall, ripped, dark hair, tanned, and . . ."

Olivia's eyes widened as her gaze whipped to the cameras and then back to Cara. "He can *hear* you."

"I know," Cara said, laughing. "Do you disagree? Do you think he's ugly? Think he's as hideous as a skankerous slug during its skin shedding?"

Olivia gasped. "No!"

Cara pointed at her, still laughing. "Your face is beet red. Almost as red as the time I hit the visor button and retracted the privacy shield on his pod."

Olivia thought back to the day. They'd been nineteen when Cara had done it. Most of the crew and the passengers aboard the vessel had gone into stasis wearing medical gowns, or even tank tops and pajama bottoms. A select few had gone in wearing nothing but what they were born in. Doctor Hoyt Cameron was one of those daring, bold ones.

Cara glanced up at the camera. "Do you remember what she did?"

"She nearly broke her neck to cover my pod until you put the privacy screen back up," Cameron said, his voice echoing through the bridge, carrying an amused tone.

Olivia closed her eyes a second, allowing them their time to tease her before looking at Cara. "Are we going to make fun of me for affording him privacy?"

"Yes," Cara said smugly. "Now, tell me you're excited he'll be up and about soon."

Olivia averted her gaze, shame nearly choking her. "Yes. I'm excited."

"Could that have lacked any more enthusiasm?" Cara tapped a hand on her hip.

"My thoughts exactly," Cameron inserted.

Cara came to a stop next to her. "Livia, do you really think he's going to wake up and totally ignore you?"

Yes, that was exactly what Olivia feared. Cam was a powerful member of the expedition team. As chief medical officer he'd be consulted on all matters. Plus, he was a member of the Founder's Council. They'd be the provisional government on Twelve. Meaning, Cameron would be so busy with everything there, he wouldn't have time for her anymore. "Everyone will demand his attention. He's very important."

"So are you."

"No," she said. "I'm not. And I fully understand everything changes when the rest of the ship wakes."

Cara sighed and touched Olivia's shoulder lightly. "Hon, you really think Doc is going to pretend he hasn't been there for you for the past ten years?"

"He's been there for all of us."

The camera lens drew back and stopped panning the room. Cameron often did this when he was checking other areas of the ship, or when he knew she needed privacy.

Cara smiled. "For us, sure. But, Livia, the rest of us don't act like a married couple. You two do."

Olivia's nose crinkled as confusion set in. "What are you talking about?"

"You know what I mean. Those couples who have been married a while. They have that way about them – they finish each other's sentences, seem to guess what the other wants, and know each other's habits."

"He's been our interface to the ship for ten years. We know him. He's watched us every day for all those years. Of course he knows us well."

"It's not *my* sleeping quarters that he's been monitoring all night as of late. It's not *me* he has long conversations with until the wee hours of the morning." Cara laughed and waved a hand in the air flippantly. "I'm not complaining. I'm just pointing out that there are dozens of us, but you're who he focuses on. I'm in charge of accessing the ship's camera logs each morning. So, uh, yeah, he does."

Olivia glanced at the camera. "Are you worried something will happen to me when I sleep? I promised to get this ship to Twelve in one piece. I've kept my word so far."

Cameron didn't respond.

Cara snickered. "Livia, you're one of the smartest people I know, but really, are you so thick when it comes to men that you don't get why he'd be watching you all night?"

Cara and Olivia were the same age, but Cara had a much different upbringing. Her mother had been a prostitute on Three. Cara had been raised in brothels on the edges of the galaxy. She knew things – things Olivia hadn't been exposed to growing up under the watchful eye of her brother, who had raised her since their parents' death when she was only six.

Olivia squared her shoulders. "Well, I've watched him sleeping, too."

Cara rolled her eyes. "That's different. He's in stasis. Anytime you go near his pod he looks like he's out cold." She glanced back to the camera. "If you don't come right out and tell the girl that you have a thing for her, she'll never catch on. She's socially stunted in the *male* department, if you know what I mean."

Olivia burst into a fit of giggles. "Right. Yeah. One of the greatest minds mankind has ever known has a thing for me. Okay. Sure. Why not? Can we stop with the teasing now and focus on the wakening? We still on schedule? Cameron is first in line, and then Oliver since he's head of security. Then . . ."

Cara put her hand up. "We're all set. And why wouldn't Doctor Cameron have a thing for you? You're brilliant too, Livia."

"Would you please stop?" Olivia asked. "He's friends with my brother, and older than Oli. He's who fixed my arm when I fell off that racer when I was nine."

"And he's been locked at his same age for eleven years now, while you've grown into a young woman," Cara reminded. "So stop using the age difference as an excuse. There is a gap, but not a huge one. He's also part-Vanesier, so he ages at a slower rate than a human. Meaning, he may be thirty-five but he doesn't look a day older than twenty-five." Cara smirked. "Of course, there is the drawback of his sight. Without the ship's interface or his special custom glasses he's practically blind. I remember meeting him when we boarded, and he was standing there, next to your brother. His glasses gave him feedback problems that day and he had to take them off. His eyes – they're silver. Freaky."

Olivia's temper flared. "His eyes are *not* freaky. How dare you say that? And because he has a neuro-mechanical implant he can interface with nearly any technology, so seeing isn't really an issue for him. And he's *not* blind. No, he doesn't see like we do, but who is to say our way is better? Plus, he's very capable of functioning without any technology to aid him. Oli told me once when I was younger that Cam would often shut off his implant and function without its help absolutely brilliantly."

Cara smacked her lips. "You talked to your brother about the doctor when you were younger?"

"They're best friends."

"And Oli just offered this info up to you?" Cara gave a questioning look. "You didn't ask him?"

Olivia blushed more. "I might have been worried about Cam once. His opti-spectrum glasses were damaged, and his backup pair hadn't been calibrated yet, so they hurt him more than they helped. I could sense how much pain he was in with them on. I suggested he take them off, and he cocked his head and stared at me for the longest time. He took them off and then kept looking in my direction no matter where I moved, or how quietly I did so."

"Hon, he was waiting for you to freak out about his eyes. It's what most people do when they see them."

Olivia tipped her head. "Freak out? Why? They're gorgeous."

Cara laughed.

Olivia groaned. "You know what I mean. They're not freaky. I like them. And without his opti-spectrum glasses on he sees the way the Vanesier race does. He sees with his mind – he gets impressions, and his senses compensate, going into overdrive, helping him get a clear idea of what is happening around him. Honestly, he probably sees more than we ever will."

Cara crossed her arms under her chest. "You're very defensive of your husband."

"He's not my . . ." Olivia groaned. "I'm done having this conversation with you."

She looked up at the camera, wondering how much Cameron had overheard. He didn't say anything, and she tilted her head to the side. "Cam?"

Still he didn't answer. Something was wrong.

Cara glanced at her. "The wakening? Already?"

Two

Olivia rushed out of the bridge, down the corridor and then into the lift to the pod levels. She knew the way to his pod by heart. She punched the button for Level 4 and waited for what felt like forever for the lift to get there. When it finally did, she pounded on the sliding doors, wanting them to open faster.

Horrific thoughts of Cameron's pod malfunctioning during his wakening flooded her mind and hit her hard. The tears came fast, and she did nothing to stop them. She ran full force towards his pod. She came to a grinding halt when she spotted Cameron's pod hatch unopened and completely intact.

She eased up alongside it, letting her fingers skim over the hard, yet clear, shelled lid. The body inside lay perfectly motionless. Olivia pressed her palm to the lid, lining up with the side of Cameron's scruffy jawline. He was incredibly handsome. There was no denying it. "Cam?"

The nearest mounted camera zoomed in on her. "I'm here," Cameron said through the pod sector's sound system. "Sounded like you and Cara could use some privacy."

She stiffened. "How much did you hear?"

He was quiet for a fraction of a second. "Enough to know my eyes don't bother you."

Exhaling slowly, she nodded as the hollow pit in her stomach eased somewhat. "True. They don't."

"Livia," he said. "My body is slowly starting the wakening process."

She'd seen others undergo it. The process wasn't always pretty to see. "I'll give you privacy and activate one of the medical droids to oversee it."

"No. Stay with me for a bit. Please."

She reached under the pod and pulled out the sliding bench seat. All pods had one. They were used as bedside tables or seats for the use of the medical droids who oversaw the crew-members in stasis. She sat and kept her hand on the pod lid. Cameron looked so peaceful. Locked in a state of slumber, so close yet so very far away from her. She bowed her head, putting her forehead to the polycarbonate-blended lid. She wanted to touch him. For too long she'd known only the feeling of cold unforgiving surfaces instead of the touch of the man she longed for.

"Do you know what I want to do the second I wake?" Cameron asked.

She kept her head against the lid. "Shower. Oli told me once that's what most crew-members want after coming out of a long stasis sleep. Some throw up. A few of Quincy's men did that."

Cameron grunted. "When I get my hands on Quincy I'm going to rip him apart. His men, too."

She looked to the camera. "You've done a fine enough job locking them in the brig for all these years. I can't believe you overrode the codes so we couldn't let anyone out."

"Quincy and his faction of followers wanted all the females dead," Cameron said, his voice hard. "Had things gone his way that is exactly what you and the other girls would be – dead. He and his men sabotaged your pods."

"I know. This isn't news to me." She sighed. "After what happened on Ten, I can't exactly fault his logic. The Omethus virus strain nearly wiped out all the women and children. And it opened the door to a war that cost us how many more lives?"

The overhead lighting flashed. A sure sign Cameron was upset. "Bloody stars, Livia. I don't care what his reasoning was. He tried and nearly succeeded in ending the lives of all the females under the age of sixteen aboard this vessel."

"Cam," she said. "That was ten years ago. We're not children anymore. We all managed to survive despite Quincy's best efforts. I know you hate him. We're not exactly fond of him either, but we don't hold the same rage you do."

"Livia."

She took a long, deep breath. "Tell me what you want to do first thing upon waking. Let me guess: wring Quincy's neck."

"No," he responded. "I want to hold your hand. I want to hold you."

She wasn't sure how to reply, so she just did her best to hide her smile. She wanted to hold him, too. Three years back her feelings for him had started to change – to morph into something more. Cara had told her again and again that Cameron's feelings for her had changed around that point too, but Olivia couldn't believe it. A man as powerful and brilliant as Cameron couldn't possibly feel anything more than friendship for her – for a pod-reject.

Doctor Hoyt Cameron watched through the surveillance cameras as Olivia stroked the lid of the pod containing his body. He could see the edges of her smile and knew she was pleased. He wanted more than anything to be free from the stasis sleep and to wrap his arms around her.

Her long brown hair fell forward, cascading over a section of his pod. He wished his body was alert enough that he could reach up and push her hair from her face, so he could see her blue eyes. They were the same color as the waters on Vanesier. When he looked into her eyes he thought of home – of the planet he could never return to but had loved deeply. Sickness and war had ravaged his homeland before his own people had turned on themselves and their planet. When they'd come across the human race, a race so closely resembling them physically, but far inferior in terms of intelligence and technology, the surviving Vanesier had latched onto them, wanting desperately to aid them in finding a suitable home world.

Livia ran her hand over the pod lid slowly. Absentmindedly, she scanned the consul screen affixed to the side of his pod. It gave a continuous readout of his vitals. Each pod had one. "I'd like it if you held me."

His state of awareness slipped quickly before returning, and he knew then that the wakening was moving ahead as planned. Soon he'd lose his sync with the ship's computer interface. His consciousness would return to his body, and he'd then fight through the chills, the shaking and the nausea that accompanied most awakenings. None of it mattered. All that mattered was getting to actually touch Olivia.

He'd wanted to come out of stasis the very second he'd realized her pod, like so many of the others, had been sabotaged. He'd wanted to help but he hadn't been able to. He was the one crew-member who had to remain under at all costs, because he was the one mentally linked to the computer systems of the ship. For ten years he'd been forced to watch the girls learn to survive on their own. They'd had to deal with Quincy's men systematically waking early from stasis sleep, and they'd been forced to take action accordingly. Their childhoods had been stolen from them. Granted, they'd all grown into fine young women, but they'd deserved so much more.

Cameron zoomed in on Oliver's pod. As Olivia's brother, and head of security on *Rhea*, Oli would not take kindly to the knowledge that there were traitors among them. Cameron had considered waking Oli years back, but Oli's kidneys had been damaged in the wars of Eleven, and he'd needed to remain hooked into the pod's regenerative healing matrix.

Cameron paused, his mind wandering to Oli. They'd been close friends since Ten, and had been through much together. Cameron had been there when Oli's mother had succumbed to the Omethus virus strain that had swept through Ten, taking most of the females. He'd been there when the wars of Eleven had taken Oli's father, leaving Oli as Olivia's guardian. Now, he would have to be there to tell him that an attempt had been made on his sister's life, that she was no longer the thirteen-year-old girl he remembered placing in the pod – but rather, a beautiful young woman now. And last, but not least, that Cameron was totally and completely in love with Olivia.

She looked up at the camera, her blue gaze moist and her dreamy, pale skin flawless. "How much longer?"

"At least thirty minutes or so," he lied. He'd held her up longer than he should. Her presence dulled the burn of loneliness he felt. "Go activate a medical droid."

She nodded and stood. As she walked away Cameron felt his consciousness slipping. It was time for him to wake. He just didn't want her witnessing it first-hand.

Three

Olivia activated one of the medical droids, and smiled as he nodded his head. From all outward appearances he looked human. Very big, but very human. It was the case with all the androids. They'd been made with synthetic genetic material, and some had even been spliced with actual human DNA. The ones on *Rhea* had some human DNA in them, making them even more lifelike than others. They had designated call numbers, but Olivia and the other pod-rejects had given them names. Granted, the names were ones thought up by a bunch of young girls nearly ten years ago, but they were names all the same.

"Hi, Rainbow," she said, using the full version of the name they'd given him, even though they'd taken to calling him Rain for short.

"Miss Olivia," he responded, very polished with his pronunciation. He was about as far from a rainbow as one could get, with his tawny skin, oversized muscular body and closely clipped hair. He looked more like the bouncers she remembered working at the drinking holes on Ten than a medical man, but that was what he was programmed to be. "Have you need of me?"

"Doctor Cameron's wakening has started."

Rain cocked his head to one side and his left eye went totally black. It was a sign he was accessing the computer interface. "Correction. His wakening is complete."

"What?" she asked, her breath squeezing out of her lungs in a fast swoosh.

"His pod emergency-exit cord was pulled." Rain continued to look out of one green and one fully black eye. "My scanners are unable to determine if the cord was pulled externally or internally."

"Quincy!" she yelled and turned, running back in the direction of the pod row that Cameron was in.

She slammed into the bay doors. They were set to open automatically when they sensed a presence. She'd never tested them at a full run before today. Clearly, they could stand to be tweaked. When they opened, she visually scanned the row of pods, her gaze locking onto Cameron's.

It was empty.

Wires hung loosely from the pod's lid. The white bed portion looked untouched save for the smallest of fading depressions. The privacy visor was drawn back. That was something that happened automatically once the wakening sequence was nearly complete. Cameron had told her he had thirty minutes yet.

Spinning, Olivia stared around the pod bay. Machines beeped, scanners blipped and everything seemed normal, except for the fact that Cameron was missing. Her mind continued to reel. In her head, Quincy and his faction of followers had sabotaged Cameron's pod, or had even abducted him upon waking. Reason said Quincy was safely locked away in the brig with the thirteen followers they'd identified to date. No one else had come out of stasis in nearly nine months. Still, she worried.

Olivia scanned the room. "Cameron?"

She found his naked form huddled on the floor on the other side of his pod. He shouldn't have tried to stand already. He wasn't scheduled for a full wakening for another hour. She rushed to his side and knelt.

Rain pushed in alongside her. "Doctor Cameron?"

Cameron grunted. "I'm fine, 17390."

Rain's expression said otherwise. "'Fine' would not leave one on the floor, Doctor."

Cameron pushed onto his elbows and glared at Rain. "You're going to make me lie here because I used your call number, not your name, aren't you?"

"I will admit I am considering it," Rain replied, with deadpan delivery.

Olivia pushed his arm. "Rain!"

He shrugged, seeming so human it made her grin despite the situation. She then focused on Cameron. "What are you doing on the floor?"

He lifted his head, his silver gaze greeting her.

"I was hoping to wake ahead of time, get cleaned up and surprise you," Cameron said, his voice tight and his body tense.

She sighed. "Cam."

"Didn't go as planned."

She shook her head and tugged on him. It was obvious she wouldn't be able to budge him. Rain stepped in and assisted, lifting Cameron with ease.

"Everything okay in here?" Cara asked, appearing at the bay doors. "Want to tell me why Doc is being held up like a naked rag doll?"

Rain stared at Cameron. "What explanation would you like me to give?"

"Go with . . . 'Because he was stupid,'" Olivia snapped. "Get him to an exam room."

Cameron shook his head. "No. I'm fine. Put me down."

Rain did, and Olivia was shocked Cameron managed to stay upright all on his own. She glanced at Cara. "You can go now."

"And miss the hot guy show?"

Olivia groaned. Cara tossed her hands up and went.

Rain followed behind Cara, leaving Olivia alone with Cameron. He was still solid muscle, just the way he'd been when he'd entered suspended animation eleven years ago. Of course, back then, he hadn't made her heart race the way he did now. She eased him to his feet and kept her gaze lifted to his face, ignoring his nakedness.

She smiled up at him. "I'll help you to the cleansing chamber."

"Thanks," he said, his hand moving over hers.

"Cam," she said softly, surprised at how much taller than her he was. "I'll miss our talks."

"They aren't ending, Livia," he returned. He nodded towards the cleansing chamber.

She helped him to it and stepped back, letting him enter. She closed the door behind him and the cleansing unit automatically kicked on. Sanitizing particles immediately filled the unit. She waited, fearful he'd fall due to his wakening weakness. Finally, the door opened and Cameron stepped out. She raked her gaze over his glistening form. Every part of him rippled with perfection. As she lowered her eyes to take in more of his body, she gulped and looked at the floor fast, embarrassed by her lack of self-control.

Cameron chuckled, appearing right before her. "Grab me some standard-issue clothing and I'll run a diagnostic on myself."

She did as she was told and handed him the clothes while looking away. After a moment, he touched her chin and she was relieved to see he had pants on – but nothing more yet. Her gaze met his, and the next thing she knew Cameron had jerked her against his powerful frame. He dipped his head and his lips crashed onto hers. She'd never been kissed before, and was too stunned to do anything other than allow him to lead. And lead he did. He thrust his tongue into her mouth and drew tiny moans from her. Her hands instantly went to his bare chest. She found herself pushing on him gently as if she wanted him to step away, yet her mouth said otherwise. Her tongue laced around his and she fell against his body.

Cameron wrapped his arms around her and drew their kiss to a sensual end. Breathless, Olivia stared up at him. She wasn't sure what to say.

He kissed her forehead gently. "Gather the other pod-rejects."

She touched her swollen lower lip, blinking up at him as if she didn't have a single functioning brain cell left in her head. "Huh?"

A certain calmness settled over him as he stared down at her from silver eyes. "The others. Gather them in the ready room. I'd like to talk to them."

"But you just underwent the wakening. You need food, rest and to be monitored for signs of the shakes," she protested, concerned for him.

He touched her cheek lightly. "Livia, do as I asked. I'll be fine. My diagnostic scan came back clean. No sign of the shakes."

"But . . ."

He swatted her backside playfully and she yelped with surprise. "Go."

She stood there watching him before she grew bold and went to her tiptoes, pressing her mouth to his. One second she was standing before him and the next he had her yanked tightly against his naked chest. There was an air of authority in his actions that excited her to her very core. She ran her hands over him, touching anywhere and everywhere she could. He, in turn, did the same to her.

"Go," Cameron whispered. "If you don't, I'm going to take you right here and right now."

Olivia steeled her nerves. She licked her lower lip. "I'm not going anywhere."

A sexy grin slid over Cameron's mouth. "I was hoping you'd say that."

Four

Cameron walked with distinct purpose down the long, dimly lit corridor as he headed to the brig. He'd waited ten years to get his hands on Quincy for what he'd done. He'd thought finding release in Olivia might curb his need to kill the man. It hadn't. As he'd held Olivia after losing himself in her for the third time, his thoughts had drifted to Quincy, and to the man's traitorous actions. Actions that had nearly cost Olivia and the other girls their lives.

For ten long, torturous years, he'd plotted his revenge against Quincy. He'd fantasized about the ways he'd destroy him and his followers. They were a faction of people who believed the new world would be better off without females, and especially without children. These were considered a burden to provide for if resources were lower than expected on Twelve. Over the many different colonization attempts, women had been an issue more than once. Alien races wanted to abduct them for breeding purposes, sicknesses affected only them, affairs and adultery left men launching wars over them. Still, none of it meant they should be wiped out. Already their numbers were lower than the males'. Women were to be cherished and protected at all costs. It was simple. Quincy had broken that rule.

Cameron tapped the side of his opti-spectrum glasses, calibrating them further. They'd been acting up prior to him going into stasis eleven years ago, and only seemed to have gotten worse with non-use and time. He'd been without them for so long his body had grown unaccustomed. Under normal circumstances, after a long stasis sleep he'd have given his body at least half an hour to get used to the glasses once more. Instead, he'd used the time to bed the woman he loved, and after that he could no longer wait to deal with Quincy.

The glasses glitched and – for a split second – everything around Cameron went dark. His natural-born abilities kicked in, giving him impressions of the surrounding area. He could function fully without the glasses, but he was rusty and not at full strength just yet. Putting a hand out, he steadied himself by using the smooth wall face until his glasses stopped acting up.

He continued onward, his boots echoing off the floor of the corridor. The boots were standard military issue and went up to just under his knees. The grays he wore were also standard issue, indicating his rank. There wasn't an officer on board who outranked him since the commander of *Rhea* had turned on them all, thus losing his rank. Quincy was a bastard and needed to pay for his actions.

Cameron stormed to the end of the hall, to the cell in the brig holding Quincy. He punched in the override codes to gain entrance to the cell. He'd been careful to keep the codes hidden from Olivia and the others. The women continued to falsely believe that each of Quincy's men could be redeemed. They wanted to see the good in their fellow man, but Cameron knew better. He knew Quincy and his followers were capable of great evil.

The door slid open and he stepped into the dark, dank cell. Scratch marks lined the walls where Quincy had used his fingers to carve images and sayings all over the place. They were the ramblings of a lunatic. Cameron had seen nearly all of them because of the built-in security cameras in each cell. Quincy's mind had deteriorated the most, by far. Stepping into the cell, Cameron glanced around, his sole purpose to end the life of the monster for good.

His opti-spectrum glasses started to glitch again. When they cut off his vision, pain exploded in the side of his head. Cameron went down hard and fast, already sensing another presence close. He kicked out, scoring a direct hit with flesh.

"Bastard!" shouted Quincy, his hot, rank breath filling the room. Cameron's heightened senses reacted violently to the smell, costing him in reaction time as Quincy struck him again.

He reached out, grabbing hold of Quincy's ankle and twisting it. The man screamed in pain and the sound of it gave Cameron great satisfaction. As his glasses continued to glitch, Cameron yanked them off and tossed them aside.

Quincy laughed. The sound was chilling and void of real emotion. "Problems seeing, Doctor? Yes, I made sure to tamper with your opti-spectrum glasses before you went into stasis sleep. I thought the droids might attempt to wake you when they sensed me sabotaging the pods. I didn't want you to be a burden. Too bad you managed to still be one."

Cameron relied on his natural gifts. He sprang up and off the floor with a speed that no doubt shocked Quincy, and punched the man directly in the face. Each sound Quincy made only increased Cameron's ability to draw upon all his senses and get a clear mental image. It was a lot like echolocation, yet more. He struck Quincy again and then grabbed him by his ratty shirt lapels. "You sick son of a bitch," he snarled, his lips curling with disgust.

"Cameron!" Olivia's voice cut through the cell, distracting him.

He was worried. "Livia, go!"

Quincy attacked then, gaining the upper hand and rushing at Olivia. He threw her across the room with a strength he shouldn't possess, then ran from the cell. Cameron's focus changed from wanting to kill Quincy to wanting to assure himself that Olivia was safe.

He moved to her side quickly, accessing her slumped body. Without his glasses he couldn't run a diagnostic on her. "Computer, send medical droid 17390 to us at once. Seal off the bay doors to the women's chamber. Report on Quincy's location."

"All bay doors sealed. One female unable to be contained. She is currently with medical droid 17390 and headed in this direction. Ex-commander Quincy is currently entering escape pod four."

Cameron held Olivia against him, kissing her temple as she groaned.

"Ouch, what happened?" she asked.

"You took a header into a wall," he replied. "What hurts?"

She sat up on her own and rubbed her neck. "Right now, my pride. Did Quincy escape because of me?"

"He escaped because I was foolish and couldn't control my temper. I should have waited until I was a hundred per cent. Had I waited, I'd have noticed my glasses weren't functioning properly." Cameron sighed. "Instead, I let my temper guide my actions. I just wanted him to pay for hurting the woman I love."

She gasped.

He paused. "Livia?"

"You love me?"

With a shaky breath he nodded and pulled her into his embrace. "Of course I do."

She wrapped her arms around him. "I love you, too."

The computer beeped. "Doctor Cameron, ex-commander Quincy has successfully detached pod four. His course, New Earth Twelve."

Olivia tightened her hold on him. He kissed the top of her head. "It will be all right. We'll find him once we reach Twelve."

"Is everything all right?" Rain asked, appearing in the doorway with Cara at his side.

"Holy stellar remains," Cara whispered. "Quincy's gone?"

"Yes," Olivia said softly.

Cara made an odd noise. "Darn. I was hoping to get to see Doc there beat the living heck out of him."

Olivia laughed nervously. "Somehow, I think you still might get to see that. I have a sneaky suspicion we haven't seen the last of Quincy."

Rain approached. "With respect, Doctor. I am sensing injuries on you. Odd, they seem to be caused by a short in something electronic."

"Quincy sabotaged my glasses," Cameron offered.

"All of them?" questioned Rain.

"All of them?" echoed Cameron, unsure what Rain meant.

"According to inventory logs, there are five additional pairs, all calibrated for you, in the lower storage deck. It will take some time to retrieve them but it can be done in transit, if you wish."

"17390," Cameron said with a wink, knowing the android didn't appreciate being called by his number. "You're all right, for an android."

"So are you . . . for a Vanesier," replied Rain. "You do tend to grow on a person."

Androids weren't known for their ability to joke. It meant the adjustments Cameron had done prior to launching the *Rhea* expedition were working, slowly, but working all the same. He grinned. "I'm the only Vanesier you know personally."

"True."

Cameron helped Olivia to her feet and hugged her again. He couldn't stop touching her. She didn't seem to mind. She laid her head against his shoulder. "Computer, open the bay doors to the rest of the women."

"Yes, Doctor."

Cameron took Olivia's hand in his. "It's time to start the wakening for Oli."

She groaned. "Do we have to?"

Cara laughed. "He's your brother."

"I know. Picture me explaining how I lost my virginity to his best friend."

Cara leaned in slightly. "Is that before or after you explain how it is you're not a little girl anymore?"

Cameron cringed. She had a point. He cleared his throat. "New plan. We let him sleep a bit longer. At least until I'm back in fighting shape and can move fast enough to duck his right upper cut."

Everyone laughed.

Red Dawn

Delilah Devlin

Planet: Mars
Farming Tract: 782
Year: 2213

Mary stood alone in the middle of a vast golden field, only her little house in the distance to break up the view of her large tract. No signs of civilization, other than her well-ordered crops. She feathered a finger across the tip of the wheat stalk she held. Stiff, but not brittle. Soon the harvest would begin.

Loneliness nagged. She hadn't thought it would bother her. The interminable days of chores and nightly reporting should have kept her too busy to notice she was alone, without another human being to talk to, other than the dispatcher who'd confirmed that this day her first shipment would arrive.

Tension rode her shoulders, boiled in her belly. Today, her life would change. Again.

Among the first who'd stepped outside the dome without a breathing device, she'd taken the chance the air was truly safe, that alien toxins wouldn't accumulate in her blood or that the newly manufactured atmosphere wouldn't smother her.

She'd had no fear. Only a sense of wonder and fierce pride that she, Mary Bledsoe from the Americas Sector, was among the first colonists of Mars.

Fifty years of terraforming the barren planet had at last produced a habitable world to replace the one they'd ruined. The Mars-Tech Company owned exclusive rights to the project, and had released oxygen trapped in the northern icecap to form an atmosphere that mimicked the former success of Earth's natural greenhouse and normalized the temperatures. They introduced animals, insects, bacteria – everything necessary to ensure the soil would be ready for the first crops. They dug canals to deliver the water beginning to melt from the icecap to the plains, where crops were sown by huge industrial machines – all in preparation for the colonists who would assume responsibility for the first harvests, and thereafter all future plantings.

Mars would feed Earth. Animals bred from the first pairs shipped from the home planet had been raised in cramped stalls inside the domes, but now would be turned over to the farmers and ranchers, further nurturing the classic model of pastoral life that was almost extinct on their own overcrowded planet.

The environmental lessons learned from past mistakes, along with strict adherence to new social rules, and an ordered reclamation of Martian resources, became a roadmap for humanity's survival.

In her own little way, Mary was part of this grand experiment, this last chance for humans to survive long enough before jumping out into the galaxy to find new worlds to populate.

Given her own plot of land as a dowry, she'd eagerly signed her acceptance of a mate, which the company would choose according to her preference profile and the attributes needed to complement her skill set. Guesswork, or messy natural selection, wasn't permitted. This she'd known before making the long journey from Earth to her new home. Since she'd had few relationships, and all had been unsatisfying, she hadn't thought twice about accepting a mate sight unseen. Better the AI matchmaker make the selection than her.

She had yet to meet her new mate, or even learn his name. However, she was notified days after she'd settled on her small homestead – with its prefab concrete cabin, fiberboard barn, canal-fed stream and pond – that he would be selected from among the new shipment of prisoners. Because intelligent, healthy men chose professions which required less physical labor, furloughed prisoners would be given a second chance to earn their freedom by becoming spouses to pioneer men and women – a fresh start for people healthy enough to adapt to the rigors of this life, and who harbored no hopes of ever returning home. A different kind of life sentence.

She hoped he'd be strong, and that he harbored no violent tendencies, but again, she trusted in the Company to choose well on her behalf. So far, all their promises had come true. She'd signed up for a new adventure, a chance to live a life outside the crowded mega-cities of Earth with their choked air and transits.

Here, she could breathe, watch a fiery sunset that had nothing to do with pollutants tainting the air, and the deed for the land was in her own name. Her crops for the next few rotations would be claimed by the Company – the hope being that after she'd returned their investment in her, she'd be allowed to sell her grains in a free market and reap the profits.

A true pioneer, she'd stepped onto an alien planet, full of hope for a new future for the human race.

For once, that thought didn't comfort her. Returning inside her home, she glanced around. She noted the grayness surrounding her, and wondered why the Company, with all its psychological studies, hadn't figured out that cheerfully colored walls could do wonders to lift a woman's spirits. But then, it probably seemed like such a little thing, and they hadn't bothered due to the expense.

She pushed back the sleeves of her shirt and set to cleaning her little home, ignoring the images from her childhood that the smells of lemon and pine pulled from her memories.

The transport arrived amid a whirl of dust kicked up from the barren yard beside the house. The gritty air nearly obscured the moon, Phobos, as it made the first of several orbits for the day. The aircraft hovered, framed by the uneven curves of the asteroid, and then set down with a thud that shuddered the planks of her front porch, vertical engines stalling then shutting off altogether. The dust slowly settled.

She'd been sweeping, preparing the cabin for the transport's arrival. As with every element of the Company's schedule, it arrived precisely on time. Although prepared, a flutter of anticipation tickled her belly. She set aside the broom, wiped her palms against the sides of her sturdy blue work pants, and descended the stairs, eager to meet the shipment.

A man dressed in a gray Company coverall climbed out of the cockpit and strode toward her. She pasted on a smile. "Welcome."

His sharp gaze swept her little cabin, the golden fields beyond it, and then finally rested on her. "You Mary Bledsoe?"

He likely wondered how someone of her stature had managed to pass the physical tests to qualify for farming. She stiffened her spine to add a few centimeters to her small, wiry frame, and met his gaze with her usual calm, chilly stare. "I am." She bit back a sarcastic *Who else do you think I could be?* Every one of the thousand colonists had been handpicked and transported by the Company – they had a monopoly on Martian transportation and industry.

His mouth twitched, but he kept his gaze steady. "I have your shipment, and I'll need your signature on the bill of lading."

She nodded. "I'll need to inspect." She'd received notice of the contents of the shipment via the comm-console situated in the cabin's main room, shortly after claiming her homestead.

Although the fields had been pre-planted and her new home fully furnished, there were still some items, especially the perishables, that needed stocking: replacement blades for the combine sheltered in the barn, pallets of foodstuffs, clothing and fuel packs . . . and her mate.

Trying not to appear overeager to see him, she waited as the transport commander's crew scurried to let down the rear ramp and roll out the pallets. With well-trained efficiency, they stacked them beside the porch. She counted the pallets with their quick-wrapped goods, signed for delivery, and then shoved her hands into her pockets to hide the fact they were beginning to shake.

The commander's mouth firmed into a straight line. "Did you receive training in the use of the B-Mod collar?"

He knew she had. Otherwise she wouldn't be here, already in possession of a land grant. She gave a curt nod. "Yes. I also signed saying I knew there were no guarantees for my safety or his willingness to work. If we don't suit, if he proves stubborn, then I'll return him."

"Just don't get too attached, ma'am. You have enough on your hands without coddling one of these rejects."

The brusque quality of his voice surprised her. *Was he truly worried? Should she be more concerned?*

He handed her the chain with the controller for the prisoner's behavior modification collar, a thin ID tag with a recessed button on one side, the B-Mod chip. She slipped it over her head and followed him to the side of the transport. The guard inside the vehicle opened the door. The prisoner scooted on the seat toward the edge, hands still in manacles, then slid to the ground beside her.

Heartbeat rising, she gazed up into a face set in grim lines. Blue eyes, cold as ice, sparked with some deep emotion as he stared back.

He was larger than she had expected. Surprisingly so. Prisoners built like this one were generally shipped to Company loading docks or to the arena. He was built like a gladiator, and she studied his broad chest and wide shoulders. His arms and thighs were deeply muscled. "You're sure he's mine?" she asked, turning toward the commander, who'd fished a key from his pocket to unlock the prisoner's handcuffs.

The commander's grunt and the flinty glare he gave the prisoner said he too had some reservations. "His collar matches the invoice. Guess they thought you might need the extra muscle."

Anger flashed at his comment. She'd had enough of men thinking she wasn't up to the rigors of Martian prairie life.

Her hand still gripped the B-Mod chip. She slipped it slowly away, remembering her training. *Show no fear.* As long as she had the chip, she had control. Lifting her chin, she cleared her expression. "Do you have a name?" An inane question. She winced inwardly.

One side of the prisoner's mouth quirked, but it might have been her imagination because he gave her a stony stare. "Colm O'Riordan."

The commander cleared his throat.

"Ma'am," the prisoner amended with a drawl.

Heat crept up her neck, but she ignored the blush threatening to suffuse her face. Turning back to the commander, she offered her hand.

His grip was strong, the look he gave her doubtful. "Good luck to you, Mary."

Not a professional salutation, but no one had said her first name, all on its own, for a very long time. She gave him a warm smile. "Thanks for everything. We'll be fine here."

A duffle was tossed from the transport by one of the guards. The bag was small. Likely only a couple changes of clothing for the prisoner. She jerked her chin toward it, knowing she was still being observed by the crew. "Bring it," she said, making her tone curt. She turned, walking toward the cabin, wondering if the lock on her new mate's door could actually hold him.

Colm followed the small woman inside the cabin. Everywhere he looked was gray. Bare concrete walls, fiber-composite cabinets. No curtains on the windows, just cheap solar-glass that turned a milky color when the sun hit it directly. Utilitarian. Ugly.

Ugly, everywhere he looked. Except the woman.

She was a surprise. Small and slender, she didn't look capable of driving a combine, much less handling a man as large as himself. But for the chip she wore around her neck, he could overcome her inside a single heartbeat. And yet, she hadn't hesitated to accept him.

Her clothing was the pioneer uniform – heavy denim trousers, a form-fitting, long-sleeved shirt, insulated to retain body heat or to wick away moisture if the air grew warm. Her small feet were encased inside clunky work boots. And yet she was lovely. And likely didn't know it.

She wore no make-up. Her bluntly cut hair – held up with a single band at the back of her head – was a pretty brown with strands of blonde and red setting it afire. Her eyes, when she'd stared up at him, had been a soft green, like springtime blades of grass. Something he'd seen in domed parks back home. Vivid and fresh, those eyes. And so unaware.

The perfect product of the Company's long assimilation program. Despite her slight stature, she'd survived the grueling testing and come to this place. But why? As pretty as she was, she needn't struggle for her survival. She'd have made some Company scion a fine mistress. Or some gladiator a concubine. He'd have taken her on, for a full month's use, just to see whether he could make that blush she'd betrayed deepen.

His loins stirred and he sighed, knowing he was concentrating on the puzzle she presented because it was better than sinking into a black hole of despair. *This would be his life until he died.*

In another time and place, he might have enjoyed the adventure: traveling years to reach this desolate planet, testing his mettle against the elements for his own satisfaction, overcoming obstacles that arose from living on another world. However, he'd left behind a mess. One he was fated never to repair. Everyone he knew and cared for left behind forever. Lost.

"Your room's in here," the woman said, her soft gaze lingering on him. She likely wondered if he was a halfwit, he'd stood there so long, staring at nothing. "Drop your bag beside the bed. You can put away your things later. We have work to do."

Colm said nothing, but stepped past her, making sure to brush an arm against her, just to see how she reacted.

Her quick, indrawn breath and startled gaze told him a lot. She was every bit as aware of him as he was of her. Satisfaction warmed him. *Here was something he could work with. Perhaps he could convince her to toss away the chip. And soon.* The memory of the sharp pains it invoked, seeming to tap every single nerve with fire and agonizing cramping, was enough to nauseate him.

A prisoner now, and for the rest of his life, he determined in that moment that he wouldn't be seen as one by at least one person on this wretched planet.

He dropped his bag beside the narrow cot. As stark as any prison cell, at least the room had a window, although the hardware surrounding it told him there would be no escape. Not that he had anywhere to go if he did manage to slip away.

However, just the thought of walking freely in the out of doors, of swimming in the stream he'd seen that perfectly divided fields of wheat from oats, was enough to keep him thinking about breaking out.

"We work until the sun sets," she said, her voice oddly gruff. *The sweet note it had held when she'd spoken with the commander was gone. But then, by the way the other man had eyed her up and down and had given her unsolicited advice, perhaps they knew each other.*

The thought bothered him more than he wanted to admit. *He was already feeling possessive of his new jailor.*

"Tell me what needs to be done," he said, dropping his voice to infer he was ready to do more than labor in the wheat fields. "I'm here to help."

Her cheeks pinkened and she turned away, bending to pick up a pack and then striding toward the door. "Let's just make sure water's making it to the plantings. We'll walk the fields."

And walk they did. Colm was amazed at the size of the tract she'd been handed. On Earth, land this rich, this verdant, was so rare only the very wealthiest could afford it. And yet here, as far as he could see, stretched yellow-and-green fields filled with fragile bio-gold.

He and his new mistress carried all-service tools slung over their shoulders, which changed with a *click* from a shovel to a pick, depending on the need. At midday, she unearthed crusty protein wafers and bottles of fresh water from the bottom of her pack.

He grimaced at the stale taste of the wafers, but did have to admit the food satisfied his growling belly. Then back to work they went, with the woman walking between neat rows to inspect plants for wilt or disease, although every grain brought to Mars had been specially engineered to suit the soil and climate.

"That's odd," she whispered, bending closer to one wheat stalk. She tipped it with her finger and drew away with a small insect.

Peering over her shoulder, he noted the frown bisecting her brow. "A ladybug?"

"This insect's not scheduled for release. It shouldn't be here."

Colm shrugged. "Perhaps it stowed away with the seeds when they were shipped."

Still staring at the tiny round bug, she shook her head. "Makes me wonder what else we might have. I'll have to report the sighting." She tucked the insect into her pants pocket.

"Do you really think the Company can control every element of this world?"

"They have to try," she said softly. "There's a fine balance here, between all elements of the environment."

"Is there no room in these plans for surprises? For a natural progression?"

Her head canted as she studied his face. "You're an odd man, Colm. Everyone knows the dangers imminent when anything is given free will."

Colm breathed deeply, pulling his gaze from her curious one. He knew she wondered about him, where his loyalties lay.

Phobos rose large on the horizon. She glanced toward it, shielding her eyes as the sun peeked around the edges of the asteroid. "That's the last orbit for the day. We should head back before night falls."

Colm's body tightened. His own indoctrination had included

training to please his new master. *Farmers must be kept happy, after all.* He wondered if she would avail herself of his training tonight or would opt to get to know him better first.

He tamped down his excitement, but already blood surged southward, thickening his cock. A chance to lie with her, to lose himself in lust, was too tempting a thought. *Could he tempt her to forget her natural reticence?* "I'm trained, you know. I could give you a massage. Draw your bath . . ."

Her head swung his way, green eyes narrowed. "Let's get this straight. I don't need a servant or a sex worker. I need a partner. You aren't obligated to pleasure me. So long as you pull your own weight, I'll be satisfied."

He suppressed a grin at her terse tone. "And what if I have needs, ma'am?"

Her jaw clenched. "You've a hand. Use it."

She stomped away, but he couldn't help smiling. He'd noted her heightened color. *He'd shocked her. Now she was thinking about the coming night and all the delightful possibilities.*

Mary eyed Colm from beneath the sweep of her thick eyelashes as he bent over the bowl of stew she'd heated for their dinner. Ever since he'd offered to pleasure her, she hadn't been able to get certain lusty images out of her head. It had been ages since she'd taken a sexual partner.

And what if I have needs, ma'am? She wished she could look at him as though he was just another machine she'd been provided with for convenience, because *dammit*, she had needs, too. Yet, even though she understood the necessity of physical release, somehow the thought of using a prisoner in that way felt sordid.

He really didn't have any choice in the matter. And even though he'd offered, he might have done so because of his conditioning, not because of any true attraction he might feel. How could she know for sure? Certainly, they were destined to mate, and they both had an obligation to reproduce. However, deep inside, she hoped they'd find some affection first. Some spark of attraction to make the act feel less like another of her daily mandated chores.

Sitting across from him, she freely admitted more than a spark existed on her side. Although his features were rugged, he was a handsome man. With a square jaw and sharp, blunt blade of a nose, his face was strong and masculine. His cheekbones were as sharp as arrowheads. When he spoke, white even teeth flashed between firm lips. Already, her nipples tightened as she imagined those lips tugging at their tips.

His size alone fed a feminine hunger to feel his weight pressing over her. Thick dark hair caused her fingers to curl against the need to comb through it. His watchful eyes inspired images of him rising up to gaze between their naked bodies as they came together.

He'd be attentive to her pleasure, his training would assure that. *But would he really want* her?

Mary pushed aside the foolish thought. His wants should be secondary to their mission. They were ordained to mate, to produce progeny and populate this planet, just as they were ordained to nurture the fields.

"Would you like to join me on the porch?" she asked. "The fireworks should begin soon."

"Fireworks?" A dark brow arched, seeming to mock her flight of fancy.

"Okay, missiles, actually. Seeding the clouds. This will be the first time I've seen the seeding since leaving the dome. Would you like to watch?"

In answer, he gathered their dishes without being asked and took them to the sink. Then they both headed to the open door and the dark porch outside. She sat atop the steps, making room for him to join her, then trained her gaze on the sky. "It's supposed to look like Fourth of July," she whispered. She angled her head to glance his way. "Where was your home, Colm?"

She was entitled to his answer, but wanted more. Not intending to pry, she glanced away in case her question caused him pain.

"Arizona," came his gruff reply. "You?"

She smiled. "Iowa. My great-great-grandparents were farmers. It's partly why I decided to apply for the land grant."

"Were there other reasons?"

She grimaced. "I wasn't the best student. No aptitude for math or science. And since I didn't want to be consigned to factory work, I volunteered for this."

"Did you leave anyone behind?"

She shook her head. "My parents died several years ago.

There wasn't anyone." Although she wasn't sure she wanted to know, she asked, "Did you leave someone behind?"

Colm drew a deep breath. Sorrow deepened the grooves beside his mouth. "My father. He was in enforcement. And my little brother. Also a cop." His mouth tightened, and then he shot her a pointed glance. "You haven't asked me the important question yet."

She swallowed hard. "What crime did you commit?"

His smile was bittersweet, a thin twisting of his firm lips. "My crime was daring to question."

Shock rattled through her. "You were a rebel?"

"Imagine that," he said, his tone filled with bitter sarcasm. "They sent one of my kind here."

She shook her head. "Were you involved with the bombings?"

"No. I chose civil disobedience. I never wanted to harm anyone."

His glance fell away and she noted the tightness of his jaw. "But you did?"

His glance fell to his hands, which gripped his knees. "I broke into a comm facility. I was the one with the skills to get us inside. We intended to divert the feed and post our own transmissions. Free radio. Tell the truth about what the governments were up to."

"Up to?" She snorted. Seemed everyone had had a conspiracy theory or two.

His gaze swung her way, his eyes cold as a Martian glacier. "You don't get it. Whole regions of the Earth were dying. Our only hope was population reduction and plantation projects. Plans were already in motion, plans every single government in the Seven Sectors supported."

She shook her head. "A grand conspiracy?"

His eyes narrowed. "How about extermination? World population extermination."

Mary studied his face. Colm believed what he said. How the hell had he gotten past the psych evaluations? "That's ridiculous. They're already practicing population control."

"It wasn't working fast enough."

"How do you know?"

"I was military, *ma'am*," he bit out. "Part of the group responsible for security around the Seven Sectors summits. I heard everything. That's why I'm here, and not in some hellhole prison camp on Earth. They didn't want word getting out before they could begin. While I slept in stasis aboard the prison ship traveling here, it happened. *It's done.*"

Cold, like ice water spilling down her spine, shivered through her. "But news feeds . . . there's been no mention. Something that big—"

"The feeds are fiction," he ground out. "To keep you happy. To keep you working and productive. The next waves of colonists are already in transit, just as dumb and oblivious. It might be years before you all learn the truth."

Mary grew still. Everything he said made sense. "Extermination . . ." She raised her glance to the sky, searching for the small speck of unblinking light that was the Earth. "I don't know why that's so shocking. It's what the doomsayers have been talking about for years. The end of the world."

"No. *New life.* That's the name of the initiative. Their comforting spin for those who were allowed to live."

Mary sat silent for a long moment, and then dragged in a deep breath. "Do I want to know how they did it?"

"I was arrested before I could find out. But it had to be fast, targeted."

Flares lit the sky above them, and then explosions sounded as the missiles blew apart, delivering their payload. "The fireworks," she whispered, trying not to imagine how the governments had cleansed the Earth.

Moving slowly, Colm placed his arm around her back. Mary sat, stiff, unyielding, then leaned close to his side, accepting his comfort. *Maybe his crime had been misinformation. Maybe he was a con man.* However, deep inside, she knew he'd spoken the truth.

"So, your father and brother?"

"Dead."

"I'm sorry," she whispered.

His chin scratched the top of her head as he folded her closer. "As awful as it is, I won't let bitterness touch you," he said, his voice filled with gravel. "My promise. What you have here, what you might share with me, is something . . . hopeful. I get that."

She tilted back her head. "This isn't an easy life, Colm. And for most of the time, we'll be alone out here. I'd like for us to be friends."

One corner of his mouth curled up, and his gaze narrowed. "Could that be friends who sleep together?"

Relieved he seemed ready to change the painful subject, she arched a brow. "Are you afraid of sleeping on that little cot?" she teased, surprised she still knew how to be seductive.

"Terrified." A hand cupped the back of her head, and she relaxed, giving him the weight of it, surrendering as bright starbursts of light filled the sky beyond him and he kissed her.

They undressed in silence. Mary was glad he didn't feel the need to talk. Her mouth was dry, her tongue thick. She thought she'd probably only manage a croak if she tried to enter into any bedroom conversation.

However, the moment he shoved down his trousers, her mouth moistened.

His cock sprang free, tilting toward the ceiling, and all she could think was how relieved she was that there was proof of that elusive spark she'd hoped for.

He climbed onto her larger bed and lay on his side, a curled hand supporting his head, and patted the mattress. A faint smile curved his lips as his gaze swept her trim body. She noted his pause when his gaze touched on her breasts, then again when it dipped to the apex of her thighs.

His cock jerked. His legs shifted, opening as he bent one to make room for his burgeoning erection and hardening balls.

Without hesitating, she lay down beside him, rolling to her side to face him.

He cupped her chin and rubbed his thumb across her bottom lip. "Are you sure you want to settle for friends?" he asked softly.

"I hope for more. I do. But for now . . ."

His thumb rasped her lips again. "Yes?"

She rubbed her cheek against his large palm. "For now, I'd settle for sex. Straight up, sweaty sex."

His smile stretched. "Yes, ma'am."

Their second kiss wasn't the sweet, chaste thing they'd shared on the porch. The moment his lips touched hers, his hand smoothed down to cup her bottom and pull her closer. His cock dug into her bare belly, and her body reacted, her sex swelling, excitement seeping from inside her as her hips flexed to bring their bodies closer still.

His mouth pressed against hers. His tongue darted out to push against her closed lips until she opened, then swept inside to tangle with her own. She sighed into his mouth, and he rumbled back.

With a quick breathless movement, he rolled atop her body, nudging with his knees to open her. When the long, thick ridge glided against her folds, she bent her knees and cupped her hips, forming a cradle for him to rock against. Her arms encircled his strong back, and she sought handholds, squeezing his shoulders, running her fingers down the deep indentation of his spine, raking her nails across his buttocks to encourage him.

When he finally rose, braced on both arms, his mouth was tight, tilted on one corner. "I could slow down . . ."

"I want you inside me. Don't make me wait." She narrowed her eyes and touched the B-Mod chip, still around her neck – but raised her eyebrows to let him know she only teased.

The growl he gave made her giggle, but she forced her mouth into a frown until he shifted, raising his hips then dipping into her with the blunt round tip of his cock. She contracted, holding him there.

Her breaths deepened; endorphins released. Her lids drifted down as the pleasure prickled her skin and liquid flowed to ease his entry.

Colm dropped to his elbows. His body blanketed hers, warming her inside and out. His movements were small, subtle pulses, enough to keep them both excited, but not so much that they rocketed toward orgasm.

"You're stronger than you look," he murmured. His sleepy gaze said how much her sexy inner muscles pleased him.

She gave him another squeeze, and then undulated her hips. "I'm not delicate, if that's what you're afraid of."

"Are you impatient?"

She shook her head, but then wrinkled her nose. "Getting there, I think." And she was. Her nipples were tight, needy beads that couldn't be satisfied with the gentle scruff of the curly hair on his chest. "Colm, please," she whispered.

"Please? You have only to command me."

"Not here. Not now." Her fingernails dug into his ass. "I need you to take me. Move now. Please, Colm."

He lowered himself further, sliding his hands beneath her

body to cup her ass, then began to drive deeper and deeper, sounds echoing against the hard concrete walls.

She moaned in his ear, then sucked the lobe between her lips and bit him. "More," she whispered.

Colm withdrew abruptly, kneeling over her. Rough hands turned her over and pulled up her hips. She got her knees beneath her a moment before he set his thickness against her and plunged inside.

Mary howled. Not from pain, but from joy. Pushing up on her arms, she rocked backward to meet his thrusts, reveling in the sensations his motions produced. Fierce, hot friction burned inside her; her bottom warmed as his pelvis slammed against it. His fingers curved around the corners of her hips.

She exploded, emitting a wail as her orgasm cascaded over, quivering along her skin, rippling deep inside her channel.

His muffled shout followed, but he continued to rock against her. When he slowed, his body bent to blanket her back. His arms encircled her in a crushing hug.

She didn't mind. Inside his strong embrace, she felt a sense of welcoming, of peace, of pleasure shared.

They fell to the bed, bodies still connected. With his arms around her, she snuggled her bottom into the cradle of his thighs and slept.

Rain pattered on the metal roof, a soothing sound that had Mary nestling deeper against Colm's chest. With a thigh trapped between his and an arm around his waist, it seemed she was every bit as content as he was.

For the first time since he'd awoken aboard his transport ship after the liquids had cleared from his lungs in the stasis cell, he didn't awaken with his chest tight with sorrow. The woman nestled so closely against him was an innocent, as much a pawn in this grand scheme as he was. *There was no war to fight. No cause to herald.*

All that was left was surrender.

As he lay there with his mistress wrapped around him, his body began to shake. Tears eased from his eyes and seeped into the pillow beneath his head. He closed his eyes and willed himself to lie still so as not to wake her.

"What's wrong?"

He couldn't answer for the lump lodged at the back of his throat.

Hands cupped his face. Thumbs swept away his tears. Then soft kisses peppered his cheeks, jaw, mouth. "Tell me."

He opened his eyes to find her soft green gaze glittering with concern. "This will be our life."

"And that saddens you?"

"God, no," he blurted, shamed by the ragged texture of his voice.

Her mouth pressed against his again, then she rose beside him, kneeling. Her hand closed around the controller chip and she lifted the chain from around her head. Without a word, she handed it to him. "I never wanted a slave. I didn't lie when I said I wanted a partner, but more than anything, I would like for you to be my husband."

Colm breathed deeply, blinking away his tears. He gave her a nod, then reached to pull her against him. "More than anything, I want to be your husband."

Her smile crept slowly across her face. Moisture gathered in her eyes, and she laughed and wiped it away with the backs of her hands.

Colm's chest expanded. Happiness lifted guilt and helpless anger from his soul – borne away by the radiance of her smile. "What shall I call you?"

She wrinkled her nose. "Getting tired of 'ma'am'?" she teased from beneath her dark lashes.

He nodded.

"Me too. I'm Mary."

A sweet name for a woman who hid all her softness behind a facade of brisk competence. "I like it," he murmured. "Do the fields need us, Mary?"

"Not until the rain stops."

He narrowed his eyes and reached up to palm a small, round breast. The nipple was soft as velvet. The tip hardened beneath the press of his thumb.

Her breath caught and held. She tossed back her head, shaking her hair behind her.

"Grow it long," he said.

"For you, I will."

"What else will you do to please me?"

She arched a brow then slowly straddled his body. "Whatever you desire."

"Am I now the master?"

A sexy grin stretched across her pretty face. "If it pleases you."

Colm raised himself on his elbows and drew a turgid nipple between his lips, not relenting until she sighed and clutched his hair.

When he drew back, he lifted her, urging her down his body.

She needed no further instruction, kissing her way down his chest, teasing his belly with gentle bites and wet kisses until she knelt between his legs and took him into her mouth.

Colm groaned as she devoured him, sifting her hair with his fingers, pinching her ears to pull her deeper. Her hands surrounded him, her sweet mouth locked beneath the sensitive ridge and suckled while her tongue lavished him with wet sliding caresses.

Joy like he hadn't felt in years poured through his veins. He gripped her hair and pulled her from him. Then forcing her to her back, he ravaged her breasts with hot flicks of his tongue and stinging pinches which caused her to yelp and giggle.

Smiling, he worked his way downward, hands caressing her smooth belly, fingers digging into her firm bottom and thighs as he opened her. Arousal, potent and spicy, filled his nose as he buried his mouth between her legs until she squirmed and bucked beneath him.

When she was breathless and he was so hard he couldn't wait a moment longer, he brought her over him, watching as she guided him inside her. She let go, leaned back her head and sank deep, gliding downward in a single stroke. She paused, swaying over him. "Do you think they planned the rain to happen today for just this purpose?"

He grunted, not fond of the Company, not wanting the big consortium to intrude into their bedroom, but what she said held merit. "Perhaps. But we had the choice of how to spend the downtime, Mary."

She began to move, slowly at first, inching up, then down. His cock warmed inside her snug hollow. When a wave of heat swept through him, he decided he'd let her savor the ride another day.

He flipped them, relishing her cry of surprise. Without pausing he stroked into her, clutching her buttocks to hold her close so that each roll of his hips tunneled deep. The push-pull of his motions drew sighs and groans. Her legs moved restlessly, inner thighs rubbing his legs, then rising higher until she gripped his waist.

Her small hands pushed against his chest, and he lifted himself, bracing on his arms, increasing the length of his strokes and giving each forward thrust a snap that shoved her body up the bed. Before long, the bed frame groaned, pounding against the wall.

Mary's breaths were shallow, open-mouthed. Sweat slicked both their bodies as they writhed together. When the first internal flutters heralded her blooming orgasm, Colm pounded harder, deeper, not satisfied until a garbled scream ripped from her throat.

Only then did he let go, giving his own hoarse shout of triumph. His thrusts slowed. Her legs eased from his waist. He sank over her, tucked his face into the corner of her shoulder and released an agonized sigh.

She giggled beneath him. "That tickled," came her throaty complaint.

He raised his head, centered her face between his palms and gave her a hard kiss. "Will you melt if you get wet?"

Her brows shot high. "Too late on both counts."

His snort jerked against her chest. "I meant, would you mind taking a walk in the rain?"

He held her hand as they walked beside the stream bank. She liked the way his large hand engulfed her own. Another reminder of his largeness, which she'd so thoroughly enjoyed.

The place between her thighs felt hot. Her nipples raw. *But she couldn't wait for nightfall to beckon them back to bed. As odd as it seemed, she was already in love with Colm O'Riordan. Head over heels – with a man who'd arrived in manacles just a day ago.*

Rain misted down on them. Their clothes and hair were soaked, but they continued to walk. She didn't mind the exercise or the comfortable silence.

"It's like we're the only people on this planet," he mused. "It's so quiet. Restful."

"The first week I was here, I wondered what was missing. Whether my ears weren't working right. I was so used to the constant noise in the dome, the hum of the fans."

They neared the bend of the stream. Mary halted, eyeing the object clinging to the edge of the bank. "Is that a tree?"

"A bush, perhaps?"

He let go of her hand and they both knelt beside the object.

"They planted orchards further north," she said, touching the edge of a green leaf.

"They aren't going to be able to control every element of this new world. Life will find a way to flourish."

"Or they'll cut it down." She raised her head. "Maybe we should replant it near the house."

A smile quirked up one corner of his mouth. "Are you suggesting we nurture rebellion?"

"A quiet one. It'll give the house shade when it's larger."

Colm laughed. "Ever practical." They dug with their hands around the shallow roots and pulled up the sapling. Then he took off his shirt and wrapped it around the roots.

With her smile warming him, Colm captured her hand again and they headed home.

Racing Hearts

Kiersten Fay

Priya stepped onto the solid metal platform of the dismal spaceport. Musty, reused air flooded her lungs, along with the scent of rust and sweat. Gripping her luggage handle in one fist, she thanked the transport ship's steward before striding forward in search of her next destination.

As she wound through a crowd of roughnecks, she noticed a pattern of stains on the dark green bulkhead to her left, probably from a recent brawl. A good one, by the looks of it.

The domed ceiling provided a murky view of space. She squinted past the thick film of grime to see another ship pulling in where hers had just departed. A few more ships were lined up behind it, waiting to unload passengers.

A masculine voice sounded from behind. "Do you need a guide, sweetie?"

She rolled her eyes and turned around, keeping her right side angled away from him. Usually, that was the side she wore her pulsar gun, but according to the rules of this particular establishment, she was not allowed to keep a weapon on her immediate person. She could, however, stow it in her bag for easy access.

In place of her security work belt she'd tied a stylish strip of fabric over her brown tunic dress, with burgundy stripes that matched her hair.

The man lowered his eyes to her bare legs and black knee-high boots with obvious interest. His features weren't terrible, but he wouldn't win any beauty contests. His nose had clearly been broken more than once. His dark hair was a mess. And when he peered back up at her face, he grinned, revealing a full set of crooked teeth.

Schooling her features, she replied, "I'm looking for a ship—"

"I got a ship," he interrupted, with innuendo buried in the layers of his voice.

An entourage of onlookers chortled. With their matching stained uniforms and equally unkempt hair, they had the appearance of grunt workers.

"A tiny one, no doubt," she countered, and then smirked when his mouth fell into a petulant downturn.

His friends guffawed and one slapped him on the back. These weren't bad men, just products of a hard life and a serious lack of civilized influence. Not that she was any better. She'd practically been raised in places like this.

"The craft I seek is about to be entered in Phase Nine. I've been petitioned to join the crew."

The laughing cut off and a round of brows shot up. Their surprise was natural, but not because she was a woman entering the most dangerous competition in the known universe.

No. Even the most hardened of men would have received incredulous looks. Few who entered Phase Nine would live to see its finish. The race had few rules and spanned vast distances of space. A ship without a good crew wouldn't be expected to last long at all.

Ah, but she wasn't joining just any crew. She would be captained by a man who had not only run the race before, but had won it. And she fully intended to be with him when he did it again.

Silently, two of the men pointed toward a corridor while the others continued to gape.

She nodded in thanks and headed in the direction they'd indicated.

After a few steps, the first man called out, "Pray, tell me your name, beautiful lady, so I can cheer for you."

Not bothering to look back, she replied with a wave of her hand, "You'll just have to watch the show." It was the thing people loved most about Phase Nine. Strategically placed cameras throughout the race would provide entertainment to over thirty planets and countless space cities. Every fifty years, it became a universal obsession. People quit jobs just to watch.

The wide passageway was crowded with people trying to get through, and she had to push her way into the crowd. After getting knocked around by a few careless shoulders, she found herself in a much larger room, where vendors offered supplies to a slew of stationed ships. She counted fifteen. The high ceilings permitted them to be flown to a loading dock at the far end.

The pungent odor of oil seeped into her nostrils. Many of the ships were in a state of disarray as workers rushed to make them ready for the long flight to come.

To her right, people lined up to register for the competition. Anyone was allowed to enter, and nearly every planet encouraged participation. It was one of the few activities that brought both the allied and disjointed sects together.

A lift vehicle rumbled by, honking as people made a path. Over the chaos, she spotted the appreciable, dark brown hair of her soon-to-be captain, Aidan. It had been cut short since she'd last seen him. He stood with a small group of men next to the open hatch of a ship. She assumed the craft would be her new home for the duration of the race.

She could hardly contain her excitement as she crossed the great room. A few months ago, Aidan had surprised her by showing up at Uli Rings, where, until recently, she'd had a nice, cushy job as head of security. The massive space city was a popular tourist destination, made up of three giant rings that spun to simulate gravity. She'd hoped to take him out for a drink and catch up, maybe offer him a job, but he hadn't had the time.

Then a few weeks ago she'd received a transmission from Aidan to get her ass to the North Star spaceport and prepare for Phase Nine.

She'd sat back in her expensive office chair, stunned to the core. An hour later she'd been shoving clothes into a large duffel bag with the tags still attached.

When Aidan caught sight of her, he rushed forward to clasp her in a bone-crushing hug. His massive arms held her up as though she were as light as a pea. "Priya! Thanks for coming."

As her feet met the ground again, she couldn't help but tease, "You know, I received three more offers, besides yours. Pretty good ones, too."

"Aw, and you chose me above all others? I'm flattered," he replied with a smirk, and offered to take her heavy bag.

Glad to be rid of its weight, she handed it over. "Don't be. I was considering not coming at all." Lie. Although she wouldn't have answered any other call but his. Or have traveled so far just to risk her life.

"Tell me," she said. "Why in the name of the gods are you entering Phase Nine under the banner of the Legura Dragon Clan? Since when does your clan mingle with theirs?" When she'd received the news, she'd been taken aback. Though their respective planets shared a solar system, their cultures were quite different.

"It's a long story," he replied, looking frustrated. "I'll tell you about it later."

At his back, three men stood observing; one of them was a stranger to Priya. With a smile, she approached Asher and Zeek. Seeing them brought her back to a time when she had been truly happy – when they had all worked together as mercenaries on a POS rust bucket of a ship. *Only one other face was missing from the reunion. But she knew if she saw him, her joy would turn sour.*

She greeted her old crewmates with big, squeezing hugs. In turn, they messed her hair with a rough, playful palm, effectively ruining her sleek braid.

She slapped their hands away with irritation and undid the tie to run her fingers through her now-tangled locks. "In some corners of space, people get shot for that," she chastised.

They only laughed.

"You two haven't changed at all," she grumbled.

"Have, too," Zeek protested. "Check this out." He lifted his sleeve to reveal dark ink against his otherwise tan skin. The tattoo was outlined in red, as if it was still healing. It was the image of a buxom, black-haired lady looking over her shoulder, hand covering her mouth as her obscenely short skirt rode up to offer a peek of white panties.

"Classy, Zeek."

He gave her a boyish grin that was accentuated by his short blond hair and stormy blue eyes.

Turning to Asher, she asked, "How about you, Ash? Any tattoos?"

She knew better. Ash's skin was as tough as metal, with the hint of a metallic sheen. Most needles couldn't penetrate it. His pewter, chin-length hair was tough as well. As a game, he used to pluck a strand and challenge them all to try and rip it apart with their bare hands. No one had ever succeeded, but they continued to try anyway.

Asher's hypnotic silver eyes pinned her with a dubious expression. "No tattoos, Priya. How about you?" He wiggled his brows suggestively.

"None that you're ever going to get to see."

Typical masculine curiosity covered both their faces. She couldn't prevent her impish grin. The third man cleared his throat, drawing her attention. She gasped. *Legura royalty?*

Aidan introduced him. "This is Prince Lear of the Legura Clan. He'll be joining us."

Lear bowed respectfully. A black strand of his hair fell over his face as he cooed, "My lady." Seeing her jaw locked in surprise, he added, "Now doona be intimidated by my rugged good looks." His accent was thick, and sounded nothing like Aidan's.

She scoffed and crossed her arms. "Have you ever worked on a ship, kingy?" She recalled learning from Aidan that the Dragons had been one of the first races to enter space. Many of the known languages had branched off of theirs, and they had connections or treaties with nearly every amiable planet.

Lear cocked his head and said confidently, "I am no' without skill. And I'm no king."

That was obvious by the way he stood. He held himself more like a warrior than royalty.

She faced Aidan. "Is this the whole crew, then?"

Aidan took on a guilty expression and ducked his head. A deep sense of foreboding dug a pit in her stomach. She'd seen that look before.

Scrubbing a hand over the back of his neck, he stumbled over his words. "Uh . . . well . . . about that—"

From within the ship's hatch, a deep voice cut in, "The craft is tight, Aidan, but needs some work."

Recognition hit her like a slap to the face and she sank under a wave of nausea. Her heart twisted painfully, and she unconsciously brought her hand over her chest as if that would save her.

Vin emerged from the hatch, wiping grease from his hands with a dirty cloth. His gray tank top was equally stained, but no matter how ragged his clothing, it could not detract from his awe-inspiring physique. *He was built like a machine. And made love like one, too.*

She forced the thought out of her mind and struggled to keep it from re-entering.

The moment Vin noticed her, he froze mid-step. His arms dropped to his sides. He seemed to deflate.

She ignored the pang that caused in her chest.

"Oh, hell, no." Priya snatched her bag from Aidan and stalked away. She didn't quite know where she meant to go. Anywhere but here would do.

"Wait." Aidan grabbed her by the arm. "I won't stop you if you really want to go, but take a day or two to think about it. The entry deadline is in three days. I'd like you both on my team."

She ripped her arm free and snapped, "You should have told me he was here." Her hand began to sting from clenching the bag, and she forced herself to ease her hold.

"I wasn't sure if either of you would show," he explained. "But if I had mentioned he might be here, would you have come?"

"No," she said honestly.

Aidan remained silent for a moment. "I've rented you a room. Promise me you'll go and sleep on it."

She ground her teeth and tightened her fist. *How could Aidan ask this of her?* This could end up being detrimental to the entire group.

Could she put away her past, the heartbreak, and work with Vin? She could say no, she reasoned. *She could walk away right now and not look back. But, out of respect for Aidan, she would take his advice and chew it over. It was the least she could do.*

And the least Aidan could do was provide free room and board for her to do it in.

Without facing him, she slowly nodded. "I'll think about it."

From behind came Vin's low and – damn it – sexy voice. "Priya, can we talk?"

"Screw off, Vin. You're good at that." Quick strides led her back the way she came.

"Run away!" he retorted. "You're good at that!"

With a swift motion, Vin whipped his damp rag at Aidan. It hit his shoulder with a *splat* before flopping to the floor.

Aidan avoided Vin's gaze as he darted into the ship.

Vin followed, letting his outrage escape through his voice. "You sent for her!"

Unperturbed, Aidan replied, "I did." He continued down the hall, coming to stop in the lounge.

"Were you ever going to tell me?"

Taking a seat at the cheap metal table, Aidan replied with a mocking grin. "I just did."

Vin threw his hands in the air. "No, you didn't. I just found out." And he had stood there like an idiot as he had gazed upon the woman he'd once loved. *Did she have to be as beautiful as he remembered?* He always liked to picture her haggard and broken with regret, like him.

What he saw instead was a sexy-as-hell redhead with the luscious curves he used to know by heart.

He ran his hands through his brown hair, wishing he'd gotten it cut. "You could have given me a heads-up! She got to look all . . ." He gestured incoherently with his hands. "While I look like a bum."

"What? You would have put on a suit and tie?"

"I would have put on a clean shirt, you son of a bitch."

Aidan grew serious. "I wanted a winning team. And that means both of you."

Zeek and Ash entered, claiming seats as if he and Aidan were putting on a show.

Aidan ignored them. "What was that fight about anyway?"

"Like I can remember," Vin lied.

Zeek lifted a finger in the air. "You bought her a tool kit for her birthday."

Through clenched teeth, Vin said, "Thanks for the reminder."

"As I recall, it was a set you'd had your eye on for a while."

Lear appeared in the doorway with his arms crossed and an amused expression in place. "I'm guessing she did no' appreciate the gesture."

Vin scrubbed a hand down his face, not noticing the oil stains covering his fingers until afterward. "I don't need a play-by-play," he replied snidely.

They didn't know the half of it. Priya had always been an easygoing chick. He could have easily fixed it. If only he'd turned right – into that flowery gift shop.

Instead, his anger had directed him left, straight into a gentle-men's club.

"Go talk to her," Aidan suggested.

"Is that wise?" Lear asked warily. "If these two have a history, it could affect their performance."

Vin spoke directly to Aidan. "Tell your prince to keep his opinion to himself or I'll shove it down his—"

"Enough," Aidan admonished. "She's the best gun hand I've ever seen. We need her. You will talk to her. You will convince her to join us. And we will all act professional. Got it?"

Everyone gave reluctant nods.

"And just so we're all clear, Lear is not *my* prince."

Ash retorted, "In my culture, when you offer vows of alle-giance to a royal family, you become their subject."

Amusement danced in Lear's eyes, and he gestured toward Ash with one hand, as if he'd made a good point.

"I only vowed to run Phase Nine in the Legura name."

Zeek chimed in. "And to do that you had to join the Legura Clan . . . ergo."

"Shut up, all of you." Aidan stood. "I need a drink."

"Me too," Vin said. "Let me clean up and I'll join you."

Zeek jumped to his feet. "Why don't we all go? It should add depth to this riveting conversation. Plus Chastity is dancing tonight." He rubbed his hands together.

"Lear, you stay here and guard the ship," Aidan ordered.

Lear nodded, uncaring.

In the bar, Vin and the crew claimed a table near a stage full of barely dressed dancers who were keeping step to a poorly choreographed number.

A waitress took their drink orders. When she returned, Vin spotted Priya, and his heart stuttered. She faced away from them, perched on a stool. A quick survey of the drink in her hand told him she was going heavy tonight. Usually she sipped those theme-cup drinks with matching straw and umbrella. *He always gave her shit for that, but secretly considered it adorable.*

Tonight, she drank something hard on ice. *Could it be she'd been just as thrown by their meeting as he had?*

Or perhaps she had changed. Maybe she was a different person now, with different tastes and different preferences in men . . . in bed.

Gods, he hoped not.

He missed the noises she made when he nuzzled her just right.
Remembering made him stiffen and he had to adjust himself.

She swiveled in her seat, and he quickly turned away. When
his gaze met the gyrating ladies on stage, he nervously shifted
again, finding himself looking straight at Aidan, who studied
him with a keen eye.

Vin stifled a growl of irritation, and scowled.

With the smallest movement, Aidan gestured his chin toward
Priya.

*How could Aidan expect him to confront her? And here, of all
places?* The location was different, but still reminiscent of the last
time he'd laid eyes on her. Only this time, there wasn't some
drunk, flirtatious working girl running fingers over his shoulders
and whispering in his ear.

He cringed.

Aidan's gaze shot past him and his lids lifted a fraction.

Vin snatched his ale and gulped it down just before he heard
her voice.

"Could you guys get any closer?"

Zeek answered. "I don't think they allow you on the stage."

"How do you know if you don't try?"

"Good point."

When Zeek pushed back his chair, Aidan snapped, "Z, down."

Zeek plopped back down with a smile and sipped his drink.

"Why don't you join us, Priya?" Ash offered.

Surprisingly, she pulled up a chair. Vin lifted his bottle to his
lips, forgetting that he'd emptied it. He motioned to a nearby
waitress for another.

"So I've been thinking," Priya said, propping one arm on the
table and resting her chin on her palm. Using her other hand, she
motioned to the entire group. "I don't think this is a good idea."

Aidan replied first. "You haven't even thought about it for a
minute."

She gestured to her half-filled drink. "I've had three of these
to think, and I still—"

"Don't say anything now. Take the night. And if you feel the
same in the morning, then Vin is out."

"Hey," Vin protested, leaning back in his seat.

Aidan leveled him with a stare. "Talk to me when you can
shoot like her."

Vin shrugged, conceding the point. *He might be a great mechanic, but Priya was a badass with a gun.*

"So what have you been up to, Priya?" asked Asher.

"I've been working security on Uli Rings."

So that's where she ran off to, Vin thought.

Ash raised a brow. "Impressive. They let you temporarily leave your position to run Phase Nine?"

She frowned. "Not really."

"You quit to come here?"

She didn't respond, but her silence said as much.

"Then you have to join us," Zeek exclaimed. "You and Vin don't even have to interact. In fact, I'll do you one better and staple his mouth shut."

She rolled her eyes. "I saw the size of your ship. We'll basically be living on top of each other."

"Mmm," Zeek replied playfully. "Thanks for the visual."

Vin knocked him in the shoulder with his fist.

"Ow." Zeek rubbed the spot. "Joking."

Priya observed the exchange with an air of indifference. She brought her glass to her lips and took a long swig. Her expression told Vin she didn't like the taste. *Maybe she hadn't changed that much after all.*

She caught him staring, and her eyes narrowed.

He tried to keep his features passive. "Can I buy you a drink? Maybe one of those fruffy ones?"

Her lids slit further.

Damn, he shouldn't have added that last part.

"I'll buy my own drinks. In fact, I'll buy the next round for the table."

Despite his glass being full, Zeek ordered another drink.

Vin leaned forward and muttered, "Priya, can we talk in private?"

She pretended to think, tapping her chin and lifting her eyes to the upper right. "Um. No. Why don't you go talk to her?" She pointed to a skinny blonde at the bar. "I'm sure she'll be real interested in anything you have to say."

A muscle ticked in his jaw.

Zeek stepped in. "I'm amazed at how non-uncomfortable this is. Am I right, guys?"

Ash stood and flicked Zeek in the temple.

"Ow! Enough with the abuse. I'll shut up."

"How about I buy you a drink at the bar?" Ash said.

"Jeez. Any more free drinks and I'm going to start questioning the cut of this blouse." He tugged at his T-shirt.

Aidan pushed out of his seat. "I need to get back to the ship and check on Lear. Some weird girls have been coming by asking to join the crew, and I'm afraid he might just let them."

Priya watched the traitors scurry away, leaving her alone with Vin. *Most likely that had been their plan ever since she'd sat down.* With just the right amount of alcohol in her, she couldn't muster up the proper amount of outrage, or the conviction to get up and leave.

She stared blankly at Vin. "Enjoying the entertainment?"

The ladies on stage reached a pivotal point in their dance, moving to the fast beat of the music. To her surprise, he didn't even glance at them.

"What are you drinking?" he asked.

"Solar orbit on the rocks."

"That's a pretty stiff drink."

"Yeah, a guy turned me on to it a few months ago. It tastes good. He tasted even better."

His fists clenched around his bottle. She waited for satisfaction to flood her, but it never did. He took a long drink, placing his attention on the stage. She studied the table and sipped from her glass. The harsh bite of liquor hit her throat, warming her body as it made its way down.

When she looked up, Vin's eyes had creased in amusement and his lips had curled into a sexy, lopsided smile.

"What?" she barked, mentally denying the desire that bloomed in her from that simple look.

"Don't you think I know you well enough to realize when you're lying?"

"You haven't known me for a long, long time," she countered.

A flicker of doubt ran across his face, but he quickly turned it into disinterest. That bothered her. *She wanted to hurt him like he had her. She raked her mind for something cutting to add, but came up empty.*

"So . . ." he said, after a moment of silence had passed. "Uli Rings?"

"As if you didn't know?"

"How would I know that's where you went?" He took another drink.

"Because I bought my ticket with your credits."

He sputtered before working the liquid down his throat. His expression danced between stunned confusion and horror, making her realize he hadn't checked his invoice before paying the bill.

All this time, the fact that he hadn't come after her had been devastating. She'd used that devastation to fuel her rage, but now she felt it escaping like air from a leaky valve. *If he'd taken the time to go over his expenses, would he have come for her? Begged forgiveness?*

She snorted out loud. Knowing him, he would have demanded it. However, the idea that he might have come after her made her hope for something she'd long since given up on.

Yet, underneath that hope, resentment still simmered.

"What's funny?" Vin demanded, still reeling. *She'd left him a trail to follow and he'd missed it!*

"I just figured you knew. You always keep track of your finances."

He mentally scolded himself. "I was a little off that day."

He remembered someone handing him a bill, glancing over it without really seeing, and then signing on the dotted line. It had been just after he had returned to their room, found all her belongings gone, and had started his panicked search for a pissed-off redhead.

Gods, he had thoroughly screwed things up between them.

Had she used his credits in an attempt at one last jab, or as a hint that she'd wanted him to follow her?

His gut clenched, and he clung to the latter idea like a dying man to his last breath. He studied her closer. There was a stubborn shape to her lips, though she leaned back in her chair, appearing completely at ease. Her crystal-blue eyes were audacious. He could get lost in their steely depths for hours. With his gaze, he followed the smooth line of her jaw, wishing he could have his nose buried in the crook of her neck while her nails scraped along his scalp . . . his back.

His need for her doubled. He would have followed her whether she wanted him to or not.

"You don't really think this will work, do you?" she asked, interrupting his thoughts.

He shrugged, feigning nonchalance. "I don't have a problem with it, but I'll understand if you do."

As expected, she bristled. "You don't think I can remain professional? You're not the center of everyone's universe, Vin."

Priya mentally laughed at the statement. *At one point, he had been the center of her universe, but his ego didn't need that particular piece of news.*

He smirked as if reading her thoughts. "Tell me about Mister Solar Orbit."

"What's to say?" she hedged. "He's nice."

"Just nice? That's it?"

"Do you really want me to talk about him?"

Him. A fabricated lie in a petty attempt to make Vin jealous – which didn't seem to be working.

"Does he make you laugh?" His voice turned rough. "Make your blood fire?"

No one did that anymore.

She gulped. "He doesn't hurt me."

He flinched and leaned back with his finger crooked around the neck of his bottle. "S'pose that's something."

The dance number ended and a new set of girls took the stage. After watching them for a moment, Priya glanced at Vin from the corner of her eye. His lips were pressed in a hard line as he glared at his bottle. She wanted to ask him what he was thinking, but that was something a girlfriend did, and that was no longer her place. The silence between them made her feel like she was still light-years away.

"I shouldn't have come," she blurted.

His head snapped up. "Of course you should have. I bet you were just as excited as I was when you got Aidan's transmission."

"*Was*," she emphasized.

His expression grew dark. "You hate me that much?"

She shook her head, feeling a shadow of gloom fall over her. "I don't hate you . . . that much. You have to admit, we'd make a pretty shitty team at the moment."

"I told you, I don't have a problem—"

"*I* have a problem with it," she snapped.

His continued insistence that he felt nothing grated on her.

She pinched the bridge of her nose. "In the morning, I'm going to get a ticket back to Uli Rings. See if I can get my job back."

"So you're just going to run away? Again."

She shot to her feet and scowled down at him. "Here," she said, giving him a handful of credit chips. "Have a lap dance, on me."

Vin discarded the chips on the table, glowering after Priya as she walked away. He'd lost his taste for lap dances the day she'd left, but her words cut him deep. *Just as she'd intended.*

His eyes dipped to her ass, swaying in that unconscious way that always drove him nuts. The turmoil inside him turned violent. A voice in the back of his mind screamed that he was about to lose her again.

Can't lose something I don't have, he reasoned.

Ash and Zeek returned to the table. Vin wondered how much of the show they had caught. Zeek offered him a fresh ale. He took it and downed half before coming up for air.

"That bad?" Zeek observed.

"Did you expect anything else?"

"Honestly, I expected chairs to be thrown across tables."

"Then from that perspective, it went pretty well." Vin sucked down more booze before saying, "She's leaving tomorrow."

Ash let out a sigh. "Aidan's going to be pissed."

"Who gives a fuck how Aidan feels?"

The two men went quiet for a moment. Then Ash inquired, "How do you feel about it?"

How did he feel? He felt like someone had chewed up his guts and spit them back out. Like his chest was about to collapse into a black hole and take this damn spaceport with it. Every muscle coiled with dread and urgency. But most of all, he felt, if he let her go this time, he would be sucked down the pit of despair that had nearly swallowed him the first time she'd walked out of his life.

Without answering, he stood and bolted toward the ship. Inside, he rushed toward his compartment and rummaged through his things, snatching a small package and stuffing it in his pocket.

On his way out, he passed Aidan.

"How did it go?" Aidan yelled after him.

"Don't know yet!"

Entering her tiny room, Priya flopped on the thin, lumpy mattress held up by the meager frame and placed her arms behind her head. The lack of color on the metal walls matched her dreary mood.

She closed her eyes and let out a frustrated breath, remembering that terrible day. The day she'd caught Vin with a leggy tramp draped over him, his gaze riveted to her generous bosom. *On her friggin' birthday!* She knew he'd seen her standing there in the doorway, and he hadn't even had the gumption to look guilty.

A knock sounded. After a short debate, she labored to her feet, knowing who it would be.

Vin straightened as she opened the door, his russet eyes wary. "Can we speak?"

She crossed her arms in answer.

Turning defiant, he pushed past her, giving her a whiff of his musky scent. He smelled of hard work and man. *She used to worship that scent.*

Stifling a sigh, she closed the door and gave him her best stubborn expression. Yet, on the inside, she was stupidly eager. *He always did that to her. No matter how angry she was, he could always make her want him.*

Bastard.

Silence filled the space, coated by tension.

Finally, he spoke. "I just came to tell you I don't want you to leave. I want to run Phase Nine with you, and I want us to win."

"Thank you for your opinion. I'll take it into consideration."

His lips thinned.

"Is that it?"

"Yup." He shrugged and lifted his palms as if at a loss.

She stepped toward the door to let him out, but suddenly found herself being pulled back by the waist. Eyes wide, she flipped around in his arms. He'd made sure she was off balance and had to grip his shoulders for support.

"No, that's not it," he hissed. "Why did you leave without a word?"

"You know why."

"I know what you *think* you saw." His words came out in a rush, as if he'd rehearsed them. "You know I was angry with you that day. I was already pretty drunk when I saw you at the club, and out of spite I let you think I was interested in that woman." Sorrow entered his eyes. He shook his head. "I never assumed you'd disappear without railing at me."

Averting her gaze, she swallowed the lump that had built up in her throat. "You told me we were finished." She cursed the quiver in her voice. "When I saw you with her, I knew it was true."

"It was never true. Never," he insisted. "Still isn't."

His eyes locked on hers with such intensity it stole her breath. Her heartbeat faltered as she registered that familiar determination she used to love about him.

Still loved about him.

He pressed his mouth to hers, and she did nothing to dissuade him. His lips were soft and warm and molded to hers, just as she remembered. Her body responded, melting under the heat of his desire.

When he crushed her against his chest, she felt something like desperation roll off him. Tilting her head, she deepened the kiss. He took her cue, slipping his tongue past the border of her parted lips.

His taste flooded her and became a drug that fired in her veins, igniting her lust. A needy sound escaped her, and she began to meet him with every sweep of his tongue. Her arms latched around his neck as she pushed her body deeper into his.

Just like that, she was lost.

The kiss became demanding, as though both were starved for each other. He inched her backwards till he had her pressed against the wall, caged by his strong arms. The cold metal rivaled the burning heat that had come over her. She gave a soft moan. He responded with a rumbling, hungry groan. His calloused hand slipped to her backside, while the other gripped the small of her back.

Then his kiss turned sweet as his mouth glided over hers, lazily nipping at her bottom lip. Slowly, he moved to the soft curve of her jaw, stopping just below her ear.

"Forgive me," he whispered. His breath caressed her skin.

Her mind cried to relent, but she held back. "You can't just kiss me and expect to be forgiven."

Against her neck, she felt his lips curve into a smile. "How about a thousand kisses?"

"Try a million."

Hard yet tender, his fingers gripped her as though he would never let go. His mouth captured hers once more. She placed her palms over his broad shoulders, bringing them down his thick arms, reacquainting herself with each titillating muscle. His smooth skin felt blissful under her touch.

Suddenly, he pulled back. "I have something for you."

She cocked her head. "What?" When he reached into his pocket, she rolled her eyes. "Don't be cheeky."

He laughed. "Where's your mind at?"

Then he presented her with a rectangular box.

She raised a brow and took it, pulling off the lid. Inside, a thin silver chain with a heart-shaped pendant sparkled.

Anger flared.

She glared at him. "There are no gift shops on this spaceport. Who did you *really* buy this for?"

He took a step back, hurt. "I've had that since the day you left. I bought it for you after I left the club. Before I knew you'd gone."

Her mouth fell open to speak, but nothing came out.

"It was going to be a please-don't-be-mad bribe. I was going to grovel on my knees, like this." He dropped to the floor, his hands skating up her legs to rest on her thighs as he looked up at her with emotion-filled eyes. "And I was going to say, 'I'm sorry I'm such an ass and if you don't like the necklace, I'll get you something else.'"

She felt her face freeze in shock. She glanced down at the box. The corners were old and worn. When she examined the pendant again, her memory stirred. A few days before her birthday, she had not-so-subtly pointed it out to him.

Her throat suddenly tightened and her response came out breathy. "I would have said you are an ass, and I love the necklace, and if you ever touch another woman again I will shove it in a place that doctors will take hours to extract it from."

He gave her a heart-stopping grin and stood to kiss her with renewed hunger. Her arms clasped around his neck and she hitched her legs around his waist. Taking her full weight, he carried her to the bed, following her down onto the mattress. He kissed her in quick succession, finding a new place each time: the corner of her mouth, her cheek, her neck, her shoulder, making his way to her cleavage.

The sensation made her squirm.

She pulled at his shirt. He sat up to shrug out of it, and then went for her dress. As he pushed the hem up her thighs, he made sure to trail his hands along her skin, making her shiver. He discarded the dress to the floor. His belt and pants soon followed.

He returned to the cradle of her thighs, and his delicious muscles covered her. He found her center and entered. They both let out a guttural sound. As he began to move, euphoria took her and ecstasy assailed her. She became intoxicated by pleasure. At first, she matched his speed with her hips, but soon his thrusts became frenzied, and she could only accept him and the bliss he offered.

Powerful jolts shot through her, and her orgasm burst out in the form of a primitive cry. He followed with a rough groan. Finally, he stilled. His weight came to rest on her while they both gathered their breaths. Her fingers trailed over his back.

Then his head snapped up. "I love you, Priya. I never want to lose you again. Marry me."

She choked on a gasp and searched his expression. He looked sincere and anxious.

"It's a little soon for proposals, isn't it?"

"Not for me. I've spent far too long without you. I know I only have a tiny sliver of your heart back, but I am going to hold onto it with everything I have. You want a ring? I'll get you a ring. More necklaces? I'll buy them all." He paused. "Being without you was like being without my best friend. I don't want to go back to that."

Her vision blurred. *Could this truly be happening? He'd made a mistake that day, a humongous mistake, but so had she. If she hadn't acted so rashly and jumped the first flight out of there – or perhaps left him a note – she might have saved herself countless nights of misery.*

"Would you really have come for me?" she found herself whispering.

"Without a second thought." His voice held no hint of doubt. "I will never forgive myself for missing your little clue."

She offered him a tentative smile, when what she really wanted to do was laugh till she cried.

Lifting her hand to the side of his face, she stroked her thumb over his cheek. "Ask me again when we've won Phase Nine."

In the Interest of Security

Regan Black

Prologue

Chicago 2092, Office of National Health Chairman Dr Leo Kristoff

"Senator, I appreciate these new penalties for smugglers. We cannot allow this contraband to continue to flow unchecked." Dr Kristoff took a long sip of his coffee while the senator rambled on through the speaker phone. "Yes, sir. It is most certainly a direct assault on the public and our core values as a society. Publishing the results of our latest studies, combined with these updated caffeine-awareness campaigns, should stem the tide of illegal trafficking among casual users."

When the call ended, he waved Captain Derrick Simmons into his office, eager to get to more important matters. "Good morning. How's your fiancée?"

Simmons gazed through the wide window that overlooked the lab, and smiled fondly at Lorine. "The hot chocolate was a great idea."

"Of course, son. Little kindnesses impress women." Kristoff checked his watch. He'd introduced the two of them, knowing Simmons was the ideal match for his niece. Their recent engagement meant he could move forward with the next stage of his plans. "You have the field report?"

"Sir." Simmons came to attention. "The supplement is improving stamina and reflexes, as well as faster run times over

increasing distances. Generally, the 'juice' is delivering everything you promised: a more obedient and lethal soldier. The
Army is pleased."

"Generally?"

Captain Simmons placed a disc on the desk and activated the
hologram. "Nine out of ten soldiers are showing the predicted
results."

Kristoff watched the holographic soldiers rush forward with
snappy salutes, eager for the next order. "Ten per cent failure
rate isn't acceptable." Kristoff was already considering adjustments to the formula.

"Not precisely a failure rate, sir." The hologram shivered and
a new image appeared. "This soldier has super reflexes, and he
hasn't lost a hand-to-hand or battle drill in over a year. He has
an uncanny ability to anticipate his opponent's moves."

"Interesting. See that he gets back into the field immediately
and keep me informed."

"Yes, sir. Though he seems less inclined to blind obedience."

"Ninety per cent gives us enough simple cattle." Kristoff
glared at the tiny representation of the odd soldier. There was
potential here, he could feel it. "Ten per cent are like this one?"

"No, sir. It seems ten per cent are variables. Some of these
x-factors you might find favorable."

Kristoff appreciated the young officer's ability to see the big
picture. It was part of the reason he'd brought him into his inner
circle, providing him with boosters of "nutritional supplements"
unavailable to the general military. In his years of genetic
research and public service, guiding policy as the Health
Chairman, he'd found an open mind the most important asset
when it came to advancing the human race.

Checking his watch once more, he walked over to the window
overlooking the lab. Lorine was slumped at her station, her head
pillowed on her hands. The sedative he'd told Simmons to put
in her hot chocolate had done the trick.

"Good work, son. Take her to the operating room."

One

Chicago, December 2096

Jim Corvin leaned back and laced his fingers behind his head as he scanned the bank of monitors. Each perfect camera angle showed him every corner of the secret warehouse compound he was charged with protecting.

Everything looked fine, but his instincts were warning him about a looming threat, and he wanted to pin it down. *Professional or personal? In his line of work it could be both.* Usually his sixth sense about risk and danger gave him a more concise picture. He chalked up the lack of clarity to third-shift fog.

He could turn on specialized equipment in any one of the private suites, but only when absolutely necessary. Without a specific lead, intuitive or solid, he wouldn't breach privacy. The boss guaranteed everyone on staff the best security at all times, and complete privacy after the probationary period.

The boss, known as Slick Micky, was the most notorious smuggler in the region, and he kept the heart of his operation in Chicago. His success was directly tied to his radical philosophies about teamwork, his rare talent for inspiring loyalty, and his trade secret of only running coffee, sugar, and nicotine, while everyone believed he ran the hard stuff.

Despite his twitchy sixth sense, Jim yawned at the complete lack of activity in the warehouse. Working third shift to cover for holiday leave used to be easy. These days, he was grateful for the unlimited availability of full-caff coffee. Pulling this detail with the government-approved half-caff would be impossible.

The door from the boss's office opened and Micky stepped inside the monitoring room. "Need a refill?"

Jim nodded and held out his mug. "What are you doing up?" With all the years between them, he no longer bothered with *how* Micky got around the security cameras. The boss had plenty of secrets, and Jim knew some were better left undiscovered.

"Couldn't sleep," Micky said with a shrug. "Figured you wouldn't mind the company."

"Sure." Experience told Jim there was more to this visit, but the boss wouldn't reveal it until he was ready. Jim watched the entrances to the warehouse cycle through on the monitors. All the guards on post were alert, though they were dressed like strung-out bums and addicts. These disguises helped conceal the state-of-the-art facility Micky had planted in the middle of a condemned urban neighborhood.

No one in their right mind got off the el and wandered into this area. It made some aspects of security relatively boring, but working with Slick Micky offered lots of other opportunities for excitement.

Jim would bet his generous pension one of those opportunities had brought the boss in here tonight.

"I've got a problem," Micky said.

Jim sipped his coffee, waiting for the rest of the story, hoping this would mesh with his prickling sense of oncoming danger.

"One of the girls wants to leave."

"Not the first time."

"True," Micky agreed. "But this one is different."

More silence, which Jim filled with speculation. Smuggling by its covert nature and Micky's unique system turned strangers into family, creating a stability most of them had never had. When one of them left Slick Micky's team – mules, security, or even a supplier – everyone felt it.

But the boss didn't usually worry. Routes and customers were easy enough to cover, and there were always more girls eager for the safety and steady work Slick Micky's operation provided.

"I want you to go with her."

"What?" Jim mentally reorganized schedules and came up with gaping holes. "If she needs help moving, we've got guys who can handle that."

"She might actually need some heavy lifting." Micky seemed to think that over. "But what she really needs is your protection."

"*This* place needs protection." Everyone on his security detail was solid and battle-tested, but he wasn't about to leave the heart of Chicago's smuggling operation vulnerable. "We're on a skeleton crew for the holidays already."

"You got a feeling you're not telling me about?"

Jim paused, his mug halfway to his mouth. "Nothing concrete." Only the boss knew about his extra instincts. They rarely discussed the weird sixth sense Jim had honed to a fine point during his years with the Army. Jim's new skill most likely resulted from the *juice*: the military's nutritional supplement that was meant to enhance a soldier's performance in combat.

Several dangers of juicing were just coming to light, and while Jim had gained the ability to predict the future as it related to incoming risk and threat, most of the reported side effects weren't as helpful. From post-traumatic stress disorder to actual mind control, thousands of warriors had been wronged by the unethical medical practices of the developer, Dr Leo Kristoff.

The pieces clicked into place. Lorine must be ready to move. The woman had joined the team of mules running sugar and coffee for Slick Micky in order to provide for and protect her young son. Just a few months ago, they'd learned that she'd graduated Harvard medical school and had once enjoyed a reputation as a brilliant researcher in her own right. Until she'd turned on her uncle to expose the dangers of his nutritional-supplement juicing experiments.

More recently, he'd heard through the grapevine that she had her eye on a rural place south of the city, so her son could grow up with fresh air and sunshine.

"So what's not concrete?"

Jim shrugged. "My radar's been humming, but I can't nail down anything in particular. Threat or target." But when he thought of Lorine, his danger sense jumped to full alert. She had one of the more complex smuggling routes, through a rough neighborhood, with high-level competition. "What are you hearing?"

"Trina caught chatter about a hit."

"Another attempt on the route?"

"No." Micky sighed. "This is personal."

"They want Lorine?"

"Not exactly. They want the *boy* alive."

Kristoff's death had not killed off his organization. Assuming Kristoff's associates were behind the hit order on Lorine, Jim couldn't see a benefit to taking the boy alive. He gingerly set his coffee mug aside before he smashed it. "Can't you just tell her it's not safe to move?"

"I *could* do that."

"You can't mean to use her as bait?" The idea turned Jim's blood cold.

"Believe me, I'm not a fan of the tactic," Micky grumbled. "Trina and I have talked the issue to death. Lorine has a plan for her life. For her son's life."

"She's a good mom."

"Agreed. But the boy doesn't stand a chance if she finds herself constantly on the run."

"So she stays here. We can keep them both safe," Jim insisted.

"No. I don't think we can."

Shocked speechless, Jim studied the monitors until each camera feed had cycled through once more. How could she not be safe here? He'd made this warehouse the safest place in the city, if not the country, through technology and anonymity. This wasn't about his security skills or systems.

"I'm not feeling a specific threat aimed right here at us."

"That's my point. They don't know – can't know – to come *here*." Micky reached over and hit the key that enlarged the day-care view. Lorine's son slept soundly, a floppy rabbit cuddled under his chin.

"She's on third shift?"

"She wanted the extra pay."

Jim shot Micky a dark look. "I should be so lucky. If someone's gunning for her to get to the kid, why are you letting her work the route?" But he already knew the answer. *Changing the routine only put the enemy on alert.*

Resigned, Jim returned the monitors to his preferred configuration. The emotional pressure of watching Lorine's son, Zach, wasn't going to make any difference. *If Micky wanted him to handle this, he'd handle it.*

"Who's keeping the wolves at bay now?" Lorine was one of his favorites because of her rare combination of book smarts and street savvy. She probably already knew someone was tailing her.

"Trina's on her."

Well, that was something. No one else could blend in like Trina. "What do you want me to do?"

"Help them move, and handle whatever develops."

"Any backup?"

"Intel, a few gadgets."

"Weapons?"

Micky raised an eyebrow as he sipped his coffee. "Like you don't already have an armory in your apartment."

True enough. "Vehicles?"

"One of the vans is being modified now. She doesn't have too much in the way of furniture. Mostly books."

"Books? The heavy, dead-tree kind?"

"Both a hobby and a necessity, she told me." Micky shook his head. "Scientists. You'd think they'd embrace technology in all things."

Jim didn't bother to comment. *How did a bodyguard serve up protection while toting an armload of books?* "Then what? I just invite myself to stay a few days after the heavy lifting's done, and wait for the attack?"

"I don't think it will take that long." Micky's intent gaze told Jim more than the words. "If the rumors are true, someone has a line on the boy that will pop as soon as he's out in the open."

"Good lord." Genetic tracking devices were supposedly impossible, but Jim had seen too much in both the Army and civilian worlds. He no longer believed in impossible. He'd designed the security net here, adding layers of signal jammers along with the other protocols. The suggestion that the boy was invisible as long as he was within the security net of the warehouse made complete sense.

"And Lorine doesn't know about a potential genetic trace?"

"Not yet." Micky shook his head. "But she'll never outrun this." He clapped a hand to Jim's shoulder and stood.

"She's due to leave day after tomorrow. I've changed the duty roster so you're done after this shift. Check in with her when you're both awake tomorrow afternoon."

Jim tried to sound happy about it. "Sure thing, boss."

Lorine Sheraton felt the tail on her. From the second el station, she'd known someone was close. Third shift played with her head sometimes, but blowing it off as too little sleep and overactive nerves didn't make it better.

Paranoia happened, but sometimes it happened for a reason. Still, she kept to her schedule, made her drops of contraband sugar and coffee, and dealt with her legitimate job at the dairy.

It was her last night with all of the above. She'd be floating on air if the tail wasn't hovering back there. Knowing her son was safe, and instructions were filed in case something did happen to her, kept her calm in the midst of what her experience as a mule suggested was serious danger.

Another subtle glance over her shoulder revealed nothing.

She checked the reflection as she passed a window and gave points for skill to whoever the tail was.

She was too close to the future she'd painstakingly planned to lose it to a street thug.

Or worse. The thought came with a shiver of dread as she settled at her station.

No, there wasn't a "worse" here. Lorine deliberately reviewed the facts. Her warped uncle had been discredited and recently killed by his own greedy power play. He'd never seen her while she was pregnant, nor had access during her delivery or recovery. Zach was a normal, healthy toddler. And he'd stay that way. Soon they'd be settled on a small slice of farmland south of the city. A quiet rural area in an excellent school district, with green spaces full of children. Her own definition of utopia, where the air didn't need to be filtered and the views weren't pockmarked with urban decay.

The daydreams got her through the boredom of her shift and eased the tension in her shoulders while she waited for someone from Slick Micky's security detail to walk her back.

Chicago had been good to her, and she'd enjoyed more than a little satisfaction hiding here and actively undermining her uncle's ridiculous regulations about sugar and caffeine.

She smiled when she caught sight of her escort back to the warehouse.

"You look like the cat who ate the canary," Trina said.

They hadn't known each other long, but Lorine considered the woman a good friend already. "Pretty much," Lorine confessed. She waited to add more until they were alone on the street. "I was just basking in the pride of a job well done."

"All your jobs, I take it."

Lorine appreciated Trina's quick understanding. "Of course. I'm glad they sent you to meet me."

"I volunteered," the redhead said with a wink.

Lorine frowned. "Is everything okay?"

"Sure. Sometimes I just have trouble sleeping."

"Mm-hmm." Lorine didn't believe it but she let it slide. "I'll miss you when I move."

"That's mutual. Though I feel obligated to add we'll probably miss Zach more," Trina teased.

"He *is* the most adorable child ever, in my completely unbiased opinion."

Trina's light laughter faded too quickly. "So why did you call for security?" The dark edge in her voice worried Lorine.

"Someone tailed me from the el, all the way through my route."

"Anything distinctive?"

"No. That's what creeped me out. It's third shift and the route is too short for a big team. I did everything I've been taught and none of it worked. Sorry."

Trina waved it off as they climbed the stairs to the el station. "Sometimes I think the talent is getting better in this town."

"That's unsettling." Of course, "talent" probably meant different things to each of them. Her uncle had specialized in programming talent into the genetic code of embryos headed for in vitro fertilization. She shuddered, thinking of what he might have done to Zach if given the chance.

"Can I ask a personal question?"

Lorine nodded.

"Does this move have anything to do with Zach's father?"

"Not at all." Lorine pleated the strap of her purse. "The man's most likely dead by now. He was a soldier who got addicted to the juice." She'd called off the wedding when she'd discovered his addiction to the toxic formula and his inexplicable loyalty to Kristoff. The pregnancy test had turned positive two weeks later.

The substance had terrible side effects, a few were known already, and Lorine intended to work to reveal more in the coming years.

"And you still got pregnant?"

"Yup," Lorine said with a smile. She considered Zach a miracle, as the health department had admitted a link between juicing and infertility.

Their trip was uneventful, and Lorine felt a little silly for calling in the support. "Maybe it was third-shift paranoia," she said as they neared the warehouse.

"Men are paranoid. Women are intuitive."

Lorine chuckled. "I like that."

"Professional philosophy. Besides, it's better to be safe about these things. You've got a little one relying on you."

"Don't I know it." Lorine picked up her pace. "I'm going to peek in on him, then sleep for a few hours." They passed the sentry doing his best squatter impersonation and entered the long corridor that dropped under the street and into the next building.

When she reached the day care, it took all her resolve not to scoop her son into her arms and cart him back up to their apartment. But she needed rest, and the staff here would keep him entertained in the morning when he woke up full of energy. So she brushed his silky hair behind his ear and indulged in a sentimental moment before she headed out to her own suite.

The lingering glow of maternal joy and the odd twilight of working third shift distracted her so thoroughly, she collided with the person trying to exit the elevator when the doors parted.

Big palms landed hot and heavy on her shoulders. "Steady, there," Jim said.

"Ex-excuse me," she stammered, going stiff under the touch. She felt her face heating with embarrassment. How long had it been since a man had touched her? "Lost in thought." She tried to smile, but knew the relief was all too obvious when he lifted his hands.

"Me, too." Jim shoved his hands into his pockets. "I was just doing the last rounds. The boss says I'll be helping you move."

He was built like Zach's dad. Too big, too much . . . everything. She suspected he'd been a soldier, though no one in Slick Micky's employ was addicted to anything stronger than full-caff coffee.

"Oh?" She cleared her throat. Jim defined safe and trustworthy. Micky had told her he'd arrange for help, she just hadn't expected him to assign the head of security. "Thank you. There isn't much." She skirted around him to call the elevator back.

"Whatever you need."

"I, uh, appreciate that." *When would the door open, and why was she acting like an idiot?*

Jim tipped his head in the direction of the day care. "Is he okay?"

"Oh, yes," she said. "He always has a blast with everyone there."

Jim cleared his throat, but the elevator's arrival stopped whatever he might have said.

Making sure she didn't repeat her collision with someone else, Lorine paused before stepping inside. "I guess I'll see you soon."

Jim nodded.

Two

Knowing the place was wired from the rooftop atrium to the second sub-basement, Jim wondered if the boss had used the elevator to interrupt him when he was talking with Lorine.

He wasn't going to talk her out of moving. Well, he wasn't going to push the issue. Not really. He'd been hoping to get some information about the boy. Any information would be better than nothing, and yet the boss was essentially sending him in blind.

Why?

When Lorine had requested a protective escort after her shift, Jim was pleased she had trusted her instincts, even if it was likely Trina who'd set her off. *Why wouldn't his sixth sense cooperate?*

He stopped at the wide windows of the day care. The playroom would soon be lit up, and kids would come and go according to their mothers' schedules.

Who would help Lorine when she was out there on her own?

He started to turn away when a movement caught his eye. Lorine's boy came wandering into the dim playroom. He had the floppy bunny by the ears in one little fist, while the other rubbed at his eye. He stopped directly in front of Jim and tipped his head up.

"Sir?" he said, with a salute, like a soldier reporting for duty.

What the hell? Hiding his uncertainty behind his years of training, Jim dropped to one knee and looked the little guy in the eye. "Just checking in. Go back to bed. And stay there."

The boy nodded, did a perfect about-face, and toddled off.

Jim got to his feet, heart hammering against his ribcage. *That was no ordinary little boy.* Granted, he wasn't an ordinary man anymore. Juicing had changed him, in a mostly beneficial way. But the kid obviously hadn't served in the military, and Jim hadn't juiced since he'd left the service.

Taking the stairs down to his apartment, he tried to tell himself it was coincidence. *The little guy woke up, saw a grown-up and did the normal thing for a polite, outgoing kid. But* that *wasn't normal.*

Micky's warning about keeping the kid safe echoed in his head. Jim had witnessed soldiers caught up by the mind-control side effect. Nothing inside him had ever responded to an internal summons nor summoned another person, but he'd added signal jammers to the warehouse security plan anyway.

Precognitive episodes of potential danger were plenty to deal with. The nasty stuff interacted with every soldier differently. *Was he changing? Or was there something in the kid that was programmed to respond to soldiers?*

Lorine dreamed of church bells pealing happily, then growing more insistent. Soon her subconscious gave up the fight and she recognized the sound of the comm system.

Bolting upright, she reached for the monitor, a mother's worry pounding in her heart when she saw the day care on the display. "Yes? What's wrong?"

"Annie here. Zach's fine. I hate to bother you." Lorine blinked until Annie's face came into view. "He refuses to get out of bed. I was hoping you could say something. It's no big deal. But, this just isn't like him."

Lorine agreed. Zach rarely disobeyed. "I'll be right there."

She tugged jeans on under her nightshirt and grabbed shoes and a cardigan to put on in the elevator. Telling herself not to panic didn't help. Three-year-olds had ornery moments. Not even the best scientists could completely explain what went on in their developing brains.

Racing in would only scare the other kids and add credence to the chaotic thoughts churning through her brain. She pasted a smile on her face as she entered the day care.

It was situation normal in the playroom, but Lorine caught the concerned glances from the staff. Annie was sitting on the floor, chatting with Zach, when Lorine walked into the sleeping area. She paused and opened her arms, but her son didn't budge.

"Hi, Mommy."

"Hi, buddy. Annie tells me you don't want to get out of bed."

"Stay here."

"How come?"

Zach shrugged.

He had to be hungry. "I'm in the mood for pancakes. You want to help me make pancakes?" The mess would be worth it if it got him out of bed.

He nodded, his smile bright. She'd never seen this combination of stubborn and happy on him.

"Let's go, then."

"Hafta stay here."

"But we can't make pancakes in bed."

His face fell.

Lorine signaled Annie to give them a minute. "Can I sit by you?"

He scooted over and wiggled a little more than necessary.

"You have to pee?"

"Uh-huh."

But still he wouldn't leave the bed. She searched for the right angle to break through his odd stubbornness. "Zach, why do you have to stay?"

"He told me stay there."

Dread coiled like a snake in her belly. "We don't have to obey the people in our dreams."

"Not dreamin'."

As the potty dance got worse, Lorine resigned herself to the fight of dragging him to the bathroom against orders.

Orders. He was acting like a new recruit.

"Who told you 'stay there'?" She listed all the names of the day-care staff. He shook his head at each one, clutching his bunny to his chest. "Who, Zach?"

"The big man."

An image of Zach's father popped into her head. She dismissed that as impossible. *No one got in the warehouse uninvited, not even dead people.* The ridiculous thought only showed how exhausted she was.

She struggled for calm. "When did the big man talk to you?"

He shrugged.

"Where?"

"At the window."

She made a mental note to double-check with security. There had to be a camera with a record of the interaction. "No one wants you to pee in the bed. Go on to the potty."

"No!" Tears brimmed in his big eyes. "Said stay there."

She barely restrained her temper. "Who is a smart boy?"

"Me."

"That's right. Do the smart thing. Go potty, and come straight back here."

"Big Jim said stay there."

Jim? "*Mommy* says go now."

Lorine suffered a wealth of emotions in the long seconds Zach weighed her authority over Jim's. When her son rocketed from the bed, triumph was short-lived, quickly replaced by a quiet fury. She wanted a piece of Jim and she wanted it now.

When Zach returned, she gave him new orders, and promised him pancakes for lunch.

Leaving a happy son and relieved staff in her wake, she stormed down to Jim's apartment.

She didn't bother with the comm system, she pounded on the door until it opened and Jim's wide palm caught her fist before it landed on his chest.

His bare chest.

"Lorine? Wh— What the— " His gaze drifted down her body, lighting little fires along the way.

She yanked her hand back to her side and thought she might have exercised her intelligence by pausing to put on a bra first.

Then she thought of Zach in his dinosaur pajamas nearly wetting the bed because he was following orders, and her temper boiled over once more. "I demand an explanation."

"Huh?" He rubbed a hand over the stubble shadowing his jaw.

"My son! What did you do?"

In the blink of an eye, he pulled her inside and she was all too close to that broad chest. He slammed the door closed behind her. He had her wrist cuffed in one hand and braced himself against the door with the other. The man was too close. Too big. But she couldn't stop her eyes from taking a foolish journey over that perfectly sculpted arm.

"Explain. Slowly," he said.

"Zach." Her throat dry, she tried again. "He refused to get out of bed or cooperate with the day-care staff because you ordered him to 'stay there'." She put it in air quotes. "When and why would you have anything to do with my son?"

He scowled. Not at her, rather through her. In a rush, he dropped her hand and pushed away from the door, turning his back as if the mere sight of her offended him.

"Jim, I expect an answer," she said when she could form words. His back might be his best side, from a purely anatomical standpoint, barring the flat white scars that splashed from shoulder to hip. At some point in the past he'd been doused with scalding water. Accident or abuse? From the little she knew about him, he'd likely been protecting someone.

She shook off the surge of sympathy. His past problems or heroics didn't give him the right to upset Zach.

"I don't know what happened, Lorine."

"My son gave me the impression he was following your orders."

Jim turned, his face pale. "When I was walking by, he just showed up. I told him to go back to bed and he did."

"He was at the window?"

"Yeah."

"You're lying. I'd just looked in on him. He was sound asleep."

"Maybe you woke him." He winced under her harsh glare. "Okay, maybe not. I was tired. When he showed up, I just sent him back to bed. Seemed safest."

That she believed. Jim was all about security all the time. Something she'd been grateful for until this morning. "What else?"

"Huh?"

She wished he'd put on a shirt. *It was hard to stay mad when the man put a kick in her pulse this way.*

"Why were you near the day care?" She made herself ask the more pertinent question. "What do you know about Zach?"

He shook his head. "Nothing. Other than I'm slated to help you move." He slumped onto the couch and rested his elbows on his knees. "I'm sorry I upset your kid. I like him."

"He likes you, too." Which was probably why he'd been so persistent about following orders. "You didn't do any manly little soldier routine, did you?"

"No way." Jim shook his head, but he didn't meet her eye.

"Any chance you can go by the day care with me and confirm your orders are lifted?"

"Sure." He pushed to his feet. "Give me a second."

True to his word, Jim returned within moments wearing a gray sweatshirt and running shoes. Lorine tugged her cardigan tighter around her as they walked to the elevator.

"Sorry I came on so strong," she said as they waited.

"You're a good mom." He gestured for her to board first, and punched the button.

"Thanks. I know I'm overprotective." For good reason, she didn't add. "And I'm a little wired from working third shift."

"It happens."

The doors parted and they stepped out, but she stopped him

with the merest brush of her hand against his arm. "Why are you being so nice about this?"

"Fastest way to get to bed." He grinned, then his words sank in and his eyes went wide. "That's not . . . Aw, hell. I meant— "

She laughed. "I get it. You want to get back to sleep. Me too." She ignored the sneaky bit of disappointment that she didn't ignite his desire the way he ignited hers. She'd always been a sucker for a fine chest, and his would forever be the gold standard. Not that romance was on the agenda until Zach was grown. She refused to let her hormones lead her into a temptation that might jeopardize her son's safety.

They reached the day care and she breathed easier when she saw Zach flopped on the floor working intently on a puzzle.

"Does that mean I'm off the hook?"

Lorine was about to answer in the affirmative, when Zach turned toward them. He pushed to his feet and hurried over, skidding to a stop right in front of Jim, saluting. "Sir?"

Lorine stared as Jim dropped down in front of her son and told him he was on leave until further notice and didn't need to follow his orders anymore.

Jim was relieved his only idea had worked, when Zach beamed and ran back to his puzzle. But the horror on Lorine's face told him he wouldn't sleep anytime soon. Resigned, he nudged her out of the day care and back to the elevator. He was starting to wonder if he should take her up to the infirmary when she finally spoke.

"What *was* that? He can't possibly know what 'leave' is."

Jim agreed, but he didn't have an explanation that would make her feel better. "That's pretty much what happened last night. Only he did a perfect about-face and went right back to bed."

"No way!"

Thinking back, it had been a cute maneuver in those footie pajamas.

"Wipe that grin off your face," Lorine snapped. "This isn't funny."

No, it really wasn't.

"He's a little boy, not a toy soldier." Her voice caught on unshed tears.

"I know that." He guided her off the elevator and toward her apartment. "Why don't you catch a couple more hours of sleep and we'll discuss it after lunch?"

"But—"

He shook his head. "Lorine, he's safe." *For now.* "You should know better than anyone the value of a well-rested mind."

"Of course."

"Then we'll pick this up in a few hours."

He swiped his master key card to unlock her door. Her gasp only made him more aware of his own tired thought processes.

"Think, Lorine. You had to know I have access to all the suites." The dark circles under her eyes made him feel worse. "It's a safety issue. The boss would boot my ass if I ever abused my authority."

"You're right." She rubbed at the tension lining her forehead. "I'm being ridiculous. You're system is one of the reasons I've stayed this long." She looked up, their eyes locked, and something inside him stirred. He wasn't in the right frame of mind to analyze it.

"Get some rest."

"We're having pancakes for lunch. Zach's favorite. Why don't you join us, and we can talk about the move. Please?"

He had the time and she was officially his priority until they flushed out whoever wanted the boy. "Sure."

Her pleased expression carried him back to his own apartment where he sent an email to Micky. Maybe knowing Zach's reactions would help the boss interpret the rumors and threats against Lorine and the boy.

When he finally hit the bed, sleep came easy, but the dreams were hard.

Lorine took extra care as she dressed. She styled her hair and pinned it up and took time with her make-up. She wanted a casual effect, but something more than the bare minimum of mascara and lip gloss. Not for Jim, for her. She needed the confidence of her best jeans and a holiday sweater in a bold red.

Wringing out every possible minute of sleep, she'd asked Annie to walk Zach back to the apartment while she prepped for the pancake lunch. It wasn't just about the meal, it was making a little time for the research, too.

She wanted to believe Zach's behavior was only a matter of his observant nature and imagination, but her intuition said she needed to face the possibility of dear old nasty uncle Kristoff's tricks. He'd been on the cutting edge of genetic research, and a master manipulator of people. Her research had turned up anonymous video accounts of soldiers responding to a superior officer much as Zach had done.

Damned juice. But Zach had never been juiced. What had set off this behavior? Had her uncle gotten to him after all?

She took it out on the eggs, whipping them to a point better suited for waffles. Luckily Zach wasn't picky as long as there was syrup.

But a man like Jim didn't maintain that kind of build on refined carbs alone. And she had no business thinking of his build. On a wistful sigh, she pulled out more eggs and found a container of bacon in the freezer.

She heard the hiss and click of the front door. Jim called out, and she was startled to hear his deep voice rather than Annie's. Glancing up, her breath caught as she saw Jim filling the doorway, her giggling son tucked under his arm.

"This urchin says you'll vouch for him."

"Really? I don't know any urchins."

"Momma, it's me!" Zach shrieked between giggles.

Jim and Zach exchanged a look. In a blink, Jim was holding a delighted Zach upside down by the ankles. "How about now?"

"Hmm. He's vaguely familiar." She walked over and gave his feet a tickle. "Does it like waffles?"

"Yes!" Zach squealed.

"Then it can stay, I suppose."

Her heart skipped a beat when Jim pretended to drop Zach, then simply melted when Jim set her son down with a gentleness that belied his size and toughness.

It pleased her to watch both man and boy stuff themselves with syrup-drenched waffles, eggs, and the last of her bacon. She lingered over her coffee, listening to her son chatter, putting off the inevitable conversation.

"I was against the move," Jim said when she'd washed the remnants of syrup off Zach's face and hands and sent him off to play.

"After last night you must be eager to get rid of us both."

He shrugged.

Clearly he didn't want to discuss last night, but she needed answers to protect Zach. Topping up his coffee, she wondered how to breach a topic most retired soldiers found uncomfortable at best. "You were juiced during your service."

"Yes."

She met his wary gaze with a smile. "I've been thinking and researching," she admitted. "Last night was probably a result of juicing."

"I've been clean— "

"You wouldn't be at my table otherwise," she said with enough force to shut him up. "I've seen footage of soldiers behaving just as Zach did with you."

"Juiced soldiers," Jim muttered.

"Zach's father, Derrick Simmons, was a juiced soldier. I think it's safe to say we don't know all the ramifications or variations of Kristoff's experiment."

"I've never heard of any juicing effect passing to the next generation. Most juicers are thought to be sterile."

"True. Yet Zach is here. I imagine there's much about juicing we haven't learned. I ended the relationship when I realized Derrick was particularly close to Dr Kristoff." What had happened last night had raised her fears that she'd been used by her uncle. "Regardless, something in my son automatically responded to something in you."

She saw the hesitation again and pushed this time. "You obviously have an opinion, Jim. I'm not too fragile to hear it."

"I've seen that auto-response first-hand, but I've never triggered it. Seeing it in Zach lends weight to your theory."

She ran her finger around the rim of the coffee cup. "How did juicing change you?"

As a researcher she'd only been able to expose the most consistent damages resulting from her uncle's awful "advancements". It would be impossible to help all the men in Jim's situation. If they even wanted help.

"I've got a sixth sense about danger." He leaned back in his chair and sighed. "Think of it like an early warning system. I don't always know where or how, but I can sense a threat. Best lead time is about two days out. I went by the day care to see if I could get a reading on the threat to Zach."

She would not panic. When Slick Micky had assigned Jim to her relocation, warning bells had gone off in her head. *Why send the best security when she only needed a bit of muscle?*

"And?"

He shrugged those wide shoulders. "Nothing. Except the toy-soldier thing."

"Why did you try?"

"The boss heard a few things on the street."

A chill raced down her spine. "What do you know?"

"Not enough." He shifted and his warm palm covered her fisted hand. Instead of comfort, his touch sent a new awareness shimmering through her. "Micky heard there's a hit on you, but the goal is to take Zach alive."

Her heart leaped into her throat. "Who?"

"We only know you're the first target. It looks like when Zach's in the warehouse he's safe, but based on what happened with me, I think when he's out of the warehouse, any juiced soldier could find him pretty easily."

The room took a long, sickening spin. Without Jim's warm hand as a touchstone, she might have slid to the floor. "I bought a little farm. It was going to be a quiet, normal life."

"Not for long," Jim said. He gave her hand a squeeze. "We weren't going to leave you out there alone."

Well, that was something.

"Lorine, you can postpone the move."

She glanced over at her son playing with his trucks. "But if we don't flush the threat out now he'll never have a normal life."

Jim scowled as he nodded the affirmative. "The boss thinks if I'm with you, I'll be able to get a read on the threat. Then we can take action."

Restless, Lorine tugged her hand free and went to clean up the kitchen.

"Let me."

He was behind her, crowding her. Rather than threatened, she felt a jolt of desire stronger than any full-caff coffee could provide. "No, thank you. I need to stay busy while I think this through."

"Can you at least think out loud?"

"Sure." She loaded dishes into the sanitizer and pressed "start". "A blood test would be a good beginning. I can compare your blood with his. When Zach was born I did a full panel, looking for anything out of the ordinary."

"Smart."

She smiled. "That baseline will tell me if anything has changed recently."

"You mean, changed when he reacted to me?"

Lorine stopped puttering and studied him. His pensive frown, the sincere concern in his quiet brown eyes, had her feeling more affection than was wise. "Jim." She didn't know what to do with her hands, and crossed her arms to keep them still. When he met her gaze, she continued. "None of this is your fault. If anything, you revealed a problem I needed to know about."

His gaze slid back to Zach. "Is his father alive?"

"I doubt it. He was loyal to Kristoff beyond all reason. Though the official reports are vague, I'm sure he died trying to protect Kristoff. He wouldn't have been anywhere else."

"Who else would want the boy?"

"Considering all of this, no one with good intentions," she said with a sigh. "If Kristoff manipulated his father somehow to test-drive something new, the only way to know for sure is to give the remainder of his team a chance at Zach."

She watched Jim lean back on the counter. It was a struggle, here in the safety of her small kitchen, to keep her mind focused on the dangers waiting for them, rather than on the man who was igniting feelings she couldn't afford to indulge.

"You're awfully calm about this."

She shrugged a shoulder. "You're awfully good at security." *And awfully good with my son.* "I suppose you have other things to do today?"

"A few details to deal with," he agreed. "Thanks for lunch."

Lorine walked him to the door, and Zach joined them, bouncing up and down until Jim scooped him up for a hug.

When Jim was safely on the other side of the door, Lorine indulged in a moment's enjoyment of the girlish butterflies he sent winging in her tummy. The attraction was misplaced, ill-timed, and likely one-sided. But it was nice to know she could still experience it.

Three

Jim stalked down to Micky's office in a foul mood about the whole mess. When she wasn't angry at him, Lorine tempted him to all sorts of insanity. After his juiced days with the Army, he hadn't thought to be close to anyone for longer than a one- or two-night stand.

Respecting the house rules, he didn't look for partners among the girls who ran contraband. They were family. Practically sisters. *Keeping Lorine in that tidy box was becoming a serious challenge. Because she accepted him, or because she needed him?*

Hell, they all needed him.

Good thing she and that cute kid of hers were moving away. Once they were safe, he'd count it a job well done.

With a curt nod for the guard posted outside Micky's office, he rapped on the door. The permission was instant, and Jim walked in, closing the door behind him.

Without a word, he reached for Micky's keyboard and took the office off the surveillance grid. He wanted complete privacy for this conversation.

"You're in a mood."

Jim ignored that. "Do you know who's been hired to take the kid?"

"Not yet."

"Did you see my message? Have you found any leads?"

"Not yet." Micky shook his head. "You look rough around the edges. What's going on?"

"I've got an idea." He gave Micky an overview of Lorine's theory and the first of a couple options he'd thrown together. "I could take the two of them out on the town for a couple hours. The aquarium would work."

"Just a happy family outing?"

Jim rolled his eyes. The boss had romance on the brain since finding Trina. "Just a casual, covert exercise."

"No."

"I'll rig a jammer for the kid to wear." Jim sat back, not bothering to hide his frustration. "Whoever is after her knows she's in Chicago, and they assume the kid is with her."

"Agreed."

"How about a little recon?" He patted his pocket. "I've got a few strands of the kid's hair. If they've managed some sort of genetic trace, this might be enough to draw them out. Trina can use her powers to cast a mental illusion and make it look good."

"Only if she knows where to cast it." Micky sipped his coffee. "How about this? You take Lorine out tonight. Zach stays here. Keep the hair sample on you. Trina and I will tail you."

"What about the warehouse?"

"Got a feeling?"

Jim grumbled. "I hate it when you ask that."

Micky grinned. "I know. So do we have a plan?"

He hesitated, wondering how Lorine would react. "Double up security teams at the el and the street entrances and you've got a deal."

"No one's ever followed her as far as the el, but consider it done. Looks like we've got ourselves a double date," Micky added.

Jim didn't care for the smug expression. "A date would break protocol," Jim said, feeling more regret than he should.

"Nah. As of last night, Lorine's officially off my payroll. She's fair game."

They'd known each other for too long for Jim to take the bait. While he might admit to himself he was attracted to a woman who didn't hate him for the lasting side effects of juicing, he wouldn't admit that to the boss.

He messaged Lorine, and got an affirmative on the date, once she was assured of Zach's safety.

After making a dinner reservation, he modified a couple of security bracelets to block any signal transmissions. It was a quick job and not fully tested, but he expected them to work short-term.

Armed with a brief list of names and faces after digging through classified reports of Kristoff's death, Jim felt prepared for everything but the "date" itself.

"It's not a damned date," he muttered, staring at his closet, but the reservation required more than jeans and a button-down shirt.

He cursed Micky to hell and back because the date idea still rolled around in his head half an hour later when Lorine opened her door. She was an absolute knockout in a low-cut emerald dress that flowed over her curves, and heels that boosted her to nearly his eye level. She'd piled her hair up, so that all he could think about was setting his mouth to the delicate creamy skin at her nape. He'd bet a week's salary the pendant resting over her heart was a genuine emerald.

The simple bracelet he'd modified would look out of place. He left it in his pocket and convinced himself she'd never leave his sight.

"Can you run in those shoes?" With the tangle of desire and concern in his head, it was the safest phrase he could offer as they moved down the hall.

"Oh, I can hold my own." She winked at him and kicked up a spiked heel. "At a pinch they are excellent weapons."

"Good to know," he said, as they took the elevator to the garage level. "The risk doesn't bother you?" He recognized the signs of anticipation. The sparks she gave off weren't from jewelry or make-up.

"Surprisingly, no. I feel so ready for this." The elevator opened and she stepped out, glancing around the garage. "Where's our backup?"

He ignored the sway of her hips. "Probably out there already," he replied, leading her to the waiting car and opening her door. The only two-seater in Slick Micky's fleet, the modifications guaranteed a quick getaway if things went bad.

"You're not claustrophobic, are you?"

"Not a bit."

"Let's hope this doesn't change that."

He'd known she was strong and brave, just by making the choices that had brought her to Slick Micky's family. But this was a whole new side of Lorine, a side that made him want more than he knew he could have. Tonight marked the first step in making sure her plans for her son's future succeeded. With renewed focus on the "mission", he eased the car out of the garage and into the tunnel.

When they emerged, he smiled at her small gasp. This time of year, the city sparkled with lights and the darkness hid the worst of the decay.

He drove through the city, hoping they'd pick up a tail. As their reservation time neared, he took a detour down Lakeshore Drive, not quite ready to put her on display.

"Anything?"

"No." His sixth sense wasn't firing either. He glanced over, his breath catching at the sight of her skirt riding high on her legs. Maybe he was too distracted for his radar to function properly. "We'll see how dinner goes."

"You're sure whoever is after me will find me at a ritzy place downtown?"

"I'm not sure of anything other than someone wants you out of the way so they can get to Zach." He should tell her he'd brought Zach's hair. "If we're dealing with genetic tracking anything is possible."

"Agreed."

"The hit on you sounds more old school. Where does Zach go if something happens to you?"

"My parents would raise him. But I've already checked with them. They're safe and they haven't had any problems. Oh, wow. We're dining here?"

He grinned, pleased with her reaction as he pulled to a stop at Water Tower Place. Handing the keys to the valet, he felt the first tremor of trouble. Instinctively, he draped his arm across her shoulders as they walked inside. When they were seated, he leaned close. "What's security like at your parents' place?"

Her smile was like a fist to the gut. "It would make you drool."

"If whoever is after Zach knows that detail, they'll definitely make the grab before he gets there."

The waiter arrived, took their drink requests and hurried off.

"Why didn't you just go to your parents when things got rough?"

"Insecurity with a side of paranoia." She kept her eyes on the menu, but he knew she was aware of everything around her. "Running to my parents felt like an invitation to disaster. Even with their excellent security, it seemed like taking us all out at once would have been relatively easy." She met his gaze. "Stop frowning. Besides, I'm a grown-up."

That was true. "But living in obscurity—"

She rolled her eyes. "Might have worked if my uncle hadn't apparently outsmarted me somehow with Zach's father. Can you do me a favor?"

"Sure." *He knew he'd do anything she asked. Even beyond this evening, beyond her move, keeping his distance felt all wrong.*

"For the duration of dinner could we just pretend we're not doing the worm on the hook thing?"

Her husky voice slid over him and had him wishing they could pretend other things as well. Not trusting himself, he nodded. The resulting smile and happy light in her eyes unlocked a part of him he'd buried during his years of service.

The excellent food and service paled in comparison to the delightful company. Pretend or not, he could get used to nights like this. Beautiful and intelligent, Lorine put him at ease. It was a feeling he hadn't realized he'd missed. She flirted just enough to draw him out and make him laugh.

To anyone else, they were simply another couple out for a romantic evening. Even with his senses sounding the alarm of imminent trouble, he struggled to remember this moment with her was just a game.

When his sixth sense spiked, he blinked against the image of sunlight flashing off a windshield. In the soft glow of candlelight at the table, he winced and rubbed his burning eyes.

"What is it?"

"Trouble," he said through gritted teeth.

"Where?"

His instincts said they'd face that image during the move tomorrow, but something was closing in on them right here, right now. "I usually have more warning." He pushed his cuff back from his watch, but before he could use the comm hidden inside, the alert came through the tag pressed into place behind his ear. "Threat identified and closing in," Trina said. "We'll handle it. Get her out. Car is in the alley."

Jim didn't like retreating, but Lorine mattered more than his pride. He glanced around. *Who was the enemy? How would they attack?* "Go to the restroom," he said, giving her hand a squeeze. "I'll be right behind you, but have a shoe ready in case."

She nodded as she rose, and strolled through the restaurant as if she didn't have a care. *God, she was good.*

"Boss?" Jim spoke into the hidden mic.

The reply of two clicks told him Micky was taking down the threat. Resigned, Jim swiped his card through the reader and added the tip.

As he stood, his knee buckled in response to his sixth sense. *The enemy would go for a debilitating blow to his knee first. Too bad he didn't know precisely when they would strike, but now he would be on the lookout.*

Nearing the restrooms, he recognized the heavy thud of a body slamming into a wall. He rushed to the door. "Lorine?"

"Gun!"

He jumped aside just as a soft *pop* sent a bullet ripping through the door where his knee had been a fraction of a second earlier. His adrenaline pumping, he barreled through the door to rescue Lorine.

"Great timing," she said, a wide smile on her face and her eyes glittering with excitement. Her dress torn, hair tumbled, and her feet bare, she looked like an angry goddess thrilled with her triumph. Dragging his eyes away, he followed her gaze to the man slumped behind the door. "What'd you do?"

"Sedative hypospray in the heel." She held up the two pieces of her shoe, then clicked the heel back into place.

Impressive. "Recognize him?"

"It's Zach's father."

"Are you sure?" Maybe he'd memorized the wrong faces.

"Oh, he's had work done, but that's Zach's father." She slipped those narrow feet back into her shoes. "What do we do with him?"

"Backup is standing by." Jim punched the anonymous code into his cell card and sent the message. With the comm in his watch, he updated Micky and Trina. "We've got to get you out of here."

Handing the gun and silencer to Lorine, he dragged the dead-weight dad into a stall and cuffed him to the toilet.

When he held out his hand, Lorine rushed toward him and he savored the feel of her warm body nestling close as they moved through the kitchen and out into the alley. In the car, he flipped down the false front on the dash and turned on the signal jammers. He wasn't in the mood for more confrontation just now.

"Some date," she said when they were a few blocks away.

"It's gone better than some I've had," he admitted.

Lorine stared out the window, watching the sparkling lights fade as he sped away from the city. "Me too," she said at last.

"Really?"

"You have to admit a covert op adds an edge of excitement to the evening."

"And you wanted to pretend things were normal."

She laughed. "I should admit something else."

Jim waited. Hoped.

"I've got a sample of Zach's blood in my pendant."

"I've got his hair in my pocket."

"Oh, we're a pair." The short laugh was brittle this time. "Genetic tracking." She gave a low whistle. "If only we could write this one up for the science journals."

"This *is* a first. Better to wait until you figure out how Kristoff managed to tweak Zach."

"That's my top priority now that I know he's safe."

"We're not quite out of the woods on that one."

"What do you mean?"

He hated putting a damper on her mood, but reality was often brutal. "Lorine, do you believe your ex simply wanted custody?"

Lorine thought about it. Pressing the pendant to her lips, she stared out the window again. "No." Shifting in her seat, she studied Jim's strong profile, grateful for his expertise and logic. Adrenaline or attraction, she wanted to indulge a fantasy and forget the looming threats.

"We should go forward as if you don't know anything," he said. "I'm sorry it has to be that way."

"Your sixth sense?"

He nodded. "I believe they'll come for Zach when we're on the road."

"And they won't give up."

"No." He sounded so sad, so resigned.

"Jim, the move can wait. Zach doesn't know what he's missing. I can get my old job back."

"No." He swerved to the shoulder and put the car in park. She could only stare as his big hands flexed on the steering wheel. "You have a right to want a normal life. Zach has a right to a normal life."

"I think that ship's sailed. Derrick was convinced Zach was with me tonight." She twirled the pendant. "His confusion was my only opening. If my uncle wasn't already dead, I'd kill him myself."

"You think Kristoff planted more than a genetic trace in Zach?"

"I think he was demented and evil and anything is possible. With time and the right lab, I will know for sure."

"The boss's friends will get something out of Derrick and his pal."

"I'm sure." But Lorine didn't much care about enemies present or future. *Jim was right here, filling her senses with a longing she didn't want to deny.* She gazed up into his shadowed eyes and trailed a finger across his smooth, square jaw.

"Got a lab at your farm?"

"Not yet."

"How's security?"

Her pulse spiked at the raw desire in his voice. "Lacking."

"I could fix that."

"I'm sure." *But she didn't want to think about anything else right now. He was everything she told herself she didn't want and everything she didn't want to give up.* "There's no lab right here." She watched his dark eyes trace the path of her tongue as she wet her lips. Her pulse leaped. "And the security is great." A gentle tug on his tie brought his mouth down on hers with a heat and a joy that sent her reeling beyond her darkest fantasies.

She trembled when he whispered her name like a prayer, and under the tender caresses of his warm, strong hands she learned what it meant to be cherished.

Hours later in the warehouse lab, Lorine compared blood samples from her son, his father, and Jim. Even after debriefings and renegotiating with Slick Micky, her body still replayed her encounter with Jim.

"Planning to sleep on the road?"

She glanced up, admiring the way Jim filled the doorway. "What road?" The flash of hope in his eyes confirmed her decision.

"You're not moving?"

"In your professional opinion is it the smart thing to do?"

"Not at all." He took a step closer. "But it's what you wanted for Zach."

"Zach should grow up happy and strong, not running from whoever will use him. Here people love him, and can help me keep him safe."

Jim's expression sobered. "We're family here."

He was thinking of the standard warehouse rules. She'd cleared this with Slick Micky and yet she shivered, weighing the risk and reward of taking this next step. Her feelings for Jim, rooted in respect, affection, and desire, had deepened practically overnight to love. *Was it the same for him? She said a prayer she hadn't misinterpreted the emotion behind his actions and kisses last night.*

"We could be." She waited for her words to sink in. When his gaze locked with hers, the intensity stole her breath. "If you'll have us," she finished on a whisper.

"If I'll have *you?*"

His expression unreadable, she mentally cursed her miscalculation. She'd moved too fast, assumed too much. "It's more than the security."

"Lorine." With his startling speed, he crossed the lab and laced his fingers with hers. "Security is a good foundation."

"For love." She kissed him tenderly.

He broke the kiss and cupped her face in his hands. "For love." His mouth tilted. "You know you're getting the raw end of the deal with me?"

"Nah. Zach is still a serious security risk." She smiled as the laughter rumbled through his broad chest.

"We'll figure it out together," he said. "Your skills in here, mine out there."

As tears brimmed, she could only nod. "When the farm sells— "

"Why sell?" He leaned back. "Let me work on it. When the security's set we'll make it a frequent vacation spot."

His confidence was contagious. "You think so?"

"I promise." He tucked her hair behind her ear. "All of our children will know what fresh air and sunshine feel like."

He couldn't have said sweeter words, or given her more of a hope for a truly free future.

End of the Line

Bianca D'Arc

One

She saw the incoming fire too late to save her ship. The one-man fighter was going down, and if she didn't pop her canopy in the next five milliseconds, she was going with it.

Lisbet realized she had no choice. Hitting the CATASTROPHIC FAILURE button, she checked herself out of her ride split seconds before it blew into a million little weightless bits. Out in the nothingness of space near the galactic rim, she was in no-man's-land, where rescue was hard to come by. She had either a long wait or a slow death to look forward to in the next few hours.

The enemy Jits had won this battle, though hopefully not the war. Skirmishes on the rim had escalated in recent years as the Jit'suku empire looked for ways to gain a foothold in the Milky Way. The expansion from their home galaxy was fueled by the comparative ease of travel via an inconvenient wormhole and several jump-points – that had been created before humans had realized how the Jit'suku truly viewed the human race.

Inferior. That's what the Jits thought of humans. Inferior in every way to their warmongering race. Though they looked very human in appearance – if built on a bit of a larger scale than most humans – Jit'suku society was one that most humans had a hard time understanding.

They prized warriors and seemed to scoff at diplomats and anyone who wanted to negotiate. The only thing the Jits understood was conquest, it seemed.

Which was why they'd been fighting so long and so hard out here, on the rim of the Milky Way galaxy. Lisbet was just the latest in a nearly endless rotation of human fighter pilots who had drawn the dreaded, but vital, duty of patrolling the rim.

With vast reaches of emptiness between nearly lawless stations, dangerous jump-points, and the occasional star system, rim duty was enough to drive anyone crazy. But she welcomed the emptiness of space and the loneliness of her own thoughts after this humiliation.

She'd been on this patrol for over a week with nothing to report. Then this. A Jit'suku battle cruiser had appeared as if from nowhere, and blasted her before she could even get a message out. He'd been lying in wait behind an asteroid. Lisbet had known to be cautious, but honestly, her thoughts had been elsewhere. As soon as she had spotted the giant ship lumbering out from behind the cover of the asteroid, it had already been too late. Her signals had bounced back – jammed. A moment later, a blanket of weapons fire had appeared on her screens. She'd been blown already, and she had known it.

Popping her canopy and stranding herself in the middle of nowhere in the emergency pod had been her only choice. Not a great one, but there'd been no other way to get away from all the incoming fire. *The bastard giving orders on that battle cruiser hadn't been taking any chances that she'd get clear and report back. He'd thrown everything but the kitchen sink at her, and she hadn't stood a chance.*

"Human, this is Captain Fedroval of the battle cruiser *Fedroval's Legacy*. Warrior to warrior, I give you the choice. Would you prefer the fast death of missile fire or the slow death of suffocation when your air runs out?" He spoke directly into her emergency pod.

For a moment, Lisbet thought of ignoring the short-range communication from the cruiser. He was still blocking her long-range transmitter, but he'd allowed her enough bandwidth to broadcast to his ship. *Big of him. Damned Jit'suku bastard.*

"How do you know I'm not the advance scout of a much larger force? Could be my battalion is on my heels and will pick me up after they blow you to kingdom come." Oh, how she wished that were true. She'd get a lot of satisfaction right now at seeing the Jit'suku ship blown into a million pieces.

There was a slight delay in the answer; she'd expected one right away. *The captain probably knew she was bluffing. If he'd been hiding out behind that asteroid for any length of time, he had to know hers was merely a patrol craft on a regular route.*

"Who is this? What is your name, rank and gender?"

He sounded mad now, for some reason she couldn't imagine. And why would he ask her gender? That seemed odd in the extreme. But she'd play along. She'd be on her own out here for a long while – if he let her live after this encounter – and she was going to have a lot of time, alone with her thoughts, before her air ran out. Might as well talk to someone while she had the company, even if he was a damned Jit.

"Lieutenant Lisbet Duncan of Earth. And I'm female, not that it should matter to you. I'm a qualified pilot and graduated top of my class from pilot training."

While there had always been a lot more males drawn to military life than females, Lisbet wasn't too much of an oddity. Many women had the natural skills needed to fly shuttles and other spacecraft. She was unique in that she'd requested fighter duty. She liked shooting at things, and would've tried for a gunner position on one of the big battleships if she hadn't qualified as a pilot.

"Prepare for retrieval." The order was brusque, and the harsh voice sounded even angrier.

"Now just wait a damn minute!"

A moment later she saw two small craft launch from the battleship and head straight for her. *The bastards were going to pick up her pod. She was going to be a prisoner of war.*

Dammit!

Although . . . it was probably better than dying alone in the vastness of space. At least if they picked her up, she might have a chance to do some damage to them before she died. She didn't like the idea of being tortured, but she'd trained for it, like all the other pilots, and thought she was mostly prepared. She didn't know much anyway. She wasn't privy to any battle strategies or troop-deployment information. She only knew her current mission and those she'd been on previously. *Not much of value to the Jit'suku empire.*

Sure enough, the two craft flanked her and deployed sturdy microfilament netting that encompassed her pod. As soon as she was secure, they flew her back toward the cruiser.

The ship was even larger than she'd thought. It had the latest in Jit technology, from what she could see of its outboard arrays. This was no battered old warhorse. This ship was battle-ready and gleaming, though she could see a few spots where repairs had been made after engagements with human forces, no doubt.

The two patrol craft deposited her inside a gleaming hangar bay, bumping her only once as they set her down. The nets retracted and they parked on either side of her ship. She waited patiently inside her pod, gathering what little information she could. Her instruments told her the hangar bay was pressurized with a breathable atmosphere, and she saw big Jit'suku men working on various craft parked nearby without breathing gear.

The hangar bay had a giant force field at one end, keeping the air in. *Nice.* On human battleships, the hangar bays were kept at zero atmosphere. Pilots loaded into the canopies above and were dropped down and secured to the fuselages via a small chamber that was sealed and then evacuated of its precious air before opening to the hangar deck below.

The pilots who had caught her pod climbed out of their cockpits and moved closer to investigate. One made a sign for her to pop her lid and she shook her head, refusing. They went on like this for a few minutes, arguing via sign language through the window, until suddenly everyone on the flight deck jumped to attention.

At the far end of the long deck, Lisbet could see a giant of a man – even among the very large Jit'suku warriors – coming toward her at a fast pace. He looked absolutely furious. And handsome.

Damn. Why did she have to notice how handsome he was? She should be completely immune to men after what she'd been through. But this guy – this angry guy – flipped her switches in all the right ways.

He grabbed a piece of equipment as he went, nearly tearing it out of a tech's hands. It had to be magnetic because it clamped onto her canopy the moment he touched it to her hull. He held something on a wire up to his mouth, and suddenly his voice boomed through her internal speakers.

"Stop playing games and come out of there now, or I'll have you cut out."

Lisbet sighed. She'd have to open the hatch sooner or later.

She admitted, if only to herself, that she was scared. These Jit'suku were all massive, and everyone she had seen so far was male. She had no idea what they had in mind for her, but she wasn't looking forward to finding out. Still, she couldn't hide in here forever. *The time had come to take her punishment. Whatever that might entail.*

Releasing the hatch, the canopy popped with a hiss of equalizing air. Whirring gears indicated the hatch was rolling up and back the way it had been designed to do. As it cleared, she got her first really good look at the glowering man with the captain's insignia on his uniform.

Oh, boy. The captain himself *had come down to get her.* No wonder the crew had all jumped at his entrance. Lisbet wondered what she'd done to rate the captain's attention.

Pushing herself out of the seat, she stood within the canopy. She should have been taller than anyone on the deck from where she was, but she hadn't counted on these giant Jit'suku.

The captain's eyes met hers and time stood still for a breathless moment.

His eyes were dark. The dark of space with a hint of golden brown that made them somehow warm. His molten gaze would have been inviting in another setting. As it was, she could see the flare of gold in his eyes as his expression tightened.

He held out one impatient hand and she took it before she could think better of it. He assisted her in the big step over the canopy lip and down onto the deck of the cruiser. She was truly in enemy territory now. *Goddess help her.*

Two

Val couldn't believe what he was seeing as a small human female stepped out of the damaged cockpit. He'd almost killed her, and the guilt and anger ate at him. *What were these humans that they sent their women into battle?*

Barbarians. That's what they were.

Women were to be protected and revered. Not shot at and nearly killed in battle.

Val shuddered to think of the stain he'd almost incurred on his soul. Killing a woman in battle was considered one of the most terrible sins among Jit'suku warriors.

His men were as horrified as he was. This strange female had almost cost them all their honor.

"Have you nothing to say for yourself, woman?" Val demanded. He was so incensed that he wasn't thinking clearly. And he had yet to let go of the female's soft fingers.

As soon as he realized that, he dropped her fragile hand as if it burned him.

Her head cocked at an angle that he sensed meant trouble, though he'd seldom run afoul of a difficult female. Those few left in his family were all quite well behaved, and if they ruled the home with an iron fist, they also filled it with nurturing love. He'd been lucky with the matriarchs in his clan.

"As I told you before, I'm Lieutenant Lisbet Duncan of Earth. Beyond that, I have nothing to say."

Val felt his temper rise and knew he must not lose his cool any further in front of his men. He had things to say to this female that were best said in private. If he was going to blow a gasket, better that the whole flight deck didn't witness it.

Val grabbed the female's hand again and tugged her along with him – trying not to use too much force – as he exited the hangar. Mercifully, she followed without too much trouble. She probably had a hard time keeping up with his fast pace and longer steps, but he was in no mood to slow down, and she skipped along at his side reasonably well.

He didn't stop until they'd left the hangar far behind, passing a number of startled crew members on his way toward officer country. That was the colloquial name given to the area that housed the private quarters of the captain and his staff. There were also guest chambers that would serve his purpose, and it was toward one of those comparatively luxurious compartments that he made his way with the human female in tow.

"Could you slow down a bit? Or take shorter steps?" she finally complained as he dragged her along.

Val stopped in the wide, empty hall, dropped her hand and turned to assess her. He quickly realized she was breathing much too heavily, laboring to keep up. He'd dragged her at double-time the length of the ship. No wonder she was huffing and puffing. *Lady of Chaos!*

He'd caused her discomfort. First he had blown her ship out from under her, almost killing her in the process, then he had made her jog to keep up with him, causing her to nearly hyperventilate.

Val let her go and bowed his head, holding her gaze. "My apologies."

Some of his fury had cooled on the trek across the ship. Rather than anger, he was filled with dismay every time he looked into her pretty green eyes.

She was small and soft, though she acted tough. She had piloted her vessel well, from what he had observed as she had approached their hidden position, and she was an officer in the human armada that fought surprisingly well against Jit'suku expansion.

"You're the captain of this vessel, aren't you?" Her voice rolled pleasantly over his senses as she asked the question, rubbing her wrist where he'd manhandled her a bit.

Shame filled him when he saw the red marks his fingers had left on her pale skin. He'd tried to be careful of her fragility, but his anger had gotten the better of him.

"I am," he replied, then reached for her hand to examine the red marks on her wrist more closely. "Again, I apologize. It is not our way to harm females."

She looked at him oddly for a moment, and then pulled her hand back. He let her go with surprising reluctance. She had very soft skin now that he'd slowed enough to take notice. Smaller than most Jit'suku females, she was oddly fascinating. Her coloring was pleasing in the extreme and even her scent – female mixed with the oils and lubricants he associated with fighter craft – was wickedly attractive to him. He'd been a pilot when he was younger and even though he'd never smelled those scents coming from a female before, he found the mix strangely arousing.

"It's okay. My skin marks easily. It's nothing." She looked around the empty hall. "Where are you taking me?"

"To private quarters where you will remain as my guest until I can figure out what to do with you." He hadn't meant to reveal quite so much, but he could tell she was skeptical and probably scared behind her bravado.

"I expected torture and interrogation."

He grimaced, his anger returning slightly. "I do not harm females."

"You blew up my ship!" she countered, squaring off with him.

He was just in the mood to argue with her. Arguing wasn't prohibited, though it seldom occurred with Jit'suku females.

"I thought you were male! What kind of barbarians are your people that they send women into battle? Jit'suku women do not make war. They make—"

"If you say babies, I'm going to slug you!" she cut him off, her voice rising in intensity.

"They do that too, of course," he replied, confused by her apparent anger. "Our women are the lawmakers. The leaders of our clans. The power behind our businesses. They do not put themselves in harm's way by fighting on the front lines."

That seemed to set her back on her heels, and she looked truly confused. Adorable and confused. He really didn't understand why he found himself so attracted to this tiny female.

"Your women really have active roles in your society?" She blinked up at him as if unsure of the truth of his words.

"Of course." *What did she think of Jit'suku? That they were as barbaric and backward as her people?*

She looked away, peering absently down the corridor before returning her lovely green gaze to him. "I think the gender roles in our respective cultures must be very different. Among humans, anyone can join the military. While it's true that most women don't choose to serve, some of us do and some of us even seek out adventure on the front lines."

"You came here by choice?" Val couldn't credit her words. *Patrolling a dangerous border was the work of a warrior. It was too dangerous to risk a female on such tasks.*

"I had to apply three times before I got assigned a fighter patrol. The rim sweep isn't usually this exciting, but it is important." Her chin jutted out defensively and Val realized she took pride in her assignment to the dangerous post.

"Are you hungry?" he asked, hoping to change the subject. She'd given him a great deal to contemplate, but first he wanted to be certain she was comfortable. He'd treated her shabbily up to this point, and he wanted to make amends.

"I could eat," she replied cautiously.

"Then follow me." He walked more slowly this time, traversing the long hallway in the sector where all his staff were housed. He was looking for one portal in particular.

Raising his hand to the lock plate, he keyed in his command code, opening the door. He stepped back, allowing her to precede him.

She walked in with some hesitation and he wondered if she hadn't believed him about taking her to guest accommodations. Perhaps she still believed that he would throw her in the brig, or worse. She would soon learn that he was a man of his word. And he didn't harm females. Not on purpose.

Three

The room was spacious and fitted with high-quality furnishings. *The captain might just be telling the truth after all,* Lisbet thought, as she took in her surroundings. This didn't look like any kind of cell she could imagine and there didn't appear to be anything more sinister than a couch and some chairs placed along one wall.

"Guest quarters," he announced, moving into the room and making it seem a lot smaller all of a sudden.

Before today, she'd only seen images of Jit'suku warriors. They were all well over six feet tall and built on the brawny side. As big as the biggest human men, they towered over most civilians. But this captain was a good seven and a half feet to her five and three-quarters. And he definitely kept himself in shape. *The view she'd gotten of his muscular ass as he'd dragged her along behind him had been epic.*

If she'd been in any other position, she might have found herself drawn to the incredibly handsome warrior. As it was, she was his prisoner – though not, perhaps, in as bad a situation as she'd feared. She was certainly a captive, but the conditions didn't seem too horrible at the moment. She'd remain wary, but something about the way he'd spoken to her made her think he was as unfamiliar with real humans as she was with real Jit'suku.

All she knew was what she'd been told by her commanders and seen in the news media. She'd heard about the many battles along the rim, and knew the death statistics. The war, which had been going on for a long time, was taking a definite toll on both sides. Many men had died. Women too, of course, but the Jit'suku were very careful to only attack military targets, and the few female casualties she was aware of were women soldiers.

Based on what she'd just been told by the captain, she'd bet he hadn't known before seeing her that women served alongside men in the human armada. She wondered what he'd do when he thought through that scenario. He'd seemed truly upset to discover she was female.

"I will order food for you. It is almost dinner time. If you have no objection, I would like to share the meal with you, so that we may talk more."

"Interrogation?" She had to ask. It didn't sound like he really wanted to interrogate her – not in the way she understood the term – but he would be asking questions, she had no doubt.

"Nothing so drastic." His lips lifted at one corner in a hint of a smile that almost stopped her heart.

Damn, he was sexy when he wasn't quite so angry. He'd be devastating if he ever decided to turn on the charm.

"I wish to ask more questions of you, but I will not force you to answer. It becomes clear to me that I do not know enough about humans. I had no idea your women served as pilots. I'll have to rethink my strategy if I am to continue this mission with honor, now that I am aware of this fact."

That sounded promising. She thought over her options, coming to a quick decision.

"I'll answer what I can, but I won't betray my people. I don't really know enough to do any serious betraying anyway, so you might as well get that thought out of your mind right now." She took a fortifying breath, watching his handsome face carefully. "But I'll answer cultural questions if I think they're safe. I'd like to know more about your people too, while we're at it," she added.

"Then it is agreed." He moved toward the door. "The sanitation cubicle is beyond the light green portal, in a corner of the attached sleep chamber. I will leave you to refresh yourself for approximately one standard hour. I'll return when the meal is served." He paused by the door. "You will be locked in for your own safety. My crew is all male. I do not wish for you to interact with them at present."

She was okay with that, and merely nodded. Privacy in this luxurious suite was better than being in a cell, or being accosted by a bunch of giant men who hadn't seen a female in who knew how long. *And Captain Sexy would be back in an hour with dinner.*

Life had just gotten very interesting, very fast.

The captain returned with a team of men who brought in two floating trolleys loaded down with multiple domed platters. Both of the serving men gave her quizzical looks before departing with a crisp salute, but neither said a word.

Before leaving, the men had set the table and served the main course. The captain waited for her to be seated. So far, the dining rituals seemed very similar to human practices, which surprised Lisbet. She'd heard Jits were barbarians, and had almost expected them to be ripping meat from the bones of some large animal with their teeth.

Instead, she got gleaming, monogrammed silverware and what looked like costly china with the crest of some noble house. Her finger traced over the design on the rim of her plate.

"It is the sigil of my house. The Fedroval crest." He nodded toward her hand, still fingering the raised golden symbol as she looked up to meet his gaze.

"You said your name was Fedroval. As is the name of your ship. *Fedroval's Legacy,* right? So if this is anything like human nobility, you're some kind of overlord or come from a seriously rich family. Am I right?"

The captain bowed his head slightly, holding her gaze. "I am surprised humans have such things, but yes, to both questions. I am the Liege of House Fedroval, eldest male of the line. And yes, we as a family have more than most. Unfortunately, I am the end of the line for House Fedroval." His expression turned grim as he busied himself with the snowy white cloth napkin, placing it on his lap.

The topic seemed painful to him, so she let it drop. *For now.* She followed his lead, glad of the etiquette her mother had tried to drill into her when she was a girl.

Funny, she hadn't thought of her mother in years, but she supposed the old gal would have approved of this situation. For once, Lisbet was behaving like a lady, sitting down to dinner with a rich and titled gentleman. *Okay, so he was an alien.* Lisbet figured it probably didn't matter – her mother was long dead. Still, the thought brought a wistful smile to her face as he uncovered the steaming dishes that had been laid out for them.

The silence lengthened, but she didn't mind. There was a great deal of information to process here, and if she wasn't very careful, she might succumb to the captain's charms. He had said he wouldn't interrogate her, but she wouldn't put it past him to try to weasel out information while wining and dining her. She had to be on her guard.

"What amuses you, Lieutenant?" he asked as he poured blue liquid from a wine bottle into her crystal goblet. She watched as he poured another glass for himself. He took a sip before she followed suit.

The flavor was fruity and delicious – and intoxicating, she had no doubt.

"I had a stray thought about my mother. She always despaired of my tomboy ways. She taught me the proper way to set a table, and all the womanly things she thought important, but I always wanted to do stuff she thought wasn't seemly."

"Like flying a fighter craft?" One of his dark brows arched, and she got the impression he agreed with her long-lost mother.

"It was good enough for my older brother. Why should he be allowed to follow his dream into the sky and not me?"

"And did you truly dream of the sky, Lieutenant? Did the stars sing to you?" He stared at her over the rim of his goblet, seducing her with nothing more than the tone of his deep voice and the look in his dark eyes.

"Always. My mother despaired, but my granny knew my destiny was in the stars. She had a bit of the 'sight', and she argued on my behalf with the family. They listened to the old girl, thank goodness, and let me go. A month after I left Earth, my entire family was killed in an industrial explosion that leveled half the town."

He stilled, his expression growing very serious.

"I am sorry for your loss," he said in that deep voice, soft now with true emotion. She gazed into his eyes and met sorrow there. He understood. He'd lost people close to him, too. She knew the look. He'd felt the pain of losing those who made his life whole.

"Thank you." She dragged her gaze from his and took a sip of the fruity wine. It numbed her throat a bit and dulled the jagged edges of her pain momentarily.

"Our first course is roast waterfowl from Solaris Delta. I

believe all the ingredients used by the chef tonight are compatible with your system, but please alert me if you perceive any difficulties. I've been surprised by how much alike human and Jit'suku physiology is since I've begun my study of your species."

"Am I the first human you've met?"

"Yes," he answered with some surprise in his voice. "This ship was only completed a few standard months ago. We have only engaged with your folk from afar until today." He frowned as he cut into the succulent bird with his knife. She was lured in by the delicious aroma of the perfectly cooked meat. It tasted delicious, too. "It worries me that we might have inadvertently engaged with female pilots before now."

"Is it really that big a deal? I knew what I signed on for when I came out here. Every man and woman in the military knows they could die at any given time. We agreed to the danger when we volunteered to defend our galaxy against your empire's expansion plans."

She spoke matter-of-factly. She didn't see any reason to pussyfoot around the issue, but she also didn't see any point in getting all worked up. She was a prisoner here, for all that he was treating her like some kind of honored guest.

"Making war on women is not the Jit'suku way. Already the men under my command are speaking of what happened today, worrying that their honor has been stained by what we did to you. It is a very serious matter."

"Really?" Lisbet's eyes widened as she regarded him. *The man was serious. Wow.*

"I would not dissemble. The warrior's code is very specific and sacrosanct. We do not make war upon females, children, or each other. With so many in the warrior caste, we need these rules to keep peace among ourselves and our various colony worlds."

"Your people live in a caste system?" She was learning all kinds of things she'd never imagined about her enemy.

"Many males in each generation – usually more than seventy per cent – are born warriors. The rest are skilled craftsmen or artisans. Some have other talents that bring them to their proper caste. As is the case with our women. Is that not the way of human society?"

"The ratio is flipped. Only about thirty per cent of our men go into the military. Usually they're the biggest and strongest from each world or colony, but not always. Women who want a military career tend to end up in supporting roles – piloting shuttles, doing supply or other organizational roles, simply because we're smaller and usually can't fight hand-to-hand the way the men can. Mechanization equals things out, so women are equal with men when it comes to piloting, gunnery, et cetera. But a lot of women don't seem to go for those kinds of roles anyway. They put us where we are best suited and needed. In my case, that was patrolling the rim until you blew up my ship." A bit of her bitterness about losing her ship bled through into her words, but she couldn't regret it. He had to know she was upset about almost dying out there at his hands.

"If I had known you were female, I would never have fired upon you. Even if I had given the order, had my gunner known he was firing on a female pilot, he would have refused, and been within his rights to do so. He was very upset when we discovered your gender."

"I had no idea you guys were so touchy about women. If my commanders knew this, they'd probably recruit all the women they could to throw at you. I bet that would end the war real fast."

He frowned, his dark brows lowering as he considered her words. "Which is why I cannot let you go, Lieutenant." He sat back, ignoring his food while he studied her. "You present a very large problem for me, Lisbet Duncan, and I have no idea what to do about you."

"Who says you have to do anything? You could just let me go and jump back to your own system, where you belong."

"Retreat? That is not the Jit'suku way." His frown deepened.

"It's either retreat or fire on more women. Can your honor take that chance? I'm not the only female out here. I wasn't the first, and I certainly won't be the last." She challenged him, wanting to zing him a bit, even if her position was precarious at best.

He stared at her for a long time before shaking his head and returning to a more composed state. He lifted his fork and speared another bite of the meat, bringing it to his mouth. She watched him chew, realizing he had the sexiest mouth she'd ever seen on a man. Disconcerting and incongruous as that thought was, she felt her body warm as she watched him. *He really was incredibly attractive, even if he was the enemy.*

She took her cue from him and returned to her food as well. It was delicious, and she didn't want to waste a gourmet meal. Not when she'd been living on rations for far too long.

"You said something before about your granny having sight. What did you mean by that?" he asked out of the blue after the silence had stretched.

"My maternal grandmother sometimes had visions of the future. That side of the family descended from a place called Scotland on Earth. My mother was a redhead, which is where I get such fair skin from, even though my hair is darker. As I told you, my granny's visions convinced my family to let me fly. Little did I know when I left Earth that I'd never see any of them again."

"We hold such gifts of clairvoyance in great esteem," he said in a very serious tone. His dark gaze pinned her. "They say sometimes it runs in families."

She squirmed in her seat a bit, knowing what her grandmother had predicted for her. She wasn't sure she wanted to admit it, but perhaps her gran's predictions would help her with this compelling man somehow.

"Gran said . . ." She had to clear her throat before she revealed a secret she'd never told another soul. "Gran knew her gift would pass to my daughter. It would skip two generations, but be extra strong in my child. She said my girl would be an oracle the likes of which hadn't been seen in our family for hundreds of years."

"You have a child?" He seemed shocked.

"Not yet." Lisbet had to smile. "I've never known Gran to be wrong, but I wasn't sure I'd make it there for a while today. Somehow, though, according to my granny's prediction, I'm going to have a daughter who will be strongly gifted. She saw me having other children too, but she couldn't tell me more about them, only the girl who will carry her name."

"I find this fascinating. If we'd had a seer in my family, perhaps I could have avoided—" He stopped abruptly, as if realizing he was speaking aloud. The pain in his eyes made her reach out to him.

"What happened to your family, Captain?"

Four

"It is not fit dinner conversation." He tried to change the subject, but she was having none of it.

"I just told you something I've never told another soul. And I saw the understanding in your eyes when I told you how I'd lost my entire family. Something similar happened to you, didn't it?"

He regarded her for a long moment. "Are you sure you're not the gifted one in your family?" She noted the instant he let down his guard. His shoulders lost their tension and his expression changed.

"I am the end of the Fedroval line because no Jit'suku woman will have me. And rightly so. I was not meant to be liege of the House. I was a younger son, meant to serve in the Zenai priesthood. I was away from home when the unthinkable happened – my brothers were murdered by a rival, who has since paid for breaking the warrior's code. But the damage was done. I had to take over as liege and give up my intended path as a warrior priest. I had not been groomed for the position the way my older brothers were. I made mistakes. One was allowing all the younger females to go on a trip alone, without my protection. I failed to keep them safe, and they died. The wives and children of my dead brothers. The next generation of House Fedroval, gone in an instant."

"Were they murdered as well?" Lisbet kept her voice to a whisper, shocked at the awfulness of the story.

"It is still unclear. There was an investigation, of course, but the mechanical failure of their ship could have been accidental. There wasn't enough recovered to reach a conclusion of sabotage, though I strongly believe some of the rival family who escaped punishment for the deaths of my brothers came back to finish the job."

"Did you go after them?"

"I tried, but without evidence, I cannot make war on another of my kind. Being dishonorable myself will not negate their dishonorable behavior. No, this despicable act – whether accidental or on purpose – has well and truly ended a noble House."

"But surely you can marry and have children of your own to carry on the line?"

"Because I failed to protect my House adequately, no women

of quality or honor would be willing to submit to the nij'ta. If my true mate is out there, she will not allow me to find her."

"Wait a minute." Lisbet was confused. "What is a nij'ta?"

He looked surprised by her question as he moved the plates around, making room for a second set of dishes. He paused as he was lifting the dome off some sort of gel.

"The nij'ta is the ritual kiss. It is how we identify our perfect mate. Don't you have something similar?"

"You can find your life mate through a kiss?" Lisbet couldn't quite believe what he was saying, yet he seemed perfectly truthful.

"Of course. How do your males go about finding their perfect mate?"

"With a lot of trial and error," she admitted with a sigh. "We date." At his puzzled look, she went on. "We see each other socially, and the relationship progresses to more intimate levels if both parties are agreeable. After a time, the male can ask the female to marry him—"

"Marry?"

"It means to legalize the relationship – joining them in the eyes of the law, and of any religion either or both might follow."

"We call that 'mating'."

She nodded.

"And then they stay together forever." He stated it as fact rather than as a question, surprising her again.

"Not always. That would be the ideal, but a lot of times people grow apart, which is why they invented divorce."

"Divorce?" He looked even more puzzled, and pronounced the word carefully, as if it were totally unfamiliar to him.

"When two married people are legally divided – and no longer married," she explained.

"No longer mated?" He sounded scandalized. "There is no divorce among my kind. We mate for life."

"Really? No divorce? Never?" It didn't seem possible to her.

"The nij'ta does not lie. A man must kiss a lot of women before he finds the one that makes his blood sing. I will never have that opportunity now and it is one of my deepest regrets. I would have liked to have a wife and children."

"I really don't understand why you can't just ask a woman to marry you. Maybe she won't be of noble birth, but judging by this ship, you're loaded. There are a lot of women who would

marry you for your money, I'm sure. And you're not bad looking." She added the last bit out of sheer devilry. The man was
handsome as sin. If he weren't her enemy, she'd seriously think
about jumping his bones just to see if his lovemaking lived up to
the advertisement.

"That is not how things are done among my people. By my
prior negligence, I have proven to be careless with those I am
responsible for. No woman of reasonable station would have
me. I could father children on a mistress who might come to me
out of pity, or for the things I could buy for her, but those children could not carry on my line legally. And mating cannot
happen without the positive results of the nij'ta. I am in an
unwinnable situation, which is why I commissioned this ship
and set out on the warrior's path."

"So who's running things at home while you're here? I assume
your family still has interests that pay for all of this." She gestured
to the luxurious suite. She knew she was being nosey in the
extreme, but she was learning a lot about the aliens in general,
and this devastatingly handsome man in particular.

"The dowager. My mother. She heads the family. I am merely
the liege now that my brothers are gone. I thought I'd be a priest.
I'd given up the idea of a wife and children of my own, but now
I want them more than anything in the world, and they are
denied me. All I have left is my mission, and your presence has
brought that into question, too. The Lady of Chaos has touched
my world repeatedly, and altered my path in ways I could never
anticipate."

"I won't pretend to understand how your society works, but I
do feel for you, Captain. Losing your family is not an easy thing."
She made a move to cover his hand with hers, but checked it.
Maybe he didn't want her reaching out to him. They were
enemies, after all.

But he saw her slight motion and tilted his head, reaching out
to take her hand in his.

"We have both suffered a loss that nobody should ever have to
suffer. It changed the course of both our lives. I am amazed to
find I have so much in common with someone I thought of as
the enemy until now."

She liked the rich tone of his voice as it dipped to compassionate, almost intimate, levels.

"Me too, Captain," she agreed softly.

"You might as well call me Val," he replied in that same intimate tone.

"I'm Lisbet, but my friends call me Liz."

He reached out with his spoon, not letting go of her hand, and scooped up a small bite of the gel substance in the dish before her. He held the spoon up to her lips and smiled encouragingly. His dark gaze smoldered as she parted her lips and allowed him to feed her the small dollop.

Flavor burst around her mouth in a display of bright notes that made her lips tingle. She swallowed, enjoying the cool sensation of the sweet confection as it slid down her throat.

"That's delicious," she admitted with a grin.

"I thought you'd like it." His answering smile lit a fire in her belly that had nothing to do with dessert – or at least not the edible kind. *She'd like to make a dessert of him. She'd lick him like an ice-cream cone.*

The look in his eyes seemed like he might be agreeable to that. Before she knew what she was doing, Lisbet leaned toward him. *Was he leaning in toward her too?*

His eyes grew closer until the dark gold of his gaze was all she could see. Then his lips touched hers and time stood still.

Breathing became optional as his mouth covered hers. His arms wrapped around her shoulders and dragged her out of her chair and into his lap. By slow degrees, he deepened the kiss.

His tongue bathed her mouth in his taste, his mastery. Her body squirmed against his, not trying to get away, but wanting to be closer. Her clothes were in the way. As were his.

She wanted nothing more than to feel his skin on hers, his hard muscled body against her softer skin, his hardness mastering her responses.

But it was not meant to be.

An urgent noise from the comm panel broke them apart. Her senses were fuzzy with desire and, for a moment, she didn't know exactly where she was. In those stolen moments, Val had ceased to be the captain or her enemy. He was simply a man.

An entirely too attractive – some might say devastating – man.

Val stood, straightening his jacket as if he were uncomfortable, and went to the door. He left as if all the hounds of hell were on his heels.

Five

The captain disappeared and did not return that night. Nor did she see him all the next day. Her meals were served in silence and taken away just as quietly by a warrior who looked at her with curiosity but made no overtures toward her whatsoever. Neither friendly nor hostile, he merely brought the trays and took them away at regular intervals.

The food continued to be of gourmet quality, which surprised her. She'd understood being served the good stuff when she ate with the captain, but on her own, she expected rations. Instead, she continued to be treated as some kind of weird mix between prisoner and honored guest. She was locked in her quarters, but she had some limited access to the computer for entertainment and learning. No communications to speak of, but she was able to occupy her time discovering more about the Jit'suku culture.

Of particular interest was the concept of the nij'ta. It seemed so foreign to her, but the Jit'suku actually mated based on a single kiss. Some of the romantic fiction she'd been able to access from the computer was built around the idea of a mating based on a single kiss – even if the kiss was considered totally inappropriate socially, it had to be accepted by the respective families because true mates could not legally be kept apart. A Jit version of *Romeo and Juliet* – with a much happier ending, because nobody could deny a true mating in Jit'suku society.

It was kind of amazing. Humans really had no clue about these strange, oddly noble people.

Nor did the Jit'suku seem to have any real understanding about humanity.

So many misconceptions on both sides. It saddened her to think that countless numbers had died based on incomplete or misunderstood information. One thing was clear, though – the Jit'suku were a race of conquerors who had expanded to the farthest reaches of their own galaxy and beyond. Even had they fully understood humanity, chances are the war would still have been waged because they needed more room for their growing population, and the Milky Way was the next logical place for them to go. Humans didn't like being invaded, and Jits didn't respect those who operated on diplomacy alone.

It was an inevitable conflict. She didn't have to like it.

Her thoughts kept turning back to the sexy captain and that devastating kiss. *Had he been as affected as her? Was he thinking of her while he ran the ship and did who knew what?* She'd only spent a few hours in his company, but already she missed him.

She almost . . . pined for him. Such an odd concept for a woman who'd thought she would live the rest of her life alone. She wanted to be with him, and she didn't care that he was an alien or part of the enemy army. Lust – *or could it actually be love, so quickly?* – didn't care about such things.

All she knew was that she missed him and wanted to be with him. After only a single kiss it was like she'd become addicted to his presence, his touch, his taste.

On the third day of her confinement, the captain sent a message with her silent server, along with some clothing for her. She'd been able to freshen her flight suit using the sanitary chamber's cleansing unit, but she was getting a little tired of only having one set of clothes.

The outfit he sent her was confusing at first, until she realized it was female attire in the Jit'suku style she'd seen in images on the computer. She wondered where it had come from. Had some warrior on this ship been tasked with making women's clothes in her size? One thing was certain – she would never have fit in any spare Jit'suku uniforms.

All in all, she was glad of the new clothes that didn't make her look like a child playing dress up, even if the style was different from what she was used to. There were wide-legged pants in very soft fabric, covered by a tunic of sorts, and a jacket that tied at each hip, layered over with a wide sash. There weren't any shoes to go with it, so she continued to wear her boots. It looked a bit strange, but she couldn't very well go barefoot, and the long legs of the pants covered the tops of her boots, so just her feet showed.

Not too bad, she thought, twirling in front of the mirror in the bedchamber. She looked better than she had in a long time. The soft fabric emphasized her figure and the curves her flight uniform had hidden. She didn't look like an androgynous pilot anymore. No, now she was definitely revealed as a woman, with all the usual curves and bumps.

She looked forward to seeing what the captain thought of her new look. She knew it was wrong, but she couldn't help herself. She hadn't been so impressed with a man since her first boyfriend back in high school. She felt as giddy as the teenager she had once been, though she knew she shouldn't.

The man was an alien. An enemy. She'd been blasted out of her fighter on his order.

He was still the captain of an enemy craft engaged in the conquest of the Milky Way. She was sworn to prevent this conquest. The conflict made her heart hurt.

Somehow, this strange man had wormed his way into her thoughts, though he hadn't made any overt attempt to do so. *One kiss and she was hooked. Addicted to him.* She knew she was doing this to herself. Her fascination with the man was not normal. She'd tried repeatedly to stop thinking about him, but it was no use. Her heart seemed to be fixated.

The note that accompanied the clothing asked her to be ready after lunch. It was worded politely, handwritten in a bold cursive that she had to believe was the captain's own handwriting. Val. *He'd told her to call him Val. She'd thought a lot about that in the past three days. His family name was Fedroval, so maybe Val was a nickname for that? Or could his given name be something that shortened to Val? She'd have to ask him, if she got the chance.*

She wanted to know every little intimate detail about him. She had it bad. She was downright obsessed. *Any minute now she'd be drawing little hearts and doodling their names inside.*

Disgusted with herself, she checked her appearance one more time. It was about as good as it was going to get.

Promptly after lunch, a chime sounded near the door, alerting her, as it had for the past three days, that someone had come to take the empty tray. She looked toward the door, but when it slid open, the silent guard was nowhere to be seen. Instead, Val filled the doorway, his gaze holding hers as he walked into the room.

He stalked toward her, speaking not a word. His eyes took in her new outfit with obvious approval before returning to her face. He walked across the room and took her in his arms.

There was no hesitation in his movement. No question but that he had a right to embrace her. His head dipped and his lips claimed hers. She didn't protest. She wanted his kiss as much as he appeared to want hers. She'd thirsted for him for days, waiting for this. This moment, when he would kiss her again. Hold her as if he would never let her go. Make the two of them complete . . . together.

The foreign thoughts raced through her mind. *She'd never thought such things about a man before. She hadn't known she had such a romantic imagination. Maybe this alien was bringing things out of her that had remained hidden with the other men she'd known. And maybe her fascination with him wasn't all one-sided. Judging by the hard feel of him against her, it most definitely was not.*

Val reveled in the kiss of his true mate, glad to know the positive response to his nij'ta he had perceived three days ago had not been a desperate attempt at self-delusion. No. This was the real thing. This surprising human woman was his true mate.

Now he only had to convince her of that fact.

He'd spent the last three days pulling every string he knew how to pull. He'd contacted the High Priest of the Zenai Brotherhood. If anyone would know the legality and sanctity of mating outside his species, it would be the High Priest. What he had learned had given Val the first hope he'd had in years.

Reluctantly, he broke the kiss, knowing the time had come to speak his heart to the woman of his dreams. Would she be as receptive to mating with him as she was to his kiss? The High Priest had reminded him that the Goddess worked in mysterious ways.

Her faint protest as he pulled away from her luscious lips renewed his hope.

"There are matters we must discuss," he whispered against her lips, finding it hard to let her go completely.

It was she who moved back, going to the couch and dropping onto it with her arms folded. She'd gone from receptive to combative in a flash and Val admitted to himself that he was worried.

"What did I say to make you wary?" He moved over to the couch and seated himself sideways, facing her.

"When someone says 'we need to talk' it usually means trouble." She turned to him and he perceived hurt in the depths of her eyes. Hurt he had put there. Val couldn't help but reach out and take her into his arms, holding her against him as he spoke. He couldn't bear to see her pain.

"You're not in trouble. I might be, but you're not, sweet one." He kissed the crown of her head, loving the feel of her in his embrace. "I have kept away until I was certain we could be together."

She drew back, surprise replacing the hurt in her expression. "What?"

"I realize you are not used to our ways, but you had to feel the magic in our first kiss. It was the nij'ta. Though I didn't mean to kiss you, I couldn't help myself. Your kiss proved we were meant to be."

"Is that what that was?" Her words were soft, as if she were unsure.

"I'm not sure if it's the same for humans as it is for us, but I knew the instant I kissed you that you were meant to be mine. You're my perfect mate, Lisbet Duncan of Earth. Crazy as that may seem." He knew he was smiling, but he still couldn't quite believe it himself. "I'd given up ever finding my mate, the one woman destined to share my life. I sank my efforts into building this ship and dedicated myself to my people's cause of conquest. Without a wife or a future, I had no other recourse. But now that I've found you, everything's changed."

"Just like that?" She sounded as incredulous as he still felt.

"Just like that," he agreed, dipping in to place a quick kiss on her lips. Sparks seemed to fly whenever they touched, and he reveled in the response only she could evoke in him. "We're out of the Milky Way and on our way back to my home system, Solaris Delta. It is my right and duty as Liege of House Fedroval to quit the battle now that I have found my perfect mate."

"Wait a minute. You're taking me *home*? To your home? Don't I have any say in this?"

Her anger set him back. He moved away, facing her as they sat on the couch. "Do you wish to part from me? Do you believe you can . . . what is that human word . . . *divorce* me so easily?"

"We're not married," she said, causing pain to lance through his heart.

"In the eyes of my people, you are already mine, Lisbet. I would have you come willingly, but if necessary, I will give you little freedom and no opportunity to desert me."

"I'm your prisoner?" Her beautiful green eyes went wide with dismay.

"Only if you want to be. I'd rather have you as my bride. My loving wife. The mother of my children, if we are so blessed."

She sat back, air puffing out of her as if in shock. "This is a lot to take in."

"Don't you want to be with me?" He knew he sounded desperate, but he couldn't help the way he was feeling. He had to do everything in his power to convince her.

She looked at him and he saw the uncertainty in her eyes. "This has all happened so fast."

He tried a different tack. "Do you believe in a power higher than our own? I believe most humans call it God."

"I believe God is female." Her brows knitted, as she tried to follow his jump in conversation, no doubt.

"You do?" He grinned again. This was a good sign. One might even say a sign from the divine. "Jit'suku believe in the Goddess. It was she who allowed us to find our destined mates by means of the nij'ta. It was she who guided me to you, I now believe. I have conferred with the High Priest of the Zenai Brotherhood, an order dedicated to her service, and I've learned there is some precedent for human women being the true mates of Jit'suku warriors. Now that our races have come into contact with each other, ours is not the first such pairing, though it is the highest ranking. Still, those who came before us will ease our way."

"Other human women have been taken to the Jit'suku galaxy as brides?"

"Yes, and I will invite those who have had trouble with their mate's clans to join ours. Such things have been done in the past, and since House Fedroval has suffered such great losses in the recent past, we are well able to support a few more families under our banner. It would also allow you to have friends from your home galaxy nearby."

"Is that why you're doing this? Are you that hard up for a wife that you'll take any foreigner who happens along? I remember what you told me about being the last of your line. You said no proper Jit'suku woman would have you. Is that why you picked me?" She looked angry, and he had to make her understand.

"No, my love. If you were Jit'suku you would know, one cannot fake the nij'ta. I never expected to find a mate. I'd given up. And then there you were. Now I begin to understand why the Goddess led me on such a difficult path. She was leading me to you, Lisbet. Only to you. Always to you."

"I must be crazy," she muttered as if to herself, but he heard her. She faced him squarely and spoke in a clear voice. "I can't get you out of my mind, Val. I don't know what you've done to me, but I'm crazy about you and if you think we can make a go of this, I'll agree to be your wife."

"Thank the Goddess!" he whispered as he dragged her into his arms for their first kiss as declared mates.

A kiss that would have led to so much more if he hadn't had an interplanetary call standing by. He drew back and stood, holding out one hand to help her up. She accepted him eagerly, and he was amazed again by the blessing the Goddess had bestowed, finding him a mate when he'd thought all was lost.

"We have a few formalities to take care of before we can celebrate in true mate style."

He led her out of her quarters and to the bridge, where they would stand together in front of the comm station. Their images and words would be broadcast to all within the ship, a special few on Solaris Prime, and everyone on Solaris Delta. There would be many witnesses as the Liege of House Fedroval – King of Solaris Delta – officially introduced his queen.

Space Cowboy

Donna Kauffman

One

Dani Beckett didn't believe in aliens or UFOs. Sure, she'd cried when she'd watched *E.T.: The Extra-Terrestrial*, and she'd have taken the little guy home, too. But she'd been eight years old when she'd first seen that movie. It had been the feature flick at Lake Machapunga summer camp. She remembered lying in her bunk that night, clutching Beemer, the stuffed elephant she'd hidden under her pillow so the other campers wouldn't think she was a baby, going over in her mind exactly how she might have hidden E.T. from Aunt Teddy and Uncle Deacon while nursing him back to health.

Of course, given the three of them lived together on a hundred-acre dairy farm back then, how hard could it have been to sneak in one undersized alien dude? But the idea that she'd be the perfect care-taker, should some other poor, celestial creature lose his way and end up on her planet, had captivated her fertile little mind, and she'd spent the rest of the summer keeping a close eye on the woods around the camp. Just in case.

Twenty-three years later, she still had a fertile imagination, but, being a decidedly practical businesswoman and shop owner these days, not to mention a grown adult, she channeled any and all whimsical thoughts into the unique floral designs she created. Unlike the impressionable eight-year-old dreamer she'd once been, adult Dani knew quite well that life only handed out the fantastical to those who went out and created it for themselves.

So, when she watched – wide-eyed and slack-jawed – as a half-naked man slowly took form, particle-by-incredibly-delec-table-and-not-remotely-alien-looking-particle, right smack in the middle of her little coastal Carolina florist shop, there was only one explanation, really. Brain tumor. Possibly a stroke. Probably both.

The instant the man finished materializing, he quickly scanned his surroundings, then swore something unintelligible under his breath. If she hadn't been frozen to the spot in shock, she'd have considered ducking as his gaze swung her way. Or screaming. As it was, she just stood there, staring. *Okay, okay, ogling.* But he looked like a Greek statue, come to life. Besides, it was her stroke, after all, and the least she could do was enjoy it before her brain went completely to mush.

If he'd noticed her, he hadn't so much as blinked in aware-ness, but before she could figure out whether she'd be dialing 911 to demand they send a SWAT team to capture an alien intruder . . . or an ambulance to transport her to the nearest hospital for a full neurological workup, he shifted his gaze directly to hers and demanded, "What year is this?"

"What – *year*?" she repeated, though it came out as more of a squeak.

He strode directly to the work table she was standing behind, his expression so . . . intense, it made her instinctively swing her hands up in front of her in defense, and back up until she banged hard into the shelving racks behind her. Vases and assorted stacked pots and trays wobbled, some crashed to the floor. She ducked, hoping to keep anything hard and heavy from conking her on the head. Which made little sense if the stroke was going to render her permanently senseless, anyway, but instincts were instincts.

The fight or flee impulse was also kicking in, swaying heavily toward the flee side, but before she could put thought to action, in a move so fast it was more blur than clear motion, he leapt over the table in a single, Superman-like bound, knocked her hand to the side and pinned her wrist to the shelf rack.

"What the hell," he growled, flinging her hand away as he inspected the thick, clear ooze now dripping from the base of his palm. "What is this substance you tried to shoot me with? Is it toxic? Tell me!" he commanded, pushing his face close to hers.

Her eyes were likely as big as saucers. His, on the other hand, were the most amazing mix of blue and green. "I – I didn't shoot you with anything."

He pinned her to the shelving unit with his body, held his goo-covered hand to the side of her head. "Tell me," he said again, the threat clear. Tell him or get slimed with the supposedly deadly toxic material.

"Glue gun," she managed, her throat dry from the sudden threat, and breathless because, well, because she had a big, mostly naked guy pressed up against her very defenseless body. "I – I forgot I had it in my hand. Not dangerous. Just . . . hot. And sticky."

Dear Lord, she knew all about hot at that moment. And sticky, come to think of it.

His hair was dark, almost black, and clung damply to a fore-head and neck flecked with some kind of dirt or grime. He was deeply tanned, which made his bared teeth flash even whiter. Those eerie, laser-like, teal-colored eyes topped features that looked like they'd been chiseled from granite, including a rather hard-looking mouth and jutting chin.

He was a good half a foot taller than her taller-than-average self, with shoulders the size and width of your average Mack truck, and a chest and set of abs that looked like he modeled as a Greek god in his spare time. He was wearing dirty black cargo-like pants, sporting tears at the knees and thighs that she doubted were a design esthetic, tucked into equally worn, calf-high laced-up military-looking black leather boots. The loose fit of the pants did next to nothing to hide a powerful looking set of thighs that any NFL coach would've paid top dollar for on sight. And many women might pay a whole lot of individual dollars for, should he decide to become a stripper at any point in the near future.

"Get it off," he demanded.

She gulped. Getting off was probably the very last thing she should be thinking about at the moment, given she was either about to be killed, or go into a permanent vegetative state when her obviously rapidly swelling brain tumor imploded. She squirmed, or tried to. "You're . . . crushing my dahlia hybrids."

Really, Dani? A guy beams into your shop, like a character straight out of a Spielberg movie, assaults you, appears to be quite ready, willing, and able to finish what he's already started . . . and the best you can do is whine about your smashed-up floral arrangement?

Maybe it was just as well that E.T. had found cute little Drew Barrymore instead of her, after all.

"No time," he muttered, apparently changing his mind about . . . whatever he'd been talking about.

Dani wasn't following, mostly because she was still thinking about what it would take to get this guy off. As for getting her off, well, sadly, that didn't require any thought at all. It had been long – far too long, clearly – since a man of any size and shape had pressed himself so intimately on top of her. One year, four months, two weeks, and a couple of days, to be exact. Not that she was counting. The date just happened to stick in her mind for other, more demoralizing, cheating-rat-bastard reasons.

So, it seemed a shame, really, bordering on unfair, that when the opportunity for body-to-body contact finally happened for her again, the guy was some kind of raging psychopath, possibly recently beamed down from another planet, and more interested in the glue gunk on his hand than her womanly form, trapped beneath him.

For God's sake, get a grip! "Right, right," she muttered to herself, trying to focus on the situation at hand without going into a full-blown panic. In her defense, though, who wouldn't, really? Well, besides Drew Barrymore? Hence the thinking about hot, sticky sex, instead of . . . whatever the hell was actually happening to her, neurologically or otherwise. And, she had to admit, the guy presently molding his body to hers seemed like a pretty realistic "otherwise" to her.

Take charge, Dani! This is your shop, your business, the livelihood you worked so hard for. The one thing you have left, dammit. He can't just . . . just . . . beam down and have his way with you.

Okay, well, clearly he could. But still. "Who are you?" she demanded, hoping he didn't notice how shaky her voice was. "And . . . and how did you get here?" She wasn't sure if she really wanted the answer to either of those questions, but she had to face facts at some point. Either he'd give her a perfectly plausible, scientific explanation about how he'd magically appeared in front of her, and she'd have to deal with the fact that this was really happening and E.T. had finally shown up, after all, only older, taller, and a hell of a lot hotter . . . or he'd tell her he was Han Solo, beamed down from the *Millennium Falcon* after escaping Darth and his buddies, and she'd have to deal with the fact that her mind had, in fact, cracked. *Not in your right mind, you must be.*

She held her breath, trying to decide which response would be the better reality of the two, but he wasn't listening to her at all. He scraped his hand hard along the sharp edge of a shelf, removing most of the rapidly solidifying glue chunk, then gripped her wrist in his wide palm and tugged her along with him as he headed toward the back of the shop. "You have transport?"

"I – have a car," she said, answering before she thought better of it. *Sure, just tell him you have a car, so he can abduct you and car-jack you. Dear God, she was handling this exactly like an idiot actress in a bad D-list sci-fi flick. She'd never pictured herself as that girl. She'd always wanted to slap that girl.*

He pushed through the swinging door that led to the rear storage area, pulling her along behind him, and she finally snapped out of her shocked stupor and dug in her heels. "Wait!" she shouted. "Just—" She flung out her free hand and grabbed on to the handle of the wall-sized refrigerated unit she stored her flowers in, and held on tight. She almost got her shoulder wrenched from its socket for her troubles, but when he did snap around, she said, "Hold on a minute!"

"No time!"

"Then you're going to have to make some, because I'm not going anywhere with you until you tell me what the hell is going on." *Yeah*, she cheered herself, *that's more like it!*

He turned on her and, with one simple maneuver, shifted himself in a way that forced her to release her hold on the handle and land in front of him, where he could now pretty much shovel her toward the door. "No time means no time," he panted in a near snarl, next to her ear.

She gulped, because he sounded a lot more lethal – which she, frankly, hadn't thought possible – and, oddly, she realized . . . Australian. Had he had an accent before? Or was this just a sign that her brain synapses were in their final zenith and her hallucination was shifting accordingly?

For a hallucination, his grip on her sure felt real enough. As did the rest of him, hot, hard, and supremely male, pressing up behind her as they stumbled forward toward the door that led to the rear lot behind the shop. "Wait, I need my—"

"Stop talking." He pushed them both through the door, then kicked it shut behind him. "Where is your transport?"

It was after shop hours, and the sun had set some time ago. For late October, it was still pretty warm on the southeastern coast, but she shivered nonetheless. The small security light didn't do much to illuminate the area, but the full moon bathed the narrow alley behind her shop in a bluish glow . . . making the whole situation feel that much more surreal. "Right there," she said, inclining her head toward her green Jeep Cherokee, since he held her hands, crossed at the wrist, behind her back. "But, I was trying to tell you – my purse is in the shop."

"Purse?" He dismissed that as unimportant. "Uncloak this transport you speak of, and do it now."

She tried to swivel her head so she could look back at him. "It's right there," she said. "But we're not going anywhere in it without the keys."

"Keys?" His scowl deepened.

"Yes," she said, with exaggerated patience – which was a marvel really, considering she had the pulse rate of your average jackrabbit at the moment. "The ones you just locked inside the shop with your *Rambo* door-slam move."

He followed her gaze toward her Jeep, then spun her around so she faced him. Literally almost nose to nose. Well, nose to chin. He took care of that by tipping her face up to his, his hold on her chin just the wrong side of civil. "I have no idea what game you think you're playing, but this is no time to test me. Now, reveal your transport to me." He pulled her clenched hands up between them with his free hand, which easily circled both of her wrists. The sudden move had the very special consequence of jerking her hips up flush to his. *And . . . oh my. Why, he was no Greek god after all. Because every statue she'd ever seen of those guys? Yeah, not all that well-endowed. This guy? Exceedingly different in that department.*

He tipped her chin up further and leaned down until she swore she could see so deeply into his eyes, she—

"Give me the sequence start-up code, sweetheart, and I'll fly. I've no choice but to take it. But, look at it this way. Losing your transport isn't worth losing your life for."

Definitely Australian. She'd heard that Aussies were a bit on the wild side, but this guy was taking that reputation to extremes. "The only transport I have," she said, through gritted teeth, "is that Jeep behind you. It rolls on the ground. On four wheels. It doesn't fly. I don't own anything that flies. Or uses a start-up sequence for that matter. If you're looking for a spaceship-type thingie, I think you landed in the wrong century, cowboy."

"Thingie?" He loosened his hold on her chin.

"You know. Ah . . . hovercraft. Podracer. Whatever." She worked her jaw. "Can you tell me what's going on?" Maybe he was some kind of mental patient, on the loose. Or hopped up on drugs, though his eyes seemed pretty crystal clear to her. Besides, neither of those options would explain how he'd done that whole "beam me down" thing back inside her shop.

Once again, he wasn't listening to her. He was scanning the narrow gravel and sand alley that ran behind her shop. On the other side was a strip of overgrown weeds, then a drainage ditch. *Yeah, don't look at the drainage ditch. Good place to store dead bodies.* Namely hers, since she'd just made herself dispensable to him. "Um, maybe – we could get a helicopter. Would that work?" She knew there was a tourist business that operated down near the waterfront, where a person could pay for a coastal air tour. Of course, they were probably closed now, but he didn't have to know that. If she could get the two of them out of this alley, maybe she could figure out a way to get free of him. And check herself into the nearest mental facility.

"At least tell me your name," she said. "I'm Dani." *That's right,* she thought, *make friends with your captor, get him to think of you as a real person and not a disposable nuisance.* Besides, since her stroke was taking its sweet time in killing her off, she had no choice, really, but to go with her present reality as if it were, in fact, reality.

She looked back up at him, and was surprised to see that instead of looking all ferocious and serial-killer-like, his expression had changed to one of deliberation. And, if she wasn't mistaken . . . fear. Or, at the very least, serious concern. Something about that sudden hint of vulnerability, of . . . humanness, gave her back a bit of much-needed moxie.

"If you'll just tell me what's going on, then I'll do what I can do help you," she told him, not necessarily meaning it, but she had to get him – them – out of the alley. "At least tell me your name."

"Jack," he said, but he said it dismissively, probably just to shut her up. She wasn't even sure if it was his real name, but at least it was better than "Yo, cowboy." And, she had to admit, a part of her was relieved it was something normal, and . . . human, and didn't sound all otherworldly, like it had double consonants and apostrophes in weird places.

"Okay, Jack. If you tell me where you need to go, maybe I can help you."

He continued to scan the alley, then the sky, then the alley again. She didn't think he'd even heard her, until she felt a slight lessening of the tension in his grip on her wrists. "You can't get me where I need to go." He squinted at the sky. "How did it put me here?" he muttered.

Dani slowly slid her gaze skyward, almost afraid of what she'd find. *A huge hovering spaceship? Three moons and a big blue sun? Something to indicate she was still having her hallucination?* She almost wished something would.

Because the dawning reality that he might be exactly what he appeared to be wasn't nearly as exciting as she'd have found it twenty-three years ago. No matter how much she'd grown up. Or how hot her extraterrestrial space cowboy was.

Two

Jack looked at the woman. Dani. "This is, what, early twenty-first century?" When she frowned and nodded, he looked back to the sky. He couldn't figure out how it had gotten messed up. He'd made the trip dozens of times. More, even. Time fissures worked how they worked, and all the readings indicated that the one he'd traveled through was still quite stable. Not only did it appear as if he'd missed his target by a couple hundred years, but given her accent and the position of the stars, it appeared he was also off by a continent. Or two.

He'd never gone this far back. Not only that, he had no idea where the fissures were in this part of the world, much less where this one looped back out again, or how long it would take to loop in. More importantly, literally no one on Earth would know where the fissures were, either. It would be a good hundred years or more, from this point in time, before mankind figured out how the time-space continuum could be manipulated for travel, and many more years still before they made successful, practical use of the knowledge.

"How did *what* put you here?" she asked. "Why don't you just explain your situation, from the beginning?"

He let out a humorless laugh and looked away. "Sweetheart, you wouldn't believe me if I told you."

She took this opportunity to slide her wrists free. But, rather than run, like any smart-minded soul would do, she merely crossed her arms and gave him a good once-over. "Sweetheart," she said, in a pretty good imitation of his accent, only tinged with that butter-melting-on-biscuits accent of her own, "I just watched you materialize out of thin air in front of me. I'm thinking there's not much you could say that would surprise me."

Right. Another reason they never traveled back to any date prior to 2297, the year cellular particulant transport had finally been approved for safe use. No point in freaking out the natives. Especially when that wasn't necessary. Bodysnatchers didn't have to risk traveling this far back to do their dirty work.

"Be careful what you ask for," he told her, in lieu of a direct response. Particulant transport was the least that he could surprise her with.

"Why are you in such a hurry? And you look kind of . . . beat up. Did something happen to you?"

She sounded a lot calmer, which was, he supposed, a blessing. Hysterics weren't going to help anyone. But her eyes still held that heightened wariness. Which was smart – very smart – on her part. "I didn't have time to clean up from the last job before diving – literally – into this one."

"And your last job was . . . ?"

He was still trying to figure out how an established fissure with solid stability readings had gone so far off, and answered her without thinking. "New Guinea. 2379. Native girls are a hot commodity. None left in my time."

"Your . . . time," she repeated, and, in his peripheral vision, he noticed she took a step backward.

He looked at her fully, then lunged to catch her wrist when it looked like she was going to take off running. Not that he needed the extra baggage at the moment, but he definitely didn't need any loose ends running about, telling people about time travelers, et cetera. Not that anyone would likely believe it. "Hold on there," he told her. "Listen, you asked, right?"

She nodded, and held his gaze, but he felt the tremors running through her.

"No running. It's not safe."

"What's not safe about it, exactly? Because you don't look all that safe to me at the moment."

"Sweetheart, I'm the best bet you have going right now."

To his vast surprise, and grudging delight, she barked a laugh. "Well, then, let's hope this actually *is* a brain tumor, because otherwise, I really am screwed."

"Brain tumor?"

"What would you think if you saw someone materialize in front of you? Never mind. You apparently actually *do* see that." Her smile faded and she tried to tug her wrist free.

"Just . . . hold on, would you?" He relaxed his grip, but kept hold of her all the same. He tried to smooth some of the tension from his voice, but it was a challenge, given all the things that were horribly wrong with the situation he'd landed in. Not the least of which was whether or not the guy he'd been chasing had also ended up here. Stoecker was a nasty piece of work. And, against that particular threat, the woman in front of him wouldn't stand a chance. She might not be the exotic tribal type Stoecker was usually after, but she had the height of an Amazonian warrior and just the right kind of attitude to make her irresistible to his sort.

"That must be it," he muttered, realizing why Stoecker might have broken protocol and gone back farther in time than was legally mandated – as if the law meant anything to a man who made a living snatching women and selling them into slavery. "That must be it!"

"Must be what?"

"Stoecker's after a new, even rarer commodity. Someone must have paid a pretty penny for him to take this kind of risk, but – how did he do it?"

"Pretty penny for what? Who's Stoecker?" She tugged at his hand again, bringing his attention back to her. "Are you in danger? Is . . . someone following you?"

He looked at her, really looked at her now. In addition to being significantly tall for her gender, her other striking feature was her hair. It was long, well past her shoulders, and fell in dark

waves and curls. It was the kind of hair that encouraged a man
to sink his fingers into it. And those dark curls framed an attractive face, now that he was paying attention, with well-defined
cheekbones, and a strong chin. *Stubborn*, he thought now, given
her brief display inside the shop and out here in the alley. Her
eyes were hazel, nothing exotic, except for the intently direct
way they held his own. He wasn't used to that.

Given what he did for a living, the people he ran across usually
worked hard to avoid making any kind of eye contact with him.
He supposed a woman of her height wasn't used to feeling
threatened or intimidated in any way. *Well*, he thought darkly, *if
he didn't do something, and fast, that was about to change.*

"No one is following me," he said. "I'm doing the following."

"Who's Stoecker?"

Jack swore under his breath. If what he suspected was true,
Dani here would be the perfect target for one of the best bodysnatchers in the business. She was just different enough to get
attention at the black-market auctions, and the key part was that
she was from an era in history no one remembered anything
about. She'd be well and truly out of her element, without even
a rudimentary understanding of how she could escape back to
her time. The perfect slave. Tall, dominant in appearance, with
all that hair, that stubborn chin . . . and yet completely at the
mercy of her new owner. "Let's pray like hell you don't have to
find out."

He pulled her toward the door. "We need to get back inside." He
still didn't know for sure if the fissure had simply flung him through
to a more distant time and place, or if Stoecker had figured out a
way to manipulate the fissures already documented and cleared for
use. This didn't happen often, if ever. He'd been hunting Stoecker
too long, and he was the best there was. He'd know.

"You locked us out," she reminded him, as he tried the door
handle.

Of course, if the continuum had somehow been manipulated
to send him so much farther back than it should have, who was
to say it hadn't warped over such a long distance? Maybe
Stoecker was no longer in front of him. They hadn't been that
far apart. Jack turned back to Dani. "How long had you been
inside the building?"

"You mean my shop? I've been there all day. I closed up a few hours ago and stayed late to work on a special order—" She broke off, shook her head. "Why? Why do you want to know? Will you please just tell me what the hell is going on? I think I deserve that much."

He took a step closer to her, crowding her back up against the locked door. "What you deserved was to be left alone to conduct your business. That didn't happen."

"I – uh – well, that's very true," she stammered, her eyes widening, but her gaze still holding tightly to his own. It was damn disconcerting, really. "I mean, you intrude right into the middle of my shop, then you smash up the hybrids that took me two weeks to track down in that particular color, and if you had any idea what kind of bridezilla I'm dealing with on all that, well, the very least you owe me is an explanation—"

He covered her mouth with his hand, stopping her nervous babble. Her eyes went wider, but it was her brows furrowing in a very good show of temper that actually had his lips quirking, just a bit.

"I'll explain," he said. "But . . . no screaming."

He slowly slid his hand away, and was surprised to discover that the slide of her soft lips across his palm was somewhat stirring.

"Why would I scream?" she asked, her voice quieter, but no less intense.

"Actually," he said, "I suppose if you were a screamer, you'd have already done that."

"I couldn't scream then, I was in shock. I thought I was having a stroke, or an exploding brain tumor."

He couldn't help it, the smile threatened again. "And now?"

"And now I don't know what to think. Why don't you tell me your version of reality? Mine involves lengthy neurological testing, and possible electric-shock therapy, so I'm hoping yours sounds like more fun."

He outright grinned at that. "I wish I could ease your mind, sweetheart, but, on that score . . . checking yourself in some-where – anywhere – might be the better option."

She frowned again. "Why? Who are you? Really."

He felt her physically tense up, bracing for his response. Something about the way she shifted against him, however, had him thinking he wouldn't mind checking in somewhere there, either. She felt soft and warm, and, he was pretty sure, possibly inviting – if he could remember how to be charming. It had been quite some time since he'd needed those particular skills. Which was probably why his body was thinking it was on holiday instead of on a mission gone horribly wrong.

Well, he knew one way to snap them both out of that particular hormonal stupor. "When I arrived in your shop, I had traveled a bit farther than from Papua New Guinea."

She nodded calmly enough, but he saw her throat work. "Like, from another galaxy? Or something?"

His lips curved. "Nothing so exotic as that. I'm as human as you are."

She sighed and relaxed somewhat, even as the most delightful flush warmed her cheeks. "So, did I just imagine you appearing in front of me like a hologram come to life?"

He shook his head.

"Then . . . ?"

"I didn't travel through space, sweetheart, just through time."

She let that sink in for a moment. "So, that's why you wanted to know the year?"

He nodded.

"Which means . . . what time – year – exactly, did you travel from?" She glanced down between them, ostensibly, he assumed, at his clothing. "Not the past, surely." She looked back up into his eyes.

And he had the most peculiar urge to kiss her. He shook his head, both in response to her and his own urges. "2563." While she goggled a little at that, he turned the conversation back to the more immediate concern. "You said you've been here all day. No breaks? Did you leave at any time?"

"No, why? Listen," she tugged at her wrists again, as if just remembering he still had them in his grip. "What's going on? The whole story."

"I don't know the whole story. Yet."

"So, tell me the parts you do know." She tugged again, hard, this time, making him tighten his grip again. "Who is Stoecker?"

Her pupils flared, and her throat worked, which he told himself was fear, but his body was busy telling him that that part of her reaction was based on something else entirely. Which made him a bit more blunt than might have been entirely necessary, because given the fact she had him rapidly growing hard as a rock, maybe they both needed a bit of shock therapy. "Kir Stoecker is a bodysnatcher. He gets paid a very princely sum to travel back through time and capture women to be put up at auction for those who enjoy the companionship of the helpless and truly enslaved."

"You mean s-sexually?"

He couldn't help it, he could feel her, soft, curvy, pressed up against him. His gaze drifted to her mouth, and then back to her eyes, pupils so wide and dark he could fall right into them and never come out. "Sexually, and every other way they might want to wield their newly purchased power."

He brought his hand up and stroked the side of her face, pushing back those wild, ridiculously luxurious curls. "And you, sweetheart, would be ripe picking for his sort." He slid his hand across her hair, palm to cheek. "You'd earn him quite a bounty."

"Me?" The word came out breathy, almost hoarse.

"Tall, defiant," he said, crowding her further, tipping up her chin. Then, giving into the urge, he pushed his hand deeply into all that silky curl. "With the kind of hair a man can get a good grip on. Oh, you'd fetch a pretty price, indeed."

She swallowed hard, then her gaze drifted to his mouth, too. "And you?" she said, still looking at his mouth. Her breath was coming in shallow pants now. "What do you do?"

"Keep him from succeeding."

Her gaze lifted to his. "And do you?"

"Not always."

She gave a convulsive little jerk at that. "You don't participate in the trade. Do you?"

A smile twitched at the corners of his mouth. "Sample the wares, you mean? There are some who have been grateful to escape their fate." When her eyes widened, he lowered his mouth until his breath mingled with hers. "I always refuse."

He could feel her body tighten further, rather than relax. Her voice was hoarse now, barely a whisper. "So, you never . . ."

"Oh, I didn't say *that*." He slid his hand to the curve above her nape, and tipped her mouth up to his. "I just prefer my partners wanting me out of something other than gratitude."

She wet her lips. "Like?"

"Spontaneous, mutual desire?"

He looked into her eyes as her chin quivered. "Yes," she breathed, holding his gaze quite steadily, nonetheless. "I mean . . ."

But it was too late for quantifications. He took her mouth, intending it to be a shock of sensation for her, bringing her to her senses. But it turned out the recipient of that shock was him. Her lips were warm, and tasted both sweet and earthy, beckoning him to explore, to find out what was beneath that surface. So . . . he did. She moaned a little as he parted her lips. Her newly freed hands gripped his biceps, not to push him away, rather to support herself as her body trembled against his.

That should have been enough. Enough to jerk him out of this state he'd somehow succumbed to. Instead, like some kind of elusive jungle quicksand, it simply sucked him in more deeply. That sweet vulnerability in one so tall and strong made him want to both claim and protect. He ignored those thoughts, thoughts that never interfered when it was pleasure he sought. In fact, thoughts like those had never interfered in any instance. A man like him, a slave-trade bounty hunter, didn't lead a life conducive to lasting friendships and deep, personal relationships, so he chose his partners accordingly.

Dani here, she wasn't that kind of partner. In fact, she wasn't like anyone he'd ever encountered. Not so innocent, and yet so very, very naïve. At least about what was happening to her, or could.

And yet, those thoughts didn't stop him from sliding his hands from her hair, and down along her torso, letting his thumbs drift in so they brushed along the swell of her breasts. She jerked at the touch, moaned against his mouth. So he shifted her, just enough, to bring his thumbs back up again, only this time brushing them directly across nipples that were hard and plump to the touch.

His body was the one jerking now. *Sweet hell, it had been far too long since he'd indulged in this kind of simple, yet primal, pleasure.* She moved against him, and he was the one groaning under his breath. She was sinuously tall, so well matched for him, and oh so ripe for the taking. He felt it in her quick breaths, rapid pulse, and the way she shook when he slid his hands down her hips, then hiked her up the wall, so he could press the aching, rock-hard length of himself right where it wanted most to be nestled.

"I want to rip your clothes off and sink every last inch of this into you," he growled against her neck. He didn't know if he was still trying to scare her or convince her.

Her thighs squeezed instinctively, reflexively, around his hips as she locked her ankles around his lower back. "I – yes," she panted. "Yes."

Lost, so well and truly lost, he thought, reeling at a time when he should be at his sharpest. *Wrong time, wrong woman, wrong everything.* And yet he was undoing the buttons on the front of her filmy little sundress, sliding her higher up the wall, so he could put his mouth on those turgidly plump and oh-so-perfect nipples. Even through the sheer, pale-pink film of her bra, she tasted dark, and sweet. Her responding moan was a low keening, and she slid her hands to his head, into his hair, holding his mouth where she wanted it to stay. Her scent was sweeter still, and growing increasingly musky. His body all but howled for him to take what was being so generously and openly offered. No harm, no foul, just pulsing, thundering release.

But, before they could make a decision they would surely come to regret, they both froze as the wall behind Dani's back vibrated, followed by the sound of something crashing inside the shop.

"Shit. *Shit!*" What in the hell had he been thinking? He scooped her against his chest and ran like hell across the narrow alley, dropping her feet down as soon as they hit the grass on the other side, where it slanted down steeply toward a ditch. "Down," he commanded, brain back in focus, even if his body wasn't. Not even close. "Belly flat, don't look up."

"Jack—"

There was no time to think now, to wonder, worry, decide. Operating purely on unquestioning instinct now, he crouched down and took her face in his hands. "Trust me, Dani. Do as I say, and live. Look up, show yourself in any way, and I can't be responsible. You got me?"

She locked gazes with him, in that unnerving, intense way she did, that was so much more than a simple meeting of the eyes, and nodded. Then he did the damnedest thing. He wasted another precious several seconds to lean down, and kiss her. Hard, fast, but . . . dammit. "I'll be back for you."

"Right." Her expression was sober, as if a shield had dropped into place.

"Dani—"

"Just, don't die," she said, as seriously as he'd seen her. "You got me?"

He grinned. And something clicked, right into that empty place he'd never thought someone like him could fill. "Wouldn't dream of it, sweetheart."

Three

Dani lasted a full minute, which felt like several lifetimes, before she peeked. Not that she hadn't taken Jack's warning seriously. In fact, she quite understood that the right thing to do was to scuttle down to the bottom of the ditch, crawl her way to the end of the alley through the muck (*eww*), then run as far away from her shop as she could get. Because that was what any person in her right, tumor-free mind, would do.

But, let's face facts. She was presently lying belly down in gross, damp weeds, hiding, while a hot, time-traveling bounty hunter took on a psychopath who'd apparently also just come through time into her little florist shop, intent on abducting the nearest woman – her, for the sake of argument – for the twenty-sixth-century slave trade.

Still, why was she lying here? In hopes that her Aussie Greek god of a hero would rush in, save the day, then come back and . . . what? *Yeah, what, exactly, Dani? Make mad, passionate love to you in a drainage ditch? Then beg you to join him and go back to his time?*

And she'd been shaking her head, trying to decide just what kind of brain tumor would create such a completely involved, highly detailed psychotic break like the one she was obviously having. Something like that couldn't possibly be operable, could it? Because, if that were true, then what harm was there in waiting for her space cowboy to kill the bad guy and come back for her, because at this point, psychotic-break sex sounded pretty damn good. What little foreplay she'd had so far had been quite excellent, in fact. Win-win really, if she was going to die either way.

Which was why, when the sky over her shop exploded in a yellow-orange haze of smoke, she'd peeked.

What she saw was pretty damn impressive. Jack was facing the back entrance to the shop with some kind of small gadget in his hand, aiming it at the door, which – more or less – dissolved in front of her eyes. Then he palmed some other sort of weapon from the side of one of his boots and, crouching low, went inside the building.

Did she stay in the ditch and wait to see what happened? Or did she run to get help? Or did she go inside and make damn sure that the man who'd just kissed her like she was the last woman on Earth didn't go and get himself killed before he could finish what he'd started?

She was up and running low across the alley before allowing herself to really think the plan through. But then, she'd never been much of a sideline-sitter. Not since Tommy Decker had goaded her into diving into the lake at summer camp, despite the fact that she didn't know how to swim. But the girls in her cabin had discovered Beemer and were incessantly taunting her, and drowning felt like a potentially acceptable alternative to a summer bunking with a hit squad of mean girls. Plus, Tommy was already showing asshole-guy tendencies. So, she'd dived in. And lived. Take that, Cabin Three bitches!

Of course, she'd been right about Tommy. Turns out he'd just wanted to see her in a wet T-shirt. He'd been all of nine at the time. If only she'd been more focused on that lesson learned instead of shutting up her bunkmates, she might have saved herself from the world of grief she'd suffered one year, four months, two weeks, and a couple of days ago. Because idiot boys like Tommy grew up to be asshole jerks like Adam.

But she wasn't thinking about Adam, Tommy, or the mean girls of Cabin Three. She was thinking about the flower shop – *her flower shop, dammit!* Aunt Teddy and Uncle Deacon were both gone now, the family dairy farm long since sold off. Then, sixteen months ago, on that fateful, much recalled date, she'd discovered – as in, before-her-very-eyes – that Adam, her tax-accountant fiancé, was cheating on her with his much younger bookkeeping assistant. Whom he'd happily agreed to marry right away. This, after hemming and hawing over setting a date with Dani for four long years. That news had been capped recently when, while being maid of honor – again – for the last of her single friends, she'd overheard that the blissfully happy newlyweds were already expecting their first child.

Yeah. She was so over all of it now. Except, apparently, the

*prolonged sex deprivation. Which left her with her little fledgling
florist business and not much else. If she lost that, then what?*

She ducked behind her Jeep, straining to hear what sounds, if
any, came from inside the shop. "Like what, Dani?" she
muttered. "Gunshots?" Because, it was doubtful, given Jack had
just vaporized the door to her shop without making so much as
a whisper of sound, that whatever that little weapon thingie was,
it would make any noise either. Of course, the person getting hit
by whatever that weapon produced might at least scream. Right?

"Oh, for the love of—" She edged around the front of the
Jeep, trying to decide what her best bet was, and what she
could arm herself with. When a crashing sound came again,
like shelves – many shelves – being toppled over, accompanied by much grunting, and what sounded like old-fashioned
fists on flesh, she was on the move again. That they were killing each other was one thing, but she'd be damned if they'd
just trash her shop while they did it. She didn't think her new
insurance policy covered destruction by alien invasion. Or . . .
whatever.

She peeked around the corner of the door, wincing suddenly
as a bite of heat hit her on the shoulder. She looked down to see
that the doorframe – what was left of it – had pretty much melted
her shirtsleeve.

She edged inside the building. With the door gone, the moonlight penetrated the back room of the shop and bathed it in a
dim glow. She scanned the storage shelves for anything that
might help her defend herself and her shop. She wondered,
briefly, if this Stoecker guy would fall for the toxic-glue gun
thing, but figured it wasn't worth the risk. Instead she palmed
the biggest, heaviest crystal vase she could wrap one hand
around, then crept closer to the swinging door that led to the
front of the shop. More grunting, more crashing. More of what
sounded like fists on flesh. *Apparently men didn't change much
over the centuries. Not particularly surprising.*

Without a set plan in place, other than to help Jack so the
destruction of her shop would end before it was completely
leveled, which had the dual win of thwarting the threat against
her apparently black-marketable person – and, well, yes, she
hadn't exactly forgotten that a win against Stoecker would allow
them to get back to what they'd started out back by her Jeep

– she quietly edged through the swinging door. *Was it wrong that it was that last part that had provided the most motivation?*

She didn't have time to ponder that, as she was immediately confronted by two men, locked in mortal combat. Telling them apart was easy, even in the dim interior. Assuming it was Stoecker that Jack was currently wrestling with, the future world slave trader was as pale and blond as Jack was swarthy and dark. Plus, he had more clothes on. What he also had was a good fifty pounds and a few inches in height on Jack. He looked like a Nordic Incredible Hulk.

Neither of the men saw or heard her as she slowly moved toward her work table, intending to use it as a shield. Of course, they could probably just vaporize it, but she didn't see weapons in either of their hands at the moment. She crouched down, gripping the vase more tightly. She edged behind the table, scanning the area now – in between wincing as they sent another display, then another, crashing to the floor – for any sign of Jack's weapon.

Then she saw what looked like a cell phone, just out of Jack's reach, on the floor, and realized it was what both of them were trying to grab at, while keeping the other from getting it first. She was trying to decide how good her chances were to grab the weapon herself, when Stoecker managed to get free from Jack and palm the small weapon. He writhed to his back, and lifted it – aiming it right at Jack, who was lunging at him, making Jack vulnerable for a shot right to the chest.

Dani didn't even think, she just stood up and drilled the vase directly at Stoecker's head. Like a perfect spiral pass, the heavy crystal caught him on the temple, just as he pushed the button, sending the violet stream to the left of Jack, where it vaporized half the wall between the front and back of her shop, and a good part of the ceiling.

Stoecker grunted and collapsed, as Jack – after a quick look of shock in her direction – kicked at the slave trader's hand, sending the weapon out of his reach. Then Jack grabbed it and aimed it at Stoecker. But the man hadn't moved. In fact, he was out cold.

Jack looked at Dani. "I thought I told you to stay outside."

"You were trashing my business. And my home. I live – lived – upstairs." She glanced up, and felt her shoulders slump, even as the rest of her began to shake as the after-effects of the adrenaline rush kicked in.

"What *was* that?" Jack asked, as he pulled himself to his feet. He staggered to her work table, looking a bit more worse for wear after the fight.

"Fluted vase. Austrian crystal." She sighed. "Imported."

"Lucky throw."

She looked at him. "Nothing lucky about it. Archery and darts champ, Lake Machapunga, three summers running." She looked over at the prone form of Stoecker and smiled. "Bite me, Tommy Decker."

"Who?"

She looked back at Jack. He was holding one arm around his ribcage, and there was blood trickling down the side of his temple. Even battered and banged-up, he was the sexiest thing she'd ever seen. "Are you going to be okay? You should let me look at that puncture wound—"

"I've had worse." He shook his head when she started to come around the counter to check on him. "Stay back. I need to get him secured."

"I didn't . . . kill him?"

"Doubtful, sweetheart." But before Jack could secure him, the air around Stoecker began to shimmer. It only took a moment or two for Dani to realize it wasn't the air around the prone giant, it was the giant himself who was shimmering. "He's – Jack! Look!"

"I can see it." Moving with surprising swiftness, Jack came around the table, blocking her behind him with one arm. He was sweaty, almost hot to the touch, and despite the blood and the obvious wounds, felt sturdy, stable, and strong. "It's the fissure. It's looped back already. Must be a tight bend this far back."

"So, he's what? Going back? I mean . . . forward?" She shook her head. "Back to your time, I mean?"

Jack nodded, then turned to face her, keeping her tight in the circle of his arm. "I have to go with him, Dani. It's the best chance I've had, the closest I've gotten to stopping him for good."

"Can't you just, you know, catch the next – what did you call it? Fissure?"

He shook his head. "This is just the far end looping. No telling if it would ever come back this far again. I still don't know

how it was manipulated to do what it did. I may never know."
He looked at her, searched her eyes. "You should be safe now.
At least from Stoecker. I'll make sure of that."

"So you're going? For good?"

He nodded.

"But—"

He framed her face with his palms. "No time."

She smiled faintly. "You said that once before."

"Stop talking," he said, only this time a smile hovered over his
beautifully chiseled, if slightly battered, lips.

"That, too," she said, trying to smile, but hearing the quaver
in her voice.

"Come here." He tilted her head and kissed her firmly,
passionately, but there was something else there now. Not
simply urgency due to the situation. It was far more elemental
than that. When he lifted his mouth from hers, her eyes were
glassy and unreadable. "I've never missed anyone before. But
I'll miss you, Dani."

"Jack—"

But it was too late. He broke his hold, and stepped back, into
the aura that surrounded an almost completely transparent
Stoecker on her shop floor. Then Jack started to fragment, too.

Dani raised her fist to her mouth, determined not to say
anything, not to beg him to stay. He had no choice but to do his
job, to save those whose lives Stoecker would destroy. *Besides,
what the hell would a time-traveling bounty hunter from the future do
in a tiny, South Carolina tourist town?*

She couldn't, however, stop the single tear that tracked down
her cheek as he held her gaze, solidly, intently, until the very last
particle of him was gone.

Dani slowly gave in to the trembling in her legs and sank to
the floor of her battered and trashed shop. *Funny how the destruction didn't even seem to matter to her.* All it was to her now was
proof that the entire night hadn't, in fact, been a product of an
overactive imagination.

It had really happened. Jack was real. His commanding presence and take-charge attitude. His instinctive need to protect
and defend. His kisses, so dark and dangerous.

She lifted her fingers to her lips, and didn't even try to stop
the tears. "I'll miss you, too."

Four

Nine months (plus one week, three days, and two hours – but who was counting, really) later, Dani was working late, putting the finishing touches to a table centerpiece for the upcoming town-council banquet. They didn't go in for the exotic or whimsical, so her thoughts were wandering as she plugged in a spray of lily grass here and a random piece of fiddlehead fern there.

She was proud of herself. She'd gone a whole month now without making up reasons to stay late after the shop closed, till long after the sun had gone down, you know . . . just in case. This evening, she actually hadn't had to make up an excuse. The council order had been last-minute, to be picked up the following morning, and she needed the business.

She'd had to stay late. Possibly, if she were being honest, not quite as late as she'd ended up staying, but she couldn't seem to stay focused on the project at hand. It was a nagging problem. Ever since Jack.

She might have stopped waiting for him to materialize again, but there didn't seem to be anything she could do to stop thinking about him. Even running into Adam and his very young bride as they pushed the stroller with their adorable baby past the floral shop hadn't distracted her from her, well, moping, really. There was no way to pretty that up. *She missed Jack. Simple as that. And she couldn't even talk about him to anyone.*

The local cops had shown up moments after Jack had vanished. Apparently vaporizing the back door had set off her new silent security system, which automatically alerted the police and fire department, who had also shown up, sirens blaring. She had still been a wreck, which the responding police officers had assumed was a result of her finding her shop broken into and vandalized. That's how the report had been written up, though no one could adequately explain how the wall and part of the ceiling had been destroyed.

Thankfully, she supposed, her insurance company had settled the claim on most of the repairs and replacements. And the accompanying excitement had driven business her way. For a time. But the cost of repairing what her insurance hadn't covered, combined with a very slow winter season, had put her business on the brink of closing. If things didn't pick up fast now that summer was here – well, she tried to keep positive.

She sighed, and plunged another sprig into the arrangement. She still enjoyed her work, it was the one true escape she had from her tormenting thoughts. *What would have happened if she'd run to Jack in those last few seconds? Would she have gone with him? What did it feel like, being all particulated like that? Was it risky? Would she have done it anyway, if he'd asked her to go with him?*

She shook her head as she picked up the glue gun and started attaching small beads around the exterior lip of the base container. The council wasn't paying for the extra dazzle, but she had a reputation to maintain, and since her business was going to be listed in the program, it was important to create a centerpiece worthy of a second look.

"Ouch, dammit!" She wiped the hot glue off her fingertip and dipped it into the water pitcher sitting off to one side. *Seriously, Dani, get a grip. You're not doing your best work. And if you don't snap out of this . . . funk, you won't be doing any work. Then you'll lose the only thing you have left. The only thing that matters.*

What if there was something else that mattered? Or someone?

She lifted her head and closed her eyes. For the past nine months (plus one week, three days, and three hours now) she had been hearing her own voice in her head, but she hadn't gone so far around the bend that she'd been hearing Jack's.

"Dani."

She swung her hands up, glue gun loaded and aimed. She couldn't survive him leaving her twice. "Jack," she breathed. "Is it . . . are you really here?"

"I'm really here."

She couldn't gather her thoughts, it was all so sudden, and real. What came out next was not what she'd envisioned saying to him. "Do they still have flowers in your time?"

He frowned, even as his lips quirked. And damn if he didn't look way more intoxicatingly sexy than she even remembered. Which was saying a hell of a lot. "We do, yes."

"Then, I'm good."

"Dani—"

"Did you . . . come back to see me?"

"I – I came back because of you."

She tensed and her heart skipped a beat. "Is this about Stoecker?"

He shook his head. "He's dead."

She flinched at that.

"Not killed by you," he said quickly.

"By you?"

His nod was almost imperceptible. "I told you I'd make sure you were safe."

"So that's it. You just came to tell me that?" She steadied her stance, glue gun still held out in front of her in a two-fisted grip. "Because, to be honest with you, I haven't spent any time thinking about Stoecker."

His expression flickered, but was still unreadable. "I see."

"I'm glad he's dead, though. If he did all those things you said he did, then I'm glad."

"There will be others like him."

"Are you chasing one of them now?"

He shook his head. "I'm retired. From active duty, anyway."

The glue gun shook a little, and her composure slipped. "Are you okay? Did anything happen? Was it Stoecker? Did you get hurt, or . . . ?"

"I'm fine, I'm just done chasing bad guys."

"What will you do now?"

"At the moment, I'm still working on figuring that out. Maybe train a team to do what I used to do. Did. I can't . . . I can't seem to focus, though. It's not enough, anymore."

She swallowed. Hard. "And?"

"You didn't think about Stoecker? No worry?"

"That he'd come back?" She shook her head. "I trusted you."

"Then why are you holding me at glue gunpoint?"

"I – I don't know. Self-preservation instinct, I guess. I've—" She broke off. He hadn't given her much to work with, and she wasn't about to make a complete fool of herself by spilling her guts.

"Dani, put the gun down."

She looked up, found his gaze, and got lost in it, all over again. He took a step forward, then another. "Do you still trust me?"

She nodded.

And then he was in front of her, his hand over her shaky one. Or was it his hand that was shaky? He gently pushed the gun down, until she dropped it on the work table.

"Let me ask you one thing."

Anything. "Okay."

"Did you think about me?"

She nodded. *Every second of every day.*

"Come here," he said, his voice gravelly, but softer, gentler, than she'd ever imagined possible.

"Wait," she said. "I – I don't want—" She broke off, not sure what to say. That she didn't want him to leave her again? Did she think he was back because he was staying? Was he going to ask her to go with him? "Why – why are you here?"

"For you."

Her heart leapt so fast and hard it hurt. "With what in mind, exactly?"

"I don't know. I don't know what's possible. What you want. Or don't want. I just know that I don't want to not have you. Not for another day, another minute."

"When did you know that?"

For the first time, his expression wavered, and she could see that this stoic act was costing him. "The moment I couldn't see your eyes anymore."

She smiled, even as her eyes grew a bit glassy. "I might have you beat on that, then."

The relief she saw, the quick, sudden sag to his oh-so-broad shoulders, almost leveled what was left of her willpower. "It's been almost a year," she managed.

"That's how long it took to figure out how Stoecker manipulated the fissure. And to make damn sure it would hold up."

"Hold up to what?"

"Getting me here. Getting the both of us back."

"Is that what you want?"

"Right now, what I want is to not be standing apart from you like this. So close, and still a lifetime away. The rest can figure itself out." And the rest of his protective shield came crashing down. He let her see, for the first time, all the anxiety, the anguish, the frustration, and yes, even the fear. "Dani, sweetheart, I just want you."

And that was all she needed. She literally leapt into his arms, and he caught her, hard and fast against him. "Then phone home, E.T.," she murmured, smiling against his lips. "And tell them you're bringing company with you."

Tales from the Second Chance Saloon: Macawley's List

Linnea Sinclair

Telling her he loved her was on his list of things to do.

Dying before he had a chance to do so, wasn't.

The metal decking of Starbase Delta Five skewed suddenly under his boots. The shock wave of the first explosion blasted by him. He stumbled, slammed against the bulkhead. Debris cascaded down through the ruptured conduit panels. He swung his good arm up to shield his face and slid awkwardly to the floor.

"Macawley!" Her anguished voice called to him through the communications badge pinned to his shirt.

He almost said it, right then and there. *I love you. I've always loved you. I'm just too much of a coward to tell you.*

He ripped the badge from his shirt, threw it across the wide corridor. It skittered against a chunk of ceiling tile. If he answered, she'd try to rescue him. Even though he'd given her a direct order to pull out.

But she had a propensity to ignore his direct orders. That was one of the things he loved about her.

The station rumbled again. A large section of the corridor collapsed into the level below, taking the chunk of tile and his badge with it.

He hooked his good arm around a curved support pylon and hung on, though he didn't know why. He was already dead. A

Duvri ion lance had severed his left arm at the elbow, cauterizing it neatly. And he was bleeding profusely from a shrapnel wound in his thigh.

But none of that mattered. What did was the destruction of Delta Five. His tactical team set the charges for that purpose an hour ago. That would bring the Duvri's invasion of the Galleon Quadrant to a dead stop, like slamming into a black hole.

"A waste of a few damn fine pubs," Briony Winn had quipped just before she followed the rest of the team into the escape shuttle.

That was another thing he loved about her. She always had a quip, some little sotto voce remark.

"I'm sure you and my crew will take it as a personal challenge to find replacements," he'd shouted to her as he'd jogged backwards towards the airlock. He was headed down to the next deck to appropriate an X-7 fighter, and blow a few more holes into the station for good measure as he left.

She had the audacity to stick her tongue out at him just as the hatch was closing. "They're my crew, too, Mac!"

They were all hers now. In the event of the death of the captain, the executive officer automatically took command.

A Duvri suicide squad had greeted him at the fighter bays. They had an ion lance and shrapnel guns. He was trapped, and wasn't about to recall the shuttle and risk the lives of eight team members – and one irreplaceable Commander Briony Winn – to save his ass.

The station shuddered violently again. He heard the agonizing groan of metal stressed to its limits; the harsh snap of plasticrete as it twisted and shattered. The jagged ledge under his legs vibrated.

He had minutes. No, probably only seconds. The lights blinked out. A rush of wind drove gritty particles of insulation into his skin. He knew what it was. The station's hull had ruptured. The air was being sucked out into the vacuum of deep space.

"I love you, Winnie." It was the first time he had ever said those words out loud.

It was the last thing he remembered.

Until he coughed.

He was face down in a pile of insulation dust. It coated his lips, stuck in his throat. He coughed again, planted his hands on the ground and pushed his shoulders up.

And heard piano music. Light, tinkling, jaunty piano music.

I'm dead. And someone in hell plays the piano.

He rolled over on one hip, sat up.

Hell is a desert. Legends said the afterworld had seven hells. He didn't know which one this was. But he did know deserts. He had spent three months on Nas Ramo teaching a dirtside survival course for the Alliance. It was just before the Alliance gave him his captain's stars. Winnie was part of his team, but she was only a lieutenant.

Only a lieutenant. As if Briony Winn could be "only" anything.

He looked around. This desert in hell was less mountainous than Nas Ramo's. The scrub cacti were taller, the sand almost pure white.

And someone was playing the damn piano!

He wrenched his head to the right. A two-story wooden building stood ten feet behind him. The architecture was unfamiliar. It was painted red – fitting, he thought – and had a wide porch with a criss-cross-style railing. Three slatted chairs waited, empty, on the porch.

Perhaps hell has a check-in point?

He pushed himself to his feet, then wiped gritty hands on his pants. He felt a gust of hot wind ruffle through his hair. The sign hanging over the porch entry swayed slightly.

Second Chance Saloon.

The boards creaked under his boots as he climbed the three steps to the porch. His mouth was dry. He could remember the thick insulation dust filling his lungs, the shuddering of the starbase in its death throes.

He coughed again, his fist coming up to cover his mouth as he stepped through the open doorway. And for a moment he saw nothing. The white sands and the bright sun had bleached his vision.

His eyes adjusted. The piano music reached a crescendo and halted. A metallic-skinned 'droid pushed back the piano bench and stood.

Light applause rippled through the saloon.

"Your kindness is appreciated." The 'droid snatched a tall, wide-brimmed hat from the top of the piano and shoved it onto its bald head. Then it ambled with a swinging gait over to the bar and leaned against the counter.

A dusky-skinned woman stood behind it, polishing a wide-mouthed drinking glass. Mac could see her face in the mirror behind the bar. Her eyes were dark, slightly almond-shaped. Her hair was a deep magenta color, like rich Trelgarian wine. It was braided and wrapped with strips of patterned cloth that matched the flowing tunic covering her tall form.

"Two fingers of premium-grade synth-lube, Jezebel," the 'droid said.

The woman turned. "Sure thing, Tex. And how about you, Captain Macawley? Need something to wet your whistle?"

"You know me?"

She chuckled. "Know you? Why, child, we've been expecting you." Her voice was a rich warm contralto, as thick as the lubricant she poured into the short crystal glass. She slid it towards the 'droid, then looked at Mac, folding her arms across her chest. Rows of metallic bracelets in a rainbow of silvers and golds jangled. It was a pleasant sound.

"Double shot of Pagan Gold?" she asked.

He didn't realize hell kept track of his drinking habits. He nodded, stepped up to the bar and leaned his elbows on it.

Both elbows. Somehow the one he'd donated to the Duvri was back.

He glanced at his leg. Same gray uniform pants he always wore. But the material – and his thigh – was intact. No shredding. No blood.

Hell evidently liked its occupants in one piece. He sipped his drink, watched Jezebel pour another one. But it wasn't a double shot of Pagan Gold.

It was a pale-green liqueur in a tall, slender glass. Starfrost.

Jezebel thumbed open a small container, took a pinch of dark granules and sprinkled them on top.

Nightspice. Starfrost with a touch of nightspice.

Winnie's drink.

He whirled around. If she was here . . . then she was dead. Which he didn't want, Gods, no, he didn't want her to be dead. He'd died so that she could live, damn it!

But if she was here, if she was . . .

He scanned the tables. The saloon was full. There was a trio of pretty women, all humanoid, at the table closest to him. A voluptuous brunette with shoulder-length hair popped open a sof-screen 'puter on the table. The other two leaned closer. Petite, both of them, one platinum blonde, one a deep auburn. They seemed unaware, or uninterested, in his scrutiny.

At another table, a man and a woman, more felinoid than human, sipped something frothy from squat mugs. They wore commercial freighter uniforms, though neither bore any insignia he recognized.

Then there was movement at the back stairs. A round-faced young woman sauntered down, her curls bouncing with each step. The light from the candles in the wall sconces caught the mix of colors in her hair: honey blonde, amber red, russet brown. She held a handful of her long, lace-trimmed dress in one hand as she descended, careful, it seemed, not to catch her heels. She smiled, but Mac knew she wasn't smiling at him. She wiggled her fingers towards a young man sitting alone in the corner.

Mac turned, caught the man's answering nod.

He didn't know any of them. He didn't see Winnie anywhere.

He heard Jezebel slide the tall glass in his direction.

"Where is she?" he asked.

"Now, that's a strange question." Jezebel leaned over the counter towards him. "Most folks first ask, 'Where am I?'"

"I know where I am. One of the seven hells." He never had any illusions about going to heaven.

"Wrong. You're in the Second Chance."

"Semantics. I'm in a bar in hell. I'm still—"

"You're not."

The intensity of her tone startled him into silence.

"You're in the Second Chance," she repeated. "Which is exactly as its name implies: a second chance."

"A second chance at . . ." *Okay. I'm not dead. I'm dying. Hallucinating as I die.* Still, he had to say the word. " . . . at life?"

"No. At love."

At—?

"Love," she repeated. "The one thing left on your to-do list. The one most important thing. The one thing you couldn't bring yourself to do, until you were just about out of time."

He closed his eyes, swallowing the lump in his throat. He knew what he'd done, what he'd said, just as Delta Five turned into intergalactic debris. "I didn't tell Winnie." His voice was raspy.

"Tell her what?" The flickering light from the candles in the chandelier overhead danced in Jezebel's dark-brown eyes.

"The last thing on my list. What I never told her."

"And what did you never tell her?"

He stared at the bartender. It was clear from her tone she knew what he never told Briony Winn. Why in hell was she being so obtuse?

Frustration tinged his voice, made him narrow his eyes. "You know damn well—"

"Yes, Raphael Macawley, I do. Know damn well. But that's not at issue here. What's at issue is, do *you* know? And can you tell her? Because if you can't, there's no sense in our sending you back to her, now is there?"

"You can send me back to my ship?"

Jezebel made a tsk-tsking noise with her tongue. "Not if you can't tell her, we won't."

Tell her. Tell Commander Briony Winn he loved her. Loves her. He nodded his head vigorously. "I can."

"Good. Let's hear it."

His eyes widened. "Now?"

"No time like the present."

"But she's not here."

"For good reason. You need to practice first. You weren't born a starship captain, you know. You had to work your way up to that exalted position."

He picked up his glass, let the last shot of Pagan Gold burn down his throat. Then he drew a deep breath. "I love her."

Someone in the saloon behind him made a rude noise. Loudly.

Jezebel slapped her hand on the bar. "None of that, now! Man's a virgin here. You got to cut him some slack."

Virgin? He'd rarely lacked bed-partners. Mac almost burst out laughing, but sobered quickly as Jezebel's eyes narrowed.

"Raphael. Now, listen up."

He flinched. No one ever called him Raphael – and remained standing for very long.

"You go say 'I love her' to Briony and she's going to be looking left and right for whoever this 'her' is. You've got to say what you've got to say *to her*. Understand?"

He nodded.

"Well?"

He closed his eyes, saw Briony's quick smile. The way she wrinkled her nose. The way she fiddled with her hair when she was tired.

The way she chewed on the end of her lightpen when puzzled over incoming data, or some glitch the sensors couldn't unravel.

The way she shared high fives with the crew when a problem was solved. And that little hip-bumping victory dance he caught her doing once, down in engineering.

And more than once, a compassionate hand on a shoulder, when things were less than victorious. When just being there said more than kindly words.

He opened his eyes but still saw her, and not the rainbow of colors dancing through the rows of etched crystal glasses, or the warm tones of the ornately carved bar.

"I love you, Winnie. I love you, more than you'll ever know." His voice became thick with emotion. "More than I can ever explain. I've loved you, and always will." He looked down at his empty glass, turned it around in his hands.

Jezebel sighed softly. "There's hope for you yet, Mac."

"So how do I get back to the *Intrepid*?"

"You don't."

"But you said—"

"I said you get a second chance at love. I didn't say you can pick up your life right where you left off." Jezebel drummed her fingers on the bar. "Listen up, now. You screwed up, you admit that?"

He nodded.

"That has to be undone. Or else all your pretty words are for naught. She's convinced you're heartless, you know."

Because she knew him well. Most of his crew saw only his competence, his unflagging dedication. "A tireless compulsion towards perfection," one division chief's review stated early in his career. "A true Macawley."

But Winnie knew his compulsions were a facade. And she didn't give a damn that he was a true Macawley.

"How do I undo all that?"

She held up her hand, splayed her fingers in his face. Jeweled rings glistened. "My people have a story. It says that fate has five fingers. But we always start here, first."

She touched the center of her palm. "From there, we have choices. We say, five choices. But each choice we make only once."

She wiggled her index finger. "This was your choice, many years ago. From there, you made your next choice." She touched her index finger to the center of her other palm. "That gave you five more choices."

He understood. Each finger, each choice, was a path. A one-way street. Every decision he made – or didn't make – led to the next one.

"There was a time, a point at which telling Briony Winn how you felt about her would have mattered to her. But you didn't make that choice at that time. So it doesn't matter to her now."

Something hard constricted in his chest at her words. He'd loved Briony for so long, it was almost second nature to him. And he assumed if he ever told her, she'd respond in kind. He loved her so damn much!

But she didn't love him. Couldn't love him. He'd been a fool. In his selfishness, in his cowardice, he'd let the moment go by.

"Then why even bother with all this?" he asked harshly.

She waggled a finger in his face. "Temper, temper, Raphael. We're bothering because what is now isn't the only reality. You will get a second chance with Briony. But not with Commander Briony Winn of the Alliance ship, *Intrepid*. With Lieutenant Briony Winn, junior-grade drive tech on the *Versatile*."

The *Versatile*! Hellfire and damnation, he'd just made XO, been transferred to that damn rust bucket, and let everyone on board know he was damned unhappy about it. Including one still-wet-behind-the-ears-and-straight-out-of-the-academy Briony Winn.

He was a Macawley, after all! Of the Radley's Station Macawleys. His uncle was a senator. His grandmother, an admiral. His father took the millions his own father had made with Radley Intergalactic and made another billion on top of that.

The Winns were nobody in particular. And nobodies in particular got assigned to derelicts like the *Versatile*. Not Macawleys.

If Briony Winn hadn't been so damn good at her job, he probably wouldn't even have noticed her. Third-shift drive techs were not his usual fare.

She had been good; brilliant, in fact. And she had had a

mischievous smile and a sparkle in her eyes to go with that brilliance.

By the time he'd realized just what a priceless gem she was, she had been lost to him. Or rather, she had been totally unfazed by his pedigree, his money, his rank, and his infamous attitude.

The last of which she'd taken great pains over the years to rattle every chance she got.

Which was why he loved her as much as he did.

Because she didn't give a damn that he was Raphael Macawley.

"It won't work, Jezebel. She made it clear a long time ago that our relationship was purely professional."

"Then you're going to have to change her mind, aren't you?"

"You don't understand. At the point I met her, on board the *Versatile*, I—" He stopped as if a blinding light were suddenly flashed in his face. "I'll know it's possible for her to love me. That's it, isn't it? You send me back ten years, and I'll know—"

"You'll know everything at the moment you return, yes. But minute by minute, Raphael, you'll forget. Your memories of the past and what *had* been your future can't coexist. By the twenty-four-hour mark, you'll forget everything."

"Twenty-four hours?" He straightened abruptly. "Gods damn it, that's not fair! The first twenty-four hours I was on that damned ship were a bloody nightmare. It was chaos! The captain was stinking drunk, half the crew'd been left behind on shore leave, the sani-facs only worked on alternate decks . . . I was thrown in the middle of that and then told to expect an admiralty inspection. If I didn't get that ship at least functioning my entire career was at stake!"

"Sounds like you pissed someone off royally on your previous posting." Jezebel's deep chuckle returned. "But be that as it may, child, you're going to be here again." She pointed to the middle of her palm. "You can pursue the fame and glory of your career. Or you can pursue the woman you love."

He clutched the edge of the counter. "If you could just return me to the point where I got command of the *Intrepid*. The awards ceremony, right before that. My grandmother was there. Winnie and I—"

"No."

His heart sank. "It has to be the *Versatile*?"

"Yes."

He slowly relaxed his grip on the bar. "And if after the first twenty-four hours, I can't change her mind?"

"Then you have ten years to deep-six the plans to use an X-7 to get off Delta Five. Take the shuttle, instead. At least then you'll be there when Commander Montalvo asks Briony to marry him."

Monty? His chief of engineering?

"And you'll be there to hear it when she says yes."

"I'm dying and she says yes?"

"Death has a way of making some people face their priorities."

He understood that. It pushed his love for Winnie right to the top of the list. Then the station exploded. And she said yes to that slime, Monty.

He balled his hand into a fist, nodded at Jezebel. "I don't have any choice, do I?"

"You always have the option to turn down our offer."

"That would be abysmally stupid of me."

"You've shown a certain flair in that area before," Jezebel said dryly. Chuckles came from the trio of women behind him.

Mac bit back his comment. "The *Versatile* it is, then. How do we do this?"

Jezebel retrieved a new glass from the rack behind her, pulled out a bottle of clear liquid from under the bar. "Drink up."

He didn't even hesitate.

It took him a few seconds to get his bearings. The corridors weren't quite as filthy as he remembered. Maybe the years had added more grime and stench to the memory of his first hour on board the ageing destroyer.

But those years and all his future mistakes would be gone. He was alive, damn it! And Winnie was around here somewhere.

He turned the corner, caught his reflection in the cracked mirrored wall as he passed by the ship's gym. The wide doors were open. Stuck as usual. The man who stared back was in his thirties.

Not forty-two. Thirty-two. He took his position as XO when he was thirty-two.

He hesitated for only a second, grinned, trudged on. Damn, it felt good to be alive. Young and alive.

Gray-clad crewmembers saluted stiffly as he strode by. Not one smile, not one friendly greeting called out.

That was just as he remembered.

Of course, it was only his first day. He'd do things differently this time. Get to know the crew, slovenly bastards that they were.

Get to know Winnie.

He stepped into an empty lift. "Engineering deck."

It shuddered and jerked for fifteen seconds, then stopped, the doors squealing open.

He heard the low rumble of voices as he headed down the short corridor. Then a laugh, a throaty laugh that belonged to only one woman.

He wiped his palms down the side of his uniform pants. They were slick. His heart hammered in his chest and he regretted not stopping longer in front of the gym's mirror. Did he look okay? He ran his hand through his short-cropped hair. Everything felt normal.

He stepped over the wide hatch-tread, immediately looked left towards her station.

Briony Winn. Lieutenant Briony Winn. His Winnie. Oh, Gods, she was there and she was alive and she was even more beautiful than he remembered. All of twenty-four years old. Impulsive. Animated. Sassy. Downright sexy as—

"Commander Macawley, is there a problem?"

"No." He shook his head without looking at the officer speaking to him. He held out his hand as if to push the woman away.

Winnie, Winnie. Look at me. Turn towards me. Give me that smile. Please, Winnie.

His bootsteps sounded muffled on the latticed decking. But she must have heard, because she turned. Her eyes narrowed.

"Macawley. You're late."

Late? How could he be late? They hadn't met yet. He clearly remembered his first few hours on board, touring the ship from top to bottom, from bridge to engineering. That was where he first saw her, sitting at her tech console on the left.

He glanced over her head at the stat-board. Eleven-twenty. He'd come on board at oh-eight-hundred. That was about right.

But she called him Macawley. Not Commander. They hadn't been introduced, yet she knew his name.

He stared back at the stat-board. Eleven-twenty-one. Galactic Date 874-987.

He'd been on board the *Versatile* for three months. He'd already made three months of abysmally stupid mistakes.

"That bitch!" The words exploded from his mouth before he could stop them. But no one turned at his outburst. Winnie seemed unruffled. They were already used to him.

That bitch Jezebel had tricked him. With her sultry voice and fanciful tale, she'd tricked him. He wasn't starting at the beginning with Briony Winn, as she promised. He was—

She hadn't promised. He grabbed the back of the vacant chair next to Winnie, leaned on it. Jezebel hadn't promised to send him back to his first day on the *Versatile*. She had promised to send him back to the day that *would make a difference in his relationship with Winnie*.

No wonder the ship didn't look as bad as he remembered. He'd been pounding it back into shape for three months.

He collapsed into the chair, leaned his elbows on his knees, then ran his hands over his face. He peered at Winnie from over the tips of his fingers.

Every finger represents a choice.

What was today? Damn it, why couldn't he remember? Jezebel said . . .

. . . that he would begin to forget from the moment he got back on board. That his past and present memories couldn't coexist.

Galactic Date 874-987. What was it?

Winnie was staring at him. "You okay? Maybe you should be in sick bay."

"No. I'm fine. It's just that—" *Think! Think! What's today? Or more importantly, what happened before today?* "I need to talk to you. It's a matter of . . ." He waved one hand aimlessly in the air, let his voice trail off as two techies thumped by in their thick-soled black boots.

"Life and death?" She wrinkled her nose at him. His heart did a flip-flop. "What is it this time? Can't find a power outlet for your personal massaging recliner?"

Gods, he forgot about that. A gift from his uncle the senator.

"Winn – Briony." He used her given name deliberately. He didn't remember doing so before. He needed some way to signal to her that he was desperate. "I really need to talk to you."

The fact that she didn't come back with another quip told him she was at least taking him seriously. "I'm off shift in four hours."

He didn't have four hours. He could no longer remember the name of the bitch in the Second Chance Saloon.

"Now. Before I forget what I'm going to say. Or the rest of my life will be a total waste."

"You'll have to clear it with Admiral Wellinsky. But I don't think he's going to put up with any more delays."

Wellinsky? What would that pompous son of a bitch be doing on board?

He groaned. The Parken Random Calibration Unit test run. The PRCU was Wellinsky's pet project. Better to risk blowing the drives on the *Versatile* than on one of the Fleet's better ships. If the unit didn't work and the *Versatile* had to sit in spacedock for months for repairs, no great loss. At least, not to Wellinsky.

He glanced at the data on Winnie's console. A strange light-headedness washed over him. Wellinsky's voice bellowed at him through his comm badge but the hand that moved in extreme slow motion to tap at it in response didn't feel like it was his. The air around him felt thick as Suralian honey soup.

"I'm waiting on your release code, Macawley!"

Release code. A safety procedure. The captain and the XO had release codes to be entered at separate stations before the test could begin.

"Ten seconds, Macawley!"

Seconds. Seconds. The word echoed in his mind.

I said you get a second chance at love. I didn't say you can pick up your life right where you left off. A woman's voice, sultry, soothing.

He felt his eyes move slowly towards Briony Winn. She hadn't spoken. Then who? Whose voice was that?

His fingers touched his comm badge and he snapped back into the present. "Acknowledged, Admiral."

Hell, that was the last time he was having Oysters Galafar for a late-night snack. Felt like he was going to keel over there for a moment.

He reached for the console, keyed in his codes, saw the PRCU initialization sequence scroll down the screen. Then a flurry of activity around him as the experimental-matter conversion system came online.

Time to get back to the bridge. He didn't trust Wellinsky's tinkerings, but the chief would handle the problems – and he knew there'd be problems – as they surfaced. Plus Winnie was on duty. Whatever Chief Damaris Lagronde couldn't tackle directly he knew Lieutenant Winn would solve, albeit in some wildly unorthodox manner.

He pushed himself out of the chair and nodded to Lagronde, who was already frowning. But something made him stop just before he reached the corridor. He turned, saw the stout woman leaning over Winnie's shoulder, talking to her.

Talking to her. What was it he had to talk to Winnie about?

He shook off an inexplicable sense of edginess and strode briskly for the lifts.

He had just stepped onto the command deck when his existence shifted again.

Love. A woman's voice. That woman's voice. The one thing left on your to-do list.

Winnie. He didn't tell Winnie he loved her.

He did an about-face, reached for the lift pad.

"Commander Macawley, the Admiral's waiting for you."

Gods damn it! He spun on the young ensign in the corridor, fist clenched. He didn't have time for the Admiral's petty experiments.

The young man stepped back quickly. Mac reined in his emotions. Yes, the crew knew what he was like. Knew he was an unmitigated bastard who trampled over people's feelings like a gelzrac on a rampage. Three months and they already knew it.

So did Winnie. Because he'd brutally trampled over her feelings last night. Then downed a bottle of Pagan Gold and a dozen spiced oysters to ease the pain.

He knew now why he was here. And why he had to apologize. And why if he didn't in the next few hours, he'd never be able to. He had to get back down to engineering.

"Tell the Admiral I'll monitor the test run with Chief Lagronde."

"Sir, I don't think he'll agree to that."

"It's not your job to think!" he almost barked at the young man, but stopped. *He had to do more than just apologize to Winnie. He had to change everything about himself. Starting now.*

"No, Ensign. I'm sure he won't. And I'm sorry to put you in the line of direct fire." He twisted his mouth into a wry grin.

"But the Admiral's less my concern than this ship is. Help me out here. I'll owe you one."

He admired the young man's ability to prevent his jaw from dropping. But it did take him three attempts to get out a stuttered: "Yes, sir!"

The lift, uncharacteristically, appeared when summoned. He stepped in and, for fifteen shimmying seconds, leaned his forehead against the slick metal wall. A sense of disorientation returned. *Damn those oysters!*

The doors opened and he trudged towards engineering, shaking his head. He just left here. *But had to come back, for some reason, some important reason.*

Which he couldn't remember. But it didn't matter because when he stepped over the hatch-tread, all hell broke loose.

"Chief, we've got a full system lock-up starting in the starboard feed!" Winnie's voice carried clearly over the discordant beeping of alarms.

Mac sprinted to her station. Lagronde came puffing up behind him, swearing.

"Gods damn him! Gods damn that asshole, Wellinsky!" The stout woman glared at the data cascading down the console screen, then turned, startled, towards Mac.

"Macawley? Thought you went back up."

"I did. But then I remembered something." He slid into the seat next to Winnie's. And recognized the slight skewing in the initialization sequence codes. He'd seen it once before, but only in a sim at the academy.

"You don't want to see this in real life. Ever," his aged professor had growled.

He was looking at it now. "We've got a breakdown—"

"In the anti-matter core slough," Winnie finished for him. Her fingers flew over her console.

"A shutdown will rupture us." Lagronde yanked the datapad from her utility belt, keyed in her own commands. She slapped it into an open terminal port. "Containment field activated," she hollered over the din.

"You picked a bad time to go slumming," Winnie said to him as Lagronde hurried away. Her voice was light but he clearly heard an undercurrent of pain. And knew it wasn't related to their present somewhat critical situation.

"Actually, no. I always wanted to see a real core-slough failure. The sims just don't seem to have the same urgency." He picked up on the modification she was entering on her console, nodded in approval. Then keyed in a few adjustments of his own.

She hazarded a glance in his direction, arched an eyebrow. "I never thought dying down here with the black shoes was on the top of your to-do list. You strike me as more of the 'in the arms of a beautiful woman' type."

Her console beeped twice. "I didn't ask for your opinion!" she told it and entered another sequence. It quieted.

His mind hung for a moment on her words. His list. His to-do list. They were a regular item already: Mighty Macawley's To-Do Lists.

What was it that topped his to-do list?

Not dying on the *Versatile*. Even in the sim, he'd not been able to stop the disintegration of the slough. And that was a sim based on top-notch equipment. Not an ageing destroyer that didn't have half the fail-safes and sensitive components the newer ships did. The *Versatile* was a basic starcruiser. Functional. No frills. No—

He pulled up a secondary screen, his mind racing over the data. Somewhere, somewhere . . . there!

"We can manually override her slough filters!" He took his fingers off the pads just long enough to grab Winnie's arm.

She looked at him, startled. Then her eyes grew wide in amazement. "Damn straight! Damn straight we can."

He fed her some code strings. She segued them in, then threw the modified functions right back at him.

The first in a long row of alarm lights stopped blinking.

He tagged Lagronde's terminal, sent her the data. A few seconds later her whoop of joy sounded over the wails of alarms just now beginning to recede.

An hour later, the containment field was lifted and a red-faced Admiral Wellinsky harrumphed through engineering and out again.

Lagronde stood with her arms folded in front of the main console. A detailed re-creation of the entire fiasco scrolled by. "Lucky as hell you came down here, Commander."

Lucky as hell. But not for Wellinsky, who wanted to blame the *Versatile* for his project's failure. But this time, he couldn't. The slough didn't rupture. The evidence the PRCU itself was flawed wasn't destroyed. And Lagronde's career, along with the careers of a few other competent, and equally as innocent, black shoes, wasn't ruined. After all, who would dare find fault with *the* Wellinsky? Only the Mighty Macawley—

Who had no idea how he knew all that, but he did. Just as he knew he was standing in engineering, with Lagronde on his left and Winnie on his right, so close he could feel the heat of her body against his arm.

Winnie. He had to talk to Winnie. He grabbed her elbow, pulled her towards him as she shot him a startled glance.

"Ten minutes. Please."

That made Lagronde turn and he knew why. It was probably the first time the Mighty Macawley had ever said "please" on this ship.

"With your permission, Chief." Another first. "But Lieutenant Winn is mine. Until further notice." *Until all of the seven hells freeze over. And until the roof collapses on the Second Chance Saloon.*

He propelled a protesting Briony Winn into the corridor. The small conference room at the end was empty. He guided her inside, locked the door.

"Sit." He pointed to a gimballed chair at the end of the table.

She crossed her arms over her chest. "I'll stand, if you don't mind." A tired defiance played across her features. He knew his timing was horrendous. They were both exhausted, physically, mentally and emotionally. And not only because of Wellinsky's foolish experiment.

He had to make things right.

"I mind. Now sit."

"Give me one good reason."

He heard it in her voice. She was pissed, royally pissed at him.

He sucked in a deep breath. "My reason is that I'm going to get down on my knees and beg for your forgiveness. And that's going to be damned awkward to do if you're standing up."

She sat, her eyes wide with surprise.

He knelt before her. "I'm an idiot. A moron. An unspeakable imbecile. I know you're angry with me and I know you have a right to be. Even if I have no idea of exactly what I did."

"You don't know?"

Not completely. It was still only a sensation, a sickening

sensation; much less than a memory. Still, he could make a stab at it. "I don't know which of all the abysmally stupid things I've done tops the list."

"Besides being ill-mannered, arrogant and insufferably rude?" She pointed her finger in his face. "Berating and belittling every member of the crew? Then demanding we jump when you say 'jump', just because you're the Mighty Macawley?"

He nodded. "Besides all that."

She looked away from him. "I don't like being reduced to a name to be crossed off a list." Her voice was soft, laced with bitterness.

"This is about last night."

"Yes. No!" She turned back to him suddenly, her eyes bright with tears. "It's about your damned lists. And that one list of suitably *worthy* women that a Mighty Macawley could spend time with, and still maintain his high standards."

He reached for her hands. They were balled into small fists. She snatched them away.

"I don't meet your high standards, do I? And you made damn sure I knew that, Raphael! You figured it all out from one short kiss."

It wasn't one short kiss. It was one of the most intense kisses he had ever experienced, packed into a very short period of time. It had scared the hell out of him, made him jump from the lumpy couch in his small quarters and turn his back on her.

And then, because she couldn't see the agony on his face, say some extremely nasty, unkind things to a very young Briony Winn. Because he knew if he didn't push her away then, he was never going to let her go. And that just might affect his perfectly orchestrated, Macawley-like soar to the top. His finely honed love-'em-and-leave-'em image. *The facade he called his life. His former life.*

"I didn't mean what I said last night."

She sat very still. Some of the anger seemed to drain out of her. Finally, she shrugged, but wouldn't look at him, toyed with her academy ring instead. "It's no big deal. You're not the first guy to dump me. Probably won't be the last. I have this tendency to fall in – to pick the unsuitable."

Fall in love. He heard her almost say it. He swallowed hard. *Could you love me, Briony Winn?* He hoped so. His knees were starting to hurt.

"I'm definitely unsuitable." He reached again for her hands, grabbing hold of her before she could pull away. "An arrogant bastard. But I'm also very much in love with you."

She raised her lashes. A small tear glistened in the corner of her eye. He felt as if an ion lance pierced his chest.

"That's why I had to stop kissing you. And that's why I said what I did. Because if I didn't, I would've gotten down on my knees," and he winced as he brought his left knee up, "and begged you to stay. To give me a chance. To let me love you."

He rose – *damn, that hurt!* – and pulled her out of the chair. He held her hands against his chest and, when he was sure she wouldn't back away, let them go, and wrapped his arms around her. "I love you, Winnie. I want to spend the rest of my life telling you that."

She gave him a tremulous smile. It heated his blood like no bottle of Pagan Gold ever could.

"I've no reason to believe you," she said cautiously, but a haughty look crept into her eyes. "But then, I never thought you'd stand up to Wellinsky, either. I think there's hope for you yet."

There's hope for you yet, Mac. A woman's voice, sultry, yet now not much more than a fading whisper.

He lowered his face. "I'd like to try that kiss again, if you don't mind, Lieutenant."

She brushed her lips across his. "I think I'd like that, Commander."

And this time the Mighty Macawley didn't pull away when bolts of lightning arced across an imaginary sky, or waves crashed fiercely against an imaginary shore. Or a thousand imaginary stars exploded and vibrated in a little hip-bumping victory dance inside his heart. A dance accompanied by a jaunty piano tune, which haunted him at the oddest moments.

Like whenever anyone, other than Briony Winn Macawley, tried to fill the number-one spot on his list of things to do.

Wasteland

Jess Granger

One

"C'mon, baby," Rexa whispered under her breath as she watched the information flashing on the screens in large three-dimensional blocks of glowing blue on the inky black field. Tugging on the sync gloves that both controlled the cursor and decoded the encryption on the files, she sorted through the large cubes of information. She didn't dare turn on the lights. The glow from the screens was enough of a risk.

If Palis discovered her, she'd be dead.

After all, family loyalty only went so far, and in her clan, blood was not thicker than politics.

The box on the far left flashed like a beacon. She immediately reached out, grabbing the info-lex with the ghostly cursor floating through the air in front of her, and pulling it down to her personal screen. Her heart thundered as she read.

This was it.

She knew the bastard had sold his soul and rigged the last election.

She snatched the info-lex, simultaneously opening links to every media outlet from Udan to Calaria. All she had to do now was let go of the block of information the cursor-hand gripped so tightly, and the whole world would know her brother was a fraud.

The lights flashed brilliant white, and the screens turned black. Rexa spun around.

In the doorway stood her brother, looking at her as if she were a little girl who'd just broken his favorite toy. Two of his bodyguards edged into the room.

"Really, Rexa?" Her brother's dark hair had thinned since taking office. It only made his face sharper, more like a skulking river rat's. "I thought you were smarter than this." He flicked his wrist, and the bodyguards surged forward.

Rexa screamed, and one of them clamped a hand over her mouth. She tried to bite him, but his gloves were thick, and he was more than twice her size. When he picked her up, she thrashed her legs, but it did no good.

"Take her to the portal," her brother commanded.

Rexa tried to scream again.

Not the portal. Please. No.

She tried to wriggle out of the bodyguard's grip but it was no use. If they would just kill her, there'd be evidence, eventually her brother would be caught, and fate would be far less cruel.

Palis left the lights off and led them through the dark corridors with the small light from his sync gloves. They weren't far from that part of the complex that stored the original election files to the justice corridor. The bodyguard now carried her through the cavernous Hall of Justice. The sentencing chamber was just beyond.

At one time, anyone who broke a law was sentenced to banishment in penal colonies on the far outskirts of their tightly knit civilization. But some prisoners had managed to escape and find their way back into society. That's when the branding tradition had started, so everyone could recognize a criminal and his crime by the location of the brand. Then the portals had been invented. Once a convict was sentenced to banishment, they never came back, and crime had ceased to exist in their world.

Or at least it ceased to exist unless you had enough power and money to corrupt the system. Rexa jerked against her captor again.

The guard holding her didn't flinch as they entered the small, bare room. Rexa stared at the ominous hexagon framework of metal looming in the far corner. Palis stepped over to the controls and waved his sync gloves in front of them. The machine came to life. A wavering red light pulsed within the metal frame.

Rexa twisted her head around and caught one of the guard's

fingers in her teeth, biting down hard. He shouted and snatched his hand away from her mouth.

"You can't get away with this. Someone will know I'm missing." It was a useless thing to say, but she was desperate.

"I'll tell them you ran off with that Telaran lover of yours." Palis shrugged as if he weren't sentencing her to death.

"I don't have a Telaran lover!"

"Too bad for you." He grinned.

"You bought the election." She twisted, but the guard's arm clenched tightly around her throat.

"I only bought it by slightly more than my opponent did. That is how the game is played." His eyes were icy and cold.

"You broke the law."

"What would have happened if the Rengal clan had resumed control of the senate? Father died to see our clan in power. I'm not going to let his sacrifice be in vain. The trouble is, everything has to be so black and white with you." Palis turned and programmed the portal. It snapped and hissed as whips of bright white energy crackled within the swirling red light.

"So you're willing to sentence me to death?" She tried to kick herself away from the portal.

"It's not death, just banishment. Enjoy your life in the wastelands with the other conniving dregs of society. Goodbye."

Rexa screamed as the bodyguard pulled her up on the platform. The red light swirled and seemed to reach for her. She tried to cling to the guard, but the second one grabbed her around the neck. Choking, she felt herself fall and her vision turned black.

Burning whips of lightning and searing cold assaulted her as she dropped, falling through the red light. She couldn't breathe. Her flailing arms did nothing to stop her as she tumbled through the portal.

Suddenly, she felt as if she was being pulled through a tight vortex, spinning and spinning. She hit the ground hard.

Rexa took a minute to breathe. Pain from the impact radiated through her. Still dizzy and sick, she didn't want to move. The metal platform felt cold against her cheek. She tried to wiggle various parts of her body, hoping that nothing was broken.

Thankfully everything worked fine, although not without a good deal of pain. Cradling her side, she sat up. She'd probably cracked a rib. A gray desert stretched endlessly around her. The barren rocks and crags blended seamlessly on the horizon with the heavily overcast sky. She shivered in the cold, dry wind and pulled the collar of her jacket up around her neck.

She glanced back at the portal framework. The red light was gone. Now it was only an empty metal arch. There was no way back.

In the distance, a large mountain range rose above the desert. At least the mountains would provide shelter. But then, that was the most likely place for the other foul residents of this prison to congregate. She had no desire to run into any of them. She'd be lucky if the only people she came across were thieves and prostitutes.

Rexa touched the back of her hand to her stinging cheek. A smear of blood marred the top of her sync gloves.

Her gloves!

Her idiot brother had forgotten to take her gloves. She struggled to her feet and inspected the side of the portal frame. If she could hack into the system, perhaps there was a way to reverse the gate and send herself home. And when she *did* reach home, nothing was going to stop her from ruining her brother and making him pay.

She searched the entire structure, but there was nothing she could tap into to gain control of the blasted thing. Without a control screen, her gloves were useless, so she pulled them off and pocketed them. She shaded her eyes with her hand. To her left, some sort of gully scarred the ground.

If it was a ravine, there might be water. It was as good a goal as any.

She couldn't survive out in the open for long. She'd barely gone ten steps when she noticed bones sticking up out of the dirt. At least there were animals here . . .

Oh dear Creator, the bones were human.

The arm and leg bones had fallen at odd angles, but there was no mistaking the human ribs. Only the skull was missing.

Rexa shivered and turned away from the grim warning. She started walking.

She learned quickly that several things were deceptive in the wastelands. One of them was distance. She'd been walking for what felt like hours, but seemed to be no closer to the ravine than when she had started. Now that she looked back, she couldn't see the portal either. The only things she could see were the scraggly bushes growing like an enormous maze, and the outcroppings of black rock that rose from the brush.

She heard a rumble in the distance, a clattering noise that sent a chill down her spine. *Someone was out there.*

Climbing one of the outcroppings was a risk, but she needed to know where the noise was coming from.

A large hawk-like bird cried overhead. Rexa glanced up at it. It circled on the wind, an ominous reminder that even the animals in this place would pick her bones clean.

The rumbling came from a different direction now. Frightened, she trotted to the nearest rock outcropping and searched for a handhold, her already parched mouth painfully dry. Luckily the dark rock was layered, giving her several cracks to wedge her hands into.

She climbed, her heart beating faster. The rumbling stopped, and she thought she heard voices. Thankfully, her black synth coat meant she blended in with the surrounding rock.

Without thinking, Rexa jammed her hand into another crack, and immediately felt a sharp jab of burning pain. She gasped as she let go of the rock and fell backward, landing with a thud on the hard ground. She grabbed her wrist. Blood oozed from a nasty bite on the side of her palm. A red-spotted reptilian creature scuttled out of the crack in the rock, bared its sharp teeth and hissed at her. The frill along its back rattled in warning.

Her hand felt like it was on fire. It was already beginning to swell. She could only hold her wrist tightly and clench her teeth against the pain.

"Over here!" A man shouted. The rustling in the brush grew louder. "Sounds like a kiver got the bastard."

"Good, we won't have to kill him, then. We'll just take his head when he dies." A second voice answered. "The bounty on the Mad Man will be more than the last three combined."

Rexa closed her eyes. She was poisoned. Already the nausea set in and she felt dizzy. She was dead. Either way, she was dead.

She watched helplessly as a rusty blade cut through the brush. "Hey, it's a woman!"

Rexa tried to clear her vision, but it took too much effort.

The other man cackled. "They must have sent a whore

through the wrong portal. We'll have fun tonight. If she's not breathing, she'll still be warm."

Rexa felt them pawing at her clothing, searching for pockets, and felt the bile rise in her throat.

"Stop – stop it," she whispered, as one of them tried to hoist her up over his shoulder.

"Hey you!" A low, booming voice broke the silence of the wasteland. The hawk cried once more, the sharp keening sound slicing through the air like a knife. "You think a kiver could kill *me*?"

"The Mad Man!" One of them shouted.

The two men immediately dropped her onto the hard rock. She used all of her energy to curl into a ball.

Just then a *roar* blasted out overhead, followed by a blistering wave of heat. Rexa opened her eyes to see fire raining down around her. The two scavengers screamed as if the hand of death had just opened up to grab them.

The rumbling started up again, and with a squeal of an engine, they were gone.

"You okay?" The new stranger loomed over her. Her eyes cleared just enough to see the edge of his long, patchwork coat waving in the breeze beside the still-burning tip of a junked-together flamethrower. The bushes around them crackled as the man let out a high-pitched whistle.

The hawk swooped over the burning bushes and landed on a leather pad tied to the man's shoulder. Dark hair blew haphazardly across the man's hardened face, dark eyes, and the K-shaped brand on his cheek.

Murderer.

Rexa let her head fall, and the world turned black.

Two

She woke slowly. At first she held still, frantic to keep the nausea at bay. Her body was just as desperate for something to drink, though. She flopped her arm over her body and rolled to her side. She was on a flat pallet with a rough blanket beneath her cheek. A chain rattled as she moved.

She blinked her eyes into focus and stared down at the wrapping on her wounded hand. Although the clean bandage compressed her sore hand tightly, the color of her fingertips looked healthy. Her clothes were intact. Her ribs were still sore, but other than that, she didn't seem to have any injuries. Then she noticed the makeshift shackle on her ankle.

"You're alive." A deep, gravelly voice commented. "Good."

Rexa pushed herself against the hard dirt wall behind her. She was in a cave. Exposed wires and lights were tacked into the rough ceiling. The walls curved naturally, as if they had been carved by flowing water.

In every nook and corner, mounds of junk were piled. At first glance, they gave the impression of being heaps of garbage, but as she looked closer, all of the refuse seemed organized by size and material. Throughout the cave, strange furniture had been welded or strapped together from salvaged parts of old appliances and vehicles. This recycled furniture had even been polished to show off vintage designs. In their own way, the structures were whimsical, if not outright beautiful.

On a stand that had once been the control wheel for a Patarch War-era starfighter, the large, dark hawk roosted with his feathers fluffed in contentment and his eyes happily closed.

That's when her gaze fell on her captor. He sat at a table using a tool to pry into an electronics panel. He'd pulled the top half of his hair back and tied it, revealing the hard lines of his face and the rough dark stubble of a young beard. He was large and powerful, with wide, honed shoulders and long limbs.

Her gaze traveled back to his face and fixed on the shining scars. They formed a brand on the crest of his cheekbone, just below and slightly behind his left eye.

"What are you going to do to me?" Rexa hugged her legs tightly. She tried to fight her fear, but she couldn't stop staring at the brand.

The man frowned and rose from his seat. He stalked across the room like a large hunting cat. Rexa caught sight of the glint of metal and flinched, but when the man came forward, he was only carrying a cup of water. He towered over her, not bothering to try to make himself less threatening as he handed the cup to her.

She took it, and while the clear liquid sloshing inside the dented cup was the most tempting drug she could imagine, fear kept her from taking a sip.

"It's only water." The man returned to his chair and resumed his work on the electronic panel, as if she were no concern to him at all.

"How do I know?" She placed the cup down on the edge of the pallet. It was the only way she could defy him.

"Trust me, or don't. I don't care either way." He lifted the panel and examined it from a different angle.

"Then why did you chain me to the wall?" She pulled her leg forward and dragged the heavy chain over the blanket.

"Because I don't trust you."

Rexa let out a gasp, and almost choked on a laugh. "I'm not branded."

Her captor fixed her with a stare that could have cowed a deadly creature twice his size. "Not where I can see it, maybe. There are plenty of places to hide a brand on a body."

"I'm innocent," she hissed.

"Congratulations, you know the planetary motto." He put the panel down and walked to the other side of the room, where he lit a fire in the belly of an antique camping stove.

"So, you're innocent?" she crossed her arms. Again, he looked at her with such intensity, he forced her to glance down.

"No." He turned his back and walked into another room in the cave.

She fought a shiver, and then looked at the cup of water. Her throat clenched. "I didn't break any law. I was sent here because I was trying to expose political corruption." Rexa bit her tongue before she said anything more. Her father was responsible for a lot of the laws that sentenced people to one-way trips through the portals.

The stranger huffed and returned to the table. He chopped up some sort of tuber and tossed it into a pot. "Good luck with that."

"No kidding." She pulled on the edge of the bandage wrapped so carefully around her hand. "Why did you save me?"

He placed the pot over the heat of the fire, and then lifted one shoulder in a lazy shrug. "I don't know."

"Are you going to kill me?" she whispered.

His face remained impassive. "I don't intend to. Don't force me to change my mind."

"Rape, then." She said it as if it were a foregone conclusion. Her stomach twisted into knots of terror.

He looked at her again, but this time something about him had softened. His eyes seemed dark and deep, and no longer quite so frightening. "My brand is here." He brushed his hand over his cheek. "Not here." He brought his finger up between his eyes, where those guilty of sexual assault wore their scars.

Rexa's heart beat heavy and hard with relief, which she found troubling, since he made no attempt to hide the fact he was a convicted killer. "Then why are you keeping me here?"

He spooned some mash from the pot into a cracked bowl, and then walked over to his hawk. He gently ruffled the feathers on the bird's neck. The hawk shifted on the perch and the bells tied to the straps on his legs jingled. "You'd run."

"No offence, but it seems the logical thing to do." Rexa said, glancing at the dimming natural light slanting against one of the far walls. The light had to come from the entrance to the cave. If she wanted out, it was that way.

"Even if you cleaned me out of food and water to try to make it across the flats, you'd still be dead before you crossed Fool's Ridge. If the kivers don't get you, a pack of sand wolves will. If the sand wolves don't manage to finish you off, there are always the headhunters. And if you somehow make it past them, I'm sure you'll do fine in the city without protection or anything of value to trade."

She reached in her pocket and pressed her hand against her sync gloves. They were cutting-edge tech, and he must not have known what they could do. To someone unfamiliar with them, they would have looked like ordinary gloves.

She slowly pulled her hand back out of her pocket. He watched her with suspicion as he placed the food bowl next to her untouched water. "I don't like wasting energy, or food. When you know your limitations, and have gathered your own supplies, you can go."

"So you intend to make me work for my freedom?" Whatever he had cooked for her smelled savory and wonderful. Even though it looked like a pile of wet sand, her stomach still rumbled.

"I hadn't thought of that, but it's not a bad idea, now that you mention it." The corner of his lip turned up in what almost looked like a grin.

Rexa fought the urge to throw the bowl of mush at him. Her

tongue stuck to the roof of her mouth. She desperately needed a drink, and the bowl of mash was beginning to resemble roasted meat in her delusional mind.

"Who were those men in the desert?" She asked, poking at the steaming food. "Were they headhunters?"

Her captor nodded. "When the Red Hand Gang finally took over control of the planet, they appeased the less violent masses by offering a bounty for the heads of anyone with a brand on their face." His cheek twitched just beneath his scar. "Thieves, conspirators, prostitutes and drug-users aligned themselves with the gang under the promise that there would be no murderers or rapists in their midst."

"They got rid of their competition." Rexa mused.

"Smart girl." The man sat back down and kicked his feet up on the table.

"And these headhunters kill for money?" She knew the wasteland was a bad place, a dangerous place, but in her worst nightmares, she couldn't have imagined this.

"Trust me, the irony is not lost on me." Bitterness dripped from his voice. He looked at her, his expression grim and serious. "The really bad ones kill whoever they want and brand the face post-mortem. You were lucky I found you." He tilted his head at her unused cup. "It's only water."

Rexa picked up the cup and slowly took a sip. Her whole body cried out in relief and she hastily gulped down the rest. She waited for dizziness, some sort of sign he had ill intent, but there was nothing.

She picked up her bowl of food. She watched as he filled another bowl for himself. "What's your name?"

"Taven." He took a bite, and she did as well. The mash tasted rich, warm and soothing, with a pleasant sour bite.

"I'm Rexa." She took another spoonful. "Thank you," she forced out.

He looked down at the bowl in his hands. "You're welcome."

Three

Three weeks passed while Rexa remained chained. Thankfully, the tether was long enough that she could move fairly freely through Taven's ramshackle home. She could only get about a foot outside the mouth of the cave, though, before the chain stopped her. In that three weeks, she took great care in observing her host.

To say he was a man of few words was an understatement. In fact, since the day she'd woken up, he hadn't initiated any conversation or interaction at all. He always left it to her. At first it was infuriating. Then Rexa came to the startling realization that he was, in effect, *taming* her. Any interaction between them was always her choice. She had to seek him out.

When she did, it was often rewarding. In spite of the fact that he was quiet, she found Taven to be thoughtful, observant, fiercely intelligent and patient. On occasion, he showed a dry wit. He was even gentle. When her kiver-bite wound festered, he treated her hand with delicate care, and apologized under his breath when his efforts to clean it stung.

She still wasn't quite sure what he wanted from her, but as each day passed, she knew without a doubt he would not harm her. He earned her trust the way one would a wild creature's, and she wondered if he'd used the same method to tame his hawk, Wingman.

Any time she neared the bird, it gaped its beak, hissed at her and puffed all its feathers up in warning. She decided to give the raptor a wide berth for both their sakes.

Even after all this time, Rexa still didn't know what Taven had done to earn the brand on his cheek, but in her mind she came up with a million excuses for him. Maybe it was self-defense, or perhaps he had been trying to protect someone. She couldn't believe he would willingly kill another person in cold blood. Perhaps she was fooling herself. She'd heard stories of people allying themselves with their captors out of self-preservation, but from where she stood, it didn't seem like too bad an idea. So far, he'd proven she could trust him. She couldn't say the same for the rest of the planet.

That morning, Rexa watched him as he stood at the entrance to the cave, preparing to go out to check his traps for food. Whatever star threw light at this backward hole of a planet seemed to take pity on them that morning. For the first time since she'd arrived, a sun broke through the endless layer of clouds. In the unfiltered light, Taven's hair looked more dark brown than black, with parts that shone deep red when the rays hit them right.

He concentrated on untangling a snare. She could only see the unbranded side of his face. It was harsh, barely tamed. In that moment, he was a handsome man.

"Can I come with you?" she asked. "I could help." Her belly fluttered nervously as she stared at him. He slowly turned to look at her, his heavy lashes low, giving an inexplicable heat to his dark eyes. She knew it was futile, but she wanted to be with him on such a nice day.

He strode forward with slow and carefully placed strides, a half-grin quirked in the corner of his mouth. It reminded her of that first day. Her heart kicked up, thumping loudly in her ears, and her throat went dry. He bent down and wrapped his large hands around her ankle. With his fingertips, he deftly unscrewed one bolt, and the entire contraption fell away.

"It wasn't locked!" Rexa kicked the damn thing, and then had to hop on one foot as she nursed her bruised toe. "The whole time, I could have walked away?"

Taven shrugged. "You coming?" He held his arm out to indicate the world outside the cave.

In half a millisecond, Rexa thought of a million acts of torture she could inflict on him, and every single one of them seemed like a pretty good idea. "Damn you," she muttered. "Damn you, damn you, damn you." *And damn herself for being so stupid.*

"Too late. C'mon, before the scavengers beat us to the traps." He smiled at her, and she found herself chuckling in response.

Freedom, even such a small taste of it, felt good. The heat from the sunlight soaked into her coat as they carefully hiked down a well-worn path through the ravine. Wingman flew overhead, circling through the bronze-tinted sky.

"From this point on, you have to obey any order I give without question," Taven said, turning back to her.

"Why?" She stopped in her tracks, worried for the first time.

Taven looked exasperated. "*That's* a question." He took a careful step forward and pointed down to a thin wire crossing the path. "I've set traps all along here to keep headhunters out. Pay attention, follow my lead, and go slowly. Got it?"

Rexa gave him a quick mock salute, determined not to disappoint him. She'd never learn her way around enough to survive on her own if she couldn't keep his trust. They proceeded slowly until they reached a broad trail along a dry river bed at the bottom of the ravine.

"Keep your eyes and ears open for trouble," Taven warned. After a long, still pause where Taven watched Wingman's behavior in the air, his whole posture seemed to ease. "Do you have any experience at hunting?"

"Unfortunately, no," Rexa confessed. "I'm a bit of a city girl. I didn't even have any pets." In truth, she had been ignored most of the time she had been growing up. One of the political neophytes had always been assigned to watch her, because her parents had been too busy with their campaigns to pay her any attention. She had learned to occupy her time by hacking the tech around her, because it was there, and the only thing she really had to play with. Now that she thought about it, the stark loneliness of her childhood had been crushing. Even her brother had always seen her as a spying nuisance bent on getting him into trouble. Maybe he had had something there.

Taven seemed to have a lot of experience trudging around through brambles. They didn't have luck with any of the snares he'd set, but he carefully checked and concealed each of them before moving on again. They were able to catch some mud toads. These amphibians were immune to kivers, and Taven used them to make antivenom.

"How long have you been here?" Rexa asked, stuffing a toad in the pack.

He shielded his eyes from the sun with his palm, and seemed to consider the question for a moment. "It's been about fourteen season cycles for this world, but I don't know how many standard years that translates to."

Twenty-one. Damn.

"How old were you when you were branded?" Her throat closed up with shock as she said it. He didn't look old enough to have been a convict for over twenty years.

"Sixteen."

Dear God, he'd been a child. What had happened to him? Whatever it was, he had only been a boy. His whole life had been taken away. It didn't seem fair. But whoever he had murdered was dead. Was that fair? It was all so twisted. No matter what, she had to remember – the man who stood before her had lived most of his life in the wastelands. This place had honed him. She couldn't let herself forget it.

"Rexa, look," he said in a hushed whisper. As he turned to her, his dark eyes lit with excitement. She pushed all other thoughts from her mind and focused on the weedy patch of ground where he pointed. She stepped closer, bringing her body close enough to him that he wrapped his arm over her shoulder and directed her gaze toward an enormous, fat, muddy-brown bird resting beneath the bush.

"I haven't caught a brushrunner in years," he whispered against her ear. A shiver tickled down her neck and pooled deep in her belly.

"Do they taste good roasted?" she whispered back, as warmth spread through her limbs.

"It's the closest thing to etherium you can get around here." He pulled out a sharpened blade. "Hold still. They're strong, and it looks like the snare only caught his leg. If he breaks loose . . ."

"I'm on it."

Excitement coursed through her as he stalked around to the back of the bird. It was an ugly thing with a wrinkly bald head and a long, flappy blue comb. At the moment, its eyes were closed. Perhaps it had exhausted itself. Taven crept up behind it. Rexa took a step to the side to hide herself behind a scraggly tree.

Just then she heard a familiar rattle. A kiver hissed at her from the trunk of the tree and she screamed and leapt forward.

The bird woke with a loud "Gwark! gwark!" It flailed against the snare. Taven swore as he lunged for the thing. The tie snapped and the bird, easily the size of a small dog, barreled straight toward Rexa in an awkward, hopping run.

"Grab it!" Taven shouted, hot on the bird's tail feathers.

Rexa fought the urge to run and, instead, squatted in the middle of the bird's path with her hands outstretched as if she were catching a ball.

The ugly bird launched at her face, beating his enormous black wings. All Rexa could do was duck and cover her head with her hands.

Another sharp oath erupted from Taven as he crashed into her. They both tumbled along the ground. Fire lanced through her side from her sore rib, and the rest of her was a tangle of arms and legs. She came to a stop with her back on the warm sand and Taven pressing down on top of her.

"I'm sorry," she cried, as she wriggled beneath him. "Hurry, we can . . ."

But he didn't move. His body shook with odd jerking motions. At first she was concerned he was having some sort of seizure, but then she heard it. Low at first, as if he were trying desperately to hold it in, but couldn't.

He laughed, and the sound was far better than a roasted bird ever could be.

Rexa found herself laughing with him as they lay there in the heat and just gave in to the moment. Taven's face was transformed. Warm and bright, he seemed to glow with mirth. She wondered how long it had been since he'd laughed. He'd been alone for so long.

She reached up and touched his unbranded cheek and his gaze met hers. Tilting her chin up slightly, she smiled at him, and then let her eyes drift closed.

Her heart hammered as she waited for him to bring his lips to hers. She ached for his touch, for his kiss.

Finally, soft lips brushed hers, and his cheek scratched her warmly. Rexa had only ever heard of the effects of etherium, and the wild, free-floating ecstasy it induced in its users, but she couldn't imagine anything more mind-blowing than this kiss.

Taven pulled away. She fought to catch her breath.

"Are you okay?" His voice had turned husky and taken on a tone she'd never heard before. Her rib still ached, but at the moment she didn't care a whit. She nodded, unable to speak.

Taven rose and helped her to her feet, though he wouldn't look her in the eye and seemed uncomfortable. "C'mon, let's go home."

Rexa nodded again, feeling both dizzy and drunk from the after-effects of his kiss. "I guess it's tubers again for dinner. It's better than eating the toads."

He chuckled and led her back to the cave.

Four

Another few weeks passed, and Rexa was sure they were far more agonizing than the last ones. She had her freedom, but now her mind was in a constant state of chaos. Taven remained his usual elusive self, and to her endless torment, he refused to acknowledge that he had kissed her.

Rexa had no idea where she stood with him. Half of her felt she was completely out of her mind for thinking about it at all. It wasn't as if they could be married and live happily ever after. But he looked at her with such longing it nearly broke her heart.

If that weren't enough, sometimes they sat at the mouth of the cave in companionable silence listening to the soft sounds of the desert as daylight faded. In those moments, she really felt at peace. When they stared out over the ravine, all her thoughts and worries fell away. She could live in the present and it felt good.

She caught Taven watching her. It wasn't the first time. Usually he'd turn away, but this time, he met her gaze.

"What would you do if you could escape this place?" he asked, before tossing a kiver tail to Wingman.

"That's easy. I'd expose my brother and watch him get tossed into this hellhole." She crossed her arms and rested them on her knees.

"You really think he'd be convicted?" Taven asked.

She shrugged. "He broke the law." It was as simple as that.

Taven seemed to consider this as he picked up a knot of wires and slowly worked to untangle them. "The question is, do the people really care?"

She looked back out over the ravine. "What do you mean?"

"I'm just wondering what the point of exposing a politician is if the people are too fat, content and lazy to stage a revolution anyhow. Even if you get him, the next guy will be just as bad." He managed to work a length of red wire out and laid it in the sand.

"It's the principle of the thing." Her brother needed to pay for what he did.

Taven nodded. "I bet it's nice to have the luxury to stand on principle."

Rexa opened her mouth to protest, but then shut it again

when she realized this was one argument she had no hope of winning.

"What about you?" She tilted her head, curious as to how he would answer.

"I'd jump back to the old garbage portal that used to serve the penal colonies before they decided to throw away people." He set his lips in a thoughtful line, and then tossed a pebble into the ravine.

Rexa huffed in disbelief. "You want to go *to* a penal colony?"

"From what I understand, they're abandoned now. No one would notice strange activity at the portal, and from there I could head out into the wilderness. No one would ever find me again." He turned a second pebble over and over between his fingers before throwing it as well.

"That sounds lonely." The words came out before Rexa thought about them at all. He stared at her, his deep eyes sad and mysterious.

"It would be." He hung his head, and a lock of his dark hair fell across his scarred cheek. "I have to go somewhere tonight. Remain here. Stay vigilant until I return." Taven pushed himself off the ground and brushed off his hands.

"What? Where are you going?" Rexa jumped to her feet and followed him as he gathered some things in his pack.

"I'm heading to the junkyards. The headhunters like to patrol there, but don't worry about me. I'll be back before dawn. Stay safe." He brushed a hasty kiss on her cheek, and then turned for the entrance to the cave.

Rexa grabbed him and hauled him back. Her lips met his, and she hungrily took his mouth in a searing kiss. He caught her, holding her around the ribs. She let her fingertips slide over his neck. His mouth opened to her, and she took full advantage, slipping inside him, coaxing him to meet with her completely.

She broke the kiss, breathless. She stared into his eyes, which were alight with shock and a deep burning fire. "You come back," she demanded.

She let go.

He pushed forward and met her for a second blistering kiss, brief and fierce. When he pulled away he nodded, then disappeared into the night.

Rexa tried to catch her breath, but her heart was

pounding, and nothing seemed to quiet it. Wingman lazily flipped his wings and picked at the leather ties on his feet. The bells jangled and he fluffed his feathers as if Taven had gone to the junkyard a million times and the bird didn't have a care in the world.

Looking around the cave at all his stuff, he probably *had* done this a million times. She settled down on her hard bed and tried not to worry. It was no use.

She didn't sleep at all. After a few hours, she reasoned he couldn't possibly be back so soon. In another few hours, she fought to keep her eyes open and furiously tried to find anything that could tell her the hour. When she gave up on her search for a clock, she had to admit she was worried. When dawn finally broke, fear – deep ugly fear – gripped her.

Where was he?

By mid-morning she knew there was no mistake. Something was terribly wrong. She didn't know what to do. She didn't know where to find the junkyard. The wasteland outside of the cave was endless. What if he was out there somewhere and needed help, but she couldn't reach him? She had to do something.

"Wingman, get up!" She undid the bird's ties and pushed him on the rump, but he hunched down over his perch and hissed at her. "Damn it, bird. Taven's in trouble." She smacked him on the tail and the hawk flew out the cave opening. Taven had used the bird as a spotter. Maybe she could as well.

She grabbed an iron bar with a hooked end and Taven's box of medical supplies. Then she slung a pack with water and food over her shoulder. She ran out of the cave and looked to the sky.

Wingman was silhouetted against the gray clouds, circling and crying, beyond the ravine in the wasteland where she'd been bitten by the kiver.

If she went out onto the wasteland on her own looking for him, she was putting her life in grave danger.

She had to try.

Taven had never taken her up the trail that led to the rim. She had to be careful of the traps. Ferreting out the triggers took time, and she worried she was already too late. Once she reached the rim, she ran as hard as she could, following the circling bird. Wingman was the only guide she had.

She'd run for what felt like hours when she spotted a strange-looking vehicle with wide treads and a large, steaming tank in the back. She dove behind some brush.

Wingman had spotted the headhunters.

Slowly she peeked around the thick brush. A man with dark hair was slumped over the vehicle's controls.

Good, the bastard was dead, but there might be another. She gripped the iron bar tighter, gathering her strength. Then she noticed the familiar tie in the man's hair.

Her heart shattered.

"Taven!" Rexa rushed to him. She pulled him back from the wheel and he fell against the seat. His skin had gone gray and he'd broken out in a sweat, but he was alive. His whole shoulder was soaked in blood. Rexa pulled his shirt away from the wound. Someone or something had stabbed him, but the bleeding had stopped.

He moaned, his breathing shallow. Rexa reached for her water canteen, and brought it to his lips. "No," he whispered. "I'm poisoned. Kiver venom on the blade." *Oh dear God, he was dying.*

No! Rexa forced some water down his throat and pulled out the medical kit. In a small, sealed plastic pouch was a bright green, viscous fluid. "Is this it? Is this the antidote?" she asked, holding it up for him to see.

He nodded weakly. "You have to inject it deeply into the wound."

With what? There were no needles in the kit. Damn it! Here she was with the antivenom and she couldn't use it. She was going to have to watch him die with the cure in her hand.

She looked around desperately. There was a plant nearby covered with four-inch-long thorns. They were the closest things to a needle she could see.

Rexa broke one off. It was hollow in the middle. *Thank God.* She snapped off the tip, and then jammed it into the fluid. Pinching the pouch tight against the thorn, she squeezed. The fluid oozed out of the tip of the spine.

Swallowing the lump in her throat, she slid the spine into the wound. Taven cried out and started to shake as she emptied all of the antivenom deeply into his shoulder.

"I'm sorry, I'm so sorry," she said, as she pulled the empty pouch away, but the thorn remained lodged in his arm. Wincing, she dug carefully into the wound to get a grip on it. He shouted again as she wrenched the thorn free. Blood poured out of the agitated wound, and she staunched it with a piece of cloth. He grabbed her hand and held on. She tried to give him more water but he passed out.

Rexa struggled to stay calm. She had no clue how much antivenom she should have given him. *What if she'd just killed him?* She felt for a pulse, and breathed a sigh of relief as she found it slow and steady. She brushed his hair from his face and felt his skin. It was warm, but his color was already returning, and his skin didn't feel so clammy. The antivenom was working. They just needed to give it time.

Rexa didn't know how long they would have to remain out in the middle of the wasteland, but her fear increased with each passing minute. Cuddling in close to help keep Taven warm, she prayed the headhunters weren't watching them. They were completely exposed.

As dusk began to fall, Wingman let out a long warning cry. Rexa heard a rumble in the distance. She gripped the hooked bar tightly.

They were coming.

Five

Rexa tried to shake Taven awake. He stirred and mumbled something, but didn't regain complete consciousness. She tried to push him out of the driver's seat, but that was no use either. She had no idea how to run the machine. It was all levers and wheels. If it had a control interface, she could have handled it, but this was beyond her.

Desperate, she searched for some sort of weapon, anything. All she found was the flamethrower in the back. That thing would probably kill her faster than the headhunters would. The rumbling grew louder. She thought she could hear high voices whooping and shouting above the engines.

She threw her coat over Taven, then jumped down behind the vehicle, hiding. She forced herself to stay calm. *Panic wouldn't help her now.* She wiped her sweaty palms on her pants and adjusted her hold on the bar. She'd been pretty good with a batter-club when she'd played field ball. *Swinging a hooked iron bar at someone intent on decapitating you was hardly different from swinging at a ball, right?*

The rumbling grew louder, and then stopped, becoming a low, ominous growl. She heard two sets of boots hit the ground. "Hey, over here!" The voice sounded young.

They came closer. Closer.

Rexa let out a feral yell and ran out from behind the vehicle. The two headhunters turned in surprise. She brought the bar back and then swung with all her strength, aiming for the knee of the shorter hunter. As she connected, she felt the vibrations of his shattering bone reverberate up the iron bar. He crumpled with a loud scream, holding his broken leg.

The second came at her with a long blade, swinging it up and down in a sloppy arc. She had just enough time to block his blade with the bar, catching it with the hook. With a quick twist, she pulled the blade from his hands. Both weapons fell to the ground, bringing her face to face with her attacker.

Dear God, he was just a kid. His eyes flashed wide with panic and he lunged.

He grabbed her around the neck, choking her. Rexa struggled to kick him, but he was tall with long, lanky arms. He clenched his teeth, his face tight with fear as he squeezed the life from her. White light swam in her vision until something ripped him away. She collapsed, coughing.

Taven wavered on his feet as the young hunter turned his attention to this new threat. The hunter with the shattered leg pulled himself toward the fallen blade. Rexa dove for it, snatching the knife away at the last second and holding it over him, daring him to make her use it.

The young hunter launched himself at Taven, who fell into a fighter's stance, and with the grace of a champion, landed clean, precise, terrible blows. Taven's face had gone completely blank, as if his soul had abandoned his body and instinct alone controlled him. His hard fists landed with loud smacks on the hunter's gut, ribs and jaw. The kid was down.

They were safe. But it wasn't over.

Rexa watched in horror as Taven pulled back to strike the young hunter again and again, even though blood poured from the kid's face, and he was writhing on the ground, helpless and begging. The man she knew wasn't there anymore. Taven had become some sort of animal. And he was going for the kill.

"Taven!"

Rexa's heart thundered. Taven's bloody fist hovered, clenched in mid-air. He looked at her with wild eyes that frightened her.

His fist loosened, and he staggered backward, landing hard against the vehicle's treads. He looked horror-struck. The pain in his eyes was overwhelming. He looked down at the bleeding face of the kid he'd almost killed. She ran to him.

He panted out heavy breaths as she smoothed his hair back from his face.

"I . . . I," he stammered.

The two headhunters writhed in the sand, but neither could get up. Rexa tossed the canteen of water at them. She spoke to the one with the broken leg. "Come for us again, we won't show mercy." She turned to Taven. "Let's go home."

Taven started the vehicle and they rode across the wasteland in silence, Wingman following in the sky. Guilt and a terrible darkness had come over them.

When they reached the safety of the cave, Taven stumbled into the alcove where he had his bed. She'd never entered his space before, and remained at the narrow opening.

"Who trained you to fight?" She crossed her arms and watched him as he pulled off his boots and peeled his bloody shirt over his head.

"I'm exhausted." He let the shirt fall to the ground.

"You were trained for bloodsport, weren't you?" It wasn't really a question. Everyone knew about the illegal fights in the slums. On occasion, the loser didn't come out alive.

Squinting as if pained, he rubbed his forehead with the back of one hand. "You're not going to let this drop, are you?" He poured the contents of a bottle onto a rag, and then pressed it to his wound and hissed.

"No."

He clenched his jaw and remained silent as he tended his wound. Rexa waited him out. Finally he spoke, "My mom was arrested for drugs when I was three. The government handed me over to my uncle." He let out a bitter chuckle. "He was her dealer. They should've arrested him."

Rexa felt ill. Taven inspected the red stain on the cloth he pulled from his shoulder. She took an uncertain step into his room. She could feel his presence filling the small space as she moved closer to the bed. "What happened?"

Taven didn't answer for a long time. He sat on the thin feather mattress of his patched-together bed and folded the bloody cloth in his hand before pressing it to his shoulder again. "He decided early I'd be a good fighter, so he used any method he could to make me believe he had power and complete control. As I grew up, he deserved brands in five different places for all the things he did to me, but he never broke me. He thought he did, but he never broke me."

She sat next to him and placed her hand on his knee.

A muscle in his jaw ticked. "One day, he told me about an upcoming fight. I knew I couldn't win. He knew it, too, which was why he'd asked for my cut up front. I told him I wouldn't do it. I'd get killed. He didn't care. He said he owned me. So I hit him." She reached out and took his hand. He wove their fingers together as if he feared she'd leave. "I hit him."

Rexa felt a hot tear slide over her cheek. She squeezed his fingers tight, but the connection just didn't feel deep enough to tell him everything she wanted to say and couldn't.

Taven hung his head, his hair sliding into his eyes. "When the authorities came, I was still standing there with his blood on my hands." He looked up and met her gaze, as if daring her to claim he was innocent. "I wanted him dead. I wanted him to suffer half of what he'd made me suffer. I didn't even flinch when they gave me this." He brushed his fingertips over his branding scar.

Rexa leaned in close and kissed him there, the raised scar smooth and corded across his rough cheek. She pushed her fingers into his hair. He leaned into her, burying his face against her and holding her desperately. His shoulders shook as he fought against silent sobs. She let her own tears fall and stroked his hair.

Together they eased back onto the bed, clinging to one another. Rexa wasn't sure at what point comforting touches turned into enticing strokes. She didn't remember who exactly had peeled off her shirt so they could feel each other, skin to skin. Stroking hands turned into soft kisses. Soft kisses became gentle tugs as the rest of their clothing seemed to disappear. His skin was so soft, his body hard and hot, and in such great need of her.

She felt no fear as she surrendered to him. She ached for him, both her body and her soul. She met his hot gaze as he braced himself above her. With a gentle touch, she guided him to the core of her. With careful, agonizing strokes his body slid into hers, joining them together with such heat and intensity it took her breath away.

They moved slowly, reverently. Taven's eyes were filled with such heartbreaking wonder, Rexa struggled to keep herself centered in this storm. In the end she could only hold on, crying out and letting her tears stream down her face as they crested together. Rexa let herself be swept away, and as they clung to one another in a tangle of limbs and sleepy kisses, she felt whole.

The next morning Taven was a new man. Rexa giggled because he couldn't stop smiling, and when he tried to kiss her smirk off her face, they ended up having another much more playful go round.

Finally, weak-limbed and giddy, they managed to pull themselves out of the bedroom and into the main part of the cavern. Wingman welcomed them by tucking his head under his wing and flicking his tail.

"Good to see you too, buddy," Taven greeted.

Rexa rolled her eyes at the hawk and smiled at Taven. He turned to her. "Thank you for coming after me."

She let a soft smile play on her lips. "You're welcome. I hope that vehicle you found at the junkyards was worth it."

He straightened as if he had just remembered something. "I'll be right back." He bolted out of the cavern.

"Hey!" she called, but she didn't chase after him. She didn't have the energy, and her legs were still feeling a little wobbly. She sat at the table and looked over at the bird. "What's gotten into him?"

Wingman just ignored her as usual.

It didn't take long for Taven to come back, carrying a large chunk of scrap metal. He laid it down on the table, and turned to get his tools. Rexa examined his prize.

She grabbed it in disbelief, turning it over in her hands. It was an old-model control screen for a banking kiosk.

"Oh my God," she whispered. With enough know-how, and the right wiring, they could convert the control screen and tap into the command functions of one of the portals.

His eyes were alight with something she'd never seen in them before – hope. "I've been searching for something like this for years." Taven laid out his tools. "This is the first one I've found in good enough condition that it might work. Now it's just going to take me the next twenty years to figure out the security codes so I can program the portals." He gave Rexa a resigned shrug. "At least it's a start."

Rexa's heart flipped over and over in her chest as she reached into her pocket and removed the sync gloves. "It's more than a start," she confessed, laying the gloves on the table. "These are sync gloves. I was using them to hack into the information databases when I was caught by my brother. If we can get enough power to the control screen, the gloves should activate and I can transfer the security codes from the gloves directly into the portal's command system."

His brows knitted together. Taven seemed wary, as if he didn't dare to believe what he was hearing.

She swallowed. "If we can get it working, we're free."

Six

"Damn it!" Rexa smacked aside the bent piece of wire she was using to patch together the circuit framework on the table. They had been trying to breathe life into the damn control screen for weeks, and nothing had happened. Every time they powered up Taven's generator, their patched electrical connections would pop and hiss, but it did no good.

"We're never going to get off this damn rock," she muttered to herself as she bent back over the mechanically cannibalized screen.

"Would that be so bad?" Taven patiently picked up the bent wire and tried again. Rexa looked up at him. He'd changed so much from the first time she'd seen him. He now trusted her to shave him and clip his hair, two things he couldn't do well before, since he had no mirrors. Without the stubble on his face, his scar seemed less pronounced. There was humor and warmth in his fathomless eyes, and his shorter hair gave him a rakish quality.

"Your silence is less than flattering," he commented, humor shining in his eyes.

Would it be so bad? Honestly, in spite of the headhunters, the kivers, the terrible food and living in a cave, she was happier than she'd ever been in her life. And it was all because of him. "No," she answered. "No, it wouldn't."

She didn't have a lot of experience of love. As bad as she had it, Taven had it worse.

As she looked at him, she knew. They didn't have to say a thing. He leaned forward and kissed her tenderly, his warm lips showing – in all the ways they might never be able to say – that he loved her, and she loved him too.

He gave her a wicked smile full of promise as he flipped the switch on the generator for one more try.

The entire contraption whirred and hummed, and the screen came to life.

"We did it," Rexa whispered, so overcome with hope she could hardly draw breath.

Taven let out a victorious shout and bounded from the table. He swept her up, swinging her around as he kissed her. It was a kiss filled with joy and hope and so much fiery desire all Rexa could do was hold on.

It didn't take them long to pack up anything useful they could find. Taven's new vehicle made quick work across the desert, but at the height of the day, the risk of headhunters was very real. Finally, they arrived at the portal.

Rexa watched Taven cut the leather ties from Wingman's legs. As she finished the last connections that spliced the new control screen into the portal she'd come through all those weeks ago, her heart twisted in sympathy when Taven said goodbye and sent the bird soaring free.

The hawk let out a long keening cry that carried on the wind. Rexa took Taven's hand as they watched Wingman soar.

She tried to quell the jittery feeling in her hands by pressing them together. "Are you ready?" she asked. She reached down and turned on the generator. The control panel came to life and she slipped on her gloves.

With expert dexterity, she hacked into the coding, overrode the security systems, and activated the portal so it could draw power from the entire network of portals on the other side.

The red swirling light burst to life in the center of the frame. "I've tapped into the old portal at the abandoned penal colonies." She gave him a soft smile. "That's what you wanted."

Taven had to go first. She'd have to reprogram the portal to send her back to the capital. It was what she had wanted since she'd arrived on this planet. She'd wanted to go home.

But now?

Taven lifted her chin with one finger. "I want you, Rexa." He pulled her in close, holding her tight as if he would never let go. "Come with me."

"Taven, I . . ."

He pulled away from her and stepped to the edge of the red light. "Come with me," he said, as the light engulfed him and he disappeared.

Rexa cursed. She suddenly felt choked with an emotion she could hardly understand. She knew what she had to do. It was black and white.

She pressed her lips to the back of the control glove. Taven was right: political corruption would just roll merrily along while her brother got a slap on the wrist.

But it was the law.

She didn't care.

The generator's hum dropped a note and began to slow. She didn't have much time. She had to make her choice.

The hawk cried, and she felt the tears streak down her face. There was no choice.

She stepped forward into the red light. It surrounded her and she let it sweep her away. She didn't fight the vortex as it grew tighter and tighter.

She fell.

Strong arms caught her on the other side.

She blinked up into Taven's shining eyes. He buried his face into her neck and held her like she was the most precious thing he'd ever seen.

"I didn't think you'd follow," he whispered against her skin. She looked out on a sunrise glowing over an endless forest teeming with birds and beasts, and clear running streams. "God, I'm glad you did." He turned to her and looked at her with such awe. He kissed her with deep, fierce, true love.

She wound her fingers with his, and together they walked toward freedom.

Nuns and Huns

Charlene Teglia

One

The ship emerged from the colossal stresses of the wormhole
with all klaxons blaring warnings. Captain Althea Eudora hit the
override to silence them. If the ship's structural integrity failed,
crushing them all or perhaps peeling away and exposing them to
hard vacuum for another variation on sudden violent death, she
didn't want that cursed noise to be the last sound she heard.

But the controls responded to her frantic hands, moving
faster than her mind could, and the red warning indicators
gradually shifted to green. Death by any method became a less
pressing concern, to be replaced with the next: where were
they? And when?

Her navigator, Su Carst, spun her chair in a circle as she took
in star charts overlaying the real-time display of their current
position. "Captain, confirming we emerged from the wormhole
following the same trajectory as the exiles."

"Excellent. Comm, can you pick up their ship's beacon?"

Nia Thule frowned in concentration, long slender fingers
tapping her console. "I have the signature, but it's degraded.
Enough to indicate a significant lapse in time between their
emergence and ours."

Althea nodded. They'd all known the risk they were taking.
The trip through the wormhole was one way, and although
they'd only been a month behind when they'd seized this ship

and gone in pursuit, they'd been prepared for significant time dilation on the opposite end. "How much?"

"Over five centuries."

"So much." Althea slumped back in her seat, as much as the harness allowed. "They'll have forgotten everything, their descendants."

"Which might make our mission easier," Nia suggested hesitantly.

It might, at that. The leaders of the warrior caste their government had rightly identified as a threat had been deported without warning, shot to the far side of a newly discovered wormhole while on a manufactured training exercise. Those men, deprived of everything they had a right to, and trained to solve problems with overwhelming force, would hardly be predisposed to listen to a scientific delegation from their home world.

But their descendants wouldn't have to be reasoned with. And they would carry the same precious genetic material that had been so abruptly purged from their race, lest any future generations rise to threaten the order genetic manipulation had made possible. The very order that doomed them all, according to every projection Althea and her team had run from the sanctity of their cloistered institute based on Pangaea's third moon. The very traits that guaranteed a vibrant and adaptive race were also disruptive.

Life, Althea mused, *had such a tendency to be messy.* Biology disapproved of political expediency. So strongly that if her team proved correct, the world they'd left behind no longer existed. The will to fight ensured the will to survive. Without the very traits that threatened the status quo, their civilization had unwittingly sowed the seeds of its own destruction.

She'd tried to get their leaders to listen to reason. At first. And then she'd realized the willful ignorance that met her team's results was the only reason she remained at liberty. Before somebody suddenly started listening and recognized her team as the next threat to the ruling body, she'd plotted grand larceny, treason, and a host of civil infractions from small to great. And somehow, together, they'd done it. They'd hijacked the supply ship on its biannual run to their moon, and plunged headlong in pursuit of their hope for survival.

They'd made it this far fueled by desperation and determination.

The same motivation would carry them through the next steps. "Triangulate that signal, and then scan the nearest inhabited world for our genetic markers."

Three months later, Althea paused outside a door and tugged at her clothes, trying to ease the unfamiliar sensation of tight denim encasing her from hip to heel. The boots she wore were made of soft-tooled leather, and a plain white cotton T-shirt completed her ensemble. She was appropriately garbed for the occasion, she assured herself, even as she frowned at the sheerness of her shirt's fabric and the restriction of motion imposed by her pants. The outfit was wholly impractical, and she failed to find any esthetic value in it, either. But she'd seen dozens of similarly dressed women enter the establishment before her, and several of them had engaged the attention of her target; the bar's proprietor.

The signal they'd followed after exiting the wormhole had led them to a small, blue-green world, third in its system from a golden G-type sun. Weeks spent researching Earth's records confirmed that their warriors had wreaked havoc as the army of invaders known as Huns, a people who suddenly appeared with their own language and no prior known history. The line of descent from the man called Attila to the man known as Caleb Bronson was unmistakably Pangaean, according to the ship's scanners.

It had taken time to locate the men they sought, and even more time to learn the dominant language, copy local styles and attain enough working knowledge of the world to enter it undetected by the current technology.

But at some point, it would be time to declare an end to research and act. Althea hoped she'd struck the right balance between preparation and procrastination. And she really hoped the dubious custom of mechanical bull-riding would prove an effective way to attract Caleb's interest.

The full impact of the bar's sights, sounds and smells hit her as she crossed the threshold. She paused to adjust for a moment as the door closed behind her. After years on a moon base followed by months aboard a ship breathing canned air, the sudden plunge into so much life was staggering. Raucous music and dozens of simultaneous conversations at all volume levels were distractions she forced herself to filter out. She scanned faces and body types until her eyes came to rest on the match she sought.

His tall broad-shouldered form looked more impressive in the flesh than it had via a computerized image. His green eyes glittered with clear intelligence beneath the camouflage of hooded lids that made him appear disinterested while he took in every detail around him. Sensual lips softened the severity of his sharp cheekbones and stubborn chin. The well-defined musculature his every movement revealed showed he'd honed the physical gifts he'd been born with.

Caleb stood out amid the terrestrial males like a wolf among sheep. Althea wondered if they were aware of that on some level, because the bubble of personal space around his body was larger than that surrounding his counterparts. The man inspired a sense of caution in her, too. He had bred true to type. He was strong, dangerous, unpredictable. Exactly what she needed.

"Got another taker," Boyd Maxwell jerked his head to indicate the direction. Caleb finished pouring beers, and sent four of them sliding down the bar, where they stopped at the precise spots he intended – in rapid progression like targeted missiles of malted barley – and turned his attention to the slender redhead mounting the bar's mechanical bull.

She was worth a look even without the high-heeled cowboy boots and skintight jeans that made the most of her legs and emphasized the heart-shaped swell of her backside. The blunt cut of her straight copper-hued hair made a flattering frame for her delicate features and porcelain skin, and the fabric of her T-shirt clung in a way that hinted at rather than displayed the curves beneath.

A sign overhead invited interested parties to "Take the Challenge". Anybody who could stay on through Caleb's programmed course of bucking got a free pitcher of beer. Which wasn't usually the incentive for women to climb aboard. No, most of them were vying for masculine attention. Often, for reasons he didn't analyze, his.

The redhead seemed to sense his gaze, or maybe she'd been subtly watching him, because she raised her head to let her gray eyes meet his across the crowded, smoky bar. She studied him in solemn silence for a long moment. And then her lips tilted in a smile. She dropped him a wink as if to say, *Go ahead. I can take it.*

Her choice. Caleb pressed the button that launched the bull into action, and the noise around him shifted from general uproar to shouts of encouragement, catcalls, and carnal invitations. When she fell off, she'd have no shortage of partners ready to soothe any bruises she had gained.

The redhead wrapped herself around the bull and clung like a burr, if burrs were long, lithe, coordinated, and had nipples that thrust up enticingly against a tantalizing layer of white cotton. Her spine arched and relaxed as she moved with the mechanical beast, seemingly anticipating each shift in direction and reacting effortlessly. The shifts became more abrupt, the bucks harder, steeper, grouped unpredictably. She held firm. Her hair fanned out around her shoulders as the bull went into a furious head-down extended spin that usually unseated anybody who could stay on that long.

The stranger showed no signs of coming off. Instead, she leaned back with arms extended above her head to maximize the centrifugal force, like some cross between a ballet dancer and a daredevil, staying connected to the machine between her legs with the pressure exerted by her thighs and absolutely perfect balance.

The beast at last plunged to a halt. The stranger rose up gracefully and swung a leg over, dropped to stand beside the defeated bull, face flushed, eyes sparkling, a picture of lush sensuality, gleeful triumph and something else he couldn't define.

Caleb motioned her to him. "You win," he stated, already pulling the tap to fill her pitcher. He slid it across to her, his hand brushing hers as she accepted it. That small contact sent a frisson up his spine and made his groin tighten.

"Only if you share it with me," she responded, still grinning like a kid who'd gotten away with something. If she'd given him a sultry come-hither invitation, he could have resisted. But the impish glee resonated with him. And hell, if she could ride a bull like that, he knew what she could do with, for, and to him.

"Deal." Caleb tossed his bar towel to Boyd to indicate he was going off-duty, and grabbed two frosted glasses. Then he led the way to a table in the corner, for relative levels of quiet. But her unexpected victory had dropped the normal level of volume in the place to a dull roar, low enough to allow her to say whatever she wanted to him.

Which turned out to be, "This is delicious."

Two

She tasted the froth at the top of her glass as if sampling some unknown delicacy, then tilted her head back. The icy cold beverage filled her mouth before she took a leisurely swallow, eyes closing in appreciation. She set the glass back down carefully, as if she were used to handling delicate crystal and drinking something that cost significantly more than beer.

"It's my own recipe," Caleb stated, wondering where she was going with this.

"You're a genius," she assured him with apparent sincerity. She raised the glass for another long drink.

That wasn't the line he usually got.

"No, really," she stated, as if sensing his skepticism. "A wonderful balance of flavors, bitter and yet sweet. And the mechanical bull, that was your program, yes? Excellent tactics."

His lack of response made her brows draw together. "I offend you?"

"Most women say something like,'My place or yours.'"

She tilted her head to one side, considering. "It will have to be yours. Mine is . . . complicated."

A mixture of amusement and arousal stirred inside him, along with a curious reluctance to let the conversation come to its natural end. When was the last time he'd found it so stimulating to talk to a woman? "Aren't you going to introduce yourself first?"

"Is that a required part of the ritual?"

"Usually."

"I am Althea. You are Caleb." She beamed at him, and the suddenness of it gave him a curious shock. "We are now introduced. May we proceed to your place?"

"Slow down and back up to 'complicated'. Is sleeping with you going to get me shot?"

"Oh, no. I pose no danger to you at all."

Caleb wondered why he wasn't reassured. A complicated,

sexy, obviously intelligent woman could pose all kinds of dangers to his peaceful existence. "You're not from around here, are you?"

To his surprise, the offhand remark made her features still and her eyes widen, almost as if she were frightened. Then her face smoothed into calm. "No, but I thought I spoke your language well?"

"You do." Just, oddly. But he kept that observation to himself.

"We don't have to talk." She leaned forward and touched the corner of his mouth with the tip of one finger. "I am sure you can think of other things we could do."

Caleb gave in to temptation and nipped at the finger, lightly grazing the pad with the edge of his teeth. "Many things."

Her eyes darkened. "I would like to try them all."

Ending up at his place seemed inevitable. So did the slide of his hands through the silk of her hair, the urgent meshing of tongues and mouths, the soft sounds Althea made as he backed her up against the wall and kicked the door closed behind them. She kissed him with a mix of wild abandon and hesitation, as if she weren't sure what to do first. Or maybe she simply wasn't sure. The thought made him halt and drag his lips from hers.

"You want this?" Caleb rasped out the question in a voice roughened by desire.

Her eyes held his. "Oh, yes."

"Are you sure?"

"I rode a mechanical bull for you. Yes, I am sure."

Her exasperation made him grin. So did her confession. "So you did do that to get my attention?"

Althea gave him that impish grin that did things to his insides. "It worked."

"It did." Caleb gave up talking for more direct communication now that his conscience was clear. They were both consenting adults, she wanted him, and he sure as hell wanted her.

Her T-shirt became a barrier he lost patience with, so he pulled it up over her head, exposing a satiny expanse of bare skin all the way down to the hip bones that showed above the low waist of her jeans. He made a sound of satisfaction at the sight and then proceeded to taste her from the line of her jaw to the hollows of her collarbones, the slant of her breasts, the valley between, the pebbled nipples that tightened as he curled his tongue around them, before moving down to the soft skin below her navel. His hands gripped the rounded swell of her buttocks, drawing a low gasp from her.

Caleb paused to look up at her. Her passion-darkened eyes stared down at him, lips swollen from kissing, breath coming in soft pants. She looked wild, wanton. Wanting. With a low growl, he pulled her down to the floor and rolled onto his back with her plastered to his chest, belly to belly, thigh to thigh, far too many layers separating the lower halves of their bodies. Before he could get her pants off, her boots would have to go.

"Boots off. Now."

She struggled to comply, but the tight leather proved difficult. Caleb recognized the problem and sat up. He turned her around and kept her in his lap, her backside snug against his groin. From his new position he could grasp her boots while she pulled her feet free, one at a time. He tossed the boots aside, not caring where they fell or what they hit.

"Pants next," Caleb murmured, hands already working on her snap and zipper. "You okay with the floor, or should I leave these on you long enough to make our way to the bed?"

She gave him a confused look. "What?"

"My thoughts exactly." He hooked his fingers into her belt loops and tugged the open jeans down, then off. He paused to note the lack of panties to match her lack of bra. She hadn't worn socks, either. He put the oddity aside and decided to focus on being grateful that her choice sped up the undressing process while he stripped away the remains of his own clothes, pausing only to snag a foil square from his pocket.

Small, slender fingers plucked it from him and tossed it aside. "Not necessary."

She was on the Pill, then. Or maybe she took shots. Whatever, the opportunity to ride this intoxicating redhead bareback had him hard as granite. He had presence of mind enough to be a gentleman and take the floor while his body provided a mattress for hers, instead of crushing her into the carpet.

That was the only gentlemanly impulse that escaped the vortex of heat and need swallowing them both whole. Her satin flesh slid against his while he captured her mouth again and again, hands fisted in her hair. Her thighs parted and slid over his, settling the moist heat of her against his penis. That member throbbed in response to the contact, and the tiny motion combined with the pressure of her body against his opened her slightly as if in welcome.

Caleb reached down to stroke her where their bodies nearly joined, finding her slick and ready. He didn't waste any more time claiming her the way he'd wanted to since he'd watched her ride that wicked bull: parting her flesh, sheathing himself to the hilt again and again while she writhed and bucked against him, until they spent themselves and came to rest, panting, her small body shivering with aftershocks atop his.

"Bed next time," Caleb rasped against her ear. She gave a nod and a half-laugh. But despite his intentions, they didn't make it past the couch the second time, where her upper half rested on the leather as she knelt on the floor, legs wide apart while he thrust endlessly into her from behind. After that, the shower, where he braced her against the wall with her legs wrapped around his waist. And then the bed seemed redundant, so they made their way to the kitchen with a towel slung around his waist and one tucked neatly sarong-style between her breasts.

"Hungry?"

"Famished." Althea settled into a chair while he put together a plate of cheese, crackers and grapes. She tasted everything the way she had the beer, as if every flavor and sensation was something new to experience and savor. Come to think of it, she'd gone at him the same way.

"Drink?"

"Um." She swallowed. "Yes, please. More of your own recipe?"

Since he always kept a few bottles cold, that was an easy request to grant. He twisted the cap off for her and handed her the chilled brew. She took it gingerly, then followed his example when he drank straight from his bottle. Once she started, she gulped thirstily, so he offered her another. She accepted with cheerful greed.

"So you're some kind of illegal alien," Caleb stated, not certain he was right about her status but dead sure she was from further away than another town or state.

A peal of laughter escaped her. She raised the bottle in a salute, grinning at him conspiratorially. "You have no idea. I broke so many laws and regulations. Possibly all of them."

She was proud of her lack of visa, then. She didn't seem the criminal type, either. Curiouser and curiouser.

"But how did you know I was an alien? I pass for human perfectly as long as nobody scans my genome."

She couldn't possibly be drunk. Not on fewer than two beers. Which meant she was joking.

"You look very human."

She nodded. "So do you. That's why you all got away with it. You have for hundreds of years, so I knew we could get away with it for a few days."

You? We? Caleb's attention sharpened. "Who do you mean?"

"All of us." The hand not holding the bottle made an encompassing wave. "You and all of your genetic prototype, you've been on Earth since Attila and his men landed in their escape pods and decided to topple the local government. Their own being inconveniently out of reach."

"And who is we?" Caleb asked the question casually.

"Myself and my team," she answered promptly, taking another long drink. She paused to wipe her mouth on the back of her hand and beamed at him again. "This is so good. We have nothing like it. May I sample the molecular composition for later reconstruction?"

"Be my guest."

She removed a plain metal stud from her earlobe and waved it over the bottle. It emitted a beam of light. When the light cut off, she restored the earring to its former position.

Toy laser jewelry? Caleb decided to ignore that and stay on topic. "You were telling me about your team."

"Oh, yes." Althea turned solemn. "We're scientists. All women. We work in teams that way, segregated by gender as well as area of study. We've lived a very sheltered existence. I always thought it was to encourage us to focus on our work, but now I realize it was to keep us isolated from the general population and prevent unlicensed cross-breeding. They had to enhance our curiosity and creativity, you see, or we'd have been no good, but those traits made us a danger to the status quo. Much like your genotype."

"Mine?"

"Mm, the super-soldiers. Not just brawn, although you all have that, of course, but high intelligence, adaptability, leadership, outside-the-box thinking. Mavericks. Renegades. And that was why they realized they had to get rid of you. They were afraid you'd stop following orders and start giving them. Judging by what the Huns did, a valid concern."

"And who is *they*?" Caleb asked, wondering if this was an elaborate fiction or evidence of mental illness.

"Pangaea's ruling body. The ones who set up the genetic-manipulation program and designated every future person for their predestined role. They threw you away like garbage, jettisoned to the far reaches of space, but you aren't trash. You're treasure. You're the hope and future of our race. That's why we came to find you."

"And have wild monkey sex."

Althea blinked. "Well, yes. We hijacked a space ship with FTL drive but we couldn't steal a genetics lab, too. That limited us to natural methods. We don't have the equipment for anything else."

"You're telling me I'm an alien. And you're part of a second wave of hot alien women looking to score." It was the stuff of juvenile science-fiction fantasies, except that something about her kept him from dismissing her story entirely. Like the way she held a grape up to the light and squinted at it, studying it as if it were a specimen in a lab.

His words made her grin in delight. "You think I'm hot?"

"I did until you started talking aliens."

Her smile faded, and then became a frown. She focused on the bottle in her hand. "This beverage. This is some sort of truth serum." She let it go so abruptly that it nearly spilled the remains of its contents on the table. Her hand flew to cover her mouth, eyes wide in horror. "I have to go."

Yes. Yes, she did. But she went faster than Caleb anticipated, and in a way he never could have. She twisted the stud in her ear. A rainbow of light encased her body. When the light went out, only an empty towel on her chair was left to dumbfound him.

"Hey. Hey! Althea!" He shouted at the empty chair. "Dammit, come back!"

But she didn't. Even though he sat at the table until dawn broke outside the kitchen window. He would have been tempted to believe the entire episode was a hallucination, but when he got up and retraced their hurricane path through his condo, it ended in two sets of clothing on the floor. She'd left that much behind. Caleb knelt and gathered up her shirt and jeans, folded them neatly, and collected her boots. In the process, something caught his eye. Something small, winking in the light of day.

A metal stud. Twin to the one she'd used to vanish, taking his genetic material with her. And it was at that moment he realized why she'd told him the condom wasn't necessary.

Althea might already be carrying his child.

Three

"I jeopardized the mission," Althea repeated. Her lips felt numb. Her stomach felt like lead. "I told him everything."

"You didn't," Nia assured her. "I scanned your report. You never mentioned your favorite color, or that you slept with a stuffed koa until you reached your majority."

Althea groaned and buried her face in her hands. "I have to abdicate as captain. I've failed. You're next in seniority, you should take over."

"You are behaving irrationally," Nia said. "You're the team leader. You organized the hijacking. You have more flight experience than any of the rest of us. I barely passed basic stellar navigation. I know just enough to pilot an in-system shuttle from moon base to moon base. And you didn't fail, you engaged your target. You may have told him more than you intended, but what can he do? Report you to the local authorities? You've studied their culture. People who believe in UFOs are dismissed as crackpots."

"I don't know what he can do. That's what worries me." Caleb was dangerous and unpredictable. Precisely why she'd wanted him. She knew better than to dismiss him. If he chose to complicate her mission, he was capable of finding a way. He'd been designed to innovate on the spot, under any conditions. And to never give up until he won.

"Worry in private," Nia advised. "You're the captain."

For better or worse, it seemed she still was. She took advantage of captain's privilege and retired to her quarters. The walls seemed to close in on her after the expanse of a planet, so she took the time to synthesize the beverage she'd sampled at

Caleb's. It tasted flat. False. She sighed and discarded it. Another failure.

"You can't make it like a photocopy," a low masculine voice said from behind her. "You have to brew it. It's a process. The magic happens over time."

Althea turned slowly, not willing to believe the evidence of her ears until her eyes confirmed it. She took in the sight of Caleb, from his rumpled hair to his dark scowl, and something inside her breathed again. He was real. He was here.

Then she remembered that that was a very bad thing and backed up as far as her tiny shipboard quarters allowed. Which wasn't far enough.

"Hello, Althea. Surprised to see me?"

She licked suddenly dry lips and swallowed hard around the obstruction in her throat before she could answer. "Yes."

"You shouldn't be."

"I didn't underestimate you, if that's what you mean," Althea said.

"I'm glad to hear it. The mother of my future child should have some respect for her baby's father."

All her instincts had been right. Caleb was dangerous, and she'd given him reason to see her as a threat.

"You're angry," Althea said cautiously.

"No, I'm a little past that. You set out to seduce me in hopes of getting pregnant and then going on your merry way, taking my child with you."

When he put it that way . . . "You weren't to know. I never intended to tell you."

"And you think that makes it better?" He stalked closer.

"You have sex with strange women all the time," Althea protested. "It wasn't like I was trying to make you do something against your will. And they didn't need you like I did."

His face abruptly closed, losing all expression. "But you didn't, did you? You didn't need me at all. I was just a convenient sperm donor."

Althea lost all patience. "There is nothing convenient about you, Caleb Bronson. You were difficult to analyze, nearly impossible to make contact with. I had to go to ridiculous lengths to gain your attention and win your interest. If you knew the hours I spent in a simulator running mechanical bull programs until I could stay on no matter what the computer threw at me, you wouldn't stand there calling yourself convenient." She spoke the last word like a curse.

"If I was so inconvenient, why didn't you pick on another man?"

The question caught her off guard. "I, well, you were the ideal candidate for me."

"Really? Why? If I'm one of a batch of discarded genetic experiments, wouldn't any other one do?"

Her lower lip caught between her teeth. She began to feel trapped by more than his body and the cold panel pressing against her spine. "Your blood and tissue type, um . . ." she broke off in confusion.

"What about them?" Caleb took a step closer, and into the tight confines of her cabin, bringing him within touching distance.

Althea waved her hands in surrender. "Fine! Okay! Any other would have done for the mission." Her voice dropped to a near whisper. "But only you would do for me."

"Oh, Althea." He reached out to rub his thumb against her lower lip, tracing the line he'd kissed until the sensation made her head swim while she hungered for more. "You present me with a dilemma."

"I didn't mean to." The raw honesty was no defense, she knew. Yet it was all she had to offer.

"I know." Done with talking, at least for the time being, Caleb bent his head to hers. Their mouths met, clung, opened to taste each other more deeply. His hands captured hers, fingers tangling. When the kiss finally ended, Althea felt certain that whatever he demanded of her, she would be powerless to deny. The thought made threads of ice form in her veins, only to melt away under the onslaught of his body moving against hers.

He rasped out, "We never did make it to a bed. You have one hidden away somewhere?"

In answer, she pressed the button that made a folding bunk lower from the opposite wall panel. No matter what came next, she wasn't about to rob herself of the chance to touch him and be touched by him one last time.

Caleb swung her up in his arms and carried her to it, placing her on her back before lowering himself on top of her. Urgent hands made short work of clothing. She yanked at his, he tore at

hers, and in moments they were gloriously skin-to-skin. The
heat of him burned into her like a brand as his weight pinned her
in place.

Not that she had any intention of escaping at the moment.
Althea was all too delighted to be caught by the press of his flesh
into hers, the heady slide of his length inside her, the sensation
of being surrounded by the heat and scent of him while he plun-
dered her body like a warrior bent on conquest.

The dizzying pleasure ended in a molten burst, as Caleb spent
himself in her depths while her flesh clenched around his as if
trying to prolong the moment and prevent the inevitable with-
drawal. But it had to come.

Althea bit her lip against the protest that she had no right to
make as Caleb released her and rolled off to sit up facing away
from her.

When he spoke, his voice was hard and implacable. "Two
things. First, don't think you can settle every fight we have with
hot make-up sex. Second, I'm coming with you."

Althea blinked. "What?"

Caleb turned to glare at her over his broad shoulder. "Which
part didn't you understand?"

She gave up struggling to make sense of the turn of events,
and threw herself at the lifeline he offered. "All of it."

He rubbed his jaw as he looked down at her sprawled, naked
form. "Okay, the first part. You can't control me with sex. Well,
maybe you could. But I'd know you were doing it and it wouldn't
end well."

He thought she could control him with sex? Now there was a
revelation. "I wasn't sure I was doing it right," Althea confessed.
"I did tell you I lived alone, no men, no distractions. Just work."
The possibility that she'd bent his mind into the bewildering
dimensions he'd bent hers into delighted her as much as it
surprised her.

"You mean you'd never—?" he broke off. "Never mind. The
next part. I'm coming with you. You want a child? You can
have as many as you want. But I'm part of the package deal.
The thought of you running loose in the galaxy makes my
blood run cold."

"It does?"

Caleb nodded. "Look what you've done since you broke out

of your ivory tower. Stealing a space ship to hunt down dangerous renegades, riding mechanical bulls, going home with strange
men. You could have been killed at least a dozen ways. If I go
with you, your odds of staying alive long enough to give birth go
way up."

If he went with her, her odds of survival and success were
exponentially increased. But that wasn't what made the giddy
bubble of hope rise inside her. "Caleb. Why would you do that?
Leave the only world you've ever known?"

He shrugged. "According to you, and everything I've seen
backs up your story, it isn't even my world. And it'll be a hell of
an adventure. Think of it. The chance to explore strange new
worlds, seek out new civilizations."

She narrowed her eyes at him. That sounded tantalizingly
familiar, but she'd waded through so much background material
learning about his culture that she couldn't place the reference.
"And is that all you want? Adventure?"

"Hell, no." Caleb scooped her up into his lap and cradled her
close. "I can find adventure on Earth. And I have. What I can't
find there is you."

This must be happiness, Althea thought, dazed and amazed.
She curled into him and nuzzled his chest. "Welcome aboard,"
she said.

After that, there wasn't any more talking for a long time.

Song of Saire

Leanna Renee Hieber

One

Professor Brodin dialed back the ship's filters so that there was no mental block between himself and the whole of his surroundings. He soared inside a vaulted ship of cool steel and Gothic arches called the *Dark Nest*. The craft was the only friend and hope of survival left to his people. He had to sift out the tumult of emotions of the ship's grieving crew, and instead attempt to pierce the whole of space and time with one psychic lance. He dared to break into the mind of the woman who meant more to him than he'd ever been allowed to say.

He put his fingers to the pressurized glass and stared out at the stars.

Only in reaching out his hand did he notice how hard he shook; not because he was an elder – age was relative for a man of his power—

The pristine white tunics of the first-grades were spattered with garish scarlet blood as shrapnel tore through little bones and vulnerable tissue.

He shook for all the years he'd spent wondering if he could ever freely love her—

She was running. Hard.

He shook because a rare graft over his heart allowed him to feel her pulse in concert with his—

Choking out the stench as the training school burned; buildings, turf, human hair . . .

He shook to be truly *with* her in these terrible moments—

Hiding the surviving children – all that were left from her class – in a cave in the mountainside . . .

Success. He'd gotten through. He could sense her, see flashes of her mindscape. Her experiences hit him like swift blows to the head—

Captured by gunmen . . .

But what good did *seeing* do when he was light years away, forced to watch and wait, helpless to get her off the Homeworld that wanted her dead—

An assailant struck a blow to her side, a rib cracked in searing pain—

Brodin slammed his fist against the glass, and the cavernous vault of the *Dark Nest* cathedral of a ship echoed his furious cry. He didn't know when these flashes timed with her reality, or when he could know she was safe.

She could not feel him as he did her. Her mental fields were too tightly sealed as she did her best to mitigate the crashing waves of psychic screams transmitted as her students were murdered. But because she was unable to wholly block them, Brodin in turn was accosted by the dying emotions of children he considered his own, though they were not. Gunned down or bombed, the children faced the shock of death with the question: *Why, what did we do?* on their terrified lips.

Brodin rallied as his mind's eye watched—

A swift, psychic blow brings the gunmen to their knees. She sends what students she can onto a ship, but she couldn't get to all the survivors, so she stays behind . . .

As she watches them go, Brodin catches her stern, terse prayer, though she'd have no idea he was listening or alive:

Brodin, you and that Nest *better be up there, and you better be ready . . .*

"I'm ready," Brodin cried aloud. Hearing his words bounce back to him in the cool steel vault of the ship that had seen many miracles, he knew he meant it. In every way. He had to break through and tell her that he was waiting for her, in the *Dark Nest*, with a new planet at the ready. He had to contact her lest she sacrifice herself when there was so much to live for.

Every action heroic and selfless; that was the essence of Professor Saire.

The only woman he had ever loved.

The woman he'd not been allowed to love.

Whether she was confident in his sentiment, or what he'd done to ensure she'd stay alive, was another matter entirely. A matter that might yet cost him his own life. If she died, she would take him with her. This was no metaphor or exaggeration, it was simple fact.

Two

It had happened at last. The genocide they had prayed would never come. Their intel was wrong. Saire had been given a tip that there would be an attack the next month. But then her source was shot. There were contingency plans, of course, but as elders of the Psychically Augmented population of newly evolved humans, she and Brodin knew there would be inevitable casualties. The issue was how many.

I will count and mourn the dead later, Saire promised herself, hoping against hope that the attacks didn't extend to their brethren in space. She couldn't count on hope – she could only try to survive.

Racing back to where a few of the children had hidden themselves, she did her best to stay out of sight, but there was a hundred-yard dash she had to make out in the open. Though she might be an elder, her young physique was a contrast to the glimmering silver of her long hair and the crease of worries around her eyes. The newly evolved humans were proud that they aged beautifully, like the finest wine. So, her sprint was impressive. Especially nursing a broken rib. But it was not enough to outrun a drone.

"They won't even kill us themselves, but send robotics to do it for them? Devils and cowards," she spat through clenched teeth as the ground exploded behind her. She expanded her psychic shields. Concentric, iridescent circles of color unseen by the untrained eye bubbled up around her in a protective field that didn't keep all the shrapnel out, but blocked life-threatening bits. It was a power she was still perfecting.

Thrown against the steel door, a new shock wave of agony overtook her body. She could hear whimpers from the other side of the door. She was sure if she placed her hand somewhere on her torso it would come away bloodied from scratches and gouges. It was hard to pinpoint one injury amidst the general sea of pain. The next thing she knew the door was open. She tumbled inside, many small hands upon her.

Little blonde Franca, eight years old, was first in her face. "Lady Saire," she cried, cradling her head. A similarly small, dark-skinned boy rushed to shut the door as another drone caused an explosion outside. The room shook and the metal of the door bent in its grooves.

All four children hovered over their teacher, whom they'd taken to calling "Lady Saire". Franca had gotten it in her head that Saire *had* to have earned a title at some point in her life. They'd been studying ancient royal history. Saire hadn't the heart to tell them that the Homeworld would bestow no such honors on people like them.

Dizzy, she sat up and tried to clear the fog of pain. If the door to the unventilated storage space was as jammed as it looked – all Homeworld doors had sealed shut due to the searing temperatures of the planet – it meant they only had a few hours of air. She had to calm the children down.

"Ducklings," she said fondly. "I'm all right—"

Questions came in a torrent, about the school, about those aboard the Nests, and simply *why*.

"We are powerful beings," she responded, as to why they had been attacked. "More powerful than you even know. Watch."

She spread out her psychic fields, layers expanding and shimmering in the dim light cast by battery-powered lanterns. They breathed a sigh of wonder. She shifted an inner field outward with a subtle wave of her hand. It was all mental, but the physical gesture helped demonstrate the effect, and the children felt a cool breeze blow calmly through their agitated minds and lower their pulse rate.

"We use more of our brain than other humans. Our mental abilities as newly evolved means we are feared. Each of you came from a home that didn't know what to do with you. Abandoned, cast off, we are not welcome there any more."

"What are we going to do, then?" the smallest boy, Tynne, asked. "Where are we going to go?"

"We're going to find a new home," Saire replied.

"We're going to the Nests?" Simm asked hopefully, his dark skin glistening with nervous sweat.

"I hope so."

If there are even Nests to land in.

It was their only option, and Saire's sole goal; to get the children off the Homeworld and onto the Dark Nest. *Beyond that, the hope was to find a new home for their kind. This had been the contingency plan. But the best-laid plans . . .*

What sort of new home would welcome her? She had done her best to try to keep peace between Homeworld powers and the Psychically Augmented population, or PA for short. And still it had come to this. She'd sacrificed *everything*. For what? And what would take the shape of home if she lived to see it?

"Children, I'm going to give you something that will help you sleep."

There were protests – how could they possibly sleep? – but despite the outcry, Saire opened the medical pack slung over her shoulder and produced small disks from a metal container. "I need you sharp. So now I need you to rest. We can do nothing until the offensive cools. Then we make a plan." She sounded more hopeful than she was, but the children gave her their arms. She stuck the adhesive bandages filled with sedatives onto the crooks of their arms.

The reality was that they were in a small cave with no rear exit. So unless someone friendly broke down that door, they weren't going anywhere.

Once the four were sedated and piled together like corpses, breathing so shallowly Saire had to strain to be sure they still were doing it, it occurred to her that the children would have longer to live, a better fighting chance, if she were one less large body competing with them for oxygen.

Hadn't part of her known, in those recesses that were a part of her burgeoning powers, that it might come to this? That she'd sacrifice herself in the event of a full attack? Long ago, before they'd abandoned what they'd once meant to one another, Brodin had teased her for having a martyr's prerogative. But beneath his teasing they both knew she'd readily die for her people. After all, he'd met her when she had been standing on a ledge . . .

Three

Brodin glanced around the *Dark Nest*. It was a ridiculous flight of fancy in air, a Gothic cathedral floating through space, a beautiful feat of engineering and imagination. Its denizens were all PA, two ships having consolidated into one after a Homeworld-contrived attack. Brodin felt his people grieving collectively, a shuddering mass. They kept focus by trying to shield their remaining ship, rescue PA children, and perhaps wield a little psychic revenge.

The majority of the PA population had been sent into space to seek a new planet for the Homeworld to colonize, as their own dried to a crisp due to unmitigated environmental destruction. The Nests had found a few suitable planets along the way and had ferried the research home, secretly withholding information about one likely planet. Soon after, the Homeworld found the PA population expendable, and elimination began. The Homeworld leaders decided there was no room in the new future for cohabitation with another strain of human. The PA were seen as a threat.

Brodin always knew they were feared. He and Saire had dedicated their adult lives to trying to make peace, and mitigate the persecution of their people. At the cost of their own happiness.

As two of the first PA to be known, and Saire the first to be tested on, it was very clear that the High Council expected Brodin and Saire to be solely business associates. Not mother and father to a whole new strain. Not a family. Breeding would be discouraged. Possibly by force. If Saire and Brodin wanted a school, then it was only by the grace of the High Council and their parameters that they would get one. The alternative was that they could go back to being marginalized lab animals.

And so the training school, the unfolding understanding of their powers. The basic needs of their people always came first. The two of them were friendly. Civil. They lived separately. They did not dare discuss marriage. They did not touch.

Brodin had convinced himself that their separation was good. That way they couldn't be used against one another. They couldn't be tortured for information or bartered for ransom as husbands and wives might be.

And yet, he knew when they were in a room together, everyone felt the unmitigated tension between them. It was impossible to hide.

"Brodin," called a soft voice. He turned as a lovely, tired woman approached. Ariadne, a chief counsel, the foremost empath of her day, was in charge of ship-wide mental health. She had recently saved the minds of the entire crew during the attack. She'd have died if not for the skills of her lover, Kristov, once Brodin's star pupil.

Her selflessness and talents reminded him of Saire's, and he ached looking at this younger version. An ageless beauty of golden skin and gray-violet eyes, she resembled Saire closely, save that Saire's long, silken hair was silver with wisdom. The fact that Ariadne had been saved by love made Brodin ache all the more to be that same force of nature for Saire.

Ariadne broached the dreaded question. Perhaps sensing Brodin's pain had brought her here. "Is she . . . ?"

Brodin swallowed. "Alive? As far as I can tell. But wounded. The rescue team must go quickly to find them. Ariadne, I need you to understand. I'm sure you, like all your peers, wondered about Saire and me . . ."

Ariadne looked away, uncomfortable. "Well, you were never outwardly open or affectionate. But it was assumed there was something between you. We really couldn't figure it. You two are, without question, the king and queen to us all. I suppose we just wondered why you weren't . . . official."

"We couldn't be. From the first dealings with the government in regards to the training school, it was clear Saire and I could set no example of family, love or togetherness. They dictated everything," Brodin spat. "But the school was our mission. And you well know that business and duty often come before affection," he added pointedly. Ariadne blushed. She understood. Brodin continued gently, not bothering to hide his vulnerability from Ariadne's searching mind. "I'm not sure I understood my priorities until I came aboard this ship."

Both Brodin and Kristov had faked their deaths to rid themselves of Homeworld interference before fleeing to the Nests.

"Did Saire forgive you for your death and resurrection?" Ariadne asked sharply. "I'm not entirely sure I've forgiven Kristov," she muttered.

"She understood. But it's been a year. A year without contact, save for echoes of our thoughts."

"Why does the Homeworld think they can tear us all apart?" Ariadne growled.

"They've no right, and they won't win. They can't oppress us anymore. We are on our own, and good riddance."

The fury they felt was palpable, the desperate desire to get beyond survival and towards healing.

"I need to go, Professor. The rescue vessel is about to leave. I came because I sensed—"

Brodin grabbed Ariadne by the arms. "There is so much left unsaid. So many things she didn't know. Things I'd saved for emergencies, things I'd taken for granted . . ."

He tore at his robes. He revealed the scar over his heart. It pulsed with a thin line of blood. "*Her* pulse, I grafted it from her DNA so I could have *something* of her. Aboard this ship, I had the doctors add something else, attach a mechanism onto my heart."

Ariadne's mouth opened in slow realization. "So if she dies . . . she . . ."

"Takes me with her."

"Brodin . . . Why would you do that? That isn't what she would want—"

"I know that. But she, like you, would so easily sacrifice herself for others. If I ensure she lives by saving me, then our population keeps its queen, its goddess, the matriarch to us all. She doesn't understand how vital she is, how important she is—"

"You'd best let her know." Ariadne tapped the glass of the crypt, looking out at the stars. "Try to break through to her. If anyone can, you can. Use the ship to magnify your own signal. Tell her what you've done. She'll be angry," Ariadne said, walking back to the lifts just as the command for the rescue party to meet at the docks was issued.

Brodin grinned suddenly, holding back tears. "She's beautiful when she's angry."

Four

"Son of a bitch . . ." Saire muttered, trying to reroute the circuit to open the door. It wouldn't budge.

She glanced back at the peaceful children. If they died here, at least they'd simply slide off into unconsciousness, never to wake again. Painless. Silent. Much better than all the other deaths. She turned on a tracker with PA-only frequency in hopes a rescue crew would sweep for them.

Saire dosed herself with a powerful chemical for concentration, knowing she had one chance to try the impossible; a mental SOS relaying that they only had a few hours to live. And then she'd sedate herself with a needle on a timer to conserve more oxygen. If, by a certain time, they had not yet been rescued, a medical cocktail would allow her to slide on toward some great beyond and ensure the children a bit more time to breathe.

She closed her eyes and cast her psychic fields wide.

Saire, she heard his whisper in her mind. He was reaching out to her. Somewhere between space and time their thoughts connected. Just like the first time . . .

Brodin? Are you there? Are the Nests—

The Dark Nest *is all that's left*, he replied bitterly. *Where are you?*

Storage tunnel, south-west quadrant. Door jammed. Only a few hours of oxygen.

The ship won't make it to you in time. We have to work on the door. Together.

Saire rose and stood at the door. *I'm here*.

In secret, their top talents had been working on expanding their powers: telekinesis, levitation, defense and offensive strategies. But Saire doubted Brodin could do much from so far, unless the *Dark Nest* transmitters had truly been revolutionized. Still, she stood at the door, palms out, prepared to field whatever he could produce.

She could feel Brodin's energy, his life-force, cascade like a downpour of sizzling live electricity, the air crackling and sparking. The control panel on the door lit up and then died again. The door rumbled in its metal grooves. But it did not budge.

Saire shook her head. *It won't work. I'm breathing too heavily, taking too much air. If I'm one fewer set of lungs, these children might live—*

No, Saire. We must get you out. Or else the PA lose their founding mother and *father . . .*

What are you saying?

I know you'd easily sacrifice yourself, but if you do, you'll kill me too. My heart is attached to the pulse of yours, I grafted yours to mine.

Saire blinked at the closed door. *You selfish bastard.*

You'd die to save someone else, Brodin countered. *I'm ensuring you'll live to save me. This is no different from my desperate call to you, when you were on the ledge all those years ago. I won't die if you won't. There's a planet we found and named "Sanctuary". And you're going to see it with me. Now try again.*

Saire grit her teeth and tried again. Channeling her rage at everything the Homeworld had done to them – killing them, warping them – and drastic measures like this misguided suicide pact of Brodin's. She put one hand on the door, one hand on the control panel. Their shared conduit created quite the combination of psychic fields and focused energy.

The room shook, the door eased on its latches, sliding back enough to let bodies and air through. Success!

Then the mental surge, difficult to turn off once it had been unleashed, was so overpowering that Saire crumpled to the floor and everything faded to black.

Five

Saire was twenty-one years old when she stood on that tenth-floor ledge, ready to throw herself onto the pavement below if the governmental facility keeping her prisoner didn't stop hurting her. Tests, surgeries, probes, endless bloodletting – she'd had enough.

Just at that point of no return, a voice had called to her; a soft and timid question, like the call of a child who has turned onto a darkened path and lost his way.

She heard a young man's voice in her mind. *Is there anyone out there who can answer back? I hear everyone else's mind. Can't anyone hear mine?*

I can, Saire replied, her mental voice tiny, hopeful, shaking.

Oh. Oh thank God, he cried in relief. *Because I am going mad—*

So am I, Saire confessed.

About to kill myself—

So am I—

Don't. They said it in each other's minds at once.

I won't die now that I know you're there, he promised.

Saire stepped off the ledge and back into the hospital. A guard tried to take her arm. Glaring at him, her mind shoved him back. She ran. Ran for her life, toward the sound of that voice. She escaped other guards with psychic blows and nimble movement. That night, two young minds – alone in the dark, each running away, far flung across a vast country – vowed to meet in the middle. Saire heard a boy she came to know as Brodin crying for all he'd endured: the family that had beaten him, the utter lack of understanding, everything he was leaving behind, and his fears of what was to come.

Saire did the only thing she could think to do when someone needed comfort. She sang. She sang a song that her grandmother had taught her, before the government stole her from her family, a song she had learned from the wise old books, some ancient rite called a "hymn".

> *My life flows on in endless song;*
> *Above earth's lamentation,*
> *I hear the sweet, tho' far-off hymn*
> *That hails a new creation;*
> *Thro' all the tumult and the strife*
> *I hear the music ringing;*
> *It finds an echo in my soul–*
> *How can I keep from singing?*

But she had not moved her lips. She offered the song to him in his mind. She swore she heard the air take up the harmony. She swore a bird had her notes in its throat. That was in the days when there still were birds.

"Don't stop . . ." his voice begged. How could she deny him?

> *What tho' my joys and comforts die?*
> *The lord my saviour liveth;*
> *What tho' the darkness gather round?*
> *Songs in the night he giveth.*
> *No storm can shake my inmost calm*
> *While to that refuge clinging;*
> *Since came the lord of heaven and earth,*
> *How can I keep from singing?*
>
> *When tyrants tremble, sick with fear,*
> *And hear their death-knell ringing,*
> *When friends rejoice both far and near,*

> *How can I keep from singing?*
> *In prison cell and dungeon vile,*
> *Our thoughts to them go winging;*
> *When friends by shame are undefiled,*
> *How can I keep from singing?*

It became their private anthem.

Night by night, as they crossed the country towards one another, the need for connection, for intimacy, for understanding and for company, consumed them. Their minds entwined, they learned about their tragic pasts, and assumed others of their kind suffered too, if there were any. Saire shared what the scientists thought of her: that she was a newly evolved strain.

They knew they couldn't run forever undetected, so they decided that once they met up, they'd try and find others and create a society. They'd likely not be able to do this without the government's knowledge, and so Saire pledged she'd be a liaison and perhaps gain training and research facilities on their *own* terms. They were going to create a new world.

Each day as they got closer to one another, they kept out of sight and off the radar, their excitement building.

Finally she saw his silhouette across a barren field of dried grasses. The ruins of an old stone building, something grand and sacred with Gothic arches, stood silent sentry in the field.

Slowly they approached one another. The moonlight cast them in stark light, beautiful, heavenly light, and Saire swore she saw a halo about him, as if he were an angel. He was tall and elegant, sharp-featured and dark-haired, slightly fairer than she. His eyes were luminous, humming with the raw power of brand-new creation. And bright with desire.

They didn't say a word. He took her hand and led her into the beautiful ruins, beneath the pointed arches, into a room where moonlight cascaded in through a hole in the vaulted ceiling, illuminating a vast stone table that was cracked and settled at a slight angle. Saire moved to it, sat upon it, and placed Brodin's hands upon the buttons of her blouse.

"You've been deep inside my mind," she breathed, her lips dancing up his neck, making him shiver. "Now, my body. Let me *feel* you . . ."

Slow and tenderly, Brodin undressed her so that she lay upon the stone, vulnerable and exposed in the moonlight. He stood over her and wept at his gift, so beautiful and graceful and full of an understanding he'd so desperately craved. She could feel his appreciation both in thought and in tangible touch as his hands explored her with the wonder of a child but the needs of a man.

They could feel each other's arousal so pointedly that the entire experience of touching, kissing, caressing, was painfully delicious agony. Their bodies joined slowly, achingly. Their connection built into furious climaxes. Hours of torturous builds to transcendent releases, their ability to sense one another's pleasure drove the cycle again and again. Their minds and bodies were entwined until the sun began to rise and even then their hunger was not quenched.

They were the stars of the ancient tales, Adam and Eve, and this Gothic ruin was their Eden, and they were about to become mother and father to a whole new family. A powerful yet peaceful people whose abilities might allow them to reverse damage done to their planet, create bridges out of barriers. With abilities that resembled magic, anything was possible.

And as their bodies writhed in wave after wave of inexplicable ecstasy, they pitied the average mortal for not knowing what this kind of bliss was like; this soul-bond on a level mere coupling could not begin to match.

Somewhere deep in her unconsciousness, Saire moaned, aching again for that long-lost sacred connection. She realized she was dreaming, dead, or near dead. That's when memories make their parade . . . But Saire had the distinct impression, on whatever level her mind was able to register it, that she was not alone in this journey . . .

Six

Dark Nest counsels swarmed over Brodin, who had collapsed at the Great Well, which he was using as a transmitter, to project his mind toward the Homeworld and to Saire.

"He's dreaming, I think, lost in unconsciousness," one counsel said. "He's tethered to another mind."

"Madame Saire, surely," another counsel breathed.

"But they're—"

"Destined. Even the High Council cannot keep souls such as theirs apart forever." They knelt in reverent guard at their regent's side, keeping watch on his vital signs and willing their great mother home.

Saire watched as ground was broken for the training school. She and Brodin were granted safety and their facility was green-lit provided that an inhibitor, a substance developed during testing on Saire, was used in the construction of the whole facility. Their powers would be limited, contained. Saire balked at this but Brodin signed off.

"If it's what keeps us safe," he said to her in private. "You and I know we can do so much more. We'll find a way. We'll push boundaries in private. But on the surface, this is what has to be done. We have to be seen as harmless. There will be more persecution otherwise. As for you and I . . ."

Saire knew Brodin meant the connection the Homeworld demanded they sever. "We have to comply and do what is expected of us, to best lessen the suffering of our people."

She watched Brodin's blazing eyes cool, his jaw tense. But he nodded.

Later that day, Saire went to a doctor whom she trusted. She had missed two periods and assumed with a mounting thrill that she was carrying her lover's child. It would change everything, and they would have to rear their child in secret, but it would be their most precious treasure and a sacred defiance that the Homeworld could not take away from them.

Only to find out that due to all the tests she had endured, she could have no children.

Saire closed off her mind, kept this knowledge to herself, wept bitterly for days, and threw herself into the work of the school.

Brodin felt the weight of a great and terrible pain but did not pry. He took her cue to be stoic. They had so much work to do, and children were being dropped off at a facility that was still under construction. It was easy to lose oneself in others' lives.

How children could be so easily abandoned puzzled Brodin, as his own abuse had baffled him. Saire just took the children in without question and looked for more.

She sent Brodin out to travel the country to gather others as the rift between humans and these newly evolved beings grew wider. As she handed him his bags on the platform, checking to be sure they were not being watched or recorded on security cameras, she kissed him.

He bent to her hungrily, seizing her. "I love—"

"Always," she interrupted him before he could complete his declaration.

It wasn't a vow.

But it had somehow sufficed for countless, interminable years. Until it hadn't.

The Homeworld was planning to assassinate Brodin.

The night before he knew he would be killed, Brodin traveled the corridors of the training school and went to Saire's quarters. She greeted him with tears in her eyes, disabled the sensors in her home and led him to her bedroom.

This kill order was the beginning of a new phase of persecution. There was no going back. Their people were not numerous enough to cause a revolution, nor were they trained to do so. Their best chance to survive was to keep building and perfecting their escape vessels and ships – their Nests – so they could live and develop their powers and skills in peace.

They made love for what they both knew might be the last time. The act was careful and loving, but without the wild abandon they sometimes felt when they were both scared they might break apart, shattering into frightened pieces.

"I don't want to pretend any longer that you're not my mate, my partner. I don't want to pretend that I don't want you for my husband," she gasped against his shoulder. "We've sacrificed everything, and for what? So they could kill you in the end anyway? I swear to you, if you do not resurrect as planned—"

"I'll resurrect. I promise," he said, holding her tightly. "But it will be a long time before I see you again."

She wept that he kept his mind closed from her. To protect himself. To prepare himself, he said. Neither of them knew if he would survive the ordeal as planned, or if it would all be in vain. In her mind, she apologized for the painful things she'd never told him, but by now he must have assumed. But he didn't seem to hear her.

In the morning he was shot and there was a funeral.

Saire managed to be present at the memorial as the training

school grieved bitterly for their leader. She sang, her voice clarion, clear, magically reverberant in the close air.

> *My life flows on in endless song;*
> *Above earth's lamentation,*
> *I hear the sweet, tho' far-off hymn*
> *That hails a new creation;*
> *Thro' all the tumult and the strife*
> *I hear the music ringing;*
> *It finds an echo in my soul–*
> *How can I keep from singing?*

His coffin was laid in the ground and her tears rolled down her cheeks onto the rain-starved earth.

Internally, she kept singing for him, verse after verse, for whatever deep recesses of his mind might be listening, to bring him back to those first days when they only had each other.

There was the distant sound of an explosion and Saire's dreamscape of memories shifted into a vague, swirling darkness where she felt lost and alone.

Had the *Dark Nest* exploded? Did they have no one to turn to after all?

Come, Saire, she heard dimly in her mind. *Rise and bring your people home. No more deaths.*

They were all being killed. Exterminated.

But there was singing. Her singing. She'd just been singing.

No, someone else was singing . . .

A drop of water fell on Saire's cheek. A tear. A small body shuddered next to her. She lifted one heavy eyelid. In the dim light little Franca bent over her, splashing more tears, choking as she tried to sing the song Saire used to sing her to sleep with as an orphan at the training school.

"N-no s-storm can sh-ake m-my in-most calm . . ." Franca's sobbing voice warbled.

As Saire shifted her hand to Franca's knee, the little girl gasped and clasped her hands over her runny nose and streaming cheeks. She fell on top of Saire, arms around her neck, and in that moment Saire finally let go of the pain of never having her own child. She had countless, and they did not count for any less.

"I can't lose you too, Lady Saire," Franca cried, nearing hysterics. "I can't hear Joyie. I can't sense my sister."

"Shh, I need you calm. Joyie needs you calm. What happened? How long was I unconscious and how did you wake?"

"A voice in our mind told us to get up," replied Tynne. "It sounded like Professor Brodin. How could he do that?!" Tynne exclaimed. "It's like he's God."

"Oh, don't tell him that, it'll go to his head," Saire laughed even though it hurt like hell.

Simm rushed forward. "I heard voices." He tapped his head in wonder. "Someone from our class hid in the school. Deep in the corridors. It sounded like Zho."

"Good. We'll go to her, and that's where the crew will rescue us."

If the children heard Brodin then it wasn't just her imagination. Perhaps there was a Nest to land in after all. But they needed to survive until the transport. And patrol drones would make periodic sweeps outside, waiting for movements and heat signatures. Now that they were awake and alert, they would be targets.

"Children, I need you to be as powerful as Professor Brodin right now," she said, and allowed her psychic fields to expand around her. Everyone gasped again at the subtle beauty. "This is what you can do. Even in training school you were being suppressed. Oppressed. And now that the Homeworld has come to tell you your lives aren't worth preserving, you must use your powers to rebel. We can move underground undetected if you cast your fields wide and we move quietly but quickly."

A brief lesson, but an effective one with survival on the line, and they were out the door and towards another underground tunnel. The Homeworld had been given incorrect schematics for the tunnels and had no access to them, for the codes only responded to psychic signatures.

Saire imagined the Homeworld must have thought extermination would be far easier than it was. At this thought a fierce smile curved a corner of her mouth.

They reached Zho, who shrieked with joy to see them, soot and tracks of tears marring her smooth olive skin. She threw her arms around Simm. "Thank you for hearing my mind," she cried.

Saire ached for Brodin, hearing her past echo in the mental connections between their students.

Zho excitedly showed them stores of food she'd ferreted from the cafeteria kitchen between sensor sweeps. Everyone took hands and gathered in a circle, honoring the dead before they sat to eat.

Another round of sweeps and a few explosions rattled the ground nearby, sending dust, dirt and bits of concrete down upon them. The students panicked, but Saire cast her fields out around them like a blanket, masking their heat signatures and calming their systems. She didn't let on how exhausted and drained she was, or that she might not have it in her to hide them all again.

But she had to.

Selfish as it may have been of Brodin to tie his life to hers, it finally let her know what kind of footing she was on. They had been through so much. Perhaps there was a limit as to whom you simply could not lose and still go on. Just like that time at the ledge, that moment of possible death, when they had turned and run toward one another.

Seven

Brodin paced the Great Well, a pool of water that transmitted images from the Homeworld like a screen. Gray robes whipping behind him, little Joyie was by his side, pacing too, her elder-grade tunic replaced with deep-blue *Dark Nest* robes, all her thoughts on her sister Franca.

She stopped suddenly and looked up at him. "Were you and Saire the first? Of our kind?"

"The first to be known," he replied. "There may have been others before us who never came forward. We were the first to be experimented upon."

Joyie shuddered. "Do you think we'll ever go back to the Homeworld?"

"Not that dying crust. We'll go live on Sanctuary, the planet we've chosen for ourselves. It is empty and waiting for us to coexist with it, its flora and fauna. As for the Homeworld, our rescue team has one extra task – to leave behind a lesson, a psychic blast that will detonate in the capital. Hopefully then, should there ever be relations between our kind again, they'll be sure to know what we've been through."

"Revenge?"

"Better. Empathy."

Just then everything started screaming.

A wail came up from the Great Well, flickering images of Homeworld citizens doubling over, shrieking as if they were on fire, clawing at their faces, each of them experiencing a PA death but with no psychic shields to ease the pain.

"Franca," Joyie hissed, clutching her head. "It's agony. They can't move, they're paralyzed—"

Their own people were not immune, the blast too powerful to block. The planned psychic reckoning spun out of control. It wasn't empathy, not really. It was revenge. Revenge was hard to contain. And on the minds of untrained, "average" humans, very dangerous. The transmission seemed to increase exponentially. Perhaps the amplification meant that on some level, all humans had latent psychic powers, it just took something drastic to access them.

Images of the PA students awaiting rescue flickered into view across the Well. Brodin watched as one little boy pummeled Saire with punches as he experienced a panicking seizure. He felt the pain of her cracked rib and seared flesh ricochet up his own body.

The rescue team had reached them, but they were all useless.

"Try to cut through, Joyie," Brodin commanded the teenage girl beside him. "Tell Franca to hold on to the voice she loves. To concentrate on you. They must concentrate on something, someone beyond that pain."

"Friends!" Brodin cried, gestured wildly for the other counsels, the ones who had so graciously stood guard over him, to gather round the Well. "Help me break through. We're so close! Shelter them, bring them home!"

You shall live, this day, my children, Brodin said, transmitting through the Well and into all of their minds.

Live, my love, he said in Saire's mind as she and the rescue team dragged the shaking, seizing students towards the door. *Focus on me.*

What's happening? she cried.

Reckoning, he replied.

Make it stop! Saire growled, throwing the hysterical Tynne over her shoulder so that at least if he kept punching it wouldn't be on her bad side.

We will, just get to the transport. Sanctuary is within sight, my love. It's big and beautiful.

Tell me about it, Brodin.

It's very blue. Lots of water.

I've always wanted to be by the sea . . .

We will. You and me, love. By the water. Come home to me. We'll not see a new day unless you make it through this one . . .

A sensor sweep rained down an explosion. There were injuries but no one fell. The tethers of those they loved helped them cast their fields wide despite the strain.

And on this terrible day, the whole of Homeworld felt what it was like to be a Psychically Augmented human. Saire softly sang through the agony she relived as she sought Sanctuary.

> *When tyrants tremble, sick with fear,*
> *And hear their death-knell ringing,*
> *When friends rejoice both far and near,*
> *How can I keep from singing?*

Eight

The psychic disruption across the whole of the Homeworld offered some cover, and the *Dark Nest* helped keep them sane. But mechanical and technical systems still had to be overwritten to get them to safety, not to mention a few jumps to cross the massive miles between them and the *Dark Nest*.

As their whole team reached the ship hangar, deep in a hollowed mountain shaft, Saire went to a control panel and pressed her forehead to a small silver disk. A small red light blinked. She recorded the thought:

If you hear this, you are special. Do not be afraid. Reply to this signal. Keep quiet, keep safe. Seek Sanctuary. You are not alone.

That would be left as a low-grade, undetectable signal for those PA yet to come, in case the Homeworld didn't learn its lesson in the psychic explosion. Saire didn't feel like waiting around to find out.

Stepping into the escape vessel, she said nothing. She sat with her hands in her lap, her breathing measured, and awaited him.

Never before had she felt him so alive within her, as if his veins were superimposed onto hers, truly inseparable beings. Perhaps, after so many years being connected and yet denied one another, soul mates could grow into increasingly dynamic, even explosive, powers.

After two faster-than-light jumps, the *Dark Nest* rose before them. Everyone breathed a sigh of joy and relief.

For the first time, Saire realized that the Gothic cathedral floating in space was a testament to her and Brodin's first meeting in the flesh – the day they took on the roles of the ancients.

Tears were in her eyes. So much of their society was due to their making; the two of them. They had so much to be proud of. They had so much to mourn.

But they had so much to love.

And presently, there was nothing else in the whole of space and time but their minds.

Just like it had been so long ago.

They both could feel the other's presence approaching. Their points of view merged, like films superimposed, their entwined pulses raced. Brodin nearly floated out onto the dock. Saire felt the bump of the landing on the dock floor and held back a sob as the vessel opened and the children rushed out.

She could see him from across the room. Regal and tall, no less handsome to her eyes after all the years, gray robes buffeted around his feet in the breeze of his own power.

He saw her stand, stepping down onto the dock floor, tall, soot-smeared, scraped, bloodied, silver hair wild about her shoulders. The most beautiful creature in all the world. In any world.

Her gray-violet eyes pierced him and his breath fled.

They approached one another slowly, and Brodin realized every eye in the dock was on them, breathless, waiting to see them touch, a sight they'd never seen.

Reaching one another, their shaking hands stretched out and entwined, they sunk to their knees, tears pooling between them, their foreheads pressed against each other.

They could feel the leavening of hearts that their reunion provided. Their people wanted them to be together, in love, partners, mother and father to them all. They needed them to be the family they all craved. A show of undying love, a happy ending to star-crossed fate, did far more good than any separate show of strength.

Their minds entwined amorously with torturous promises of passion to come. A vow rose to Brodin's lips.

Don't interrupt me, he began in her mind. Saire laughed.

"I love you," he murmured aloud, for anyone and everyone to hear.

"I love you," she replied.

"Nevermore in the shadows. Never again to be denied."

In a small cottage built from hewn logs and wooden planks, Saire and Brodin gazed out over a vast body of water, a lake they'd named Eden, a lake that had been the backdrop for a ceremony officially marking their eternal bond before all those they'd helped raise, teach and care for. Their people had never before thrown such a joyous celebration. They'd never needed it so badly.

Sanctuary's days were always bright from small twin suns that rose in the east and set in the west. Stepping out amidst a bed of strange and wondrous flowers that Saire looked forward to cataloging, she gestured for Brodin to stand at the edge of Eden with her. He wrapped his arms about her waist, kissing her neck.

She sang the old ancient hymn as the suns shone upon her face and the tune carried across the lake. The words that once were so hard to believe had transformed into reality. Now their paradise had been won. The thrum of the heart that was tied in every way to hers was always near her. Now, she truly could not keep from singing.

The Noah

C. L. Wilson

"Why do we bother?"

Eve Cartwright looked up from the soil recovery auger she was using to collect core samples for testing. "What did you say?"

The shielded screen on her sister Shar's biosuit visor reflected the sunlight and surroundings, making it impossible to see her face. "I said, 'Why do we bother?' I mean . . . what does it matter? What does any of this matter?" The girl's hand swept out, indicating the vast wasteland that had once been a celebrated old-growth forest on one of the oldest mountain ranges on the planet. But that had been hundreds of years ago, before the End, the cataclysmic war that had poisoned the world and left it a barren, contaminated husk.

"It matters because this is our world. The only one we have. And even if we never walk its surface without a biosuit, someone who comes after us will. And when they do, they'll thank us for all our work." Eve stood up, wiping the knees of her clay-dust-coated biosuit. She and the girls had been struggling all their lives to save what tiny remnants of their world they could, just as their ancestors had for the last three hundred years. Yes, the task seemed insurmountable. Whether they were searching the wastes for signs of life or sampling air, soil and water to test for regeneration and habitability, most days were long, fruitless, depressing efforts in futility. Like Shar, Eve had had her moments of doubt in the past, but she wasn't made to give up, no matter how difficult the path might seem.

A bright light flashed in the sky overhead, and a boom rattled the earth, making Eve and Shar grab the nearest boulder as loose rocks shifted and tumbled down the mountainside. Eve glanced up to see what looked like a meteor streaking through the sky – through the very nearby sky.

It disappeared behind a large sand dune in the desert wastes below, then another boom shook the ground. A cloud of dust rose into the air.

"Did you see that?" Shar breathed. She turned around, her eagerness unmistakable. "Let's go check it out." She ran toward the solar-powered rover they used to transport themselves, their equipment and their samples on their expeditions.

"Shar . . . Shar! Dang it." Eve sighed, packed up her samples, and jogged after her sister.

Twenty minutes later, the rover crested the last dune near the spot where the object had fallen from the sky. Inside the spacious helmet of her biosuit, Eve's jaw dropped. Down below, half-buried in that sand, was what appeared to be a ship of some kind.

"Is it Alliance, do you think?" Shar asked.

"I doubt it. There's been no sign of Alliance or Cartel ships in three hundred years. The holovids say they were all wiped, just like the rest of the planet." For the last three hundred years, the people of Homebase had been the only survivor colony on the planet – well, if you didn't count the Ghosts, those savage bands who dwelled in the wastes. "If we're going to check this thing out, we'd better do it quick. It's getting dark, and the Ghosts will be out soon." The ship's descent and crash had been visible for miles, which meant there was a good possibility the Ghosts had seen it too, and would be coming to investigate. "Bring the rover in close. I don't want far to go if we need to make a quick getaway."

"Roger." Shar maneuvered the rover into the valley between the dunes and drove right up to the crash site.

"That's close enough," Eve advised. She hopped out of the rover and approached the ship cautiously.

The soft dune sand had absorbed the impact, leaving the ship intact. Steam vented from several places on the vehicle's silvery shell. The ship was without any external markings. Not Alliance then, nor Cartel. Unless of course either of those had stopped painting identifying marks on their warcraft.

Eve circled the vehicle, looking for a way in. The ship seemed too large to be an unmanned drone, and if the pilot had survived the crash, she wasn't going to leave him without offering assistance.

The more she examined the craft, the more confused she became. The ship was like nothing she'd ever seen before. The silvery shell looked more like layers of crystal than metal, and now the setting sun had cast the bottom of the valley into shadow, what she'd thought was sunlight glinting off the ship's highly reflective metal surface now resembled pulsating light trapped in some sort of translucent shell.

What was this thing? Where had it come from?

"Stay back, Shar," she cautioned, waving a hand in a sharp, imperious gesture when her sister's curiosity got the better of her. "In fact, stay in the rover." She didn't think the ship was going to explode. She couldn't see any sign of a fuel leak – for that matter, she couldn't see any sign of an engine! – and based on the readouts from her gas chromatograph the venting was primarily water vapor. She made another circuit of the ship, moving in closer this time. The entire surface of the craft appeared seamless, as if the whole object had been formed from a single molded piece of . . . whatever the ship's exterior substance was. *What in the name of heaven was she looking at?*

A loud whooshing noise and the sudden jetting of vapor clouds made Eve jump and Shar scream. Eve spun around to find that the previously solid surface of the ship had pulled back, revealing an opening into the interior of the craft.

"Maybe this wasn't such a good idea," Shar called. Her voice sounded tight. Afraid. "Come away, Eve. The sun's gone down."

The Ghosts would be out soon, scavenging for food – and sticking around when they were on the prowl was definitely asking for trouble. But this was the first time in three hundred years that any sort of advanced life form had been spotted in the wastes. The first time in three hundred years that anyone in Homebase had had proof they were not the only non-Ghost survivors on the planet. Eve wasn't about to leave now.

"One more minute." She detached the disruptor from the belt

of her biosuit. No one in Homebase liked weapons – after the End, who would? – but the wastes were dangerous. Too many of Eve's people had died at the hands of Ghosts while taking samples and conducting experiments in the wastes. Wearing a disruptor when exiting the safety of Homebase was standard operating procedure now. Even Shar knew how to charge and fire a weapon.

"Eve . . . please."

"Shar, stop. You know I have to check this out." She worked to stay patient, not to snap. Shar was only twelve, still a child in most of the ways that mattered.

She had reached the craft's opening. The inside was a pale, luminous blue-white. It was surprisingly tidy, considering the way the craft had crashed to earth. As if the craft's hull had absorbed most of the shock of the rough landing. A movement to her left made her spin. A figure in a shimmering silver biosuit and helmet was pointing a weapon at her.

Eve was faster on the trigger. The disruptor fired. An energy field enveloped the stranger. The pilot dropped like a stone as the equipment nearby sparked and sputtered.

"Eve!" Shar's voice crackled through Eve's in-helmet audio unit. "I just heard wails, and I'm getting movement on the sensors about two kilometers out. The Ghosts are coming. We need to leave."

"The pilot's alive but unconscious. Bring the rover to the door and come give me a hand." She pulled several plastic binding ties from the thigh pockets of her biosuit and used them to bind the pilot's wrists and ankles. Moments later, Shar was there, and the two of them managed to drag the pilot outside and into the back of the rover.

"So? Is the ship Alliance?" Shar asked, as Eve vaulted back into the passenger seat and the rover took off. They drove by heads-up in-helmet display rather than the rover's lights. The people of Homebase had long ago learned the folly of using lights at night in the wastes.

"I don't know. We'll keep the pilot in quarantine until we find out." Alliance or no Allliance, she wasn't going to leave any human being to the mercy of the Ghosts. The wildlings who roamed the wastes were not kind to the humans they found, torturing them in all manner of vile, obscene ways. Ghosts thrived on human agony, probably because it fed a deep-seeded need for vengeance. She couldn't think of a more horrible way to die. Alliance or not, that wasn't happening to the craft's pilot.

The ride home was swift and, thankfully, uneventful. The outer airlock door closed behind the rover and sealed shut. Shar parked the rover on its landing pad and locked it down. Together, she and Eve unloaded their equipment, samples, and the pilot, and stood waiting, arms spread, as decontamination sprays soaked everything in the airlock. When decon was done, they loaded the still-unconscious pilot into a sealed quarantine gurney and placed that alongside all their boxed samples and equipment on a conveyor belt that ran along the left side of the airlock. While the conveyer carried its burdens through an infra-red bath and sonic shower, Eve and Shar walked through the secondary airlocks that subjected them to the same treatment. They removed their helmets and biosuits in the third airlock and hung them up for a final decontamination in a heat bath before pulling on loose-fitting tunics and trousers and slipping their feet into shoes.

Everyone was waiting for them when they stepped out of the third airlock into the carefully conditioned atmosphere of Homebase. Everyone, meaning the rest of Eve and Shar's family: gray-haired Nonna, her younger, but equally gray-haired, sister Dre, and four-year-old Misha, the baby of the family. There had been one other – Eve's older sister Beri – but she'd been lost to the Ghosts ten years earlier.

Nonna and Dre stared at the bound body inside the sealed gurney with identical looks of concern. Misha stood on her tiptoes and peered into the glass cover with wide eyes.

"Ghosts were coming," Eve replied to Nonna and Dre's unspoken concern. "The ship was unmarked, but I couldn't very well leave the pilot behind. I'll take care of it," she added in response to Dre's frown.

"I'll help you," Nonna offered.

"No." The pilot had confronted her with a weapon. She wasn't going to endanger her family any more than she already had. "I'll do it alone. Our visitor remains locked down in quarantine until we're sure she's no threat. You can take care of the samples for me, though. I don't know how long I'll be."

Leaving the others to take care of the samples and equipment, Eve pushed the sealed gurney down the corridors to the quarantine lab. Once inside, with the doors sealed and locked behind her, and wearing the protective quarantine lab biosuit to protect herself from potential contamination, she lifted the glass lid on the gurney and activated the hydraulics that lifted the prone figure from the gurney tube to the examination table. The table didn't come with restraint straps, but Eve improvised with more plastic ties. She dragged the scanner down the length of the pilot's body, looking for broken bones or internal injuries. Finding none, she set to work removing the pilot's biosuit.

Beneath the helmet and outer suit was a humanoid. Tall, thin, but well muscled. Lean. Under the silvery cloth of the biosuit, the pilot wore a thin, form-fitting tunic and pants made from some sort of shimmering blue fabric. Eve examined the fabric. The weave was as fine as any she'd ever seen, but its composition didn't feel like any cloth she'd ever touched. She cut the clothing off the pilot's body and saved a small square of the interesting material to put in her analyzer. Eve was a woman who liked mysteries for the challenge of solving them.

When she turned back to cut away the pilot's pants, her breath caught in a little hiccup. She reached a hand out but stopped before touching. She held her hand there, hovering a bare inch from his flesh, trembling faintly. Her head cocked to one side. How odd. *Why did the man make her hands shake?*

Perhaps because he was the first man she'd ever seen in the flesh? Or because he was the most beautiful man she'd ever seen, period?

Nothing in the holovids about the world before the End had prepared her for him.

His hair was silky and golden, the color of sunlight shining through clouds. It was cropped close to his skull, except for a slightly longer fringe on top that feathered across his forehead and filled her with the absurd desire to brush it from his eyes. His skin was a pale golden-brown shade, too, much lighter than her own. His face was beautiful. Straight nose, square jaw, well-defined cheekbones, full lips. Eyelashes long, thick, and straight lay against his cheeks. His body was completely hairless, the skin porcelain smooth and so soft to the touch even through the gloves of her biosuit that she could stand there, stroking him, for days without ever losing interest. Baby soft. Possibly softer. She tried to remember what Misha and Shar's skin had felt like when they were newborns, and couldn't remember it being like this.

From the waist down, with the exception of the hairlessness, he had all the same parts as the men she'd seen in holovids, but somehow seeing a man up close and personal was very different from the clinical introductions offered in an anatomy lesson.

Eve wet a cloth with cleansing liquid and began stroking the antiseptic, decontamination solution across the pilot's skin. She washed him more slowly than strictly necessary, letting her fingers explore and linger. She'd never known a man. By the time she'd been born, the men in Homebase were all gone. He was her first. He was fascinating. She continued the decontamination cleanse down his legs and feet. Hands, feet, five fingers, five toes. He appeared perfectly human, a living replica of the men she'd seen in the holovids. Except, of course, that he had no navel.

"Who is she?"

Eve jumped a little at the sound of Misha's voice, then laughed at her own ridiculousness. She'd been so caught up in her discovery, she hadn't realized her youngest sister had followed her to the quarantine unit. Misha was standing just outside the unit, her small face pressed against the glass wall.

"'He', darling. This is a man. You call him 'he' not 'she'." Eve smiled at the little girl. Familiar love swept over her in a rush. Misha was so adorable, with her big brown eyes, silky, coffee-colored skin, and the black hair Eve had lovingly braided and decorated with shiny crystal beads just this morning. She was only four, and full of curiosity. Her favorite word was "why", followed closely by "how" and "what".

"What's a man?"

"A person, like us, only a different gender. You've seen men before, on your training vids." With Misha there watching, Eve's strange, almost trancelike fascination with the man had faded. She completed the decon wash of the man's skin and hosed him down with a spray nozzle. Sudsy water poured off the examination table onto the floor and trickled down the slight slope in the floor to the gravity drain in the center of the room.

"Why is she – *he* here?"

"I don't know, darling," Eve said. "That's what we're hoping to find out when he wakes." She ran the drying tube over the gurney and drew a sheet over the man's body, tucking it beneath his arms in much the same way as she tucked Misha into bed each night.

"Where did he come from?" Misha did a little dance on the tips of her toes, and ran her fingers on the glass near the man's hand.

"I don't know."

"He's very pretty. Why is her skin like that?"

"'His', dear. His skin. And I imagine that's what his people look like."

"You mean there are others like her?"

"Him. And yes, I'm sure there must be."

"Where are they?"

"I don't know."

"How did he get here?"

That, at least, was one question Eve could answer. "He came in a ship. It crashed in the dunes near Mount Carallon." She took blood and tissue samples, setting each on the sterilized tray beside her.

"Is he Alliance?"

"Not that I can tell."

"Why did he come here?"

Eve sighed and then had to laugh. "You already asked me that, darling, and I still don't know. Until he wakes, I won't have any answers for you, so why don't you go help Nonna and Shar with the soil samples?"

Misha's big brown eyes never strayed from the stranger's face. "I don't want to. I want to stay here. Do you think he wants to be friends?"

"I hope so." He'd pointed what appeared to be a weapon at her when she'd boarded his ship. Now, possibly he'd only been being cautious, not threatening, but Eve was taking no chances. From every holovid she'd ever watched in her life, men were violent at heart. They were the ones who built weapons, who started wars, who murdered, raped and brutalized. She should remember that instead of being so drawn to his alien beauty.

"When will he wake up?"

Eve sighed again and reached for the deep supply of patience one needed when faced with Misha's curiosity. The child had more questions than the world had answers. "I'm not sure, darling."

"Well, *will* he wake up?"

"He should. I'm doing everything I can to make sure it's possible." She tracked the scanner over the man's head again, going more slowly this time and watching the monitor as she did so. There was no sign of a cracked skull or brain swelling, which was amazing considering the force of the crash. Other than a few cuts, scrapes and bruises – and being knocked unconscious – he seemed to have emerged unscathed.

But would he, upon waking, be friend or foe? She hadn't thought about that when bringing him back to Homebase. Foolish of her, perhaps, but with Ghosts approaching rapidly, getting him to safety had seemed more vital than worrying about what sort of threat he might pose when he awakened.

She finished up with the rest of her scans and samples, and packed up her kit. She exited the quarantine unit and waited in the decontamination airlock for the required three cycles, following protocol even though there was no indication the pilot posed any sort of biological or chemical threat. When the airlock opened, she shed her quarantine biosuit and stepped into the corridor to join Misha. "I've got to get these samples to the lab."

"Can't I stay here?"

"No, dear." She ushered a pouting Misha out the door. "Not until we know whether or not it's safe."

"But he's sleeping. I won't bother him."

"It's not you bothering him I'm worried about." She locked and sealed the quarantine unit doors, activated the motion sensor from the console in the center of the adjoining room, and checked the video feed on her portable comms device to be sure she'd be able to keep an eye on their guest.

The quarantine room was the closest thing to security they had in Homebase. The clear, eight-inch-thick walls were bullet-proof, the door locks unbreakable, and the containment system would allow her to flood the room with neural gas, or she could suck all the air out of the room with the touch of a button. If the visitor was a danger to them, she would be able to neutralize him before he had a chance to do any harm.

"Come on, Mimisha. It's time for lessons."

The little girl pouted. "I don't want lessons. I want to stay here."

"Time for lessons, all the same. You mustn't neglect your education. He'll still be here when you come back."

That seemed to mollify the child. Misha put her plump little hand in Eve's palm and allowed herself to be led back to the schoolroom. Eve helped the little girl into her learning chair and lowered the teaching helmet over Misha's head.

"Comfortable?"

The child nodded, and gave "thumbs-up".

"Good. Enjoy your lessons." Eve patted the helmet and pushed the button to activate the instructional program. As the tape began and the sound of Misha's sweet, childish voice began speaking answers to the training questions being posed by her helmet, Eve's heart swelled with love. Misha was such a beautiful, precious child.

Eve thought about the pilot, about the weapon he'd pointed at her, about the possibility he was from the Alliance or Cartel. She had saved him from the Ghosts. Rescued him despite the weapon he'd pointed in her direction. And she'd brought him here, to Homebase, to mend any wounds he might have sustained.

But if he threatened Misha, Eve would kill him without a second thought.

"So, you're awake." Eve put her hands in her lab-coat pockets and regarded the stranger with her head tilted to one side. It had been an hour since she had finished her initial examination. Her tests had all come back negative for any chemical or biological contaminant that might pose a hazard, so she'd left her biosuit hanging in the locker outside the quarantine chamber.

The man's eyes opened, and Eve received yet another shock to her senses. His eyes were blue, the rich color of deep seas she'd only ever seen in photographs. She already knew that, of course, having checked his pupils for dilation when he was unconscious, but noting the color when he was unconscious had nowhere near the impact of meeting that deep, arresting blue gaze head-on.

Her pulse rate increased, and her breathing grew shallow. Eve moistened her lips. Her palms were sweating. What a strange reaction. She didn't understand it. He was naked, strapped to an examination table. He posed no threat to her. And yet her pulse still raced, and she could feel the adrenaline coursing through her veins.

"What is your name?" she asked.

The man looked at her blankly, started to sit up, then stopped and glanced down at his restraints.

"You pointed a weapon at me when I boarded your ship. You'll stay restrained until I find out who you are and what you're doing here. Do you understand me?"

He frowned at her, regarding her as if she were some sort of odd puzzle he didn't understand. It occurred to her that he might not understand her language at all, but then he spoke.

"I understand."

His voice was low and possessed a stirring, musical quality. The sound of it penetrated her skin and vibrated deep in her bones. She shivered, tiny, trembling little quakes that shuddered through her as she stood there. *Good heavens. It was all she could do not to press a hand to her thundering heart.*

"What is your name?"

The man tugged against his restraints then fixed his gaze upon her. "Release me."

Eve stood her ground. "Not until you tell me your name."

"I will not harm you. That is not my purpose." And his gaze remained so steady, so penetrating upon her, that she could not look away. It was mesmerizing, that look. It made her feel light-headed and calm all at once. Was it possible for him to control her mind with just his eyes and the sound of his voice? The scientist in her started to scoff at the idea, but thoughts were just energy. Sights and sounds were energy, too . . . just different wavelengths detected by specialized centers in the brain. Audiovisual stimuli had long ago been proven capable of putting the brain in different states.

She forced herself to turn away, and the broken connection let her regather her wits. "You pointed a weapon at me when I boarded your ship. That seemed like a threat of harm to me."

"You pointed a weapon at me, too. You fired yours."

"I—" She stopped the apology just before it came blurting out. *What did she have to apologize for? And why in heaven's name was she blushing?* "And I saved your life. The Ghosts were on the way. Believe me, you wouldn't want to meet them."

"Then I thank you for my life and I ask you to release me."

She ignored the request as if he hadn't spoken it. "You said you're here for a purpose. Are you with the Alliance? The Cartel?"

"No."

"Then who are you with? Are there other factions?"

"I am not of this world. I am the noah of it."

She crossed her arms. "You're trying to tell me you're – what? An alien? A little green man from another planet?" She gave a bark of disbelieving laughter. "Right."

"I am alien to this planet, yes," he replied, "but I am neither little nor green." His expression remained completely deadpan. "I am the watcher of this world. The preserver of its life."

"Right. Well, if you're a preserver of this world's life, you're a few centuries too late," she scoffed. "Most life here was extinguished three hundred years ago."

"Yes, I remember."

That got her attention. Her gaze slammed into his as forcefully as if it were hitting a concrete wall. It left her reeling. "You . . . uh . . . you *remember*? Remember is a word that implies you created a memory engram in your brain of an event that you personally experienced. You mean you remember reading about it?"

"I understand the nuances of your language. I understand the nuances of all languages of this planet. And I did not read about the End. I witnessed it. I told you, I am the watcher of this world. I am its noah." He nodded to the sink in the corner of the room. "May I have a glass of water?"

Feeling a little dazed, she went to the sink and filled a plastic glass beneath the faucet. When she turned back to the pilot, she screamed and dropped the glass.

The man had somehow freed himself from his restraints and had crossed the room to stand directly behind her – well, now in front of her. In a swift move that left her blinking, he caught the falling glass without spilling a drop. She stumbled back against the sink and gripped the porcelain with both hands as he tilted the glass to his lips and downed the water in four swallows.

"Your restraints cannot hold me, and I choose not to be

immobilized." He reached around her to set the glass on the edge of the sink, then returned to the gurney and sat on its edge, his arms folded across his chest.

He seemed not the least embarrassed by his nudity. Indeed, he seemed unaware of it entirely. But she was not. Eve wondered at the strange fluttering in her belly. She had seen many photographic images and many holovids of men. She had studied the differences in their bodies, their musculature, their voices, their skeletal structure. But she'd never experienced this strange ache in her lower abdomen that made her groin feel heavy and tight.

Stop, Eve! He is a man. You cannot forget that. Men were fascinating creatures, but driven by aggressive, hormone-powered tendencies. The holovids had made that perfectly clear. Men were destructive. It was men who had made the wars and the weapons that had ended life on the planet. Yet here, standing before her, was a man who could clearly overpower her, but who instead exercised restraint and claimed to be a preserver of life. A noah, whatever that was.

"A noah collects archetypal samples of all native organisms from the worlds he watches," the man said, his intent gaze never leaving her.

"So, what, you're some sort of alien biologist cataloging all life in the universe?"

"Not exactly. When the time comes, I transplant the organisms I have harvested to a world of the creator's choosing so that life may begin anew."

"The creator?"

"The entity you call God."

"Ah." *Humor the man, Eve. At least he's talking. And staying on that side of the room.* "So you were sent to this world to harvest samples of all life and transport it to a new world?"

"Yes, that was my purpose." He looked down. He interlaced his fingers and steepled the thumbs. "But I find I can no longer perform the duty for which I was made." Abruptly, the noah's belly rumbled and he glanced down at his abdomen in surprise.

"Are you hungry? Would you like something to eat?"

"Eat." He frowned, as if he had to process the information. "Yes, to eat would be good."

"I'll bring you something." She started for the door.

"There is no need to confine me. I am no danger to you."

"Yes, well, that remains to be seen." She dialed the lock code on the touchpad and waited for the sound of the seal pressurizing and the lock bars sliding into place. Then she dialed another code to release a mild sedative into the controlled space. "I'll be back shortly."

True to her word, she returned thirty minutes later. She carried folded clothes and a plate of grilled vegetables and soybean curd in her arms, a charged disruptor in her lab-coat pocket. She wasn't going to make the mistake of entering the quarantine room unarmed a second time, not even with the sedative she'd pumped into the chamber. Not so long as her guest, the noah, was so adept at freeing himself from his bonds and moving with such astonishing speed and silence.

The noah was sitting on the floor, slumped in one of the chairs near the gurney. He was still conscious – she'd been careful to keep the sedative dose mild – but he wasn't going to be making any sudden moves on her this time. Eve dialed the code to filter the air, then opened the quarantine chamber and entered.

She needed to hurry. Misha would be done with her current training session in ten minutes, and Eve knew the child would make a beeline for this part of Homebase as soon as the training helmet lifted. The visitor would draw her like a magnet. After all, he drew Eve the same way. But until Eve understood exactly who the man was and what he was capable of, letting Misha near him while was conscious seemed like a very bad idea.

"I brought you a change of clothes," she told the noah. "They should fit. I used your own clothes as a measurement. Once that sedative wears off, eat your food and get dressed. I'll be back in an hour to check on you." She started for the door.

The drugs in his system should have kept the noah too lethargic to move for at least another ten minutes. Instead, the moment her back was turned, the man erupted from the chair. One second he was slumped over in a chair in an apparent mild trance, the next he was pressed against her back, pinning her to the wall, one hand slapped against the glass on either side of her.

"I was made to walk among your kind, but I am not of your kind," he said. "My body does not process your drugs as your own does. Nor do I lie, as your kind has always done. Next time, when I say I am no threat, believe me."

Eve's heart was in her throat. He was very tall, and very strong. And every inch of him was pressed against her back, hot and hard and intimidating. His mouth was pressed close to her ear. She swallowed heavily. "If this is your idea of non-threatening, you are not as familiar with the nuances of my culture as you think."

The noah pulled one of his hands away from the wall and slid it down the side of her waist. The hand moved around the front of her belly and went slower still. Eve's mouth went dry.

"What are you doing?"

He thrust his hand into the pocket of her lab coat and retrieved her disruptor. "I let you shoot me with this once. I will not do so again. It *hurts*."

He'd *let* her shoot him?

"I have shown you how quickly I can move," he murmured in her ear. "Yet you still doubt me? I had not counted you for a fool."

"I'm not. I'm sorry." Oh, God. He had the disruptor. He had just proven how easily he could overpower her. If he got out of the quarantine space into Homebase . . . he could kill her easily. He could kill them all.

The noah gave a frustrated sound and grabbed her hand. With a yank, he spun her around and pushed her towards the center of the room. "I will not kill you. I do not kill. I told you, I am a preserver of life, not a destroyer of it." He cupped the disruptor in his hands and squeezed. Eve heard a crack and a sizzling pop, then he tossed the charred, smoking chunks of metal on the floor between them. "There, do you see? I no long have the disruptor, and you can no longer shoot me with it." He rubbed the spot on his naked ribs. Her earlier blast had left an ugly bruise.

"Do you read minds?" *How else would he have known what she was thinking?*

"Thoughts are energy. I am skilled at manipulating energy. And just so you know, I only remained in this room to put you at ease. You cannot hold me here except by my choice." He touched the lock on the door behind him, and with a snick and a pop, the seal depressurized, the lock turned and the door swung open. "There is no technology you possess that I cannot manipulate." Instead of walking through the door, he stepped back, hands open, palms up in an unmistakable gesture of surrender. "But I will stay here, in this room, to prove that you have nothing to fear from me."

"Good, then I won't have to shoot you myself." Nonna stepped into the open doorway, a much larger disruptor in her hands. Dre stood at her back, also armed. Despite their gray hair, they both looked deadly.

Eve watched the noah's expression go blank. For the first time, the humans had managed to surprise him, it seemed. Those brilliant blue eyes of his darted from her face to Nonna's, then Dre's. "You are the same," he said. "You are the same woman, but different ages of the same."

"The technical term is clones," Eve said. She walked forward, putting herself between the noah and her family. "It's all right, Nonna, Dre. He has proven that if he meant to harm us, he could easily have done so by now." She waited for the two women who looked like older copies of herself – who, in fact, were exactly that – to lower their weapons.

She turned back to the noah to find him watching them with a mix of surprise, curiosity and bemusement.

"Remarkable," he said. "It is a rare day that humans can still surprise me."

"Clearly, you've never met the daughters of Eve before," Dre said.

"Clearly." The corner of his mouth tilted up in the very faintest of smiles.

"Eat your food, and I will explain," Eve said.

"He can put some clothes on first," Nonna commanded sharply. "Our baby's almost done with her training vids, and she doesn't need that particular anatomy lesson yet." She nudged the tip of her disruptor towards the noah's groin, indicating the penis that had been in a rather impressive state of semi-arousal since the moment the noah had pinned Eve's body to the airlock door.

"My sisters and I are all genetic copies of Dr Eve Cartwright, a scientist who lived and died before the End."

Eve and the noah were sitting at a table in the dining hall, the remains of his meal pushed off to one side. Shar, Dre, and Misha – who after a slightly heated discussion with Nonna had been allowed to join them – were there as well. Nonna had absented herself, saying she had too much work to do.

The noah had donned the tunic and trousers Eve had brought earlier, and though she would never admit it out loud, she missed being able to covertly admire his lean, muscular beauty in its natural state. She didn't think she'd successfully kept that thought to herself, though, because every few minutes he would shift in his chair and stretch in a way that drew her eyes to his chest or arms or elsewhere, and she would feel his eyes on her. It was very distracting.

"Dr Eve Cartwright and her father saw what was happening between the Alliance and the Cartel, and they knew where the escalating tensions would lead," Dre said, picking up where Eve had left off, as she had been doing every time Eve lost her train of thought. "They understood the destructive potential of the doomsday weapons the Cartel and the Alliance had amassed. So they bought an abandoned government bunker and refitted it to serve as a survival enclave and a laboratory, and among other things, they stored five thousand embryonic clones of Dr Cartwright so that her work would continue beyond her own human lifespan."

"And it has," Eve added. "Every twenty-five years, two new embryos are gestated and raised by the others. Nonna and Dre are the seventy-fourth generation of Eve's daughters. I am the seventy-fifth. Shar and Misha are the seventy-sixth."

"What work is it that all you generations of Eves are continuing?" The noah crossed his legs and leaned back in his chair. Eve sighed and tried to smother images of running her hands across his chest.

"The survival of our species and our world," Dre said. "Come. Let us show you."

Misha held out a hand to the noah. She beamed a huge, beautiful smile up at him when he took it, and she skipped happily by his side as Eve escorted him through Homebase.

"Homebase is a self-sustaining, geo-thermal-powered biosphere," Eve informed him. "We cannot support a large colony of life, only about a half dozen adults at any given time. So that is why each generation of Eves gestates only two more sisters for the next generation. We live together, teach each other, keep Dr Cartwright's work alive and going – and with her work, her hope for renewed life on this planet."

She escorted the noah through the laboratories and living spaces of Homebase. "Each of us record our discoveries, observations, thoughts into the Mind of Eve, the mainframe computer that operates all aspects of Homebase. And each successive generation of Eve's daughters is imprinted through the neural trainers with the memories and life experiences of all the Eves that came before. In this way, each generation continues where the other left off. No discovery is ever lost. Our collective consciousness continues to expand and grow."

She opened a door into the large brightly lit conservatory that had been designed to look like a forest meadow, complete with a waterfall tumbling down rocks into a small stream. "We maintain four of these conservatories, as well as two gardens where we grow our own fruits and vegetables. The plants all came from seeds and seedlings that Dr Cartwright and her father collected before the End, with the intention of sustaining life in Homebase and ultimately re-seeding the world. Once the planet becomes habitable again, which should be in another few hundred years, we will begin gestating the other embryonic lifeforms the first Eve and her father collected."

"You have made yourselves into noahs," he observed when the tour was done.

"You sound surprised. Did you think we would not want to save our own species?"

"No," he answered honestly. "In my experience, your kind has been hopelessly bent on its own self-destruction."

"Then you have never experienced the love of a mother holding her newborn child," Eve said. She ran a hand over Misha's braided hair. "I assure you, she would do anything in her power to *stop* harm from befalling her child."

Misha gave a huge yawn. "I'm tired."

Shar stepped forward, bending down in order to pick up the child. "I'll carry you to bed, Mimisha."

"No." With a fractious scowl, Misha evaded her sister. "I want *her – him –* to carry me." She pointed at the noah and held up her arms in clear invitation. Her pearly teeth beamed up at him in a beguiling smile.

Eve leaned against the doorframe, watching as the noah succumbed to Misha's charms and tucked the little girl into her

bed for the night. He was so gentle with her. Tender and attentive. Even Nonna had to give her grudging approval.

A pensive smile played about Eve's lips. If ever she started to
think there was no purpose to life, if ever she started to think the
struggle was too hard, too pointless, she had only to look at
Misha's smiling face, hear her small, pert, girlish voice, and
Eve's heart filled with overwhelming love and determination.
Hard, the struggle indeed might be, but for Misha, it was worth
it. Anything was worth it. Because in Misha, the beauty of life
glowed with its most enchanting promise.

Since the moment Eve had first held the wriggling infant in
her hands, she'd known such love as she never knew existed –
never knew *could* exist. She'd spent so many nights wide awake,
just lying beside the baby, staring at her absolute perfection,
marveling at each incredibly tiny finger and toe, the plump
perfection of her rosebud lips and tiny, curling black eyelashes.
And Eve had known in those moments that life was worth any
hardship, any sacrifice. Life was the greatest gift in the universe.
The one never to be squandered. The gift that made everything
else worthwhile.

Through Misha, Eve had discovered what Nonna and Dre
had learned before her. Unconditional love. Complete selflessness. Having Misha, holding Misha, caring for her every need,
teaching her, loving her, watching her grow . . . those moments
had given every other moment in Eve's life meaning and purpose.
She had looked upon Misha's tiny, newborn face, held her tiny,
newborn hand, and known she would fight for Misha to her last
breath, suffer for her gladly, die for her without a qualm.

She wondered, as she watched the noah brush a broad hand
tenderly across Misha's brow, if he had ever known such a love.

"No," he said half an hour later, as she and he wandered the
trails in one of the conservatories. Shar, Dre and Nonna had also
turned in for the night, but Eve was too charged from the day's
events to consider sleeping.

"No what?"

"No, I've never known the kind of love you feel for Misha."

She cast him a sideways glance. "You really should stop reading people's minds. Thoughts should be private."

"I always find more truth in thoughts than words."

She didn't doubt that for an instant. "How old did you say you are?"

"Thirty thousand of this world's years."

"Thirty thousand." She shook her head. She could still hardly believe it. "And in all that time, you've never known love?"

"No."

"You never even thought about it? What it would be like to have a wife, a child of your own?"

"I am a noah, a watcher. My duty is to tend the worlds in my care, not to tend my own desires. Besides, I have seen what becomes of worlds, of love and families. Why would I want to subject a family of my own to such a fate?"

She was starting to get an idea of what his existence had been like, and she wasn't liking what she saw. He'd been alone. Utterly alone. Alone in a way she'd never known. She'd always had her sisters, Nonna, Dre, Beri until she'd died, then the little ones Shar and Misha. There might not be anyone else alive in the world, but they'd always had each other. The noah, he'd never had anyone. Ever. The mere thought made her want to cry. No one should ever be separated from the rest of the world for so long.

"I'm sorry," she said, laying a hand on his arm. His skin felt so smooth and warm.

He stared at her hand, a strange expression on his beautiful face. "I do not understand. For what reason are you sorry?"

"No one should ever have to be that alone." Those perfect, drowning blue eyes captured her again. If there was a heaven – and she believed there was – its skies would be that particular shade of blue. A blue the oceans would envy. A blue a woman could happily drown in.

He shrugged off her hand. "To be a noah is to be alone. I knew my purpose. I did my duty."

"I'm sure you did." She could see the topic made him uncomfortable, so she took pity on him. "Tell me what this world was like thirty thousand years ago."

"Much greener."

She laughed, and was rewarded by that faint smile that lurked along the corner of his mouth. It softened him, made him look younger, more approachable, a little mischievous.

"It was . . . peaceful . . . but also savage. Before men built their civilizations, before they made their machines, survival was their goal. Their lives were short, as you can imagine, with no medicine or technology. But there was a certain beauty to the simplicity of their lives. Of all the ages, that has always been my favorite. Because in those ages, the people . . . needed each other, much the same way you and your sisters need each other here. Of course, even then, they fought. For territory, for females, for food and resources."

"All creatures fight for survival. It's instinct. A bit like the way you don't like to be caged, I imagine."

Blue eyes glanced sideways. "I spent a lifetime – thousands of lifetimes – confined to my ship. When I am away from it, no, I do not like to be restrained."

"I can understand that." They'd reached the waterfall. The terrarium lights had darkened, simulating night, and the softer silver lights reflected off the water in the stream. "And those more primitive humans from the ages you admired . . . did you . . . harvest . . . them the way you did the plants and animals?"

"No. My duty is to preserve whatever life is in danger of extinction. They never were."

"And now? Did you come here to harvest us?"

"I came here to die."

"What?" She stared at him in shock. "Why?"

"I no longer see the point in my existence. Nothing ever changes. The patterns are fixed."

"But . . ."

"There are no others on this planet besides you Eves. The men who engineered the End did their work very well. And when I saw it happening, I watched and I did nothing. I did not harvest human archetypes to carry on to the next world I had prepared for them, because I knew they would only destroy that world, too. And now, this world does not have much time left. What the final war did not destroy, an asteroid will in four months' time. This world will be wiped clean. It is inevitable."

"Inevitable." Eve had never believed anything was a done deal. She came by that honestly – an inherited family trait. If the original Eve had believed in inevitability, she wouldn't have built this place. "My sisters and I may be scientists, but we deal in hope, not inevitability. Homebase is deep enough to survive an impact. And being geo-thermal-powered, even if the ejecta from impact were to remain in the atmosphere and lower global temperatures for a decade, we could survive it."

"To what end?" he challenged wearily. "I've seen your thoughts. I know why you and your sisters incubate only females. But you cannot sustain a population on the clones of Dr Eve Cartwright forever. And you cannot replicate yourselves indefinitely, either. Eventually, you will have no choice but to turn to your cache of stored embryos to create a self-sustaining population of males and females. The problem is, once you do that, you lose the control Eve Cartwright built into her system. Once your civilization grows beyond a small, tightly knit tribe, you will reach the beginning of the next End."

"Why would you think that?"

"Because I've seen it. Over and over and over again. Every human world ends the same, in violence and self-destruction. Again and again, I have watched civilizations grow, watched them turn on one another and rip each other apart, watched them create bigger, stronger, more powerful weapons until they destroy not only themselves but the very planets that sustain them. It is always the same. Not just on this world, but on the dozens of others I have watched as well. There's no point in hoping for a different outcome. It is always the same. So it has ever been, so shall it ever be."

"You're wrong. Things can change. Your very existence is proof of that." She nodded at his look of disbelief. "Think about it. Why else would the creator send noahs to harvest the seeds of life from one dying planet and transport them to another? Don't you see? You are humanity's chance to try again, and to keep trying until we get it right. What else would you call that, if not hope?"

The noah bowed his head, shoulders slumping forward in an expression of pure weariness. "Foolishness," he whispered. "To try the same, failed experiment again and again, that is foolishness."

He looked so discouraged, so beaten down by the many disappointments of his long existence. He was such an ancient soul, but at this moment, he reminded her of Shar the time she'd fallen down a cliff during one of their expeditions and broken her leg. Hurt, wounded, in need of love and comfort. Eve's hand reached out instinctively to brush back the fall of golden silk, as she'd been itching to do since she'd first uncovered his face.

He stiffened at her touch, spine going rigid, shoulders squaring.

"The experiment has too many variables to ever be the same," she told him. "You and I have never met before, have we?"

"No."

"There, you see. The experiment is already different." She smiled. And then, because he was so beautiful, so sad, so alone, and because she knew that once he left, this chance would never come again, Eve did what she'd been wanting to do since she'd watched him tuck Misha into bed.

She leaned forward and pressed her lips to his.

His mouth was silky soft and warm, his eyes wide open and locked intently with hers. She brushed her lips against his, nibbling a little, touching her tongue to his lower lip. Tendrils of heat curled in her belly. Tingling sensations gathered in her breasts and groin. She drew back, smiling at the way his lips followed her, and knelt over his lap, straddling him so that they were face to face, chest to chest. Comfortable, feeling bolder, she wrapped her arms around him and pressed her body tight to his.

"Beautiful, beautiful man." She smiled into his eyes and stroked the golden hair back off his forehead. "You've been alone so very long." She cupped his face in her hands, loving the silky smoothness of his skin, the contrast of her darker flesh against his lighter, more golden tones. Bending closer, she feathered kisses across his face. "Don't you think it's time to come out of the cold?" She breathed the last into his ear, and followed it with an impulsive flick of her tongue.

He shuddered. His arms came up, locking her in a tight embrace. His head tilted to one side, mouth slanting across hers with sudden fervor. His hands found her hips and pressed her down against his lap, against the rock-hard bulge beneath the clothes she'd given him.

Eve gasped as dizzying sensations swept through her in rippling waves. The edge of his teeth scraped down her exposed neck. The moist heat of his breath warmed her skin. Lips and tongue tracked burning trails down her chest. His hand caught in her dense curls, and he pulled her head back, baring her chest, her breasts to his mouth and teeth and lips and tongue.

"Dear God!" Just that fast, she was on fire. Breath heaved from her lungs. His teeth closed around one nipple through the thin cloth of her tunic. She sobbed and ripped at the fabric, wanting those teeth, those lips, on her naked skin. Cool air kissed her breast, turning dark brown nipples into hard, pebbled points as she flung the tunic away. And then his mouth followed the caress of the breeze, suckling with strong, hard pulls. The feeling ignited a taut, fiery cord that reached from each nipple straight down to her core. She moaned and thrust herself against him, pressing her breast into his mouth, clutching his hair in tight fists and pulling him tight against her.

Then they were ripping at the rest of their clothes. Who tore what from whom, she would not remember, nor did she care. All she cared about – all she wanted – was the pure, sensual fire of his naked flesh pressed against hers, rubbing against her, driving her wild.

"I've never—" She gasped. "Never – ah!" His fingers had found a spot between her legs, and sensation exploded across every nerve ending. Hot creamy moisture drenched her, making her body slick and steamy.

"Nor I, Eve. You are so beautiful. I never . . . knew . . ." He guided the thick, hard length of his erection to her. The wide, silky-soft head pushed against her, into her, pressure building, stretching . . . The tendons in his neck stood out. His muscles flexed and trembled.

She panted, rocking against him, biting her lip to stop from sobbing. "Don't stop . . . don't . . ." Her eyes squeezed shut. Something gave way. She registered a sharp pain, but then he was full inside her, hot and throbbing and filling an emptiness she'd never known existed. He moved his hips, and gripped hers to raise her up, then brought her sharply back down upon him.

"Oh, my God . . ." Stars exploded across her vision. There was a word for this moment: ecstasy. But she'd never understood the magnitude of what that word meant until now. It swept her up in a firestorm, flung conscious thought to the winds. She wasn't Eve Cartwright, scientist. She wasn't Eve Cartwright, sister. Not even Eve Cartwright, mother.

She was just Eve.

Woman.

Born for this moment, for this man.

He moved inside her, above her, through her, body and soul. He moved, and her world moved with him, following his lead every shuddering, breathtaking, mind-shattering step of the way. Her nails scraped across the broad, strong blades of his shoulders as her feminine core clenched tight around him, suckling him with strong, rippling quakes. He flung her onto her back and crouched over her, hips pistoning, driving his body deep inside her in swift, hard, rhythmic thrusts until she screamed and exploded yet again, and then his body went rigid, as hard and unyielding as steel. He shuddered against her, and thrust into her one, two, three final times before collapsing to one side, his chest heaving like bellows.

"Dear God." Eve gasped and flung an arm across her face. She struggled to catch her breath. "You may not think much of the human race, but you can't honestly tell me *that* isn't worth saving."

One eyelid cracked open. One stunning blue eye peered at her. He laughed. And the rich, deep sound of it nearly made her climax all over again.

Overwhelmed with emotion, humor fading, Eve brushed her fingertips against his jaw. She couldn't believe this was real – couldn't believe *he* was real. "You said you came here to die. But would you consider something else instead? Like staying here to live? With me?"

He propped himself up on one elbow, his expression turning serious. With his free hand, he brushed the sweaty curls away from her temple. His gaze swept slowly over her face, as if drinking in the memory of her at this moment. For one, heart-stopping moment, she thought he was going to say goodbye, but then the corner of his mouth tilted up in a wondering smile, as if he had just discovered an unexpected treasure.

"Yes," he murmured. He bent down to kiss her, lips brushing against hers with exquisite tenderness. "Yes, Eve, I think I would like that. I think I would like that very much."

The rover flew over the dunes of the wastes. Eve gripped the steering wheel firmly between her gloved hands to keep from constantly touching the man sitting beside her. In the back seat of the rover, Shar and Misha clung to the roll bar and laughed with a joyous abandon Eve had only ever seen on holovids of long-dead families from before the End.

The noah had decided to stay. He would take Beri's place in Homebase and add his collected samples of their world to their own. Together, they would bring life back to their planet. They were going now to fetch his ship. He had assured Eve that the outer hull of the ship had absorbed the bulk of the energy from the crash, and he was certain he could pilot it back to Homebase, where they could work on a way to transfer his biological storage units into their warehouses.

Like the children, Eve was bubbling over with happiness. She'd lived her whole life with just her sisters around her, but now that the noah had come, she couldn't imagine a life without him.

Nonna, who wasn't big on change – especially change involving the presence of a man in their midst – hadn't been as enthusiastic as her younger sisters, but she had come around after the noah offered her full access to his ship's computers and his vast organic library of plants and animal life long since extinct on their world. Science was her weakness, and it didn't take the noah long to ferret out how best to win her over. Mind-reading definitely had its benefits.

"You know, you still haven't told me your name." Eve maneuvered the rover around a rocky outcropping. The green lights on her in-helmet display showed the map she was following to the coordinates of the noah's ship. "I can't go on calling you 'the noah' forever."

"I have no name. I and my brothers are just the noahs. There has never been need for more."

"Well, there's need now. We could call you Noah, if you like."

He considered it briefly, then shook his head. "No. A noah is what I was, and what I am no longer. Now, I am just a man."

"Then we'll come up with a name for you. We'll have to give it some thought. Names are important things. You wouldn't want to be called something horrible like Englebart or Euphaestus." When he didn't answer, she darted a worried look his way. He had lifted the polarized visor on his biosuit helmet, and through the glass faceplate, she saw him mouthing the names and frowning in consideration. *Oh Lord, what had she done? He was seriously going to pick one of those.* "No. We are not calling your Englebart – and not Euphaestus either. That was a joke."

"But I think Eve and Englebart has a nice sound to it," he protested.

"No, it doesn't. Believe me. It absolutely doesn't."

White teeth flashed in a mischievous grin and she realized she'd been had. Then he laughed, low and deep, and the sound rippled through her body, bringing back visceral memories of last night and all the hours of shattering pleasure.

"Oh, God." Eve gripped the steering wheel harder. "Stop that. Don't laugh like that. You know what it does to me."

"Yes," he agreed. "I do." He sounded smug, but in an utterly adorable and sexy way.

"What does he do to you, Eve?" Misha piped up.

It was a good thing Eve's biosuit covered her completely, because she did a full body blush. "Er . . . nothing, Mimisha. The noah is just being silly." To the culprit in question, she muttered, "Down, Euphie. Behave. The kids are in the car." Then, louder, in tones of exaggerated brightness, she exclaimed, "Oh, look! We're here." The rover rounded the corner of the last dune, and approached the crash site.

As they drew near, Eve's good humor evaporated. The ship was still there, where she'd left it, but the area around the ship was strewn with wreckage and riddled with large, charred craters. Several bodies lay sprawled in the sand.

"Ghosts." Eve maneuvered the rover closer, her gaze sweeping the area for any hint of movement. "Girls, stay in the rover." Though she spoke in a low whisper, her tone left no room for debate. "Shar, charge your disruptor and keep it handy."

"Roger." Shar moved closer to Misha. "Get down, Mimisha. There's a good girl."

Eve climbed out of the rover, disruptor in hand, and crept toward the ship. "I don't understand. Ghosts don't have advanced technology, but these craters look like laser fire."

"They are." The noah crouched down beside one of the Ghost bodies and turned it over. The lumpy, misshapen face with its lipless mouth and bared, sharpened teeth snarled up at them. There was a charred hole in its chest. "My weapon – the one I had when you found me – did you take it with you?"

Eve thought back. Much had happened in such a short time. "No, I didn't. You think Ghosts did this?"

"The Ghosts may be more beast than man, but their ancestors were human. If they found my weapon, it wouldn't take much for them to figure out how to fire it." He headed for the open door in the side of his ship.

"What are you doing?" Eve chased after him. "Wait! They could still be in there."

"No, the ship is empty." He disappeared into the ship.

Swearing, Eve followed. And what she found inside made her heart sink. "Oh, noah, I'm sorry." The interior of his ship had literally been torn apart by scavenging Ghosts.

The noah ignored the mess and headed to a console near the pilot's seat at the front of the craft. Lights were still flickering. The ship still had power. He punched a button, and a flat panel display emerged from a console. Lights flashed in patterns Eve did not understand.

The noah's finger moved swiftly, typing and tapping at the display, bringing up several screens filled with more flashing lights.

Suddenly, he swore and took off at a fast stride to the back of his ship, stopping beside what looked like a flat, crystal panel shimmering with more lights. Using his fingertips, he dragged four of the lights around in an intricate pattern, then slapped his palm flat. The wall opened, revealing a rack of metal objects.

"What's wrong?" Eve asked.

"The weapon that made those craters out there had several other settings. The Ghosts have it and they've managed to put it on the highest setting." He pulled several flat, egg-shaped devices from one of the shelves and stuffed them in the thigh pocket of his biosuit. With his other hand, he reached for a much larger, silver cylinder set with a blue-white crystal at one end. He clipped a strap to the cylinder and slung it over one shoulder.

"So?"

"So, I checked the locator on the weapon. The Ghosts are headed for Homebase, Eve."

Fear shot through her, and for one long minute all she could do was stand there, paralyzed. She'd seen her sister, Beri, slaughtered by the Ghosts. The image haunted her to this day.

"The Ghosts have followed us back to Homebase before," she said. Somehow, she managed to keep her voice steady. *Breathe, Eve. Just breathe. Hysteria helps no one.* "The walls are steel-reinforced concrete, twenty feet thick, and the outer airlock doors are solid titanium. They can't get in."

He gave her a grim look. "If they fire the weapon on its current setting, I'm afraid they can."

Eve's calm evaporated. She bolted for the door. "Shar, get on the comms! Call Homebase! Hurry!"

She raced across the debris-strewn sands and leapt into the rover's driver's seat. She slammed the gears into reverse and slapped a foot on the accelerator. Sand spat out from beneath the tires. The noah leapt into the passenger seat as she was pulling away.

"What is it?" Shar cried. "What's wrong? Nonna and Dre aren't answering. Why aren't they answering?"

Huddled on the floor of the back seat, a frightened Misha began to cry.

"Keep trying, Shar." Dread filled Eve's veins with icewater.

"I'm sorry, Eve," the noah said. "I should have returned to my ship as soon as I regained consciousness to ensure it was locked down. This is my fault."

Fear for her sisters made her lash out. "Why do you even have weapons aboard your ship if your mission is all about preserving life? Or was that a lie?"

"I have never lied to you. I never will. I am a noah, and my mission *is* to preserve life. But not all lifeforms in the universe are peaceful. Sometimes, even a noah must fight to protect the worlds he watches."

Behind them, Shar continued to call out on the wide-area comms, "Rover to Homebase, come in. Rover to Homebase, come in. Nonna! Dre! Answer me!" Her voice cracked.

They'd reached the edge of the wastes, and the ride got bumpier as the rover sped over rocky mountain terrain. Eve kept up a desperately whispered mantra as she drove. "Please, God, please God, please, let them be safe. Please, let them be safe." But when they reached the base of Mount Nuru and saw the smoke hovering in the air above the entrance to Homebase, Eve knew her prayers had gone unanswered.

A pack of Ghosts were huddled in the middle of the road near the blackened hole that had been Homebase's solid titanium airlock door. Their hands and faces were smeared with blood, and they were fighting like feral dogs over something that Eve feared to look at too closely.

The noah stood up in his seat, slinging the metal cylinder atop his right shoulder. The crystal at the front of the cylinder began to glow a vivid blue. Then there was a blinding flash, and the pack of Ghosts disapppeared in an explosion of blue-white light.

Turning, the noah fired another blast toward the side of the mountain, taking out another seven Ghosts hiding among the rocks. "Eve, you and the girls take cover by that rock over there. I will go look for Nonna and Dre."

She shook her head. "No. We're coming with you. We're safer if we all stick together."

For a moment, she thought he might argue, but then he said "Fine!" and reached into the pocket of his biosuit. "Here, take these." He held out two of the flattened-egg-shaped metal objects to Eve and Shar. "To fire, put your thumb in the depression here and your fingers in the depression here on the underside, then just point and squeeze." He demonstrated with the third device, and made them do the same to show they understood. "Good. And be careful. The beam will vaporize whatever it touches. Misha, you stay between the three of us at all times. If you see a Ghost, let us know right away. Understand? Then let's go."

Together, the four of them walked through the charred airlock into Homebase.

What met them inside was total destruction. The airlocks had been vaporized, the rooms and equipment torn apart. The Ghosts hadn't destroyed the power station yet, because the lights were still on, but sparks sputtered from torn wiring and smashed electronics. No room had been left untouched. Even the plants in the conservatories had been ripped up by their roots.

There were splashes of blood on the walls and over a dozen Ghost bodies littering the floors of several rooms. Nonna and Dre had clearly put up a fight, but of the two eldest Eves, there was no sign.

Then they entered the room that housed the Mind of Eve. The computers were shredded and sparking like mad, their torn surfaces splattered with red.

"Misha, Shar, get behind me," Eve whispered. She raised her weapons – disruptor in one hand, the egg-shaped device in the other.

Growls and snarls and wet, smacking noises were coming from behind one of the destroyed computer banks. Eve and the noah had started to creep around the corner when Shar brushed against the edge of one of the computers and dislodged a torn faceplate. It fell to the floor with a loud clatter.

Shrieks erupted. Half a dozen Ghosts leapt up and over the computer bank, claws extended, bloodied maws filled with sharpened fangs. Misha screamed. Eve, Shar and the noah fired. A blinding light flashed and the wall beside Eve simply disappeared. Eve turned to see an enormous Ghost holding the missing weapon from the noah's ship in one massive, blood-soaked paw. The Ghost pinned its savage gaze on her and pointed the weapon again.

"Get down!" The noah shoved Eve and the girls to the floor just as a second blast took out the spot where they'd been standing. The noah hit the ground in a roll and came up firing. His laser enveloped the last Ghost, vaporized it in an instant.

The ensuing silence was broken only by the sound of sparking wires and Misha's muffled weeping. The noah stood up and began a final sweep of the room. Eve and the girls started to follow, but when Eve caught sight of a bloody femur stripped of flesh lying on the floor where the Ghosts had been congregated, she gasped and grabbed the girls, holding them against her body so they could not see.

"Noah . . . is that . . . is it . . . ?"

He rounded the corner. She heard him take a deep breath, and knew what he'd found.

"No." Tears sprang to her eyes. "Oh, no. No."

"I'm sorry, Eve." He pointed his weapon and fired one last time, vaporizing the remains of her oldest sisters. Then he returned to gather them all into his arms. "I'm so sorry." And he held them all until their tears were spent, then gently guided them out of the ruins of their home into the rover, and drove them back to his ship.

Once he closed the door and re-established a breathable atmosphere inside the vessel, Eve helped the girls out of their biosuits and tucked them into the noah's berth, staying with them until their tears ran dry and exhaustion dragged them into sleep.

She walked back to the front of the ship. The noah had tidied the worst of the mess and was standing with his palms flat against the walls of the ship. Glowing light flowed from his palms and tracked along the walls, and as she watched, the damaged surfaces began to repair themselves.

He took his hands from the wall and turned to hold out his arms. She went to him without hesitation, surrendered herself to his embrace, and let her tears flow.

"What are we going to do?" she whispered when the storm of grief finally passed. "Homebase is destroyed, and without it, we can't stay here."

"No, we can't stay here, but I know a place where we can go." He stroked her hair, kissed her tear-dampened face, and held her tight. "If you are willing, Eve, I will be a noah – *your* noah – one last time."

"The girls and I have decided on a name for you." Eve cast a teasing smile at the beautiful, golden-haired man sitting in the pilot seat of the noah's spacecraft. The wide vidscreen before them showed the video feed from the ship's cameras as they descended to the lush, green-and-blue planet the noah had said would suit them as their new home.

Two weeks had passed since the destruction of Homebase and the deaths of Nonna and Dre. Although sadness for their lost loved ones still frequently overwhelmed Eve and her sisters by surprise, resulting in sudden bouts of weeping, they were finally beginning to laugh again. The resilience of the human spirit was fighting back against despair.

"Oh?" the noah asked. He arched a brow, magnificent blue eyes twinkling. "I thought you'd already settled on Euphie."

"That was just for fun, silly," Misha chided, her grin so wide Eve wondered why it didn't split her cheeks.

"We chose an Old Tongue name for you," Eve said.

"Yeah, you're always saying how you're done being a noah and are ready to be just a man," Shar added. "So that's the named we picked for you."

"Adam," Eve said. "It's the Old Tongue word for man."

"Adam." He rolled it around experimentally on his tongue, then nodded. "I like it. Very well, Adam it is." He leaned over to plant a lingering kiss on Eve's lips.

With a quiet hiss, the landing gear deployed and the spacecraft lowered itself gently to the ground. Adam punched a few lights on the command console, and the side door opened with a slow whoosh.

"Eve, Shar, Misha, welcome to your new home." Adam held out an arm, escorting the three out of the ship and onto the sweetly fragrant grass that grew in abundance beneath the magnificent branches of the forest trees. "I call it Eden."

Written in Ink

Susan Sizemore

"I wasn't in a post-apocalyptic mood when I got up this morning."

"Too bad, cause that's where you're going today."

"I knew that when I was issued this charming outfit of jeans and hoodie as my ensemble." Frannie settled into the TC and got comfortable before she looked back at her controller. "Why the Ruin Times?"

"You're supposed to ask 'where', which often gives a clue to 'why'. Even better, you're supposed to sink into the mission file."

"If I do the homework all by myself there'll be no reason for you to have a job."

"You are not as amusing as you think you are, Lady of the Elite."

Frannie frowned at the use of the title, as the controller knew she would. She might be an Elite, but she worked for a living. She could see her reflection in one of the TC's blank screens and knew she certainly didn't look like an Elite. Physical perfection attracted too much attention in the places where she spent most of her time. She had brown hair and brown eyes and skin tone, and features that were altered slightly depending on where and when she went. Today she just looked like herself.

She didn't need physical disguises for a visit to the grungy, grubby, post-apocalyptic past where nobody wanted to live, let alone go.

Frannie sighed. She punched the file into her wrist implant, closed her eyes and got on with finding out the specs of the mission.

Oh, Lordy, it looked like the Starshine Group was at it again. Someone was supposed to get killed. It had to happen. She needed to stop an attempt to stop the death while at the same time observing – the records didn't really say much more than that this death ended the beginnings of a proscribed movement. Proscribed meant that the scholars had decided that this was one of the points in time that absolutely couldn't be fiddled with.

So, she was off to save the future of the present.

She liked the jobs where she just went back into the past and observed. Bringing back accurate data was a proper job for a historian such as herself. She liked keeping her scholar happy enough to keep getting her choice assignments. She didn't think of herself as an actionwoman sort of special agent to the ages. But the Starshine hippie idiots had infiltrated the Historical Search Project a few years back, stolen highly classified technology and were now making sporadic and totally stupid idealistic efforts to change the past in order to make the present into the world they wanted to live in.

Frannie was of the opinion that attempting to save the world was a fine ambition, but – it was all so much more complicated than that. And ethically and morally really weird. She herself had actually saved Hitler's life on one of her assignments to stop the Starshiners, and she still felt like a traitor to all humanity for making that necessary choice. Saving the world was a dirty job. She hated it when her bosses picked her out of the time-travelers pool to do it.

"It's not right to try to change history," she said after she'd finished absorbing the assignment. Unless history was coming at you with a big ole sword.

"That's easy for an Elite to believe," her controller answered.

Frannie glared at the cyborg she'd worked with for years. "Are you developing Starshiner sympathies?"

"Going to turn me in if I am?"

"Turn you in to who?" she asked. "We live in a perfect world, where all opinions are respected, if not sanctioned."

The controller snorted, which was an odd sound coming from a voice synthesizer. "Ready to go?"

"Yes."

"Comfortable?"

"Yes."

"You won't be for long."

How well she knew that. "Make it a go," she said.

Riding time was not a pleasant way to spend the morning. Or any other increment of one's lifespan. But if you wanted to go from now to then you learned to put up with the suffering. No one said you had to suffer in silence, though.

Frannie screamed the whole ride down the timestream. She was still screaming when the bright blinding lights faded back down to normal. She began swearing as soon as she was finished screaming. She didn't open her eyes until the flow of words ran out. She wondered if her reaction to the wrench of the change was as professional as her HRP colleagues' as she looked around. She suspected she was more ladylike.

She was not surprised to find she was sitting on a filthy mattress in a filthy room where a filthy rat sat in a corner boldly looking back at her. Then again, perhaps the rat wasn't filthy. Its dark fur looked rather shiny and healthy. That couldn't be said for the watery gray light outside the dirty window. At least there was glass in the window to be dirty. Bullets, rocks, bodies, all sorts of things destroyed the most fragile signs of civilization in this corner of time. She could hear gunfire in the distance. And close by. Firefights were a fact of life back here.

She got up to see how far her grungy arrival point was above the city street, careful not to stand directly in front of the window as she looked out upon the blasted world her ancestors roamed in well-armed bands. Well, not her ancestors. Hers had managed to save themselves from all the dystopic anarchy going on below. At least eight floors below, where she had a bird's-eye view of two groups of ragged people firing guns at each other from the flimsy cover of rusted cars and piles of garbage. There was no mistaking the rattling fire or banana-shaped bullet clips of the Kalashnikovs most of the fighters were using. Typical for the time.

She didn't give the skirmish below much thought, because after a moment a metal structure in the distance caught her attention. The sight caught her like a blow to the gut.

"Oh, no. This is not good."

She knew when she was, but this wasn't the right where.

The Eiffel Tower was so not in New York. It had been in Las Vegas at one point in the past, but that had been a much smaller replica of the one she could see outside the unbroken window. Her internal sensors hadn't completely adjusted yet, or alarms would be going off. She clicked all her orientation implants but the chrono to neutral to avoid the coming hysterical buzzing in her head. She could manage to be hysterical all on her own, but she only allowed herself a few seconds to pound through that reaction. Her clock told her she'd arrived four days ahead of schedule. The time differential was within the mission window and perfectly normal. Precise downtime landings were something that happened in ficvids. Reality was so much messier and harder to predict; a little wiggle room was actually a good thing.

She immediately had suspicions about what had gone wrong, but the important thing wasn't to place blame but to correct the huge mistake that had left her in the wrong town.

"I'm under a bit of a time constraint here, so how do I get out of here without getting shot?"

The rat tilted its head, as if it were actually considering her question, then it jumped up on the windowsill. Frannie took a cautious look outside, and as she did the rattling firing of the AK-47s abruptly halted.

It took her a moment to spot the lone man standing in the no-man's-land between the warring groups. He was dressed in a long black leather drovers' coat, and thick hair as black as the leather hung in a braid down his back. He was imposingly tall and broad-shouldered, but didn't appear to be armed. She couldn't understand why no one was trying to kill him, or why both armed groups dispersed at his gesture, but Frannie was delighted that she seemed suddenly to have a chance at safe passage. At least out of this Paris neighborhood.

"Paris," she grumbled as she moved to check the contents of the pack of equipment that had arrived down the timestream a few seconds after her.

The silence in the street continued, so Frannie took the time to make a thorough check of her supplies. She had a long way to go and wasn't sure how she was going to get there. She considered activating the recall implant, but that would be wimpy.

Time agents who ran home to hide in under three days on a tough assignment were mercilessly teased by their peers, and could look forward to a future of being given the most boring trips into the past. She might be in dangerous territory, but she was giving herself the traditional seventy-two hours to make things right.

She was more interested in the defense cache she found than the packets of food and survival gear. She had her own implants for any computer assistance she might need. Her weapons consisted of the standard-issue stun gun with extra charges, and other small, non-lethal defenses she was glad to find. She was downright delighted to discover that her controller had thoughtfully added her own non-standard-issue, completely contraband and potentially lethal 9mm Glock handgun, ammo and knife to her supplies. These were ever so much more helpful accessories in the sorts of situations her journeys threw her into.

The first rule of time-traveling was that YOU DON'T KILL ANYONE down the timestream. You were allowed to defend yourself, but had to be willing to die to preserve the past. It was a fine, idealistic rule, and every time-agent obeyed it for at least the first few years on the job. After watching a colleague get torn to shreds in a Roman arena or being the only member of a team to escape a medieval mob, or appearing in the middle of a battle instead of an observable distance away, your attitude changed. You tried hard not to do any harm, but when it came down to killing your potential grandpa or letting the smelly barbarian that might be important to history take your head off with his axe, you made sure to be the one to shoot or stab first – to do whatever you had to do to stay alive. Travelers and controllers didn't discuss unauthorized additions to packs, but the travelers' "personal property" tended mysteriously to come along for the ride. And most of the scholars just wanted the data, no questions asked.

Frannie repacked her supplies, and made sure to conceal all of her weapons. Just as she finished, a deep voice spoke behind her.

"How did you get in here?"

As she whirled around to face him her translator told her that the man spoke almost unaccented French, but was not a native speaker, and suggested she reply in the English of the era.

She opened her mouth to answer as she faced him, but ended up staring for a moment. "You're the one who stopped the battle!" At least the words that burst out of her were the suggested language.

He looked past her shoulder out the window. "Hardly a battle."

She noted that he had remarkably blue eyes. A long scar marked his left cheek, but it didn't mar his striking good looks.

"But how'd you do it? Why didn't they kill you?"

"If they kill me who will they have to read for them? Who'd write their letters for them, and make sure they get delivered?"

"You're a mailman?"

He nodded. "Archivist. Librarian. Living memory. Who the hell are you?" he added.

But before she could answer he was across the room. This reminded her that the mailmen had started their lives as a military genetic-engineering experiment. They'd been enhanced super-soldiers who had rebelled against their creators. And won. They were too damn smart to sacrifice their super-bodies and intellects in the endless conflicts of this time. As civilization and communication broke down they found a peaceful and profitable purpose for their exceptional skills.

He grabbed her right arm and pushed up the sleeve of her sweatshirt to examine the inside of her wrist. "Elect," he said. His tone was scornful, but his touch was surprisingly stimulating as he ran his thumb across the skin surrounding the small implant plug.

"Elite," she blurted out. "That old Elect term is so—"

"Evil? Selfish? Morally repugnant?" His blue eyes glittered with anger.

She didn't scare easily, no matter how big and hostile he was.

"I was going to say old-fashioned. We saved civilization," she added.

"It's taking you long enough."

At least he hadn't picked up on her use of the wrong tense. Even as she justified her ancestors' actions a sane part of her that was not viscerally reacting to this stranger's touch was swearing at her for completely forgetting years of training and behavior. Speaking the truth to a downtimer could be more dangerous than killing one.

But this wasn't any ordinary local, was it?

Frannie calculated her options and came to a decision that wasn't going to be easy to explain on her report, justifiable though she judged it to be. "I need to get to New York," she told the mailman. "I want to hire you to get me there."

"I don't deliver people," he answered.

She sensed that this wasn't an outright refusal, but the opening of a negotiation.

"I'm not interested in working for anyone who broke into my place to get my help," he went on. "What are you doing out of your hole, anyway?"

"Observing," she answered.

"You people have your own routes and roads."

"I don't. I'm lost."

She wondered if her controller had dumped her here for that exact reason. Maybe there hadn't been a glitch in the machinery, but roundabout was the only way to get her to her assignment. Another possibility was that this was somehow part of another Starshiner plot. And maybe she was being paranoid, because why would anyone get her involved in an operation that it would be her duty to stop?

She showed him her implant plug. "You deal in information exchange. I have lots of information to trade."

His expression remained stony. "Why do you need help to travel?"

She laughed and gestured toward the window. "It's not like there's any public transportation available. There are no scheduled flights, no trains running, not a lot of gas for cars."

"And there are scavengers and wolfsheads every step of the way," he added. Even a sneer didn't look bad on his handsome face. "There are guides you can hire. Armed guards are available for rent."

She laughed again. "You know the safe routes. You're left alone." She knew the history of this period as well as anyone could. "Most mercs sell out their clients the second things get dicey on the road. Coyotes treat the refugees they move through borders like animals. Those who try to travel on their own get killed or trafficked. I have no intention of getting killed, squashed into a cargo container without food or water with a thousand other people, or dead. I'm going with you."

"We're not dating," he answered. He sat down cross-legged on the floor and pretended she wasn't there.

"Oh, yes we are." She sat down in front of him and thrust her wrist under his nose. "You know you want it."

He looked at her with deep, dark hunger in his eyes. They held each other's gaze for a long time. He finally shrugged. "You have a name?"

She was hopeful at the sign of softening. "Francine. You?"

"Rakesh." He stroked the skin around her implant. "I'm on my way to New York anyway. You can plug in and download when we get there."

Yes, she could. The jacks from this era were the prototype that every generation of data-transfer tech had been built on.

"And until then?" she asked, because she wasn't silly enough to think there wouldn't have to be a down payment on his help.

He pulled a worn brown leather bag to him, flipped it open and took out a painted wooden box. He took out a shallow bowl, a container of dark liquid and a short stick with what looked like a row of viciously sharp teeth attached to one end.

"Are those needles?" Frannie asked, trying to hide any sign of dread.

"Yes."

Just what sort of payment did this mailman have in mind?

Rakesh peeled off his leather coat, then rolled up his left sleeve. Rows of numbers and letters in various colors marched up the skin of his arm. Tattoos.

She gestured toward the markings. "What's that all about?"

"Mnemonic," he said. "It's how I remember and retrieve data." He dipped the tattoo needles into the ink, and poised the device over a bare space on his skin. "You've got a head full of information, Elect. Give me some of it."

He was certainly correct about the vast amount of info stored on microscopic chips connected to her brain. Some of that information was fictional. Fiction from this time from the vast library her ancestors had saved and hidden away in underground lifeboats along with themselves. There was no harm to the future in sharing a story that was already part of this time. Maybe it even existed somewhere out there in a library that had escaped burning.

She called up a book from her cache, and started to read it out loud. "It was the best of times. It was the worst of times . . ."

She kept her eyes averted from the mailman's gruesome aid to memorization while she continued to talk.

The first part of the journey turned out to be in the back of a coyote's truck after all. They boarded the truck in an alley behind the shell of an abandoned cafe. Who had time for a baguette and cup of coffee anyway?

"He's a friend," Rakesh said when she protested about dealing with a human trafficker. Which meant Rakesh got to sit up in the cab with the driver.

Of course it wasn't pleasant in the back. She hated being packed in body to body with more people and their raggedy belongings than the back of the trunk could hold. It wasn't so much that she minded the stench of fear, desperation and outright dirt of the gaunt refugees piled in closely around her. She'd spent time in a walled city besieged by Mongols. She hated the sense of futility and frustration that memory called up. Not to mention guilt. Guilt because that had been the first time she'd broken the rules of observation. Guilt because her nursing and feeding those people hadn't stopped them all from being massacred when the Mongols had broken through the city walls.

She'd gone uptime, safe and sound, and that was that. Frannie hadn't even gotten much satisfaction out of killing a half dozen of the invaders to get safely to her up point. It was when she was offered self-editing software by her controller to keep certain details out of her reports – for a price – that she began to understand that the system wasn't perfect, it certainly wasn't pure, and those who didn't bend rules became broken and washed up. She liked her job too much to leave, but she still lived by the rules ninety-nine per cent of the time.

She couldn't do anything to help the people squashed in around her now, and she hated the reminder so much it made her stomach roil and her head hurt like hell.

She didn't bother observing her fellow passengers. She kept her head raised toward the tarpaulin roof and didn't listen to anything that was said. Not that the refugees did much more than try to hide their fear and conceal what little hope they had to cling to. Never admitting to having anything that could be exploited or snatched away was the best way to survive this time and place.

Frannie could only thank the All-Seeing that the descendants of these people would have an easier life. Not that it would come for free. And not at all if the Starshine fanatics' attempts at good deeds got in the way of how the future needed to roll.

At least the trip in the back of the truck didn't last more than a few hours.

It was very dark outside when the truck stopped its slow, swaying, bumping gear-grinding progress. A shiver of worry went through the occupants, replaced by indifference when Rakesh lifted the tarpaulin over the back and called, "Francine."

She squeezed her way through the crowd to the exit, and got no help from Rakesh jumping to the ground. She landed in a puddle and stumbled. Without night-vision implants she wouldn't have been able to see the figure of Rakesh already walking briskly off into the darkness. She hurried to catch up with him, and then got her bearings. She checked GPS to find out where they were. The answer came as no surprise.

"Please tell me we aren't heading for Sangatte," she said when they were striding side by side.

Sangatte had started as a refugee camp a century earlier. It was so much worse than a wretched place for displaced people in this time; it was more like the first circle of hell. Over the decades it had been closed, closed again, burned, and there had been at least one massacre trying to drive everyone out. The place simply wouldn't go away. It couldn't go away. It was a final resting place just one step out of the grave for thousands with nowhere else to go.

"We're not going in," he answered. "We'll stay at the supply station two kilometers out."

"You have deliveries," she guessed. "To and from?"

"That's right."

She could also guess what he was carrying. "Forged visa chips for countries that still let people in?"

He gave her a hostile look. "You going to report me, Elect?"

"Elite," she reminded. "Hell, no. There's few enough spots on this planet that are safe. I don't begrudge anyone getting to them who can."

"Good to know your opinion," he said. "Because I was going to kill you if you went all righteous on me."

She was fully aware that he'd started life as a super-soldier.

She gave him a smile without a hint of bravado in it. "I would so love to see you try," she told him.

As far as she could tell, Rakesh took no part in the buying and selling of false IDs; he was a courier. He delivered a package to a tent on the outskirts of the camp outside Sangatte, then settled down at a table in what could best be described as a den of iniquity and waited with a glass of dark liquid by his hand while word went out that the mailman had arrived.

Frannie received an annoyed look when she sat down beside him. "My presence will keep the hookers off you," she told him.

"Who says I want to keep them away?" He gestured. "Not that the stable roams around freely in here."

She glanced under her lashes at a row of skinny girls and boys lined up along a side wall, waiting. They each stood beneath a crudely painted number. Every now and then one of the pimps conducting business at a nearby table would call out a number, and one of the sex-workers would leave with a buyer. Everyone involved seemed more bored with the transaction than anything else, even the customers.

Of course there was no prostitution in her time. Not that people didn't pay for sex, they just didn't have it with each other. It was all very virtual and virtuous and nobody died from STDs. People still made a profit on it, of course.

What was the matter with her? She shook her head, trying to clear out at least a little of the cynical mood that had descended on her since her arrival downtime. She lived in a Utopia. Almost a Utopia. As close as humans could get to a Utopia. The population was stable, everyone had food, clothing, shelter, employment, education, leisure time, medical care. Not everybody was equal, but everybody was fine. The planet wasn't completely healed from the dark times yet, but it was being made greener every year. All right, there was a stratified social order in place, but from her spot at the top she couldn't see all the way down to where the dissatisfaction with things as they were bubbled and brewed.

"There's no way the world can be perfect," she murmured. "But it's sure as hell better than this."

"What the hell are *you* doing out here, then? Slumming outside the CERN hole when the whole world's a slum?"

She wished she hadn't spoken. For a man who didn't invite conversation Rakesh was fired up for one now. Confrontation, more like. "I'm not from the CERN Enclave."

In fact, she was a Hillbilly. Her ancestors resided underground at the Appalachian Enclave. CERN was where her profession originated, as the place had been home to scientists who fiddled around with physics while waiting for the apocalypse to calm down.

"Why are you here? Why do you need to get to New York?"

"I was under the impression you didn't ask questions about your delivery jobs. Why do *you* roam the world?"

"Because I can."

"See, that's the kind of bullshit answer I'd expect from a macho war-fighter type. I thought mailmen were trying to save the world, doing what they could to keep civilization going."

Apparently she was up for a confrontation too.

He said, "I do what I can. Don't lay that macho military shit on me. I walked away from war, but I didn't leave the world. What do the Elect do to help anyone but themselves?"

"Elite. We saved the knowledge."

"Let it free. That's what we need."

She leaned in close to him to keep the conversation private. Not that anybody in this place would pay attention to anything less than a gun battle breaking out, and then only to duck, or to scavenge the bodies. He smelled of dust, sweat and ink, and she found the combination rather intriguing. Their gazes met and held, and she saw how deeply he cared about *everything* burning deeply in his eyes. And his gaze burned deep into her soul. She was goddamned stripped naked all the way through, with no interest in trying to hide anything from this man. He knew her insatiable curiosity, her doubts, her regrets and hopes.

Well, she learned about him, too. But before either of them could pounce on the other's vulnerabilities a couple of clients showed up with business for the mailman.

Frannie settled back in her chair. She finished drinking Rakesh's whisky. Alcohol wouldn't affect her, but she appreciated the burn of the stuff going down her throat. She watched the way he dealt with people, and was surprised to discover he had a ready smile and a charming manner toward someone who needed him. Interesting fellow, this Rakesh.

For the shy, arthritic elderly woman who was his last client he wrote a paper letter, and coaxed specific directions on where in London to deliver it. Frannie observed his behavior with all her sensors. She didn't know if the scholar who had commissioned her research would be interested in the routine of a mailman, but she wanted a record of this. She wanted a memory of Rakesh, she supposed.

When the old woman was gone he put away the letter then set out his tattoo equipment and rolled up his sleeve. His attitude had returned to grudging neutrality. "Continue," he said when he was ready.

She returned to Charles Dickens.

It didn't take long for a group of English speakers to gather around to listen to the story. Frannie felt the pressure of their attention on her. She felt hunger deeper than any physical hunger trying to eat her up.

The pimps and the bartender were the only ones who didn't look completely enthralled with the storytelling. Why should they when it interfered with the entertainment they provided? She was certain the only thing that kept them from pulling weapons was fear of crossing a mailman, but it was coming soon. Restraint was not a common virtue of this era. An itch between her shoulder blades warned her that this could get bad.

"I'm done." She stood. "Let's go."

There was a collective disappointed sigh from the crowd, but they instantly turned away. Rakesh looked up in irritation, but he took her hint when she gestured her head slightly toward the pimps' table.

He put away his gear and they went on their way. Their path led along a torn-up railroad track.

Frannie looked toward the refugee camp when a wisp of smoke drifted around them. A portion of the night sky was flame-lit and the roar of angry, frightened voices came across several miles' distance. Frannie just shook her head and kept on. Something as common as a riot wasn't worth observing.

Frannie had hoped they'd be meeting a boat when they reached the coast at Pas-de-Calais, but of course it wasn't going to be that easy. Oddly enough she recognized the ruins of the town because they reminded her of similar destruction she'd seen wrought on the French coast during a trip back to June 1944. She'd enjoyed that trip, even if it had been into the middle of a combat zone during a world war. At least it had been a war where right and wrong had had some real meaning. Good guys and bad guys were much harder to define most of the time.

Never mind nostalgia for the Allies storming the Normandy beaches, she guessed why Rakesh had brought her here and she didn't like it. "You are not seriously going under the English Channel?"

"We are," he answered. "Pirates have been busy in the Channel lately. So many boats have been captured or sunk, the Chunnel is the safest route at the moment."

She knew very well that the partially flooded remains of the Channel Tunnel, while a gaping abandoned hole on the French side, were cordoned off and tightly guarded where the tunnel ended in Folkestone on the English side.

"It's a two-hundred-and-fifty-foot-deep, thirty-mile-long dead end. A leaking one, at that. How can you possibly— ?"

"Are you coming?" He turned his back and walked toward a screaming mouth of a hole in the ground.

Frannie settled her pack more comfortably on her shoulders. "Yeah. Sure," she grumbled, and followed Rakesh into the Chunnel entrance.

Frannie gazed into the heart of the tiny campfire, feeling wonder at the place she and Rakesh had ended up to get some rest. They were dry and warm, surrounded by other groups and other small fires. Several of the travelers seemed to be Rakesh's friends. There had been smiles and nods and a few invites to join groups. Rakesh returned the greetings, but settled down at an empty firepit with her.

They'd traveled for many miles in the main tunnel. Frannie had been grateful that they both had genetically enhanced night vision. The way was dark and wet, vermin-infested, and crazies and cut-throats lurked in the shadows. They'd had to swim in freezing, filthy salt water a couple of times. They'd fought off a trio of robbers, leaving bodies floating face down in streaming water and their own blood. She'd appreciated Rakesh's deadly speed and skill, and had considered it a compliment when he'd conceded she was damned good with a knife. Neither of them had commented on how good it had felt to be standing body to body, back to back. But the awareness had continued to sing through her long after they had continued on their way.

After a long, hard slog they had come to a blank spot in the wall that had seemed like every other blank spot in the wall. "This is the entrance to the Dry Way," he had told her, and clicked the latch to a hidden door. After another long walk, feeling their way in darkness that was nearly complete even with enhanced vision, faint light had appeared ahead of them. Rakesh had led her into the side tunnel that held this encampment. There were working air vents near the roof, taking out smoke, bringing in salty air. She'd love to see a schematic of just how those worked.

"I guess there's a lot about this world I don't know," she said now, still not quite over the surprise of the secret path and this protected place.

"Well, if you came out of your hole more often . . ."

She glanced up across the fire at Rakesh. He was toasting chunks of bread on skewers for them. "Give it a rest," she advised.

"Am I just supposed to appreciate that you're trying to find out about the world? Are you going to take the knowledge and use it against us, Elect?"

"Elite. And who exactly is us?" she asked. "I'm one of us. Besides, neutrality is one of the things that keeps the enclaves safe from warlords and crusaders. And their mercenaries," she added, giving him a significant look. She reached out a hand. "Stop throwing stones and give me some food."

He accepted her point and passed over some toast. "Ex-mercenary," he said as their fingers briefly touched. A smile didn't touch his lips, but she saw it in his eyes.

Frannie was considering moving closer to Rakesh when one of the other mailmen, a woman, actually, came over and took a seat in the area between them. The woman slapped Rakesh on the shoulder, so hard that he almost dropped his bread into the fire. He gave the newcomer a glare.

Which she ignored. "You're on your way to the meet, aren't you?" the woman asked. "I know you said you weren't interested when the general's call went out, but I knew you'd change your mind."

And so it was that Frannie found out who she was going to New York to watch die. "General Dehn, the man who led the super-soldier mutiny. I thought he was dead." Frannie just barely caught herself from saying *already dead*.

"He led our fight for freedom," Rakesh said.

"Now he's asking more from us," the woman said.

"I already know his speech by heart, Salome," Rakesh said.

Frannie wanted to say, "I don't," and find out more, but she had to keep out of this. Just observe and hope some useful data was forthcoming.

Salome grinned widely and clapped him on the shoulder again. "But you've decided to listen to him in person this time. A lot of us have. We're beginning to believe. That's a good sign."

"I've got deliveries in New York," Rakesh said. "But I'm thinking about being there. Don't." He jerked aside before the woman could hit him once more.

Salome laughed. "You'll be there. Knowledge is power," she added, then moved back to her own campsite.

Frannie was hoping to get an explanation, but instead Rakesh said, "It's been a long day. Let's get some rest."

She couldn't hide her surprise. "Don't you want me to read?"

He put a finger to his lips, looked around at his fellow mailmen, then whispered. "Knowledge may be power, but you're not something I'm ready to share."

Frannie decided to take that as a compliment, and broke out her sleeping roll. She also took it as a good sign when he settled beside her and they ended up sleeping together spoon fashion.

"How are we getting to New York?" Frannie asked once they were safely out of the secret Chunnel that let out at the bottom of a tall white chalk cliff. They moved quickly to a narrow path that led up from the seashore. Smugglers had been using this coast for hundreds of years.

"Flying," Rakesh answered when they reached the top of the cliff.

Rolling green, empty countryside spread out before them.

"Thank goodness you have access to a plane. I feared we'd be snorkeling across the Atlantic."

"There are still a few flights from Gatwick. If you have the right contacts. And the price," he added.

She frowned. "How much is this going to cost me?"

"More data."

She tapped her forehead. "I've got some Laura Ingalls Wilder in here I'd be happy to share with the pilot."

He touched the same spot her finger had. "Save the story for me. I'll take care of your ticket."

"When do we leave?" she asked. She had a time constraint to consider.

"We have to deliver Mrs Bledsoe's letter first."

Frannie had figured that was coming. She wondered if he noticed he'd said *we. Oh, yeah, he had.*

"Bad neighborhood?" she asked.

"Worse than most."

"Where you go I go," she said. A true statement wasn't a promise of help if his delivery turned dicey. But of course she'd have to help, because she needed him to get to her assignment. And she'd hate to see anything happen to his handsome ass.

"The mailing address is Paddington Station."

Frannie took a shocked step back. Rakesh caught her before she could take a fatal fall backwards. He kept his arm firmly around her waist as they talked.

"Paddington's a quarantine zone," she said.

"I already know that. I'm immune," he added. "I'm betting you are too."

"Yes. But that's not the point. Brit security strictly enforces the zone around the area. Maybe you can sneak in, but getting out isn't so easy. And the conditions inside . . ."

"Gangs, gunfights, the usual stuff. Only a bit more concentrated."

"Zombies," Frannie added.

That was the common, if incorrect, name for those few who survived the engineered biological weapon that terrorists had set loose in London. Not that the scarred, brain-damaged ones who lived through the original sickness survived more than a year or so after the so-called recovery. They were crazy mean while they lived. Frannie knew she couldn't catch anything from them, but the thought of being scratched and bitten by a stinking husk of human did not appeal in the least. And they were bound to be attacked if they went into Paddington Park, as the place had come to be called.

"Hardly anybody inside the cordon is sick anymore. Most people packed in there are healthy, but they won't be let out. Mrs Bledsoe wants her daughter to know that the kids she got out before the quarantine are safer than their mom will ever be."

Frannie cringed. "You're trying to make me feel sorry for people," she complained.

"Is it working?"

She relaxed against him. "Yes." She sighed. "Let's get this delivery over with."

Rakesh hugged her before he let her go. "You're not so bad, for one of the Elect."

"I'm considered a rebel at home," she told him. Which was sort of true. Rebel without a cause, or a clue, she guessed.

They traveled to London on bicycles retrieved from a hidden smuggler's cache, much of the way along a forgotten Roman track. And then along another ruined railway line that once led directly into Paddington Station. They had to abandon this route within a few miles of their destination, leave the bikes in another cache and move cautiously toward the security cordon on foot.

As things went in this time, London was a fairly civilized place. At least the gangs that ran the various areas of the city mostly kept to an agreement that kept them from killing the people they exploited. The government spent its time either chasing the gangs or leaving them alone, depending on the current policy on bribes and corruption. The one thing the official security forces were good at was enforcing the quarantine. It kept the streets safe for the official gangs to go about their business, and the threat of ending up exiled to Paddington Park was a great incentive to keep the populace docile and tax-paying.

Of course Frannie and Rakesh sneaked toward the quarantined area at night through a city under curfew. But it wasn't like sneaking was that hard for either of them. Frannie just wished that Rakesh didn't have an affinity for traveling in the sewers. It got them dirtier than they already were, and it kept them safe a while longer, but it still didn't get them all the way to their destination.

They emerged on the edge of Hyde Park and ducked into the entrance of the abandoned Lancaster Gate tube station. They paused long enough to clean off as much as they could in a lavatory that had a trickling water faucet.

"I don't suppose you have an invisibility cloak?" he asked when they headed back out into the dark street.

"They'd still smell us coming."

"Okay. I guess we'll just have to do this the old-fashioned way. Cover me," he said, and walked boldly up to the nearest checkpoint gate.

Frannie stayed in the shadows with her gun out. She felt terribly exposed, even if her implants made sure she at least couldn't be picked up by infrared security cameras. She waited and watched in her hiding spot—

While a bribe passed from Rakesh's hand to a guard's.

Hey! That wasn't fair.

She was furious when Rakesh waved her forward. "Why didn't you just ask her to deliver the letter?" Frannie asked after they were clear of the checkpoint.

He was affronted. "My job is to deliver the mail, and I do exactly that."

She was unwillingly impressed, and mollified, by Rakesh's professional integrity. Or possibly it was willful, stubborn insanity. She still kind of liked it.

"Now that we're in, how do we get out?"

"We'll think of something."

She'd suspected he'd say that. He took her by the hand as they walked into the abyss. She made sure her Glock was in the other.

There was no curfew inside the crowded tangle of streets cordoned off with the ruined train station at its center. Most of the multistoried, close-set buildings around the station had been small hotels and pubs in the days when there were tourists in the world. Now it was an overcrowded tenement neighborhood that reminded Frannie of Whitechapel in the days of Jack the Ripper. Only not quite as safe.

There weren't many moving on the dark street. Greedy-eyed people were gathered on steps and seated on curbs, looking up as they passed, gazes following. Some were sharks, most of them were scavengers who could easily form into packs. Walking in a place like this was an art form that took total spacial awareness and cold confidence. Rakesh was as adept at the do-not-fuck-with-me dance as she was. They made good partners.

The street had a way of clearing of people as they walked along. Which didn't mean Frannie and Rakesh weren't followed, or word of outsiders' presence didn't spread along the streets and alleys. It was only a matter of time.

There was no electricity in this part of the city: only the occasional flicker of a candle or oil lamp behind a window throwing out faint puddles of light. It came as no surprise when a tall man with a large gun stepped into one of those puddles ahead of them.

"Welcome to my territory. Why should I let you live?"

Frannie sighed, not because of this threat, but over the fact that the people trapped in this slum had access to high-tech weapons but no way to make light bulbs work. Rakesh dropped her hand and stepped forward to confront the gunman. Frannie stayed in the shadows and watched his back. Further into the dark, others watched her.

Rakesh showed the gunman his leather courier bag. "I have a delivery to make. Can I take anything out for you?" he added.

Rakesh sounded so polite and helpful Frannie had to hide a smile. But it worked.

"The mail has to get through, eh?" the gunman asked. He thoughtfully scratched his bearded jaw. "Heard about you lot." All the bravado had left his voice.

"Just shoot him and take what he's got," a watcher in the dark called.

Frannie turned enough to make sure her gun was visible to the watchers. She caught the glitter of eyes. "Kindly keep out of this," she suggested softly.

"He's a mailman," the gunman called to the others. "Remember what happens when the mail doesn't get through."

The troublemaker took a step out of concealment. "Who'll know, if he's dead?"

"They'll know," Rakesh said. There wasn't a hint of doubt in his voice. He didn't bother to look at anyone but the gunman. "I'm on my way to Paddington. I'll come back this way. Be waiting here if you have anything for me to deliver. Francine." He gestured her forward.

"What the—!" The troublemaker lunged.

The gunman shot him before Frannie could. The man's angry shout turned into a scream that nobody paid any attention to. The blood that flowed onto the ground was just one stain among many.

"I'll be here," the gunman said. "Watch out for the Zs," he called out as Frannie walked away with Rakesh.

"So, you peace-loving ex-mercs retaliate when something happens to one of your own," she said once they were away from the gang.

"I've heard that rumor," was his cool answer.

When they reached the main entrance of the ruined rail station she asked, "How are we finding Mrs Bledsoe's daughter?"

He took out a handheld puter and used the keypad. "Easy. Mrs Bledsoe had her daughter chipped when she was a kid."

"Ah. Of course." She kept her attention on the dark street and the shadows by the surrounding buildings while Rakesh used the primitive tracking function of his puter.

She supposed the old lady's daughter would be in the age range for that particular endtimes app. Identity/tracking chip implants had been all the rage for children back when civilization began seriously to fall apart. Even members of the Elect communities had used them. Frannie supposed the IT chips had been the first tech enhancements her ancestors had used.

After a minute or two he lifted his head and looked to the left. "This way."

She accompanied him around a corner, into an area of tents and shacks set up on the street. They stopped in front of a tent, where they found a very surprised middle-aged woman who burst out crying when Rakesh gave her the letter. She said no when Rakesh asked her if she wanted him to bring an answer to her mother.

Duty over, Rakesh and Frannie headed back the way they had come. They exchanged a glance to acknowledge they knew they were being followed as they approached the spot where the gunman had said he'd meet him.

The gunman was there all right, a piece of mauled meat, with a pair of zombies kneeling on either side of him, munching away. The gangbanger had warned them to look out for the Zs, but had ended up a victim of the hunt himself.

"Because he was alone," Rakesh said. "Waiting for me."

The Zs sprang away from their kill, toward them.

"Two more coming up behind us," Frannie answered.

"Aim for the head," he said as she span around.

"I know!"

Her irritated shout was drowned by the roar of the Glock as she fired. The bullet went into the Z's forehead with a horrible thud, blowing a much bigger hole in the attacker's head than it should have. Stinking brain fragments flew away into the dark.

Her next shot went through the second zombie's shoulder. He slammed into Frannie without slowing at all. This one had enough intelligence left to grab her arms and wrench them so hard the Glock was forced from her grasp. She held the Z away from her while he snapped at her face. She brought up her knees from beneath him.

But a knife sank to the hilt into the zombie's head before she could lever him off.

Rakesh flung the body away before it collapsed onto her. He pulled her to her feet. A quick glance told her Rakesh had taken out the other pair of zombies. No one else was around.

"I owe you one," she informed the mailman.

He gave a curt nod. "I'll hold you to it. Keeping promises and returning favors is the right way to live," he added. He sounded like he expected her to argue.

"Well, yeah," she answered.

They made their way back to the sentry post. Frannie had wondered if getting out would be as easy as getting in, but the guard was waiting there for them. She let them through and pressed a tiny bag into Rakesh's hands. Mailmen had the run of the world, Frannie decided. What they did was just too useful to keep them from making their rounds.

She and Rakesh spent some more time in the sewer, but were met by a smuggler's van at the spot where they came out. It was just after dawn. The van took them deep into the hangars beyond the collapsed terminal buildings of Gatwick Airport. A well-maintained private jet was parked inside the hangar. They were taken past it, up a flight of metal stairs to an office/living area. A tall, thin man came from behind his desk to greet Rakesh, arms held out for a hug.

He stopped inches away from the mailman and made a gagging noise. "Oh, God, you stink." He went to a door in the back of the office and gestured them through. "Get cleaned up. There'll be food waiting for you when you're done."

Not only was there running water in the bathroom shower, but it was hot! Frannie stripped off her clothes and plunged into the steaming stream of water with her face turned up and her eyes closed. Heavenly!

It wasn't long before her rapture was interrupted as a naked Rakesh squeezed in beside her. "To save time and energy," was his comment. He began to rub her skin, leaving a trail of lather and tingling pleasure. "I brought soap."

She gathered up soap bubbles and returned the favor, her hands gliding over his chest and hips and down his thighs.

"We both know how this is going to end," he said.

"Uh-huh." Frannie leaned her head against his shoulder, put a hand on his hip to steady herself and wrapped her leg around him, welcoming him inside.

"What is it you want from me?" Frannie asked Rakesh. She didn't turn away from watching the clouds below the airplane window, but she was acutely aware of him in the seat beside her. They'd both slept on the flight. When she woke up she found his head resting on her shoulder. She watched him for a while, then turned toward the window when he woke up.

She held her wrist up, showing her implant. "I can't offer you every bit of data I can access at the retrieval point. I certainly can't download everything there is in the database into my one little brain. I'm letting you name what your help's been worth. And it has to be something accessible at my security level. I ain't no hacker, hon."

He looked skeptical. "You're just a simple little expendable scout roaming the outside world? Is that it?"

"I wouldn't say expendable."

He patted her shoulder. "Of course you wouldn't. Everyone is, for the right reasons."

She thought about the man she was about to observe die. What really disturbed her was knowing that Rakesh would also see the man who'd been his leader, the one who'd led the mailmen to freedom, fall before an assassin. Then again, maybe it wasn't a murder, Maybe General Dehn was about to have a fatal heart attack or stroke. There was no definitive proof of how the man had died. She was here to find out and bring back historical fact.

Frannie showed her wrist again. "What can I get for you?"

"Medicine," he said promptly. "I want the formulas for cures, vaccines that I can get to chemists."

"There aren't any chemists outside the enclaves."

"Who do you think does the processing for the drug cartels?"

She shrugged in acknowledgment. "There's no cure for the zombie plague," she said. Not in this time, and anything she gave him would have to be from this era.

"Give me the AIDS vaccine, aspirin. Anything to keep people alive."

She appreciated his desperate need to help, and kept silent about everything she'd been taught about overpopulation being the cause of civilization's downfall. The Elect even called what was going on in the world right now the "hinning of the herd". But the Elect didn't come out of their enclaves to witness the horrible process in action. She believed her ancestors would have had more compassion if they had.

"Medicines," she said with a decisive nod. "I'll get you what I can."

Would giving away a few formulas be breaking the rules? She suspected Rakesh's compassionate request would only lead to an intensification of the drug wars that raged along with all the other wars infecting the planet. Rakesh believed he could do some good, and her admiration for him was such a strong, burning emotion that she suspected it was more than admiration.

The plane landed in Newark. It had been a very bumpy landing, but not much rougher than one into Newark she'd experienced on a 1990 observing trip. The difference now was that the airport wasn't officially operating anymore. The jagged ruins of the New York City skyline were visible in the distance. None of the bridges linking New Jersey to New York still stood.

"Almost there," Rakesh said after they climbed down the ladder that got them to the ground.

"Almost," she told Rakesh. They paused long enough to smile at each other. She was going to miss him when she was gone. They held hands. It was becoming a habit. "Let's head to the ferry dock."

The boat was approaching the Battery Dock when Frannie's mission log kicked on. "Your GPS indicates you have reached physical objective. Stand by."

She blinked and sat up straight. She'd been leaning against Rakesh, warm and relaxed, enjoying the ride. All of a sudden she was back in her real world.

"Francine," her scholar's voice spoke inside her head. "If your controller has done his job correctly you have traveled from Paris to New York in the company of one of General Dehn's commando force. As you are already aware but do not acknowledge, your controller is a member of the Starshine Group. What you do not know is that I am also a Starshiner."

Frannie gasped.

Rakesh asked, "What's wrong?"

Her scholar went on speaking. "I arranged your assignment, not because I want you to observe a murder, but because I want you to prevent one. The Starshiners want to save General Dehn from the assassin sent by the Elect to kill him. You have a sense of justice that you try to hide. Use that sense of justice. Stop a murder. Help the people. You have spent the last several days traveling through a blighted world that your own ancestors did a great deal to create. You have witnessed first-hand the damage the Elect fostered to achieve the world you and I and your controller live in. You have been taught all your life that the residents of the enclaves were neutral, that they hid themselves away and did no harm to anyone, other than to fend off attacks from the outside. Lies."

Did her scholar think he was surprising her with that revelation? They'd had the right to defend themselves from attacks. Did the Starshiners – her own scholar – really believe the Elect had been murderers as well?

She was surprised at his political sympathies – which could get her in a lot of trouble. "You're one of the Elite, too," she said.

"What?" Rakesh asked.

He turned her to face him. She looked through him, her attention on what she was being told by her mission log.

"The history you know states that General Dehn died while he was giving a speech. This fact is a tiny footnote in what we call the Ruin Times. We claim to have very little information about the time you are in. Because, after all, the Elite were closed up in the enclaves while the world burned around them. Have you noticed how few missions have been sent back to this era? Because the Elite would love to place the whole era under interdiction, but that would rouse suspicions."

She'd assumed scholars just weren't that interested.

"I have evidence that Dehn will be killed to keep him from organizing a movement that could become dangerous to the Elects' policy of letting the world go to hell until it is time to come out of the enclaves and take complete power themselves. I want you to save Dehn. His movement might not be able to save the world, but I think anyone who tries to help in the Ruin Times deserves a chance to try. You have to make a choice now, Francine. Let Dehn die or save him. That is all," the mission log ended.

"Oh, fuck."

"Francine?"

She found herself looking into Rakesh's worried face.

Anyone who tries to help in the Ruin Times deserves a chance.

She put her hand on his cheek. It was warm, faintly rough with new stubble. Alive. Real. He was so alive and real and – good.

Damn it! She hated using that word. She was cynical, jaded, just a little corrupt. She was an observer, not a doer.

She hated having witnessed how this one mailman's acts of kindness had added to what passed for civilization back here. She hated that she remembered these acts with fondness, and pride. She tried telling herself that he wasn't doing any good, really.

But he wasn't the only mailman out there, was he? They hadn't started out as peaceful couriers, had they? What was Dehn planning for them? Would they follow?

Could he change the world? Save it?

"Do you want to save the world?" she asked Rakesh. "Do you really think you could?"

"I am saving the world," he answered. "One delivery at a time."

"You're saving your soul," she spat back at him. "You're trying to make up for your mercenary past."

"That too," he agreed. "What are you doing to save your soul?"

"Nothing. Nothing at all."

Her own words took Frannie completely by surprise. She'd

been so set up, and she knew it. It hurt. Instead of making her angry, it hurt. Pain stabbed all the way through her, from her head to her heart and all the way down to her toes. *And why didn't she doubt for a moment what her scholar told her?* She'd always had a nagging belief that her ancestors were callous about the chaos outside the enclaves. Their writings had claimed there was nothing they could do to save the world but what they did. She'd believed their sins were of omission not commission. Now she'd had her nose rubbed in that lie.

What was she going to do?

Why was she even asking herself that? She should go home and turn the Starshine traitors in. She should cover her ass. She should—

Rakesh brushed his lips across hers, a gentle angel's kiss. Her head swirled with confusion and she began to cry. *She never cried!* He held her close and she cried on Rakesh's shoulder while the ferry's hull ground up against the side of the dock. She was vaguely aware of the other passengers moving around them to get off the boat.

"It's time to go," Rakesh said.

She reluctantly moved away from him. She nodded. "It is."

This is a con, she told herself as she accompanied Rakesh into the wreck of Lower Manhattan.

"When's your meeting?" she asked after her mind ran around in circles too long for her to take it anymore.

"I'm not sure I'm going. I can guess what the general wants. I don't want to be talked into it."

Right. He'd really only come to New York to make deliveries. He wanted to believe he was doing as much as he could.

"You'll be there," she told him. "You won't be able to stay away."

"Yeah. Probably."

"I'm coming with you," she said. That wasn't a surprise. Her scholar had authorized her to be at the meeting no matter what he really wanted her to do. What surprised her was when she added, "It's a far, far better thing I do . . ."

"What?"

Frannie drew Rakesh into a deep doorway and held his shoulders. She took a deep breath and spoke very fast. "The truth is, I am not from one of the Elect enclaves – not from this time period. I was sent from the future to save the world. It wasn't my idea, but there it is. Actually, your general and you mailmen are supposed to save the world. My job is to save your general. I can't do it by myself. Are you in?"

Of course he looked at her like she was crazy. Then he looked thoughtful. He reached up and took her wrist to turn it and look at her implant. "I thought this looked odd," he said. "And I've never heard one of the Elect calling herself Elite. And how did you get into my place without getting through my security? And what Elect would have sex with one of the riff-raff?"

"Very enjoyable sex," she said.

"Good. We'll do it again." He kissed her palm. "What are we going to do to save the general?"

"God, you're easy," she told him.

"I'm also good at taking orders I believe in. Tell me what we're doing?"

"We're running," she said. "I'll think of something along the way."

The meeting place was in the lobby of the Chrysler Building. It was the only skyscraper still standing in the city. Not in very good shape, but it was still standing.

There was a group of mailmen already in the lobby when they got there. Frannie recognized Salome. Several more came in while Rakesh and Frannie caught their breath.

"What's up, bro?" Salome asked, coming up to them, along with several others who were happy to see Rakesh.

"Hey, Colonel," somebody said. "I lost a bet over your showing. Glad I did."

"The general will be glad to see you."

Frannie wasn't surprised when Salome clapped Rakesh on the shoulder, but she didn't like Salome touching him. Any more than she had in the Chunnel, she admitted.

Frannie left Rakesh to explain to his comrades. "The Elect are going to kill the general. Here and now."

This was all the information the mailmen needed. They believed Rakesh instantly, and waited for him to give them orders.

"Riff-raff, eh?" Frannie asked him.

He gave her a crooked smile. "Your turn," he told her.

She couldn't demand that the general not give his speech.

History said he was killed giving it. Some bits of history had to go the way they were supposed to, even if the details got changed.

She turned slowly, taking in a growing crowd of black-haired, blue-eyed people in the lobby. People were still coming in. Most of them were in duster coats, carrying mailbags. They were a homogeneous genetically engineered lot. On the periphery of this group some of the former soldiers had already turned to form a perimeter. To protect her? Keen glances were surreptitiously scanning the rest of the crowd. A pair had peeled off and were casually making their way toward the elevator alcove. Frannie supposed the general was waiting there. *Damn, these guys were good.*

"The assassin will look like you," she told them. "There's probably more than one. Rakesh, is your puter battery still charged?"

"Of course."

"Do all of you carry handhelds?"

Puters appeared from beneath duster coats with the speed of fast-draw pistols.

"Search for ID chips," Frannie told the mailmen. "The Elect of the right age for this mission will be the right age to have been chipped as kids."

Rakesh was scanning for the IDs before she finished her explanation. Yep, the mailmen were good. Especially Rakesh.

"Got one," he whispered within moments.

"Got him," Salome added. She started to move away.

Rakesh grabbed her by the elbow. "Wait for it." He looked back at the puter screen. "There's a second one moving toward the alcove." He looked around at the watching mailmen. He made hand signals they understood and Frannie could guess at.

Several mailmen moved to block the alcove. They started shouting at each other and a knife fight broke out. This blocked the Elect heading toward the general.

It also drew the attention of the assassin closer to the entrance.

Rakesh headed that way while the Elect was momentarily diverted. Rakesh's knife was drawn. Frannie went with him. But the mailman was just a little bit faster than she was.

The assassin's throat was slit before she had the chance to suggest he be taken prisoner. *At least there was still one more they could interroga—*

"Go!" Rakesh spun away from the falling body, just barely avoiding a spray of blood.

The mailmen moved on the man near the alcove. And there was no one left to interrogate.

Oh, well, it had been a thought. Frannie didn't really mind the lost chance at gaining intel. General Dehn's movement had all of her considerable knowledge at their disposal. Because she sure as hell couldn't go home now. When Rakesh put his arm around her waist, she knew she didn't want to.

General Dehn stepped out of the alcove as soon as the bodies were hauled into a corner. He moved onto a low platform and gestured. The mailmen gathered around. Rakesh drew her forward with him into the group. He held her tightly pressed to his side, and she put her arm around him as well.

She knew that her retrieval point and its data outlet hidden at the United Nations ruin would have to be secured fairly quickly, before the disruption in the timestream caused it to disappear. They needed the info dump before this successful Starshiner operation was detected back home. But for now she stood solidly with Rakesh and the others, and waited to hear what the general had to say.

Nobody's Present

Marcella Burnard

"Ms Selkirk?" A young man poked his head through the doorway. Though he looked in my general direction, he wouldn't meet my gaze.

I put the science brief I'd been pretending to read back in my case and rose.

The damned guy's eyes went straight to my legs. My one-time sorority sister, Jill, had insisted I wear a skirt for the interview. I'd let her talk me into it when every instinct had screamed "slacks". It isn't that they aren't nice legs. They are. I work for them to be nice legs. But it was late December, barely a week before Christmas, and I wasn't interviewing for pole-dancer.

This was a shot at a private space program. I'd done my research, and I wanted in. I was ready for a long-term project with potential worldwide impact. But I didn't want it said I'd gotten in on the value of my stems.

"Ma'am, the comman—" he broke off and flushed. "Mr Carrollus will see you now."

"Thank you," I said, giving no outward sign that I'd noticed his slip. But I cataloged it and felt the first tingle of warning drip down my spine.

'Commander,' he'd tried not to say. *Interesting. Not in a good way.*

He swung the door open, keeping it between us as if I might start shooting at any moment. I hesitated at the threshold, trying to sense what I might be walking into.

Office. Immaculate. Big. Bright. Typical, distressing, unidentifiable color of commercial carpet.

The smell of fresh coffee lingered in the room, but I caught no hint of any other odor beneath it. Not even of furniture polish or carpet glue.

In one corner, a fake Christmas tree glittered with tiny, multi-colored lights and ornaments. Fancy baskets filled with poinsettias and other plants dotted the room. They were lush, green, well-cared for. Built-in white display cases were arranged with gleaming books and art pieces.

Below the cases, a brown leather love seat and a matching armchair were fronted by a glass coffee table set with a polished silver coffee service. Steam curled from the spout of the pot.

Almost as an afterthought, a rich cherrywood desk sat tucked behind an exuberant ficus near the window.

To my relief, the holiday elevator music that had been piped into the reception area didn't intrude into the office.

At the wet bar stood a man pouring an iced seltzer with a twist of lime that sent a burst of spicy citrus across my olfactory receptors. Commander Carrollus, I presumed. Tall, dark, and out of uniform, unless Armani was building his own, well-dressed, pinstriped army.

My mouth watered. The lime? Or the man?

"Sir," the young man hid behind the door, "Ms Selkirk."

Carrollus turned.

I had to combat the effect of gravity on my jaw. Tall. I'd said that. But, really. I'm five foot ten in my cute little "rocket scientist to my toes" socks. In my sensible but passably sexy pumps, I pushed six feet. I still had to tilt my chin up to look him in the eye. Broad shoulders, strong arms, narrow waist, all of the classic descriptors of male beauty present and accounted for. But that face. Cheekbones and nose carved by a master sculptor, check. Lips that instantly reminded me I hadn't entertained an unclothed man in over a year, check.

But none of those good looks mattered to me. Much.

It was the grave weight of responsibility in those midnight blue eyes, the sense of power. He had command presence. And that scared the crap out of me.

So I smiled, strode into the office, and extended a hand. I couldn't escape the thought that no matter how much I hated the holidays, I'd be happy to find him under my tree. *I could* so *get into unwrapping him.*

His gaze swept me, lingered on the damned legs, but rose again nearly quickly enough that I might not have noticed had I not been studying him. I thought I detected a flicker of appreciation in his gaze and in the quirk of his faint smile. He shook my hand and squeezed gently.

Warmth zinged across each nerve fiber in my body, putting every single biological system on high alert. As if I hadn't already processed the fact that he was far too attractive for my peace of mind.

His eyes widened, and he glanced at our clasped hands.

I took marginal comfort in knowing I wasn't the only one affected.

"Unexpected," he murmured.

"No kidding," I said.

His gaze flicked to my face and he frowned. "Explain."

I awarded him the same bland look I turned on my high-school students when they gave me the "what assignment?" line. "I teach physics. Not chemistry."

The corners of his eyes crinkled in amusement before he wiped all expression from his face.

"Ms Selkirk," he said in a smooth, rich voice with just a hint of dialect.

The sound shot another burst of "Hey, stupid, he's sexy" hormones into my already overly-aware body.

"Won't you have a seat?" He nodded at the sofa. "May I offer you something to drink?"

Needing both the distraction and the fortification, I asked, "Is there real cream to go with that coffee?"

He stepped in beside me, and tucked my hand – the one he'd never released – into the crook of his elbow to escort me across the room. "I believe so," he said with the air of someone who knew precisely that no one would dare bring coffee into his office without real cream in the frosty creamer.

He released me.

Mr Carrollus sat in the armchair and poured coffee for both of us.

I sank to the edge of the sofa, and settled my briefcase against the coffee table. A surreptitious glance around the room assured me that the receptionist had vanished. I was alone in a room with a man who made me feel small and dainty as he filled my china cup with steaming coffee.

"Thank you for taking the time to meet, Ms Selkirk," he said. "The holiday season is meant to be shared with family."

I met his eye, my chest tightening, and my hand frozen near the creamer.

"Ms Selkirk?"

Damn it. I pulled in a breath, but couldn't force my hand to move. At least I couldn't feel it shaking.

"No family," I managed to say in an even tone. "Just me."

He studied me with a gaze that felt as if it might be burning through my skull to get a look inside.

I couldn't break free.

"Yes," he murmured. "My HR department is thorough. I believe I saw mention of an accident."

I found myself nodding. Since my folks had died in a car crash two years ago, I'd felt as if most of me had shriveled and died, too. Holidays were a sharp reminder of the fact that I'd buried my heart with my family's remains.

"I'm sorry," he said. The flicker of pain in his eyes told me he meant it.

I blinked. My eyes stung. It was beyond time to change the subject.

"Mr Carrollus—" I said as I poured the cream.

"Trygg," he countered.

I paused, mid-stir, to glance at him.

"If you don't mind, I prefer a more informal approach to interviews," he said. "Your résumé is intriguing, but it doesn't tell me who you are. I'd like you to call me Trygg."

So that was it. Put the interviewee at ease and find out whether or not she could play well with others. Psychological battery. *Been there, done that*. I should have recognized the set-up.

I nodded, but couldn't talk myself into standing down the alarms still jangling my nerves. "Trygg," I repeated, straightening my cup and saucer. I studied him a moment.

He held still, his expression bland as if he were allowing me to look my fill.

"Scandinavian," I said. "Isn't it?"

"It means 'true'," he said, nodding. "My mother's choice,

though I never understood why. The family isn't Scandinavian. Your name. Finlay. Celtic?"

"Yes." I took a sip of coffee. My toes curled in delight. "Oh, that's excellent. Bonus points on the coffee."

He lifted one jet eyebrow. "Do I need bonus points?"

"Depends on the answer to my original question."

"What question is that?"

"The one I didn't get to ask because we got sidetracked by names," I replied.

His gaze followed my every move as if he were a cat and I the mouse he was thinking of pouncing upon.

The thought curdled the cream in my mouth. I swallowed hard and set the cup and saucer down with a clatter. So much for my poker face.

"Why did your assistant trip over himself to not call you Commander Carrollus?"

"I am active reserve," he admitted. "This is a separate venture, however, reporting to no one but me. I will not have this venture flown into the ground by political wrangling and financial mismanagement. It's too vital to me and to my . . . to the people with a stake in this endeavor."

I found myself nodding. That felt true. It was the first unvarnished statement I'd gotten from him, even if he had stumbled over not saying "my investors".

"Okay," I said. "Where does that leave us? If I had to guess, I'd say you had this office staged today."

Interest gleamed in his gaze again, and he leaned closer. "What makes you say that?"

The question felt like a caress. I jumped and had to fumble for my train of thought. "It's too clean. There's not a speck of dust on anything. It doesn't smell right. Without looking, what's on the shelf just over my head?"

He grinned. The corners of his eyes crinkled.

My heart skipped a beat.

"You do think on your feet, don't you?" he murmured, smile dying as he took my hand again. He lifted it and pressed his lips against my fingers. "Well done. I have no idea what's on any of these shelves."

Heat rushed into my face. "Trygg." It came out a croak. I cleared my throat and tried again. "My hand, Trygg. I need that."

"Do I frighten you, Finlay?"

Of course he did, but I'd eat that dusty, dry science brief I'd been reading in his fake reception area before I'd admit it.

A wave of dizziness slammed me. I held my breath and frowned, willing it to pass. A buzz filled my ears and I noticed two things at once.

One, Carrollus watched me far too intently, an odd, avid gleam in his eyes. Two, he hadn't touched a drop of his coffee.

Fear burned a path straight down my throat to my stomach. I tried to jump to my feet and ended up wavering to them instead.

"You unbelievable bastard," I gasped. I grabbed the spoon. I'd had two sips. Maybe I could stick the handle of the spoon far enough down my throat to trigger a gag reflex. My numb fingers refused to cooperate.

The spoon hit the carpet with a *thunk*.

I bolted for the door, except, of course, I moved as if I waded through hip-high mud.

Carrollus snaked an arm around my waist.

"Oh, no," he murmured at my ear.

He swept me into his arms as if I weighed nothing at all.

I couldn't protest.

Heat joined the dizziness. I felt the fine sheen of sweat on my face. My breath wheezed when I drew it.

"Lieutenant!" he snapped at the receptionist.

"Sir?"

"Alert the medical team," Carrollus ordered. "She's having an adverse reaction."

He'd poisoned me, yet he had the gall to sound concerned.

"Aye, sir."

"Hang on," he muttered to me. "I'm not willing to lose you, Finlay Selkirk."

Something dinged. Doors opened. He stepped in.

I groaned. "God, not an elevator." An insipid muzak version of "Jingle Bells" on sax.

"Close your eyes," he urged. "It'll help."

It sounded like a good idea.

He pressed cool lips to my brow.

Surprise and a tendril of pleasure pushed back the dizziness for a split second.

"My everlasting regret is that I can't have you myself," he said in a voice that led me to believe I wasn't supposed to hear him.

Then the buzzing in my ears rose to a deafening shriek and it occurred to me it sounded curiously like my own voice.

I woke in a bed not my own. I couldn't call it too soft because it was exquisitely comfortable, but it cradled my body in a way my bed never had. It was nice. If only because I felt like an entire tank squadron had driven through my head. From the rumble in my brain, I gathered they might be circling for another pass.

I hadn't had a hangover since the single ill-fated experiment with alcohol I'd undertaken at my first and last party at nineteen. What on earth had possessed me this time?

Ah. That's right. Poisoned coffee and Commander Carrollus had. Not literally. At least, I didn't think so.

Just as well. If there were going to be bad things done with those lips of his, I wanted to be awake for it. Could I ask for something like that for Christmas?

Unfortunate that those lips were attached to someone I fully intended to prosecute. Commander Carrollus in prison for slipping me a mickey. The thought shouldn't have made me smile, but it did.

Someone shifted.

"Finlay?"

Carrollus.

My eyes snapped open and I gasped at the searing array of fabrics and colors surrounding me. "Dear God. You drug me, kidnap me, and bring me to hell?"

I was tucked into an enormous Gothic horror of a canopy bed hung with sheer, gauzy fabrics that vibrated with combinations of saffron, teal, crimson and violet. The nightmare curtains had been drawn back on one side to show me the rest of the room, decorated with the same Marquis de Sade flair. Padded leather handcuffs dangled from a chain attached to the ceiling. A bitter tendril of fear slithered into my chest.

I had no idea where I was or how long I'd been out. *Why* kept rolling around the inside of my skull, accompanied by an unsettling feeling of helplessness. *Stop it, Finlay*. First rule of running a psychological battery: put the subject off guard by any means possible.

Commander Carrollus had succeeded.

I suppressed a shudder.

He appeared to be sitting vigil at my bedside. Sweet, in that "the jerk who poisoned me gives a shit whether I live or die" kind of way. He'd deserted Armani's army. Even though I didn't recognize the black uniform he wore, that's exactly what it was, and it fit far too well for my comfort.

"Finlay?" Carrollus, again. "Are you all right?"

"No, I am not all right. Could you turn down the melodrama in the room? My eyes are about to bleed."

His lips twitched like someone who wanted to smile, but knew he wasn't supposed to. "You're feeling better."

He'd won this round. I'd be damned if I'd let him win another.

"I'm better enough that you can start explaining," I grumbled as I struggled to free myself from the bed.

"There are explanations to be had. It is not my place to give them to you. If you're able to dress, I'll escort you to my CO."

I knew it. Goddamned military op. I was pretty clear that my government wouldn't have spent the cash on a military op that dealt in negligees like the one I discovered I was wearing when I rolled out of the bed and stood. My hair swung down my back, free of the French twist I'd so carefully put it into.

A low, inarticulate sound came from Carrollus. "Finlay, you are beautiful." He sounded grudging, as if he thought he ought to explain his growl of appreciation, but didn't like the fact that he'd reacted at all.

Heat suffused my skin. I glanced down at the lace and pink silk barely covering me, then met his gaze. Irritation put lines in his forehead. What annoyed him? The fact that I was still standing there half-naked? Or was it the desire clouding his blue eyes that troubled him? For that matter, shouldn't it bother me rather than make me tingly all over?

I lifted an eyebrow.

He had the grace to flush. His gaze slid away. "Mary insisted you'd be more comfortable like that. You'd better dress."

"Fine," I said. "Where are my clothes?"

"You'll find clothing . . ."

"*My* clothes," I growled. I sounded like I meant business. I wished all over again I'd worn slacks, but the stupid skirt, blouse and jacket were the closest thing to a power suit I had at the moment. And something told me I'd need a bit of power to get out of . . . whatever it was I'd gotten myself into. Trying to face a military kidnapping while dressed in a pink nightie didn't bear thinking about.

"Your clothes are around the corner," he said.

I marched past him and into the alcove he'd indicated. A curtain of the same colorful fabric covered the wall in front of me. I spotted my clothes neatly folded on a vanity, my shoes on the floor as if waiting for me to step into them.

I felt his gaze follow my every move, the weight of his regard like a caress against my bare limbs. My body heated and I gritted my teeth against the sensation. Biology apparently didn't care that I was heartless and cold. *The fact remained,* I reminded myself, *that no matter how solicitous and gorgeous my captor, I was a prisoner.*

Where did that leave me? To my horror, hot prickles ran up the backs of my eyes.

That pissed me off.

Hoping for a clue as to my location, I glanced surreptitiously at my surroundings. To my right, an arched doorway opened onto a bathroom tiled in deep blue and green and gold. It reminded me of a stained-glass window I'd once seen in one of Europe's oldest cathedrals. To my left, another archway led into a closet.

I could be anywhere. I slid my skirt on over the insubstantial silk negligee. No help for it. I'd have to strip before I could put on my bra, shirt and jacket. At least I had my back to Carrollus.

I yanked the nightie off over my head and hurriedly fastened on my bra, then put on and buttoned my white silk blouse.

"You're taking your situation very well, Finlay," Carrollus commented.

Meaning what? That he'd expected me to weep and gnash my teeth? The thought made me shudder. I should have found something heavy and knocked him flat.

"If by 'my situation'," I sneered, tugging on my jacket, "you mean 'being kidnapped', I assure you I am not taking it well at all."

He risked a glance at me.

"You are bigger than I am and I don't have a gun," I clarified.

Amusement sparked in his eyes a moment. "You need a gun to take me out?"

My smile in response felt tight. "No, Commander, but a gun would make a satisfying mess, and I'd get to hear you scream when I shot you in the kneecaps."

He grinned.

My breath caught.

What was he playing at? Weren't kidnappers supposed to be mean, vicious thugs with missing teeth and psychopathic tendencies? How was I supposed to respond to a sexy commander exuding power and authority? Especially when he smiled at me as if I'd surprised him into enjoying himself?

"You're a disciplined woman, aren't you?" he said.

I blinked. "Disciplined? No. I am not."

"You have so many questions," he observed, closing the distance to stand directly in front of me. His frame blocked out the rest of the room and I had to look up to meet his eye. "I see them running circles in your eyes. Yet you don't ask."

"You said the explanations weren't yours to give," I breathed. "But if the whole kidnapping thing isn't enough of a power trip without me begging for information, then I can oblige. Where am I? Why me? Because I have no family? Is that it? You imagine I don't have a life?"

My voice wavered.

He scowled.

I should have listened to the instinct whispering at me to keep my yap shut and my eyes and ears open. The fact that I hadn't been hurt didn't mean I couldn't – or wouldn't – be.

And it certainly appeared that I'd ceased to amuse him.

"Our world was at war with the Orseggans," he said. "We were hit by a biological weapon. The bio-agent enhances sex drive."

I frowned. *Weaponized Viagra? Why not take advantage of that with one another? Why kidnap me?* The blood rushed from my head and I stumbled into the curtained wall. Rage drowned out rational thought. Shoving off the surface at my back, hand clenched, I punched Carrollus in the stomach.

His breath went out in an audible rush. He didn't quite

double over, but I wasn't looking up into his face anymore and that felt *good*.

Temper stoked, I cocked back for another blow.

Gasping for air, Carrollus rushed me. His shoulder took me in the ribs, driving me back.

I hit the curtain-shrouded wall. One foot twisted beneath me. Fabric tore and I slid to the floor.

Carrollus followed me down.

When my butt hit the floor, I found I had enough leverage to shove him off of me. It felt like trying to shove a freight train.

"You son of a bitch," I wheezed. "You're infected with a sexually transmitted disease and you kidnap people from Earth to assuage the symptoms?"

He crouched in front of me, posture wary, guarded; but curiously, I saw no anger in his face or body.

"Your species cannot be infected," he said. "Our medical staff made very certain before we began recruiting from your world. We could not ethically sacrifice another species to save our own."

"Medically necessary sex?" I sneered. The burn behind my eyes spilled over. "That has to be the cheesiest line I've ever heard."

"Finlay." As if he couldn't help himself, Carrollus rose to his knees and reached for me. One warm hand on my hip set my nerves alight, the other cupped my damp cheek. "When both sexual partners are infected with the bio-agent, it activates, killing both partners. If an infected person doesn't have sex often enough, the agent activates."

I sucked in a horrified breath. "But . . . condoms?"

He shook his head. "Whenever two infected people are intimate, regardless of barriers to sexual fluids, the bio-agent activates. It's as if their immune systems cancel one another out. It was a genocide weapon. One that worked. Our population was devastated until we worked out the disease mechanism."

The waterworks evaporated. I believed him. Awareness of him rippled through me, tempting me to melt into the feel of his skin on mine.

"When you worked out how the disease spread, it ripped families and loved ones apart?" Visions of lovers torn from one another ran through my head. Mothers wouldn't have been able to nurture their own children. Sympathy made my breath catch.

He blinked at me.

I thought I detected the first inkling of respect in the softening of the lines around his mouth.

"Yes."

"You don't look sick."

He shook his head. "We're not. Sex with uninfected partners keeps the bio-agent in remission. Our medical people believe there's something in the human immune system that bolsters ours."

"So what does that mean? If you don't have sex what? Every week? Every day? You'll die?"

"Each of us has to work out our interval," he replied. "Most find that two or three times a week is sufficient."

I bit my tongue to keep from asking him his.

"Does this mean that because of the bio-agent, your people can't reproduce?"

He nodded. "Hybridization is our only option."

My mind reeled trying to work out how many alien babies might already be walking around on Earth.

"You don't hit like a girl," he noted.

"Sorry." I sounded sullen.

"I earned it," he said, smoothing tear tracks from my skin. "If it's any comfort, Finlay, we mean you no harm."

I twisted out of his too-soothing grasp and barked a laugh. It sounded vaguely unhinged.

Scrubbing tears from my face, I climbed to my feet.

"You mean me no harm?" I parroted. At least my voice sounded even again. Mostly. "Too damned late for that, isn't it?"

"Finlay."

The weight of that single word turned me back to face him.

I noticed the porthole in the wall. It had been revealed when we'd ripped the curtain while we fought.

I don't remember how I got there, but suddenly, I found my fingers gripping the chilly frame of the porthole hard enough that my knuckles went white.

I stared out into the starry expanse of dark night sky, empty, except for the big, blue, gleaming jewel of a planet hanging in the lower third of the porthole arc.

My breath froze in my chest.

Earth.

I was looking at my planet from such a distance that I could barely make out any of the land mass beneath the cloud cover.

Dizziness swept me. Carrollus gritted out something that sounded like a curse. It wasn't one I knew. Or in any language I recognized.

He surged upright, took hold of my upper arms, and turned me gently away from the view.

It didn't matter. The vista had been seared into my memory. I'd heard astronauts say that happened. That in the instant you look down from space on the world that gave you life, you *changed*. You were marked in a way that meant you'd never be the same. The only way you'd forget what you'd seen, what you'd experienced, would be to close your eyes in death.

I finally managed to order my eyes shut, but still saw my home hanging miles and miles below my feet. Disorientation rushed from my feet to my head. Or maybe it had gone the other way, but suddenly, my feet *knew* they no longer had ground beneath them.

Only the warmth of Carrollus's body heat merging with my own kept me anchored.

I'd started the day interviewing for a space program and ended it on an actual spaceship. Kidnapped by aliens disguised as humans?

I cracked one eye open. My head and my feet seemed to have agreed that the floor made a fine substitute for ground. Dizziness faded and I risked opening the other eye, too.

I turned back for another look.

"No," he said, preventing me.

"Let go," I turned away from him. "Every kid dreams of seeing Earth from space. Now that the shock has worn off, I want a better look. You must get a terrific view of the Northern Lights."

He chuckled and escorted me to the porthole as if I might still fall over. "One of the many charms of your little blue world. When we first arrived, we thought your civilization was more advanced than it was because of the electrical interference at the poles during a solar event."

I felt as if the floor had lurched out from under me. I stared at him. *When we first arrived?* Blowing out a steadying breath, I forced myself to focus on his statement about electrical interference at the poles. *That* I could wrap my mind around. "Ship's sensors can't punch through the aurora?"

He met my gaze, his own searching. "You've seen too many *Star Trek* episodes."

"Undoubtedly," I replied.

The smolder of desire in Carrollus's hooded gaze rushed heat through my body.

A self-satisfied smile touched his gorgeous lips. He traced his right hand down my arm to claim my hand in his. Bringing it to his lips, he pressed a heated kiss to my palm.

Pleasure zinged through my blood, settling between my legs. I stifled a gasp. Palm unsettlingly connected to genitalia. Who knew?

"You are remarkably resilient. The questions are back in your eyes," he noted.

Unable to trust my voice, I nodded. *Questions in my eyes and a promise of some kind in his. Did I imagine that? Did I dare hope that I could convince him to return me to my home?*

"Come with me," he said, releasing me. "You'll be able to ask your questions of my commanding officer."

His commanding officer. Interesting distinction. One of the only things I felt I could process in this morass of quicksand – or airless vacuum – beneath my feet.

I eased out of his grasp and turned back for my shoes. Mary had been so careful when she'd undressed me that I could account for every single hairpin I'd used earlier in the day. She'd even left a comb, which I applied to my tangled hair.

"Which military?" I asked, stepping into my sensible brown pumps. My attempt at a casual tone didn't even fool me.

"One you won't be familiar with," he replied.

A military I wouldn't know, and that hint of dialect flavoring his words – clues that ought to add up to something useful. Who had the kind of technology that could put me on a spaceship hundreds of miles above the planet without a spacesuit? For that matter, why weren't we floating in zero-g? Since we *weren't* floating, did I know for a fact that no one on Earth had the special effects budget to mock up something like this?

I didn't. But I couldn't imagine anyone going to the effort and expense. It wouldn't make sense. Again, my thoughts circled back to *why*.

Impatient with the disorderly whirl of conjecture in my brain, I slapped down the comb and coiled my hair into another French twist.

Light and heat thrummed through my blood. Carrollus tangled his fingers with mine before I could reach for the pins to secure the coil.

"Leave it," he commanded, pulling my hands away as if I wasn't resisting.

Hair spilled down my back.

He had strength in spades, and he had me trapped between him and the dressing table.

A split second of fright trailed ice down my spine.

"Your hair is beautiful," he said, folding my arms around my middle so that I stood, confined within his embrace.

Every piece of my biology arced to life at his contact. The reaction shook me. I'd never known that I could feel so much, so strongly.

"Mousy," I corrected. My voice sounded small. Scared.

"I've yet to see a mouse with strawberry-blonde hair," he countered, humor deepening his accent. "It's beautiful and unruly. Like you."

I shook my head.

"Leave it down," he urged.

I shivered at the caress of his warm breath against my ear. While I had little inclination to indulge his whim, I couldn't control my body's runaway response to his persuasion. Goosebumps erupted over my skin.

"Fine. Yes," I choked. Anything to get my body back under my control.

He chuckled, released me, and walked away.

The note of triumph in his laugh made me clench my teeth. Stiffening my spine, I tugged my jacket straight, turned on my heel, and marched to the door.

Assuming I wasn't locked in, I'd walk out the door, and wander around until I found someone else and demand to be taken to their leader.

I left the bedroom and walked into a tiny, Spartan compartment, little more than a glorified closet, really. It had a kitchenette on one side and a scarred desk on the other. Odd. So much space devoted to a bedroom and so little to the rest of off-duty life.

The door opened at my approach. I had expected a *whoosh* sound effect, but it opened and closed silently.

I wasn't locked in. Fine. It didn't change the fact that until I learned interplanetary flight and navigation, I was more effectively a prisoner than any Earthly lockup could have made me.

"This way," Carrollus said from behind me.

He led me through a maze of corridors, any of which could have been found inside military facilities the world over. Except that this one was *over* the world. By miles.

I was on a spaceship! Or was I? Could I be on a base? Or a station? Did it matter? I'd left my planet, something I'd never dreamed would be possible, much less likely. I had to fight to keep a giddy grin from my face.

We paused at a junction where several corridors met at what looked like a central elevator shaft. I felt his gaze on me.

"If I were going to hide a spaceship, which I assume you're doing, since I haven't heard about UFOs outside of the regular conspiracy theory circles, I'd put myself in orbit inside the asteroid belt. Just another space rock," I noted, slanting him what I hoped was an innocent look.

A shadow passed over his perfect face. It looked like uneasiness.

Score one for me. If his expression was any indicator, I'd nailed that.

"To stay hidden, you'd have to dodge the craft that get lobbed out past lunar orbit," I went on.

The uneasiness drained out of him. He waved a hand. The elevator door opened and Carrollus gestured me inside.

Either he'd gained control of his poker face or I'd gotten that last bit wrong. I entered the compartment and propped one hip against the wall.

He said something. It wasn't English. Again. *Native language? A non-Earth language?*

The elevator started up.

If they weren't avoiding spacecraft, they'd have to find another way to conceal their presence, which suggested tampering with the signals in some way.

"You're tapping the data streams of everything that could see you, and scrubbing your ship's image?" I marveled, forming the hypothesis as I spoke it. *Of course. It made sense. With the*

technology I'd seen so far – like the fact that I wasn't floating through
the corridors – it might be a trivial matter to splice in . . .

Carrollus crossed the tiny space in a single stride, slapped his
hands against the wall on either side of my head. An odd combination of anger and regret sparked in his eyes. "Stop. No more
synthesizing observations. Your hope of returning home dimin-
ishes the more that you know."

My fleeting sense of satisfaction at having hit so close to home
evaporated. I clenched my fists. "I'm a scientist. I can't stop."

He spun away from me.

The rigid set of his shoulders warned me to watch my mouth.
I took the caution to heart. Studying him, it hit me.

He looked human. I'd naturally assumed he was human.
At first. *How far had they come? From which star system? Why?*
Was it a quirk of genetics that allowed them to pass as human?
Or had they modified . . . The elevator stopped and the door
opened.

He led me through another short maze of corridors to a set of
double doors. He muttered another incomprehensible command.

The doors opened. Bright lights blinded me. I squinted
against the glare.

Either the place was huge, or it had been soundproofed. Our
footfalls disappeared into the quiet. I smelled . . . *Did expectation*
have a scent? I drew in a breath and knew that other people filled
the room.

As my eyes adjusted, I caught several things at once.
Uniformed, young men stood at attention in front of instrument
panels. The oval room was terraced, personnel and equipment
arranged in descending concentric horseshoes down to a central
floor. An enormous table of what looked like black glass domi-
nated the lowest point.

Definitely not an office. A command center? Or a coliseum?

Carrollus and I paused on the top tier where the horseshoes
opened into a broad aisle up the steps.

A thin, brittle-looking man with white hair, a hawk nose and
rheumy, pale-blue eyes watched us. A blue uniform hung on his
frame. No visible rank insignia. On any of them. Including
Commander Trygg Carrollus.

"Ms Finlay Selkirk," Carrollus said, "may I present Orlan
Grisham? Sir, Ms Selkirk."

"Captain," he didn't say. But it was obvious.

We sized one another up.

In the deep frown lines around his mouth and eyes, I believed I saw a despot.

"Ms Selkirk." His tone dripped with misgiving.

"Captain Grisham."

Frozen silence.

Crap. First words out of my mouth, I'd messed up. As if Carrollus hadn't warned me to guard my tongue. I attempted an innocent smile. I don't think any of us bought it.

"Did I guess the rank system incorrectly?" I inquired. "Commodore? Admiral? Or is it that I pegged the military thing?"

"Finlay . . ." Carrollus growled.

I quelled and slid my gaze away from the older man.

"Perhaps we should refrain from interviewing academics," the old man said to Carrollus, his tone flat.

"You'll want to broaden that to anyone with an IQ over fifty," I muttered. *How should a captive address her kidnappers? Bravado? Caution? Diffidence? Did I know how to pretend that last one?*

"My apologies if I've offended protocol in some fashion," I offered. "Am I to understand that I might be permitted to ask a few questions of you pursuant to my presence here?"

He narrowed his eyes at me, then glared over my shoulder at Carrollus. "Definitely no more academics."

The asperity in his voice made me bite back a grin.

"We require your assistance, Ms Selkirk." Grisham said. He'd thrown his shoulders back and straightened as if trying to assume a more commanding presence.

He had the act down pat. I pasted a neutral expression on my face and nodded.

"We have need of men and women with good hearts and quick minds," he said.

Irritation flashed through me. *Quick minds, my foot.* "You're capable of interstellar travel. Yet you've come to a world that hasn't managed to land manned craft on its nearest planetary neighbor, and you've shanghaied a high-school physics teacher. You're blowing sunshine up my ass, not telling me the truth."

The at-attention onlookers gasped.

I swallowed a curse. *Mistake number two, Finlay.*

The old man blinked. His upraised palms fell.

"Interstellar?" he repeated.

I shrugged. "It's plain you aren't from around here."

Grisham tipped his head and eyed me as if sizing me up for a vivisection table. "What makes you say that?"

Throwing my arms wide, I snapped, "The fact that I'm standing a couple thousand miles above the surface of my planet was a real tip-off."

The old man spun on Carrollus and jabbed a finger at him. "You let her—"

"There was no 'let' to it!" I yelled.

"Ms Selkirk discovered our orbital position on her own," Carrollus said. He looked troubled when I tossed him a glance. "Sir, I think we'd be best served—"

"I know what you think," the captain snapped. "You've been overruled. As you were, Commander."

Fury leaked past Carrollus's glacial mask. It made my blood run cold.

Grisham turned his rheumy gaze upon me and attempted a paternal smile. "May we first beg a single boon of you?"

Alarms rang in my head at the captain's antiquated phrasing, painfully polite though it was.

Wary, I said, "You want to trade for information? What coin?"

"No coin, Ms Selkirk. We aren't mercenaries. Choose a man," he directed, waving a hand in a wide sweep to indicate the soldiers lining the tiers, "or as many as you want to sample, from amongst those assembled."

"Not mercenaries"? "Sample"? My mind twisted in on itself. I winced. "You did *not* just tell me you kidnapped me for sex."

"That is precisely what we did."

"Wow. We are all going to be so disappointed."

The old man blinked. "Excuse me?"

"Put me back," I said.

"You're inhibited?"

"What? No! Yes! Who the hell cares?" I squawked.

"We care. Let these men help you," Grisham said, his entire demeanor overtaken by sudden concern and compassion. *The old faker.*

"Why?"

"I beg your pardon?"

"Why?" I repeated. "What do you stand to gain from this?"

"What makes you think we harbor ulterior—"

"Kidnapping stirs up an awful lot of trouble," I noted.

Grisham frowned at me. From the corner of my eye, I caught Carrollus studying me.

"It's no trouble," Grisham countered, shaking his head.

"So you burned down my apartment?" I prompted.

"Of course not."

"Destroyed my computer files and my backups?"

"We've done nothing of the kind," Grisham said.

Carrollus shifted, drawing my gaze to his. He scowled.

"Do you believe the police will secure a search warrant for your home", he said, "where they will find your computer with your résumé files and the address of the building where we met?"

I held his gaze for several moments. "They'll find my briefcase with my belongings still where I set it against the coffee table, yes."

"Release your cares," Grisham urged. "Cast aside your culture's notions of morality. We value physical pleasure. These men want to fulfill your every desire."

My every desire? Did I have any? Other than going home and maybe kicking Jill repeatedly in the ribs? I shook away the vision.

"Are there no women in your crew? Is that why you're kidnapping sex slaves?" I asked.

The captain jerked upright, glaring. "That, madam, is a grave insult. We have never and will never force anyone—"

I frowned. "You put back the people who refuse?"

"No one has ever refused."

"No one—" I echoed before clamping my mouth shut.

"Pick a man," he coaxed. "Give us thirty days, then we'll talk again."

I stifled the urge to put my spike heel through his foot. Even *I* knew that would negatively impact on my captivity.

"'We'll talk'? Oh, no. You want me to play this game? Give me something to fight for. Swear you'll put me back when the time is up, and then I'll pick someone. Otherwise, we're at an impasse. You've been kind enough to say no one will force me. I'd like to return the courtesy. I do not want to have to force your hand."

Every man in the room stared at me. *That's right, boys. Long legs, short skirt, cute pumps. Harmless.*

"You have no means to carry out that threat," the captain scoffed.

"Look up Gandhi," I said, pressing my voice flat. "Then look up 'hunger strike'."

"You would destroy yourself?"

"You've destroyed my freedom," I said, "my career, and now you're threatening to destroy my life. I'm clear that getting your soldiers laid is vital to you. It's also clear that you won't tell me why. I may have little interest in dying, but I'm less interested in being kept as a sex slave. So many willing, young, fertile women in the world. Why me?"

His breath hissed in between his clenched teeth.

"This isn't slavery," he snapped. "Thirty days. If at the end of that time you still wish to return, I swear we'll find a way."

"Deal." I noticed that he hadn't answered my question, but I had a possible road home. If the old man could be trusted to keep his word. "Tell me the rules."

"Choose one or as many men as you please from those assembled within the limits of the oval, then enjoy yourself."

Enjoy? Could I?

"*My everlasting regret is that I can't have you myself.*" Carrollus had said that when he'd thought I couldn't hear.

He'd kidnapped me.

If I had anyone to blame for this mess, it was he. I could use him. I straightened and smiled.

"You've chosen?"

"Sure," I said. I spun and jabbed a finger at Trygg. "Him."

The room held its collective breath while Carrollus rocked back on his heels, shock in the widening of his midnight-blue eyes.

I grinned, a careless, I-dare-you – and maybe slightly vengeful – grin at him.

Protest erupted from the testosterone line-up. Carrollus thundered for quiet, got it, then turned a baleful glare upon me.

"I am disqualified. You may not select me."

"I just did."

He shook his head. "No—"

"Let me get this straight," I said. "Your captain laid out the rules. I followed them, and now you refuse to abide by them? You're already taken, is that it?"

"Yes."

The way he pounced on the out I'd offered him made it obvious. He was lying.

I nodded. "I believe this invalidates our thirty-day agreement. I'm ready to go home, now."

His expression shifted and my heart skidded into uneasy thudding.

He looked intrigued.

"He was not a part—" Grisham growled.

"'Choose one or as many men as I please from those assembled within the limits of the oval'," I quoted back to him. "Your rules. He's in the oval."

The old man scowled. "Then keep him. The agreement stands, with the caveat that you leave me no choice but—"

The lights dimmed.

Carrollus swore in his language. I thought I heard an audible alarm somewhere in the distance.

Men scrambled for stations. Several young women, also in uniform, burst through the door and raced for empty chairs.

The alarm died.

"Sir!" one of the women called. "Enemy ships entering the solar system!"

"Enemy ships?" I echoed. "I thought you were hiding from Earth."

"We are," Carrollus said, cold rage coloring his voice. "We *were*. Until now."

I froze, awful awareness tripping my pulse into high gear. "You're refugees, aren't you? You thought you'd escaped. But you drew your enemy after you."

Carrollus gripped my arms and pulled me around to face him. I shivered at the chemistry that bubbled through my system at the contact. "They want us," he said. "Your world is in no danger."

But *I* was, by simple virtue of being on board their ship. "How did I get here? A shuttle? Teleportation of some kind?"

Carrollus nodded at the last one.

"Is it working?"

"No time," Grisham barked. "There are too many of you. Commander!"

Carrollus accessed a panel, studying the data that answered his summons.

Too many of us? What did Grisham mean? Too many people to evacuate to the safety of Earth, presumably.

"The sensor embedded in the New Horizons probe indicates a pair of Orseggan scouts inbound to our position. Weapon status?" Grisham thundered.

"Offline, sir," a young officer replied.

My heart bumped against my ribs.

"Shields?"

"Offline, sir," yet another officer answered.

"Interstellar drive?"

"Offline!"

I pressed shaking fingers against my temples.

The ship was defenseless.

"This is the second time today you've tried to get me killed," I snapped at Carrollus.

"This was unanticipated!" Grisham protested.

My humorless smile felt icy. "Like an adverse reaction to a drug?"

Carrollus glanced up from his panel to pin me with a grim stare. "You have a right to be angry. I can't change what's happened. But we have time. They do not yet know we're here."

I frowned. "You have the time to bring weapons and shields online?"

"No. We were badly damaged at the end of the war. The Orseggans saw this ship escape," he said, "but they clearly didn't know where we'd gone."

"They've been hunting for you since," I finished for him. Any question of who was the good guy and who was the bad guy vanished from my head. My allegiance was dictated by the fact that I stood on the defenseless ship.

"Yes," he said, looking back at the illegible data. "Now we need options, not distractions."

Anger and shame burned me, but he was right. What did a high-school physics teacher have to offer aliens who'd mastered physics to the point that their space travel broke all the rules as I knew them?

Unless.

Data I'd picked up from the morning's internet space-weather blog to present to my students flashed into my head. They would know this stuff already, right? Or was it too much to hope that space aliens would keep up on internet blogs?

"Do your enemy's sensors work the way yours do?" I demanded, meeting Carrollus's hard look. "You told me you thought Earth was more technologically advanced than it is because of the electrical interference at the poles."

"Yes," he said.

"Would the energized thermosphere obscure your enemy's sensors, too?"

A light went on in his face. "The Orseggans? Yes."

Grisham was already shaking his head. "It does us no good—"

"Solar-flare activity spiked a day and a half ago," I said, as if the old man hadn't spoken. "The aurora should be lighting up the northern half of the planet as we speak. Take the ship down under the Northern Lights. Blind the Orseggans with neon."

"Do you think we haven't already considered and discarded the option as unworkable? Exposing us to the people of your planet will *not* get you sent home," Grisham snarled at me.

"You're smarter than I am. You have interstellar space travel. But this isn't about any one earthly phenomenon protecting your ship. This is my planet. Maybe you've studied it, but it's clear you don't understand it or the people who live on it," I retorted.

I turned to Carrollus. "Can you land this thing?"

"We can," he rumbled, striding down the stairs to the center of the oval. He gestured at me to join him and brought up a three-dimensional hologram of Earth. "It isn't a trivial task, and if I read you right, you mean to complicate it further. Give me details."

As I descended to the pit floor, nerves fluttered in my stomach. I wobbled down the steps in my heels. "You'll be seen. The US military doesn't like being blindsided. The phased array systems are going to spot us. I know of a few in Alaska, but if this solar storm packs the punch the data suggests it does, their communications systems will be useless. The danger will come from spotting stations south of the storm."

"Beale?" Carrollus guessed, naming an Air Force base in California. "They'll scramble fighters."

"F-15s out of Elmendorf if they can get a call through," I agreed. "If they can't, they'll move south until someone hears them. The fighters will get coordinates for first point of contact and a vector for our trajectory. Then they'll fly into the Alaskan wilderness in the dead of night, in the middle of one of the hottest solar storms to hit in two decades."

Carrollus flashed a grin at me that nearly stopped my heart.

"Meaning they'll be deaf and blind."

"Their navigation systems will go Tango Uniform," I agreed.

Amusement and anticipation lit Trygg's blue eyes. Okay. So he not only knew the names and locations of military bases, he understood my reference to TU. Clearly, he'd spent time inside the US military. What did that mean?

"Their communications will be dead, too," I said. "Without radar or GCI to talk them in, they'll have no hope of vectoring on the ship."

"We'll have to leave the planet surface before the atmospheric disturbance dissipates," he said.

"The minute we're on the ground," I added, "you'll have to power down the ship's systems."

"Are you mad?" Grisham barked, stomping down the stairs. "We'll have no oxygen generators!"

"We have hours of air without them," Carrollus answered before he glanced at me. "You propose we run silent?"

"To hide the ship from ground observation, we have to look like part of the landscape. That means no heat signature and no engine vibration," I said. "Come into atmosphere mimicking a meteor. Leave behind some space rocks for the government types to find after the fact. You'll get written up in a document so classified not even the president will see it. The official news story will say 'meteorite'. To avoid casual observation, we'll look for a wind storm. Preferably, a really strong one. We want blowing snow that will cool and coat the surface of the ship."

"Physical camouflage?" Trygg said, his tone dubious.

"We call it hiding in plain sight."

"It's a recipe for genocide," Grisham huffed.

Carrollus spun on his captain and snapped, "We have no shields, no weapons, and no other, viable ideas, sir. Ms Selkirk is trying to offer us the opportunity to finally stop running."

Is that what I was doing?

"As Ms Selkirk has so charmingly reminded us," Grisham retorted, "we drugged and kidnapped her. What makes you think she's remotely interested in helping us?"

I stared at him. "One: do you really think I blame every man, woman and child on this ship? Two: I can't help but notice that if I sit on my ass doing nothing to help, it gets vaporized, too!"

"Finlay, what else?" Carrollus prompted.

I turned my attention to him. "Do you have a topographical map?"

A lieutenant with spiky brown hair and green eyes manned the table's controls. "Lieutenant Vran, ma'am. And yes. We do."

The map appeared.

"Can you make this section bigger?" I asked.

Carrollus reached past me and expanded the map where I'd indicated.

I hoped no one detected the tremor in my hand as I gestured at the image suspended above the black table. "This is an aerial topography map of the region where I propose you put down."

Captain and commander came closer, peering at the lines and colors hovering in the air before them.

"Alaska," Carrollus said.

Pointing out a broad swathe of the interior of the state, I said, "We'd aim for this region. Low population density, violent winter storms, intractable wilderness. There's one added element in our favor. Lieutenant? Do you have access to magnetic anomaly data? I'll also need current weather conditions for this region."

"Yes, ma'am."

The map lit up with color.

"Alaska aligns low population density with high-intensity magnetic fields at the mountainous regions best able to hide the ship. It makes landing trickier, because the magnetic disturbance will wreak havoc with shipboard instruments."

"Our technology doesn't rely on magnetic fields," Carrollus replied.

"Good," I said. "Earth-based technology *does*. Our navigational instruments are impacted by both magnetic anomalies and by the electrical noise produced by a strong aurora event."

He nodded.

I pointed to a mountain range on the map. "Right here, we have both things going on at once. That'll make life tough for anyone trying to navigate there, except us. Weather reports indicate winds in the region blowing snow and ice in excess of twenty-five miles per hour. That's not as strong as I would like, but given the snow-pack reports, we should find the blowing snow adequate to our needs."

The captain peered over her shoulder at the map.

"If anyone sees us coming in, they'll think we're a meteor coming down in the wilderness. No one will wander into the worst of the magnetic anomalies at night. Most humans won't willingly venture into a strong magnetic vortex at any time. Something about intense magnetic fields induces dizziness, nausea and skewed perception. I may be affected, even aboard this ship. Once the ship is on the ground, chances we'll be seen are low."

"Vortices?" Grisham echoed, disdain in his tone.

"You've seen some of the New-Age claims regarding them, I take it," I said. "Whether magnetic phenomena are at the root of the New-Age vortex mythos, I cannot say, but I can say that magnetic phenomena were of significant interest to the US military at one time."

The captain studied me, calculation in the narrowing of his eyes. "How do you know?"

"My father was a physicist with the Air Force. He specialized in magnetic fields. He used non-classified data to spark my interest in science."

"The military wanted magnetic weapons?"

"Shielding," I countered. "Magnetic fields can make something close look far away, distort an object's true size, thus throwing off targeting. I'm suggesting using naturally occurring magnetic fields to our advantage."

Grisham looked skeptical, but he nodded.

"When you take off all hell will break loose," I went on. "The military will see the ship, and they will scramble jets again. You'll want out of atmosphere as quickly as possible, and you may need to take up position behind something of size to avoid having all of Earth's telescopes pointed at you. Assuming you choose to remain in this solar system."

"If this works," Carrollus said, "this solar system will be the safest place for us."

"Not for much longer," I replied. "With the current speed of scientific advancement on Earth, you won't be able to hide indefinitely. When our measurements become accurate enough to detect your mass influencing the orbit of nearby bodies, you'll have real problems."

"We have to survive the Orseggans, first," Carrollus said.

"Agreed," Grisham weighed in. "Analysis."

"Without shields or weapons," Carrollus said, "our options are run or hide. If we leave the solar system, the Orseggans have a shot at picking up an exhaust trail. We'd abandon hundreds of our people planetside, not to mention destroying years of intelligence work spent infiltrating native governments."

Interesting. They'd put agents on Earth? Surely I could use that as a bargaining chip. Somehow.

"Chances we could bring weapons online before the Orseggans reach sensor range?" Grisham demanded.

Carrollus shook his head. "The real question is whether we can destroy the scouts before they detect us. This crew hasn't faced battle. The lack of experience both with weapon systems and combat tactics gives us very low chances of ambushing and destroying them before the Orseggans fire off a distress call."

Grisham grunted. "Thereby confirming our existence and our location."

"Hiding is our best option."

"What if the Orseggans decide to investigate the aurora, see if they can punch through?" I prompted, wanting all the contingencies on the table.

Lieutenant Vran answered. "If we go dark, as you're suggesting, and if the hull has cooled in the wind and snow, we will look like part of the landscape at best. At worst, we'll resemble one of the military installations dotting the region, assuming the Orseggans would risk detection and destruction by pressing into the atmosphere for a closer look."

"Destruction?" I echoed.

"An F-15's payload would penetrate the scouts' hulls," Carrollus explained. "Scouts are built for speed, not combat."

"If they come poke you with a stick, they'll have the US Air Force swarming them in short order," I mused. Uneasiness gnawed at the inside of my breastbone. Making my species aware of aliens in the solar system could be a disaster. Chaos and panic would result. We'd made and distributed too many science-fiction movies in the past several decades to hope humankind would welcome men and women from Mars with open arms.

"Sir?" Carrollus turned on the captain.

Grisham sighed. "If we fail, it will mean the end of our kind. And the deaths of people we've taken into our protection."

Reaction rippled around the command center. Even I felt it.

I began to understand. They'd already lost. Big time. "Genocide", Grisham had said. Did that mean they were the last surviving members of their kind?

I imagined I could see the cost of everything they'd given up in order to survive defined by the lines of sorrow carved into their faces. Sadness surged within me as if in answer. I'd buried my folks. These people had likely lost wives, husbands and children. If I looked around the room, how many other faces would mirror my wounds?

"Commander," Grisham said as he tore his gaze from mine. "Take us in."

"Yes, sir!"

Carrollus issued orders in the language I didn't recognize. The lieutenant at the table bent over the console, packing and sending all pertinent data to the rest of the command crew.

Grisham mounted the steps to his post, where he sat and keyed in commands on his panel. "Ms Selkirk, join me. We don't have the time to secure you in quarters before we hit atmosphere."

He nodded at a seat beside his. I strode up the steps and sat down.

He pressed a colorless button on the arm of my chair. Webbing that seemed to have a life of its own snaked up over my lap and around my torso. Trepidation shot through me, but when the animate seat belt stopped moving, I wasn't pinned as I'd feared. I could still move and I could still breathe. I noted he wore one just like it. That was vaguely comforting.

From the vibration rattling up my spine, I gathered the engines were already firing, already breaking orbit.

From the center of the floor, Carrollus called, "Permission to institute tactical alert?"

"Granted."

The bright lights illuminating the command center died.

I gasped and dug my fingers into the arms of my chair. The floor had vanished. I was sitting in space. From what I could deduce, the entire command center projected from the main body of the ship. The hull, so opaque in bright light, disappeared entirely in the dark. It looked as if every single station hovered in the vacuum.

My heart thundered in my chest. I'd never imagined a front-row, first-person view of my return to Earth. We'd barely begun moving and I was giddy with anticipation.

I'd been right. The ship edged away from a particularly large asteroid, crossed Mars's orbit, and then swung toward the far side of Earth's moon.

Disappointment stung me. I'd hoped to get a first-hand glimpse of the red planet.

Carrollus paced the central floor, flinging commands and acknowledgments to the staff manning the stations lining the now-invisible tiers. Tension stood out in the rigid set of his shoulders and in the fire I caught burning behind his eyes when his gaze sought mine for a split second.

The ship arced, altering trajectory, turning us toward Earth. Stars blurred and turned to streaks of light. I slid sideways in my seat before the webbing caught and held me.

Carrollus steadied himself with a hand on the table.

The tug to the right eased, but I pressed back into my seat. I assumed that meant engines were hurling us at Earth.

I couldn't see the planet. For several irrational moments, I couldn't ease the panic clenching my gut over having misplaced home. We were aimed right at the sun. The planet had to be there, somewhere.

"We're coming in above the ecliptic plane," Grisham said.

Had my scanning the sky been that obvious?

"And we're coming in fast," he went on. "When we slow for descent, the planet will be below us and to your right."

As if on cue, our trajectory shifted. I lifted out of my seat. The web caught me, and I was glad Grisham had made me strap in.

I slammed into the chair when the ship slowed. Earth appeared right where Grisham had said it would. We were directly above the North Pole. As the planet loomed swiftly larger and grew to dominate the field of view, a flowing, multicolored sea of light danced in the upper atmosphere. In places, the light curled out into space as if beckoning us.

I caught in an enchanted breath and leaned as far as my restraints allowed so I could watch the play of light and color. Sure, I knew the display was the result of photons emitted by ionized nitrogen, or by nitrogen and oxygen atoms in an excited state returning to ground. It didn't change my sense of awe and wonder in the slightest.

Some native people called the aurora the "Dance of the Spirits". I thought I understood why. The light moved like a living, breathing thing. The ship would drop down through the seething sea of color and the aurora would protect us. Watching the light show from space, I could almost believe in magic.

The thought made me smile.

As we plummeted nearer, the ship shuddered. First contact with the exosphere. Or was it entry into the thermosphere?

I glanced at Carrollus to find him watching me. Rippling green, white, blue and red light illuminated the faint smile on his face. My cheeks flushed.

"We haven't seen a show this intense and vivid in a very long time."

"If ever," Grisham agreed with his commander.

The ship bucked.

I glanced back at Trygg, wanting to ask whether or not I'd been set up.

His feet left the floor. Or maybe the floor left his feet. I couldn't be sure which. My stomach turned over. Fear spread a bitter chill through me.

He caught hold of a rail. It saved him from being thrown over the tier one stations.

"Commander!" Grisham thundered. "Station and secure!"

Carrollus, hand going from one rail to the next up the tiers, climbed to our position and took the chair on the other side of me.

Once he'd activated his restraints, his thigh rested against my leg. Little curls of heat reached from his body to mine as if our individual electromagnetic fields exchanged secrets while we sat strapped to our chairs.

Electricity jolted me. My awareness narrowed to Trygg Carrollus, despite the turbulence rattling the ship.

I forced myself to wonder how the ship would handle the heat of re-entry. As far as I knew, spacecraft didn't enter atmosphere at anything approaching the speed of meteors. On purpose.

In the blink of an eye, we were in the midst of the aurora, and even though I knew the supercharged particles couldn't penetrate the hull of the ship, pressure built inside my sternum. Was the red glow cresting in front of us the Northern Lights or the atmosphere heating the hull?

Voices rose as crew members called out information in their own language over the creaking and groaning of the craft. Anxiety and tension edged high in the clipped phrases.

It surprised me to find how much I could deduce of message content from the tone of the speaker's voice. While I didn't actually know what was going on, I had to give Grisham points for affording me a front-row seat for the Northern Lights and the subsequent landing.

Our descent slowed and the pile-up of red in front of us dissipated even as the jolts rocking the ship intensified. *What layer was this? Mesosphere? Stratosphere?* I clutched the arms of my chair tighter, as if my grip alone could hold the ship together as we hurtled through the sky of my home world.

We'd hit weather in the troposphere, the final, thickest layer of Earth's atmosphere. *Did they know? Surely Carrollus did. Could their instruments tell them when wind would present an additional challenge to navigation?*

"Entering stratosphere. Eight miles above the Arctic Ocean!" Vran shouted above the clatter of the ship.

"Watch for commercial aircraft!" I hollered.

"Negative contact on sensors, ma'am!" a young woman replied.

"Leveling off," another young officer yelled, "for glide to designated landing zone!"

"Ground station communications outages confirmed," someone else called. "Comm silence on all channels used by native technology."

My interest piqued. They had communications tech that would cut through the geomagnetic storm? *Good.* It might be the only way to know what the Orseggans were doing.

"Tropopause and the North Slope!"

"Engines to minimum. Stand by braking thrusters," Carrollus called.

I didn't know how he did that, speaking so that everyone heard him, yet without sounding as if he'd bothered to raise his voice.

"Engines at minimum. Braking thrusters, standing by."

To my surprise, the ride smoothed out as we descended. I shot a glance at Carrollus, who concentrated on a holographic panel readout projected in front of his seat.

"Fire braking thrusters," he ordered.

"Firing braking thrusters."

I fell forward into the webbing holding me.

The ship slid sideways in the sky, leaving my stomach far behind. Wind shear. Looked like my twenty-five-mile-an-hour winds had increased over the mountains.

"Get us on the ground!" Grisham bellowed.

"Yes, sir!" several voices answered in unison.

We slowed. Vran counted down the distance to touchdown. At zero, we hit with a jarring crunch. The nose of the ship tipped down and we slid and spun ninety degrees.

Heart in my throat, I gasped. A few people screamed. The ship slid to a halt.

I think we'd all stopped breathing, as if afraid the slightest twitch on our part would send the ship plunging into a crevasse.

"Hull temperature?" Lieutenant Vran said.

Even though the answer was ostensibly in English, the number and temperature measurement were meaningless to me, and I had no idea whether or not we'd cool fast enough to hide.

"Permission to power down?" Carrollus requested.

"Granted, save for planet-side monitoring," Grisham said. "Get me a feed from the ISS chip."

Naturally, they had a sensor on the International Space Station.

"On your screen, sir!"

A piece at a time, with every system that powered down, the ship drifted into slumber. Stillness settled over the vessel.

For no good reason, adrenaline flooded my system. I hated waiting.

"Sir?" a young woman said into the silence. "The scouts are on approach."

I glanced outside. The command center remained transparent in the power down. We'd set down on a slope. It appeared that we'd triggered at least a partial avalanche. In the brilliant glow of the aurora overhead, I could see where snow had cascaded past the nose of the ship. I hoped we were too big to be buried.

"The scouts are coming in fast, not masking their arrival," Grisham said, his voice hushed. "Crossing Saturn's orbit."

"They'll be seen by ground stations," Carrollus replied. "They may afford us some distraction."

Even the enchantment of the Northern Lights faded as I waited for the scout crafts' arrival. If they weren't fooled by our ruse, we were sitting ducks.

Grisham marked the scouts' approach by each planetary orbit they passed. Jupiter. The asteroid belt.

As the Orseggans approached the orbit of Mars, my breath stumbled in my chest. The aurora had suddenly dimmed. Without the particle activity in the atmosphere, our last defense was gone. The scouts would see us.

Then it hit me. The aurora wasn't dying out. It was the snow. The hull had cooled, and blowing snow had begun accumulating on the hull as hoped. I relaxed.

"They're approaching Earth from behind the moon," Grisham said. "Damned sloppy. I'm surprised they haven't been detected by ground-based personnel."

"Monitor the Twitter feeds of the conspiracy theorists," I offered. "They break all the UFO reports first."

"Here we go," Grisham said, ignoring me, but leading me to believe he had a line on Earth-based communications, even from within the aurora field. "First query away."

"I hope they don't set up camp," I muttered. "We'll be effectively under siege."

"They won't," the captain replied. "Your world isn't desirable."

"We like it," I protested. "And you certainly seem to have found a use for it."

"We like the world, Ms Selkirk, but your species is crazy."

I bit back a laugh.

"Second query from civilian telescopes. The Orseggan sighting is being escalated to military channels." The old man leaned back in his chair.

"Ms Selkirk," he said, "I can scarcely believe it, but it appears your scheme has worked. The scout is reversing course to the asteroid field. I expect they intend to use it as cover to round the sun and have a sensor scan of each planet on their way out of the solar system. They clearly didn't expect us to be in system. They aren't looking that hard."

I grinned at the muted cheer that went up. Something sharp lodged in my heart, making the backs of my eyes burn. Was that happiness?

"Merry Christmas," I said. I met Trygg's gaze and played my trump card. "Now, open a door and let me walk away?"

Carrollus scowled and tensed beside me. "No."

I bridled.

"The cold and the terrain would kill you within minutes, Ms Selkirk. Commander," Grisham said.

Desperation shot through me. "Teleport me home!"

"Ms Selkirk!" Grisham snapped. "Our orbital position is no impediment to returning you!"

"No time like the present," I shot.

I didn't realize I'd dug my fingers into the arm of the chair until Carrollus covered them with his warm hand. "Returning you is power-intensive. If we send you home now, we can't lift off for hours."

Recognizing that the danger to the ship now came from my own planet, I slumped. The unhappiness in Trygg's voice convinced me he was telling the truth.

"Was this a set-up?" I blurted out.

He frowned. "A set-up?"

"To make me feel – I don't know – like I'd contributed?"

"Humans are still arrogant," Grisham muttered. "At least some things never change."

I flushed.

"I wish it had been a set-up, Finlay," Carrollus said. "Then we wouldn't have had to risk exposing ourselves to your world. A risk we're still taking."

I believed him.

"Lift," I said. Defeat by my own moral code – that insisted my concerns take a back seat to their survival – tasted sour.

"You heard the lady. The ISS sensor has lost the Orseggan scout behind the sun. Put out some rocks to simulate a meteor landing and wake us up in preparation for departure," the captain commanded.

"Yes, sir."

Systems woke slower than they'd gone to sleep. Grisham estimated the Orseggans had passed Neptune's orbit by the time Carrollus issued the command to fire the engines and take us out of atmosphere.

Acceleration hit, pressing me into my chair. I gathered that some property of the ship buffered us from the worst of the g-forces. I could still breathe.

We were pointed right at the rippling river of neon light twisting like a living thing above us. The ship shook, squeaking and protesting at the mistreatment.

"We've been spotted," Vran said, "doesn't look like the fighters will overtake, though."

Despite the assurance, I waited, nerves tingling in anticipation of a missile strike. The magic of the Northern Lights would shield us again, if we could get to the other side before the F-15s closed.

It seemed like hours before Vran yelled, "Exiting atmosphere!"

"Get us under cover!" Grisham ordered. "Keep us out of sight!"

"Yes, sir!" several voices answered.

We leveled off and the ride smoothed out.

Grisham released his restraints and rose.

Carrollus unfastened his, and then leaned across me to press a series of buttons on the arm of my chair.

The web holding me to my seat released me.

"Ms Selkirk," Grisham said, "you've saved our lives. I doubt you'll ever know what that means to us."

Registering the regret in his voice, I levered myself to my feet. The icy pulse of fear in my gut made me waver.

Trygg closed a hand around my upper arm to support me.

The resulting shower of internal fireworks annoyed me.

"Don't you dare tell me I've seen too much and that you can no longer afford to send me home."

"That is the problem," Grisham said.

"It isn't," I countered. "Do an internet search on UFO abductions. Have a look at how the people who report them are treated. No. Wait. I'll demonstrate."

On autopilot, I stuck my hand in my jacket pocket. My cell-phone was still there. Why?

Commander Carrollus didn't strike me as careless. He'd have searched me. Why leave me my phone? Had he assumed it was useless on the far side of the moon?

We weren't out that far, yet.

I yanked the phone out of my pocket and lit the screen. One bar. Must be a satellite still in range. Lucky me. I hit "quick dial" for Jill, and then punched the "speaker" button. The line clicked twice, and then began ringing.

I caught the concern in the old man's face and, shaking off Carrollus's hold, I put distance between us.

Jill picked up mid-ring.

"Fin!" she said, her voice carrying through the room. "How'd the interview go?"

"You're on speaker," I said.

"So I hear. The interview. Spill."

"About that," I said. "Turns out the interview was a front for a bunch of aliens who've kidnapped me for sex. I'm not going to make your Christmas party."

Alarm spiked in Grisham's face. It warmed my heart.

"Ha, ha, very funny," Jill grumbled.

I turned the phone and an I-told-you-so glare on the old man.

Carrollus, trying not to smile, seemed abruptly to find the toes of his boots fascinating.

"I really won't make the party," I said.

"It went that well?" she prodded, her tone riding high on excitement.

"That remains to be seen. I can't say much."

Jill gasped. "You're under NDA already?"

"I suppose a non-disclosure agreement is one way to look at it," I said. "Look. Jill, you aren't going to see me for a while."

"This isn't you trying to get out of the holidays, is it?" she grumbled. "You aced the interview and now you're holed up in some secret lab? That had better be some damned fun research."

Carrollus stared at me.

"I can't answer that," I said. "And this will be the only call I'm allowed. I'll have to give up the phone in a minute."

"How long will you be gone?" she demanded.

I pinned a meaningful look on Grisham. "Unknown."

"You have to be back in time for Christmas," she protested.

"I'm nobody's present, Jill."

"Because you're afraid to care for anyone, again. That's your Christmas gift from me to you, my professional, psychiatric evaluation. No charge. Finlay. What do I tell the school?"

"Nothing."

"Your students will think—"

The phone went dead.

I rubbed my forehead and tried not to see the sudden concern crinkling Carrollus's brow. I handed him the phone.

"You misled your friend about us," he noted as he took the cell, pulled the battery, and pocketed both, one on either hip.

"A demonstration. You can put me back without fear because no one will believe me if I say I was abducted by aliens."

"The demonstration is not lost on me," the captain said, his tone grave. "You ceded us thirty days. Allow us to use that time to thank you properly for your assistance. Commander? Escort Ms Selkirk to her quarters."

All the words were right. He insinuated that he'd send me home, but something in Grisham's tone told me he didn't intend ever to let me go. I swallowed a huge, jagged lump of fear.

"Finlay—" Carrollus said. He took my hand and placed it in the crook of his arm.

My heart nearly tripped over itself. Damn biology.

He ushered me through the doors of the command center, back to the elevators, waved one open, and escorted me inside.

When I attempted to draw away from him, he tightened his grip on my hand. He gave a verbal command I assumed equated to a floor number.

"You've put me in a difficult position," he noted as the elevator began moving.

Guilt lurched through my chest, but I mentally strangled the emotion. I turned to face him.

"Funny," I said when I could be sure my tone would remain neutral. "I could say the same of you."

He met my eye with a direct gaze that unnerved me. "Yes."

"Especially since your captain doesn't intend ever to let me go home." I refused to back down, even as my body heated.

His gaze shifted to my lips.

"I've been ordered to ensure that when your thirty days are up, you will not want to leave us."

Liquid fire dumped straight to my lower belly. I clenched my teeth to keep from telling him that his job wouldn't be so hard.

"I get the impression you'd put me back, if it were up to you," I persisted, my breath suddenly in short supply, "even though you brought me here in the first place."

As if unaware of what he did, he smoothed a strand of my hair where it fell over the collar of my jacket. He wound the curl around his finger.

I held my breath. The subtle electricity of his touch smashed into my senses.

Desire darkened his eyes, even as he frowned. "Yes."

He didn't *like* being attracted to me.

Despite his reluctant response, or maybe because of it, arousal slid hot and wet into my lower body. I gasped. *Did I really want someone who didn't want to want me?*

"So put me back," I forced myself to rasp. "You could pick any number of women who'd be less trouble than I am."

He smiled, but lines that looked like pain creased his forehead. With a gentle tug, he freed himself from my hair. "Not possible. Not now."

"Why not?"

The elevator stopped. The doors opened. He led me out.

"What you said to your friend on the phone," he said, glancing at me, "'I'm nobody's present.' What does that mean?"

"You heard her assessment," I said, pressing my voice flat.

"You're afraid to care? You have no one?"

I detected no sympathy or pity in his tone, just straightforward curiosity. "No."

I felt the look he ran over me as a caress, and had to suppress a shiver despite the hurt gripping me. "Look. I buried my heart a long time ago. That makes me no use to you."

"Heartless? Is that what you think you are?" Carrollus murmured.

Hot blood flooded my face.

"You aren't. I'll prove it," he said, disengaging his hand from mine. "I'll be right back."

He ducked into a door that closed behind him.

Beneath my feet, the vibration of the engines eased to the point that they became undetectable. Orbit achieved, I gathered.

When Carrollus emerged, he carried a rumpled package in one hand. He held out his hand to me. "Fewer than thirty humans have seen the far side of the moon. If you can keep it a secret, I'll make you one of them."

I gasped at the unexpected thrill. I think I bounced as I tucked my hand into his. "Yes!"

Chuckling, he led me through a maze of corridors to a point low on the ship. He unlocked a door. It opened on what looked like a glass bubble.

The pockmarked lunar surface spread out before me, a slender crescent illuminated by the sun, the rest cast in shadow. It looked close enough to touch. For a split second, I hesitated, overwhelmed by the sheer wonder of seeing something only a handful of humans in the history of my world had seen.

Then, like a kid at the zoo, I plastered myself to whatever substance made up the see-thru hull and stared. My breath didn't even fog the surface of the window.

The door closed. I heard Carrollus lock it, and he pressed in close behind me, trapping me between his heat and the cool hull.

I sucked in a sharp breath at the want twisting my gut. I'd met him not twenty-four hours ago. How could I want him so urgently?

"What I told you about the bio-agent?" His voice vibrated through his chest into mine. The sound and the warmth of his presence curled around the cold, dead space where my heart should have been. "There's more." He threaded one arm around me, as if he needed something to hold. "My parents were among the first to die."

"Which one of them was your captain's child?" I asked.

Carrollus stopped breathing for a moment, then his diaphragm kicked in a laugh I couldn't hear. "How did you guess?"

"When you're angry, you and Captain Grisham look remarkably alike."

"My mother was his only child."

"I'm sorry." I felt awkward and inadequate saying the words, but they were all I had to offer.

He tugged my shirt tails out of my waistband, and threaded his hands under the fabric to caress my stomach.

The muscles jumped. I gasped at the firestorm his touch

ignited in my body. Leaning into him, I breathed, "What are you doing?"

"Something I shouldn't be doing," he murmured at my ear. "I need the touch of your skin on mine. Do you mind?"

Sensation shot heat and moisture through me. I dropped my head back against his shoulder. It dawned on me – I could no more avoid him than the moon could escape Earth's gravity.

"I don't mind." I had no idea how I got the words out.

His hand splayed against my ribs just below one breast. The other hand followed the contour of my hip bone.

I felt the hitch in his breathing as my own. With his touch as catalyst, want gathered like a storm in my blood. I'd never felt anything so overwhelming.

It sat right on the edge of scaring the life out of me. My heart couldn't decide whether to tremble with longing or with terror.

"I—," he began, and then cleared his throat. "I had a wife."

"A wife?" I echoed, dread and horror freezing my blood.

"She was pregnant with our first child."

I closed my eyes as if I could shut out the rest. My heart slid to my toes.

"Ikkari's only wish was to save the baby. We tried. Nothing worked. I lost them both."

He fell silent for a minute.

I opened damnably watery eyes.

"I'm sorry," I choked again. "Why did you tell me this?"

"You deserve to know," he said against my ear. "Most of this crew has been taught that everyone on board is their family. They were young enough to internalize the change."

"You weren't?"

"No. I haven't taken a partner since Ikkari died."

"How long?"

"I've lost count of the years."

"She was a lucky woman," I murmured.

"Finlay. You care," he prodded. "You care. You care about the people on this ship, and you care about a dead woman and baby you never even met."

Yes. I did. And I didn't comprehend how that could have happened. My crumbling defenses scrambled to close the gaps against Trygg Carrollus. I didn't know what to say.

"I'm not so selfish that I imagine I'm the only one who's lost someone," I finally spoke.

"Perhaps you haven't lost as much as you think," he said. He offered me the package he'd brought with him into the room.

I stared at the clumsy wrapping job and knew he'd done it himself. That warmed me.

When I glanced at him, he looked . . . lost.

A tendril of fear touched me. Hand trembling, I took the gift.

"Thank you," I said. I tore paper.

It was a picture frame.

I'd opened it so the picture wasn't facing me. I turned it over. I felt as if I'd been kicked in the gut. The breath left me. My mouth opened, but I couldn't force air past the painful constriction in my throat. Tears burned my eyes. A sore place in the center of my chest tore open.

A picture from my parents' wedding. I hadn't seen the photo since before the flood that had destroyed the house we'd rented in rural Louisiana when I'd been ten years old.

"I'd forgotten." I whispered because I couldn't force my voice past the lump of unshed tears choking me.

Warm fingers touched my cheek. "They look so happy." The wistful note in his voice raked my raw emotions. "Your mother is beautiful. You look very much like her. And your father looks so proud."

I breathed a ghost of a laugh. "When he saw her walking down the aisle toward him, he was so overwhelmed, he nearly passed out."

"He has my complete sympathy."

"My God, Trygg." I choked. "Thank you for the picture. Where did you—?"

"Newspaper archives from the town where they were married," he said. "I'd had you under surveillance for several months before we brought you in. I contacted the paper and explained you'd lost both the pictures and your parents. They were happy to pull the negatives."

I threw myself at him, wrapping my arms around his shoulders, aware I didn't care where, when or how. I only cared that a lost part of my family had been restored. My tears spilled over. Embarrassed, I realized he hadn't returned the embrace. I ducked my head and tried to back away.

He caught me, eased the picture from my hands, and pulled me tight against his chest. He tucked my head beneath his chin and held me until the emotional storm passed. He didn't try to quiet me with false assurances that everything would be all right. He simply held me and accepted my sadness. That felt oddly like another gift – one I'd never before been offered.

I'd gone from slugging my kidnapper in the stomach to taking comfort in his arms, all within a twenty-four-hour time frame.

When I finally straightened, he wiped moisture from my cheeks with shaking fingers. I registered the pressure of his erection, hot against me. Intrigued by the notion of stripping Trygg Carrollus out of his austere uniform, I flexed my fingers on his hard thighs, seeking to slide a hand between us to stroke him through the fabric.

"No," he rasped. He caught my wrist. A sharp sliver of hurt lodged in my chest.

"Don't," he ordered, when he looked at me. "If I have you, I won't be able to do what I know is right."

"And what is that?"

"To take you home," he said. "Isn't that what you want?"

Pain expanded inside my chest. I could barely breathe around it. Confusion rocked me. "I – yes. No."

The skin between his brows puckered. "I don't understand."

"You'd be disobeying another direct order," I said.

"Yes."

"What happens to you then?"

He shook his head. "I don't care."

"I do. Come with me." I said. Where the hell had *that* come from? "You were right. I care what happens to you. All of you. But you, specifically. When you look at me, I feel so much it's—"

He drew closer with each breathless confession until I couldn't eke any more words past my lips.

"I want you," he said, "but I won't rob you of your freedom."

"I don't want to lose – whatever this is—" The words stumbled out. I hated that I sounded like a love-struck teenager, and I loathed the waver in my voice.

He nodded.

I recognized the twist of pain in his eyes. Part of my heart tore.

"Why does this have to be an either or proposition?" I demanded.

"You come to Earth. I know you do. You know too much about the US military to not be involved regularly. Why couldn't I stay here and still go to work every morning? You could stay with me when you're on assignment infiltrating governments."

He chuckled. "You don't forget anything, do you?"

"Not if I can use it to get what I want."

Hope lit in his eyes until it hurt to meet his gaze. "You'd do that? Live here and work on Earth?"

"You do."

He picked up my parents' wedding picture to run his fingers over the glass. "I do. Before she died, Ikkari urged me to be happy."

"You haven't been?"

"I hadn't given it much thought," he confessed. "It didn't seem possible. Much less relevant."

His observation touched off a sense of recognition within me. I'd felt something similar after my family had been killed.

"You've driven me mad with wanting from the moment I met you," he said. "I think that was my grandfather's plan all along when he sent me your file and ordered me to take up surveillance. He hasn't given up hope that he'll hold another Grisham descendant before he dies."

Longing arced hot and sharp through my body. He'd planted the image of a dark-haired, blue-eyed infant in my brain and in my heart.

"I want what your parents had, and I want you, Finlay Selkirk. If I have to call in all my favors at the Pentagon to keep questions from being asked, I will," he swore.

"Then help me get my things," I ordered, grinning. "You can come with me to Jill's party three days from now. Then we can take turns playing Santa."

Interest sparked in his eyes as he looked me up and down. "I can hardly wait to unwrap my present. Are you going to make me wait for Christmas morning?"

"Of course," I replied, thoroughly enjoying the buzz of arousal bolstering the easy teasing.

"Not if I have my way," he promised, taking my hand and pressing a kiss to my palm. He chuckled when I gasped and squirmed.

I so hoped he did get his way. Soon.

"Ms Finlay Selkirk," he said, mischief in his tone. "You've aced the interview. I'd like to offer you the job. Effective immediately."

"Reporting to you?"

"Only to me."

"When do we talk compensation?" I teased.

His dead sexy smile turned my insides to water. "When we've completed transport to your apartment. We'll discuss it. In detail."

Author Biographies

Regan Black
Regan crafts action-packed stories so paranormal fans can enjoy a fantastic escape from the daily grind. A recipient of a 2011 Paranormal Romance Guild Reviewer's Choice Award, she is the author of the futuristic Shadows of Justice series, the light-hearted, contemporary Matchmaker series, and the Hobbitville young-adult series.
www.reganblack.com

Marcella Burnard
An award-winning author writing science fiction romance for Berkley Sensation, her first book, *Enemy Within*, was a national bestseller on its debut in November 2010. It won the RT Reviewer's Choice Award that year and was a double RITA finalist. The second book in the series, *Enemy Games*, was published in May 2011. *Enemy Storm*, book three, is in the works. A short, erotic novella set in the Enemy universe was released by Berkley as an E-Special in April 2012.
www.marcellaburnard.com

Cathy Clamp
USA Today bestselling author of the Tales of the Sazi paranormal romance series, she also writes as Cat Adams for the Blood Singer urban fantasy series. Cathy is a recipient of the RT Book Reviews Career Achievement Award for Paranormal Romance.
www.catadams.net

Bianca D'Arc
Critically acclaimed author of paranormal, science fiction and
fantasy romance, Bianca has twice won the coveted EPPIE
Award. Her background includes degrees in biochemistry,
library science and law.
www.biancadarc.com

Delilah Devlin Delilah is a national bestselling author of erotic
romance, with a reputation for edgy stories and complex characters. She has published over one hundred stories in a variety of
sub-genres and formats with publishers like Avon, Berkley,
Kensington, Cleis Press, Black Lace, Kindle, Running Press,
Atria/Strebor, Ellora's Cave, and Samhain Publishing.
www.delilahdevlin.com

Kiersten Fay
Kiersten combines paranormal and sci-fi elements in her
romance – along with a healthy dose of humor – and is author of
the steamy, paranormal/sci-fi series Shadow Quest. Often, she
can be found guzzling coffee and lurking around Twitter @
Kierstenfay.
www.kierstenfay.com

Jess Granger
National bestselling author of dark and intense futuristic
romance novels.
www.jessgranger.com

Jamie Leigh Hansen
Jamie builds engaging worlds filled with sexy vampires, were-
wolves and more.
www.jamieleighhansen.com

Leanna Renee Hieber
Trained as an actress and playwright, Leanna adores writing historical and futuristic fantasy with a focus in the Victorian
era. Her debut novel, *The Strangely Beautiful Tale of Miss Percy
Parker,* appeared on Barnes & Noble's bestseller lists and won
two 2010 Prism Awards (Best Fantasy, Best First Book). "Song
of Saire" is part of her Dark Nest futuristic fantasy series

published by Crescent Moon Press, which won the 2009 Prism Award in the novella category.
www.leannareneehieber.com

Jeannie Holmes

Jeannie fears spiders, large bodies of water, and bad weather. Therefore, she moved from rural Mississippi to the Alabama Gulf Coast where all three are in abundance. She's a member of Romance Writers of America, International Thriller Writers, and Horror Writers Association. When she isn't spending time with her husband and four neurotic cats, she writes the Alexandra Sabian series.
www.jeannieholmes.com

Donna Kauffman

USA Today bestselling, award-winning author Donna Kauffman has seen her books reviewed everywhere from Kirkus to Library Journal, Entertainment Weekly to *Cosmopolitan*. With over fifty titles in print, her work has been translated into twenty-three languages worldwide. Her current Cupcake Club series has received starred reviews, and was named both Pick of the Week (*Sugar Rush*) and Top 12 Spring Romance 2012 (*Sweet Stuff*) from *Publisher's Weekly*. Donna lives just outside Washington DC in the Virginia countryside with her family and a growing menagerie of animals.
www.donnakauffman.com

Michele Lang

Writer of paranormal and futuristic romance, and the historical-fantasy series Lady Lazarus, published by Tor.
www.michelelang.com

Mandy M. Roth

Mandy is fascinated by creatures that go bump in the night. Her books have won numerous awards, including a Romantic Times nomination for Best Paranormal Erotic.
www.mandyroth.com

Patrice Sarath

Patrice is the author of the highly acclaimed sequel to *Pride and Prejudice*, *The Unexpected Miss Bennet*. She also writes fantasy and science fiction, and her latest novel is *The Crow God's Girl*, a young-adult novel set in her Gordath Wood series of fantasies.

www.patricesarath.com

Linnea Sinclair

Winner of the prestigious national book award, the RITA, Linnea is a name synonymous with high-action, emotionally intense, character-driven novels. *Starlog* magazine calls her "one of the reigning queens of science fiction romance". *The Down Home Zombie Blues*, published in 2007 by Bantam, has been adapted for the screen (re-titled *The Down Home Alien Blues*) and will appear in theatres in 2013. A former news reporter and retired private detective, she divides her time between Naples, Florida and Columbus, Ohio.

www.linneasinclair.com

Susan Sizemore

Susan Sizemore is the *New York Times* bestselling author of the Vampire Primes paranormal romance novels, and the urban fantasy series Laws of the Blood. Her futuristic novels include *The Gates of Hell* and *Dark Stranger*.

www.susansizemore.com

Charlene Teglia

Charlene's novels have received Romantic Times Book Reviews Reviewer's Choice Awards, have been translated into multiple languages and have been selected for inclusion by the Rhapsody, Doubleday and Literary Guild Bookclubs. When she's not writing she can be found hiking with her family or opening and closing doors for cats.

www.charleneteglia.com

C. L. Wilson

New York Times bestselling author of richly imagined romantic fantasy novels filled with action and emotion. She has won numerous awards including LifetimeTV.com's Best Paranormal debut of 2007, the Gayle Wilson Award of Excellence, two National Reader's Choice awards, the Colorado Award of Excellence and the Holt Medallion. The honored recipient of the PEARL award for Best Debut Author of 2007, she also won another PEARL in 2009 for best Romantic Fantasy novel. *www.clwilson.com*